Bondbreaker

First Printing, 2023

To request permissions, contact the publisher.
srgeorgewriting@gmail.com
Paperback ISBN: 979-8-218-26802-2
eBook ISBN: 979-8-218-26801-5
Edited By: Amanda Mulvaney
Cover Art and Page Spacer Art By: S. R. George
Cover Art and Page Spacer Art Copyright © S. R. George

Dedicated to:

To those of us who are afraid to chase their dreams.

Take the leap.

And those of us who want handlebars on our men.

Trigger Warnings

Bondbreaker may contain triggering content to some.

Trigger warnings include but are not limited to:

Graphic Violence, Human Trafficking, Sexual Assault (both mentioned and depicted), Torture, Kidnapping, Imprisonment, Gun Violence, Drug/Alcohol Use

If you or someone you know is in trouble, please reach out.

Help is Available

Human Trafficking Hotline: 888-373-7888

Sexual Assault Hotline: 1-800-656-4673

Suicide Hotline: 988

Playlist

Tales of the Night Forest – Black Hill, Silent Island

Dead Man Walking – JellyRoll

Make Believe – Memphis May Fire

@ My Worst – Blackbear

Rush – The Score

Call Out My Name – Seraphim

Dark Side – Sam Tinnez

Federkleid – Faun

Mine – Sleep Token

Shivers – Ed Sheeran

The Fear – The Score

Follow You – Bring Me the Horizon

Headstrong – Trapt

It's Called: Freefall – Rainbow Kitten Surprise

Even if it Hurts – Sam Tinnez

Feel Invincible – Skillet

Hard Feelings – Palisades

Fall into Me – Forest Blakk

Bondbreaker

S. R. George

Prologue

I cannot breathe. My heart is thundering. My head is spinning. I cannot get my eyes to focus. Is this what death feels like? Some murky abyss that sings the song of revelry. My body feels foreign to me; the lightning-sharp pain across my back tells me that I was lashed again. That wicked man takes the greatest pleasure in my suffering. I can hear screaming, laughing, crying, the crackle of that bonfire that alights the courtyard in bright summery hues. Hues that I have missed for so long. Will that sorrow ever ease? Will her death stare haunt me forever? Something cool touches my brow, patting gently at the sweat there. Who are you? Damn it all, why will my eyes not focus?

"It's okay." She whispers. It is the new elf girl that that monster has purchased. I feel a cool relief as she uses magic to stitch my skin together. "They are preoccupied with a faery right now."

I try to find my limbs, but my bones are soft. I rasp. "You—you should not do that."

"Not every being here has to be cruel." She says, pressing a sweet kiss to my brow. My vision clears and I can see her squatting next to me. She is pretty, but fairly plain for an elf woman. Her hair is straw-like in color with tinges of copper, her eyes bright blue and warm even as they resemble a cold ocean. She is lithe, too young to be dressed as she is. The scrap of fabric that covers her is sheer, leaving her on display.

"You will get hurt helping me, girl."

"Then I will take it." Her voice is soft as a finch song but firm. "No one should be treated as they treat you, slave or not. Beast or fae or human."

I huff into the bloodied dirt before me. "You have lofty thoughts, given your purpose here."

"I am no whore." There is a sharpness to her voice. A fire in her spirit I hope she never loses here, but I can smell her fear.

"That is what you will be, whether you wish it or not. The master is not above tying maidens down to have them."

She paled slightly, "I—I do not wish to be here."

"Neither do I, fair one."

"Tummilia. Tummi is what my sister, Katrel, has always called me."

"Tummi." Her name is a bell that tones at dawn.

"Beast, what is your name?"

"I—" What had I been called all those years ago, by that fire-haired witch, by the family I had long lost? "Niratap. I am Niratap."

She smiles sweetly stroking my face. "Nira."

I feel my lips move to match her smile, but a boot knocks into my ribs, my breath leaving my lungs in a whoosh.

"Beast, the fair elf girl is not for you." A guard fists Tummi's hair and pulls her off the ground. "Beautiful as she is, the master will not take your beastly seconds."

He runs his hand along her ribs, pulling at the fabric, and paws at her small breasts. She yelps, tries to kick at him. He just laughs at her. I push off the ground, a growl that I have not used in a long while crawling from my throat. It earns me a kick to the neck, my face finding the dirt instead.

"How dare you growl at me, beast. The master will hear of this." The sole of his shoe presses my face into the dirt. "I am certain that he will take great pleasure in teaching you both your place."

I glare at him. It has been so long since I have been defiant to those who hold my chains. So long since I have had this urge to protect anyone. "Let her go."

"Subjugare. Obedire. Submittere."[1] The lord hollers our direction.

The iron collar around my neck glows as do the matching cuffs around my wrists and ankles, magical thorns digging deep into my skin. I snarl and thrash against the suffocating sensation as the magic tightens around me. The heavy chains anchor me to the ground, and I fight the fire choking me.

"Insufferable beast, you will obey me." The lord's boot finds its mark against my ribs.

"Leave the girl alone," I snarl at him with all the venom I can muster as the subjugation magic acts as a noose, cutting off my air, and making my head swim. The whip cracks a lightning strike on a cloudless night, and it bites viciously across my face. I can taste my blood's coppery tang in my mouth.

The lord fists my hair, pulling my head back to glare at me, his dagger pressing into my throat. "If you value your pathetic existence, then you would be wise to shut your mouth. I am not above flaying you for fun. Do you want to live, beast?"

I swallow and look away. "Yes."

"Yes what, beast?"

"Yes, master."

"Then obey." He throws me down into the dirt, his guards laughing. He speaks to the guard holding Tummi. "Bring the brat I need some relief."

Their footsteps fade under the roar of the fire, the crackling of the logs the only sound in the silence for several long moments. I curl into myself, bracing as the laughter of men rises as does the bile in my throat. Her screams keen over the crack and pop of the logs. I wonder if it truly is the logs that I hear or if it is her bones. What horrible things are they doing to her? I press my hands over my ears. Coward. When did I become so cowardly? When did I become so

[1] "Subjugate. Obey. Submit."

weak? Even with my ears covered I can still hear her screaming, begging them to stop. Please just stop.

"Stop!" Shouts a female voice from the woods.

I uncurl at her voice, both desperate and so full of rage. Blood stings my eyes, but I can see the young elf woman, dressed like a man, her hair braided back and a sword dangling from her hand. Her features are much like Tummi's, but where Tummi was a warm summer day, this figure was a smoldering autumn night.

The master laughs from his seat between the girl's legs and purrs. "Now, now who might you be?"

The girl brandishes the sword at the master. "Release my sister, you fiend."

"And who might your sister be?" He thrusts into Tummi. Her yelp of pain echoing into the night.

"Release my sister now, or I will release your member from your body." The would-be elf warrior snarls.

"Now, now girl. Do you even know who I am?" He coos.

"You are a dead man if you do not release my sister."

The master frowns. "Men, grab the wench. She will be fun to torture. I cannot wait until I can smother that fire in her."

The men surround her, all of them laughing mockingly. I rise to my knees, watching. The master shoots a glare at my movement, and I ease back sitting on my heels, averting my eyes from his gaze. The girl holds up the sword and lunges, but she has no experience with the weapon. The guards laugh even more as they disarm her and bind her arms together before her. They drag her before the lord, who has tucked himself back into his pants.

"*Glaoim ar na heiliminti. Talmh, tine, gaoth agus farraige—*"[2]

The master's hand careens across her face. "None of that, witch."

---

[2] "I call upon the elements, earth, fire, wind, and sea—"

A large glass cauldron carried between four guards is set before the crude dais built opposite the fire. Filled with a clear liquid that smells pungently of vinegar but carries the macerated smell of chemically cleaned bones. Acid. The master claims his spot upon his throne, crossing an ankle over a knee, and ganders at the defiant girl before him.

"Now, what to do with you?" He asks, his voice flat, but with a sinister edge. "So wild and defiant. Maybe a dip in an acid bath or defiling your noble womb will tame you."

"No!" Tummi ran onto the dais, prostrating before him. I can smell her blood and tears. "I will do anything, my Lord, anything please just let my sister go."

The master smiles. "Anything?"

"No, Tummi!" Her sister screams.

"Anything." Tummi concedes.

"Come here, child." He waves two of his fingers for her to come nearer. She keeps her head down, and crawls before the master. Fisting her hair, he pulls her between his legs. "Now, sweet girl, clean your filth from me and I will consider letting your sister live. Bite me and you both will die."

"Yes, master." She whimpers but does as she is told.

My stomach curdles as he waves to the guards around her sister. She screams and fights as the men each take a limb and hover her over the cauldron. The cruel smile dons the master's face before he speaks.

"Dunk her."

The guards obey, submerging the poor girl's back into the clear liquid. Her screams rattle through me. Break a part of my sanity and heart that I thought had long since died. The master's hand holds Tummi's head to him, whispering to her. The sounds of the acid as it devours Katrel's clothes and skin, burn on my own skin. I cannot take this. I cannot watch these innocent girls suffer. I cannot be a slave any longer. I pull against the magical chains holding me back, and the cold metal bites into my skin.

"*Manere.*" [3] The master says, waving a bored hand. The chains tighten, but I will not yield. The master narrows his eyes.

"*Submittere.*" [4] He growls at me. The magical thorns dig into my throat, wrists, and ankles. I dig my claws into the earth. I will not yield.

"*Subjugare.*" [5] He shouts and tendrils of blood trickle over my chest and hands. He throws Tummi backward off the dais. The guards drop her sister on the ground beside her, drawing their weapons to face me.

"*Cede.*" [6] He screams, tucking his clothes back into place. Heat builds between the binds and my skin. I will not. I cannot. The enchanted metal groans as I fight them.

"Insolent creature!" He bellows, stalking towards me, cracking the whip at his side. "I did not have the pleasure to break you. This newfound willfulness of yours will be entertaining nonetheless."

"I will no longer be a slave."

"*Obumbrata camporum creatura mihi es obligata. Ad voluntatem meam inclinaberis.*" [7]

Magic blue fire radiates from the metal, the smell of burnt flesh and hair coats my nose. I cannot give in. I cannot submit. I cannot yield. I must break free. I must save them. I must end this. I reach mentally into the ether and call upon the magic that has lain dormant for hundreds of years. Shadows crawl from the darkness of the forest and silent manor. They slither and slink over my skin, shielding me from the bite of the magical fire trying to consume me. I feel my muscles shift, my bones elongate, and hair grows over my skin. My senses sharpen as I rise from the ground, the

---

[3] "Stay."

[4] "Submit."

[5] "Subjugate."

[6] "Yield."

[7] "You are bound to me, creature of shadowed plains. You will bend to my will."

manacles of servitude fall from my body and turn to dust at my feet. I am free.

The man who mere seconds ago was my master pales then glares swinging back his arm, whip in hand. He says. "Let the breaking begin."

He slings his arm forward, the whip slicing through the air, the metal tip glinting in the firelight, and across my chest.

I feel nothing. There is no blood or splayed flesh, only the shadows that ebb over me. A shield that I have summoned to myself, I realize, to rend from this world the darkness that had hallowed mine. I growl. As I settle onto all fours, long claws come from the shadows, weapons against tyranny. I scent their fear, the guards, the once master. They are afraid of me. Of the ending that I was promised to bring. That makes me angry. How dare they be afraid of the monster they created? How dare these men ever hold sway over me. Control over me.

My blood is roiling through my veins. All sounds hit me at once, roaring in my ears; or was it me roaring? I raise my clawed paw and the men begin to scream, fleeing at the sight of me. One of their own is flayed, the rich earthy taste of man flesh on my tongue. One after another I slay and devour parts of each guard as they flee in a painfully slow progression to the manor house, lights coming to life in the windows. I burst through the door and slay indiscriminately, devour indiscriminately. The head of the waitstaff screams of panic, the only one I hear as I bite through her throat. The master's wife is pushed down the stairs by the master himself, a sacrifice for his survival.

The master's children are the only lives in the slaughter that will haunt me. The master's son, much nobler than the father that had shoved them from the safety of their room, holds a dagger before his sister behind him. His death is quick. The master's daughter, still so young, so young smiles up at me, eyes filled with tears. She is afraid, but not of me as she embraces the slithering mass of shadows and fur that had just slain her brother.

"I told you." She weeps as my claws dig into her back. "I told you that you would be free one day."

I cannot stop the bloodlust as my claws sink into her tiny body, sliding between her ribs, and through her heart. I feel it beat twice over the talon that had punctured it before she falls limp in my hands with a sigh. Yes, these deaths would haunt me for the rest of my existence. Silence hits my ears first. When did the screaming of guards and wait staff stop? I look behind me. The hall is coated in blood, bodies cooling where it pools. I had slaughtered them all in my quest for vengeance. I shake my head, looking at the door where the sniveling man who had once controlled this house hid. I push through the doors and there he is, cowering in the corner of the room.

He peers past me at his children who lay dead in the hall. "You killed them. You killed all of them, even the children."

I stalk toward him, bloodlust and vengeance my only goal, but my head is no longer clouded. "Yes."

"You are going to kill me."

"Yes." The shadows waver on me and pulse with my heart.

"Please no."

"You are a weak man." I growl in a voice not fully human in sound. "You preyed upon those who could not protect themselves. You sacrificed your own wife to save yourself. You sacrificed your children. No longer."

Hot tears roll down my face. He had sacrificed them, yes, but it was I who had killed them. I had snuffed them from existence, just as I was about to do to the man that I had watched for almost a decade do the same thing. His death was not drawn out, it was mercifully quick. I did not eat of his flesh, my stomach full and nauseated. I made it back to the entryway of the house before I lost all of its contents, the shadows falling away and slithering back to their homes.

The girls sat on the stoop and did not flinch as I came and sat between them. I was covered in blood, my body weary, but at least they had survived the slaughter. The tears still streamed freely. We sat there looking over the grounds where the bodies of guards lay strewn, in pieces.

"You slayed them." Katrel said softly. It looked as if Tummi had healed her to the best of her ability, rippling burn scars covering her back, much like the ones that had taken residence at my wrists and ankles.

"Yes."

"Even the lord?" Tummi asked.

I swallowed my throat dry. "Even the children."

Tummi nodded sadly, she had met the lord's children, but she placed a gentle hand on my arm. "It was merciful."

"We are free." I said to her, solemnly.

"What now, beast?" Katrel asked, her tongue sharp but weary.

"He is no beast." Tummi said. "He is the Bondbreaker."

Chapter One

Niratap

Present Day

The smell of rot and decay made my stomach turn. How these vermin could stand to live and work in this chasm of stone and death was beyond me. The sounds surrounded me and echoed around the walls of the alley, whispered conversations, cries of beings seen and unseen, and heels on the wet cobblestone rang sharp in my ears. Most of the whispers were about me as the crowd parted around me. Lord Niratap joins the fray of monsters searching for something; what will he purchase and take to his sanctuary; what manner of the beast has drawn him to our street? I heard it every time I came here, along with seedier beings debating whether my patronage was worth more than I was. They were just words because none of the people here were brave or stupid enough to try to subdue me.

The slave traders were talking about the beauties they had captured as I passed by the brothel, Nocturnal. Women were a commonly trafficked commodity in these dark causeways. I paused, a sweet scent permeating the air. What was this sweet fragrance that pulled me towards the small entryway, to the traders' den, where the two men stood, dressed in black, one wearing a hoodie against the night's chill?

"L-l-lord Niratap." One of the traders sputtered. "What do we owe the pleasure?"

I swallowed, the sweet scent calling out to me from around the door. "I wish to peruse your wares for the evening."

"Is his lordship in the market for a wife, plaything, or incubator?" The other trader asked.

I glowered at the term. "I have not decided. I wish to see what you have."

"Enter then, my Lord, the bidding is about to begin."

He opened the door, which I had to nearly bend completely over to walk through. The sweet scent pierced through the smells of sweat, sex, and fear that permeated the air. Where was it coming from? I nudged a chandelier away from my antlers as I came back to my full height so as to not get tangled in its dangling crystals. The walls were carpeted in a wine-colored velvet over a black marble floor, and before me was a slight elven woman in a body-tight black dress with a plunging neckline, a silver enchanted collar, and cuffs around her throat and wrists. I adjusted my own shirt cuffs to hide my discomfort, the sickening smell of their magic tingling on the back of my tongue.

"My Lord." She curtsied. "I am to be your hostess for the evening. Which part of the club do you wish to partake in?"

Dance music came from the doors on either side, but the smell was coming from behind where she stood.

"Where does each door lead?" I asked. I already felt like I was suffocating in the tight space.

"To your right is the dance lounge, where we would wait on you and your vices, whatever they may be. To the left is the escort hall which is lined with women ready for your pleasure."

"And the door beyond?" I motioned to the door behind her with a bob of my head.

"That is the way to the auction lounge, my Lord."

"Then lead the way, my dear."

She flushed slightly. I smelled the fear radiating off her, but she did not tremble as she nodded and turned to the door. "Very well, my Lord."

I followed her through the door, bending again to allow clearance for my antlers. The room was a large auditorium with private booths strewn throughout. Most were set up with semi-sheer curtains, and others were one-way glass rooms. All the better to see and not be seen. She led me to a large alcove close to the stage, where I could only assume whoever this sweet scent belonged to would be brought for auction. She adjusted a dial in the velvet wall and the floor before the lounge dropped, steps coming from the floor, and I knew this was where they entertained creatures of the more inhuman variety. I sat in the lounge. It was a welcome feeling in the outside world to be accommodated for my size. She pulled the gossamer curtain across the entry and gave a small bow.

"Can I get you anything to drink, my Lord? We have an extensive bar, including various other beverages for our guests." I didn't need to ask her what she meant by various beverages; I could smell the metallic tang of blood.

"What is your selection of vintage red wines?" I wanted something to cut through my dry mouth.

"We have one vintage red, an Italian I believe; would you like me to fetch it for you, my Lord?"

"Yes, please, my dear."

"Anything else, my Lord?"

"A scotch, Irish, high shelf, neat, and your name."

"M-my name?" Fear permeated her again.

"Yes, I would like to know it."

"Eloimaya. Eloimaya Daeleth"

I met her gaze. "Thank you, Eloimaya. I will wait for your return."

The scents of this place were giving me an ache between my eyes. I reached behind my mask, closed my eyes and pinched the bridge of my nose. The burn of alcohol would hopefully ease the pressure on my senses. Hushed voices grated on my ears, and my name on the tongues of many who were hidden in the private lounges. Eloimaya's heels clacked across the marble as she returned, and she paused just past the curtain.

"I-I didn't realize that was a mask, my Lord."

"Many don't, and I would like to keep it that way, my dear." My voice sounded more menacing than I intended, but she was unfazed by it.

"Yes, my Lord. I will not tell a soul."

I looked at her now. She had toed off her heels, dimmed the lighting, and come to stand before the steps. She placed the tray of drinks on the table beside the sofa. I snatched the scotch, taking a hard swallow of it. It ignited a fire and numbed my throat to the choking sensation of magic around me. Confinement and binding magic had always tasted bitter on the back of my tongue, taking me back to dark memories from long ago.

"My Lord, not to be forward, but you seem to be on edge. I remember that your kind of beast has hyper senses. Is it overwhelming to be here in the city?"

"Very." I said, adjusting the mask back into position. "Smells and sounds are particularly grating after a short time."

"Then why come into the city at all? Especially places like this."

I sat forward resting my elbows on my knees, hands clasped in front of my face. I pointed to the spot directly in front of me. "Come here."

She swallowed, fear painting her features, making her sapphire eyes widen and her breath quicken. To her credit she didn't shake, though I knew every instinct she had was telling her to run. She came to stand between my knees, her face level with mine in the position. I reached out my hand, extended my claws, and wrapped my hand around her slim waist. She didn't resist as I pulled her close, and disgust bubbled in my stomach at the notion that she had become accustomed to this in the care of her captors. She placed her hands against my chest, her head falling to my shoulder.

"My Lord." Her voice quaked in my ear, a whisper of defeat lining it. "Do you wish for me to undress?"

A growl rumbled in my chest. "No. You do not need to fear me *acushla.*[8] I Niratap *saor agus scaoilfidh ti o do ngeibhean, ionas go siulfidh tu go saor on ait seo agus an draiocht a chuir srian ort."*[9] There was a click as the collar and cuffs unlatched and fell into one of my hands, the other cupped her face, her cheek wet with tears.

"Why would you do such a thing?" She asked, her hand coming to rest against my own.

"That is why I come to these wretched places. To free those like myself who have fallen into bondage." I sat back against the back of the sofa, setting the cuffs on the table.

"My Lord, I am nothing like you."

"You are more than you know," I reached behind my head and untied my mask, letting my shadow armor drop. My face wasn't monstrous in this form, save the scars that sliced across my eye and throat. She gasped at the sight of me. The smoky shadows that I wrapped around me to hide the evidence of the darkness of my past coiled, waiting to shroud me again. She bowed deeply before me, her fine blond hair sweeping over her shoulder like a cascade of sunshine.

"You do me the highest of honors, my Lord. How will I ever repay you for this?"

I placed an elongated finger under her chin and brought her face up. "Tonight, you will aid me in my reason to be here. Then I will purchase you from these evil men and take you away from here. After we leave the city, you may choose if you wish to stay with me or return to your home from before. Either way I will place my protection upon you

---

[8] "...darling."

[9] "I Niratap free and release you from your bondage, so that you may walk freely from this place and the magic that has confined you."

and no monster, beast, or man will harm you as you have been here. *Cosaint uathu siud a chaitear faoi scath.* [10]"

"Yes, Lord Niratap."

Silence fell in the auditorium, and I could see that a man in a black suit had walked onto the stage. He was middle aged, his dark grey and silver hair swept back in waves. Gold rings choked every finger and a thick chain lay around his neck, a tumbler of amber liquid in one of his hands. He cleared his throat and Eloimaya stood straight and walked to the edge of the curtain, giving a sad smile as she stood there.

"Welcome! Welcome my friends." His voice had a heavy tone to it, an Italian. "Tonight is like any other night in the auction lounge at Nocturnal. For those of you who have never graced these walls, we proceed as such. Firstly, we bring out those who have fallen on hard times, and who are looking for work. Next, we bring out our assortment of male and female consorts that you may look at and purchase to share your company for the remainder of the evening. Then we bring out our ripe women, prime for breeding, and lastly, we bring out the new wares that we have acquired throughout the week. We have some lovely products in the newest shipment, so don't spend all your money before then. Your hostesses will initiate your bids for you so you may keep your anonymity. Favorable roads, my friends, and let the evening begin."

"My Lord, what is it that you are searching for?"

"I do not know. I only have their scent, an intoxicating scent that I must take away from here."

"Of course, my Lord. Just let me know."

Unease weighed heaving in my gut as I watched the vile show begin. We both watched as men and women of all ages were paraded across the stage, in their ratty garments

---

[10] "Protection from them that are cast under a shadow."

smelling of the allies outside this establishment. They were bid on and purchased in silence. Then the consorts came out across the stage, heavy perfumes clinging to their sweaty bodies, clad in sequins and glitter to attract the eye of worthy owners. The next group was just young women, naked, all with wide hips and large breasts. I turned away as they were all bought by strangers in the darkness to be used as cattle.

The scent thickened as they brought the last group of bodies out. Shackled together, blindfolded and bare they all reeked of fear, but I could smell it. I could smell her. A beautiful curvy girl no more than twenty-five. Her mahogany skin glistened under the lights above. Her fluffy cloud-like hair bounced as she tried to keep pace, pulled by the gold-colored chains she was placed in, that make her skin warm.

I stood and came beside Eloimaya. "Her. I want her no matter the cost."

"The dark human girl?" she asked to clarify.

"Yes, and I want her now."

Eloimaya walked past the curtain, her voice ringing clear. "My patron will pay over any bid on the dark-skinned human."

"Oh really." A voice calls from the audience. "And who would your patron be?"

She looked back at me for my response. I just nodded and waved a dismissing hand.

"My patron is lord Niratap. He wishes to take the mortal now."

Whispers erupted from the auditorium, and an older woman in a tight purple dress stormed across the stage, snatching up the chains and yanking my girl across and down the steps. Before she turned toward my shrouded alcove, hatred burned in her eyes at me. A very dark feeling rose in

my body as I replaced my mask. A need to protect the flower
I had picked.

Chapter Two

Shasha

Why do I never listen? Why? If I had listened to my mother, I wouldn't be here. I just wanted to come to the city, go to school, major in mythology and monsters, and live underneath the neon lights. It rained that night after my orientation, I wandered from my dorm and walked the city streets in awe. The green and blue reflecting off the concrete and glass painted me in an ethereal glow. That's what I wanted to be, ethereal and real in a place full of monsters, but not like this.

I stood there basking in the glow of the neon lights, eyes closed letting the rain fall on my face, not caring how frizzy my hair would be afterward, in my over-sized sweater and corduroy skirt. I felt someone approach me from the shadows. I opened my eyes and attempted to turn and face him when a black silk bag came over my face, my screams muffled by his hand. He didn't say anything, just picked me up over a muscled arm and carried me down the alley, kicking and screaming. No one was going to come to my rescue, I decided as I disappeared into the shadows. I was a foolish girl a week into living in the city, and I got kidnapped doing the one thing my mother told me not to do. I started to cry, I'm so sorry mom.

I don't remember when I fell asleep, but I awoke to being sprayed with ice-cold water. I screamed, the silk hood stuck to my face, and I had to pull it away from my mouth to breathe. I gasped as the calloused hands of two men lifted me from the floor. I tried to pull free of their grasp, but their grips only tightened on my arms. I felt claws on my left, knowing now that I would not be able to escape. I relaxed in their grip, and they allowed me to stand on my own. A woman removed the hood from my head, she stood in a purple pants suit, her silver hair done up in a tight bun atop her head, a riding crop in her hand.

"Where am I?" I ask.

"Quiet." Her voice was sharp, and she walked around me, eyeing my body. I was painfully aware of my nipples pebbling under my thin sweater that was clinging to my curves. "You did well Mandrake, she will fetch a nice price at auction."

"Auction?" I asked and the slap of the crop against the stone wall made me tense.

"Speak again girl and you will feel the crop. Boys, I want to see her more."

The smaller man grabbed my other arm. He was an orc with soft grey-green skin, his expression unreadable in his dark grey eyes, as he pressed my back against his chest. The other man, Mandrake, was an ogre. His face was marred with a jagged scar, both his hands grabbing the collar of my sweater.

"Please no," I whispered as he ripped open my sweater, exposing my chest to the three of them. He then yanked my skirt down my legs. The woman came before me and ran the crop down my chest between my breasts.

"She is fairly symmetrical, skin unmarred, yes, a nice price for the master indeed. Display her."

"What? No!" I fought the men as the ogre grabbed my ankles, and they carried me to a stone table. Each trades a limb so they held me spread eagle for the woman.

"No, please stop!" I screamed, tears rolling down my face, as she brought the riding crop down on my hip.

"Silence girl, the more you fight me the more you suffer." Tears continued down my face, and she placed a cold hand on my hip, "I know it's scary, but this is what we must do."

She produced a small knife, and I squirmed as she ran the blade under my underwear, slicing through the fabric, exposing my core to the cold air.

"Now child are you on birth control?" I looked down at her, as she pulled on white medical gloves. "Speak child."

"I-I have been taking a pill."

"Good, that will make this easier." She pulled a speculum from underneath the table. "You understand that if you fight me on this, it will be painful."

I closed my eyes, tears streaming over the sides of my face. I nodded, going limp in the men's hold. She did a thorough pelvic exam, and they released me to sit at the edge of the table. The orc bowed to the woman before he spoke.

"Matron, what cuffs do you wish for me to bring?"

The woman looked at me before she responded. "Bring a set of gold ones, they will mark her as a worthy prize for any of our guests."

"Yes ma'am. Do you want me to bring Dolan?"

"Yes, she won't fight us anymore."

"Yes, ma'am."

He exited out the door swiftly, it clicks quietly behind him. The ogre picked up the scraps left of my clothing and added them to the trash bin that the woman had tossed her gloves into. I couldn't get my tears to stop, they trickled down my cheek and dripped onto my exposed thighs. The orc returned, a black case in hand, with a man in his mid-thirties who I could only assume was Dolan. He was dressed in a fine ash-grey suit that washed out his skin and tawny hair. The orc opened the box, and I could see the shining gold cuffs and collar.

I had read about this once, beings sold in the sex trade were often bound to such jewelry, and each establishment had different markers on them to show who they had been bought from. I always found such a practice barbaric, and now I was living it. They all approached me, the orc and ogre placing cuffs on my wrist and ankles. They felt light and delicate, but my soul felt their weight. The matron came before me and lifted my chin, the orc placed the gold collar around my neck. It wasn't tight but sat snugly against my skin.

"A perfect fit as always, Mrak. Dolan?"

The man came in front of me, smiling. "She will definitely fetch a high price at the auction tonight. *Ceanglaim thu ar chach geilleadh. Deanaidh tu fonamh don te lena mbaineann tu gan cheist. Seala me na bannai seo thu go dti go mbeidh do sheirbhis no bas criochnaithe agat.*"[11]

As the spell fell from his lips, his eyes glowed an eerie sickening green, and a fine chain manifested between my ankles, another between my wrists, and a final chain descended between my breasts and connected to the one between my wrists.

"It is done." He said, closing his eyes and standing.

"Mandrake, Mrak take her to the holding cell, the auction is in a few hours. Gag and blind her in preparation."

The men nodded, the ogre taking hold of the fine chain and tugging. A sharp tingle at the back of my neck urged me to follow. We walked down unimpressive halls, and I felt my fight waning. I was trapped here. We came to a cell. Mrak grabbed my chains from Mandrake and walked in with me. From his pocket he pulled a thickly folded black kerchief and a gag that matched the gold bonds I had been adorned with. It was a metal bit, with leather straps, and decorative chains to dangle over my face. He expertly refolded the fabric and tied it around my eyes.

"Don't take it off."

His gravel voice bounced off the walls of the tiny room, thinly veiled with menace. I heard the clink of the fine chain. I pressed against the wall, my heart fluttering in my chest as I sank to the floor.

"Don't fight me with this; it won't make it easier." I feel him loom over me, his knees coming down on either side of my hips. "Now open."

I quivered, and I kept my mouth shut.

---

[11] "I bind you to obedience. You will serve whoever you belong to without question. I seal you to these bonds until you have completed your service or death."

"Don't fight me." He pushed the bit to my lips, but still, I resisted.

"Mandrake, come here and hold the bit in place."

The ogre grunted and heavy footfalls came across the room. I felt them shift, the ogre pressing the bit against my lips. Mrak shifted beneath him, planting his knee between mine and parting them.

"I will give you one last chance, girl. Submit."

I didn't want this, and I refused to try to turn my face away from the onslaught.

"Suit yourself."

Mrak's clawed hands grazed over my skin, making goose bumps crawl across my body. A heavy pit of fear settled in my stomach as his hands grazed over my breast and down my stomach, his fingers sinking through my curls and parting my flesh. I would have tried to flee, but I was beneath the two men. Mrak's claw grazed my clit and I had to fight the urge to vomit as lightning seared through my skin, a fine sweat coming to the surface. I felt Mrak lean close, his breath smelling of moldy grass.

"Submit, girl. I may not be allowed to fuck you, but I will have fun if you continue to resist."

I pushed my hands against his chest, tears coming to my eyes, trapped behind the blindfold. His tongue flicked across my pulse point, and another shot of lightning slammed my body. Hands touched me, fondled my breasts and sought access to my core. I squirmed and fought to push, trying to get them away. Mrak grabbed the fine chain and yanked it to the side.

"Stop resisting." He snarled. I hear the frustration building in his voice.

I bucked underneath him trying to get my feet underneath me. The click of heels down the corridor reached our ears.

"Mrak, what is taking so long?" The matron.

"She won't stop resisting the gag."

"You trying to coerce her?" Her voice was clear as she came to stand at the door.

"Yes, madam."

"Move boys."

They moved away and I pulled my knees to my chest hoping to shelter myself from whatever she was about to do to me.

"It's too late for me to drug you because I have banked tonight on your showing. No one wants a damaged product either, so I can't torture you. What I can do though is throw you to the flairs. They could violate you in ways you cannot comprehend, and I can still sell you tonight."

"No." I cried. Flairs were dangerous creatures that could infiltrate your mind and do things to you without touching a hair.

"Then open your mouth and take the bit like a good girl." I lifted my head and her finger slid under my chin. "Submit child, there is no escaping this fate."

I opened my mouth. What choice did I have anymore? She placed the bit in my mouth and there was a sharp metallic taste to it. She secured the gag behind my head. Then she took my wrists in her hands and tapped them together three times. I felt magic swirl around me.

"There now you won't be able to undo those on your own. I'll be back in an hour to take you to the stage."

"Madam." An unfamiliar voice calls down the hall. "The bitarog is here."

"To buy or sell?"

"He is here to buy."

"Interesting. Who is his hostess?"

"Eloimaya."

"She is braver than most. She will do well. I wonder what drew the beast here." Their footsteps left the room and the door shut. Their muffled voices grew fainter as they went. What was a Bitarog?

Chapter Three

Shasha

Time is an enigma when you cannot see or talk. It is hard to sit with your thoughts that long, remembering all your shortcomings to that point. I mostly thought of my mom and how she would react on Tuesday when I wouldn't be able to call her because I was property. My heart broke for her, over and over again. She would search for me, for a long time at that, and then she would mourn me for even longer.

Footsteps brought me to the now, the door opened, and a hand wrapped around the chain, tugging me to my feet. They led me at an unkind pace, pulling me behind them. They came to a sudden stop, hooking me to a larger chain. I wrapped my hands around it.

"Listen, my pretties." The matron spoke loud and clearly. "You will be pulled onto the stage as a unit and paraded once. If you are purchased, you will be collected by your keeper's hostess after the auction. If you are not purchased, you will be returned to your cell and sorted tomorrow for future auctions or work."

I smelled perfume and heard the giggling of courtesans as they walked past us, and I wondered how long they had been in servitude here. We moved forward roughly, and I almost failed to keep up, only able to make small strides. I felt the heat of the stage lights and wondered how many people sat in the crowd, shopping. We came to a stop and there was a long moment of silence before a light female voice broke the air from the left side of the stage.

"My patron will pay over any bid on the dark-skinned human."

"Oh really?" a voice called from the other side. "And who would your patron be?"

"My patron is Lord Niratap. He wishes to take the mortal now."

There was an eruption of whispers cascading from the audience, based on the matron's quick instruction this was not something that they did. I heard the matron's heels click loudly as she stomped across the stage coming to a stop before me. They were talking about me? The matron disconnected the chains and yanked me behind her.

"May god have mercy on your soul, child." She whispered before pulling me down some stairs and marching in the direction of the voice. "Eloima- Where are your bindings? How?"

"Lord Niratap will also be purchasing out my service." The light melodic voice said.

"Unheard of! He must know that he has broken many rules, the only reason he is getting what he wants is because Dravin is scared of him."

"Then let Dravin be scared."

"I have the mind to tell Niratap to just leave with his purchase."

I heard a curtain shift across the cold stone floor, and the matron gasped, dropping the chains as a deep rumbling growl came from directly in front of us. I felt it travel through my body and vibrate the floor below me. The room went silent, and a deep and menacing voice followed.

"It would be unwise for you to stand in my way, Matron."

"Sh-she is yours." I heard the matron's footsteps as she backed away and quickly fled.

I stood in terror and awe as the creature that had purchased me sniffed my hair. What manner of beast was this lord Niratap? My curiosity had me reaching up to cup a very human-feeling cheek, soft velvet snakes brushing my fingers as I caressed him, a rumble vibrating through my body. His large hands came to rest against my hips before lifting me from the floor and he carried me back behind the curtains. Whispers and quiet laughter filled the auditorium, the threat of bloodshed gone.

"*Is liomsa tu.*" [12] He says, his voice heavy and thick like a warm blanket.

He set me down, and I heard a small groan as he sat, whatever piece of furniture protesting his size. I reached out into the ether before me finding fabric with my fingers. I worked out that it was his leg as my hand came in contact with his knee which came up to just below my navel. He was easily eight feet tall with legs like these. He cleared his throat, pulling me from my thoughts.

"I will remove the gag from your mouth now."

I gave a small nod. His large hands came behind my head and made quick work of the knots there. His fingers touched my chin and I let my jaw relax, the gold bit rolling into his hand. I reached for the blindfold, but he grasped my wrist.

"Not yet." His voice was stern, and I found myself dropping my hands. "I do not wish to scare you more than I have. Drink."

He tapped a glass to my lips and my mouth was coated with a velvety wine. It washed the metal taste from my tongue and warmed my chilled body on the way down.

"What did you say?" I asked, finding courage.

"*Is liomsa tu.*"

"*Is liomsa tu?*"

The light voice spoke from behind me. "It means 'you are mine'."

A shiver ran down my spine and the reality that I was just purchased by a beast rocked my mind. I swayed on my feet, but his hands came to my waist, steadying me. His hands ignited both fire and fear in my belly.

"I wish to look upon you." I said, finding that curiosity again.

"You are a brave little thing, aren't you?" His breath rolled over my shoulder smelling of scotch and wilds.

"Or very foolish."

---

[12] "You are mine."

He chuckled. "Very well."

He untied the kerchief and let it fall to the floor, I stared at it there and took a few steadying breaths as he shifted back against the sofa. He was wearing black dress shoes that looked handmade, his slacks were black with pale pinstripes to make him appear even taller. I let my eyes travel up his form, his jacket matched his slacks, a black shirt beneath it, and a red tie around his neck. The mask greeted me. It was an animal skull, looking like a hybrid of a deer and wolf elongated with sharp teeth. Shadows danced and wavered across the skin that should have been exposed, below the mask, casting him in darkness. His hair was long and black coming down well past his shoulders. Grey—no, silver eyes glowed from behind the animal mask, serene but searching my face. Large nine-point antlers came from the top of his head. Those alone made him over my eight-foot guess.

"You impress me. Any other would run from the sight of me if they were wise."

There was something about him that hypnotized me, even though my heart was beating like a rabbit's. "Like I said, very foolish."

"May I?" He asked, bringing a hand close to me, but not touching me.

"You may." I swallowed, the words jumping from my throat before I could process what he was asking. His hand went to my side and ran up my ribs causing my heart to pound even more fervently. Then it traveled down over my hip causing warmth to seep into my core. He scented the air and a rumble resonated through us. His hand went to my ass, cupping the softness there and pulling me to him. My hands fell to his thighs, the rumble intensifying as his other hand cupped one of my breasts. His long-clawed fingers teased my nipple.

The elvish woman cleared her throat. "My Lord, we should be off soon."

"Right, right." He closed his eyes a moment, before taking the slim gold chain that dangled from my collar in his hand. "I hate seeing you like this. *Titeann na bannaí seo ar shiúl. Níl tú faoi cheangal ach domsa.*"[13]

The cuffs on my ankles and wrist fell away, leaving the collar around my neck and the thin chain wrapped around his hand. At that moment I was not afraid, I was mesmerized by this creature, who had claimed me as his own. He finished the last swallow of wine in the glass on the table before standing. He was indeed easily eight feet, and at least nine with his antlers. His stomach was level with my face, and I looked up at him, wishing I could read his face through the shadows beyond the mask.

"How tall are you?"

"I am eight foot four from foot to top, ten feet with the antlers last I checked. At least in this form." He tugged the chain up, so I had to stand on my tiptoes. "I'm sorry, but I have nothing to cover you with."

I had forgotten.

---

[13] "…these bonds fall away. you are only bound to me."

Chapter Four

Niratap

Her scent, both floral and honeyed, wild and calming, was clouding my judgment. She brought primal needs out from places where I had long since locked them away. I wanted her, in all senses of the word. Her voice was musical, and small like she was. Shy, but she seemed to be fascinated by me. Her eyes, an intense mocha color, met mine with no fear.

"You impress me. Any other would run from the sight of me if they were wise."

"Like I said, very foolish."

I needed to touch her. I reached out and hesitated. "May I?"

She does not pull away. "You may."

I placed my hand on her side running it up along her ribs, her skin was soft rich cashmere under my fingers. She was cold. I ran my hand back down, trying to cap my raging emotions. A heady summery scent hit me. My hand went behind her, cupping her full ass and bringing her toward me. Her hands fell to the top of my thighs, a rumbling building in my chest. My other hand traveled up her chest to palm her full breast, her head lulled back, and I could feel my restraint waning.

Eloimaya cleared her throat. "My Lord we should be off soon."

I closed my eyes trying to center myself, taking the fine chain in my hand and wrapping it around my fingers, "Right, right. I hate seeing you like this. *titeann na bannaí seo ar shiúl. níl tú faoi cheangal ach domsa.*" [14]

The cuffs fell from her ankles and wrists, her gaze never leaving my face. I wondered if she could see me

[14] "…these bonds fall away. you are only bound to me."

beyond the shadows and smoke. I finished off the glass of wine and stood. Her body was pressed to me, her gaze both soft and piercing as she stared up at me.

"How tall are you?"

"I am eight foot four from foot to top, ten feet with the antlers last I checked at least in this form." She was curious about me and that tangled my thoughts more. I tugged the chain upwards, watching as she shifted to her toes, breasts swaying with the motion. "I'm sorry, but I have nothing to cover you with."

Her full lips parted, almost like she had forgotten. It was a delicious sight and my body responded to her in ways I didn't know were possible. It was the first time in a long time that I had felt excitement. And fear.

"You will have to lead her out of the lounge my Lord." Eloimaya said. "There is no way to cover your purchase. She will have to follow behind you."

The rumble in my chest returned. I did not want to parade her through the market, though I realized that was exactly what I would have to do to take her to safety. I bent down and grabbed the kerchief from the floor. She stiffened as I crouched before her, the fabric in my hand.

"Please, no." Her voice was so small, fear staining her scent with copper.

"No harm will befall you in my company. You have my word *blath milis.* [15] However, blindness in the dark will protect you from fear and shame."

She looked down, nodding. Trusting me to keep her safe. A single tear rolled over her cheek as I tied the kerchief behind her head. An ache settled in my chest at the sight of her and then rage surfaced because I knew she had suffered. I did not know for how long, but she had suffered. I lifted the mask from my face and kissed the tear away.

"I will protect you in the darkness." I said, meaning it with all my being. "Eloimaya, I am ready. Lead the way."

[15]"...sweet flower."

"Yes, my Lord." She gave a bow, slipped on her heels, opened the curtain, and headed back the way we had come. I could feel the eyes watching us from those who still inhabited their booths. My skin crawled at the invasion. Once through the auction lounge door, three men blocked the exit, and instinctively I pushed the girl behind me. One of them was the older man who had come onstage to announce the auction, to his left was an orc who gave me a small nod, and to his right an ogre who gave nothing. My beast hissed under my skin, writhing for justice.

"Lord Niratap." He extended a gold-clad hand. He smelled of Cuban cigars and fear. "Dravin Cirano, but you may also know me as Fat Cat. It's a pleasure."

I didn't take his hand, my irritation growing. "I doubt that sincerely. I can smell your fear, so this pitiful attempt to show respect isn't going to work. I have paid for my purchases and am leaving. Whether you live another day or not will entirely depend on how quickly you get out of my way."

The man's hand fell, and he and his cronies moved out of the way. As we passed, he said. "You realize you have made enemies today in the underground."

"The underground has always been my enemy." I responded, exiting through the door.

The sun was starting to rise, and the market had gone quiet. I reached into my pocket and retrieved my cellular phone, calling Allipo, my house manager. Eloimaya stood beside me, a smile warming her face.

"It has been so long since I stood under the sun." She whispered.

"My Lord."

"Allipo, bring the car to the entry of the market."

"Right away. Did you find any treasures, my Lord?"

I looked over my shoulders at my new beauty. "The most amazing treasure I have ever found."

I lead the girls down the alleyway to the entrance, Allipo already standing at the door waiting for me. His soft honey eyes widened at the sight of the girls, a soft smile gracing his features before he bowed. Allipo, a satyr, dressed sharply in a teal suit and tie; he always insisted that color made him easier to approach. His black ram horns nested in his salt and pepper curls atop his head.

"My Lord."

"Allipo, Eloimaya will sit with you in the front. I have freed her from her servitude, and she can decide whether she wanted to stay or leave on the drive."

"Yes, my Lord." He opened the passenger door for Eloimaya. "My dear."

She walked to the car and turned before climbing in to bow to me. "Thank you, my Lord."

"Say less, my dear, you have a decision to make."

When she was situated, Allipo shut the door and turned to me, tilting his horned head at the girl. "She is quite lovely, my Lord."

My urge to protect her from sight rose, but Allipo went to the trunk and returned with a warm grey cloak. Passing me without fear, he draped the cloak over her shoulders, fastening the front with the manor moniker pin. His hands cupped her face, placing a sweet kiss on her forehead.

"You are safe now, sweetling." He said before returning to the car to open my door and bowed again. "My Lord."

"Thank you, Allipo," I said, climbing into the vehicle. Allipo aided her in behind me, before shutting the door. The privacy window was already closed.

She stood before me, her hand finding my knee to guide her to me. The cloak parted and gave me a secret view of her soft clay curves. Curves that I would love to explore. I reached forward and untied the kerchief again. She blinked against the sunlight. When the car began to move and she fell against me, I made no move, not knowing if I could control myself.

"Who is Allipo?" She asked, kneeling before me, her eyes finally finding my face.

I felt like I was looking at prey when I looked at her like this; my eyes shifted to look out the window. "He is my house manager for the manor. He keeps me and my affairs in order and takes care of our home."

"Is that where you are taking me?"

"Yes." She sniffled and my eyes flew to her face, tears falling as she choked on small sobs. "Why do you cry?"

She tried to wipe the bubbling tears away but sobbed even harder. "It's been a rough few days and I am overwhelmed. I am ashamed. I am scared. I don't know where I am. I don't know where I'm going. I don't even know what day it is."

"I am sorry that this was the road you have had to walk. You are in Boston. We are going up to my manor in the Appalachian Mountains. Today is," I checked my watch to make sure I gave her the right day, "Monday. Now come sit beside me. You need not kneel before me."

"What are your intentions, my Lord?"

What were my intentions? I had had a singleness of mind in finding her and now that she was here, I did not know what was next. I wanted to feel her. I wanted to devour her. I wanted to know her. I wanted her to want for nothing. I just wanted her to intrude on all aspects of me. It was a strange and unusual feeling.

"I do not know." I answered honestly.

She shifted then, hopping up to sit beside me, scooting close to shoo off the cold. I leaned forward and adjusted the dials and vents to blast us with hot air. She sighed as it warmed the cabin. I leaned back and wrapped an arm around her.

"Thank you." Her voice sounded tired.

"You are welcome."

"My Lord," Allipo's voice came through the intercom, "do you need me to grab anything before we head out of the city?"

"I am fine. Do you need anything, my dear?" I asked the girl.

"I am hungry, and some clothes would be nice."

My face heated as I turned away. "Get her what she needs, and we can be off."

"Right away, my Lord."

In the time between then and when we entered a shopping district, she had fallen asleep. The car came to a stop in a parking garage turning off, and I heard both of the doors open and close as Eloimaya and Allipo left the vehicle. Walking away into what I could only assume was a shopping center. I shifted, shrugging out of my jacket and draping it over her small form beside me. She mumbled a small thank you. I relaxed a little, loosening my tie and letting the weight of the night roll off my shoulders. My eyes fluttered closed and I fell into a light sleep.

Chapter Five

Shasha

I opened my eyes, finally warm after so many days of being anything but. I was nestled against someone, his heart a slow, but steady thud in my ear as he slumbered beside me. I looked up at his face, the mask still in place and darkness behind it. I wondered what was beyond the mask he wore. I sat up, his suit jacket sliding onto the seat. Had he placed it on me to keep me warm? I stood stretching, looking at his sleeping form, the form of my new life. The tension of an animal ready to strike was gone while he slept; like he had relaxed next to me. I did not understand what manner of beast he was, but I knew I had no way of escaping this fate either. I wondered if he would let me call my mom. If he would let me go to school.

They were questions I would have to ask, but for now, I was mesmerized by him. His tie was loosened and the top button of his shirt undone, the shadows that rested there shifting only when he breathed. Was he just a shadow, or was there a being beneath them? I stepped forward putting myself between his legs again. I reached up, my hand coming close to his face. His eyes snapped open, and he pinned me to the floor beneath him, his movement so quick he knocked the wind from my lungs. A feral snarl resonated between us as I lay there, his mask looming over my face. One hand had captured both mine and had pinned them above my head, exposing my flesh to him. Heat and fear bubbled through my body.

He scowled and then his eyes softened. Bringing his face down beside mine, he breathed "Very foolish is what you said, correct?"

His voice tangled my thoughts. "Correct."

He purred in my ear. "It's very dangerous to approach an animal while it sleeps."

"My Lord, I did not know." His free hand came to my side stroking me, tangling my thoughts even more.

"My sweet flower." His tongue swept my pulse, making my heart pound, a gasp escaping my lips. A possessive growl rumbled through his chest. I felt hot and excited at his touch. How did he have this influence over me? "What is your name?"

"Hmm?"

His fangs grazed my shoulder, his breath hot across my skin. "Your name? I wish to call you by it."

"Shasha. My name is Shasha."

His voice was gravelly. "Shasha."

"My Lord." I gasped as he nipped at my collarbone. "I wish to know your name."

He paused, coming to look at my face, eyes searching. He released my hands, pulling me to my feet, and the movement made me lightheaded. He was kneeling in front of me, and we are face to face. He tugged gently on the thin gold chain dangling from the collar around my neck and it disappeared with only the collar remaining. Then he spoke.

"I go by the name Niratap. In public and when talking to those who serve me; you may address me as my Lord or Lord Niratap. In the privacy of home, you may call me Nira."

"Not master?" I questioned.

He growled. "No. Never master."

"Nira." My hand extended. I hesitated before I touched him. "May I?"

"You may." He purred.

I let my palm come to rest against his jaw, the shadows dancing around my finger, a kiss of softness. He had a defined jaw; I could feel his pulse beneath my fingers. I ran my hand back into his hair, the silky strands slipping through my fingers.

"May I see your face?"

His eyes narrowed, grabbing my wrist. "Not today. You have seen enough terror of late."

My brows furrowed and I was disappointed. "Alright. Nira, you never did tell me what your intentions are for me."

"I honestly had no intentions to be in Nocturnal last night, but your scent is unusual, and I had to have you for myself. It pulled me in through the grime of the alley. To be plain with you." He said, shifting back onto the seat. "I want to understand why you smell so delectable and why that makes me want you."

I swallowed, heat pooling in my core. "You want me?"

He swallowed. "Yes, in more ways than we both expect."

I had never been told I was wanted before, I stood on my tiptoes getting close to his face. I was interrupted by a knock on the window of the door. I could have sworn I saw him scowl at the door, before he spoke.

"Spying, Allipo?"

The door opened and a satyr stood in a deep bow. He was nicely dressed, in a teal-colored suit.

"No, my Lord. Eloimaya and I have returned. My dear, we have brought clothes for you and some food for you both. It is a long drive up into the mountains." His voice took on a mischievous edge. "I'm sure the lord will show you the best sides of him on the drive."

"Allipo." A warning in his tone.

"My apologies, my Lord. Here are the things Eloimaya thinks will be best suited for now and your food."

He placed a large bag from a designer store on the floor of the car and another two bags, as well. I could smell a cheeseburger and my eyes found the brown paper bag.

"Thank you," I said, reaching for the paper bag that had to hold a cheeseburger.

"My pleasure, dear. Will there be anything else, my Lord?" The satyr asked with a polite smile on his face.

"Thank you, Allipo, and no. Let us head for home."

The satyr bowed deeply. "As you wish."

Chapter Six

Allipo shut the door, I had had in mind to wipe that smug smile off the satyr's face, but Shasha had already dived toward the bag of food, hungrily digging for the cheeseburgers I could smell. I would give modern mortal food that, it was tasty. She pulled the sandwich out of the bag and unwrapped it, taking a large happy bite. I smiled. It was nice to see her happy.

I reached in one of the bags, pulled out a bottle of water, and opened it for her. She looked up at me as I held out the water.

"Thank you." She said through a mouthful of food.

I sat back, crossing my legs, watching her. How had such a beautiful girl fallen into the market? My hand tightened into a fist, realizing that she was an innocent human who was probably taken from the street unawares. If I ever found out who took her into my world, I would personally skin them alive. A gentle hand rested against my fist; Shasha stood next to me with concern on her face.

"Is there something wrong?" Her voice was soft.

I relaxed. "Nothing you need to worry yourself with."

"You seemed upset by something. I wanted to make sure that you were okay."

Her concern for me was something I did not expect, especially after how we had come into each other's lives. I placed my hand on her cheek. "Really, my dear, I am fine. No need to fret."

She frowned but offered me the paper bag she had dug the burger from. "There's a burger for you too."

"Thank you," I said, taking the bag.

She went over to the other bag, getting the hang of walking while the car was in motion. She brought it over to where I sat and plopped down on the floor in front me, while she went through the bag. She pulled out some olive sweat shorts, a pair of simple panties, a black tank top, and a grey hoodie. She stood looking over her shoulder at me sheepishly, before snatching up the panties and slipping them on. My gaze was blocked by the cloak. The shorts came next easily going on. She was still for a moment, before she turned to me, the cloak parted, giving me a delicious peek at her breasts.

"Will you help me? I can't get the pin free."

I reached for the pin, tugging her by the cloak into me, the friction not helping the dark turn of my thoughts, "The clasps on these are always sticky."

The pin released and the cloak glided off her shoulders, exposing her to me. In the light her skin glimmered, as if golden stars danced under her skin. The olive shorts hugged her curves well; they sat low on her body. Her arms came to her chest, and I realized I was staring. I quickly looked out the window, the city traded for farms.

"My apologies, I didn't mean to make you uncomfortable."

Her cheeks turned rosy, and she looked away. "It's not that you make me uncomfortable, I just don't know what my future looks like anymore, and when you look at me like that, it makes me think I'm dinner."

"I don't plan on actually eating you if that is what you fear. I have long since left the practice of consuming humans." I said, turning towards her again. She tensed at my words.

"Meaning you used to." It wasn't a question, but I felt compelled to explain.

"It was a long time ago; it was necessary for my survival."

Concern knitted her brows together. "It should never have to come to that."

"I agree, but it's not always that simple."

My heart hurt, I knew she didn't understand or even know what I had gone through. The torture. The pain. The suffering I had felt at the hands of man. Maybe someday she would, but she would have to trust me first. Even though I had saved her from much crueler fates, I had still purchased her, and despite my lack of intentions, she had no reason to trust me. I looked back out the window at the yellow fields of wheat and green fields of corn, as she finished dressing and sat beside me looking out the opposite window. I didn't know what was going to come of this, many things weighed on my heart and mind. I did know that she was mine; I had no intention of letting her go. I knew that I would sacrifice more than I already had to keep her, but I didn't know why.

Chapter Seven

Shasha

It was unnerving, the silence that sat between us. Did I offend him with what I said earlier? That hadn't been my intention, but the way he had looked away so forlorn caused my chest to ache. I shouldn't feel this way about my purchaser, but something in his voice makes me want to. Something in him that sounds sad and melancholic. He glanced at his watch before pushing a button.

"Allipo, are we going to make it to the manor before dark?"

"Yes, my Lord. We will arrive at the manor, barring any delays in the woods, thirty minutes before sunset."

"Thank you, Allipo."

"Why do we need to be at the manor before dark?" I asked both curious and concerned.

"The woods around the manor are filled with creatures that I have purchased to protect them from scalpers on the black market. Most of the creatures are harmless, but there are some that can be quite troublesome to run into if we are in the woods at night."

"Like-like what exactly?"

He pondered my question, "There are a few basilisks, a jorogumo, and a chimera to name a few. The basilisks are the most troublesome and like to hunt on the road to the manor."

"How many is a few?"

He considered momentarily. "Six."

"Six." My stomach turned. "Why so many?"

"Basilisks are notoriously rare, but they pose a severe threat to humans as well as other beings. They are harvested on the black market for their venom, which is often weaponized. However, they were mostly hunted out about a century ago. Two of the basilisks that are in my care are old-world, meaning they were captured before the mass execution. The other four are new world basilisks, meaning that they were hatched after the mass execution and under a hundred years old. Which makes them more unpredictable."

"I knew that basilisks were near extinction, but I didn't realize that they were such a common problem."

"They're not. Basilisks are not social creatures, and their natural habitat is usually very far from humans. The fact that there are so few left in the world should put people at ease. Dangerous yes, but not directly dangerous if they are left alone. However, they regenerate and those who wish to profit use that fact and harvest their fangs knowing that they will grow back in time. Basilisk fangs carry the world's most potent venom, and it has often been used to rewrite the way the world works, at least politically, and subdue creatures."

"Don't they reproduce? Having six would make me think you would have more secretly running around?"

"Sadly no. All of the basilisks that are in my care are male. females are hard to find even in the wild. They slumber for large quantities of time and only wake for a meal and to lay eggs."

I pondered that and looked back out the window. "How do you keep the creatures in the wild and not roaming the manor?"

He made a sound kind of like a laugh. I turned, and he leaned in close to me, almost looming over me. His shadows crawled and lifted from his body. "My dear you are looking at the scariest creature in the forest."

I swallowed, fear twisting my gut and making me freeze. The vehicle lurched and came to a stop. He turned from me and pressed the intercom button.

"Allipo, what is the meaning of this?"

"My apologies, my Lord, there will be a delay."

"What kind of delay?" He asked with a growl.

"The human kind, my Lord."

"Handle it quickly, Allipo."

"Of course, my Lord."

Niratap sighed leaning back into the seat. I asked. "What does he mean by the human kind of delay?"

"The sheriff of the area closest to the manor likes to try to make my business his business. He's not a threat, just an annoyance."

A figure looked through the window at us, and Niratap raised his hand in an annoyed greeting. The man tapped the glass, pointing a finger at me, then motioned for the window to go down. Shadows slithered across the floor, and I had a feeling this interaction would not go well for the man, still Niratap compiled by rolling the window down.

"Beast, what are you doing with the girl?" My skin crawled at the roughness of his voice.

"That is none of your concern, Rodger."

"Everything that happens in this community is my concern. Now answer the question." The sheriff, Rodger, was a man in his forties who looked worse for wear. He had sun-tanned skin with deep wrinkles and a bushy lampshade mustache. His eyes were hidden behind mirrored sunglasses.

"She has recently come into my care, and you would do well to let us continue our journey home." There was a growl forming in the words.

"Girl, are you in danger? Please exit the vehicle, and I can get you somewhere safe."

I stared at this man I did not know and pondered whether or not I was safe. If I went with him, I would still be bound to Niratap, a collar still marked me as property, and if I was seen on the street I would no doubt be dragged back to Nocturnal and sold again. "No thank you."

The man seemed taken aback and blinked several times before continuing. "You can't seriously mean you are in the vehicle willingly."

"Is that so surprising, Rodger?"

"Please, child." The man reached a hand toward me, oblivious to the threat to his life as his arm extended beyond Niratap's face. "Come with me."

"Sheriff." Allipo spoke from outside of the vehicle. "I would ask that you leave the lord and his charge alone."

"Satyr, I will do as I deem fit. This young girl is obviously in danger."

"Sheriff, the only being truly in danger is you." Allipo cautioned.

"Is that a threat?"

A hiss resonated in the cabin as Niratap spoke. "It is a promise."

The man wrenched his hand from the car quickly. He looked from Niratap, who was looking forward to where the sheriff's hand had been. I gave him the most convincing smile I could, scooting closer to Niratap. I made an obvious show of setting my hand on his thigh. Niratap didn't flinch, but I could feel him coiling like a viper under my touch, his muscles hard and primed.

"Sheriff." I said in my sweetest voice. "I appreciate your concern, but I am completely comfortable with where I am at. Thank you again, but we would like to return home before dark."

"But miss." He pleaded and Niratap clenched his fist.

"Really, I am perfectly fine. Lord Niratap has shown me nothing but kindness."

Niratap looked at me then. Though fleeting, he seemed shocked by my words. I was, too, but besides staring and pinning me beneath him he had been apologetic and kind.

The sheriff took a step away. "Well then, I-I guess I'll let you be off then."

"Thank you, sheriff. Good day." Allipo said, climbing back into the car as the sheriff walked back to his cruiser.

Niratap rolled up the window, then the cabin became encased in shadow, and in the darkness, I only saw Niratap's glowing eyes. I closed my own eyes preferring the darkness to the intensity of his gaze. His breath danced across my throat, and I resisted the urge to scream. His tongue, long and wet, came across my pulse point.

"You amaze me." His voice was raspy and breathy.

"H-How so?"

"No being has ever come to my defense."

"People fear what they don't understand."

Clawed hands came to my waist slipping underneath my hoodie. "Ah, yes, but you are afraid of me now. Yet you do nothing. You refuse to scream. You refuse to run."

His hands pushed the hoodie up, claws sending tingling electricity through my body. "Yes, I am scared. Like all beings I'm scared of the unknown."

"I am definitely an unknown." His hands went to my back, claws caressing my spine.

"Yes." I gasped as his teeth grazed against my throat. "But you do much more than scare me."

"Do I now?"

He pulled me forward and my hands came to his chest, covered in soft velvety silken fur, much like the hair on his head. I ran my fingers through the soft fur, making him purr.

"Yes." It came out like a moan, his hands lifting me into what I assumed was his lap, the friction delicious against my core. I brought my hand to my mouth, trying to sequester the sound. His hands traveled back up my spine, he was warm and so soft.

"Please tell me." He cooed, before he lapped and suckled my neck.

I pushed against him trying to create space for myself to think. The words poured out of me. "You fascinate me. What manner of creature are you? What are your abilities? Are you fae or something else? How old are you? How did you become a lord?"

He pulled back the shadows receding into him, "That is quite a few questions, many of which you will probably not like the answer to. If I am honest."

He adjusted, setting me back on the seat, and fixing my clothes as he did. A gentle hand came to my cheek, and back in place were his dark suit and the mask.

"Would you lie to me?"

He sat beside me, and it almost looked as if he pondered the question before he spoke. "Yes."

"Why?"

"Because there is darkness not made for the world of men."

Chapter Eight

Niratap

She did not like my answer. It was plain as day on her face, even though I had not outright lied to her. I had omitted aspects of the truth, which in all the wisdom I had gathered was the same as lying. I had the unyielding desire to tell her everything, but truths about me, about my life, put her in danger. Hell, the way I purchased her had put a target on her, and I undoubtedly made more enemies.

She turned from me staring out at the forest, a pang of sadness evident in the air between us. I wished I had words to soothe her, but I do not. Of all the things in the world she should want to know about, she chose me. Sharing things about myself, even my species had for as long as I could remember spelled danger.

"So will you tell me nothing then?" Her voice was almost a whisper.

I stared at her before I said. "Even if I lied?"

She turned to look at me, shock glistening in her eyes, "I-It would be better than the silence."

"You would rather fill the silence with lies."

"No, that is not what I meant." She was frustrated, and it made me think she hadn't interacted with other beings much.

"You have to be specific, my dear. There are many beings that exist in this world that will twist what you say, to suit their needs."

"Are you one of those beings?"

"I can be." It was the truth, especially if my survival depended on it. If her survival depended on it.

"How does one earn your trust not to be lied to?"

How odd a question. "Time."

"So simple an answer for something so complex."

"Yes. I've survived as long as I have being this way."

"But how many of your staff do you own?"

She was trying to paint me in a way I did not like, "I may be a beast, but I am no monster. To answer your question, none. Those who serve me do it because they wish to. I compensate them financially and offer protection."

"Then why purchase a human? What is to be my purpose? Even though you have been kind to me and saved me from a much worse fate I am still bound to you as property." She pulled at the collar around her throat.

"I will ponder a purpose for you if that is what you wish." The vehicle slowed. I glanced out the window to see where in the woods we were. Not quite to the manor, I reached for the intercom, but Allipo's voice broke the silence.

"My Lord, the fae have a question they wish to ask you."

"Of course." I magicked the chain into my palm and looked at her putting as much intensity into my gaze as I could, pulling her to me. "Stay close, stay silent."

She looked like she was about to protest, grabbing the chain, but when she met my gaze, her hands fell to her sides before she scooted closer to me. I took a steadying breath before I rolled down the windows. A smell akin to spring meadow dew and freshly bloomed roses filled the cabin. A lithe woman appeared in the seat across from us, she was wrapped in a dress of woven spring grass, gossamer wings tucked tightly against her back. Her face was pleasant, but ethereal bright over-sized blue eyes greeted my own.

"Windflower? What do I owe the pleasure?"

"There have been whispers in the wind that the one of shadow has rescued a sister and a delectable prize from the underground."

My hand tightened on the chain at her words. "I have."

"Eloimaya has chosen to continue to serve you as thanks for saving her."

"If that is her decision you know she will be well taken care of in my home."

"Yes, yes." She waved a dismissive hand at me. "We are more interested in the one who smells of all the flowers of the seasons. The one who is rose and peony, sunflower and lavender, oak and burr, yew and holly."

"Yes, yes, yes." Cheery voices echoed from outside the car, and Shasha pressed herself to me. Time had taught me that her fear was valid.

"She is mine."

"Come now, shadow in the night, let the one of flowers come play with us."

"No." Shasha flinched at the volume, but I wanted them to know not to cross me. "She is mine. She is not a new toy for anyone."

Windflower appeared in my face. "Very well, the darkest part of the forest, don't let her wander or she may run wild with us."

"My senses are keen creature; you would be wise to mind the fence."

She scowled, kissing me on the forehead before she vanished, a strong spring wind carrying her scent away, and the smell of moss and heat returned. I relaxed letting the chain slide from my hand and disappear again, there was a tight feeling in my chest as she scooted back across the seat. What a strange sensation, I rubbed my sternum to try and ease the feeling. Shasha was shaking, fear evident on her face. How was she more scared of a faery than me?

"The fae are wily creatures, but they should leave you alone now."

"Should?"

"Yes, all threats aside, they may try to trick you. So, it is best that you keep your guard around all fae creatures, even those among my staff."

"Like Allipo?"

I sighed. "Especially Allipo. Damned Satyr is chaos incarnate."

"But he runs your house?"

"He does, but that does not mean he doesn't make other aspects of my life difficult. He takes his job seriously, our friendship not so much."

She smiled at my exasperation, "Understood Nira."

I liked my name on her tongue, I wondered what her kiss would taste like. "Have you ever interacted with fae creatures before today?"

She glanced back out the window. "That is a personal question and since you refuse to answer my questions of you, it is only fair that I refuse to answer."

I narrowed my eyes. "A trade then?"

She smiled sweetly. "A question for a question?"

I held out my hand. "Deal."

She shook my hand, sealing it, and I hoped I would not regret this.

"The town that I grew up in is very small and there weren't very many creatures or fae families in the area. We had some house fae at most and a family of dwarfs, and everyone else in town was human. So, to answer your question, no I have not been around wild fae ever."

"They are more difficult than house fae that is for sure."

She peeked at me through her lashes. "What manner of creature are you?"

I sighed. "I am a bitarog. We are an ancient monstrosity. Much like the basilisk, we were hunted to near extinction. However, our numbers are far less than that of the basilisk and of those of us that remain, half are feral, and the other half are similar to myself or being held in captivity. What was your family like?"

"Small. My dad left my mom when I was very little, so for the vast majority of my life, it's just been the two of us. How did you become a lord?"

"Time and violence. What is your mother like?"

"That's not really an answer, but I'll leave it for now. She's a mom, she has worked as an accountant for the farms in my hometown my whole life and at the Post Office. She's kind of a helicopter mom, and we had many fights about me moving away, but I needed to get out of my small town. I wouldn't be in this situation had I listened to her. Would it be possible to call her?"

"Yes, we can arrange that. Do you regret coming to the city?"

"No, I regret not listening to my mother about going out at night alone. I made it one whole week before screwing everything up. Do you regret being a lord?"

What a question, "Yes and no. I enjoy the freedom that it has given me. However, having status has just as many risks as being wild. What brought you to the city in the first place?"

"Neon. School was the reason my mom let me go. NYU was my ticket to freedom. Was your life hard before you were a lord?"

"Yes. What are you majoring in?"

She blushed. "Monsters and Mythology, but now it seemed like it was a waste. Were you treated badly before?"

"Exceedingly." I got the sense that she was not happy with my short answers, but I was not ready to expose the trauma that had been my life. "We could arrange something, so you could continue your studies."

"You would let me continue going to school?"

"Education is a cornerstone of society, though the field you have chosen can be dangerous. I find it interesting. Though I don't like the idea of making your commute, it's nearly a two-hour drive. I have a connection at NYU who I can contact. I can do that in the morning if that is what you wish."

"I would like that very much."

The vehicle slowed again. "We are home now."

Chapter Nine

Shasha

I peeked out the window and was greeted by the opening of an iron gate. As we pulled up the drive, the forest gave way to lush long grasses full of wildflowers. A full garden composed of all sorts of flowers. The manor was a three-story slate grey building with a large fountain, almost three dozen windows, and large stone steps leading up to large red double doors.

"This place is beautiful."

"Thank you. You may have free access to the grounds during the day as well as the manor with the exception of the back garden and the aviary. The woods and basement levels are strictly off limits."

"Why?"

"Because even in the safety of my home, there are still dangers."

"I find it interesting that it is our home when it's safe and yours when it's not."

He fisted my hair pulling my head back to look him in the eye, his voice a snarl. "You will obey my rules."

I wished I wasn't afraid, but I was. His breath was hot on my face. I didn't know him well enough to spout off, but I wanted to. Instead, I submitted. "Fine."

He growled but released me. "Dinner is served around sunset every night. It is expected that you eat with the rest of us, but not required if you do not feel comfortable. It is required that you respect my staff; they work hard, harder than they must for me. They come from places similar to that which I found you, so be kind."

The car came to a stop, two elf women came down the stairs. Going to the back of the car as Allipo came to my door, opening it with a bow, offering a hand.

"Welcome home, my dear."

I took it and let Allipo lead me out of the car. Nira got out of the other side unassisted, a distant look in his eyes. Looking back at the marvelous house, I saw a line had been formed by different creatures to welcome us. Allipo led me up the line, introducing all of them. There were the two elven women: Katrel who had chestnut hair and dark copper eyes set in golden brown skin; she was dressed in a cream-colored tunic and tan pants, and Tummilia whose hair resembled warm wheat fields and her eyes a tumultuous deep blue cradled in porcelain skin, she wore an elegant periwinkle gossamer gown that flowed to just above her ankles. The sisters stood at the bottom, and they were part of the cleaning staff for the manor. Next was a beautiful woman with long black hair braided on either side of her face, clay-colored skin with freckles dotting her cheeks with brown eyes so dark they were practically black, a selkie named Dorilody Stormswind was the head housekeeper.

Then an orc man, Durgash Day, who was almost as tall as the lord with thick arms of corded muscles and a round belly. He was dressed in blue and white striped shorts and a rough-hewn tunic covered by a white apron with various stubborn stains. The sides of his head were shaved, and the rest of his dark hair was in locks and tied back in a high tail. His eyes were a steely grey set deep in his dark grey skin, which was only disrupted by thin scars here and there, red tribal tattoos wrapped around his arms and neck. An orc woman, Rogmesh Day, Durgash's wife was about a foot shorter than her husband and just as muscled. She had long hair twisted into hundreds of tiny braids down her back, she had a friendly smile that shone in her starlight-colored eyes, it pinched at the cross-shaped scar on her cheek. Her skin was a warm shade of dark green covered in similar red tribal tattoos, she was dressed in dark color pants that were caked in flour and a cream-colored shirt. They were the kitchen staff, and I was informed that their son also worked for Lord Niratap, but he was away. Echo Wildmoon, a lithe fae woman, had pale grass green skin that shimmered in the light and large iridescent pearl eyes, her dragonfly-like wings folded delicately behind her over the flowy white top and dark green pants she wore. She was the gardener and gave me a gentle bow as we passed. A faun Dheg Podzol was the groundskeeper, he had long goat-like legs, suntanned skin, bright goldenrod eyes, and warm brown hair that had a copper sheen to it. Two horns poked through the wavy shoulder-length hair that he had pulled back in a bun atop his head and two smaller horns poked out above his brows. He was dressed in a pink paisley shirt and long dark blue shorts that had mud caked on the knees, work gloves poking out of the pockets.

Lastly, a woman, Mitta Rask, a Rakshasi, the head of security, dressed in dark leather pants and a plain white tunic belted at her center. She had a sharp angled face that was the shade of the warm sand of beaches that you could always find in calendars. Dark, rich umber hair was woven tightly in a braid and equally dark eyes were sharp and seemed to scan everything wildly. Each of them bowed and said hello to Eloimaya and me. When I was at the top of the stairs all of them turned and bowed to Niratap, who had waited for introductions to conclude.

"Welcome home, my Lord." They all said in unison.

"It is good to be home." The frustration was gone from his voice, but it still showed in his rigid shoulders. "Durgash, Rogmesh what have you prepared for dinner this evening?"

"We have prepared a pork stew." Rogmesh said excitedly.

"We had many fine veggies today from Echo's garden." Durgash spoke.

"We also have a fine herb crusty bread." Rogmesh added.

"And we made your favorite dessert." Durgash said.

"Sounds like a fabulous meal." Niratap said. "Allipo, will you get Shasha settled in her room, the ochre suite. I'm going to freshen up and we can eat."

"Yes, my Lord." Allipo bowed and led me into the manor, Eloimaya following close behind, bags in hand.

The foyer was bright, the crystal chandeliers bouncing the golden light from the sunset. A grand staircase leads up to the second floor, it's wood a warm mahogany that matched the floor under my feet.

"Marvelous, isn't it?" Allipo asked.

"Yes."

"I'm sure the lord will give you the grand tour, but the dining room is in the east wing, off the base of the stairs."

I nodded as we headed up the steps and down one of the long halls.

"I hope you find the room hospitable for you, the ochre room is one of my favorite rooms in the house."

"How are the rooms named in the manor?" Eloimaya spoke from behind me.

Allipo smiled wistfully. "Painstakingly by myself. I matched each room with a true-to-history color, with safer paint of course. Then decorated the room to fit each color scheme."

"Fascinating."

"I know. Ochre is a color that- "

I smiled, I didn't understand the importance of color, but the way Allipo spoke made me warm inside. He was passionate about color-scaping, and interior design. He chatted happily with Eloimaya about some of the finer classical pieces he had acquired for the manor and more about what colors complimented each room. I just admired the pale blue walls of the corridor and the fine ornate vases we passed.

"Here we are, my dear."

Allipo opened the door to a warm yellow room with black and teal accents and dark wood furniture. The room was very pleasing to the eye. Everything from the gossamer-hung canopy bed to the plush sitting chairs by the fireplace was beautiful and far more decedent than I was used to.

"Are you sure this is the room?" I asked, overcome with the luxury.

"The ochre suite, per his lordship's request."

"This is too much."

"Do you not like the suite, my dear?" Allipo's ever-present smile faded.

"I love it, but it is way too much for me."

"I assure you Miss Shasha this is where the lord wants you to be. You are more than deserving, especially given your recent lodgings." Allipo assured me, tugging me into the room, "the on-suite is through that door, and you do have a balcony, but be mindful of the guard rails. It's on the to-do list, but I am yet to find a craftsman willing to travel all the way out here."

Eloimaya followed behind us and began tucking clothes into a wardrobe before hanging a black maxi dress on the front.

"When you're ready. I think this would look nice for dinner." She said, giving me a genuine smile. "Allipo, I love the work you've done."

"Why thank you." Allipo's face brightened instantly. "You would be surprised how much of my work goes unnoticed in this place. It's refreshing to have someone who cares for the work as much as me."

"Will you tell me all about the other rooms on the way to my room?"

"Oh, why of course my dear."

"Now do you prefer baroque or colonial?" Eloimaya asked as she looped her arm through his and guided him to the door winking at me as they slipped out the door; it closed with a soft click behind them.

As their voices drifted down the hall I sat on the plush bed. He wanted me to have this, and I felt like a princess. I was fairly certain my mom's whole first floor of the farmhouse would fit in the bedroom. I hoped she was doing okay. I would have to get Nira to let me call her tomorrow, though I didn't know what I would tell her.

Chapter Ten

Niratap

I let the hot water run over me in the shower. This girl was both fascinating and infuriating, almost like she knew exactly what buttons to push and when. She would rev me up, excite me and just as quickly twist a knife in my heart. I needed to reign in my desire. Both because I didn't want to scare her and because I didn't want to take that frustration out on my staff. This is why I stood in the shower, cock in hand trying to ease the tension coiling in me like a cobra. I envisioned her soft supple body against mine. The taste of her skin on my tongue, would she taste just as sweet below. There was a knock on the bathroom door before Allipo's voice broke the silence.

"My Lord, both of the ladies have been seen to their rooms and are settling in."

I held back a growl and said. "Thank you."

"Would you like me to pull some attire for dinner?"

"No Allipo, I can manage on my own."

"Damn, I thought for sure I could get some color on you. I like these girls, my Lord. Shasha is sweet and will be great to have around. Eloimaya is eloquent, she is well-versed in color theory and design. I would love to have her as an assistant if you haven't already decided on a position for her."

I sigh, damn this satyr. "I have an idea for Eloimaya; however, she could also be your design assistant if you wish."

"Why thank you my Lord. And what of little Shasha, is she to be a companion for you or will she serve on your staff?"

"I haven't decided yet."

"You like her, my Lord."

"What I like, Allipo is time to myself, now if you please." I growled.

"Right, right. Dinner is to be served in thirty minutes."

"Thank you."

The click of the satyr's feet leaving was a relief of its own. What am I even doing? I pondered what Allipo asked, what was I going to do with Shasha? I could make her part of the staff, and give her a job, but part of me did want her as a companion. Thanks for nothing, you meddling creature. I wanted her, yes. I wanted to touch her, feel her, be inside her. I wanted her to want me more than anything. More than freedom. More than wealth. More than air. She was consuming my thoughts and even though I wanted all that, was it fair to her to demand those things of her and her body? I came, watching the shame of it swirl down the drain. It neither took the edge off nor staved my desire. Fuck, I needed to get control of myself.

Outside the shower, I dressed in slacks and a black dress shirt and looked at myself in the mirror, as I pulled shadows over my skin. Hiding what was the most acceptable part of myself, a human face. How could she want a monster like me? How could anyone come to love a monster?

I combed through my hair before braiding it down the back of my head, it would keep it free of food while I ate and kept it manageable until it dried. I sighed. Tonight's dinner would be hard, but I had to pull it together.

In the dining room, the grand table was set, though it was something more a family table than a lord's table. The house ate at least dinner together, if not the other meals, it was something everyone agreed on. Allipo sat on the right of me. Dinner was where we usually discussed matters of the house, so he always sat beside me, but the rest of them had shifted down so the seat to my left where Mitta usually sat was empty and Eloimaya was sitting next to Allipo.

"Rearranging the table Allipo?"

"Everyone agreed that Miss Shasha should sit next to you, my Lord."

"Really, Allipo, what makes you think that I want her there." I did, but this satyr was driving me mad.

"My Lord." Allipo's voice took on that seething fae edge to it. "No offense, you may cloak yourself in shadow and darkness, but I can see the way you look at her and you're either going to eat her or bed her and for all our sake I hope the later because the moping is driving us all crazy."

I felt my beast bristle, my voice a quiet growl. "What?"

The room fell dead silent like everyone held their breath expecting me to lash out violently. It had been a very long time since I had lost my temper, but Allipo was testing me.

"You heard what I said Niratap." Allipo's voice matched that of a disappointed father, "You wouldn't be upset if it wasn't true."

"Allipo." My rage was building.

Eloimaya placed a hand on my arm speaking in a hushed voice as she passed me. "My Lord, you and Allipo can argue the semantics of your feelings at a later time. I know you do not wish to frighten the girl so I will say now is a time to calm yourself and sit, because your audience has grown."

I looked over at the entryway, where Shasha stood. She had changed into a modest knee-length black dress that hugged her curves. The bright gold of her collar the only other adornment, and despite it, she was radiant. Though my beast cried out for vengeance at Allipo's words, I calmed down and went to pull out her chair.

"Come sit here, Shasha."

She walked sheepishly towards me. "As long as I'm not taking someone's seat."

Allipo brightened. "We adjusted for you, my dear."

How I wanted to wipe the smile off his face as I tucked her into her seat. "They thought you would be most comfortable here, but if you would like to sit elsewhere you may.”

“No, it's fine. I didn’t want to put anyone out.” She smiled up at me, that knife twisting in my heart. I tried to force warmth into my eyes, but she looked down at the table. I glowered at Allipo who smiled brightly at me in that wild fae way that made my skin crawl.

I stood at the head of the table, and there before me was the group that was the closest thing to family I had ever had. Everyone gathered here as often as we could, the work that had brought us together often left us apart. The stew pot was sitting in front of me, and the ritual of dinner was more symbolic anymore. I served everyone and they served me. Picking up my bowl, I pondered all the wins and losses that we had had, the fight to stand where I was, a bittersweet smile came to my face.

I cleared my throat. “Blessings on the blossom. Blessings on the fruit. Blessings on the leaves and stems, and blessings on the root. Blessings to our family.”

“Blessings to you, my Lord.” the table responded, faces alight. It had been a long time since I had blessed a meal.

I ladled the stew into the bowl, and moved to pass it to Shasha, her eyes glittering in the chandelier light as she watched me. I instructed her on what we did. “Take your bowl and pass it down. The bowls go all around the table at least once and we serve each other. Whatever the meal may be.”

She nodded, passing her bowl to Mitta and reaching for the bowl in my hand. “This smells lovely.”

I smiled, “Wait ‘til you taste it.”

We went around the table. Dorilody buttered bread for everyone, Durgash dropped a boiled potato in each bowl, Katrel added a glob of sour cream, and Allipo garnished with a sprinkle of cheese. When everyone had a bowl full of food I sat, tucking in my chair to the table. I watched as everyone started to dig in, my eyes coming to rest on Shasha. She stared into the bowl of stew as if it was a crystal ball that would divine her future.

"It helps if you stick your fork in it." I said to her.

She looked at me, pink dusting her cheeks. "This isn't what I expected."

I took a bite of the stew, chewing the tender meat and her words before I spoke. "And what did you expect?"

"To be honest, I don't know what I was expecting, but it's like you are a family."

"We are." Mitta said, her voice high and bell-like. "Don't let The Lord's brooding nature tell you otherwise."

I narrowed my eyes, but Shasha giggled. "Is he really broody?"

"Definitely." Allipo answered, giving me a pointed look before I focused back on my stew, not enjoying being the topic of conversation. The stew was earthy and warm on my pallet. It tasted like home.

"My Lord." Allipo pulled me from my thoughts. "We need to discuss some things."

"Right," I responded, thoroughly distracted watching Shasha take a bite of stew. Her eyes went wide as she chewed a small smile forming on her lips, before she wiggled in her chair.

"My Lord?"

I looked at the satyr, who had a knowing grin on his face. "Apologies Allipo, what were we in need of discussing?"

"Well, Dheg was wondering what you thought of adding some rose hedging on the west fence line. Durgash wanted to ask about funds so he and Rogmesh could hit the fair circuit, to purchase protein for the year. Mitta had some security ideas to run by you. I would like to finalize the budget for the balconies. We also should figure feed for the horses and look into breeding the milk cows."

"That is quite an extensive list, Allipo."

"Yes, my Lord." Allipo said around a hunk of bread. "We have been away for some time."

"The black-market circuit never rests, Allipo."

"I know, my Lord."

"Dheg, what does a new hedge entail?"

The faun straightened in his chair, setting his wine glass down. "My Lord, I would like to take cuttings from the roses on the east side of the house and root them. The process should only take a couple of weeks and then my hope is to get them transplanted and ready for winter."

"And I take it there are other aspects of the grounds that would be neglected while you did this project?"

"Yes, my Lord, but it is almost the season to let things become overgrown."

"Very well, I approve. Durgash whatever you need to feed us. That is all I ask."

"Yes, my Lord, I find it important and prudent to ask."

"Very well. Mitta?"

She wiped her face on the back of her hand. "We can discuss it tomorrow; we'll need to go to the server rooms for what I have to propose."

"Very well." I shift my tone to seriousness. "Allipo, I don't know what more there is to discuss about the budget that I gave you. It is more than adequate for you to hire a craftsman and decorate modestly. As for the horses, we did run lean on grass last year so I would say to order at least another two-ton. Echo is also well aware that it will be time to breed the cows soon, so you bringing it to my attention has little bearing on it being discussed. Echo?"

"Yes, my Lord?"

"I trust that you have already reached out to your bull contact to breed the cows."

"Yes, my Lord, Copperhead is to bring bulls in a couple of weeks."

"See, Allipo, there is nothing to worry about, things have been settled."

"But my Lord." Allipo protested.

I stood throwing my chair back as my hand came down on the table. "Enough, Allipo. You can goad me as much as you like, but we are done discussing this now."

The table had gone completely silent, and tension wrapped around the room. I became very aware of the shadows slicking off me and the wispy acrid scent of fear that danced through the air. I didn't chance a glance at Shasha, I knew her face would kill the small amount of restraint I had left. I picked up my bowl and left the table.

"I apologize for my outburst, everyone, please enjoy the rest of your meal. I am going to retire for the night. Allipo, we will speak later."

"O-of course my Lord." Allipo answered as I walked up the steps to my quarters. I'd done it again hadn't I? Fuck.

Chapter Eleven

Niratap slammed his hand on the table, and I jumped and slipped back into my chair as he snarled at Allipo. I didn't understand their dynamic enough to interject on his behalf. The shadows off Niratap's body crawled across the floors and walls. there was something in his voice that caused terror to rattle through my chest. He didn't look at me as he picked up his bowl and left the dining room. Something in his voice sounded sad as he left, remorseful about what had just transpired. After Niratap's footsteps faded the tension began to ease and the others began to speak.

"Geeze, Allipo." Mitta growled. "Why do you have to rile him up so much?"

"Right." Rogmesh agreed. "If you didn't poke at him so much, we might actually get to spend time with him."

"Now, now." Allipo protested scowling at the women. "If he would just open up for a change, I wouldn't be compelled to torment him."

Echo sipped her wine, before her voice filled with an uncanny edge. "Really Allipo, if you would ease up, we could get through at least one dinner with the lord in a good mood. I would say that I can't believe you, but history has shown me otherwise."

"Echo come on." Allipo whined. "If he would just-"

"Enough, Allipo." Dheg spoke out. "Picking on the lord is not something any of us like to watch. Your incessant need for chaos really puts a damper on the whole house and ruins it for everyone else."

"You all can't fault me for wanting him to grow up a little." Allipo continued.

"But at what cost." Durgash growled.

"Yeah, don't you think the lord has been through enough as is?" Tummi snarled.

I swallowed, asking. "What do you mean by that?"

The table fell silent.

I was irritated now. "What do you mean by 'been through enough?'"

Tummi blushed and glared at her stew. "I'm sorry, Miss Shasha, but going back there is hard. All of us at this table have gone through hardship. We've all been used or abused. Tortured, but."

Tears began to roll down Tummi's face and my heart began to pound in my chest. "But?"

Allipo cleared his throat, his face somber for the first time. "But out of all of us Lord Niratap had it the worst."

"Wha- "I began but Allipo held up a hand.

"It is best if you get that story from him." There was sadness in Allipo's eyes.

"Oh. Okay."

Allipo stood, placing his napkin on the table before he spoke. "Well then, I guess I will excuse myself for the tongue-lashing that I'm sure to get."

"Too bad the lord is too kind to give you an actual lashing?" Katrel said under her breath.

"Too true." Mitta agreed.

"It's just my luck isn't it." Allipo smiled. "Goodnight, everyone."

I sat there quietly while everyone finished the meal in silence. Durgash righted Niratap's seat and the others started picking up the dishes.

"Are you done, sweet one?" Echo asked me.

"Oh yes." I said, handing her my bowl. "Are they always like that?"

"Who?"

"The lord and Allipo?"

"Unfortunately, most of the time, yes. Satyrs are known for causing chaos and even though Allipo is probably the most responsible satyr I have ever met; he still carries that propensity."

"Satyrs give all hybrids a bad name." Dheg chimed in. "Even so Allipo is a good man and he and I have similar stories."

"Really?" I asked, curious about the world I had entered.

"Yes, Allipo and I were both being forced to fight in underground rings. Pans and satyrs are strong, so that's often where we end up in the black market. Allipo was a fighter though; I was bait."

"Bait?" I placed a shaking hand over my mouth.

Dheg shuddered. "Yeah, they would use me to try to entice the more ferocious beasts to fight. I got fairly lucky overall. It was mostly black dogs and hellhounds when I was in the circuit. Allipo told me of several times when he had to fight a hydra or a basilisk."

"That sounds terrible."

"It was." Mitta said leaning in the doorway to the kitchen. "Underground fighting is bloody and dangerous. Many of my kind have also been sacrificed in those rings."

"Were you?" I asked.

"No, I was enslaved by a warlord that used me as a mount, when he rode into battle. It was more glamorous than some of the stories I've heard."

"Aye." Durgash agreed, wiping his hands on his apron. "Rogmesh and I were enslaved as coal mine laborers. Starved and beaten all the time. If it hadn't been for the lord, we would have died in that hell hole."

"Not all of us wish to relive our traumas. You should be wise of that." Katrel hissed, her face sad as she looked out the window. Her beautiful face was illuminated by the moon.

"I'm sorry." I said quickly. "I didn't mean any harm. I just-I've never seen this side of the world."

"Ever?" Tummi asked.

I shook my head. "No, I grew up in a small town that was mostly human."

"So, we are really your first glimpse into the wilds?" Dheg asked, leaning over the table.

"I'm sorry you have all suffered, and I don't mean to cause you pain, but I feel like I am both meant to be here and stuck here, and I want to learn." The words were honest to my core.

"Come, my dear." Eloimaya spoke. "We've had a long and arduous day. How about we head to bed?"

I yawned. "I didn't even think I was tired."

I took Eloimaya's hand, and she led me to my room. The day had definitely caused me fatigue, but after what had transpired at dinner, I wanted to check on him. I paced through my room, debating on wandering the house to find his room. What would I even do when I got to his room? I imagined his hands on my skin, I wanted that fire more. Just thoughts of him made my skin tight and made the heat pool in my body. I needed to know if he was okay. I needed him.

Chapter Twelve

Niratap

In my quarters I resisted the urge to topple the mahogany furniture that decorated my room. I wanted to scream and yell and break things, especially things that Allipo loved. The knock at my door was soft, almost like Allipo didn't want to speak with me, didn't want to continue telling me how pathetic I was.

"Enter." I said, deciding to sit in one of the lounge chairs instead of throwing it.

Allipo entered the room and came to stand close to me, out of arm's reach, but close. "My Lord."

"You embarrassed me, Allipo."

"My Lord, to be frank, you embarrassed yourself."

My hands clenched fists and jaw. "Why would you push me to that point?"

"Niratap, you need to grow up." Allipo said like it was the truest truth.

"I am grown up." I knew he wasn't talking physically. "I don't understand why you must continuously bait me and test me."

"Because it is the only way you will learn to control your emotions. You need to work on finding joy instead of being angry at the world all the time. This girl is going to force that growth in you regardless, at least if she is brave."

"Leave Shasha out of this, Allipo."

"It's unlike you. Eloimaya made sense, she was used much like Tummi, but purchasing her? A human, who more than likely sold herself? And for the amount my Lord."

"No." I leaped from my seat and with a predatory speed, I closed my hand around Allipo's throat. To the satyr's credit, he kept his composure, even though I could feel his heart thundering in his body. He looked up at me as I released him, his expression unreadable.

"Am I wrong, my Lord?"

I took a breath. "Yes. She was abducted off the street."

"Fresh market goods?"

I stepped back, flexing my hand as I went to the window. "Yes."

"Why her? Why a brothel?"

"I know she has not suffered as the rest of us have suffered, but- "

"But what Niratap? She is pretty, yes, but she knows nothing of our world, nothing of the underground. She was unfortunate, yes, but I don't see her being worth the three million dollars you spent on her, before buying her clothes."

I looked at Allipo, his face severe and angry. I didn't have a defense for the amount I had spent on her. I didn't have a reason that would assuage Allipo's rage. Just my truth.

"I needed her, and you can be angry with me all you like Allipo, but I needed her. It is beyond my own understanding. She pulled me into the brothel by her scent alone and I followed. She captivates me."

"That's not what we do, Niratap. That's not what you do."

"Do you think I don't know that?" I snarled, "I don't know what drove me into that brothel and I don't know why I needed her. I just did, it was just instinct."

"Well, I hope, for all our sake, that this crazy instinct of yours doesn't spend all our finances."

"Three million is chump change in the world we're in, with what we are trying to accomplish. We spent nine on that basilisk we purchased at the beginning of the year."

"True, but you wasted three million on a human."

I ran my fingers through the top of my hair. I was tired and angry. "Leave her be Allipo. She didn't choose any aspect of this."

"Then let her go."

"No."

Allipo's eyes widened. "Just because you are a lord doesn't mean you can keep the girl a prisoner. She serves no purpose beyond catching your fancy. Fuck her and let her go. Or eat her, but keeping her bound to you is unfair. You of all beings should know that."

"You don't have to remind me, Allipo. I know what I went through. I know what you went through. It wasn't my intention to bind her to me, it was instinct. This whole thing with Shasha has been instinct and restraint. I don't need to be reminded of what that kind of servitude is, but- "

"You couldn't leave her be."

I scowled. "No, I couldn't."

Allipo sighed, rubbing his neck. "I don't understand it, but I can't fault you for making rash decisions. I am after all a satyr. I apologize for antagonizing you, not for what I said, just when it was said."

I gave him a curt nod and shook my head smiling at myself. "Half-apology accepted."

He smiled. "Very well. I know you don't care for the numbers, but we need them in order to further our goals. Without them, we won't have the influence we need to cut down the black-market trade."

"I know, Allipo. I know that the grander goals and our survival take precedence, but you can't tell me she doesn't fascinate you."

"I think the fact that she fascinates you is enough for all of us."

I chuckled and sighed. "Fine."

"Are you going to show her the best of you?" Allipo asked as he walked to the door.

"I don't know what you mean?"

He chuckled. "A millennia-old and still you are just a child."

I pushed off the wall and stalked towards him. "What do you mean, Allipo?"

"That's something only you can answer, my Lord." He opened the door and paused. "She brings something out of you, something I have never seen in you before. I'm curious to see how it will play out. Please don't scare her away with that darkness you cling to in your heart."

"Allipo."

"Goodnight, my Lord, I hope you find the answers to your questions."

With that he slipped out the door, and it clicked quietly behind him. What did he mean by the best parts of myself? I growled and began to pace the length of the room. My clothes stifled me, and I disrobed. What even were the best parts of myself? I was a monster, a beast with sentience, what was good about that? I had compassion, yes, but there was rage still seething under my marred skin, even after all these years. Allipo knows that his talking in riddles maddens me. There was a soft knock at the door.

"What," my voice came out of me as a half snarl, but no one responded. I stormed to the door, a growl echoing off the walls. Her scent flitted under, and it eased something in me. I spoke more calmly to her. "Shasha, are you in need of something?"

Her voice was quiet, "I wish to speak with you."

"Can it not wait till morning?" I was still angry, and I didn't want to take that out on her. Allipo's words twisted my thoughts.

"My Lord, I-I don't think it can." Her voice was stronger and more defiant.

I hissed, the scent of her summery arousal dusting my nose from under the door. Maddening was the smell of her, my form shifting closer to my beast. "Very well."

Chapter Thirteen

The wood floor of the hall was cold against my feet as I slipped out of my room, fueled by the heat that had been building within and my own burning curiosity. The soft creaks and groans of the house caused me to pause at every corner. The pale light of the moon illuminated patches of the floor in an otherworldly glow. I paused at the intersection of the front hall and the long hall leading to the rest of the house. Where did I go from here? A hand appeared over my mouth and pulled me to the shadows there.

"My, my little flower, it's very rare when someone other than myself is roaming the halls at this hour." Allipo cooed in my ear. "Are you lost?"

He removed his hand and released me from his hold. Still encased in shadows, he stood, moonlight danced across his honey irises, and made it look like fire glowed behind them. Would he answer honestly or lead me astray? "I want to see Lord Niratap."

He smiled mischievously. "What does the little bloom want with the lord so late in the night?"

I straightened my back, decided he would definitely trick me. "I wish to speak with the lord. Point me in the direction of his chambers. Please."

Allipo tilted his head, an impish gleam in his eyes. "The lord's chambers are straight back down this hall."

"No half-truths?" I asked, unease slipping into my stomach.

"Not tonight. I will leave it to the lord to lead you astray tonight. Good evening, little flower."

With that Allipo bowed, turning around and continuing down the other hall. I turned down the hall and mulled his words in my head. How would Nira lead me astray? Was what I was doing putting me at risk? The end of the hall came into view, a large set of red double oak doors, much like the front doors of the manor, intricate designs of oak and ivy danced across the wood. I placed a palm on the door, was he even in here? Had I been tricked by Allipo already? If I had, I'm sure that Nira would not approve of my being so trusting. I swallowed, trying to quiet the swirling thoughts running rampant in my head, telling me to just go back to my room. I knocked.

"What." He sounded irritated, and my voice froze.

There was a growl, and his footsteps approached the door but did not open it. His voice softened. "Shasha, are you in need of something."

I swallowed. Come on, Shasha, you can do this. "I wish to speak with you."

"Can it not wait till morning?"

Was he going to dismiss me that easily, as he had earlier when he had left me wanting things I did not understand? The memory of his hands on my skin reignited the fire that had driven me from my room to his door. "My Lord, I-I don't think it can."

A hiss emanated from behind the door. "Very well."

The door cracked and I was greeted by darkness, the shadows pouring across the floor. His shadows. I took a deep breath, inhaling the heady scent of petrichor from beyond. I stepped into the darkness, the door shutting sharply behind me. His clawed hand pressed me back into the door. He buried his almost canid muzzle into the crook of my neck, inhaling deeply. His tongue was hot on my skin, the sensation stirring the heat pooling between my legs.

"My Lord." my voice sounds heated and breathy. "I-"

His teeth grazed my throat, his voice reverberating. "You?"

I pushed at him; I needed space to think. "I need-"

His hands scooped me up and tossed me back onto a plush bed, his voice near a growl. "I can smell your need."

He looms over me, the delicate silver glow of his predatory eyes dancing over me. Bravery or foolishness, I wanted him to want me. "I want you."

"That is a foolish request, my dear." His voice rumbles over me.

"It may be foolish, but my body is on fire at the memory of your touch. Please." I reached for him. What would his kiss taste like?

He came down upon me, the bed dipping at his weight, but he hovered above me, his hands on either side of my head. His tongue found my throat again, his canines grazing my skin, the sensation had me arching up against him. My hands reached up, tangling into his long hair. A gasp emanated from me as he growled against my neck.

"Do you understand what you are asking of me?" His voice was strained like he was holding himself back.

"No." I answered honestly, panting. "But I want you."

He growled his hands coming to my thighs, where the nightgown was ridden up with my squirming. They were hot and firm against my skin as he stroked. His voice rolls over me like hot rain. "I cannot guarantee your safety, my control is not something I have the best hold of, and as of late it has gotten worse with you."

"I am not afraid." The words were true, and I didn't know if that scared me. "Destroy me if you must, but please."

He pressed his forehead against mine. "As you wish."

He fisted the nightgown, pulling me off the bed, his claws shredding it off my body exposing me to the darkness. His tongue and hands explored my chest, and the heat continued to coil through me. I cried out, the licking and sucking, palming and pinching sent me spinning. He purred against my skin, it sounded hungry and half-crazed as he traveled down my body. He was panting, clawed hands hooked the edge of my panties, my legs parting for him on instinct.

"I wish to taste you." His voice was thick against my thigh, breath hot. He was asking permission.

I groaned, shocked by the desperate sound of my own voice. "Yes."

His claws made quick work of the small piece of fabric. A hiss escaped him as he scented me. His breath was both hot and cold against my core, and I arched back in response. He pulled me down to the edge of the bed resting my legs on his shoulders. His tongue slid across my sex, a keening moan tore from my body. He nipped my inner thigh, and I quivered under his touch. His hands came to my breasts, teasing my nipples. I could feel his canines come to rest on top of my stomach, his tongue deliciously tasting between my folds. My body coiled at the onslaught, and when the tip of his tongue flicked my clit, it was like lightning through my body. Breathy hot moans danced through the rafters of his room. He had a tilt-a-whirl effect on me, my body trembled violently under him, his name a cry on my lips.

He pulled away licking my thigh as he left. "I am not finished with you."

He flipped me with ease, situating me on the bed, my ass in the air completely exposed to him. I groaned as his claws danced across my skin. A hand around my throat, careful around the collar so as not to bite it into my skin, pulled me back against him, his fur and shadows soft against my back. He slid his member between my legs and rubbed the swollen monster against my core. He was massive. His tongue and teeth worked my neck, his free hand stroking my breasts.

"Eileoidh me tu chorp agus anam siorai."[16]

I didn't understand the words, but my chest tightened at them, deepening my need for him. "Please be gentle with me, Nira."

"Why should I be?" His voice sounds crazy.

I swallowed, fear finally making my heart spasm uncontrollably in my chest. "Because you would be my first."

---

[16] "I will claim you body and soul eternal."

Chapter Fourteen

Niratap

I froze, her body quivering under my hands and over my cock. I had to get a hold of myself. I couldn't take her like I wanted, savagely and primal like the beast in me needed. It would be a disservice to her. I wanted her in all the ways I could have her, over and over again, but not at the cost of her body, not at the cost of her trust. Head spinning, I lifted her and laid her back on the bed, and I stepped back taking some shaking breaths. The sight of her splayed before me was maddening, legs and lips parted for me.

"Nira." Her voice desperate. "Did I do something wrong?"

"No." My voice tight, coiled like my body. I tried to regain some control, but it was lost with her smell and her taste. It was all I could do to stand my distance. "I don't want to hurt you."

She sat up, her breasts bouncing with the movement. My mind was tangled with her delicious warm summer wine dancing on my tongue, her intoxicating honeyed floral scent crowding me, clinging to my body. I needed air. I needed to drown in her.

"Nira?" Her voice is small, disappointed. "I can go if you want."

"No." I breathed, betraying my desperation.

She paused, half down from the bed, silhouetted by the almost nonexistent moonlight. fuck me. I forced my body into my human-like form. All that remained of my beast was my tail, antlers, and height. I crashed against her; her lips were velvet soft against mine. Did she taste herself on my tongue? Did she like the way I tasted? Her hands came to my face, tracing my jaw, my throat, and my chest. I lifted her from the floor, her soft supple legs twisting around my waist, bringing my member against her core. I gasped against her lips and growled.

"Nira." My name a breathy moan from her.

I laid her back down on the bed kissing any spot of flesh I can find. This form sat perfectly between her ample thighs, my cock resting next to her soft bed of curls. I placed a tender kiss on her forehead and rested my own there. Our breaths came in heavy pants.

"Are you sure this is what you want?"

"Yes."

"I will be as gentle with you as I can."

"Thank you." She whispered.

I kissed her again, before running my hand down her side, hooking her behind the knee, and opening her to me. I poised myself at her entrance, and I looked up at her once more, our eyes meeting. Mine asking. Her's pleading. She gasped and I groaned as I slowly slid my length into her tight core. She whimpered as I stretched her. She winced and I froze.

"Did I hurt you?" My voice somewhere between strangled and a growl.

"Yes and no. You feel so good; I feel full." Her head lulls to one side, her neck exposed beautifully. "Please, I need all of you, it's easing this ache in me."

"As you wish," I repositioned, using my tail to pull her leg over my shoulder. seating myself inside her completely, she shuddered around me and both of us groan.

"You have a tail." she says dreamily.

"I do." I chuckled, letting her body relax to my invasion.

"How did I not notice that?"

I kissed behind her knee, "I hide it well. Are you ready?"

She looked at me, her eyes glistening with need. A part of me ached like she saw deeper than the glow of my eyes and shadows, like she saw me. "Yes."

I pulled back and groaned. Her flesh was hot and wet against me. This was a deliciously agonizing test in control. She moaned beneath me, back arched, changing the angle, letting me in deeper. Her hands tangled in the sheets. She both ethereal and carnal. I could spend forever surrounded by her scent. I began to thrust gently, the friction was amazing on my member, and she ground against me. I dropped her leg from my shoulder, laying over the top of her, slowly and sensually fucking her sweet body. I licked the honey sweat from her throat, and her hands came to my back, nails scraping over my shoulders. I shivered, trying to stay focused, hoping she didn't feel the old, raised scars that covered my back. I took hold of her hands, pinning them above her head. She arched in my hold, pressing those precious breasts against me. Her body was starting to tighten and spasm against me.

"Nira."

"Come for me, Shasha."

It was as if my permission was all she needed, her body exploding around me, she cried out loudly. I pulled myself from her, my hand finishing me, and I came gracelessly onto the floor. Part of me was glad, but another part of me was disgusted with the loss. She would be a great mother to my offspring. I shook my head, leaving her there on the bed, going to the washroom for a rag. She wouldn't want that; I was a monster. I returned to where she was splayed out on my bed, her body glistening with sweat and pleasure. I would take her again, the smell of us together making me want more, but as she shuddered, I could feel her fatigue.

"This will be a little cold." I warned her as I took the cloth to her sensitive flesh, cleaning up the mess I had made of her. She shuddered, riding the gentle waves of our lovemaking. After I finished with her, I wiped up the floor.

"Nira." She was reaching for me.

I took her hand in mine, kissing it before promising. "I'll be right back."

I went to the bathroom again, discarding the cloth in the hamper, sliding on clean shorts, and letting the shadows slide away to stare at myself in the mirror. My human face was staring back at me, a strong square jaw, defined cheeks, attractive enough even with the thin scar that runs down my left cheek, a lucky break. I wondered if I could let my guard down with her. I wondered if she would continue to want me, even though I had taken her. I wondered if I could harbor her and protect her, especially from myself. I sighed before I splashed my face with some water. What was I doing? I could not be this tied up with my emotions, these were things that could get me killed. Then who would protect her?

Back in the bedroom, she had crawled into my comforter, her head nestled on my pillow. I relaxed and called forth my shadows, half shifting in case she woke before I could then I lifted the blanket and slid in beside her. It wasn't that I didn't trust her, she had just given herself to me. Begged to come to bed with me. It was that I had her so close; I didn't want to scare her away. She would expect to wake next to a shadow. Her hands grasped me, and she snuggled close. I wrapped a protective arm around her. The desperate need replaced by a sense of wonder. When she spoke, I could hear the disappointment in her voice.

"You changed your form."

"Yes."

Her hand rested on my chest. "What are you afraid of? I'm not planning on going anywhere."

That tightness that she kept placing in my chest made it hard to breathe. I grasped her hand. "So much more than you know. Now go to sleep, my dear, I will be here in the morning."

"Promise?"

"Yes, I won't leave you tonight."

She placed a sleepy kiss on my shoulder. "Then goodnight, Nira."

"Goodnight, Shasha."

Chapter Fifteen

Niratap

The warmth of the morning sun crept across my face, waking me from one of the deepest, most restorative sleeps I had ever had. I began to ponder that, stretching in my bed. Then her scent tickled my nose, phantom memories of the night, tangled in my sheets and draped over my skin. I rolled to where she had slept beside me but found the bed empty. A jolt of panic flooded my body, and I sat up hunting for her, finding her wrapped in my discarded shirt from last night perusing the books that lined the shelves. I sighed, flopped back down, and covered my face, not ready to leave the bed.

"Good morning, my dear." I said, peeking at her from under my arm.

Shasha turned, the shirt haphazardly buttoned. "Good morning."

She walked to the bed and sat beside me, pulling both legs up. "Did you sleep well?"

"Yes." Her voice was light, and its sound warmed me, "Did you?"

Did I tell her? "Yes, best I've had in a while."

She smiled. "Good. Thank you."

I sat up, perching on my elbows. "What are you thanking me for?"

Warmth danced across her cheeks. "For listening and for taking care of me. For saving me from a fate where I wouldn't continue to be myself."

A tear rolled down her cheek. I wanted to wipe them away. "Why are you crying?"

"You and your staff have just been so kind to me. I have not suffered like they have, and they still treat me so well."

"Ah, I see. Some of them shared their stories last night."

"Yes. They shared, but Allipo said that you had had it the worst. And I know that I haven't earned that truth from you, but I want to know."

I'd kill that satyr. "Not all souls want to share that kind of trauma."

"That's what Katrel said." She looked at me then, her eyes glistening in the morning light, tears bubbling there, but also fiery defiance.

I sat up fully and reached for her, resting a clawed hand on her cheek. She deserved my vulnerability. My honesty. "I-I am not ready to share those parts of me, but you have earned my trust, for what it's worth. *Titim amach banna an chuing.*" [17]

Her eyes widened, as the collar around her throat fell away. "Are you not afraid of me running?"

A knife of doubt plunged into my heart, but I kept my body neutral. "You are still bound to me, just not as a slave."

"Then what am I?"

I considered. "What do you wish to do?"

"I-I can't cook very well unless you want to eat copious amounts of mac and cheese."

I chuckled. "Okay."

"I don't know anything about plants or animals."

"Echo and Dheg have plenty of help from our wild neighbors anyway."

"I can clean."

"I don't think Tummi and Katrel want assistance. Dorilody may have some things that you can do, but it won't fill your time here, even with going to school. which reminds me I need to make some phone calls." I sighed. I did not want to leave this bed. I did not want to leave her.

"Could I call my mom today?"

I had said she could. "Yes. We can arrange that later. Firstly though, are you hungry?"

"A little, I usually don't eat in the mornings though."

"Why is that?"

"It's just how I've always been."

"Well, let's change that," I swung my legs over the edge of the bed.

"Nira, I don't have any clothes."

I looked at her, and lust burned through my body. I shifted into my human shape, shadows hiding my skin from her view. I stalked to her predatorily and came to kneel in front of her. My hands rested on her knees.

"I wish to have you."

[17] "Fall away bond of the captive."

Her eyes widened, face flushed. "Right now?"

I leaned into her, kissing her neck. This was better, no collar to kiss around. Her arousal warming me, I thought *I want you forever.* "Yes."

Her hands came to my shoulders. "Nira, I wish to have you."

My hands hooked under her knees pulling her to rest against me, I groaned, and I could feel her wetness through my shorts. I undid the buttons of my shirt on her exposing her beautiful breasts. Her skin was a tapestry of various shades of purple from last night. I kissed every mark I had left on her skin, the daylight telling me how I had claimed her. She moaned as I took her nipple and sucked it. Her hands cupping my face bring it to her lips, her kiss sweet and sensual.

"May I see your face?" She asked, breaking the kiss to breathe.

My heart strained, why would you want to gaze upon a monster. "Why?"

"I wish to see the man who holds me."

I frowned, eyes narrowing as I dropped my hands, stood, and step back, my voice harsh in my own ears. "Shasha. I am not a man. I am a monster in human skin. I could eat you just as easily as I could fuck you."

Her body was flush and her summery scent ready for me to take, but she needed to understand. She had to realize I was dangerous. She slid off the bed and comes to me, the button-up hanging haphazardly off one shoulder.

"Then do it."

Her words strike me, giving me pause. "What."

"Eat me, if that is your desire. Consume me or fill me Niratap. I don't care, but I need you. In more ways than I am ready to admit. I want to see your face. I want to trace its lines and commit them to memory. I can see that you have a hard time being vulnerable. I do as well." Her fingers hook into the top of my shorts.

"Shasha."

"Shush, we can talk about it later, right now I want you to fuck me like you wanted to last night."

I growled, lifting her, and her legs wrapped around my waist pressing my cock into her core. I crawl onto the bed, while she wiggles the shorts down my legs with her toes. I pulled them the rest of the way off and tossed them across the room. I sank into her in one thrust and groaned. She was hot and slick.

"Fuck."

She arches, deepening my reach, her voice light, reverent. "Yes"

"You really have no sense of self-preservation, do you?" I said, licking her neck.

"Not when it comes to you."

Her words told me things that I wanted to explore, but she squirmed underneath me, craving friction. I pulled back and she groaned with lust, her body already quivering. Thrusting into her, burying myself as deep as I could was a freeing sensation. She grasped my neck and pulled me down to kiss her. My hands clutched her face, she tasted of heaven and my instincts screamed to take her. I pulled away and she cried out in longing. I placed my hands on her hips.

"May I take you?"

Her eyes were dewy as she looked at me. "Yes"

I flipped her, letting my beast come forward, clawed hand pulling her back against my chest. I sucked on her neck and shoulder, sliding my length against her core, preparing us both for it. She wrapped her hand as far around the shaft as she could, and I hissed, her palm igniting a fire in my gut. She stroked me and a possessive growl started in my chest.

"Do you not like that?" She asked, releasing me.

I licked her neck, sending a shiver through her. "I like it, but you are playing a dangerous game with my control."

"How dangerous are we talking?" She ran her finger over the tip, spreading the fluid over me.

A choked growl crawled out of me. "Very."

I pushed her forward and positioned myself at her entrance. I looked at her before me enamored by her beauty.

"Are you ready?" I asked.

"Yes." She is confident.

I pressed against her, easing my beastly cock into her soft and willing body. She moaned and then groaned as I sank deeper and deeper into her. Her body was stretching and stretching trying to accommodate me. I paused letting her breathe, and she whimpered as she panted an iron-like smell hit my nose. I froze.

"I've hurt you." I moved to pull out, but she hooked the back of my thigh with her hand.

"No, don't go." She pleaded. She looked back at me, her eyes heavy-lidded with need. "I just need a moment; you are much larger than I thought in this form."

I ran a soothing hand over her back. "I should have prepared you better."

She stroked my leg lightly. "It's okay. I want all of you."

I peered between us, only halfway inserted. "I don't think you can take all of me, sweetness."

"I can, I just need to adjust."

So confident. She scooted back a little bit, easing me in another inch. I watched as she panted, slowly and painstakingly taking me deeper, inch by inch. I grunted as she pushed, and I felt the head press against her cervix. A soft strangled moan came out of her mouth.

"That's enough, love. You don't have to seat me completely."

She sniffled, and I was about to pull out when she rocked back hard, and I felt myself sink even deeper until her ass came to rest against my hips. She was panting and I was amazed, stunned at all that she was. Her body relaxed to the invasion, and I'm wrapped tightly in her warmth.

"See."

"I'll be gentle." I said rubbing her back.

"No, prove to me you're a monster. Take me like you mean it." This girl was my undoing.

I pulled back past her deepest gate and almost completely out. The sight of her blood on me made my body queasy, and my heart skittered in my chest.

"Niratap." I looked up at her, her gold-toned brown eyes languid. "Please."

A growl resonated within me. "Very well."

I took a breath and sat myself in one thrust. She cried out and I did it again, the speed and pace increasing. I hooked my hand around her hips, holding her still against me as I buried myself inside her. She unraveled for me, her body quivering around me. I flipped her over plunging into her again. I watched her face as I moved inside her; her head lulled to one side watching as I pounded her soft body into submission.

"You are so beautiful." I said to her, her gaze piercing me. As I edged closer to climax.

"You are beautiful." I reiterated, prayed to the being before me. "I can't wait to get to know you."

Her body squeezed mine, and I went to pull free, but the vixen wrapped her legs around my hips and pulled me in. My eyes flew up to her face just as she arched, a moan dancing across the rafters. "Fill me."

She didn't know what she asked of me, but the instinct-switch flipped in my brain and two long thrusts later, I felt myself lose control of my body and I came violently in that deepest depth. My knees shook, my heart thundered as I collapsed over her. I wrapped my arms around her back, so I didn't crush her, panted heavily in the crook of her neck. She kissed my cheek and rubbed my sides. My whole body felt foreign to me, spasms appearing in every muscle.

Her voice was breathy with joy. "See I told you I'd be fine."

I chuckled, kissing her neck.

"It felt good for both of us." I could hear the smile in her voice.

My voice was ragged when it came out. *"Is bronntanas thú nach bhfuil tuillte agam. Ba mhaith liom tú a líonadh mar seo go deo. Ba mhaith liom tú mar maité."* [18]

"That sounds beautiful. What language is that?"

"Irish. It's the tongue of my homeland. It's an old tongue that carries magic in its sound."

"I see. That's why you use it in your spells."

"Precisely."

She wiggled under me the sensation electricity through my body. I groaned into her neck.

"I am starving now; can we go eat?"

I lifted myself to look at her face. She has a dreamy quality to her that makes my chest ache with alien feelings, I didn't understand.

"What?"

"Nothing." I shifted back, my feet finding the floor. She winced. "You, okay?"

She caressed my cheek. "Yeah, just go slow please."

---

[18] "You are a gift that I don't deserve. I want to fill you like this forever. I want you as a mate."

I pulled myself from her warmth with an agonizing slowness. The smell of me and her was perfection, but the iron scent of blood twisted my stomach. She had taken me as a monster, begged the beast to come forward, and teased it out of me like fire from kindling. She sighed when I slipped out of her completely, our combined fluids oozing from her. I shifted into my human shape before scooping her off the bed and carrying her into the bathroom. I sat her down on the toilet seat as I started the shower.

"I could have walked." She said.

"I doubt that." I smiled while she tried to stand and didn't manage it.

"Okay, fine." She said with a grimace.

When the water was warm, I crouched in front of her. "Okay sweetness, grab on."

"You going to hold me in there too?"

"No there's a seat but let me help you."

She huffed but wrapped her arms around my neck. She gasped as the water hits us, the spray warm and inviting. I sat her on the stone bench and adjusted the shower head, so it hit her better. She settled against the marble wall. I watched her breathe lightly before she gazed up at me. A little stream of pink fluid is oozing from beneath her and down the front of the stone.

"When you look at me like that, I think you're going to eat me."

I blinked, grabbing a rag and crouching in front of her. "Like how?"

"Just so intensely, it makes my heart flutter."

"I am a predator by nature." I said easing myself between her legs and pulling her to the edge.

Her voice was playful as she poked me in the nose. "Boop, you're not a predator."

I chuckled, focusing on cleaning her up. She freed my hair, running her hands through the wet strands. It was as if she was entranced by me. As if I was her air and water. I liked the way it felt, warm in the center of my chest. The gift of her attention was freely given. I froze at the words that leave her mouth.

"When can I see you?"

I took a breath. "Is it necessary that you see what I have hidden?"

"Don't speak in riddles. I have given you the canvas of my skin freely. I just wanted to know if there was a chance, we could even the field."

I sighed, kissing her cheek. She didn't know. She didn't understand. "Not today, sweetness."

She opened her mouth like she was about to say something but closed it looking away eyes full of melancholy. "Fine."

I stood when she was cleaned up, rinsing myself off. I wondered how long it would be until I did have to show her my scarred and marred body. As a beast, hair covered most of the evidence, save the scar on my face. I should offer her my face as a boon for her offering me her body, but shame poisoned my gut.

"Is this to be my purpose?" Her question caught me off guard.

"What?"

"You did purchase me at a brothel, so I guess it makes sense."

I paused, resisting the urge to fist my hands. A familiar feeling blackened my heart; I knew she couldn't love me. "You do not have to lie with me if you do not wish to."

"That's not what I said." Her voice is hard.

I let my head fall back, letting the water fall over my chest trying to ease the ache. "I did not purchase you as a toy. To be entirely frank with you I didn't buy you for any legitimate reason. Something about you, your scent, pulled me from the rot of the alleys into the brothel, and apparently everyone thinks I am crazy for doing it. I don't expect anything from you, but to follow the rules I laid out yesterday. You don't have to bed me. You don't have to work."

"Then why keep me at all?"

I groaned, dipping my head under the spray, I asked no one in particular. "Why is everyone so concerned?"

"I take it I am the reason you were so angry last night?"

"Yes and no." I answered truthfully, closing my eyes and rinsing my face.

"Why both?"

"I am not mad because of you. Others are mad at me because they think you are a waste of resources, and that by purchasing you I have greatly subtracted from our cause."

"Ouch." she grunted trying to stand.

I stuck my arm out catching her. "Be careful. You are probably going to be quite sore for a while."

"How did you do that? Your eyes are closed."

I opened my eyes and looked at her, clinging to my arm. "Instinct."

The door opened to the restroom, and Allipo strolled up to the shower. I pulled her in front of me as he approached, my frame protecting her from his view.

"Allipo, what do I owe for this intrusion?" I half snarled.

"My Lord, Eloimaya is looking for your new plaything, and I wanted to see if she is still in your company and has not fled the manor."

"She is very much in my company, Allipo." His name left my mouth in a growl.

"Ah, I see that now my Lord." A lascivious smile curled over his face. He leaned over and peered at Shasha through the glass to address her. "Did he show you the best sides of himself?"

"What do you mean by that?" Her tone was suspicious.

"Oh, nothing, in particular. I'm sure he performed his best for you, my dear."

I roared, and the glass of the shower rattled. Genuine terror painted his face before he turned and ran. Part of me was satisfied with that outcome, but there was a shame; I hadn't done something like that to my staff, my family, in a very long time. I glared over my shoulder at the space where he had stood, rage making my heart pound loudly in my ears. How dare he.

Her hand came to my face. "It's okay. I'm okay."

I stared at her, her eyes were bright and full of sunshine. I pressed a kiss to her forehead. "I must have frightened you."

"No." She kissed my chin. "Somehow even when you are truly terrifying, I feel very safe with you."

"You are a roller coaster for me."

"What do you mean?"

"It's nothing." I kissed her again, before I turned the water off. "You must be hungry."

She gave me a perturbed expression. "Being vulnerable isn't your thing I take it?"

I smiled sadly to myself wrapping a towel around her. "No."

Chapter Sixteen

Shasha

"Where is everyone?" I asked as we went into the dining room.

"Probably hiding from my outburst." Niratap answered as we opened the door to the kitchen. Durgash stood at the counter cutting vegetables and Rogmesh was at the stove stirring various pots.

"Okay, maybe not everyone is hiding."

"What reason do we have to hide?" Rogmesh said.

"We are not the ones who angered the lord to that extent." Durgash said.

I smiled. "What are you making? That smells divine."

Rogmesh gave me a toothy grin. "I am just making stock. It's a long process, but it will be for tomorrow and Durgash is cutting vegetables for tonight."

"I take it you have finally come down for a meal my Lord." Durgash asked, setting the knife down to wipe his hands.

"If it's not too much to ask." Niratap answered kindly. "I can manage eggs well enough on my own, if you are busy."

"Nonsense." Rogmesh chuffed. "We can make you breakfast I will not have so many extra hands in my kitchen. Go sit and we'll get to work."

"Coffee my Lord?" Durgash asked.

"Yes please and thank you, Durgash."

"Little lady?"

"Yes please."

"What you like for breakfast, my dear?" Rogmesh asked, pulling bowls down from a cabinet.

"Pancakes? Or French toast? Both sound delicious."

They both chuckled. "Very well."

Niratap placed a hand on my shoulder, guiding me back through the door. "We'll be on the terrace."

"Yes, my Lord."

Niratap led me through the dining room and out a door that I hadn't noticed the other night. On the shady side of the house, the terrace was full of life with pots overflowing with blooming flowers and greenery, butterflies and bees happily going about pollinating. The view of the vegetable garden and beyond it the pasture, where a few horses grazed and chickens scratched reminded me of old pastoral art that hung in museums. The sounds and smells reminded me of home, so I asked.

"Could I call my mom?"

"Oh, yes, of course." Niratap handed me his phone. "I trust you know her number."

"Yes," I paused looking at the screen. Did I tell her the truth, or did I lie? The trouble was if I lied, hell hath no fury like my mama, but the same was true for the truth. I sighed.

"Something wrong?" He asked as he peered over the land.

"What do I even tell her? If I tell the truth, she will demand my location and will want to come to fetch me. If I lie and she finds out, she will unleash the fury of hell upon me."

"She's your mother. I doubt she will unleash the gates of hell on you."

"You have no idea."

He chuckled softly. "I don't, but it would be quite dangerous for your mother to come here. The mountain road is winding and then there are the beasts that roam the forest."

I grimaced as Eloimaya came out the doors to the dining room. "Got it, lie to my mom."

"Good morning, Eloimaya. Sorry to worry you this morning."

Eloimaya set a tray with coffee and fixings on the table. "It's alright, my Lord. I did not know that she was in your care. Allipo didn't say anything when I told him this morning. He cackled and just barged into your rooms."

"Where is Allipo anyway, Eloimaya?"

"He is in the vault, my Lord, cataloging."

"Will you tell him I would like to speak with him later?"

"Yes, my Lord." She bowed and walked back to the house.

When she was back inside, he asked. "Are you going to call her?"

"Yes." I said exasperatedly, dialing her number. My heart thundered in my chest, making it hard to breathe.

"Hello?"

I took a breath to start myself. "Hey, mom."

"Shasha, what's going on sweetie? Where's your phone?"

"It's back in my dorm. I'm using a friend's." Niratap huffed and shook his head. I held a finger to my lips to shush him. He chuckled.

"Well then, I'm glad you've made a friend. What is their name?"

"Nira."

"Interesting. Is that foreign? Where are they from?"

I glanced up at him, his eyes glowing in their ethereal way, mesmerizing and unreadable. He nodded an okay. "He's from Ireland."

"Shasha. A boy really?" Niratap laughed, stirring sugar into his coffee.

"Yes, mom he's been super helpful. Helping me find my classes and making sure I'm not getting lost. He's even buying me breakfast today."

"Well, you just have to be careful, okay? Those boys are never trustworthy. If they were, your daddy wouldn't have walked out on us."

"I know, mama." I rolled my eyes, every single time the opposite sex was brought up, without fail my vacant father came up. "Anyways I was just calling to let you know I was getting settled and that I am doing well."

"Well thank you, sugar. You know I worry about you in the big city."

"I know, mama." Durgash and Rogmesh came out the terrace doors each caring a tray. "Okay mama I gotta go. Our food is here, then I have class in a couple of hours. I'll call you next Tuesday, okay?"

"Okay, baby stay safe. I love you."

"I love you too, mama. Bye."

"Bye, baby."

The sound of the phone disconnecting was a gift. I slid Niratap's phone back to him exhaling hard.

"Was that difficult?" He asked, his voice sounding genuinely curious.

"Yes. I've never lied to my mom before."

"So, lying about where you are and what you're doing is a big deal. Thank you." He said to the orcs as they placed the food before us. A large tray of pancakes, eggs, and bacon. The other held an assortment of fresh fruit.

"Is there anything else that I can get for you?" Rogmesh asked me.

"No, I'm okay. Thank you." I said reaching for the cream to put in my coffee.

"I'm good as well." Nira agreed.

Both gave a nod and went back into the house. I made up my plate of cakes that smelled of vanilla and fresh fruit. Niratap was all grace as he dished his own plate with eggs, bacon, and a pancake. He decorated his pancake with the butter and passed it to me, then poured a small amount of syrup on his plate. He took his fork and knife to cut his cake, dipped it in syrup and brought it to his mouth, pausing only when he had closed it into his mouth behind the mask, to look up at me.

"Yes, my dear?"

"How did you learn to look that elegant eating a pancake?"

He chuckled. "Observation in a time long past."

"How old are you?"

"One thousand one hundred thirty-two give or take five years." He said nonchalantly, cutting his egg. "Yourself?"

I choked on my bite of pancake. "What?"

"I asked how old you were?"

"I'm twenty-three. Are you really over a thousand years old?"

"Yes." He said before taking a bite.

I looked at him in awe, and felt a wicked smile come across my lips. "You fuck very well for an old man."

It was his turn to choke and cough. "That is no way to speak over breakfast."

I shrugged, popping a grape into my mouth. "It's a good way to talk to your lover, though. Why do you wear the mask?"

"It hides my human silhouette." The answer was noncommittal.

"But?"

"But what?"

"Uh," I put my hand up to the top of my head.

He seemed to ponder that for a moment then shrugged. "That is a fair point. Antlers are quite noticeable. The mask comes from a time when I didn't have control of the magic that I do now. It was necessary back then, now it has just become a habit."

"Okay, I can understand that. How do you make money?"

"Initially it came with the manor, but in the last few hundred years, we've invested in stocks. What made you want to study monsters?"

"Lack of exposure, for the most part, and the reading I did my whole life. My dad used to read me stories, legends, and whatnot. It has always stuck with me."

"Have you had contact with your father since he left?"

"No. Mom tried initially, but it was like he just disappeared. She couldn't reach him at all. When will you tell me your story?"

He poured himself more coffee. "You really just want to open old wounds, don't you?"

"That's not my intention." I meant it. I didn't want his story at the cost of his heart or peace of mind, but because I wanted to understand why he stood where he did. "I just want to know you. I was a sheltered kid, and this experience, even though it has been traumatic and dangerous, finding you had only made me want to know more, about you, about monsters in general."

"There is really not much to know about me."

I looked at him defiantly. "I doubt that very much."

Chapter Seventeen

Niratap

She was cross with me, but what was I to tell her? I had spent a third of my life wild, scraping by and barely surviving, a third in captivity where I had lost many parts of myself at the hands of man, and a third as I am now, a benefactor in the darkness trying to destroy it before it destroyed me. Would she want to know those things, the things I had suffered, the things I had endured? I wasn't ready to share that. I didn't know if I ever would be. So many of the things I had survived all those many years marred the skin beneath my shadows. Not to mention the heartbreak and loss. No, I wasn't ready to share those parts of myself with anyone. No one knew my story in its entirety.

"You may be right, but that is my story to tell."

She huffed, finishing off her pancake, but didn't speak. I would have to give her something eventually, but I wasn't ready. I pulled my phone out and dialed Vrorlin. I needed to get her things squared away regardless.

He answered on the third ring. "Lord Niratap, what a surprise."

"I have some things I need to get arranged and you are my in."

"I work at a college now, my Lord."

"I know." I looked at Shasha who was giving me a quizzical look. "I have had a student come into my care, and I need to arrange for her to become fully online. So, I can keep her safe and out of the city."

"Who are you talking to?" Shasha asked. I held up a hand to signal for her to wait, and she glared at me. She really doesn't like the word no, does she?

"What is her name?"

"Shasha."

"Her full name, my Lord."

I didn't know. Guilt gripped my heart. I had fucked her without knowing her name. "What is your last name, my dear?"

"Dion."

"Her name is Shasha Dion."

"Ah, you're in luck, my friend. She is in my program, and it will be easy to get her fully switched to an online format. I would just need a couple of hours. She should be ready for class today, and if not today definitely by Friday."

"Thank you. I'm going to send Allipo in for her things, will you take him to her dorm?"

"Yes, I can do that. My Lord, I can infer how she came into your care, but why her? She's only human."

"If I had an answer for you, I would give it."

"Ah. The heart wants what it wants, got it."

"Stormchaser, I don't know what you mean by that."

"You'll learn soon enough. I'll get her transferred for you and be ready when Allipo gets here."

"Thank you, Vrorlin."

"Of course." With that, he hung up.

"Vrorlin Stormchaser is your in at the college, my department head?" She asked incredulously.

"Yes." I answered before finishing my coffee.

"How do you guys know each other?" She asked, that curiosity of hers was going to get her in trouble.

"The same way I met almost everyone else in the manor." It was the truth, just not the full story.

She groaned, collecting the dishes and stacking them on the tray. The clicking of the dished grated against my ears.

"Are you done with your coffee?" She asked, her tone sharp.

"Yes." She snatched the cup from the table. She was angry. "You can leave the dishes. Rogmesh will come to grab them."

"No, I got it." She barked, picking up the tray and plopping it on her shoulder holding it with one hand. She curtsied, picking up the edge of the grey knee-length skirt, and bitterly said. "My Lord."

The display made my blood boil. "Shasha. Tread lightly with that tone."

"Or else what? I'll be locked in a dungeon?" She sauntered off.

I saw red. I stood, charging behind her and snarled. "I don't have to let you go to school. I don't have to let you be connected to your family outside. I don't have to let you have freedom."

She stopped and I froze, my own words giving me pause. She sniffled, her hand on the doorknob. "If that is what you wish, I really don't have a choice in the matter." She opened the door, slipping inside, and shutting it in my face.

"Fuck." Had I really spoken that way to her? Me of all people who valued freedom for everyone. Me, the Bondbreaker, threatening her as one would a slave. I took a breath and followed through the door. I could hear Shasha crying in the kitchen, but came face to face with Rogmesh, rolling pin in hand at the door.

"I can't believe you!" She snarled, swinging the rolling pin at me.

I stepped back, to avoid being hit in the face. "Rogmesh, I can explain."

"Can you?" She swung again.

"I didn't mean what I said. She was angry with me and-"I bumped into the dining table. She swung at me again and I caught the pin in my hand; the blow stung through my bones. Tears streamed down her cheeks.

"You said something to hurt her because she hurt your pride. You threatened her freedom because you are so full of yourself. You threatened her with bonds like the bonds you broke free from. You realize that don't you?"

My eyes widened, a knife in my heart at the full realization of what I had said to her. "No, Rogmesh, I did not.

They were spoken out of frustration, and yes they were
intended to cause harm. I'm sorry."

"Don't apologize to me." She pointed to the open
kitchen door. "You march your ass in that kitchen, and you
apologize to that poor girl. Who has been through enough the
last few days and doesn't need your shitty disposition adding
to it."

I looked past Rogmesh and saw Shasha curled tightly
into Durgash's chest, sobbing. He rubbed her back, trying to
soothe her, something I should be doing. I should be the one
comforting her. Instead, I had hurt her. I looked towards the
foyer, I could go to my study and let someone who hasn't
victimized the poor girl tend to her wounded heart.

"Don't you dare run, either. Don't you dare be a
coward." Rogmesh hissed, her words are another knife in my
chest.

"Okay." I took a deep breath and walk into the
kitchen. Durgash glared at me. "May I?"

"Honestly, I can't believe you. After everything."

I couldn't look him in the eye. I chose the floor
instead, "I know, I know Durgash. May I?" He stepped away,
and Shasha's hands moved to cover her face, tears slipping
between her fingers. I came to my knees in front of her.
"Shasha."

She shook her head and turned trying to leave, but I
caught her around the waist with my hand, guiding her to my
chest. She buried her head against my shoulder, and I rubbed
soothing circles on her back.

"Shasha. I am sorry."

She wrapped her arms around my neck. Her teary
face wet against my skin and sobbed into me. Each sniffle
and hiccup cut me to the core. Fuck. Fuck. I had done this
with my words, just because I didn't want to be honest with
her completely, maybe I wasn't being honest with myself.
Just because I suffered didn't mean I should make her suffer.

"Shasha."

She sniffled, her voice cracking when she speaks. "You're not going to, right?"

"Not going to what, my sweet." I rub her back as she choked on a sob.

"You're not going to keep me locked up here. You're not going to keep me from going to school or talking to my mom."

"No, darling." I gave her a squeeze. "I spoke without thinking. I was frustrated by the interaction, and I failed to take your emotions into account."

She tugged on my braid. "You're a jerk you know that right."

"So, I've been told."

"A childish jerk."

"Yes." I was. I had never pondered what a relationship could be like. Not after everything I had survived. She twisted my feelings in all sorts of directions.

She pulled away, wiping her face. "I just want to know you. Is it really that hard to open up to someone?"

I sighed. She wouldn't let up. "We have known each other for just over twenty-four hours my dear. I-I have had a long and not-so-kind life, and I would much rather get to know you in the now, than in the time lost in the darkness of my past."

She placed a gentle hand on my cheek, and internally I flinched, expecting her to strike me. She didn't; she stroked my cheek and stared straight into my eyes. I knew it wasn't what she wanted, but I needed time to sort through things and prepare my trauma, so it didn't traumatize her. I placed a hand on her cheek.

"Okay." She says simply.

I blinked. "Okay."

A sad smile takes up residence on her face. "I don't like that you won't tell me things, but I understand that life hasn't been kind to you. Terrible things happened, and to be honest I'm not sure if I'm ready for those terrible things either."

"I appreciate that you understand. It's not that I necessarily want to keep things from you, but you have been through enough without me dumping my trauma on you."

A tear rolled over my hand as she spoke. "Okay. What were our plans for today?"

"Well, I'm going to send Allipo and Eloimaya to collect your things. If you want, you could go with them, or I haven't had the pleasure of giving you a tour of our home."

She smiled, really smiled, and I expected her to say she's going to go with Allipo, but instead she says. "Show me our home."

Chapter Eighteen

Shasha

I hooked my arm in his as he guided me into the foyer. "Well, we'll start here. The manor was built in the late 1700s by a terrible man who deserves to be forgotten to history. After his death, I took control of the manor, and it has been my home ever since. The east wing is where you will find the library, the solarium, and my study. The west wing is primarily the dining room and the kitchen, but there is also a ballroom."

"A ballroom? Somehow, I don't see you holding a ball."

"Very true." There was a sorrowful tone to his voice. "Would you like to see it?"

"Yes."

He led me down the short hall to the right of the grand stairs. The hall opened to a large ornate room, the walls decorated with maroon velvet curtains and marble carvings. The floor was the same mahogany as the rest of the house but laid in an intricate swirling pattern. There was a small dais on the other side that had a grand piano underneath a dust sheet and the far wall had glass doors that must have led out to the terrace.

"This is beautiful."

"It is." Nira adjusted his tie as if it was too tight. It was like this room made him uncomfortable.

"Show me the library next." I spun us around, taking his hand in mine.

He laughed tightly. "Alright."

Together we walked back through the foyer, and another small hall on the opposite side of the steps caught my eye. "What's that?"

He followed my gaze, "Through there is a security room, it's Mitta's space for the most part, and a medical room. Beyond that is the basement which is restricted from you."

"Why is that?"

"Because there are dangerous things both inside and outside this manor and my goal is to keep you safe."

I frowned as he tugged me gently behind him to the east wing. The hall was lined with windows that peeked out over the front gardens. Dheg was outside trimming roses, a serene look on his face.

"Does everyone look so peaceful?"

"Hmm?" He asked as I paused, watching Dheg through the window.

"He just looks peaceful."

Niratap leaned over my shoulder resting his chin there and peered out the window. "I don't force them to do what they do. They choose their jobs. Fauns are nature spirits, so it makes sense that he is happiest with his plants."

"I see." My hand came to rest on his cheek. A purr-like sound emanated from his chest. His hand came to rest along my ribs. We stood there in the hall watching Dheg trim roses and lay the long-cut stems in a basket.

"We were heading to the library, yes?" His voice was heavy in my ears.

"Yes, I am really excited to see the library. That's what I did as a summer job my junior year. I shelved books and helped read to little kids. I enjoyed being surrounded by stories."

"That sounds like it was rewarding."

"It was. I miss it, but I needed to get out of my hometown. Living in a small town is really hard. You grow up with everyone and you know everyone's business; it's suffocating, and heaven forbid you can't make friends in kindergarten because then you are alone until you graduate."

"Were you alone?" His voice sounded softer, almost as if he wasn't trying to verbalize the question.

"Yeah, I was. Going away was a chance to make some semblance of friends."

He cleared his throat. "I am sorry that I have stolen that from you."

"It's fine. You can't really miss out on something you've never had." My chest tightened with a familiar pang of sadness.

He wrapped a hand around my shoulder and pulled me close. "I understand loneliness. It numbs the heart to many things. Ah, here we are."

He turned, opening a double set of oak doors. A two-story library full of books is brightly illuminated by a large bay window. There are a couple of stacks on the ground floor, a comfy sitting area by a fireplace, and a couple of desks with lamps. It was like stepping into history.

I gasped. "This is even better than the ballroom."

"I'm glad you like it, past the stacks is the door to my study." He said stepping into the room as Allipo came past the stacks.

He bowed low avoiding eye contact. "My Lord."

"Allipo, I have an errand I need you to run, take Eloimaya with you as well."

"Of course, my Lord. The errand?" The satyr lifted his head but refused to make eye contact.

"I need you to go down to see Vrorlin and collect Shasha's things from her dorm."

"Yes, my Lord, about this mor- "

"Be back home before nightfall. We'll discuss your antics this morning when you return."

"Yes, my Lord." Allipo bowed again, leaving the library without looking at me. Niratap exhaled, rolling his shoulders in frustration.

"Not to irritate you further, but- "

"Shasha, the satyr's need to poke and prod at me is not entirely why I am irritated."

"But it is." I spoke matter-of-factually.

He turned and looming over me, his hands clenched into fists. He growled. "You do not understand."

"What do I not understand, Nira? That Allipo made comments to you about me or that he likes to push your buttons because there is obviously something between us?" I took his fisted hands in mine as I spoke. "Allipo already has seen my body, so it wasn't my nakedness that you were trying to hide, I'm fairly certain it was the little purple bruises that have started to sprout up all over my skin from your kisses and touches."

He closed his eyes, his expression unreadable behind the mask and shadow. His hands relax, defeated by my words. "I'm sorry."

"It's okay." I pulled him lower so I can kiss his cheek. "I understand enough to know you're being foolish."

He huffed in my ear. "That's rich coming from you."

I kissed his neck reaching for his tie. "Why? Because I have no sense of self-preservation"

A rumble rolled though him, his hands coming to my waist. "Exactly."

Heat began to pool in my body and despite the bruises that were blooming flowers all over my body, I needed him again. I nipped at his neck, "I like the taste of danger."

My back came into contact with a wall, Niratap lifted me at the waist, pressing his girth against me. One hand held my leg against his hip and the other cupped my face. Though shadows and the mask covered his features there was heat in his eyes as they burned into me.

"Shasha, you drive me mad." His voice was heavy and heady.

I stroked his arm. "Do I now?"

He growled hungrily. "Yes. You are maddening. Every aspect from your voice to your taste."

I reached for his tie, pulling him in. "Tell me how maddening."

He leaned against me, pressing hot kisses against my neck. "Your scent is intoxicating. Your voice is a siren's song. Your skin welcoming velvet to my touch."

His breath was hot on my skin, but not as hot as my flush. "Tell me more."

"I want to give you things that I give no other. I want to claim you at every opportunity."

My hand slipped into his hair; his tail slipped away from his waist curling around my other leg. His name a whisper on my tongue. "Nira."

He lips crashed into mine, our tongues demanding of each other. I traced the shape of his sharp teeth, even in his human form he had fangs. Those very teeth had pricked against my skin last night and driven me insane. He tasted rich like black coffee and whiskey. His hands supported me, even though I knew he wanted to use them to explore my body again. My hands found the edge of his vest seeking the button of his slacks, wanting him to sink into my bruised flesh. He lifted me from the wall and carried me through the doors beside us. He sat me on the edge of a desk. His mouth never leaving mine.

I finally released his swollen flesh of the trousers, taking his velvet softness into my hand. He groaned, fisting my hair to pull my head backward deepening the kiss further. I stroked him, my hands exploring the ridges and veins of his very human length. He sighed into me as I ran my thumb over the head. He left my lips, his eyes impassioned with need as he straightened before me.

"Shasha." My name was a harsh whisper on his tongue. "May I."

My heart was thundering and in just as harsh a whisper I breathed, "Yes."

He descended to my neck, kissing and licking and sucking and nipping at a maddening pace. His hands came to my knees, feather light as he caressed up my thighs, hooking my panties and sliding them off in a smooth movement. He sat them on the desk beside us, his eyes hungry. He reached behind me, shifting things on the desk before he eased me back on the hardwood. He pulled me to the edge, hiking the skirt up to my hips. He paused, his eyes taking me in, a softness coming into them.

"Are you okay?" Tenderness softened his voice.

"Yes, more than okay." I came up to my elbows to see what had him pausing. Dark bruised handprints covered my thighs, they must have set in after I dressed.

"I didn't mean to be so rough with you." There was a tinge of regret or maybe sorrow in his voice.

"I wanted you; I still want you. I need you Niratap." I laid back down on the desk widening my legs for him.

He crouched before me, kissing the bruises tenderly before he moved to the apex of my thighs. He lifted my thighs onto his shoulders, making eye contact with me, silver eyes devouring me, asking for permission.

"Yes, violate my body however you wish."

Something flashed in his eyes, but he didn't comment as he lowered his head pressing a kiss to the top of my mons before he slid his tongue deliciously between my folds. He lapped at my core languidly, causing me to pant and writhe beneath him. I twisted the fingers of one hand in his hair and the other found its place on a prong of his antlers. He growled possessively, pressing himself deeper, his tongue finding my depths.

"Nira." I cried, my body turning into layers and layers of knots. "Please."

He removed my hands from their claims and easily flipped me, positioning my knees on the desk and he rose to his full height. "You are a delicious treat, Shasha."

He positioned himself at my entrance and eased into my tender flesh slowly, grunting as he entered me fully. I winced and moaned at the same time, the pain also bringing pleasure.

"Nira." His name rang like a bell off my tongue.

"Shasha." He groaned. Gentle at first, easing in and out of my slowly before devolving with need, his thrusts becoming more urgent, more desperate.

I came and then came a second time while he searched for his climax, at one point he flipped me over so he could kiss me deeply. I tasted myself on his tongue both sharp and floral. His hands palmed my breasts and stroked my neck. I felt my body begin to shudder again, my screams of ecstasy bouncing off the walls of books.

"Shasha."

"Come for me, Nira. Fill me."

"Shasha." He kissed me with his final thrust, his mouth hot and desperate as he filled my body with his seed. He moved from my mouth kissing my face and neck, his kisses delicate and loving. He pulled away, righting his appearance, and fixing his clothes. He watched me, exposed and open sprawled across his study desk.

"You are the most transfixing creature I have met in my lifetime." He came between my legs again, lapping at my core.

I let my head roll to the side, my strength gone. I watched his head bob, tasting the results of our lovemaking. I wanted to see his face, to truly know how he felt, beyond the words he gave me. What would he look like? I knew he had a strong square jaw, high chiseled cheekbones, a proud straight nose, and full lips but what honeyed shade was his skin? Why did his smile pinch at one side? Why hide behind the shadows at all?

When he was finished, he slid my panties back on over my legs and helped me to my feet, fixing my skirt. He grabbed my face and kissed me, his lips salty, floral, and sweet. He broke the kiss and stared into my eyes; his silver irises glowed. He held my gaze, and I almost asked for his face, but I knew he would reject it no matter the terms of the moment. I looked away down at my hands.

"I don't know what to say to that."

"You don't have to say anything, my love."

He looked down at the floor as his computer beeped on the desk. I wondered if he was embarrassed by the way words came out of him. The small glance at the softer parts of his heart warmed me. I liked that he called me that. Liked that he wanted to claim me as his, his name very much tattooed on my heart already. He walked around the desk, sitting in the seat.

"Vrorlin emailed me. He says the schedule program is down and he won't be able to get you switched until later. He's giving you a pass for today, just says to read the first chapter of Mythos Defined. Which I assume is one of your textbooks in your dorm?"

"Yeah." Walking around to stand beside him. "I guess it's a good thing you are friends with my professor."

"I guess it is." He said turning his chair, fitting me between his legs "I get you all to myself for the day then, don't I?"

I smiled. "I mean, I have to wait for Allipo anyways."

"My Lord?" Mitta's voice came from the doorway.

"Yes, Mitta. I'm in the study."

Chapter Nineteen

Shasha

She came around the stack dressed in black leather pants, a matching under-bust corset, a light puffy sleeve tunic, and flexible leather shoes. It was the kind of outfit I pictured a pirate wearing or a swordsman. Her nose flared and scrunched before she bowed with a sweeping arm, her fluffy dark umber hair pulled back tightly in a braid down her back.

"My Lord, I hate to intrude on your time, but you did say when you returned from your trip we could draw, and I also have some things in the security office I need to go over with you."

"Right." Niratap did not sound enthused, but he stood. "Well, let us get to it then, I guess."

"Shasha, you are welcome to join us." Mitta invited me.

"Of course, I would love to see your space."

Mitta smiled warmly. Other than the Days, she was the only one warm without the hint of doubt that lingered in the eyes of the others. "I would very much enjoy that."

"What do you mean by draw?" I asked her, coming to walk beside her and she looped her arm through mine.

"Well, in the name of preparedness, I have taken to stocking medical triage items, and I draw blood from everyone a few times a year to keep it stocked. Given the nature of what Lord Niratap does, there are always risks."

"What is it that Lord Niratap does?"

Mitta looked over her shoulder before she answered, checking with Niratap. "The lord's goal is to disassemble the black-market trade of magical creatures and parts, but to do that he must remove the creatures and parts from the market. So, he purchases an assortment of dangerous creatures to get them out of the hands of those who wish to use them."

"Interesting, that is quite a goal. Do you want to draw my blood as well?" I asked.

"If you are so inclined." She said with a smile.

"Mitta." Niratap's voice is calm but serious.

"What?" I said peeking over my shoulder at him.

"I don't think that that will be necessary."

I frowned at him, pushing irritation into my voice. "In the name of preparedness, my Lord."

Mitta smiled wider but said nothing as we came out of the hall and crossed the foyer to the unassuming grey door that hid behind it some of the mysteries of the manor. She released my arm as she opened the door.

Through the door, there was an open room with plain white tile and walls. Sinks, fridges, a couple of gurneys set in a seated position, and lots of storage. Opposite the door, there was an open hall with several doors down it.

"Each of you take a gurney and I'll grab the supplies." Mitta said, going to one of the storage closets. I could see now that each door was labeled, so anyone could find the supplies quickly.

"I like how organized you have everything."

"In case I'm the one who gets laid up. I need it to be easy. Especially for Echo, she's very sensitive to blood and gore. Surprisingly, considering her species of fae aren't known for being kind or squeamish."

"What kind of fae is Echo?"

"She is a grassy knoll pixie." Niratap said as he undid his cuffs and rolled up his sleeve, the shadows hugging his skin. "They are a vicious breed of pixie that is known for tearing unsuspecting people to ribbons. Echo was chased off by her own kind because she has a delicate disposition."

"That's terrible." I said feeling sorry for her.

"Echo would not appreciate your pity, Shasha." He said as Mitta set a small table and tray beside him, "She has come to terms with that part of her life."

"Besides," Mitta said. "Echo prefers to grow life rather than take it. She is amazing in the garden and has a softness with the animals that Dheg cares for."

Mitta sat on a rolling stool beside Niratap, wrapping a tourniquet around his bicep. I watched her expertly poke him, even through the shadows. Once she was satisfied she removed the tourniquet and the blood flowed freely through the tube. Niratap looked the other way through the whole process. Mitta then rolled to the counter, grab a second tray and table and rolled back to me.

"Have you ever had your blood drawn before?"

"No."

"Ooo, fresh meat. Which hand is your dominant?"

"My right."

"Okay." She rolled my left arm over and poked at the crook of my elbow. "I'm just seeing if there is a good vein on your non-dominant arm first, just so you're not super sore. Though it looks like you are already covered in bruises."

I blushed, noticing the deep purple bruise on my upper arm. "Okay."

She wrapped the tourniquet around my arm and poked me with the needle; I didn't even feel it as she got it all set up as she did with Niratap. "Perfect."

"I didn't even feel that. You have a feather light touch Mitta."

"I've had plenty of practice. So, I'll take two pints of blood for storage from you. It'll take about twenty minutes. Let me know if you start feeling light-headed or woozy."

"Okay."

"Do you know your blood type?"

"No. I think my mom is B+, but I'm not sure."

"It's fine I can type your blood too, so you know. It helps in case you're not here; you can tell the hospital."

"Gotcha." I smiled lightly. "Have you guys ever needed to use any?"

I felt Niratap's eyes on me, but Mitta answered, "Once in the last ten years; the harpies in the aviary went after Dheg. He got knocked unconscious and was on the aviary floor for an hour or two. Echo found him, and it took him a while before he felt comfortable in the aviary again."

"I've read that harpies can be vicious."

"They are." Niratap said, his eyes fierce. "That is why you need an escort if you wish to visit."

"Understood." I said. "Mitta, I wanted to say I like your outfit."

"Oh, this." She smiled. "These are my training clothes. I wear them when I spar."

"Who do you spar with?" I asked fascinated.

"Everyone, depending on who is free. Most often it's Allipo or Katrel."

"Do you spar with Lord Niratap?"

"On occasion. The lord is very busy. Everyone knows at least hand-to-hand combat, given the nature of business."

"Can you teach me?" I asked.

"If the lord permits it."

"Please, Nira-I mean my Lord."

He chuckled. "I don't see the harm in it, but not today. Giving blood takes a toll on the body, especially if you've never done it before."

"There you have it, we'll pick a day you're free next week and we can start." Mitta said, flashing her bright smile.

"I'm excited."

"Mitta please be gentle with her." Niratap says.

"I'm only mean to you, my Lord."

He laughed, laying his head back on the gurney, closing his eyes. If someone walked by, they would probably think he was relaxing, but they wouldn't notice his hand squeezing the bars of the gurney. His skin was cloaked in shadow, but I had a feeling that beneath it his knuckles were white. I wondered why he was so uncomfortable in his own home.

"What kind of training do you do, Mitta?"

"Hand to hand mostly. Once in a while, I get to practice sword fighting with Katrel. The rest of my combat training I can do on my own."

"How many combat skills do you have?"

"Well, I know an array of martial arts, swordsmanship, archery, handguns, and knives."

"So, you're literally a weapon." I said only half kidding.

She laughed with a shrug. "It's what I'm good at, being security for the manor, and Lord Niratap requires the skills."

"Not to sound rude Mitta, but does the lord need protection?"

"Not entirely, but there are times we all feel more comfortable with me tagging along. The lord is not without enemies."

"I'm sure I have made more." Niratap said, not opening his eyes. "I broke plenty of etiquette expectations and rules to get you, Shasha."

"You said that."

"What exactly did you do, my Lord?" Mitta asked.

He looked at the two of us, eyes serious, "I broke the auction code to guarantee my success, threatened the matron, and disrespected that vermin, Dravin, who owns it."

"Fuck." Mitta groaned, covering her face with her hand.

"I'm sorry Mitta. It would probably be wise to take you next time I go to the market. What I know of Dravin is that he is very underhanded, and only has his reputation from killing and trafficking the competition."

"Do you know when the market will pop back up?" Mitta asked, undoing the draw line and wrapping my elbow.

"Not yet, granted it has only been two days. As soon as one of us on the outside knows something, we'll know."

"How many people work for you Lord Niratap?" I asked, watching as Mitta wrote my name and the date on the bags and stored them in a fridge. She then took the small bit of blood in the tube to the counter and pulled some chemicals from the cabinet above.

"A couple of dozen outside of the manor. They mainly run reconnaissance on the movements of my enemies and the market itself."

"Will you move someone into Dravin's operations?" I asked genuinely curious about what was going on in his world.

He eyed me, his answer vague. "No, I was already watching Dravin for other reasons."

"Like?"

He sighs, pinching the bridge of his nose beneath the mask. "Dravin is involved in the creature trade as well as the sex trade. That interests me more."

"Because it directly affects you?" I asked because he was in fact a creature that historically was traded. There was a deadly edge to his gaze when he looked at me.

"Among other things."

I could tell he was uncomfortable, so I stopped. Mitta came back over and smiled sadly at me. "You're B + my darling, don't mind him either, he's always grumpy when we draw blood."

"Mitta, I am not grumpy." He growled.

"You just don't like needles." She said pointedly looking at him.

His eyes widened and then he scowled. "I don't poke at anyone, yet everyone pokes at me. Why is that Mitta?"

"My Lord, to be frank with you, it is because you don't."

He didn't say anything, just closed his eyes and laid back. It was a tense few moments while his blood draw finished. I watched Mitta as she wrapped him in the same fluid manner, with ease and grace. Niratap rolled his sleeve down securing his cuffs; he was meticulous about how they sat against his skin.

"Mitta, what other things do you have to show me?" He asked once he was satisfied with his cuffs.

"I'll show you, my Lord." Mitta said from the blood storage fridge.

I went to stand and Niratap appeared next to me, his arm out. "I'm fine."

"I just don't want you falling." He said softly.

"If I did, it would be the perfect place."

He huffed something like a laugh but whatever expression his face held didn't warm his eyes, something has shifted his mood. Together we followed behind Mitta as she turned down the hall and through the first door. This room was full of monitors and keyboards, as well as two gun safes and an array of knives and swords. I couldn't imagine the cost of this room alone without the weapons, it was state of the art.

"Firstly," she said, tapping on a file to open it; a video feed came up on the large screen in the middle. In the clip you could see striped spider legs moving in the background of the video. "The jorogumo is migrating closer to the road. I figured you would be interested in knowing, since Allipo is trying to get work done."

"Noted. What else?"

She moved to another file and brought up a video that showed farmland beyond the forest, and a deer carcass, or what I could only assume to be a deer carcass, strewn at the edge of a field. A few men were gathered around it including the sheriff I had met yesterday.

"Shit. When was this?" Niratap asked as the feed played.

"The day before you returned. They left the carcass there, but there's no telling if it was one of your wards or if it was something wild."

"That would explain the sheriff's need to be on my case yesterday."

"I'll beat him up for you." Mitta offered in jest.

"No, it's fine Mitta. The sheriff is just an annoyance. I'm more concerned with whatever creature did that. Did you catch it on the feed?"

"I looked." Mitta said, rewinding the tape, it made me a little ill watching everything move backwards. I looked down at the floor and Niratap set a steadying hand on my shoulder.

"Here's the deer and there's nothing," Mitta said, and I looked up to see a young stag walk into the frame. A few moments later the camera went dark, encased in shadow. When the trees came back into view, we couldn't see past them into the field. "Any ideas my Lord?"

"A couple. I'll go sniff around this evening."

"Okay. I'll go with you."

"I planned on it. Anything else?"

"Just that we need to update some of the cameras, and I want to add to the east side forest. The creatures are getting edgy as we get closer to fall and I want to track the deer some to make sure the basilisks don't try to bolt."

"Understood. Whatever you need is yours, Mitta." Niratap turned to usher me to the door. "We'll be off then; I was in the middle of a tour."

I was in the hall when I asked. "Where do the other doors go?"

Niratap looked down the hall, and I wasn't sure he'd answer me. "The first door is Mitta's room, the second is storage for cleaning supplies, the third is the laundry, and the last door is the basement whi—"

"Which is restricted. I understand." I said quickly, before turning to Mitta. "Can I see your room."

Mitta smiled sweetly. "Of course, darling."

I twisted from Niratap's grasp and walked down the hall with Mitta. She was kind and her interests fascinating, I found myself wanting her to like me and be my friend. She opened the door to a room much smaller than my own room. The room was painted a cool grey, furnished with a large bed the covers unmade and in a pile on the floor, a worktable that had a variety of knives on it, and a writing desk that had papers strewn about it as well as a small television and laptop on it.

"I know it's not much, but that is what I prefer." She said standing in the center of her modest room. "I like being close to my work."

I smiled. "I can respect that."

"You're free to come to visit me whenever, this is where I usually am."

"I will for sure."

"Good, I'll hold you to that." She smiled and I noticed she had longer canines. "Now run along, the lord would prefer just your company."

"I'm sure." I said, turning out of her room and walking down the hall.

I walked towards the tall, severe figure who was leaning against the wall before the door to the foyer. His eyes were closed. His profile with the mask was a menacing shadow that for some reason I felt like I was starting to fall for. Wisps of lust and excitement flowed through me, and in my heart, I knew that he was what I had wanted the entire time I was trapped in my hometown. Yes, I had wanted to bask in the neon lights, but I had wanted someone to sweep me off my feet and hold me close. I wanted him to love me, but how could someone like me be loved by him?

Chapter Twenty

Niratap

Infuriating and beautiful this was all this girl was to me. She twisted knives in my chest, and whether she intended to or not, she made me want to confront the demons of my past. Even as she smiled at me so warmly, I couldn't help but be wary. Would she uncover all the dark things about me and decide that I was not worth her time and presence? I wanted her to choose me, but what is the real cost of that? Was her love worth my self-destruction? Was I worthy of her?

She came up next to me, her sweet scent warming my blood. "Where to now, my Lord?"

I looked at her with that warm smile she had. "How about the solarium and the gardens? Get out of the manor for a moment."

"Sure."

I was really just hoping the fresh air would help clear my head. She seemed unfazed, by the things that she was learning about my work and myself, taking it all in stride, and somehow, she was also holding back. There were questions in her eyes as we walked down the hall to the door to the solarium. why did she hold back?

"What is on your mind, my dear?" I asked trying to hold my curiosity out of my voice.

"Things that I want to know about you." She answered immediately, not looking up at me.

"What things do you wish to know?"

She smiles to herself, laughing at her own thoughts. "Everything, but I have come to realize that you have much hidden for a reason. Whether you think it is for my safety or for your own I am not sure."

I pondered her words as I opened the doors into the solarium; they are a bright stained-glass mosaic of the rising sun. "You are quite intuitive, my dear."

She beamed up at me. "I am just good at reading people, my Lord. This is beautiful."

The solarium was bright in the early afternoon light with an array of plants from massive monsteras to the lotus in the pond. There were several cream-colored sitting areas dotted throughout the large space. I walked behind her and let her explore amongst the plants. She was bright and happy, though I did not know if it was because of my company or because she enjoyed my home. She stopped, sniffing some snow-white lilies.

"What caused you to want to dismantle the black market?" she asked.

"I have told you that everyone here at one point or another has been bought and sold. Including myself."

"So, it's like a personal vendetta so no one else suffers?"

"More so just that no one else has to experience what I have."

"Is that why you hide behind the shadows? To hide the proof that you were once property?"

The hairs on the back of my neck stood on end and I paused, fighting to keep my eyes neutral. "One of the reasons."

She looked up at me, her deep brown eyes endless. "Why hide what you are?"

"It has become necessary as time has progressed. There are fewer and fewer who know of what I had to do to escape my bonds. It has become safer to keep the story of my skin hidden from those who would use it against me." I had never been that honest with anyone, but those eyes of hers captured that vulnerable part of my heart and held it hostage with their warmth.

"So, another aspect of you that takes time and trust." It wasn't a question.

"Why are you so keenly interested in me? My appearance?" I was curious.

"You." She paused and looked away into the flowers before her. "You fascinate me."

Something in me cried out for her, wanted her to fill my very being with the light that shone from beyond those brown eyes. "You find me fascinating?"

"Yes."

"How so? Is it because of what I am? Or is it because of what I do?"

"All of it."

Her answer had me shaking inside; how could a creature as beautiful as her find all aspects of me interesting? "Well, I guess we have all the time in the world then."

"What do you mean by that?" She asked, looking up at me from the lilies. I couldn't believe what I was about to do.

With a large sweeping bow, being mindful of my antlers I asked, "What is your name, young miss?"

She smiled brightly and giggled, the sound made my heart flutter. "My name is Shasha Nicole Dion, and what might your name be, sir?"

"I am called many things, but you may know me as Niratap Bondbreaker."

"Bondbreaker?" She asked, the afternoon sunlight bouncing off the flecks of gold in her dark depthless eyes.

"It is a moniker for who I am and what I do." I said to her, summoning the delicate chain that bound her to me. I stood tucking my other hand behind my back, gently tugging her to stand before me. "It is my hope that we can grow a bond that doesn't need to be spelled. However, for now, this keeps you safe from others, and keeps us connected."

"I would like that." She said warmly, but I could not discern if she was talking about being free of the chains or bonding with me. Something must have shown in my eyes because she clarified. "I would love to forge a bond with you, my Lord."

My heart fluttered again, a smile coming to my lips that I knew she couldn't see, and the chain faded between us. "Where would you like to start?"

"You were about to show me the gardens."

"Why yes." I said walking past her. "I would love to show you the gardens."

The gardens that Echo and Dheg kept were vast and lush in the waning summer. The flower garden was alive with the hum of bees and other insects, roses and peonies lined the walkways with splashes of hydrangeas and lavenders every now and again. Dheg liked it as a mix of wild and tamed; it made the gardens feel alive. Defined walkways and gazebos and benches were swallowed by climbing ivies and flowering vines. Shasha frolicked through soft grasses and around mossy trees, at home here in the mountains. I could smell the autumn wind and a cool breeze at the end of August. Many things would be happening in the coming weeks, and I hoped that I wouldn't have to leave anytime soon, so I could watch her flower.

"Niratap." She called happily, finding a rope swing hanging from an oak tree.

I chuckled following her over the stones. "Yes, my dear."

"Will you push me?" She asked, smiling wide, as she sat on the old swing.

"I can, my sweet." I said coming behind her and pulling the swing back. I let her glide through the air, her laughter light and melodic. More laughter that came from a shadowed part of the hollow sounded out. I looked into the shaded space, seeing only little trees hiding there.

She planted her feet and looked in the same direction as me. "What is it?"

"Naiads and dryads, I assume." I said, trying to assuage her fear that sparked at the sound.

"Naiads and dryads." She said standing and walking towards the shadowed place. I almost reached for her, but the creatures were peaceful as long as one didn't trample the wild plants they grew or poisoned their water. She called out, "Hello."

More giggling erupted from the trees, and I could see Birch, Maple, and Rowan laughing behind an oak tree ahead of her, shifting before she came to them. She pouted slightly and the giggling continued; they were having a goodhearted laugh at Shasha's expense. I strode to where she stood surrounded by the giggling dryads.

"They're hiding from me." She said and more giggling ensued.

"Girls, our newest addition would like to meet you." I said, voice playful but firm. One by one the six trees in the glade in which we stood, became beautiful women and girls.

Oak, the eldest, stepped forward and bowed gently in her mossy dress, "It seems the lord has found a sweetie to brighten the grounds."

"The scariest thing in the forest has a new pet to bring him joy." Maple cooed and the others giggled.

"Now, now." I said, getting the girls' attention. "Shasha is not a pet, and she would like to meet you. These are the dryads that live here on the manor grounds, oldest to youngest are Oak, Rowan, Hawthorn, Maple, Birch, and Willow."

Each of the dryads bowed at the sound of their name, smiling warmly at us.

"You are all very beautiful." Shasha said.

"The dryads help Echo and Dheg manage the trees on the manor grounds. They play pranks at the worst but will not treat you poorly." I said knowing the dryads would understand the boundaries I set around Shasha. They nodded in response. Hawthorn stepped forward and offered Shasha a sprig of her blooms.

"These blooms are from my body, and as long as I live, they will bloom for you, softener of shadows." She said.

Shasha looked up at me and smiled. "I think the shadows have always been soft. The world has just made them look solid."

The girls giggled at her words, but it warmed my heart to hear her think that I was soft. That the world had just made me look hard and cruel. She said her good evenings to the dryads, grabbing my hand and whisking me away behind her to one of the many reflection pools in the garden. Koi fish swam languidly in the clear water. Shasha sat by the pool, the waning sunlight dancing against her skin, reflected from the pool.

"Thank you for today." She said, her voice sounding content.

"You are very welcome, my dear."

"Can I ask you something? I realize that I might not get an answer, but- "

"Ask away, my dear."

"Do you miss Ireland?"

"Yes and no," I said. I missed the rolling green fields and moors to run in. I missed hunting deer with my sister. I missed the girl that had first shown me kindness all those years ago. I did not miss the constant state of war. The smell of blood had long stained the earth. I did not miss the sounds of slaughter.

"What is it that you miss the most?"

I sighed, taking a seat beside her on the edge of the pool. "It's not a what, but a who that I miss."

"Can you visit them?"

A pang of sorrow worked its way deeply into my heart. "No, she died a very long time ago."

I felt her gaze on me, I could tell she was searching my eyes for something before she spoke. "I'm sorry."

That pain in my chest deepened, but this story I could tell her. "It's okay. She is just a memory now, but there are times that I long for her company."

"Who was she? When did you meet?"

"When I was younger and wild, I met my first human. Her name was Deirdre, and she was as fiery as her hair, a flame in the forest, but kind to all things that breathed, even monstrous beasts like myself. We met on a foggy spring morning in the woods, her flaming locks captivated me, her sweet singing voice calling out to all manner of spirits there. I followed her song and even as I stalked her, she smiled and sang. When I finally approached her, she stuck out a trusting hand and pet me. She was fearless. I shifted into this shape with her. I- "Remembering her brought an old longing in my heart, "I fell in love with her. We laid together under the moon and she loved me, in all my feral wild she did."

"What happened to her?"

I swallowed. "At that time Ireland was, as it always has been, filled with bloodshed and warring. The Irish people were being converted to the ways of the Catholics, the English invading and taking the land from the old people. Deirdre was considered a witch to them, a pagan who refused to be anything other than a beautiful wild flame in the forest. They burned her village, because of her. People died because she existed and loved them. I- "

Shasha placed a gentle hand on my own, tears I had thought long since dried threatened my eyes. She didn't need to say anything, she just offered comfort freely. I took a steadying breath.

"I was with her the night they came hunting for her, the men of the church. They found her with me, clad only in moonlight. They laughed at her wildness, laying with a beast as one would a man. They pointed their weapons at me, and Deirdre pleaded that they let me live, that they let me free. She walked up to the man of the cloth and begged him to spare me. I was frozen, watching her plead for my life when she herself was being hunted. I didn't notice the men that surrounded us. I didn't notice the ropes and chains that they carried. The man promised her that I would be spared and when she turned her back to him, her eyes were bright with happiness, then fear. They captured me, roped me in this form, and spelled chains that kept me from shifting."

"Why would they do such a thing?"

I swallowed, the shadows slithering over my skin. "She was different than them–too wild, too free, closer to the earth than the god they tried to shove down her throat."

"That is terrible and sad, did they kill her?" Her voice was so soft, like she was treading on the edge of a knife blade. Her wide eyes reflected in the pool before me.

"Yes, but first they tormented us. The men tortured me in front of her, whipping and stabbing me into submission, breaking her heart, and spilling my blood. More men broke her body; they raped her over and over in front of me, but I had lost too much blood and didn't have the strength to save her. The man of the church was the last to violate her body with his own, and when he was done, he fisted her hair and forced her to look at me, bleeding and subjugated. He told her I would live a long and painful life in confinement. He told her I would be beaten and beaten and beaten again until no memory of freedom existed in my body. That I would be his slave and a slave for the church. I would live, a prisoner, until I drew my last breath. Then he slit her throat, and with her last breath, she told me she loved me, and my spirit was broken as I watched the life drain from her eyes. The men took us back to the burned village and hefted her body onto a pyre filled with the bodies of the villagers. They set the flame of the forest alight, and part of me died that day."

I couldn't look at her directly; I hadn't realized that this wound from my past had yet to heal properly. In the reflection pool, I saw Shasha place a hand to her mouth and tears streamed down her cheeks. She shed tears for me, for Deirdre. I rubbed the center of my chest hoping to ease the ache that had taken its home there.

"So." She started her voice dewy. "Your first love is how you became a slave. That is why you are so guarded with who you are, with being vulnerable."

I worked up the nerve to look at her, wet cheeks, and wide brown eyes with that sympathetic look on her face squeezed my heart. I wiped the tears from her cheeks. This beautiful creature mourned for me.

"Yes. I lost her and lost my freedom for a few centuries. That man's promise of pain was my existence and eventually, I was purchased by the owner of this manor and brought to the states. He was a cruel man who enjoyed torture."

Fresh tears rolled down her cheeks. "I'm sorry."

What she apologized for I did not know. "Don't cry for me, Shasha. It was a long time ago, many human lifetimes, they are just scars and stories now."

"But they are terrible things that deserve justice."

"There has been justice my dear. I am alive and I am free. None of the people who harmed me in my life still live."

She was still crying, but she nodded. I took her hand and led her back into the manor. She brightened when we bumped into Echo, tears were forgotten, and she chatted happily about how beautiful the garden was. She was kindness incarnate, just like Deirdre had been. My phone buzzed in my pocket, there were two messages there. One was Allipo letting me know they were home and had put Shasha's belongings in her room. The other was from Bastion, my eyes in Dravin's operation, the message simply said: I need to see you.

"Are you ready, my Lord?" Mitta asked through Shasha's cracked door.

"Yes."

I looked down at Shasha's sleeping form. She had curled herself against me as she had read pages from her textbook that now lay open in her hand limply draped across my lap. I dogeared the page and set the book on her bedside table, slipping out of the covers and tucking them around her. Mitta watches me from the doorway with her feline way of assessing everything.

"Yes, Mitta?" I asked as she steps back from the doorway.

She bowed but there was something cunning in her voice. "Nothing, my Lord."

I shook my head walking down the hall. "Somehow I think it's more than nothing."

She fell into step beside me with a cat's smile on her face. "You are most definitely correct, my Lord."

"Enlighten me?"

"I think I will keep this to myself for now." Mitta said, folding her arms behind her back.

I harrumphed. "Fine. Please enlighten me when you deign to share."

"I might." She teased.

I shook my head turning down the stairs. "Everyone has opinions, I take it?"

"Oh, most definitely."

The late summer night was muggy, making our clothes stick to our skin as Mitta and I traveled down the road to where the deer carcass lay at the edge of the forest. The forest itself was quiet, like the creatures that roamed the woods had hidden themselves. Either from this new development or myself, I did not know. The smell of carrion and the buzz of insects feasting on the remains, hit our senses after we turned into the farmer's field. The carcass was a revolting sight.

"Poor thing met a gruesome end." Mitta said, circling the carcass. "I smell humans and decomposition but nothing else, and whatever it was didn't leave any tracks."

"I also don't smell anything." I said kneeling by the carcass. "Whatever attacked this deer was definitely preternatural. There is barely any meat left on the bones, it was skinned perfectly, and the organs are gone."

"How peculiar."

"Yes, and you're sure it wasn't a computer error?"

"I'm offended that you even ask."

I smiled. "Apologies. I was just touching all the bases. Whatever killed this animal left no trace of itself and ate all but the skin and bones. Even wraiths and ghasts leave trails. Unless it's something I have never dealt with, we are out of logical options."

Mitta frowned. "Damn it. And that busybody of a sheriff will blame the house for this."

"That he will." Scanning the ground a pit entered my stomach, "I'll give Vrorlin a call and see if he knows of another that could do this."

"Maybe he can find something we don't know about. Whatever it is, I don't like it." She says, rubbing the gooseflesh from her arms. Nothing rattled Mitta but the unknown.

"Agreed."

"Let's go back home. Whatever it is, I don't want to be out here when it comes back."

"Spooked, Mitta?" I asked, smiling to myself, though I understood her unease.

"Are you not? Something unknown is dangerous."

"It's definitely something to watch. I'll call Vrorlin tomorrow. He doesn't really work for me anymore and I've already asked a lot of him as of late. I don't think he would be very forthcoming with information or his time."

"What is she to you, my Lord?"

I gave her an assessing look as I came to her side walking back to the road. "What kind of question is that Mitta?"

A frown graced her lips. "Why bring a human into our midst our life is full of danger, why subject someone like Shasha to it, to us?"

"Why is everyone concerned with her living with us? Why is she being in my company not acceptable by anyone's standards?" I growled, irritation growing.

"I'm just saying there has to be more to it than the fact that she smells otherworldly and lets you rut her like an animal."

I snarled. "I don't rut her like an animal. We have had consensual sex that we both enjoy."

"Oh, please. Don't lie to me, it's been two days." She gave me a knowing look. "Most everyone in the house has sensitive hearing first of all. Plus, your scent clings to her like a tattoo."

I clear my throat, straightening my tie. "Touché."

"It's not like you, is really all I'm saying. You rescued her, but at the same time you bound her to you like a prize. It's not like you to seal others to you because you understand the repercussions that can have."

"It's not my intention to keep her bound to me forever, Mitta. For now, it's for her safety. The binding keeps others from seeking her out."

"But she is out here, and coming here would be a Hail Mary effort anyways."

"I know, but there is something otherworldly about her that I can't shake. Something that calls to me and I don't want to lose that to a vampire or succubus. I made more enemies that night than we both probably realize."

"Damn it." She ran a hand through the top of her hair, "I like her and don't want anything bad to happen to her. I can see she sparks joy in you. A joy that I haven't seen since Bas was a baby. I just hope you won't be her destruction."

I paused, horror crawling through my veins. "I-I don't want that either."

Mitta stopped and sighed heavily. "You need to tread carefully, my Lord. Be it hunger or lust or whatever, you could be the end of her. Remember that."

A tightness curled itself around my heart. "I don't need to be reminded that I'm a monster, Mitta. I am fully aware."

"That's not what I mean, and you know that."

"Then what do you mean, Mitta?"

"I mean just be careful. You don't know each other and are just as likely to fall in love as you are to hurt each other."

"You don't know though, Mitta." My hands tightened into fists. "You don't know what will come to pass. Very few beings have such gifts truly. I know what the risks are. I know the risks of keeping her bound to me. The risks of bedding her. The risks of- "

Her hand pressed softly to my cheek, and I looked into her eyes. They had silvered around the edges. "I know you know, my Lord. I know you don't want to cause undue harm to the girl. I'm just saying to be aware."

I swallowed. "You don't think that I am?"

"I didn't say that. It's just a reminder to not get lost in the moment."

I sighed. "Okay."

"Good."

Her words dogged me as we walked back up the road. I was well aware of the risks I posed to Shasha mind, body, and soul. I was well aware that the world I had pulled her into and the risks that it posed to her safety. I was aware that I had put her in just as much danger as I had taken her from, but I had wanted her. I had wanted her badly enough to take the risk and I would do it again.

Chapter Twenty-One

Shasha

The night after Niratap told me about the girl from long ago, I dreamed of her. A fire-haired, fair-skinned woman with sun-kissed cheeks and shoulders led me through old forests so lush and green. She smiled even though tears streamed down her cheeks. There was a beast stalking us silently and I watched as the monster became a beautiful man. Young and bright were his eyes and smile as he lifted her and twirled her around. His body was all lean corded muscles beneath tan skin. I knew it was Niratap, but I did not know if it was what I dreamed he looked like or if it was actually him. She took his hand and led him through the forest, and I followed behind.

Through thickets and trees and over a babbling stream they roamed, bedding down as the sun began to set in a quiet nook blanketed with meadow grass and moss. He told her of the mountains they could run to, where they could hide from the men that hunted them. She just told him she loved him, kissing his full soft lips and coaxing his body to hers again. Almost as if this was her goodbye. They fell asleep there, tangled lips and limbs and my heart broke knowing this was how they ended.

I smelled the torches, the sulphury burn the smoke caused in the back of my throat as they came through the woods where they lay. Two dozen men armed and ready for whatever they came upon. A priestly man at the head of the pack as they close in. Wolves in the night.

"What savagery is this witch?" The man said and the couple came to stand as he laughed.

"Father James." The woman's melodic voice said, as she pressed a hand to Niratap's chest, stopping him from coming to stand before her, his brows knit together.

"Deirdre." His voice is pained.

"No, *mo grá,* stay. They'll kill you if you attack first."[19]

"Witch, we have come to collect you for our savior. Your wickedness and wildness will end tonight."

He fisted his hands as the men pointed spears and pitchforks at them. She stepped past them, her fiery hair a stark contrast to her porcelain skin.

"Father James." She says again. "Spare the creature, he has done nothing to you and yours. I will come with you willingly, just let him live."

The man looked at Niratap; there was cruelty in his eyes, and he smiled at the girl. It twisted my stomach to I see the men circling around his back. Trickery, because his focus was solely on his love.

The man relented, sagging with false agreement. "The beast may live."

She turned a bright smile as she was about to tell him to go. Then horror came over her face as ropes descended over Niratap's neck a roar escaping his lips as they pull him to the ground. Brave foolish men charged in with metal shackles that had an ethereal glow to them. Father James grabbed Deirdre as she tried to go to him, holding her to him.

"He shall live, but he shall be no more than a slave."

"Deirdre!" Niratap reached for her, straining against the chains and ropes as the whip came across his back. His tan skin was flayed open by the vicious weapon.

"Niratap!" She wailed.

I closed my eyes to his screams trying to will myself to wake, but I was trapped in the memory made dream. I felt tears roll down my own cheeks, his cries breaking my heart. Soon he quieted, only the crack of the whip and the weeping of Deirdre echoing through the woods. His back was in shreds, blood staining the soft grass below him.

"Enough." Father James shouted as he tosses her before a circle of men. "The beast will not fight us now.

[19] my love

Witch, do you repent your evil ways? Do you give yourself over to Christ as your savior?"

Deirdre huffed at their feet. Hatred burned in her eyes as she glared at the priest. She spat at his feet before she spoke, "Fuck you, fuck all of you, and fuck your god."

"You heard her, men." He said and with a snap of his fingers the men descended upon her pinning her to the ground. She kicked and fought, but she was outmuscled and outnumbered. The men took turns violating her, one man smeared Niratap's blood over her body. The red far too bright, too offensive against her white skin.

The whole while, Niratap's voice weakly begged. "No, Deirdre. No."

At some point during the assault, she stopped fighting the men releasing her, laughing and taunting the two spirits that they had broken. The priest descended upon her, filling her with his pious seed. When finished he fisted her hair at the scalp and turned her limply to Niratap, who was still reaching for her, bloody and beaten.

"He will live, but it will be a miserable existence."

"No, free him." She wept.

"Yes, he will live a long and painful life in confinement. He will be beaten over and over and over again, until there is no memory of you or his freedom."

She reached for him. "Niratap, my shadow."

"Deirdre."

"He will be my slave and a slave to the church I serve. He will live, but as a prisoner for the rest of his days, until he draws his last breath."

"No."

"Look upon him now and know this is the last you will see him, and this is all he will ever be because of you. Subservient to the lord."

"Deirdre!" Niratap cried.

The squelching sound of her throat being slit, and the gurgling of her last words would haunt me. Her mouthed 'I love you' caused my chest to ache, but Niratap's wail, as the light faded from her eyes-that sound shattered me.

I shot out of my bed and ran to the restroom, barely making it to the toilet before I threw up. The roast chicken from dinner tasted sour in my mouth the second time. Why did those terrible memories that were not my own flood my dreams? If that was the truth of what happened, the terrible loss that he had suffered so early in his very long life would now haunt me. Did she visit him in his dreams? Did she sing sweet lullabies to him at night before his eyes drifted shut? Did he think of her when he was with me? Did he have that nightmare, reliving that night over and over again?

I felt a strange sense of jealousy, at a woman I didn't know, a woman who had long since been gone from the world. I sighed, flushing the toilet, and curled up there on the cold tile of the bathroom floor with tears running down my face. I felt so silly. I had known him for two whole days. Who was I to feel jealous of anyone who occupied his time before me. But still my heart throbbed painfully in my chest.

I didn't know when I had fallen asleep there on the tile but awoke to a cool rag being dabbed against my face. Eloimaya crouched next to me, a sad smile on her face.

"My sweet I don't think the bathroom floor is a good place to sleep. Have you been here all night?"

"No," I said. My mouth felt like I'd been chewing on cotton. "I had a terrible dream and woke up sick. I guess I must have dozed off here."

"I'll run you a nice bath to warm your bones. Okay?" She stood and went to the luxurious bathtub, large enough to be a hot tub, and I sat up, resting my back against the glass wall of the shower.

"Thank you, Eloimaya."

"My pleasure. The lord tasked me with being your caretaker. It's an old-fashioned practice, but I enjoy the work well enough. Since I've mostly been with Allipo, and the lord has taken care of you that is." She flushed brightly.

"Eloimaya, you don't have to wait on me, especially if you are much happier with Allipo."

Her flush deepened. "But the lord said."

"He can deal, besides I'm a latch-key kid anyways. I'm self-sufficient." I gave her the biggest smile I could muster. I didn't think it was as convincing as I hoped.

"Very well, my dear." She smiled sadly.

"Unless you really want to help me, I guess."

She gave me a sideways glance. "I don't want to be a bother."

"How about," I said smiling at her, "we just be friends."

She smiled. "I-I would like that."

I watched as she poured sweet smelling bath oils into the water and smiled when she had the perfect blend. She turned the water off before she walked into the bedroom, coming back with a pair of sweats and a t-shirt.

"Mitta mentioned this morning in passing that she wanted to bring you down to train. She wants to see what you can do."

"Okay." I said.

"I'll make sure there is warm food for you when you're ready."

"Thank you, Eloimaya. I really appreciate it."

"Anytime, Shasha dear. That's what friends are supposed to do right?"

I smiled. "Yeah."

She left; a wide grin painted on her face as she shut the bathroom doors. I sank into the hot water. The warmth making me realize how my body ached, as it slipped into my joints and muscles. A sigh escaped my lips. I soaked there until my hands were pruned and my water had gone cold. As I dressed there was a knock on the door.

"Hello?"

"Shasha." Niratap's voice calls from beyond the door. "I wanted to see you before I left."

Weight filled my chest as I opened the door to his tall, lithe body. He was finely dressed as always, today in a dark brown suit with thin line pinstripes. It was much like the suit he wore the day we met. "Where are you going?"

"I have a meeting in the city that has come up." His voice was edged with something that caused unease in my body.

"Is Mitta coming with you?" I hoped the concern wasn't as evident as it felts.

"No, I am meeting with an ally. Mitta will stay here, and you can have your sparring match." He cocked his head and sniffed the air. "You smell lovely."

"Thank you. Eloimaya poured oils into my bath." I smiled up at him, but my heart ached. "Will you be home tonight?"

"That is my hope, but we shall see." His voice was distant, and I wondered what troubles lay on his heart.

I walked past him into my room and to the chair by the fireplace. I sat pulling on my running shoes. "Please come home soon. I'll worry about you if you are away for too long."

His gloved hand caught my face, and he pulled my chin up to look at him. "I will be home as soon as I can. *Guím ar mo shaol neamhbhásmhar go bhfillfidh mé chugat.*" [20]

I knew he was making a vow and as he kissed me, I felt it snap into place. "Be safe."

"I will try. May I take you to breakfast." He offers me his arm.

"I would like that." I said taking his arm, letting him guide me from my room and downstairs. Before we walked into the dining room Mitta came out of her space with a pistol in her hand.

---

[20] "I swear on my immortal life that I will return to you."

"Mitta, I told you—"

"I fucking know." She snarled, holding the weapon out to him before her voice softened. "Please, my Lord, take it and ease my mind."

I had never been very keen on firearms, but Mitta must have thought this meeting was risky enough to warrant him carrying a weapon. I spoke softly, "My Lord, it would ease my mind as well if you took Mitta's advice."

Niratap looked between us and shook his head but took the gun. I watched as he ejected the magazine, and checked the chamber to make sure the gun wasn't loaded. slid the magazine back into place and locked the safety before he tucked the gun in the waistband of his pants behind his back. "Satisfied, ladies?"

Mitta grimaced at him, and I just gave him a small nod. He took my face in his hands, pressing a gentle kiss to my forehead.

"I will be safe." He said. His eyes held mine, but I found no relief. Allipo walked from the dining room in a fine teal suit.

"My Lord, are you ready to depart?"

"Yes, Allipo." He pressed another kiss to my lips. "I'll be home soon."

"You better be." I said and he chuckled. I watched as he left behind Allipo, heading out to the car. When the door shut behind him, I wanted to follow, but I knew I wasn't welcome on this journey. Mitta sighed beside me.

"Foolish man." She grumbled before she looked at my face. "I'm sure he'll be fine. My dear. He's not stupid, but I think it's foolish that he can't just talk to Bastion on the phone."

"Who is Bastion?"

"He's an orc who's undercover in one of the crime rings. He's a decent guy, but it bothers me when Niratap leaves unexpectedly like this. Emergent situations are always rushed, and sometimes things slip by."

"What things?"

Mitta's brows knitted together. "People get followed, covers get blown, people get shot, people die."

I gasped at her words, but she soothed me. "Allipo is also armed, I didn't have to fight him with it, either. Niratap is in good hands, and he is powerful and strong. He'll come home."

I took a couple of steadying breaths. He would come home to me, he would. I smiled at Mitta, before I spoke, "What are we doing today?"

"Well, I'm going to see what you are capable of, strength-wise, and if you have any fighting skills at all."

I swallowed. "And if I don't?"

"Then we start from the beginning. Firstly though, let's get you some breakfast, you are going to need it today."

Breakfast was protein-heavy with eggs, bacon, ham, and toast, all of it was savory and delicious. Everyone chatted quietly, a heaviness hanging over the table at the missing occupants. Eloimaya made a face at the discussion of firearms and weapons training. Everyone knew a good deal; even lithe Echo was deft with a dagger and knew how to fight hand to hand.

"Why is this even necessary for those of us who stay at the house? Why should Shasha and myself learn how to fight and shoot?"

Mitta finished her coffee and smiled at Eloimaya. "It is all in the name of being prepared for anything. Knowing how to defend yourself, defend each other, defend the manor."

"But why?" Eloimaya asked again. I knew what she was implying. Who would risk an attack on Niratap?

Mitta scowled, her voice serious, and she rose from her chair, "Because it isn't a secret where we live, who our lord is, and what kind of things are in his possession. What if, like now, the lord is away? Or worse if he were injured and unable to fight? Who would protect us?"

Eloimaya went ghostly white. "Has—has that ever happened?"

Mitta sank back into her chair. "Thankfully no, but the risks are still there, and they only grow every time he goes to market."

The room was deathly still. He would come home to us. He had sworn, but the reality of him being hunted and being hurt were very real. I stared angrily at the piece of half-eaten toast.

"Mitta." I said harshly.

"Yes?"

"I need you to teach me. Make me strong enough to defend him."

The table had gone eerily quiet, I looked up and everyone was looking at me. Eloimaya had a horrified look on her face, but everyone else held some kind of reverence and pride.

"Weapons are unbecoming of a lady." Eloimaya said with bitterness in her voice.

Katrel laughed and wiped tears from the edges of her copper-colored eyes. "What courtly nonsense. I haven't heard that shit since we left the elf kingdom."

Eloimaya flushed. "I—I only—"

Katrel cut her off. "No, if you are not willing to learn then you should go back to whatever court, wherever you are from. We don't have time or resources to waste on those who are not going to apply themselves to our cause. You need to be tough. You need to be strong. "

"Katrel." Tummi chided her sister.

"What? It's the truth!"

Tummi threw daggers of ice at her sister, who in turn huffed and stormed from the dining room. Tummi looked back to Eloimaya, her face and voice softening. "Eloimaya, love, forgive my sister, she forgets sometimes that there are those who still hold court values. She lost those a long time ago when our father sold me into slavery, for no reason other than to be rid of me. When she took up a sword to save me."

"Tummi—"

Though tears edged at her eyes Tummi smiled broadly. "Don't cry for me, Eloimaya. Had Katrel not taken up a sword, had she not braved the human lands, had she not been the perfect edge that Niratap needed that terrible night, I would be dead, so would she and probably our fearless lord."

Tummi words hung heavy in the air, I wanted to ask, to pry, but instead I looked at Eloimaya. "Will you learn to fight with me?"

Her head shot up at me. "What?"

"Will you learn to fight with me?" I repeated, her bright sad eyes cutting me.

She held my eyes a moment longer, then nodded. "Yes."

Dheg chuckled and nudged Mitta as he walked past to the kitchen. "Looks like you got two newbies."

Mitta smiled. "Looks like I do."

The gymnasium was above the ballroom and was fully stocked with all manner of equipment. Mitta smiled at the two of us as we stood before her. Eloimaya had donned leggings and a t-shirt, though she looked rather uncomfortable.

"Alright, ladies. Square up, let me see what you got."

"What do you even mean?" Eloimaya asked.

"Your fighting stance." I said, spreading my feet and raising two fists. "Like this."

Eloimaya copied the motion and Mitta came up to us.

"Your idea is good, Shasha, but pull your fists closer to your face. Tuck your elbows in closer to your body; that will protect your ribs. Spread your feet wider. Good. Eloimaya. Thumbs over, not in the fist. You punch someone like that, you'll break your hand. Elbows in and widen your stance. Good. Spend a little bit practicing that form. Relax and then pull into it again."

We did that over and over and over again, Mitta occasionally correcting placement of elbows and hands.

When we held our positions well enough, she guides us through some footwork. She tells us to imagine digging our toes into the ground and keeping our knees and ankles strong but loose, and even as simple as it sounded it made my legs wobble with the effort.

Eloimaya had the balance and flow naturally with her lithe body and elven grace. I had to focus hard on my stance, remember to keep my knees relaxed and remember to breathe. My body was already sore after holding the stance for ten minutes and completely drenched in sweat. I didn't know how I could make it through this, but I would for him. I would fight for him, this man who would had saved me. Who may have won my heart.

Chapter Twenty-Two

Niratap

We waited anxiously at the cafe, sitting inside away from the prying eyes of any passersby. However, where we sat, the cozy space had quickly cleared out, and I knew it was because I unsettled many of them. I wondered sometimes if it was the shadow magic or just a natural air of predator that had the humans and other creatures fleeing. Everyone was hesitant with one around. Everyone, that is, but Shasha who wanted nothing more than to be in my presence, to know me. She made me feel things I hadn't felt for almost five hundred years. A huff danced out of my mouth at my coffee, had it really been that long since Deirdre? Allipo glanced up at me from his tea; a question danced in those eyes.

"Bastion is late." Was all the satyr said.

"He'll be here soon."

I trusted Bastion, but the crime circuit he had infiltrated was vast and hostile to those who wanted to jump rank. It had been at least three years since he had made it home. Though he was missed at the table, he understood the need to get closer to the beast trade. We all did. The simple fact he wanted to meet in person said enough. My phone rang and pulled my attention away from the traffic outside.

"Vrorlin, you got my email I see."

"Yes, my Lord. I looked over the details that you sent me, and I honestly don't have any idea of what it could be. I will have to look into it and explore with my colleagues."

"Please, keep me abreast if you find anything."

"Of course. Lord Niratap I would not approach this creature before we know what it is."

"I agree with you. Thank you again, Vrorlin." Allipo straightened. I assumed Bastion was finally here. "I have to go, Vrorlin, but I look forward to hearing from you."

"I will notify you as soon as I can."

With that Vrorlin hung up, and I kept my body neutral as I watched Bastion purchase a coffee and wander our direction. He was a younger orc. Fair-faced, Durgash had said when the boy had been born. His light grey-green skin and tempest grey eyes would have been one of the reasons he would have been sold off or killed. Durgash had explained that most orcs were proud to be ugly, a warrior race that valued the ability to intimidate. Fair orcs like Bastion were considered weak. He casually asked to sit in the tan wing chair that was next to the two couches that Allipo and I had commandeered.

Allipo lazily flipped a page of a magazine. "Were you followed?"

Bastion pretended to scroll through his phone. "As far as I am aware, no. It is getting exceedingly harder to slip away. Dravin always has work for me to do."

"It must be serious." I said, still lazily glancing out the window.

"I haven't confirmed anything a hundred percent, but—"

"Then why request a meeting if you don't have all the information?" Allipo huffed, a hard line appearing between his brows. "You put the whole mission at risk, not to mention asking us to meet you in a public space."

"I know, but this wasn't something that I could tell you from Nocturnal."

I nodded. "What's going on, Bas?"

Bastion swallowed and a sense of dread entered my heart. "There is a rumor that a bitarog is coming to market."

Allipo's eyes snapped to Bastion. "Impossible."

I tightened my grip on the shadows I wielded. It was as much to keep from exploding as it was to make us seem unbothered. There was a hard edge to my voice. "When?"

"I do not know. I've only heard that it's alive and contained. Nothing more has been shared. There has been a lot of shifting in the market, too, since you were last there."

"I figured." Cool, icy rage flooded my veins.

"Dravin increased security, but he entrusted those tasks to Mandrake, not me. It doesn't matter that I am his third, he gives nothing freely, much like you expected my Lord. He's been pushing me into aiding his wife." Bastion shivered. "That woman is vile."

"I gathered that when I met her." A thought crossed my mind that I couldn't hold back. "How often are you helping the madam with her work?"

Bastion scowled at his phone. "Off and on the entirety of my time there, but pretty much about seventy percent of my time is spent doing her bidding right now. She is the key to his legal business, and the bridge into the sex trade. Which is where he tends to stay, however he has acquired several basilisk fangs and is having his new science cronies doing something shady that I'm not even privy to. He's hired more guys on, too."

Bastion met my gaze; something flickered in his eyes for a moment. Questions and guilt about what I was about to ask ran through me when shots rang out shattering the window behind me. A shot hit Bastion in the shoulder as he headed for the floor. Beings screamed and fled in all directions as Allipo flipped the couch, slipping into a crouch, hand tucked in his jacket.

"My Lord?"

"I'm fine," I said, pulling my own pistol, crouching below the window. "Bas?"

"I'm hit." Bastion groaned. "Through and through in the shoulder. Hurts like a bitch but I'll be fine."

"Do you sense anything, my Lord?" Allipo asked.

I scented the air and find only fear, blood, and gun smoke lacing the air. My ears only caught screams and distant sirens. I peeked over the edge of the window, and saw people running, cowering, but no evident place where the shots had come from. I moved to Bastion's side. "No, there's nothing beyond what you would expect. We need to leave."

"Out the back, my Lord. I'll cover you guys."

I turned, pulling Bastion's good arm over my shoulder. He winced but was relatively okay. "Allipo, we don't know where they will be."

"I parked the car just around the back. Just through the door. Just a sidewalk away."

I shuffled across the floor to the back hall of the cafe, Allipo at my back watching and listening to every tiny sound. In the hall we froze, hearing voices coming from the main area of the cafe.

"You're sure that was Dravin's third?"

"I'd recognize that orc jackass anywhere. I'm telling you; the boss would be pleased if we dragged Stormcaster's corpse back home."

I stiffened. Whoever these men were, they were enemies of Dravin. Bastion's cover wasn't blown, which was good for us, if we could get out. I eased us to the door, Allipo at my back. It was an emergency exit that hadn't been opened. The thugs were growling at one another in the kitchen of the cafe.

"Allipo, an alarm will sound as soon as I open this door." I whispered.

"Alright, we be quick," Allipo dug in his pocket, gaze locked on the doorway to the hall. I heard the car unlock on the other side.

"On three?"

"Yep."

A scream from the kitchen.

"One."

Shouts and footsteps fleeing out the front.

"Two."

The thugs were laughing at someone; the smell of urine dusted my nose.

"Three."

I shoved the door open. The alarm was excessive for a little restaurant at the edge of the city. We swiftly darted out to the car. I threw open the passenger door, tucking Bastion into the seat. Footsteps sounded beyond the door. Allipo had opened his door. I told Bastion to duck down as I shut his door. I got around the back end of the car. The door flew open. Shots fire at me. I took one in the hip, and one flew by my face. Allipo fired four rounds. The thugs tucked behind the door, allowing me a moment to duck into the car. Allipo pulled away from the curb and glanced back.

"My Lord you're hit." There was concern in his voice as I come to Bastion to check his shoulder, first aid in hand.

"It's through and through. I'll heal up shortly. Bastion is worse off."

"Am not, mine was through and through, too." He was hunched over, his back devoid of blood.

"Well, the lack of blood on your back tells me otherwise."

"Fuck."

"When do you report back?"

"I don't." He hissed as I ripped the sleeve open, "Today was my day off. I can catch a few extra if I tell him I was shot in the city by some thugs."

"It'll be on the news soon enough, anyway." I said.

"Did you hit any of them?" Bastion asks Allipo.

"No. It was just the building I hit."

"Damn it." He cursed as I poked his back, which was almost black, as blood pooled under his skin.

"I think I can feel the bullet. I can pull it out if you trust me with a scalpel. However, I think your shoulder blade might be busted."

"Just get the fucking thing out, and Mitta can do damage control."

I slather my hands and his back with iodine. The smell burned in my nose. I grabbed the scalpel, bracing as Allipo took a sharp turn heading to the freeway. I took a deep breath and dragged the scalpel across his skin. Blood oozed from the wound, but not spraying or squirting which was good. I spread his incision open, taking the forceps and pulling the bullet free. His scapula is definitely broken in at

least two places. I wiped the blood away, placing a bandage
over his incision and twisted him forward.

"Still shadows and darkness, huh boss?"

I smirked. "Still practicing bad humor Bastion?"

He winced as I poured iodine over his chest wound.
"Got to, especially with the kind of shit you have me doing."

I chuckle, placing the bandage. "You do it willingly."

"Greater good, you know." He attempted a shrug, his
injured shoulder not moving. "Got anything for the pain?"

"Sadly, nothing that will help you, just ibuprofen in
here. Mitta hasn't checked this one in a while."

"Damn."

"Just relax. We'll be back at the manor in an hour with
how Allipo drives."

"Well, I want to get onto the highway, before the
glamour21 wears off. Police will be looking for a purple
hearse and not a black SUV."

"Smart man. How long do we have?"

"Probably about a half hour if we're lucky."

"We'll be clear of the search radius by then."

I settled back against the seat, uncurling my tail,
which thankfully had no damage. Untucking my shirts, I
could see the soft tissue wound edges already starting to knit
together. I sighed in relief. I did not want to spend any time
on Mitta's table. The city faded into small towns and
farmland and my thoughts were about the beautiful girl at
home and how her first lesson with Mitta was going.

21 Glamour is an enchantment that fae can use to hide their
    appearance or alter the way things around them are
    viewed.

Chapter Twenty-Three

This lesson was not going well. After getting a handle on our forms, Mitta ran us through a gauntlet of foot work, trying to teach us to anchor through our toes while keeping our body loose. I was sweating and panting as she had us do planks, pushups, and crunches. After four hours of training, we were stretching out and focusing on our breath. Mitta walked between us and told us when to inhale and exhale.

The gym door opened and Allipo's voice echoed off the walls, "Mitta, we need you in the infirmary."

"What happened?" She shouted at him. "We're done for the day, girls. Allipo tell me what happened?"

"Is Lord Niratap hurt?" I asked, my pounding heart skipping a beat.

"Yes and no. He was hit, but—"

I was on my feet running past him and thundering down the stairs despite my aching limbs. Niratap was standing outside of the infirmary talking with Durgash. I could hear Rogmesh verbally digging at whoever is in the infirmary. Niratap was covered in blood, his dark brown suit stained practically black and splotchy, shirt untucked and rumpled. There was a hole through his jacket on his hip. He looked up at me, his eyes widening as I wrapped my arms around his middle.

"Shasha."

"You're hurt."

"No dear, I'm okay. Most of this blood isn't mine."

"Allipo said that you'd been hit."

He tugged me close. He was warm and dry. "I was. It was through and through and it's already healed. I'm okay. I promise."

I gave him a squeeze.

"What did I fucking tell you?" She snarled walking past us into the infirmary.

"If it makes you feel better." Niratap snapped after her. "They weren't shooting at me."

"It doesn't." She snarled.

"If you and Allipo are okay, who's hurt?" I asked.

"Bastion. Some thugs saw him walk into the cafe. Enemies of Dravin's. Decent shots if they were trying to take him alive."

"Damn kid has always been a lucky bastard." Rogmesh grumbled coming out of the infirmary. She leaned into Durgash who wrapped his arm around her. "He gets it from you."

Durgash laughs. "You sure about that, my love?"

"Yeah. Luck and stupidity both from his father."

"So, Bastion is?" I pried.

"Yes, Bastion is our son." Rogmesh said.

"Is he okay?"

"He'll be fine, bullet through the shoulder, shattered his scapula. It'll be a month or two of him healing at most." Niratap said to me.

"Can I meet him?" I asked.

"As long as Mitta hasn't knocked him out yet, I figure it's fine."

We walked into the infirmary. The young male orc was sitting with his back to the door as Mitta examined his injuries. He was light skinned, for an orc, a pale grey-green that reminded me of mint candy. He chuckled and something about the sound caught my heart. I stopped, Niratap bumping into me. He asked if I was okay. I couldn't speak as I gaze at the young orc whose face was so fresh in my mind. His eyes widened as he recognized me. Gone was the coldness and cruelty in his face, but this was him. Mrak, the orc who brutalized me, I could still feel his hands on my skin.

"Ima be sic—" I turned away and lost whatever contents were left in my stomach. Niratap rubbed soothing circles over my back.

"What is wrong Shasha?"

"My Lord." The young orc's voice is softer than I remember it being.

"Bastion?"

"My apologies, my Lord, but the young lady I—" he swallowed.

"You what?" Niratap's voice was a growl, both near and distant.

"I had to process her for the auction." His voice was tight; guarded maybe even afraid.

"You what?"

"I told you they had me working with the matron. She had me processing beings for auction. She was the last one, Saturday before the auction."

Niratap took three deep slow breaths before he scooped me into his arms. I was shaking. "Bastion?"

"Yes, my Lord?"

"I want a full report after you get patched up."

"Yes, my Lord."

He made to leave but Mitta called after him. "You're sure you're okay, my Lord?"

"Physically, yes."

Mitta didn't say anything else as Niratap carried me from the infirmary, up the grand stairs, and sat me atop the plush edge of his bed. I could feel his eyes searching my face before he left, disappearing out the door. I could feel the petrified tears rolling down my face and I was once again in that cold cell. The orcs hands on my body, trying to force me into compliance. I stood and wandered to the bathroom where I rinse out my mouth in the sink and rest my back against the cold tile of the wall.

"You, okay?" I started, Niratap's voice echoing off the tile. I hadn't heard him come back.

"No." My voice sounds heavy.

"Here." He holds out a bottle of water.

"Thank you."

I took the bottle and looked up into his pools of moonlight. They narrowed, almost wary as he asked. "Will you tell me what happened? What happened before?"

I looked away from those pools of silver, swallowing.

"Okay." He sighed. "I'm going to shower, get the blood out of my hair and off my skin."

I looked back up at him, and whatever he saw there caused him to pause. He kneeled in front of me, his hands coming to rest on my face, his eyes searching and searching for what I didn't know.

"I promise you." He said finally. "That I am okay. I don't know what horrors that Bastion subjected you to, but I do know that he is not that person you met there, and I also know that saying that won't fix the past."

I only managed a noncommittal nod in response. He sighed again as he stood and went to shower twisting the knobs. I watched as he undressed, skin kissed in shadows as he stepped under the spray. I moved to stand by the doorway of the shower, watching as the water ran red before swirling down the drain. The shadow magic that hid him hugs tightly to the toned body they protect. He turned, starting slightly at my silent approach.

"Where were you hit?" My voice still sounds strangely hollow.

I watched as his hand drifted to the spot right above his hip. "Here."

I took a step into the shower with him, my hand coming to rest over his. "Already healed?"

"Yes."

He watched me carefully, assessing my every move. He dropped his hand and mine came to rest against the satin shadows. He tilted my chin up, gazed into my eyes, and I felt the shadows slide away under my fingers. My eyes widened, but I didn't look down. I could feel his soft skin over strong toned muscles; there was a raised bump under my thumb. I stroked it and his eyes flinched.

"Did I hurt you?"

He closed his eyes and shook his head. "Just bruised."

"Did it hurt?"

"Probably, I really didn't notice. Adrenaline makes it easy to ignore pain, and pain is something that I am very accustomed to."

The shadows slithered back into place under my hand, and I rested my head against his wet abdomen, looking up at him. "I'm glad you're okay."

"I am also relieved." His hand cradled the back of my head. "Are you okay?"

"I mean I am, it's just—" I took a shaky breath. "Just seeing him brought me back to that place. I could feel his hands on me and smell the dank cell I was in and taste that gag, and I just couldn't."

"It's okay. I understand that. Your clothes are going to get wet."

I shrugged. "They were sweaty anyways."

He flashed a toothy smile that didn't touch his eyes. "You are not going to tell me, are you?"

"No."

He sighed and then ran his head under the shower, the water now running clear. Even encased in shadow, he was a specimen to behold.

"Well, if you're going to be in here with me, you might as well shower too." He said, reaching for the edge of my shirt. A giggle came out of my mouth as he peeled away the sopping garment and discarded them outside the shower with a plop. He angled his head to avoid jabbing me with his antlers. He nuzzled my neck, planting sweet kisses as his hands tug down my sweats, which I kicked away towards the door. His hands skated over my skin, each caress, each kiss causing my insides my ache.

I let my hands explore the planes of his chest and abdomen. Lean muscles of a predator contracted at my touch. A sound echoed through me, a soft vibration from Niratap. I pressed a kiss to his collarbone, the vibrations tickling my lips. A purr, he was purring at my touch.

"Niratap, what manner of creature are you? I know you are a bitarog, but what even is a bitarog?"

He pulled away from my neck, cocking his head to the side much like an owl would do to observe its prey. "Well. Bitarogs are an old sub-fae beast monstrosity. Something not wholly fae or animal or human or beast."

"What does sub-fae mean?"

"Sub-fae is a term used for sentient creatures that aren't quite fae."

"What makes something fae?"

He poured soap on a loofah, twisting me into the spray, rubbing the suds over me as he spoke. "An affinity for magic defines fae. Fairies, pans, satyrs to name a few. Beasts are beings that can change shape but don't have natural magical affinity, were-beasts and rakshasi. Monstrosities are old creatures that feast on the others, most of them have been hunted down and only pockets of them exist anymore, basilisks for example. Then there are high fae creatures, which may or may not have a magic affinity, and were typically nobility; elves, dwarfs, and orcs."

"But what about beings like Dorilody? Selkies, kelpies, and the like." I asked turning so he could wash my back.

"There are subcategories in there as well, hybrids, fae-beasts, undead-fae. Selkies are considered fae-beasts and kelpies are the same."

"So, you're a sub-fae beast monstrosity because you are sentient, have magical affinity, can shape shift and are an ancient predatory species?"

"Yes. In the simplest of terms."

I turned to face him, rinsing my back. "How many shapes do you have?"

"Three, however, I can shape-shift in a spectrum meaning I can control what parts of my anatomy shift, like clawed hands." He demonstrated, his fingers elongated and came to sharp points then just as smoothly black encased fingers reappeared.

"Have I seen all your forms?"

"No, just two of them, and you really haven't seen my forms either because of the shadows. This form, the closest thing to human I can manage, and the halfway point between beast and man. I rarely take my full-beast form anymore, it doesn't suit my goals."

"Why is that?"

"Because the war I fight right now is one of words, wealth, and thinly veiled threats. I cannot communicate any of those in my wildest of shapes."

"I would like to see it, sometime."

"Someday I might show you."

"I'll take that." I said wrapping my arms around his waist, my hands interlocking just above his tail. He brushed an unmanageable curl from my face.

"How do you manage this?" He gestures to my hair.

"Very carefully. It's going to be hella frizzy soon if I keep neglecting it though."

His head tilted again. "Why is that?"

I chuckled. "You want me to explain the full-time job of taking care of curly kinky hair?"

He grimaced at that. "Well at that, not particularly, but I am curious."

"I'll show you one of these days. It'll be a lot better than telling you."

He turned the water off and offered me a plush towel, "I would like that. How did your lesson go?"

"Ugh, I'm exhausted. I didn't realize how little I knew."

"Mitta was trained for battle; there is a lot you don't know. She's a good teacher though." He said as he wrapped a towel around his waist.

"I don't doubt that at all." I said following him out into his room. "I'm just surprised that it was so much."

He chuckled. "You'll be a warrior soon enough. If that is what you want?"

I flashed him a smile. He hadn't been there to hear my declaration. That I had said I wanted to be strong and skilled enough to protect him. This creature no, this man before me who in a few short days had saved me, ravished me, worshiped my body beyond what I could imagine, and treated me not as a lesser being, but as an equal even when I had no real skills to offer him. I watched him towel off, drying his straight hair. I wondered again what his skin would be like beneath those shadows.

"What sort of spell are the shadows?"

He pulled on black boxer briefs, "It's part natural ability and part cloaking spell."

"Natural ability?"

"Yes, as a predator I have a natural camouflage ability to help blend in with my surroundings."

I sat in a chair by the fire, warming my chilled toes in the small blaze. "What other abilities do you have?"

"So full of questions." He snapped his fingers and clothes from my room appeared in the chair next to me. A soft mustard sweater that was well worn, the edges of the cuffs starting to fray and loose-fitting black pants.

"Well yes-how did you do that?"

"Affinity for magic." He waggled his fingers, before starting to button up his shirt.

I smiled sliding into my underwear. "So, abilities?"

He sighed, sliding his long legs into a clean pair of black slacks. "Don't you have classes today?"

"No. Tuesdays are a free day and I'll call my mother later. I'm your problem now. Abilities?"

He chuckled, fiddling with his cuffs until they sat just right. "Well, there is strength, stealth, camouflage, dark vision, shape shifting, and a magical affinity specifically to shadow magic."

"Magicking me clothes is shadow magic?"

"No."

I watched him then, well dressed, clean lines and the mask appeared in his hand. It's bone white stark against the blackest of shadows slid into place over his face. Bright silver eyes watched me, predatory, hungry, but we just stood there appraising each other, time frozen.

He cleared his throat. "No, it's a modified teleportation spell."

I took a step toward him. "When can I see you?"

"Whenever you please, I'm right here." He said plainly, adjusting his cuffs again in that meticulous way that he did.

I took another step. "That's not what I meant."

He closes his eyes. "Shasha. Not now. I—" He shook his head and took a step to the doors.

"Why not?"

"Because regardless of your feelings for me I cannot afford to expose myself that way. Too many things hang in the balance, including your life." With that, he stepped through the door and the soft click seemed to echo across the room.

Chapter Twenty-Four

Niratap

I shut the door quietly, anxiety made my hands shake as I moved from the door. What had happened to her in the hours before I had found her? Bastion caused a strong metallic scent of fear to pour from her, fear so strong that she had thrown up at the sight of him. I knew Bastion only did what he had to, compliance was the key to surviving undercover, the key to staying hidden. Bastion had infiltrated mid-level in the beginning, but being a grunt didn't get him the information we needed. He had become the poster boy of a motivated villain and even though I knew he was good, how many bad deeds and days did it take to become the person you pretended to be?

In the infirmary I found Mitta cleaning up the gurney, Shasha's vomit already mopped up. Everyone else had left her to it.

"They dispersed." Mitta said, moving to the sink to wash her tools. "Bastion will be sore for a few days, but he should be fine afterwards."

"Thank you, Mitta."

"It's the job I have given myself so no need. Are you going to pull him?"

I looked down. "I don't know. It would take forever to plant another set of eyes on Dravin. Let alone get to a place that would actually glean any information."

"It is a dangerous game you play sometimes. What if his cover is blown?"

"If his cover is blown, then I'll pull him. Dravin is already an enemy, so it won't make much difference except tracking his movements."

She sighed. "He's in the study. Be kind to him, he was just doing his job. You can't fault him for that, no matter how terrible he was to our girl."

We'd only known her for a few days, but she was our girl. The fact that they had accepted her warmed my heart. I smiled to myself. "I'm glad to hear you've all taken a shine to her. Glad that only Allipo really thinks that it was a misuse of resources."

"Oh, it definitely was a misuse, but she is good for us, for you."

I nodded. "I'll go speak with Bastion. See what our next move is."

"Remember what I said." She called behind me.

"I will."

"No, I'm good boss." Bastions voice filters from the study. "Yeah, I got hit and am a little banged up but I'm alive. Yeah. If you insist, boss. I can take a week off to recover. No problem. Thanks boss."

He hung up. He was sitting in the window seat overlooking one of the gardens, his lips a hard line. He is in a clean shirt and a sling to support his healing shoulder.

"Your covers not blown?" I asked as I go to my desk and sat behind it.

"No, Dravin is pretty sure it was an enemy trader looking to cut down his left hand." He sighs again, coming to sit across from me. "Got lucky the punks didn't recognize you."

"Indeed." I leaned back in my chair pondering how to go about this.

"You're angry with me." It wasn't a question.

"Yes, but for reasons I don't fully understand myself. I want to know what you did to Shasha. I want to know why she is so scared of you."

"My Lord."

I held up a hand. "I'm not finished. I realize that whatever happened between you two was because you were undercover. I understand the implications of being compliant. More importantly I am the one who sent you into Dravin's circle, so I will take that responsibility; but before we discuss this how sure are you about a bitarog coming to market?"

"As sure as I was about the basilisk you bought at the beginning of the year. Dravin was pissed he lost the bid on that by the way."

"Good. Him feeling beaten makes the fact I'm going to rend his circle all the more enjoyable. What about the location for the next market? Have you heard?"

"No, but it is that time of year again. When the beast trade slows down significantly and it's a fifty-fifty shot that there's another sale before the end of October. The sex and drug trades are the only ones that rotate year-round."

I leaned forward, folding my hands together and resting my chin atop them. "Thank you, Bastion. Now what happened to my girl?"

Bastion told me of the process of preparing beings for the sex trade. He told me that he didn't take any pleasure in what he had done to Shasha. That it was sick what he had to do and act, that it was expected of him to lust after the product and treat them less than. I had to hold my breath as he described the placement of the gag with Shasha. I saw red, but Bastion was a good kid. Knowing that made the pill easier to swallow, the blow softer to my heart. The fact that she fought and resisted strengthened my resolve.

"Just to verify what I've heard; you didn't intentionally try to cause harm of any kind to the girl, and you only acted out of need to secure information and keep yourself undercover. Correct?"

"Yes, my Lord."

I sighed leaning back in my chair and pondering. "You're free for a week, then you have to report back?"

"Yeah. Dravin says they're not planning on moving any new product this week so me not being there causes little harm, and it will trick the competition out."

I nodded. "I don't know how well that will go. Though I suppose I don't know if the short amount of time you do have will sway Shasha to you either."

"You care for her."

"I am fascinated with her."

A knowing smile swept over his face. "You love her, don't you?"

"How can you love someone if you have only known them for a few days?" I scoffed. I was getting quite annoyed that everyone seemed to know me better than me.

"Love is a mysterious fickle thing, my Lord." I glowered at him, and he just laughed softly.

"Anyways, take it easy and try to show her who you really are. Show her you're not the monster she thinks you are."

He nodded grimly. "Easier said than done, my Lord."

"I know. Now go help your parents: I know they'll find something easy for you to do while you heal."

"Yeah, I can still clean with one hand. Mom's going to give me a tongue lashing; you know that right."

"Oh, I guarantee she will."

We both laughed at that and as Bastion stood, he was smiling ear to ear. He paused at the door to my study, glancing back at me before he spoke. "Regardless of what you think, my Lord, you are a good leader and good person."

Then he left, the words hanging in the space he vacated, clanging through that self-hating part of myself. I shook my head trying to clear the cobwebs and dust that seemed to settle over my brain. Bastion what do you even mean by good? Eventually I stalked through the manor aimlessly, pondering everything that was on my purview. Between Shasha and Bastion, my thoughts had drifted far from the goals that we were pressing towards. A bitarog coming to market was a dangerous thing.

Chapter Twenty-Five

Vrorlin's lecture on *The Histories of Mountain People* was mind-numbing at best, and mental suicide at worst. I knew the vague histories of dwarves, orcs, and ogres, but Vrorlin had spent the last hour and a half talking about how the first dwarf king, King Durinn first of his name, foolishly started his kingdom above the home of a sleeping dragon. The story in and of itself was probably very interesting, with the foolish king mining into the dragon's lair and waking the beast which then rained fire upon the dwarves, but it had been an hour and a half retelling. Most of which had been an account of the dwarf king's many conquests before settling on the mountain and then his escapades trying to sire an heir. It took everything in me to not just lay my head down and fall asleep. A guy about my age in the in-person class raised his hand. He was some kind of hybrid.

"Yes, Cooper?" Professor Vrorlin asked.

"Professor, how much of the histories will we be required to know for the duration of the class and why do we need to know so much about the first dwarf king?"

Someone in the class chuckled and Professor Vrorlin rested his hands on his hips. "Well Cooper, considering your major is the study of mythical creatures, I'd expect you to at some point have the stories and lore memorized. Especially the mythologies of how races began and how they have carved their way through history for our society to be shaped as it is now. I expect that by the end of this field of study, you would understand that the histories of different races vastly change how they interact today. For example, since I'm not yet done with the history of dwarves, did you know that King Durinn first of his name was one of the first of the dwarves to grow a long, luscious beard? All of his seven sons also grew luscious beards and so on and so forth and now today it is a tradition that dwarven men grow long beards. There are seven honorable trades to the dwarves because King Durinn first of his name had seven sons. Each son was adept at one of those trades: miner, jeweler, warrior, blacksmith, bard, dragon slayer, and artificer. Those trades make up the skill sets that most dwarves decide to use in today's world. The knowledge of how things began for a people tells you a lot about how they have evolved through time to be where they are now and how they continue to interact with the world. Does that clarify it for you?”

Cooper's cheeks became stained a rosy color, but he nodded, “Yes, professor.”

“Alright then. Now King Durinn first of his name was a brute of a man, but he brought his people together, by uniting the thirteen dwarven clans. He took a wife from each clan and bore many children with them—” Vrorlin went into a long list of children and by the time the next hour of the class had ticked by we knew the names of all twenty-seven daughters, and finally, twelve o’clock released us.

“Your homework.” Vrorlin called around the shuffle of notebooks and bags. “For the next week is to look into the seven sons of Durinn and their trades. There will be a quiz next week.”

After everyone had left the video call and the classroom, I cleared my throat; I had some questions for my professor.

“Shasha, did you need something, my dear?” Vrorlin asks as he walks to his desk.

“Professor, I wanted to ask how you knew Lord Niratap.”

“Well, my dear, the same way I assume you came into his care.”

“He purchased your freedom?”

Vrorlin nodded. “Yes indeed. Centaurs are stronger than plow horses and historically have been used as such, because overall we have an agreeable nature and are not fond of pain. Easily subjugated, I guess.”

I frowned. "How long ago was that?"

"Hmm, I would say it's probably been a good fifty years since he pulled me out of slavery. The following couple of decades, I acted as a liaison between the free centaurs and the lord. After a while, centaurs were replaced with machinery and my services were no longer needed. Occasionally he drops information my way, in case I ever need it to avoid trouble."

"I see. Have you ever seen his face?"

Vrorlin leaned forward to glance at me through the camera, "Sweet girl, there are some things that belong in shadow, and though I have the utmost respect for the lord, he is a creature of darkness and nightmares. I would be careful where you dig, because you might not like the results."

"I—"

"Trust me child." Vrorlin's face sobered like I was asking him to slaughter a lamb.

"Okay, I'll see you Friday then, Professor."

"Have a good day, Shasha." With that he ended the video conference and left me to ponder my own questions.

I shut my laptop with a click and stood, stretching my aching legs. Welcome pops sounded from my tight lower back. Yesterday had left me raw, I rubbed her face and looked towards my door. The dark mahogany door, the only thing that was keeping me from the rest of the house, from exploring, from them. Niratap. Mrak. Bastion. His real name was Bastion, and he was Rogmesh and Durgash's son.

I sighed and flopped into the neatly made ochre bed that Eloimaya insisted on making when she had brought my breakfast. She didn't press me about not coming to dinner, even as she gathered the dishes this morning. Niratap hadn't come to my room to see if I was okay, either. Though I would love to see him, the cryptic end of our conversation yesterday afternoon had followed me the remainder of the day. I don't fully comprehend what he meant, that seeing his face could cost me my life. The rap of knuckles upon my door had me sitting up unexpectedly.

"Hello?" I called.

"Uh, I know you probably don't want to see me." A male voice that chilled me said beyond the door. "The lord wants me to try and fix the damage I caused you. You don't have to open the door, but I would like to speak with you if you'll let me."

I slid from the bed to approach the door. I took a steadying breath and cracked the door. "Why would he want that?"

The young orc started, surprised that I had even opened the door, "The lord didn't say, just asked me to make the effort to show you that I am truly just Bastion. Mrak is just my alias to spy on Dravin. I don't enjoy preying on women, but that is the part I have to play in order to glean information for our cause."

"Does Lord Niratap know what you do?"

"Yes. He doesn't like it either, but the pros of me being in the market outweigh the cons. It's the same with the others who are in deep cover." He shrugged tightly as if to ease the building tension, then leaned against the wall.

"How many of you are in deep cover?"

"I don't know that. Only the lord and Allipo know."

"Does it scare you?"

His head rolled to the side, his eyes a deep tumultuous grey so dark they were almost black. "Yes. Every day."

I chewed on my lip. "Do you want to come sit by the fireplace?"

He lifted off the wall. "If you're inclined to let me."

I opened my door so he could come in. "I think I am."

He stepped into the room and paused. "I heard Mitta was training you, you're not going to stab me are you."

I chuckled. "One day of breathing, stretching, and footwork does not make a killer."

"That sounds like something she'd say." He gave a tentative smile. "I'm sorry. For what it is worth, if anything. When I saw you with the lord, I knew you would be safe. Regardless of how he views himself, he is a good man."

"I don't think I'm quite ready to hear that apology, but I agree with you about the lord. He is a good man."

A genuine smile came across his face, he raised a hand between us. "My name is Bastion, I have made a terrible impression and would like to rectify it, if you would let me."

I clasped his hand; his palm is calloused but soft. "My name is Shasha. It's nice to meet you, Bastion."

That smile danced in those dark eyes, his lips parting in what I could only deduce was his true smile full of teeth and his well-maintained tusks. I couldn't help but give him a guarded smile in return. We sat in the yellow tufted chairs by the fire and just talked. He was trying to show me his true self, a young orc who was playing a dangerous game to keep his family safe. He was self-conscious of his fair skin that made him easy to find but loved that he had his grandfather's eyes. A man who he had never met, but who he was named after. He loved his mother's cooking, but his favorite food was microwave mac and cheese. His favorite color was violet, and favorite smell was the apple ale his father made. He used his free time away to play video games and excelled in online shooter games. When he was away, he missed his mom the most, even though every time he visited, she gave him hell for something.

We talked for hours, laughing until tears flowed freely over our cheeks. He was just a boy, like any boy my age. It was only when Eloimaya knocked, cracking the door to ask if I was going to come to dinner tonight that we realized the time. The two of us linked arms, chatting as we walked towards the dining room. The table was set and almost everyone was present, except Niratap. Bastion released my arm and went to his seat by his parents, Rogmesh pinching his cheek.

"Where is he?" I asked Eloimaya as she walked past me into the space.

"The lord is still in the study on the phone with someone. It sounded quite heated, so I didn't bother him."

I frowned turning from the room. "I'll go fetch him."
"Be careful he sounded quite upset."
"Don't worry. He won't hurt me."

I could hear him snarling, when I entered the library.
"No, you don't get to just fucking do whatever you like. No, you can't risk the rest of us like that either. I know that. I know that. Yes. I'm sorry. I wish I could. No, I can't come get you out."

I poked my head through the study door. Niratap was standing by the bay window, the moonlight the only thing illuminating the dark study. One hand holding the phone to his ear the other pinching the bridge of his nose, he looked tense, and I got the sense that he was both angry and scared.

"You're across the country, Navin. If you can get out, I'll get you a flight home. Don't get arrested. Of course, I would bail you out if you did, but you would be at their mercy while I got that organized. No if your cover is at risk, leave. I don't want you dying."

He paused as he saw me peering through the door. His eyes glow lightly in the dark room. His tie was loose, his suit jacket tossed over a chair, his sleeves rolled up, the portrait of a businessman after a long day. He gave me a small nod, as he went to the desk and sat.

"Yes, I understand. Of course. If you want to lay low, you can come stay at the manor. Okay. Yes. Yes. Okay. Call me when you get out. North or south? Okay, I'll look at Sacramento airport then. Of course. Be safe, friend. Yes. Of course. You can give me a full brief when you get here. No, I'll have Allipo pick you up from the airport. You know I don't venture in unless I have to. Okay. Talk to you soon."

He hung up, setting the phone on the desk and picking up a crystal glass with a dark colored liquor in it. He downed the whole glass, before leveling a stare in my direction.
"Yes, my dear?"

"I came to fetch you for dinner. Its ready and everyone is waiting for you."

"As sweet as that gesture is," he turned to the computer, the screen illuminating the room in an eerie glow. "Allipo knows that I am busy. They have probably already started eating. You should go though; eat with everyone else. They missed you the last few meals."

I leaned against the doorway. "What was that call about? It sounded serious."

"One of my undercover agents thinks that his cover is about to be blown. The gang that he is in, has gotten in some kind of turf war with another rival, and they are looking for a worm. He's scared and I don't blame him, so he's going to try to flee, and I need to look at flights for him to come home."

"Is he in danger?"

"He might be, by the sounds of it though there are multiple worms in the organization anyway. Their main leader was assassinated a few weeks ago and the second is looking for whoever put in the hit. Whoever gave up his brother for the pickings."

"What kind of organization is it?"

He glanced my way, silver eyes narrowing slightly. "A leveled one much like Dravin's. Legal front is in the tourism trade in L.A. They sling drugs instead of sex and most importantly—"

"Deal in monster trade."

He blinked and then nodded returning to the screen. "Yes, the monster trade."

"I would like to have your company at dinner." I paused as his eyes came back to meet mine. "That is if you will have me, my Lord."

His eyes softened and he sighed. "Shasha, let me look at these real fast and I will come to dinner with you."

"No need, my Lord." Allipo spoke from behind me, making me gasp. "We made you and miss Shasha each a plate."

"Allipo." Niratap said as the satyr walked past me and set the two plates each covered with a cloche on the desk and pulled one of the chairs closer for me. "I will have an errand for you tomorrow."

"Of course, my Lord."

"Navin thinks his cover is blown. He's attempting to flee north to Sacramento and then fly home. He supposed to call me when he is out of their territory and let me know. I will keep you in the loop."

"Of course." Allipo walked to the chair where Niratap's suit jacket was tossed and picked up the garment walking to the wardrobe to hang it. "Let me know what airport you want me to pick him up from."

"I will. Thank you for bringing us dinner."

"My pleasure, I figured you and Shasha had some things to discuss, my Lord." Allipo sketched a bow and left, giving me a mischievous smile as he passed.

I closed the study doors behind him and took a breath. "What did you want to talk to me about?"

"Come sit. We can discuss this while we eat."

I turned to find him in the cabinet behind the desk pulling out a couple wine glasses, a bottle of wine, and a couple candles. He lit the candles with a wisp of magic, before he popped the cork with a clawed finger and poured us both a glass of dark, rich wine. I sunk into the plush tufted chair Allipo had pulled to the desk as Niratap lifted the bells from the plates. Dinner consisted of some kind of red meat, twice-baked potatoes, and some buttery asparagus.

"Something tells me that this isn't what everyone else had for dinner."

He chuckled. "I can assure you that this is. Braised lamb, twice-baked potatoes, and buttered asparagus is one of Bastion's favorite meals."

"Funny, he told me it was microwave mac and cheese."

Niratap paused, reaching for his knife. "You two spoke?"

"Yes, he came by my room after my class was over and we talked the entire afternoon."

He smiled too-sharp teeth on display. "Bastion is still alive, right?"

"Just because Mitta and I have had one training session does not make me a killer."

He chuckled at that. "What did you talk about?"

"Just ourselves. Our favorite colors, favorite foods, he told me about growing up here and I told him about my small town. Basic icebreaker stuff."

"I'm glad that you got to meet the Bastion that I know. Not the orc that hurt you, but the man and family behind it."

"I didn't doubt what you said. I was just scared. I saw him and I was back in that place. In that cell."

He breathed a sigh. "I'm sorry that you had to experience what you did. Even more so that it was someone I trust that did it to you."

"Bastion was just playing his part. He extended an olive branch."

"I'm glad you accepted it."

I watched him take a drink of his wine. "You told me of Deirdre and how that was when you became a prisoner."

He looked at me with a frosty expression floating in his eyes. "Yes."

"How long were you a prisoner?"

He took a deliberate bite of potato, chewing slowly while he did the mental math. "About three hundred years."

My heart skipped a beat. "By the church?"

"It started with the church, but they eventually decided that I was more trouble than I was worth. They sold me for a hefty sum to a lord and then I was passed around by lords and dukes. A showpiece in their courts after the first great bitarog hunt." He shrugs.

"You didn't fight?"

"I did. After the initial shock and grief of Deirdre's death subsided, I fought like hell. But I was just barely into my maturity. I hadn't mastered any of my magic. I was starved, beaten, tortured, and more. By the time I was sold off my wild spirit had been broken.”

I took a sip of my wine. “How long were you in the church’s control?”

“One hundred years.”

“I’m sorry.” I didn’t know what to say besides that, the words sounded hollow.

“It’s my past.” He said with a shrug. “Most of my time as a captive is a blur of chains, stone walls, and bloody wars.”

“How did you escape?”

“That’s not solely my story to tell.”

“You had mentioned that I guess.”

“You’re full of questions tonight my darling.” He said leaning back and sipping from his wine.

“Sorry.”

“It’s nothing to apologize for. I guess given the circumstances I would also want to know the story of the person I was living with.”

“I would. Not just because of the circumstances, but because I like what’s between us.”

He went still, predatory grace taking over his body. “And what. my dear, is between us?”

“Well, you said I wasn’t a slave.”

“You’re not.”

“You don’t just want me for sex.”

He blinked and shifted in his seat. “That is also correct.”

“But having sex means we’re more than friends.”

“I would assume so.” There is a smile in his voice.

“So, I don’t want to put a name to what we have yet, because we have only known each other for a few days. I want to get to know you, in all your facets.”

He watched me, assessing what I had said before he set his wine glass down on the desk. “I am not going to lie to you, a lot about who I am and what I do are not nice things.

Most are actually very dangerous things. I'm not going to sugarcoat my life to make it more palatable for you."

"I never expected you to."

"I'm not home for great spans of time and have to travel frequently. I won't always be here."

"Then take me with you, and if you can't, I'll wait for you."

"There's a chance I won't come back."

I swallowed at that, fear twisting my gut. "I would mourn you."

He considers me a moment. "That scares you? Losing me?"

I chuckled to myself. "More than you realize, probably more than even I realize. It's just—I—I feel so right when I'm with you. Like everything makes sense. Like it doesn't matter that I'm young and naive; you answer my questions to the best of your ability and when you can't you are honest. I think my heart wants to fall in love with you." I threw a hand up to cover my mouth.

He stood and came to my side of the desk, twisting the chair, and crouched before me. "Say that again."

"I—I think my heart wants to fall in love with you."

"Why is that?" He sounds astonished.

"I feel fulfillment when I'm with you. Like—like I have everything in my hands."

He cocks his head to the side. "Interesting."

I moved to stand. "I'm sorry. I—I've said too much."

His hand came to my thigh pressing me into the seat. "Oh, I think this is just the beginning of it."

"Beginning of what?"

"The beginning of us, for I think that I have fallen in love with you."

The candlelight danced in his eyes, and that mask obscured the rest of his face. I palmed his cheek. It was warm under my fingers, and the satin shadows there wiggled between them, but beneath the shadows, I could feel that strong jaw and angular cheek.

"I know you will tell me no again, but I want to see you."

His eyes softened with something akin to guilt and he kissed my palm. "Not today, my dear, but I will show you soon."

I smiled as his hands found my cheeks. There was such sweetness in that touch, and I watched as heat filled his eyes. His hands eased down my neck and across my back. He nuzzled my neck, laying soft wet kisses against my throat and pulse. My hands pressed against his chest at the defined muscles there. His hands slid under the waistband of my leggings and up the hem of my shirt. There was a soft vibration coming from him.

"Are you purring?"

He froze.

"I mean I like the way it feels, I was just curious."

"Yes." His voice had taken on that roughness that promised, no threatened hot sex.

I found the top buttons of his shirt, undoing them to gain access to the hard planes of his body. He growled as my hands found his chest, the shadows dancing around my fingers. His heart beat under my palm and he pulled me into his lap. I gasped against his hardness where our hips met, and he groaned against my throat with the friction there. His tail wrapped along my waist holding me in place as he leans back to pull the mask and shirt off, discarding them haphazardly on the floor. He pressed his lips to mine; he tasted of sweet red wine and the wild of the mountains.

He parted the kiss and breathed against my lips. "Only you, in the long life that I have had, elicit these things from me. Only you."

"Nira."

He gave another small kiss, more tender. "Only you, drag this kind of instinct from me."

"What instinct is that?"

"To claim you as mine and mine alone." There is a lethal edge to the words that make goose-flesh dance across my body.

"Then claim me. Make me yours. Make me all those things that we haven't spoken about."

He pulled back to look at me with those quicksilver eyes. Always assessing. Always pondering. "Do you understand what you just said?"

"Enough to know that it's what I want." I ran my hands down to his chest and hooked my fingers in the top of his pants.

He cocked his head to the side, that predator's grace in every move. "You are a dangerous creature in your own right."

He waved his hand the candles going out at his command. In a swift movement he had me bent forward over the desk and my leggings down around my ankles. I felt his eyes appraise me. His hand gently caressed my hip. I felt him lower his face behind me, his breath cool against my folds. His tongue glided along my slit in a long, luscious movement, eliciting a moan from me.

"You taste so delectable."

Another pass had me begging. "Nira. Please."

With another pass of his tongue my knees were buckling. He purred against me. "Now, now, don't come undone just yet."

"Niratap please."

He ran his hands over my hips, calloused palms tickling my skin. He parted from me, and I peered over my shoulder to watch him undo his pants. His long, elegant fingers made quick work of the task. He stepped out of his pants, his long lean muscled legs coiled for the attack. He paused eyes, watching me watch him. He smiled white teeth stark against the shadows, fangs on display.

"How would you like me, my darling, as a man or as a monster?"

He was large either way, and I just wanted him. "I don't care, please Niratap."

I watched him slide out of his shorts, his hard length a black spear of night, and my body quaked in anticipation at the sight of it. His silver eyes glowed through the gloom, an amused chuckle coming from him.

"That's not how it works, love." He stroked himself for show.

I swallowed. "Take me how you like to. Shifted and wild."

He growled his approval. He shifted before me. His cock became more canid and thickened a few inches. It was fascinating to watch the shift, my body wetting at the thought of him inside me. I licked my lips with need as he stepped closer.

"Do you hunger for me?" He asked, voice hot with need.

"Yes."

His hands wrapped around my hips and rubbed that glorious length against my folds; both of us groaned heavily.

"You are so wet for me." He shuddered, hands tightening.

"You don't have to hold back."

His eyes locked with mine. A battle of restraint, concern, and lust in them. "No. I have to."

"But I want you that way."

He leaned over me pressing a gentle kiss to my lips. "You may want me that way, but your body won't be able to handle me like that. No matter how much desire we have."

"How can, you be sure?"

His eyes softened. "Because I am a monster, my dear."

"You say that like it's something to be afraid of."

He rubbed against me again and I shuddered. "Because it is."

He pressed the head at my entrance. "Well, I'm not afraid of you."

He paused and I glanced back at him. There was an emotion in those pools of moonlight that I couldn't place.

"*Is stór thú.* I don't deserve you in my life."[22]

I smiled at him, not knowing what he said, but understanding the emotions in those eyes. "I would say the same of you."

He slid into me slowly, a soft grunt coming out of him as he seated himself to the hilt. My body graciously accommodated his girth into the deepest parts of me, already on edge and ready for that sweet friction he would give me. He bent over me, kissing the hollow of my neck. His hands roved over my sides and under my shirt, his calluses causing goosebumps on their journey. His touch was soft but desperate as he began to thrust. He pulled me to him, my back pressed deliciously to his abdomen and chest. I could feel the hard muscles quiver with each movement.

He palmed my breast and pressed his cheek to mine. I turned my head and kissed his cheek tenderly. He pulled away to look at me, eyes hooded. I could see the hard angle of his nose and cheek silhouetted in the moonlight. He must be painfully handsome under the shadows. He leaned in and kissed me slowly. I could feel his love for me in that kiss. I hoped I could keep this up. I hoped that he would stay. Men had never stayed long in my life.

[22] "You are a treasure."

Chapter Twenty-Six

Falling in love is kind of like drowning. It's being sucked under and held there, but not wanting to surface. Just as traumatic as actually drowning, but different. Just as water fills the void of my lungs so the emotions fill the void where I thought nothing could survive. A burning ache of salt water in my soul. She was an ocean I would sink to the bottom for, her body the rhythm of the tides, pulling me closer and closer to oblivion.

With our bodies pressed together like they were, it was hard for me to remember restraint. Hard to remember that she was human. Even harder when her delicious scent, full of arousal for me, clouded my mind. I pressed my face against hers, greedy for the sweet little sounds she made when I plunged into her depths. She kissed my cheek; such a tender kiss that it caught me off guard. I looked at her, eyes dewy with pleasure. My heart pounded wildly in my chest. I was doomed. She was my air, my water, my light. I kissed her then, passionately, and I hoped it conveyed what was in my heart. She shuddered around me, and I never wanted this to end. I broke the kiss and licked her neck; a beautiful, luscious moan came from her. Her back arches and I drove deeper into her, a groan echoing off the study walls.

"You feel divine, darling."

"Niratap." My name was a desperate cry. "Please."

I slipped from her, and she cried out in protest as I stood her up and flipped her around. I kissed her deep, her hands grasping at my shoulders and hair as I lifted her into my arms and turned to a wall. Her legs curled around my waist as I propped her between the wall and myself. I parted our kiss in order to glance down and guide myself into her slick heat.

She panted against my neck as I tested the new position. Her legs vice-like around my hips as I gave her small gentle thrusts, finding our rhythm again. Thrusting deep into her, her nails scraped my scalp and shoulder as she lost herself in us. One of her hands wrapped around one of my antlers and she pulled my face to hers. I met her gaze and felt desire curling tighter and tighter in me. Her cries carried me into a frenzy and as her body spasmed around me, I lost myself in her, finding the sweetest of release.

My legs shook and I braced a hand against the wall behind her. Her body shuddering against me and I was undone again, my body emptied inside of her. I lay my forehead against hers, panting. Her eyes were such deep dark pools I wanted to fall into them and just drown. Never to resurface. I pressed a kiss gently to her lips. This was dangerous.

"You are magnificent." I breathed.

She smiled sweetly. "You are the magnificent one."

I shifted back a step letting her unwrap her legs from around me and slide to the floor. I pressed a kiss to her forehead as she clung to me.

"Don't let go." She whispered.

"I won't. Are you alright?"

"Yeah. More than alright, just seeing stars at the moment."

I chuckled at that. "Me too."

"I don't know why." She giggled "You did all the work."

"Doesn't mean you didn't utterly destroy me."

She smiled shyly. "You flatter me, but the person with the room spinning is probably the one who was destroyed."

"I never said it wasn't spinning for me. To be fair, if I tried to stand without a brace at the moment my legs might buckle."

"You're kidding."

I chuckled again, the laughter in her voice warming me. "Probably not."

"Well, I guess if we fall at least the study is warm, but the fire would go out." She shrugged. "Eventually, someone will come to pry our frozen bodies off the floor."

I laughed, a deep belly laugh. It felt strange and caught me off guard. I wondered how long it had been since I had genuinely laughed. I tested my legs and said. "Let's hope they don't have to."

"You're okay." She grabbed me at the waist to steady me.

"More than okay." I cupped her cheek. "Can you walk on your own, or do I have to carry you?"

"I don't know."

I took a step back, the muscles in my calves and thighs quaked, protesting at the movement. She took a tentative step. Then another. I watched her beautiful full-ass teeter towards the desk. She looked over her shoulder at me. A wicked smile came to her face.

"Niratap?"

"Yes, my darling?"

"Do you hunger for me?"

I swallowed. "Always."

Her wicked smile grew, showing her white teeth. She bent at the waist, her glorious sex on full display for me as she leaned against the desk. She picked up the wine glass, taking an idle sip. She was my undoing, and I stood frozen as she taunted me. My body responded, growing hard once more, to the sight of her wet sex, dripping, our combined release leaking down her thighs. My scent on her felt like home, a flower meadow after a fresh rain. I came to her side, let my shadows wrap around her perfect legs, and hold her in place.

"Now, why would you do that?" She asked, looking at me through her lashes.

"Because I don't want to chase my dinner." I said leaning to her shoulder and placing a gentle kiss there.

She shuddered as I brushed my fingers down her spine, my lips and tongue working their way along it. Her skin was sweet and salty over my taste buds. She wiggled in my grip groaning at the illicit sensations that I gave her. I hooked my arm around her waist, my fingers teasing that bundle of nerves at the apex of her thighs, and she bucks against me. I let my tongue taste along her spine drawing idle circles over her skin, savoring her breaths beneath me. I crouched behind her, kissing the backs of her thighs and teasing her further. She looked back at me with those warm brown eyes, heavy-lidded and sex addled, but begging me to continue. Her scent was maddening to my senses, but to taste her was a gift of hot musky earth. Wildflowers and rain on the hot sand are us together. The taste took me somewhere far away, wrapped up in her, hypnotized by the sounds that echoed from her in a lost breathy voice. My favorite sound was my name as I plunged my tongue into her, her body quaking across it and I drank down every ounce of her that poured over me.

Her knees buckled and I scooped her up in my arms. I wrapped us in shadow, smoke, and darkness, pressing my lips to her. I carried her wrapped in the night to my room. I wanted to be a tangle of limbs and hearts. Her fingers played with my hair and my heart was thundering in my ears. I set her onto the bed and went back to tasting her luscious skin, I sucked at her pert nipples, and greedily took handfuls of soft curves making my feast cry out beneath me. her nails dug into my shoulders to the point of pain. She was a euphoria that I in my very long life had never experienced. I penetrated that sweet hot place again and she whimpered beneath me, her hand cupping my face, her eyes searching mine as I made love to her. Sweet long thrusts that made us both pant with an intensity I didn't know was possible.

"I want more of you." She says breathlessly.

"How do you want me?" I ask, my voice rough and foreign to my ears.

"Lie on your back." She instructed wiggling free from under me.

I obeyed her demand, laying back across the bed. She crawled over me, her hips straddling mine. Her cloud of hair framed her face as she kissed me. My lips, my cheeks, my chest, her tongue flicked my nipples as she found them in the darkness, air passing my teeth in a hiss at the sensation. She drug her nails down my body. I arched at the touch, and I was hers. She grabbed me firmly as she guided me between her folds. She slowly slid my length into her and both of us groaned as the angle plunged me deeper into her, somehow stretching her further. I gripped her hips hard enough to bruise as she started to ride me. I let my head fall back over the edge of the bed letting the euphoria of her consume me.

She leaned forward bracing herself with a hand over my stomach and I felt her losing herself. I held her above me and arched into her pounding her deeply. Her nails dug into my skin, and I smelled my blood, the iron smell triggering something savage in me. I finished with a roar, her body quivering around me over and over. She fell onto my chest panting, baby hairs sticking to her face and neck. I shifted, positioning us into the correct orientation on the bed. She curled into my chest as I pulled the blanket over us, pressing her ear to my chest like she was memorizing the sound of my heartbeat. It was then that I had a realization that I would always want to be tangled with her. The thought both filled me with joy and terrified me. Could I protect her like I needed to?

"Do you think they do that on purpose?" She asked as she stroked my chest.

"That who does what on purpose?"

"Allipo and the others putting us in situations where we end up intertwined in one another."

I smiled to myself, chuckling. "You know I wouldn't be surprised if Allipo did that. He has always wanted to play matchmaker, but most everyone else isn't interested in it."

"So, he wants to decorate people's relationships like he does rooms then."

I laughed again; my heart ached with it. "Exactly like that."

She looked up at me, her round brown eyes framed by her thick beautiful lashes, "I love hearing that sound."

"What sound, my darling?"

"You laughing. It fills me with a bittersweet kind of joy."

I cupped her face. "Why bittersweet?"

"Because I feel like you haven't laughed very often in your very long lifetime."

"That would be accurate." I said, guarded, and I hated the sensation of walls coming up between us. "I haven't had many times in my life that brought joy. Sometimes I wonder if you are just a dream."

"I wonder the same." She said pressing her ear to my chest again. "Then I hear your heart beating and I know it's not."

"You amaze me."

She kissed my chest and sighed. I just enjoyed existing in her presence and as her breathing eased into a deep restful sleep, I fell in love with her even more.

The next morning Navin called. I peeled myself from Shasha's beautiful form that had molded to my body in the night. Allipo had roused me only after he had finalized things, got Navin on the soonest flight in and let me know the time when he would land. My brain was sex addled and the satyr used that to his advantage to dig at me.

"The study had an interesting scent this morning."

"Allipo." I pinched my brow as he handed me my mask.

The satyr chuckled. "Love looks good on you, my Lord. However, copious amounts of sex makes you quite crabby in the morning."

"I am always crabby when I'm awoken after four hours of sleep."

He continued to chuckle. "Anyways, I'm going to take Durgash and Eloimaya with me into the city. Durgash has a grocery list a mile long and Eloimaya has a small list of things that is from Shasha. Did you need anything, my Lord? Another bottle of that fine scotch that you favor?"

"That would be to my liking Allipo. I cannot think of anything that I need."

"Alright." Allipo sketched a bow. "We'll be off in an hour. Go back to bed, my Lord."

The week that Bastion was home was full of laughter from the entire house, but the solemn air settled as we took him back to the city. He promised his mom that he would be careful, and even though we all knew that he would, he was always at risk out there. Durgash told me before we left that his son was growing up into an orc the ancestors would be proud of, and I wondered if he realized that those were the same ancestors that had gotten them enslaved. The pride of the orcs was their greatest strength and greatest weakness. I had seen such foolish ancestors in my earlier life.

Shasha busied herself with her studies as fall took over for the summer. Her days were spent in lectures and under Mitta's tutelage. Mitta gave me reports weekly on her progress, and to say the least, I was impressed that she was excelling in hand-to-hand training, even though I hoped she would never have to use it. Shasha dutifully called her mother once every week, filling her in on lessons and the friendships she was making in the house. How she and Echo picked squash and tomatoes until the sunset and how Dheg had let her brush out Sirius the unicorn that was a resident of the stables. There were evenings when I poured over reports from everyone that worked for me across the world, and she sat in the plush chair working on her homework across from me. Some of those evenings when both of our eyes burned from screens, we would romp there in the study. Finding all the surfaces covered in her scent was not assisting in my need for her when she wasn't there with me.

At the end of September, I traveled to the city to meet with a trader. He was from outside the circle, and even though I was armed, and Allipo with me, I had a sinking feeling about the meeting. I had not been mistaken, either. We met in a secluded alley with a dead end. I scented his fear, standing face to face with death promised. In the dead of the alley, he was fidgeting, unable to make eye contact, and I knew the second that he glanced past me and nodded that it was some foolish attempt to trap me. A knife was plunged into my back. Allipo rushed to my aid, knocking five of the twenty men unconscious, as I slaughtered the rest. It would take much more than a knife to take me down. I returned home angry with myself for allowing them to attempt to capture me and angry that I had walked into it willingly just for the tease of information about a bitarog. How could I allow such a paltry possibility of information be that big of a lure for me? Mitta had also not been impressed with my foolishness, fussing over me like a mother hen.

The following week the market met again in the filth that was New York City. All big cities had this suffocating scent of refuse and exhaust that always lingered no matter the season. The market didn't yield any beasts; the purchase of women and parts flowed freely though. At one of the market stalls, a foolish man was trying to purchase a basilisk fang, trying to haggle down the vendor. I purchased it from under him, paying almost twice the asking price to secure the weapon. The man protested saying that throwing away money wouldn't secure me in the market. I told him that small men didn't survive the market long and I walked away. Whether it was the purchase or my words that fueled it, the man followed me through the market watching me exchange cash for parts, another basilisk fang solely to keep it from his hands, a bottle of phoenixes down, two unicorn horns, and a petrified shadow wraith which was better suited in my keeping than in the streets.

Leaving the market, he stopped me and demanded that I part with the fangs. He held his fists up at me like he thought he stood a chance. I pushed past him and dropped the collection of items into the car, telling him he was more foolish and desperate than I had thought initially. Overconfident that cruel words would be enough to scare the man off, I turned, and his right hook met my left eye. A gruesome sound reverberated through my skull. The unarmed man stood no chance against me as I half shifted and snapped his arm in my jaws in a quick movement. Allipo hadn't made it out the door before it was over. The man lay in a whimpering heap at the edge of the alleyway, alive, but he would probably never be able to use that right hook again. It was enough of a punishment to be even for my fractured orbital bone. Mitta said that the shiner and headache that lingered was enough of a punishment for being lazy on the defense, but the true punishment was when Shasha had lovingly cupped my face in her hands, and I flinched from the touch. She couldn't see the bruise, and her eyes were full of fear and pain that no number of kisses or caresses could heal; no amount of apology and explanation could remove those things from her gaze.

The beginning of October had me on a flight to California to meet with two of my eyes. The week seemed to stretch on forever without Shasha to warm my life with her pure embodiment of the sunlight. I wondered if she had ever seen the vastness of the country, she lived in. I wondered if she would love the desert with its stark contrasts or the plains full of waving grasses. We talked every night, and she told me of Mitta's grueling training, Rogmesh teaching her to make the crusty bread that she loved, and Dheg and Echo starting to teach her to ride on the tamest horse on the grounds. I smiled and laughed at her stories, but my heart ached that I couldn't be there to see her trying to climb the ceiling rope in the gym, or her bread coming out flat because she forgot to feed the yeast or watch her try to find herself on Rhythm. The meetings were boring compared to what waited for me at home, talk of shipments of drugs, gang wars, and movements of wild beasts. Allipo asked more questions than I did, clarifying things that should have been my concern, but I just wanted to be home and buried deep in the scent of all the flowers of the seasons.

Chapter Twenty-Seven

Shasha

I often floated through the manor with my nose in a book now, occasionally lifting my head to see where my legs had taken me. Most of the time I ended up in the solarium, or in Nira's room. I needed it more when he was away, the smell of petrichor soothing the ache when I missed him.

Today I was reading a novel, the second in a series that Dorilody had recommended, instead of my textbook or assigned short stories. The story was a fantastical story about a world divided between the fae and the humans and a great war hanging on the horizon. Where I was in my meandering, the main character was trying to save her man from dying of poison. It was an intense scene and I paused trying to figure out where my feet had taken me.

The crossroad of the hall I was in was dimly lit with sconces, and there were alcoves with benches on both sides of all four halls. There was a set of double doors at the end of one hall that were unfamiliar. From where I stood, I could tell that the doors are carved. Curiosity steered me down the hall. When I was close enough, I could see the faces of people screaming. I took a step back, my heart thundering. Where was I? Something whispered to me just past the door, a quiet, near silent sound. I pressed my ear to the door.

"Pretty one." A hissing whisper of a voice summoned me.

"Hello?" My voice sounded so loud in the silent hall.

"Come in." The voice beckons. "Come in."

I didn't know why, but my hand found the black oval handle on its own, twisting of its own will, and the massive door swooshed quietly over the floor.

"Yes, come in, pretty one." I took a singular step into the room.

"Hello?" I called again into the blackness of the room. "Who's there?"

"Come and see me, child? Come in. Come in." I took another tentative step.

"I—I can't see anything."

"Come in, child, the lights come on once you enter far enough." Another step.

"Who—who are you?" My heart was thundering, part of me wanted to go forward, and another wanted to run.

"I am nobody of importance." The voice said, a strangled pause in the middle of nobody.

"Do you have a name?" I took another step.

"I have been called many things throughout the ages. You can know me as, friend."

I laughed uncomfortably. "Friend isn't a name."

"Isn't it?" I took another small step.

"Shasha." Niratap's voice called from back down the corridor I had wandered from. There was a panicked edge to his voice.

"Sha—sha." The voice in the shadows coos, splitting into more voices and the hair on my arms stood straight. I took a step back.

"Shasha!" Niratap's voice rings around my head. I fought my body and took another step back.

"Come play little one. Come play with us Shasha."

"Shasha!" I tried to call out to him, but I couldn't find my voice.

"The shadow of the forest has come to ruin our fun. Come play with us." Soft tendrils of shadow caressed my face. I felt fear grip my heart full of stampeding horses.

"Shasha!" I couldn't move, but I could see him at the crossroads of halls, his silver eyes glowing in that dim light.

When he saw me, he turned. Faster than I could see he was pulling me from the shadows and the door snicked closed behind him. He was clutching me tightly as the voices beyond the door whispered.

"Come back and play with us, Shasha. We would love to play. Oh, shadow, let her play."

"Enough!" Niratap's voice was a boom in the too-quiet hall, his fist banged against the door. "She is not for you."

There is a hiss at his command then what the voices said next chilled me to my core. "We were only going to feast on her, lord of shadows. Only going to chew her bones for the marrow of her soul. Only going to fill her mind with nightmares and feast upon them. We are so hungry for the suffering of innocents."

"No." He growled, his voice tight and sharp. "You are trapped down here to starve. So, starve."

Keening wails shattered the silence as Niratap carried me from the screaming door, through the maze of halls, and up the stairs through the infirmary. The basement. How had I made it into the basement? Niratap continued to his quarters and gracelessly tossed me on the bed. He paced past me a couple of times, before he turned on me, there were too many things floating in his eyes for me to pinpoint a singular emotion. Rage. Fear. Relief. He stalked toward me, pushing me back on the bed planting his hands on either side of my face.

"Are you hurt?" His voice had a lethal edge to it.

"No." My voice was still a whisper, a small fraction of tension released from his shoulders as he sighs.

"Are you stupid?" His question set my blood on fire; he was mad at me.

"No!" I snapped back, angry that he would ask me something so ridiculous.

His eyes narrowed as he stepped back, his voice a knife. "If not, why were you in the basement? I have told you on repeated occasions that it is restricted."

"I know." I said sitting up and looking away down at my book. "I was wandering while I was reading like I do all the time. I don't know how I got into the basement. I don't even remember going down the stairs."

He reached under his mask pinching between his eyes as if he was getting a headache in my presence. "So, you mean to tell me that you just wandered, nose planted in a book, into the basement and opened the cell that contains a pack of man-eating shadow wraiths."

"Mostly." I said, sliding off the bed. "I went to investigate the door when I pulled out of my book for a moment, however, whatever those creatures were spelled me to open the door."

He half growled and half groaned. "You are the most infuriating creature in the house."

"Excuse me for being distracted, Mitta was busy today so I couldn't train, and you were still gone. Wandering while I read is an exercise for my body and mind." I made for the door, I was done being yelled at, but he came to stand in front of me blocking my exit from his chambers. I looked up at those intense silver eyes and something in my core was set ablaze. He scented the air and I watched, fascinated, as his cat-like pupils dilated, a low growl between us. His hands ever so gently came to my shoulders, stroking gently. He cleared his throat before he spoke.

"I missed you."

"And I you." I replied, my hands tossing my book to the side and sliding around to rest at the top of his ass, my thumbs grazing his tail. "Painfully so."

He swallowed audibly; lust heavy in his eyes. "May I, have you?"

"I thought you would never ask, my Lord."

He bent to scoop me up, his tongue finding the soft apex between my neck and shoulder, and I arched against the touch. His strong hands cupped my ass and lifted me off the floor, his already hard, monstrous length pressing against me through our clothes; we both groaned in desperate need of release.

He laid me on the plush carpet before the fire, his hands roving over my body, beneath my shirt at the edge of my pants. I fervently kissed that face of shadow and mystery, a face that I could only imagine as lovely as it was in my dream. He could only be as lovely as that beautiful, sorrowful soul. His tongue finds my pulse and I shivered beneath the touch, goose flesh alighting my body. He pushed up my shirt and bra kneading my soft flesh.

There was a flash of white of his sharp teeth as they found purchase on my breast. I arched against him, his name a gentle plea on my lips. He sat back undoing the buttons of his shirt, showing the shadows that lurked beneath. He discarded both the vest and fine shirt to the floor, no doubt something Allipo would despise seeing. He undid his pants, his monstrous sex, dark with the shadows that danced there; I knew his skin there would be so soft. I undid the button of my jeans and wriggled out of the rest of my clothes. We delayed there a moment basking in one another. He pulled the mask free, setting it on the side table; dark shadows still encompassed his face, still obscured from my view.

He descended upon me in fervent kisses, his tongue demanding entrance, its devilish length exploring every inch of my mouth. One hand threaded through the thick kinks at the base of my skull angling me so he could deepen his kiss, and the other palmed my breast, teasing the nipple with flicks and pinches, and eliciting moans muffled by his thorough exploration. He lifted me and then carried me to the plush of his bed. I was molten and drenched with the need for him, his cock so close, but out of my reach. I pushed against his chest in a feeble attempt to create space so I could express my needs. He pulled back, eyes heavily lidded and questioning.

"Am I too much?"

"No." My voice sounds hoarse and sultry. "I love kissing you, but it's unfair that you can touch me, and I can't touch you."

His teeth flash in a predatory smile. "How is that unfair?"

I pouted, wriggling underneath him, scooting down until his member caressed my entrance. I gasped at the friction. "I need you."

"I can see that, my dear." He rubbed his length against my core.

"Fuck." My head fell back. Nira licked and sucked at every ounce of skin before him.

"*Níl tú tuillte agam. Conas a tháinig tú isteach i mo shaol?*" [23]

My hand grasped the back of his head, fingers twining through the gossamer strands of his hair. His breath skated over my skin, evoking lusty moans. All while he continued brushing himself against my core, the friction delicious, building my need to have him.

"Nira, please you're tormenting me."

He chuckled his voice a growl. "Patience, love. I need you slick so I can have you."

"I need you." I pleaded.

"I know." He cooed, and I could hear the mischief on his tongue.

"Please."

He slipped the head through my folds. I gasped needing more. "You like that. Sweetness."

"Yes." I moaned.

He pushed another inch. "How badly do you want me?"

I panted. "Nira."

Another inch. Another tease. My back arched as those fingertips edged in shadow trailed across my skin.

"Nira, I'm going to explode."

"Not without me, you're not."

He eased his massive knot deep, my body spasming around him at the stretching and filling sensation of his length inside me, him pushing painfully and slowly into my womb. I came around him, my voice keening across the rafters. He kissed my throat, and when my body relaxed, he started to thrust, building us both up again. His breath was

---

[23] I don't deserve you. How did you come into my life?

hot on my throat, a caress as we barreled to climax. I groaned, my body growing tight, nails digging into his back.

"Say my name." He growls into my throat.

"N—Nira."

"Again. Call out my name."

"Nira, you feel so good."

A rumble of pleasure. I raked my nails over his shoulder as his thrusts became near rabid.

"Shasha." He groaned.

"Come with me Niratap."

He roared with release, arching back my nails digging into him as my own pleasure washed over me. He laid over me, resting his head in the crook of my neck, his breath coming in hot puffs against my throat. I wrapped my arms around him and idly played with the strands of his hair. He pulled himself free, rolling me and laying behind me, pulling me close to him, his heart thundered behind me. Its beat brought me back to earth, and my mind racing to curiosity.

"Can I see your face?"

"Not now." He said as he lazily rubbed my stomach and hip; I loved the feel of his hands on me.

"But it's been months, and you said soon." I said' rolling onto my stomach.

He sighed, shifting so he could look me in the eye. "What does my appearance have to do with us?"

"Everything and nothing." I said looking into the beautiful pools of moonlight. "I know that you care for me regardless, and I care for you."

"That sounds like there's a but." He shifted even more, sitting up. The shadows shifted around him.

"But" I take a deep breath, "I don't just want to love you at face value. I don't want to love just the happy parts and angry parts of you. I want to love the sorrowful and painful parts of you too."

"And if I don't want to give you those things? What then, Shasha? Am I unlovable because I won't share my darkness?" He stood and pulled on a pair of pants.

"That's not what I said, don't twist the meaning of my words."

"Regardless, I am not sharing those parts of myself with you."

I sat up on the bed. "Why not? What else about your past is so terrible that you won't tell me what happened? What is so terrible about the shadows? I've given you everything. My body, my soul, my secrets. What more could the cost of knowing you be? What more could the cost of knowing what you look like be? What more could the cost to love you be?"

He picked up his shirt, crumpled from being discarded on the floor. "Everything but your heart it seems. It's not that easy and that is something I don't want to have to force you to understand."

"But I want to." I yelled, exasperated, placing my hand over my heart. "I want that." I hopped off the bed and stormed over to the fireplace, where my clothes were discarded.

"Do not raise your voice at me." He growled, it was an order, and I could feel the magic warm the skin of my throat as I slipped the shirt over my head and then stepped into my jeans. I didn't want magic forcing me to do anything, so I lowered my voice when I spoke again.

"I just want to understand you. I want—"

He cut me off. "Your desire to understand will not make me any easier to love. The fact that I want you to love me does not change the fact I am a monster."

"I don't care that you're a monster, Nira. I just want to know the being that I want to love. If you weren't so fucking stubborn."

"Mind your tone. Why won't you just let it go?" He pleaded as he pulled on his mask.

"Because I want you. All of you."

"There is a cost for that, Shasha."

"That's what you keep saying." I said bitterly, thoroughly over this conversation and the sensation of my heart breaking. "What is the cost for you anyway? I have given you everything I have of value, but you are too fucking stubborn to share the vulnerable parts of yourself."

"Tone." He corrected again. "The cost is too great. I won't subject you to that."

"You won't let me, you mean. You won't even let me try. I have given you everything, every part of me could be yours by my choice."

"Shasha, it's not up for debate my answer is no. That part of me has cost me more than I want. People I've cared about have died because—"

"I'm not Deirdre." I interrupted, coldness sinking into my voice as my heart continued to crack.

"I never said that I compared you to her." His voice was both cold and tight.

"But you have." The ache in my chest sliced through all reason. "Fuck me. I'm sorry I'm not the fair maiden of your dreams. I'm sorry that you had to watch her sacrifice herself and die for you."

"Shasha—" His tone sharpened and the magic around my throat had started to itch.

"No. I'm sorry. I'm sorry that I wasted your lordship's valuable time. I'm sorry that I have been wasting my time trying to love someone. I'm sorry that I've been wasting my time trying to love you."

"If it's been such a waste, why come to my bed?" He snarled, fisting his hands.

"Fuck you." I spat.

He froze before he spoke, predatory grace coming over his body. His voice was quiet and dark. "What?"

"You heard me." I said stalking towards the door. "Fuck. You."

He was growling. I could feel the rumble in my chest as he effortlessly came to stand in front of me, barring my exit from his quarters. "Where do you think you're going? We are not done speaking."

"Away from you." I jabbed my finger into his chest. "And yes, we are I don't want to talk with some selfish jerk who knows every aspect of me but won't share his face. Fuck you and fuck your ego and fuck your fragility."

"You will not speak to me that way. You can't mistreat me just because you can't have your way."

"That's rich coming from you." I try to push around him, but he is blocking the knobs.

"What is that supposed to mean?" He snarled, tail flicking like a cat.

"You know exactly what it means. You get to have everything you want, and when you don't you snarl and bark to get your way, just like a child."

"Like what you are doing right now?"

I felt my cheeks heat. I glared at him, my throat filling with venom. "Fuck you."

"Shasha." My name sounded thick like velvet and full of malice. "You don't want to do this."

"Do what? Prove a point? Leave? What terrible secret do you need to keep that I can't have you?" I could hear the desperation in my ears.

He gently grabbed my hand, bending to kiss my fingers. "You have me."

I yanked my hand away and my voice grew into a yell. "No, I don't. All I have is what you want me to have, which is nothing. I get to have tea with a being I don't know. I get to crawl into a stranger's bed every night and feel his body but never see it. I get to talk casually about the terrible things that happened to me with a wall. So, fuck you."

"Enough." He yelled, rattling dust from the rafters.

"No, you will listen to what I have to say. I don't care if it hurts your pride."

"You don't care?"

"No, why would I care about a stranger!" The magic at my throat had squeezed, but I was so angry that I pushed through.

"I do not have to listen to this." He made to move, to walk away, but my blood was boiling. I reached up and grabbed the mask, yanking it roughly. It pulled his head toward me, our eyes locking as the tie ripped and the mask flew across the floor and shattered somewhere. We stood there a moment glaring at each other before his hand slapped across my face. I was stunned for a moment as the cut on my cheek began to bleed and my mouth tasted metallic. He hit me.

"You don't understand the consequences you have unleashed." The threat was deadly quiet.

Defiance filled my chest. "No, you do not understand."

I swung at him, and he caught my wrist. "That is foolish. We both know you are not stronger than me."

"I don't care. Let me go." I kicked at him, and he lifted me off the floor by the arm.

"No, I own you girl, or have you forgotten?"

"You have a great propensity to remind me that you bought me when we're fighting, master. Let me go."

His scowl deepened. "Well then if that is how you—"

I spit in his face, not letting him finish that horrible thought. He dropped me and I can see him shaking in rage.

"Shasha."

"Fuck you, master."

He roared and the whole house seemed to shake as I pushed past him and flew out the door. He continued to roar. I slipped on some flats at the base of the stairs and threw on a cloak. Fuck him. Master or not he was not going to keep me locked up like a breeding cow. I rushed out the front door of the manor not caring that it was left ajar, and I ran toward town. Into the woods.

Chapter Twenty-Eight

Niratap

"Fuck you." Her words were knife-sharp.

"Shasha, you don't want to do this." My voice was controlled, level at best. My frustration was masked as anger.

"Do what? Prove a point? Leave? What terrible secret do you need to keep that I can't have you?" Her voice broke, an edge of desperation in it.

I clutched her hand kissing her fingers. I hated being the thing that brought her pain. "You have me."

"No, I don't." She snarled, ripping her hand from my grasp. "All I have is what you want me to have, which is nothing. I get to have tea with a being I don't know. I get to crawl into a stranger's bed every night and feel his body but never see it. I get to talk casually about the terrible things that happened to me with a wall. So, fuck you."

"Enough." I shout. I don't want to fight like this.

"No, you will listen to what I have to say. I don't care if it hurts your pride."

"You don't care?" I asked my voice a frustrated growl.

"No, why would I care about a stranger!" Her words cut me to the core.

"I do not have to listen to this." I tried to move, to walk away, to cool my head so I didn't do something I would regret to the woman I wanted to love me. She didn't let me, grabbing the bottom of the mask and wrenching it, and my head towards her. The fastening band snapped, and the mask skittered with force across the floor, hitting a piece of furniture and shattering. We stood there for a moment glaring at each other. I was both enraged and shocked. I reacted before I could think, and I struck her across the face. My stomach curdled as I saw my claw had cut her cheek. Her eyes go wide, and so did mine. What have I done?

"You don't understand the consequences you have unleashed." My voice had a hard and brittle edge, but it was quiet and menacing.

"No, you do not understand." She said defiantly before she swung at me.

I caught her wrist easily, but there was undeniable strength behind it. "That is foolish. We both know you are not stronger than me."

"I don't care. Let me go." She tried to kick me, and it made me angry that she was fighting me. I lifted her off the ground so I could get something into her head. She had to understand she couldn't love me as we both wanted.

"No. I own you girl, or have you forgotten?"

"You have a great propensity to remind me that you bought me when we're fighting, master. Let me go." The word master left her tongue tinged with hate.

"Well then if that is how you—" I didn't get to finish the thought as she spat in my face, my body began to shake, and I dropped her gracelessly on the floor.

"Shasha." She does not know she has wounded me, but I felt my heart is breaking.

"Fuck you, master." That word is a knife.

I roared, these emotions were too much, and I wanted to destroy things. I wanted to watch the world burn. I didn't notice as she slipped out the door, fleeing from me. I would run too. I stalked across the room and toppled the two chairs by the fireplace, drowning in both anger and heartbreak. Why? Why? Why? No matter how hard I tried to pull us together we explosively launched each other in opposite directions. Fuck. I swept the top of a table by the wardrobe, a vase breaking a few feet away. I collapsed to the floor, clawing at the hardwood, hot tears stinging my eyes. Fuck.

The others came through the doors, and frantic voices bounced around the room.

"My Lord?" Katrel.

"What happened?" Tummi.

"I don't know, I heard yelling and came running." Dorilody.

"Shasha, where is she?" Eloimaya.

"What's going on?" Durgash and Rogmesh.

"What happened? Shasha ran past me in the garden crying, and I smelled blood." Echo

"My Lord?" Allipo placed a cautious hand on my shoulder. His steady hand makes me realize I was shaking. I felt like I was being strangled. I wrapped my arms around myself trying to quell the panic that had risen in me.

"You need to breathe, my Lord." Allipo rubs soothing circles on my back.

"My Lord!" Mitta's voice breaks into the room. "Oh, what's going on?"

"We don't know." Tummi said sheepishly.

"What is it you need, Mitta? It sounded serious." Allipo's voice was clear. Why can't I get my voice to work? Why couldn't I move? Why couldn't I get air into my lungs? I shivered violently as I remembered numerous times where I had been in this position.

"There was a disturbance on the east fence line, but the cameras are down on that side. It was one of the things I discussed with the lord the other day."

"Could it be a basilisk?"

"No, there is a deterrent to keep them from leaving the grounds."

"We have a problem" Dheg joined the fray, his voice high with panic.

"Dheg?" Allipo sounds steadfast, but I heard the fear in his voice.

"Shasha ran into the forest. I tried to chase after her, but I lost her. She's headed toward town, but the basilisk nest is between us and the town."

"Shit," Allipo swore and came to kneel in front of me. I wondered what I looked like to him. A shadow in shock. "Niratap, my friend, I need you to come back."

"What have I done?" My voice sounded foreign and hollow.

"Niratap, I need you to come out of it. Shasha is in danger, and you are the only one that can save her."

The shadows slithered across the floor and crawled over the furniture as they melted off me. I reached for him, and my body wouldn't stop trembling, "Allipo, what have I done?"

"I do not know what you have done, my Lord, but you have to pull it together and go get the girl."

I looked at my scarred arms and I could smell her blood. Panic was making me delusional, they said where she was, but I couldn't seem to remember, "Where is she? Where is Shasha?"

Cool hands came to rest on my face, Katrel and Tummi have come to crouch on either side of Allipo, the girls my longest companions. Together they spoke.

"*Go bhfuil do chroí socair mar an sruth ag caoineadh. go mbeadh d'intinn soiléir mar an spéir gan scamall. bíodh d'anáil réidh mar ghaoth an tsamhraidh.*"[24]

Everything centered itself on their command. My heart slowed, my mind eased, my lungs expanded and then girls moved back, sitting on their heels. My body was clammy from the experience and still shook. I pressed my forehead onto Allipo's shoulder while the tremors slowed then ceased. His hands wrapped around me in a gentle hug.

"It has been a long time since we lost you like that."

"Not a shining moment." I still sounded strange in my ears; I take a couple of deep breaths before I looked up at the girls. "Thank you."

"Our pleasure, my Lord." Katrel says.

Tummi wrapped her arms around herself. "I hate when you look so helpless and trapped in yourself."

"Are you okay now?" Allipo asks.

---

[24] "May your heart be calm as the babbling stream. May your mind be clear as the cloudless sky. May your breath be gentle as the summer breeze."

I nod, "Yes. Where is Shasha? I—"

Allipo pressed a hand to my shoulder. "This is alarming, and I don't want you back peddling on us. You two had a fight, by the looks and sounds of it a bad one. She ran off into the woods. She's heading towards town, but you know as well as the rest of us that the basilisk nest is between us."

I felt the panic rise, but I took a breath before I looked up at Dheg. "Dheg."

"Yes?"

"You're certain you saw her go into the forest."

He stands straighter. "As certain. As the sun."

I rose to my feet, my legs still shaky. I need to focus. "Very well then. Mitta prepare for the worst."

"Yes, my Lord."

Eloimaya came to stand next to me, her eyes full of fear. "My Lord, what is the worst?"

"The worst is this being the last time you see me."

Her eyes widened even more if that was possible. "Then what happens if?"

"Allipo and I have discussed it at length." I said looking at my friend. I was immortal, not invulnerable. I wrapped my arms around Eloimaya embracing her before whispering. "You will be safe regardless of if I am here or not. Allipo seems to fancy you anyway."

Her hand came to rest against my skin. "Bring our girl home and you come back to us."

I smiled sadly, the reality that both of us could die was very possible. "I'll try."

With that, I looked around the room looking at my family and remembering their faces. I didn't want to die, but just in case, I wanted to have them with me. Especially with them all looking so hopeful and brave. Then I walked out of my quarters and disrobed before I fully shifted into my beast. Blasting through the main doors, I scented the air. The irony tang twined with Shasha's lovely floral scent twisted a knife in my heart. Please be safe, I asked, then took off in the direction of town, following the scent of all the flowers of the seasons and shame.

Chapter Twenty-Nine

Shasha

I stopped running and sat down by a small stream to catch my breath; my face had finally stopped bleeding. I had run like my life depended on it. I wrapped my arms around myself. I was scared, and the October breeze chilled me to the core caused me to shiver. This endeavor had been stupid. I didn't know where I was, and the town was hours away on foot. I doubted that I would get there before dark. I looked around and though the spot I had found to rest was peaceful, I realized that I made a grave error running into the forest. I didn't know my way, I had never been outdoorsy growing up either, preferring the safety of library stacks to the mountains. I hadn't been paying enough attention as I fled the manor to know my way back. I was lost.

"Fuck." I muttered to myself as I stood. "Why did I run? Why did I even ask again? Every time it's the same answer. Now I'm alone in the forest, full of creatures that would find me delicious. Very foolish indeed."

I picked a direction and started to walk. If I could find the road, I might be able to find my way back home. Which home, I did not know. Would Niralap come to find me, or had we burned each other for the last time? Would he use this opportunity to teach me a lesson? Would he find me alive, or would he leave me to the beasts? I tripped over a stone and stumble down an embankment, landing hard. Pain shot up my leg and my ankle started to swell, sprained. I curled into myself, resting my head on my knees.

"I'm sorry, Nira. I fucked up and now I don't know where to go. I don't know if I'll see you again."

"See who?" A soft feminine voice asked. My head flew up and I was greeted by a beautiful woman, in a light gossamer dress. Her feet were bare, and the bottom of her hem was dirty.

"Who are you?" I asked, knowing the fae would know who I am.

"I am Yuki, and who are you?"

Shit, not fae. "I am Shasha. What manner of creature are you?"

"I am no creature." Her lithe voice feigned offense. "I am just a woman lost in the woods, and I have been lost for a long time. I am so hungry."

She came to stand before me and in a puddle, I saw her true form reflected. Long black and yellow spider legs came out of her back, and her face was contorted by large fangs that hung from her mouth. I swallowed fear, taking hold of my heart; a jorogumo, I had to get away from her.

"Lord Niratap would be quite displeased to find me out here in the forest, conversing with a jorogumo."

"Ah, you must be the new being that the shadow of the forest brought home. The fae have not stopped prattling on about you. I seem to agree with their consensus that you smell delicious." She loomed over me.

"I thought your race only ate men." I clawed at the muck, preparing a handful.

"We do, but men don't wander through the shadow's woods. I miss the taste of man flesh. I wonder if woman will taste the same."

"Unfortunately, I have to go."

I hocked the mud into her face and scurried away, my ankle burning as I forced it to work. I ran and I heard her screeching behind me. I needed to find a place to hide. Down an embankment I slid in a crack of a craggy rock face. I hoped she didn't see me. My ankle was throbbing. Her voice came from above.

"Where did you go, sweet treat?" She hissed and I pressed myself deeper.

A hiss emanated from the other side of the rock, and the jorogumo fled. I watched as she ran down the embankment disappearing from view. I wondered if the scariest thing in the forest had come to my rescue. I shimmied out of the rock, coming around to him.

"Nira, I'm sorry I—" It was not Niratap that hissed at the jorogumo.

Before me was a hard-scaled lizard the size of a pickup, munching on a doe that hung out its mouth. It looked at me, its yellow eyes glowing in the fading light; had I really been out here this long? It swallowed the last half of the deer, hissing at me as it rose on its six legs. I was in danger. I turned in my heels and ran, the throbbing in my ankle almost forgotten as adrenaline kicked in, I heard it thundering after me.

"Somebody help me!" I screamed into the ether. My own voice echoed back at me, tears streaming down my face.

I jumped over a fallen tree, losing my footing and I landed hard. I gasped for air and shimmied as close as I could to the tree. Fuck. I was going to die here. I wouldn't see Niratap or my mom again. It was her fault I was so fucking stubborn. Tears streamed down my face. I covered my mouth trying to stay quiet as the basilisk came over the log I was cowering against. It slunk over my head, scenting the air and ground in front of it. Maybe I could sneak back over and find a better hiding place. I stood reaching for a branch to pull myself up. The branch I trusted failed me, I landed hard on my ass and the basilisk had spotted me. I scooted back against the trunk. I had nowhere to run. Nowhere to hide.

There was a snarl from the other side of the clearing. A large wolf-like creature came stalking purposefully through the bramble. Its fur was grey with a black streak over the ridge of its back, antlers graced the top of its head, a long lion's tail at its rear, dark green-blue scaled forelimbs ended in black menacing talons. I made eye contact with the beast's bright silver eyes, the smell of petrichor filling the air. Niratap had come to save me.

The basilisk snarled at him, long black fangs on display. Niratap returned with a roar, stalking toward me. The basilisk saw this and turned completely on Niratap. It was a show of dominance, the beast claiming me as his prey. Niratap just shook himself, as if this basilisk is just an annoyance to him and continued to me. His eyes never left me. The basilisk turned on him and snapped its jaws at him, earning a snarl as Niratap dodged the attack.

In a last bit of defiance, the basilisk charged me, its gaping maw of serrated teeth coming right for me. I closed my eyes in horror. This was it. There was a high-pitched yelp, but the basilisk didn't sink its fangs into me. I opened my eyes to Niratap pinned under the basilisk; the beast's jaws clamped firmly over his shoulder. He needed help, but what could I do?

Chapter Thirty

Niratap

I was following her scent, but it had gone all over and in circles. She was lost and I hoped she was safe. The scents of basilisks, fae, and the jorogumo were thick here. Fear and worry made my chest hurt, please be safe. The breeze shifted and I caught a fresh trail of her scent. The light was fading as autumnal dusk settled over us. I did not want to be hunting her in the dark; it was much more dangerous as the basilisks became more active.

"Somebody help me!"

It was Shasha screaming. I pushed my legs faster and harder. I needed to get to her, before whatever made her scream. I found her hiding; a basilisk scenting for her as it crawled over the log. The basilisk licks the ground, snorting, I pushed forward and froze as Shasha stands and tried to pull herself up over the dead tree, trying to flee. The branch snapped, the crack echoing off the trees, and she landed hard. She pressed herself to the bark, out of options for escape.

I snarled from the other side of the clearing, drawing their attention. I made eye contact with the Shasha, recognition coming over her face, tears falling freely from her face. The basilisk snarled at me, it was Murdoch, an old-world basilisk, and I roared in return stalking toward her. The basilisk saw this and turned on me as I challenged him for what he thought was his. I shook to tell him not to mess with me. I didn't want to fight him for what was most certainly mine. The basilisk snapped its jaws at me. earning a snarl as I dodged the attack. You will not have her.

Murdoch looked between us and charged at Shasha, hell-bent on having his prey. I charged forward. Putting myself between him and Shasha, acid-like pain lit up my shoulder as his fangs sank into my skin, a yelp escaping my throat at the impact. He rolled me under him, pinning my legs as he chewed viciously, pushing venom into my skin.

I stole a glance at Shasha; she looks frozen in fear, then her gaze dropped to the fallen branch beside her. I kicked and thrashed at the basilisk. I needed to get free before she did something foolish. She ran past me and swung the branch as hard as she can against the basilisk's face. A hiss emanated through my chest as he moved from her, dragging me farther underneath him. She swung again making contact with the creature's eye and I took the opportunity as his mouth loosened. I wrench myself free, my flesh tearing, and the scent of my blood tinged the air. I could feel a fang broken off in my chest. Shit. I summoned the shadows and roared at Murdoch, putting myself between him and Shasha. I snapped and snarled at him, rising up and thrashing my claws at him. She is mine.

Murdoch stole a fleeting glance at Shasha before he backed away, slinking back into the shadows of the forest. I partially shifted wrapping my wound in magic to keep the venom and bleeding at bay. I embraced Shasha and pressed her into me. She was almost safe.

"Nira, I'm sorry." She sobbed.

"Shh, not here, sweetness. Let's get home first. I'm going to shift back, climb on and hang on tight."

She nodded, stepping back. There was definitely a fang crammed in my chest. As long as the acid flowing in my veins already didn't start hitting me until we got home, she would be safe, but I didn't know about myself. I crouched so she could climb onto my back. She gripped the fur tightly and a gasp came from her mouth.

"Niratap, you're bleeding,"

I grunted at her. *Just grab on.*

"But."

I pawed the ground. We didn't have time to argue.

Her fingers curled tightly into a fresh patch of fur, and she clutched herself to me. I took off. We were thirty minutes from the manor and every second counted, for getting her to safety and getting me help. I didn't feel the fang sinking deeper or loosening, it must have been stuck between my ribs. This was bad.

After ten minutes I gave my head a shake, trying to free my eyes of the cobwebs that started to form in my vision. After twenty my legs were starting to feel like Jello. I stumbled, then evaded a tree that was my path. Shasha's grip tightened as we narrowly missed it. The hedge line came into view, and the magic that was holding me together slipped as we passed through the hedges. I needed to get to the manor before my form failed me.

I lost my footing just before the steps, panting heavily. I could feel the magic dam give way, the venom lighting fire anew in my veins, blood oozing from my wound. Shasha jumped off, terror on her face.

"Niratap, your wounds—"

I felt my shape give way, and my voice sounded of carnage, "I don't matter. You're safe."

"Nira—"

I came to all fours again, my breath labored I pressed my forehead to hers, drawing on the last of my magic. *"Thug tú beatha thar cuimse dom agus fiú má rachainn thar fóir beannófar thú le sábháilteacht mo scátha."*[25]

"Nira, I—"

I left her, forcing my failing legs up the front step. I needed to get to my room and wash the wound. I wasn't going to die in front of her.

---

[25] "You have given me life beyond measure and even if I shall pass you will be blessed with the safety of my shadow."

Chapter Thirty-One

Shasha

Blood. There is so much blood. The puddles of dark crimson on the snow-colored marble steps take my breath away, as he pushes himself through the door. How had he gotten us home with such wounds? How was he still going?

I didn't know how to help him as his body contorted. A human limb became beastly, another stuck in between. I stopped as he climbed the grand stairs, cresting the top step and slinking down the hall. The others had pooled at the entrance to the dining room, all with wide eyes and fear on their faces. Mitta pushed out of the fray and rushed through the infirmary doors, and Allipo came to me, wrapping me protectively in his arms.

"Are you okay, little flower?"

"Niratap. He's wounded."

"Yes, my flower. We'll take care of the lord." He was trying to lead me away to the dining room.

"But Nira, he's hurt. It's my fault." I tried to walk up the stairs. Allipo's grip was tight on my wrist.

"No love, he knew the risks. Let's get you checked out."

"Let me go." I wrenched my hand from Allipo's grasp. "He's alone and he needs me."

I bolted up the stairs following the trail of blood to his quarters. Furniture was overturned and there was broken glass across the floor. The deep crimson trail led into the bathroom, the door was cracked, and I could hear the shower running. I pushed into the bathroom and saw his dark grey tail poking out beyond the partition. I took a deep breath and stepped into the shower. Before me was the man that saved my life. His back was to me, and he was curled under the spray of the shower. My hand came to my face. His back was a patchwork of scars. Scars over scars, bright cream on his tan skin. There was a six-inch gouge in his shoulder. He groaned, rolling slightly, exposing the jagged wound caused by the serrated teeth across his chest.

"Niratap." I went to sit by his head, mindful of his antlers. I pulled him into my lap, the cold water soaking through my clothes.

His handsome features were pulled into a grimace, he was breathing heavily. He had a strong angular face, an Irish nose, and full supple lips. A fine long scar down the right side of his face from just above his eyebrow to the bottom of his chin. I pulled his hair out of his face. He opened his eyes slightly; they were bloodshot and cloudy.

"Shasha." His head flopped uselessly to one side.

"Shh." My hands were shaking. "I'm here."

Mitta came into the bathroom and crouches beside us. "Shasha."

"It's all my fault." Tears started streaming down my face, hot against the icy spray.

"Shasha. Sweetheart. I need you to tell me what attacked you. What attacked Lord Niratap?"

"He's so cold, Mitta." Panic slipped into my voice. He was cold and hot. His skin fire below my fingers chilled in the cold shower.

She placed her hands on my face and forced me to look at her. "Shasha. I need you to help me help him. What attacked you?"

I felt as if I were still there in that clearing waiting for death to find me. My heart was pounding. "Basilisk."

She stood quickly, rushing out of the bathroom calling for others to come help. When she returned, she had a large syringe in hand, a viscous grey liquid inside. I felt a lump form in my throat as she plunges the needle into his chest. Her eyes flicked up to me.

"It's antivenom."

I nodded as she stood and grabbed the shower wand, spraying between the flaps of skin that were his wounds. She turned the water off and sniffed him; her face was drawn.

"Damn."

"What?" I felt my voice hitch with fear.

"Infection is already starting to set in. Niratap, I need you to wake up." She patted him on the face. He opened his eyes, which were still cloudy and unfocused, and groaned.

"Niratap, is there anything I need to know?"

He placed his hand over the wound, wincing. I noticed the burn-like scars over his wrist, a match to the scars across his throat and other wrist. His voice sounded so weak, far away even with his head resting in my lap. "Fang. Broken. Chest."

"Shit. Allipo, Dheg, I need you in here now." They both walked into the bathroom, Allipo had his sleeves rolled up past his elbows, both of their eyes wide.

"Okay, we need to get him out of here. Dheg take his legs, Allipo take his top." Mitta instructed before she shouted into the bedroom. "Dorilody, lay a clean sheet down on the floor so I can keep this back wound clean."

Allipo came next to me. "Let me take him, okay? Mitta will get him taken care of."

I let him come in front of me and scoop Nira out of my lap. His head lulled to one side limply and it made my stomach turn with. I followed behind them, hovering as they laid him down on a sheet. He groaned softly. Hot tears are in my eyes.

"My Lord, I need you to stay with me, okay?" Mitta hissed.

His head flopped to the other side, eyes cracked in her direction, unseeing. Mitta frowned and filled another syringe with antivenom before once again plunging it into his chest. He groaned again; a grimace came to his face as he tried to move.

"My Lord, I'm going to feel your wound and find this fang. Okay?"

He gave a small nod and sucked air through his teeth, Mitta's finger slipping between the folds of skin feeling for the fang lodged in his chest. When she found it, her brows knitted together, and she tried to pull it out.

"Durgash, Rogmesh, we'll need your help. Dheg, Allipo, grab a limb. My Lord, I know this is going to be opening old wounds, but this fang is lodged between your ribs, and it requires some force to remove. Though I care about your trauma, I can't help you if you try to kill me and this fang has to come out, so it won't be continuously envenomating you."

Another small nod and he took a shaking breath as the others picked a limb and pinned him to the ground. He was shaking, and his breathing became shallow. Mitta looked at me and saw me standing there scared.

"Shasha, come help."

"No." Niratap protested weakly.

"She's seen everything now, no point in being ashamed. Go hold down his head. Use his antlers and just sink your weight down on them. It will keep him from biting me."

I nodded and went to kneel between the antlers, grabbing the base of them and leaning over him. There was panic in his eyes.

"It's okay, I'm here."

His eyes softened even though his breathing didn't. He closed his eyes, and pain seeped through my heart. Mitta straddled his stomach so she could get the leverage she needed, taking a large set of forceps and clamping them over the fang.

"Okay, everyone hold him down," and Mitta leaned back with all she had to free the fang from his chest. He thrashed underneath all of us trying to get free. Once the fang was out Dorilody appeared with a jar and Mitta drops the fang into it. She sets the forceps on the floor and plunges her fingers into his wound. He roared bucking off the ground, trying to throw us off.

"I'm sorry my Lord. I had to make sure it hadn't punctured your heart or lungs."

Dorilody brought a tray with several syringes on it. Mitta expertly took each one and injected them into Niratap.

"More antivenom. Morphine. Antibiotics and a sedative." She said to no one in particular but pointedly stated. She must be feeling my eyes on her work. She dumps iodine into the wound to sterilize it. "I'm going to have to bandage this wound. I'm not going to be able to stitch any of it, your skin is just too shredded. Dorilody, will you run down to the medical lab and bring me some of his blood from the bank? Katrel, will you go with her and bring me the IV supplies?"

The women nodded and took off out of the room, their feet thundering down the stairs. Niratap was panting, his skin clammy and pale.

"He's lost so much blood."

"Yes. I know. Durgash, Allipo, will guys prop him up?" She asked them.

I moved out of the way, so they could sit him up. I stood grabbing hold of his antlers, so his head didn't swing wildly.

"Thank you," Allipo said, a tine of the antler close to his face.

"Yeah."

Mitta dug around in a grey bin set by the door; she folded gauze and rolled bandages under her arm. She came back, setting all sorts of bandages down on the sheet beside him. She took the bottle of iodine and poured it over the wound on his back. He winced but didn't move.

"Mitta, I—I can't feel my limbs," his voice was quiet.

"It's just the sedative I gave you. It will help your muscles relax and let your body heal. You're probably going to be on bed rest for a few days, at least."

"Damn it." He growled.

"Quit trying to fight it," she growled back, pressing sticky bandages to pull his wound closed. After they're in place she begins to wrap around his body ducking under his arms and pulling it over his shoulders. When she was satisfied, she pulled back and looked at her work.

"I'll let you rest a couple of days before I change the dressing. Put him in the bed guys."

They gently lifted him, and I supported his head as they tucked him into the bed. He groaned, his lids hanging heavily over his eyes. He was fighting the sedative still. I brushed some of his hair back and tuck it behind his fine pointed ear. His eyes drifted to me, and I couldn't help but smile sweetly at him and press a kiss to his brow. The women returned and brought the supplies to Mitta, who sets everything up with expert skill. She slipped the needle into his arm and hung two bags of blood.

"That should help with his blood volume. And then I'll run an IV when the blood bags are done."

"Is he going to be, okay?" I asked, my voice breaking a little.

"He should be fine. As long as we can head off a big infection. He just needs to rest. Are you hurt at all my dear?"

"Nothing I can't live with."

"Well, at least let me check you out. The lord would skin me alive if I didn't at least clean you up."

"Okay."

I sat up on the bed, pulling Niratap's hand into my lap, careful not to yank his IV, and stroked his long, elegant fingers. Mitta cleaned up the cut on my face, superficial at worst. She cleaned up the palms of my hands and knees which were scraped from falling all over the place.

"You sprained your ankle, pretty good, kid." She said pulling off the flat and manipulating the joint, a fiery ache taking refuge.

I winced, "Yeah, I fell down an embankment because I wasn't paying attention."

"The adrenaline is wearing off, I see." She wrapped my ankle snugly so the joint could heal. She nodded her head toward Niratap, who looked to have finally lost the fight with the sedative. "Stay with him. I'm going to clean up and I'll be back in a half hour to check his vitals and switch him to the IV. Okay?"

"Okay."

Mitta left and we were alone. I hadn't realized that everyone had drifted out of the room. Even Allipo whose worried glances had been shot my way all evening. I moved to the other side of the bed and curled into the covers with him, laying my head in the crook of his arm.

"Nira, I'm sorry." I tried to swallow the lump forming in my throat. "For everything. I feel so stupid. You could have died. You're hurt and it's all my fault."

"No." The word a soft rumble in his chest.

"I thought you were asleep." I said, wiping the tears from my face. He tried to shift a grimace coming over his face. "Don't. Just rest."

He settled back down speaking slowly. "Fine, but don't apologize. I am the one who is sorry. I—I don't know how to be vulnerable. In my very long-life vulnerability has gotten me captured and tortured."

"The scars—" I couldn't finish the sentence and it hung in the air between us.

He sighed. "May I have some time to organize my thoughts and recover, before we open old wounds of mine?"

He was asking me. His face weary, the day catching up to both of us.

"Yes. I'm okay with that." I said curling into him. "I'm just glad to be home."

Chapter Thirty-Two

I slept lightly and I woke often. Every sound and shift that Niratap made woke me and every hour Mitta came to check his vitals, add medicine or change his IV bag when it was low. She told me everything she was doing each time like she knew I was being protective of him in his fragile state. Sometime in the night, he started to get a fever and it caused me to worry. Mitta had said that it was a good sign. That even with all the trauma he had endured, his body was fighting.

The fever continued through the entirety of the following day, and he remained unconscious. I wondered if it was the sedatives or the trauma. How had I fucked up so royally that I had to pull him down with me. Part of me wished that the basilisk should have just eaten me. I dabbed the sweat from his brow and that handsome face. Why did he hide it? He said to hide his identity from the market, but I wondered if it was also because he didn't like the way he looked. That somehow all the scars that ravaged his body were reminders of traumas that he couldn't forget, failures and near misses that haunted him.

That second night, I slept a bit better, but I woke to the sounds of clacking. I shifted from my cozy spot in the crook of Niratap's arm to his face contorted and his jaw working. My heart skittered with panic, wondering what could cause him such pain or distress. Mitta entered the room a moment later, her brows furrowing at the sound.

"Why is he doing that?" I asked in a whisper.

"He's having a nightmare." She said quietly, frowning as she came to the edge of the bed with her tray. "They used to be much worse; he'd wake in the night screaming or shift and wander the manor looking for threats that didn't exist."

"Does he have nightmares often?"

"Less now and they rarely rouse the rest of the house anymore." She gave me a sad smile before she lifted her hand pressing her pointer finger and middle finger to where his brows were knit in discomfort, *"hvíldu herra minn. þeir eru aðeins draumar sem hrjá þig. ekkert meira."*[26]

A blue light emanated from her fingers and Niratap's face relaxed. She sighed; her face drawn as if the spell had expended a lot of her energy.

"What language is that? I thought rakshasi didn't have magic affinity."

"Icelandic." She smiled at me even though it didn't touch her eyes. "That is where I was born. Not naturally, but some can learn to use simple spells."

"Do you miss it, your homeland?"

"Sometimes," she said as she checked his pulse, checked the dressing, and pressed around the dressing to see if he'd react. When he winced, she frowned. Turning toward her tray she said. "But for all the things I miss, I am blessed to have the life I do. Blessed to have this family."

I smiled at that. "I think I agree there."

She smiled to herself drawing medicine into a syringe. "His body is burning through the painkillers fast, but I want him to keep this temperature for a while longer."

"Why is that?"

"His body is fighting the residual venom and infection. A fever is a natural response to that, as long as it stays like this, maintained, it makes the body a hostile environment."

"So, the fever is a good thing?"

"For now, it is. I gave him a half dose of painkillers and another round of antibiotics. He should be fine till morning now." She yawned, "I'm going to get a few hours of sleep and you should try as well. I'll check in at eight."

---

[26] "Rest my Lord. They are only dreams that plague you. Nothing more."

I glanced at the clock on the wall. It was four in the morning. I yawned to match her and laid my head back down. "Okay. Sleep well, Mitta."

"You too, Shasha."

Sunrise bathed the room in caramel-colored light, warming my face as I woke. Niratap was covered in a sheen of sweat, telling me his fever had broken. He didn't stir as I crawled out of bed to the restroom. I grabbed one of the downy hand towels and wet it as the door to his quarters opened. Mitta and Allipo went to stand beside the bed chatting quietly.

"How long do you think he'll need sedation?" Allipo asked, brows stuck with worry.

"I'll probably keep it light during the day, enough that he doesn't try to overdo it and as long as he sleeps through the night, I won't fuss much with it."

"You're going to keep him sedated?" I asked, sliding back onto the bed beside Niratap and dabbing his face with the rag.

"The lord has trouble listening to anyone regularly." Allipo said.

"It's even worse when he is hurt." Mitta finished. "He is very good at overcompensating for the fact that he is wounded. Sedation keeps him from hurting himself further."

"That does sound like him." I said quietly, looking at his ethereally handsome face, calm, at ease and wondering how frequently his face was haggard or strained.

"He will be okay." Allipo said sweetly, a sad smile painting his face. "If anything, else just from sheer stubbornness."

I smiled at that. "He is definitely that."

"Allipo?" Eloimaya said from the doorway. "Can you come to take this call in the study?"

"Sure. Are you good if I take that, Mitta?"

"Yeah, go ahead. He's still sleeping so it's okay. I'd rather him be conscious to change his dressings, but resting benefits him just as well. I'll let him sleep."

"Alright." Allipo gave her a gentle nod and then followed Eloimaya to the study.

"Does it happen often?" I asked as Mitta drew medicine.

"What happen, my dear?"

"Nir – the lord getting hurt?"

She gave me a knowing smile. "Well, in the time since you've been here, he has been shot, stabbed, been in a fistfight, and this."

Two months. In two months, he had sacrificed so much, risked so much. I swallowed, my brows knitting together. Mitta ran the medicine into his IV. She checked his vitals and smiled sadly.

"I know it's not fair to you, Shasha, but he's been rather reckless since you joined us. You smell different than other humans; I can see how that would lure any creature to you. He put everything, everyone, at risk to pull you from the trade." Her voice was sharper than I was used to, and it caused me to tear up. "But I know he is quite smitten with you. You're tenacious, vibrant, and in my own opinion you are good for him in all the ways that matter."

I felt a tear roll down my cheek, and Mitta's hand wiped it away.

"Don't be ashamed of being you. My observation has no bearing on the quality of your character. However, our lord is definitely doing much more to try and keep you safe. Even risking his life."

I nodded, but words failed me as Mitta began to pack up. Niratap cared for me. Eloimaya poked her head through the door again.

"Shasha, will you come down to the study?"

"What is it, Eloimaya?"

"Umm, well Vrorlin is on the phone and he's demanding to speak to the lord. Allipo keeps saying that he is unavailable. Allipo told me to come to grab you because Vrorlin told him that if the crazy woman in his office wasn't dealt with, he'd be coming for him."

I paled, "What day is it?"

"Friday."

"Fuck."

"Who is it?" Mitta asked, giving me a sidelong glance.

I pinch the bridge of my nose. "My mother."

"Don't you call her once a week?"

I slid off the bed, gripping Niratap's hand, "Yes, but I didn't this week, after training Tuesday I was exhausted and laid in bed, and Wednesday I wandered the halls and—"

I didn't need to finish the sentence as I looked down at the sleeping figure next to me. Mitta understood the things that I meant had happened. I hesitated.

"I can stay with him while you talk to your mother. He's stable. If anything, he'll wake up. Go."

I gave a small nod, giving the back of his hand a kiss, before setting it down and following after Eloimaya. As we neared the library, I heard Allipo's voice.

"Vrorlin, Lord Niratap is currently recovering from injuries, he can't speak with you or the viper."

No truer words had been spoken about my mother.

"I don't care if she has you cornered in your office demanding where her daughter is. You know the lord would have both our hides if she came here unaccompanied, especially with the beings in the forest being shaken and roused by the scent of blood."

Rounding into the study Allipo was sitting in Niratap's chair, his head in his hand, fingers curled into his hair. He didn't lift his head as we entered still listening to Vrorlin. He sighed then glances up at us, his face pained, irritated at the centaur on the other end of the line.

"Vrorlin, he can't. No, you idiot, it's not that he won't, he can't. Shasha is here. I'm going to put the phone on speaker so be kind to the poor girl."

Vrorlin's voice was near frantic as he comes through. "What do you mean he can't, Allipo? No measly misgiving would keep him from dealing with an issue, and this is an issue."

My mother's voice was faint on the other side of the line, but I could hear her rage. "Who the hell is this lord you're speaking of? Who is this Allipo? Where is my daughter?"

"Professor." I spoke in a shaky voice. "Lord Niratap was severely injured in a fight with a basilisk and cannot talk with you or deal with the issue of my mother. Now before you either put the phone on speaker or hand it off to her, I want to apologize for her barging into your office screaming in search of me."

"I disparage being attacked in my office. but I appreciate your apology, And my energy to the lord's speedy recovery. Allipo wouldn't tell me about the manner in which the lord was—" he paused mulling over what to say, "indisposed. I'll put the phone on speaker so we can discuss this. Ma'am, it's your daughter."

There's a pause and a beep, I took that second to take a breath. This was not going to end well. "Mama?"

"Shasha Nicole Dion." She snarled over the line. "Where on god's green earth are you?"

"I'm safe, mama. That's what matters. Why are you at my school, accosting my professor in his office?"

"Shasha Nicole, I asked you to do one thing. One thing to ease my worry. I reasoned with myself; she's probably just studying for a test. She'll call me tomorrow when she's free. Then last night I called. I called probably a hundred times and not an answer, not even a text to tell me you were okay."

"Mama I'm fi—"

"Don't interrupt me, girl. So, I called your friend and granted you only used his phone once, but I held on to the hope that he would answer. That he would tell me you were with him and safe. Though I don't approve of you being so close with men. He didn't answer either. So, this morning I drove into the city-and you know how much I hate the city. I went to your dorm, knocked and you weren't there. They had put someone else in your single. I stormed down to the dorm office, and they told me that you had been moved out at the beginning of the semester. They told me that two people came and cleaned out your things. I was beside myself in a panic. So, I went to your department head and grilled him about your whereabouts. This centaur tells me that you are with a lord in a far-off manor in the mountains. That you belong to him. Now, baby girl, tell me why are you in the possession of some lord in the mountains and not at the school you have been telling me you've been at for the last couple of months? Because if I hear one more lie out of you, I will hunt you down and drag your ass back to Afton!"

She sounded almost feral, her voice rising in pitch at the end. I took another breath, "Mama, I would love to tell you about the goings on in my life, but it's not a conversation to have over the phone."

"Then tell me where you are, baby."

Allipo shook his head and even though it wasn't his place to tell me what I could and couldn't tell my mom, I agreed. I knew my mother well enough that she would come after me if she knew where I was. I wouldn't put her at risk. I needed time to talk to Niratap and figure this out. "Mom, I love you."

"I love you too, baby." Her voice sounded teary, but I knew a crocodile was crying them.

"Mom. I need some time. I'm not at school, but I am still attending. My grades are good. I need to discuss some things with Lord Niratap before we can have a face-to-face conversation, and I know that's not what you want to hear, but there are many more factors involved than I am at liberty to discuss."

"Shasha."

"Mom." I raised my voice. She was not going to bully me. "I'm okay. There are other things that are going on that are more important than worrying about me. I am well cared for where I am. I'm fed, watered, and nurtured. I am still going to school. I am doing everything I told you I was doing. I'm just not where I said I was. I'm sorry that I had to lie to you, but I didn't have a choice. I love you and want to tell you about the adventures I've been on, but it's not a conversation to have on the phone. Now please leave my poor professor alone and go home. I'll call you next week."

"Baby-girl I—"

"No mamma, go home. Vrorlin, with everything going on today, I will miss class."

"Understandable I will email the reading and the recording in case you wish to watch. Do you know when I'll be able to speak with the lord?"

"Shasha." My mother's voice whimpered.

"Mama. I love you. Go home." I forced as much authority into my voice as I could muster, and I still felt like my heart was breaking. "I don't know, Vrorlin, he'll be down for at least a few days."

"Very well, I will escort your mother to her car. Take care." With that, he hung up and I felt for the man who was about to take my mother to her car. I sat in the soft ruffed chair I favored and sighed.

"Well, that was lovely." Allipo said humorlessly.

I glared at him. "Don't."

"Don't what, my flower?"

"Just don't. I'm going back up to Lord Niratap's quarters." I stood walking to the door of the study. "My mother may be a viper, but she is still my mom."

I walked through the door expecting the sleeping form I had left. I felt his eyes on me, and sure enough sliver pools had locked with my eyes.

"You're awake?"

He cleared his throat before he spoke with a rasp. "Yes. Though Mitta keeps pumping me with these drugs that make my limbs heavy."

"Stop whining." She growled. "If I didn't you would be trying to move around without assistance and overtax your body. Again. Just let us help you."

I came to the side of the bed I had inhabited for the last few nights. He turned his head wincing a bit at the movement; the wince itself was restrained and only showed in the small dip in his lips that he quickly replaced with a soft tired smile.

"Mitta said there was an issue with Vrorlin. What was going on?"

I shook my head. "Don't fret over it; my mother just knows I'm no longer living at the school. She is still probably grilling Vrorlin as we speak, but at least she's leaving the school."

I flopped back onto the pillows; he chuckled. "You weren't kidding when you said she would hunt you down if you missed a phone call."

"I told you." I sighed exasperatedly and he chuckled again.

"Well, it was bound to happen." He grunted as he tried to sit up. My hand went to his shoulder, helping him into a sitting position.

"You're incorrigible." Mitta growls, grabbing a stack of pillows from the linen closet, and stuffing them behind him. I let him settle back against the pillows.

"You can't expect me to stay here for two weeks, Mitta. A week, maybe, but not two." He mewled at her.

"Yes, I do." Mitta huffed. "You need to rest, a majority of the venom may have been neutralized, but I did give you eight doses of antivenom and the last check I did of your blood there is still a fair amount of venom in your body, slowing your healing. Plus, the sedatives, painkillers, and antibiotics all of which are taxing your body. That wound could have been fatal, my Lord. Fatal. You are lucky to be conscious right now because I was half tempted to leave you in a medically induced coma."

He arched a dark brow at her, before he sighed. "Will you at least allow me to work? I'll stay in bed if you'll allow me that."

Her eyes narrowed but relented. "Only in bed, On reduced hours. I really do want you to rest, you stubborn fool."

"Scouts honor." He made a show of crossing his heart over the bandages.

"You were never a scout, so don't even."

He smiled. "Mitta."

She rolled her eyes. "I'll go talk with Rogmesh and have her make you guys some food. Both of you are probably starving. Then afterward we'll check your wounds and change your dressings."

"Sounds joyous."

She shot him a glare before she stepped out the door. It snicked shut and he chuckled to himself.

"You're feisty." I said looking up at him.

"Oh, you can only imagine." He smiled; it was a sweet look on his defined angular face. It pitched on the left side where he had a small scar through his lip, but his face was one I found myself fascinated by. He arched the right brow at me, the one that had the long scar that ran down to his chin.

"What is that look for?" He asked cautiously.

"I'm just trying to memorize your face before it is hidden from me again." I said honestly. Though the members of the house weren't shocked by his handsome features that he hid, the scars he hid, I had a feeling that they also wondered when their lord would hide away again. I also had the feeling that he was the only person who cared about them.

His cheeks colored under my gaze, and he cleared his throat, turning his head away. Shadowy stubble lined his jaw, and I watched as the apple of his throat bobbed in a swallow. "I know it's not pleasant to look at a scarred face."

"You would be mistaken. I find your face very pleasant to look at."

He whips his head back to me, closing his eyes against the spins. Once steady again his eyes open and he said. "There is nothing pleasant about this face, and there are very few things that are pleasant about me."

I came to my knees and cupped his face in my hands. "You are not the most pleasant person I have ever met, but you have the most pleasant face that I have ever seen because it matches the handsome gracious soul that it belongs to. Yes, there are some scars and dark spots, but it is true to the wearer."

"Shasha." He turned, kissing my palm, eyes still locked with mine. "I don't deserve you."

"Everyone deserves to be loved. Everyone deserves happiness." I said earnestly. "You are a hero to so many. Why would you not deserve me?"

"Where I have saved one, others have fallen through." He blamed each life he wasn't able to save on himself and every time he revealed a portion of those broken pieces of himself, I fell in love with him more.

"That happens with all crusades, my love. You are not the only one who has missed something or someone. Not the first and not the last."

He nuzzled his head into my palm kissing it again, his stubble catching on the callouses I was developing. "Except when I miss something it ends up with someone hurt or worse. The stakes are too high for me."

"They don't always have to be." I said, caressing his cheek.

He gathered my wrists in his hands and sighed. "But they always have been."

Durgash and Rogmesh came into the room, Durgash holding a large tray with steaming bowls of some kind of porridge, a tea kettle, cups, and a plate with eggs and bacon.

Rogmesh had two wooden trays that she carried under her arm.

"That smells delicious." I said and Rogmesh set the trays on the bed, one over Niratap's lap and the other at my side.

"We figured you would both be hungry after yesterday's shenanigans. Durgash was up extra early in the morning to make something tasty but easy on the stomach. He made chicken congee, an Asian rice porridge. I also made eggs and bacon for you, Shasha."

"No eggs and bacon for me?" Niratap griped.

She pinched his cheek as she set the congee in front of him. "Something easy at least for a few days. The congee will be easy; you're always trying to push your luck."

He chuckled. "I have to keep you on your toes."

Durgash harrumphed. "I wish you wouldn't. Nearly gave us a heart attack."

Rogmesh poured the tea and smiled. "We are getting too old for antics, my Lord. Please just rest and stop pushing."

There was a sadness in her voice that made my heart ache. Niratap just looked down at his porridge, his brows knit together in what I could only assume was shame.

"Thank you for breakfast." I beamed. "I can bring the dishes down later if you like."

"It's okay we'll bring lunch up and take the breakfast dishes then." Durgash said. "Both of you just rest. We'll leave you to eat."

He wrapped an arm around Rogmesh as they headed out the door, I smiled at the warm, loving gesture as the door closed behind them. Niratap blew out a breath looking after them. Gingerly he picked up the spoon, scooped up the hot porridge, and blew on it. He made eye contact before he took the bite, looking away almost sheepishly.

"You okay?" I asked.

He swallowed. "Besides the obvious?"

I narrowed my eyes sitting straighter. "Don't avoid my question."

"Shasha."

"No." My voice is firm. "I don't care what excuse you have. I want the truth. You don't need to coddle me. I can handle it. What is bothering you?"

He straightened, his own eyes narrowing defensively. "Shasha. I don't—"

My eyes softened, pleading. "Tell me."

He sighed glaring down at his congee. "I feel like a failure. Like I've failed them."

"Because you got hurt?"

"That is part of it."

"What's the rest?" I said scooping up a spoonful of porridge.

"I hate having their son out there. He's their only child, and I know Bastion volunteered as soon as he was old enough to help, and honestly, my dear, I'm scared. I'm scared that I'll lose him. That I'll lose everything I have fought so hard for and that everything I do is a step backwards. Everything with these beings that I have called family for so long. Everything I have built on the legend of the Bondbreaker. Everything with you that I have had for so short a time. Too short a time." His eyes were bleary and he gestured to himself, "I feel like I'm one fuck up from losing it all."

"I can't guarantee that there won't be losses. I've picked up rather quickly that the world I'm now part of is dangerous. However, you give yourself too little credit for the things that you have accomplished." I picked up my bacon and took a bite, pondering my thoughts while I chewed. Niratap took another bite of the congee, eyeing the bacon in my hand. I swallowed and said. "I know that expressing these kinds of feelings is hard for you, and I want you to know that I appreciate that you shared them with me."

His face is neutral as he stirs his congee; pondering what to say next. I watch as he empties the bowl, then sips his tea. He sets the cup down, his face drawn as he takes a deep breath. "I don't know how to do this."

"Do what?"

"I." he exhales, leaning back against the pillows pinching the bridge of his nose. "I don't know how to be the person you need."

"What do you mean by that?"

He runs his hand through his hair, wincing at the stretch. "I don't know how to be the person you deserve. I don't know how to be a loving and doting partner. I don't know how to prove that I in fact am not all the things that I said. To prove I'm not the person who struck you." His eyes are full of regret and pain.

I finish my eggs and take a sip of tea before I speak. "What makes you think that way?"

"A man should never strike a woman, call it old fashioned if you must. I was cruel to you. Something I have to be in the life I have decided to live, but not something that I want to be with you, to you."

"I was cruel to you as well, Niratap. I said things out of anger and hurt. I attacked you. If anything, you were just defending yourself."

"Shasha. I—"

"Neither of us is perfect, we are bound to make mistakes and I hope we never are because that would be boring." I smiled to myself. "Besides that. I love you. You are the only version of you I need. So, what if we do or don't deserve each other? We can choose to defy those things and just be."

He smiled though it was tinged with sadness. "I will try to be better for you. To you."

I held out half a piece of bacon for him. "you're perfect the way you are. I just want you to talk to me and open up so we can actually know each other. I don't care about anything else. I don't care about the things that you had to do to get here. I don't care about your darkness. I just want to know you."

Chapter Thirty-Three

I took the half strip of bacon she offered me, letting her words sink in. How did this magical being come into my life? I knew what had happened under the circumstances of our meeting, but what a gift the universe had created. She just wanted me. She wasn't concerned about my titles and monikers, my wealth and business. She just wanted to have me in the truest sense of the word. I never knew that I would want something the way I wanted to have that. She wasn't concerned about the bad parts of who I was, or the bad things that I had done. She didn't care about my baggage, didn't care what I was, or who I had to become to survive.

I swallowed. "What do you want to know?"

She had the dishes stacked on a single tray and was walking across to the desk to set it down. She asked. "About what?"

I took a deep breath, "About me?"

She turned and beamed her sunlight smile at me. "Everything."

I chuckled. "Everything?"

"Yes, everything."

"You do realize how old I am, right?"

"I do." She smiled again, coming to take my tray. She folded it and set it by the bed. "I want to know about the wilds you used to roam. I want to know how you freed yourself. I want to know what you are most proud of. I want to know what keeps you up at night and what gets you out of bed each morning."

I smiled. "And let me guess, 'you' can't be the answer for everything?"

"That's not an answer." There is a knock at the door, and she hopped onto the bed at my side. "After Mitta checks you out, we will have this conversation."

She was wise beyond her meager years. "Okay. Mitta, you are permitted."

Mitta, Katrel, and Tummi came into the room holding tubs of medical supplies, Allipo followed holding a stool, his sleeves rolled up to the elbow.

"I take it I am not going to enjoy this." I said trying to push as much humor into my voice as I could.

Mitta didn't smile as she sets the bin on the floor. "I don't think you have ever enjoyed having dressings changed. I figure he's starting to heal closer to his normal pace with him cracking jokes and wanted to check for infection before it has a real chance to set in."

"Jokes don't mean anything when it comes to healing." I said.

"True, but attitude does. Allipo is gonna help you up and we'll plop you on the stool. The girls are going to help me out because they are worried about you."

Shasha was watching me closely and I knew that she picked up the almost imperceptible change in my expression. I sighed partially to hide it and partially to relieve the tension growing in my body. "Okay, let's get this over with."

Allipo was at my side as I shifted in the bed. Shasha was also there, hands outreached for my hand. I let her take it as I try to twist in the bed. My abdominal muscles ached at the motion, and I let out a grunt at the effort. Shasha placed herself between my knees as my feet found the floor, giving my hand a squeeze, I look at her face, her cheeks rosy.

She whispered. "You're naked."

Allipo chuckled next to me but didn't say anything.

"Does it bother you, my dear?"

"No." she said, looking away. "I just wanted to make sure you were comfortable."

I pressed a soft kiss to her cheek. "Nudity doesn't bother me; besides they have all seen what I look like. Mitta is the manor's medic after all. Allipo is my second and has been there with me, bloodied and bruised. Bare to the world is how slaves were typically held and that is how the sisters met me."

I felt her withdraw as her hand slid to my elbow. "Okay, let's get you standing."

I wanted to ask her what made her pull away, but I had a feeling it would evolve into another fight and neither one of us needed that right now. "Right."

They lifted me up, Shasha helping Allipo with lifting and steadying my shaking legs. I marvel at the strength she had developed working with Mitta. They eased me down onto the stool Shasha clinging to my arm to make sure I didn't fall backwards off the seat. I wrapped my tail around her back, pressing her to me. She looked up at me and I pressed a kiss to her forehead. She smiled, but it didn't meet her eyes as Mitta approached with the scissors.

"Now then, I can't guarantee that there won't be pain and I might need to debride the wound if there is any necrosis."

"I understand, Mitta. It's not the first time I've come in contact with the dangerous side of a basilisk."

She sighed. "Probably not the last knowing my luck."

I chuckled, as the scissors tucked between my skin and the gauze. "Probably not."

I hadn't realized how large the wound was until Mitta's scissors cut through the end of the gauze and brushed my navel. The bite had been the most severe of the wounds, but there was a gouge in the top of my belly from Murdoch's claws when he had pinned me. There was a pungent scent coming from under the second skin Mitta had placed over the wound, that she was now peeling away. The serrated teeth of the basilisk had shredded my skin and left a large gash in my chest. Shasha covered her face, whether it was from the sight or the smell I couldn't tell.

"The basilisk got you good." Katrel said, trying to lighten the mood in her own way.

"Well, there's definitely an infection. Tummi, will you bring me the bottle of iodine?" Mitta growled.

"Why is it always iodine with you?" I asked her.

"Because it's cheap and potent." She winked at me. "Maybe your dislike of its smell will get you to be more careful."

"You are definitely cruel." She irrigated the wound and I hissed at the sting. She poked and prodded with her tools, checking the edges of my skin. "How does it look, doc?"

"Don't call me that." She pointed her scalpel at me. "It looks good for what it is, blood flow is good and there doesn't't seem to be any necrosis. I am going to have to keep you on antibiotics for a while, at least until this smell dissipates. If we can keep it moist, I hope we can avoid necrosis. It would slow your recovery quite a bit."

"To be honest with you all." I said as Mitta went behind me to check the wounds on my back. A heaviness settled over the room. I could feel that heaviness in my limbs not completely from medicine, or the aching in my body. I understood the fear that laced everyone's eyes. I could have died, and they knew it. I cleared my throat. "I am surprised I am still alive; I am both blessed and proud to call you family."

"My Lord." Tummi said, her eyes welling with tears.

"If it had not been for all your efforts, I would not have survived this injury."

"You would do the same for us. "Katrel said as she looked away, hiding the silver that was lining her eyes, and to occupy her hands in the bin of gauze.

"Katrel, will you hand me the box of Tegaderm and three rolls of gauze?"

"Yeah."

Mitta stuck the sticky bandages to my skin, covering my larger wounds, then began wrapping my body in gauze, Shasha helping pass it around my torso. I needed to ask the girls something important before they left, needed their permission for what I needed to tell Shasha. I swallowed before I spoke.

"Katrel, Tummi, I have a request."

"Yes." They said.

I cleared my throat. "I would like your permission to tell our story."

Katrel's eyes hardened where Tummi's softened, they had always been the antithesis of each other. Katrel asked. "Why."

I wanted to look at Shasha but knew better than to make her a target of Katrel's wrath. "Because I wish to tell my namesake story, but it is not solely my story. I am asking for your permission."

Tummi looked at her sister. "Kat, let him. It's the past and it sucked, but we have grown from it."

"I don't need everyone knowing that I." Tears rolled over her cheeks. "That I was weak."

Shasha stepped from my side and went to Katrel taking her hands and when she spoke her voice was firm. "I would never think that you were weak, Katrel. I know that you risked it all to save your sister, and that is braver than I have ever been in my life. You shouldn't let the shadows hold you back."

Katrel's eyes widened at her. "You think I was brave."

"Yes. It's brave to try new things, go new places, and face things that scare you." She said, beaming that smile.

Katrel wrapped her arms around Shasha in a hug, something that she only saved for her sister and even then, on rare occasions. Katrel was stoic at the best of times and spent most of her free time in the training ring. I had never thought that the wounds from then had reached so deep into her heart. She looked up at me past Shasha's cloud of curly hair, her copper eyes soft.

"Okay." She says softly, so softly that I almost missed it.

My eyebrows raised. "That easy?"

She glowered all the warmth vacating her gaze. "Don't push your luck, my Lord."

"Me?" I smile mischievously, knowing full well Katrel could me beat in hand-to-hand on a good day. "I would never."

Mitta jabbed a needle into my arm and my stomach flip-flopped. "Knock it off. You're in no condition to get your ass kicked."

"Ow, that's gonna bruise."

Mitta sighed. "That's all the abuse you get, at least for now."

Shasha came back to my side resting her hand on my elbow, ready to guide me back to the bed. "Don't push her, they were talking about sedating you."

"She still might just for some peace." Allipo said, a hand on my back to keep me supported, knowing my body probably would have flopped around without it. I braced as they hefted me up, my chest and abdominal muscles screamed in protest at the movement as they helped me into bed against the pillows.

"Rest, my Lord. I'll come check on you in the afternoon, unless you have need of me."

I nodded. "With all sincerity, Mitta, thank you."

She bowed her head taking up one of her trays, Tummi and Katrel taking up the others before they left out the door. Allipo tucked his arms behind his back, his eyes serious when he looked up at me.

"Yes, Allipo?"

"Mitta, didn't want to alarm you." He paused, swallowing. "But that shadow creature came back."

"Human casualties?"

"Not that I'm aware, but there was another carcass outside the barrier, farmers found it. I think it was a calf, but it's impossible to tell."

"You checked yourself?"

"Yes, after the sheriff left. Whatever this creature is, it's savage. The body was mangled beyond recognition and there was no trace scent or anything that would indicate anything that I know of. Even wraiths leave dust in their wake."

Fuck. I took a breath. "Has the sheriff come up the road at all?"

"Not yet, but you know he suspects us. Even if we have no desire to release the monsters in our care."

I nodded. "Thank you for letting me know, Allipo."

He bowed deeply. "I know you want to be kept abreast of those kinds of developments." His face softened before he continued. "Rest my Lord."

Allipo exited the room leaving just Shasha and I in the room. She watched after Allipo her brows furrowed and her face serious.

"What is troubling you, love?"

"What is it?"

"What is what?"

"The creature, is it the one that Mitta showed you back in August?"

"Yes, it's the same creature."

"What is it?"

I cleared my throat and her fathomless eyes met mine. "We don't know. Vrorlin was looking into it for us, but he hasn't had much luck."

"Is it dangerous?"

I placed a hand on her cheek. "The unknown is always dangerous."

She placed a hand on my cheek, her fingers warm against my skin. "Sometimes it's not. Sometimes the unknown is what saves you."

I smile sadly. "That's not always the case, my dear. I wish it was."

"Then tell me the story, that makes you known to me truly."

"That is a long story." I said, wincing as I shifted in bed.

"You're tired, you should probably rest." She said, letting her hand fall from my face.

I didn't want to sleep, but the exertion of moving in and out of the bed had tired me. "A nap would be a fine idea."

"I'll go—" I grabbed her wrist, a tightness settled in my chest.

"Don't." I took a deep breath. "Don't go."

Her eyes softened. "Okay." She climbed into the bed and curled in close to me. "I'm not going anywhere."

I settled against her warmth. "You must think it very foolish of me to desire something like this."

"It's not foolish. You desire me, don't you?"

"Every moment of every day."

"Even when you're angry with me?"

A hand squeezed my heart. "Especially when I'm angry with you."

"Then definitely not foolish, because I feel the same way. Go to sleep and I'll be right here."

I kissed her forehead. "Okay, my love."

I can't breathe. No that's not it. Pain is radiating through my chest. It's so cold. I try to shift, there's a tinking sound of metal on metal. I'm chained. Caged. Panic seats itself in my heart. How did I get here? I can't remember. I can't stand, chained down by my antlers. I can smell blood and close my eyes. *Breathe Niratap, get a hold of yourself.*

One breath.

Two breaths.

Three breaths.

The sharp edge of panic softens. I open my eyes and the room this cage is in is dark. Silver eyes like my own pierce the darkness and I smell the mountains and moors of home. I pull on the restraints, but I can't get free. My strength is gone. I struggle against the chains, the tang of binding magic dances over my tongue. Fuck.

"It's no use." A strangely familiar feminine voice says, belonging to the silver eyes watching me.

“Who are you?” I snarl.

“Someone who you have forgotten about for a long time Bondbreaker.”

“Who are you?”

“Who I am doesn't matter if you don’t remember.” The voice changes, shifting becoming melodic and the eyes change to a deep forest green.

“Where am I?”

“Is the cold kiss of shackles not bringing you home?”

I roar at the voice.

“Temper. Temper,” The voice chides. “Your sweet flower would be so disappointed.”

Shasha. “Leave her out of this. If I am the one you want, you have me. Leave the girl alone.”

“Oh, I don't intend to leave her out of this. Besides, she is the reason you're here.”

I leapt at the voice, straining against the bonds “Leave her alone!”

The voice shifts again becoming masculine and disjointed, the eyes become a bloody crimson. “Now why would I do that? She smells absolutely delicious.”

“No!” I thrashed against the bonds.

“I wonder if she will taste as good as she smells.”

I roar again and the voice just laughs.

Chapter Thirty-Four

Shasha

Niratap shifted beside me, pulling me from my sleep. "Nira?"

His face was pinched in a grimace. He shifted again, turning his head away from me, a growl growing in his chest.

I placed a hand on his chest; his heart was pounding. "Nira. It's just a dream. I need you to wake up."

He twisted toward the edge of the bed, and I grabbed his arm, pulling back to keep him from falling out of the bed. He snarled and started thrashing. I laid over the top of him holding him down on the bed.

"Niratap." I screamed. "I need you to wake up."

The bedroom door opened and Allipo shouted. "What's going on?"

"He's having a nightmare, and I can't get him to wake up." Niratap shifted again beneath me, his antler catching on one of the pillows, feathers danced around us. Allipo came to the bed, pressing down trying to hold him being careful not to press into his wound.

"My Lord." Allipo shouted.

"No." Niratap roared, loud enough to shake dust off the rafters.

Mitta came into the room. She was shouting something, but I couldn't hear her. My ears were ringing. Niratap was fighting us—no not us, but whoever or whatever was in his dreams. I inched up his chest, cupping his face, pleading that I could get through to him. I pressed my lips to his. His body continued to contort, but I stroked his face, willing him to settle, to wake up. His eyes opened, but they are unseeing as shadows danced along the room. He threw both Mitta and Allipo off as he sat up, his hands coming to my arms, claws digging into my skin through my sweater.

"Shasha." Allipo shouted, picking himself off the floor.

"Get away from him." Mitta called, coming to stand against the wall of windows.

"Wait." I said calmly, pain rippling through my arms in his grip. "I'm okay, I just need to wake him."

I laid my hands against his cheek and leaned into him, pressing a kiss to his furrowed brow, "Niratap. I need you to wake up. I know you don't mean to, but you are hurting me. I need you to wake up."

I kissed him. His eyes fluttered closed again and his grip softened.

"That's right, my love. Now I need you to wake up."

The shadows around the room dissipated as he opened his eyes. "Shasha?"

"It's okay. It was just a nightmare."

He releases my arms, his hands starting to shake. "Shasha, you're bleeding. What happened? What did I do?"

"It's okay, it's just a scratch." I knew for a fact it was much more than a scratch, but I could feel his heart pounding erratically, terror freezing him beneath me. "I'm okay."

"But you're bleeding." His eyes were wide, and he looked at his hands. "Did I?"

"It's okay. I am okay."

Panic seeped into his voice, his breathing hiking up in tempo. "Shasha, I—I hurt you. Why would you tell me you're fine?"

"I am fine." I said keeping my voice calm. I needed him to calm down. "You are also bleeding."

He looks down at his chest, the gauze-stained red. "I—how—what happened?"

"You just had a nightmare, love. Let Mitta check you out, and I'll go clean up. I'm okay."

I made to move off the bed and go to the bathroom, but he pulled me to his chest. He shuddered underneath me. "I'm sorry."

"It's okay, love." I said stroking his hair. He shuddered again, it was a rush of hot breath at my neck and probably the closest to a sob he had had in a long time. "I need you to let me go, so Mitta can check you out and I can get cleaned up, okay? I'll be right back."

His grip eased. Looking me in the eyes, his are bloodshot and rimmed with silver. "You are fine?"

I cupped his cheek. "Yes."

His grip loosened, and I eased out of his arms. Allipo caught my arm, he was shaking, and eased me away from the bed. "I have her, my Lord. You're both safe."

Mitta came around the bed and gently started to unwrap the gauze as Allipo guided me into the bathroom and shut the door.

"Are you okay?" Allipo asked.

"I am fine." I said, peeling off my sweater to peek at my arms. Both had five deep puncture wounds from Niratap's claws. Four on the back of my upper arm and one on the inside close to my armpit. Allipo wet a rag in the sink to wipe away the blood to examine the wounds.

"I don't think you'll need stitches." He said, his honey eyes sweeping up to my face through his lashes. "Were you scared?"

I furrowed my brow. "Why would I be?"

The satyr smiled mischievously. "Not even a little bit?"

I frowned at him. "Not for me. Whatever he was experiencing was terrifying and we don't even know what it was. When he came out of it, he was scared and confused. That scared me, how terrified he was. I don't know if you saw it, but he was holding back sobs Allipo. Whatever he experienced shook him to tears."

Allipo's playful face faded, and he wrapped my arms in gauze. "I did. I have seen him worse than that. You have no idea how your jaunt in the forest and altercation affected him."

My heart pinched. "I hate how that whole day was a nightmare."

The door opened and Mitta poked her head in. "Are you okay, darling?"

"I'll be fine." I said standing and walking toward her. "Is he?"

"He'll be okay, he just opened the wound up a little." She said stepping back so I could see into the room.

Dorilody was standing next the bed, sweeping feathers away and the sisters have him in one of the wing-back chairs by the fireplace. They had eased him into some loose pants and shirt. Both girls looked toward me, their faces grim. Niratap was hunched in the chair, his head resting in his hands, his dark hair a curtain around his face. My heart recoiled at the sight. I drifted to him without thinking, and sank to my knees in front of him, being careful of his antlers. I reached to cup his face and lift it to meet my gaze.

"Are you okay?" I asked him.

His eyes were still bloodshot, his face wan. He blinked, taking in my wrapped arms and gives a small nod. "Yes."

I frowned at the sorrow in his voice and asked. "Can we have the room for a little while?"

Everyone looked to Mitta who nodded softly. "Just call out when you would like some help getting him back into the bed. Don't let him try to fool you into letting him try on his own, that is too strenuous on his body."

"Thank you."

Once everyone had stepped out of the room and the door snicked shut, I turned back towards him. "Tell me."

"I—" He closed his eyes, his brow furrowing. "I don't know what it was."

"I don't care, tell me."

He leaned back in the chair with an effort pinching his brow. "My flower, I don't understand it enough to share."

I stood taking his face in my hands, "I don't care, just—" I sighed. "Just tell me please."

His lips twitched. "I'm not going to get out of this, am I?"

"No." I stroked his cheek with my thumb.

He sighed; eyes sad. "I was being restrained, in a cage. I felt funny, heavy and I didn't have any strength." He stared into the shifting fire. "There was an entity in the room, I couldn't really see them, but they spoke to me like they knew it was all my fault. They spoke in voices both familiar and foreign at first. They said that I had forgotten them, that that was why I was there. I snarled at them, and they said you would be disappointed in me." His brows dipped in rage. "I told them to leave you out of it, and they told me that you were the reason I was there. they said that—" His hands twisted into fists, his face contorting in a snarl. "They said they wondered if you tasted as good as you smelled."

"That's terrible." I said dropping my hands. "Why would anything say that?"

He smiled sadly. "I wondered that myself. If—"

"If what?" I took a step back from him.

"I wondered." He swallowed, looking away. "I wondered if you tasted as good as you smelled."

I looked away to hide my horror, and a strange heat rolled through my body. "I doubt humans taste good at all."

He scoffed. "I didn't think it was off putting if—"

"Don't tell me that you?"

He looked at me as he interlocked his hands and leaned forward. "That I what, my dear?"

"Don't tell me that you—" I sucked in a breath and whispered. "Have you eaten humans?" He had told me that once before, but I hadn't taken it seriously.

"I have, and it's a long story that you have wanted to hear for a while, my dear."

"Why would you eat—" I felt like I'm going to be sick.

"Sit and I'll tell you a story. A story that will make me known to you truly."

"Truly?"

245

"Yes. What do you want to know?"

"I want to know everything."

"Everything?"

"Yes everything."

"Just the highlights or do you want my whole life story?"

"Might as well just tell me the whole story."

"Well, I was born in what is now known as the Sperrin mountains in Northern Ireland a very long time ago. At that time the Vikings were constantly raiding the coastal villages of the Gaelic Irish people. I vaguely remember the sight from one of the ridge lines of several villages on fire, black smoke against the grey sea. When I was that young, we kept mostly to the mountains as far away from the humans as we could. And for the first century of my life, it was like that. My father, mother, sister and I hunted and survived on deer and wild goats. We migrated around the mountains. following the deer like predators do.

"Then one winter was especially harsh. We ended up in a forested valley but so did other predators who had fled the ice of the mountains. My father had a run in with a basilisk over a deer. He won the deer but lost his life that night. He either bled out or succumbed to venom, He died curled around us, still protecting us even though he was dying."

"Do you miss him?" I asked.

He pondered that for a moment, "Sometimes, but I have very few memories of him. Time has that effect."

"I feel that way about my own father, I don't remember his face, but I remember him holding me and reading me stories of the fantastical world we live in."

He nodded, "That is understandable. He left when you were very young, I take it?"

"I was five. I remember sitting by my door listening to the fight. I remember my mother calling him a spineless coward for walking away. He said he had no choice, but part of me wonders if that was true."

"Only he really knows." He said giving me that sad smile that made my chest ache.

"Okay, you can continue telling me your story."

"After my father's passing, we kept to the forests and moors. My sister and I were still young and most of the time we just played while our mother hunted and kept us fed. It was around then that the first bitarog hunt happened in Europe, ordained by the church like all monster hunts, and we fled through mountains that were once our home, through another valley, and into another mountain. Towards the end of that hunt, we ended up in a cavern, tucked deep in the recess of a cliff face. Our mother left and never came back."

"What happened to her?" I asked.

"We didn't know. My sister and I never found her. We spent three days in the cave without her before hunger drove us out. My sister was mature, and I was about fifty years shy of maturity."

"How old is maturity for bitarog?" I asked the question falling from my lips before I could stop myself.

"Somewhere around two hundred seventy-five for females and three hundred for males."

"Interesting, continue."

He smiled. "We struggled at first, but goats, wild or not, aren't very fast. Hunting goats often lead to altercations with humans. It was after one such altercation with a shepherd that my sister and I got separated. I haven't seen her since. Alone, I thought I would die. Then one day I was taking a drink at a loch and that was when I first saw Deirdre. She was a child then, but her fiery red hair caught my eye. I went to that lake every day after, which in hindsight is probably why she was so brave when it came to me."

He paused as the door opened and Durgash and Rogmesh came in with another tray of steaming food. I hopped from the chair, pulling the tea table from across the room, and sitting it between the two chairs, scooting mine closer.

"Lunch is chicken noodle soup and tea. There is a chill outside, so we made something warm." Durgash said setting the steaming bowl in front of Niratap.

"Thank you. It smells amazing." I said.

Rogmesh beamed a smile. "Do you need anything, my Lord?"

"Not at the moment. Thank you."

"Okay." She said, placing the breakfast dishes on the tray. "Let us know, we want you to get better quickly."

"Thank you." Niratap said, reaching for the teacup. I watched him meticulously add three sugar cubes to his tea and stir it gently. He glanced up at me, silver eyes piercing, pinning me to the spot before he spoke to them. "I appreciate all your care. Will you have Allipo bring me my laptop and phone in a couple hours?"

Durgash bowed as his wife flitted out the door with the tray of dishes. "Of course, my Lord."

The door closed with a click, and he sipped his tea. "Where was I?"

"You and Deirdre." I reminded him, bringing the hot soup to my mouth. It was herbaceous and rich, and I could taste all the love that they poured into it.

"Right." He stretched in the chair and sipped his tea. "After a couple years, Deidre got braver and would bring me scraps of food and sweets she smuggled from her home to the edge of the woods. She would tell me of all her woes in the world and she was all the fire of her hair in those moments when she told me of how the church men visited and wanted them to talk with their god. She'd pace in front of me and stomp her feet with rage. She'd ask me what did Danu and Cernunnos ever do to them to make them hate us so much." He chuckled at the memory. "Time passed and she told me all sorts of gossip from her village, how she toed the line enough to stay her wild self and avoiding the priest that kept coming to the village. She told me she was most at peace while she was with me at the loch. She knew what I was, what I was capable of doing to her and her people, but still she brought me a snack every time she came to talk. No rain or snow or fog would keep her from meeting with me."

"When did you change your form?"

He cast a curious glance as he pondered, "It was her seventeenth birthday. She was late one day, and when I saw that flare of fire stomping towards me, I knew something was wrong. When she crossed the road and hit the edge of the glade where we met, I could smell blood on her. She flopped down beside me and harrumphed. She said she didn't have a treat for me that day, that the village boys, who had started to fancy her mind you, had dumped the slice of cake she was bringing me. They danced around her and laughed. The priest's son, for the clergy had taken up residency in the village, had asked her to bed him." He frowned at that. "She slapped him in the square and she said she would never bed a Christian. He slapped her, so hard she fell and whacked her head on a stone in the square. She had told me a story before this instance where the priest had done such a thing to his wife in the square. So, it didn't surprise me that the son of such a man would do the same."

He took a couple bites of soup. "She lamented that no one was as kind to her as I was. She petted me and queried as to how a monster could be so much better than man. Lamented that she would rather run wild with me than be a birthing womb to create more men like them. I took her deeper into the forest and when we were far enough from the village, I willed myself into this shape. She was giddy and asked me to speak. I said her name and she jumped with joy, wrapping her arms around me. Told me I put all the men in her village to shame with how handsome I was. She kissed me. I kissed her back." He gave me a tentative glance. "I bed her there on the forest floor surrounded by the moss and lichen."

I shifted in my seat taking my cup of tea, sipping it as he finished off his soup. It was a rich tea full of licorice and mint. He sounded sad when he spoke again. "You're jealous that I was with another?"

I sighed. "Is it that obvious?"

He tapped his nose. "I can smell it."

I blushed. "I feel like that's cheating."

He laughed, the sound a rumble like far off thunder, "Do you now?"

"Yes, I don't have a keen sense of smell. I don't know what you're feeling by the slightest change."

He smiled sweetly at me. "My sweet flower, I don't think I have control over my senses. especially my sense of smell."

I looked into the fire and sigh. "Continue the story. We can talk some other time about how silly I am for being jealous of someone who." I placed a hand to my throat, remembering the story of Deirdre and my dream.

"Someone who died such a long time ago." He finished for me.

I closed my eyes and nodded.

"It was a long time ago, my flower." He takes a deep breath. "We continued together for two years. She became my daily sweet. We would run through the woods and moors, finding soft beds of long grasses and pines. It was probably the simplest of times in my entire life. It was on her nineteenth birthday that her village was set ablaze. When she was rent from this world, and I was captured by the church." He looked deeply into fire. "I have already told you those bloody details and honestly, I don't want to relive those moments again. I was broken after her death; it was so violent and tragic. We played into their hands. The priest wanted to know where she ran off to everyday, what pulled her into the wilds and not to the church, other than his lascivious nature. He was made into an archbishop, and we traveled to the Vatican. I was housed in a dungeon there, beaten, starved, broken. When they decided I was docile enough, they used me as a weapon. In those times there was always war; The Crusades, The German Peasants War, The Thirty Years War, Wars of the Three Kingdoms, Savoyard-Waldensian War, Toggenburg. I wasn't used as a weapon in all of them, but I was a deciding factor in all the ones that they used me. Eventually battle beasts became less of a necessity and it was after the Toggenburg war that I was sold off to a member of the aristocracy, to generate funds for the church. A few years after that when that noble grew bored, I was sold to a different noble, then a string of them until I was purchased by one, William Atton and brought to the new world. He was the owner of this manor. I built this manor, toiled in these halls, and worked this earth. Atton was a cruel man, he delighted in torture. I was whipped often as were others in his care. His wife was cold and though she didn't have the stomach for her husband's kinds of pleasure. she turned her back on those cruelties. He would hold parties to show others his creature conquests, apparently having a bitarog subservient to you was quite a draw. They would travel the treacherous roads to the manor no matter the season, to witness his hold on me. Watch me serve him. Watch me bend to him. Watch as I was whipped and beaten to begging or unconsciousness."

"That was why you seemed so uncomfortable in the ballroom."

He nodded. "That was where he hosted such events; my blood has been spilled too often in that part of the house. Even though I am here, and he is gone. I can't shake it. Every time I walk into that room I feel the whip at my back, the binds on my limbs."

"That is terrible."

"Yes, it was. I didn't give up, because there were small kindnesses in that part of my life. The lord's young daughter had a fondness for creatures. There was a party where I was beaten down and I lay in a corner of the ballroom, occasionally ogled by those there to sight-see. The music and dancing had started, and the young miss snuck through the crowd and brought me water. She was a sweet thing, who spoke softly to me as if she was afraid, she would startle me. She told me that night that she knew one day I would be free of the bonds that held me prisoner."

"What happened to her?" I ask.

The firelight danced across his features, sorrow crept into his eyes, "There was a night, after a ball, the revelers had gone home, and it was just Lord Atton and his guardsmen enjoying the torture of servants and creatures. I had been whipped unconscious in the dirt and left there. Tummi came to my aid, she was a newly acquired toy, but a faery servant had spilled the lord's wine, and they were raping her and tearing off her wings, so Tummi was left unnoticed. Tummi had healed the wounds on my back, but there were so many both fresh and old, that it left me with many scars. A guard saw her talking to me and intervened; he was not kind to her. I snarled at him and even though the lord preferred his toys to look appealing to the eye, said that it made anguish a much more pleasurable sight," His hand went to the long scar that trailed down his face. "He sent the whip across my face for my insolence and used the bidding magic to bring me down. They did terrible things to Tummi, they held her down and raped her. She was still a child at that point, by elf standards at least."

His face twisted in rage. "Then Katrel shouted from the tree line, brandishing a blade to retrieve her sister. She was ferocious, but as a princess she was untrained and the men circled her, disarmed her, and bound her before the lord. Atton had this crystal vat of acid; he used it for only the sickest of displays. It didn't matter to him, human or not, he had dropped many souls in that vat. He had his cronies hold her over the acid and Tummi pleaded for mercy, throwing herself before the lord. He had her take him in her mouth, held her there as he had them dunk Katrel in the acid."

I covered my mouth, horrified that something like that could happen to anyone. Tears welled in my eyes. Niratap closed his own and his hand resting against his throat, where the violent burn-like scars lay matching ones at his wrists. "Katrel's screams, they broke my heart. I was enraged at the cruelty. I fought against the binds, against the words of subjugation that Atton threw at me. I fought against the magic, the shackles and their magical thorns tore at my skin. The guards dumped Katrel on the ground. Atton dumped Tummi next to her. He took up the whip and he said to me 'I did not have the pleasure to break you. However, this newfound willfulness of yours will be entertaining nonetheless.' Magical fire both hot and cold, cut into my wrists, neck, and ankles. I broke free and he swung the whip across my chest." He looked at me solemnly. "That was the first time the shadows came to me, that I called them forth. It was the first time I half shifted. It was the first and last time that I ate humans. The lord fled from me, and I slayed every man, every woman save the mistress of the house who the lord himself threw down the stairs to try to stop me." Niratap closed his eyes as the weight of what he was telling me came down on him. "I slayed the children after their coward of a father threw them from the room. The young boy tried to defend his sister; he was so much more of a man than their father ever was. The lord's sweet daughter embraced me and told me that she knew I would be free someday. Then I slayed the lord, coldly, without mercy. I made it through the carnage I had created and threw up in the foyer. The girls sat on the steps. Tummi had tried to heal her sister, but her magic wasn't strong enough. Katrel's back matches my wrists and neck. That was the night I became the Bondbreaker."

"I understand why Katrel doesn't like to tell her story." I said, trying to digest what he had just told me. That he had slaughtered those who had held him. That he had slaughtered children to get free.

"She is sensitive about her scars, as am I." He said, staring into the fire.

"I think they make you look formidable." I said stacking the bowls on the table.

He scoffed, shifting in the chair with a grimace. "Only you would."

"Are you doing, okay?"

"Yes." He groaned. "Just sore and stiff like an old man."

"Do you need me to get the others, get you back into bed?"

"No, Allipo will be here shortly."

"If you're sure. I can let you rest."

"No, I'm alright my dear. More than alright with you here."

"Okay." I said but worry eased into my heart. "What happened after?"

"After that we held the manor during the war. That was when Mitta joined us. We talked often of freeing others much like the rest of the world spoke of doing at that time and after about a century we figured out how we could. We used the wealth that Atton had left behind. Dorilody was freed from a freak show. The Days from a coal mine. Allipo from a fighting ring. Echo from prostitution. Dheg from a different fighting ring and many others before you."

There was a knock at the door.

"Come in," I called. and Allipo entered the room.

"Just set them by the bed. Allipo." Niratap said.

"Of course, my Lord."

Niratap scooted forward in the chair bracing his hands on the arm rest. I couldn't get to him fast enough as he tries to heft himself up out of the chair, a painful sounding yelp coming from his lips.

"You idiot!" I squawked. My heart raced as I looped my arms around his waist.

"I am okay, my dear." He grimaced trying to stand.

"That sound you just made tells me otherwise."

"My Lord." Allipo pleaded. "Please let us assist you."

"I am not a child that needs to be coddled." He snarled, trying to stand on his own. Even in the great pain that he had to be in, he was extremely strong.

I held on tightly, desperation slipping into my voice, "Niratap, we're not. We just want to make sure you heal quickly. Please just—just let us help you."

I felt him tense, then rest his hand on my shoulders. "Okay."

I sighed against his chest and my voice broke. "Thank you."

Allipo came to our side and together the three of us trekked across the room to the bed. Niratap sighed. "I'm sorry, Shasha."

"What for?"

"For being difficult. I am not entirely accustomed to being taken care of and when I am I—I lash out because I don't know how to accept it."

"Let us more often, my Lord." Allipo piped in. "You would be surprised at how much we wish you would let us."

"Everyone needs help sometimes." I said as we settled him on the bed.

"Even monsters?" He asked. I looked up at him and there was something in his eyes that I couldn't read.

I cupped his face. "Especially monsters."

Chapter Thirty-Five

Niratap

"Even after all that you have heard?" I asked her. My face hovered inches from hers and even now after everything she had learned about me, she still came to my aid.

"Especially now. Your past is part of who you are now and even though I can't save you from those nightmares, I am here now to save you from the new nightmares."

I kissed her. Her tongue slid delicately over my lip, and I welcomed it by parting them. She explored my mouth greedily, sliding over my tongue, grazing over my teeth, gingerly running it over the tips of my fangs. A low rumble came through my chest. The kiss was warm and tender and parting from her was like parting from a piece of my soul.

Her thumb stroked my cheek. "I don't want you to be afraid of losing me. I'm not going anywhere."

There was a tightness in my chest that I didn't fully understand. Her words had a profound effect on me. Allipo cleared his throat, pulling my attention away from Shasha.

"Yes?" It came out more of a growl.

"Do you need anything else, my Lord?"

I opened my mouth to snap, but Shasha cut me off. "Would you mind grabbing my laptop, and phone from my room, Allipo? I have a paper to finish writing."

"Of course. My Lord?"

"No, Allipo. I think I am in very capable hands."

Allipo nodded, "I agree my Lord."

The satyr smiled at me before he bowed and turned to leave the room.

"Allipo."

"Yes, my Lord?"

"Don't forget to knock."

He chuckled, stepping out of the room, "Of course, I will go get lost for a while."

"That won't be necessary, Allipo; they're both on my desk. He can behave himself for five minutes." I chuckled and after the door closes, she turned a glare on me. "I am fairly certain what you are wanting counts as strenuous activity."

I chuckled. "It doesn't have to be."

She laughed, helping swing my legs into the bed and tucking them into the covers. "You're incorrigible."

"Am I?"

"Yes." She laughed again; the sound filled me with a warmth that I had missed for a very long time. "What is your paper on?"

"Oh, it's a paper on the anatomy of hybrids."

"Interesting. What is your favorite thing that you have learned about hybrids?"

I looked at me, pondering what she was going to say. "I think my favorite thing that I have learned about hybrids is that most of them have a very similar origin point."

I nodded. Most hybrids save a few came from the area around the Mediterranean, a fact that none of them forgot. "Allipo would tell you all about his life in Greece if you let him."

"Considering its an anatomy paper, I think I'll pass."

"Well then before you work on your anatomy paper, maybe you can come and learn more about my anatomy."

"Nira!" she swatted my knee playfully. "Mitta said no strenuous activity."

"That kiss tells me I'm not the only one, who would love an anatomy lesson." I said as she sashayed to the fireplace, dropping a couple logs on fire. "Getting my heart going would probably help with the stiffness."

She scoffed a smile curling on her face. "Maybe the stiffness at your waist."

A deep belly laugh fell out of me, sharp lightning pain radiates across my ribs and the laugh turned into a hiss. "Damn it."

She scowled at me. "See what I mean?"

"I don't have to move for me to please you." I said laying back against the pillows.

"Oh really?" She said still poking at the fire.

"Yes." I sighed, hearing the near silent clack of hooves outside the door. "Allipo don't creep."

The satyr poked his head through the door, a mischievous smile on his lips. "My apologies, my Lord."

"Right." I grumbled. "Just set them here with mine. She does need them right away."

"How do you know?" She said placing her hands on her luscious hips, the poker still in hand.

"Because my sweet, I have other plans. You can go, Allipo. Don't hover by the door either."

"My Lord, I would never."

I gave him a knowing look. He smiled, bowed and exited, damn that fucking horny old goat. Shasha shakes her head, bringing the lap tray to the bed.

"Are we going to work or are you going to try and convince me to fuck you?" Her voice was light and playful, and I wanted nothing more than for her to use it when I was inside her.

"Do I need to convince you?"

She laughs. "Not really, but I am worried about the—" she looked at the ceiling pondering, "logistics."

"Logistics?"

"Yes." She leaned the tray against the bed and crossed her arms over her chest. "You can't stand without assistance right now, how are we supposed to do the deed?"

I shifted carefully to the center of the bed. "Now, my love, you just have to get naked and come get me."

She laughed. "You can't be serious."

"Deadly. Not tactful at the moment, but I do believe it will release some of this tension in my body."

"Tension, eh?" She cocked her hips to one side, her mouth twisted into a coy smirk.

"Yes, tension." I smiled at her.

"And what if I say no?"

My heart pinched at her possible rejection, a sharper pain than my injuries. "Then we can work. I won't force you to, even though it is quite obvious right now that I couldn't."

Her smile softened as she untied her sweats slowly keeping her eyes locked with mine as she shimmied out of them. Next was her shirt exposing her small supple breasts to me in a quick movement. The canvas of her skin was something I would never tire of exploring, with its delicious rolls and texture. In the few months that she had been here she had toned the muscles in her arms and legs and her waist had tightened though her belly still remained soft.

"Have you not been wearing a bra this entire time?"

"Well," She started, sitting on the edge of the bed in just her panties. "It's not comfortable to sleep in a bra, and there really is no point in wearing one if I'm going to lay in bed all day, making sure you behave and follow Mitta's orders."

"I thought strenuous activity was off limits from the doctor's orders."

She crawled up to me, "I thought you said this wouldn't be strenuous."

"For me." I growled, desire making my voice thick. "You on the other hand may break a sweat."

I reached for her as she came close, pulling her up my chest and kissing her deeply. My tongue invaded her mouth as I guided her to straddle me. She gasps as she came to rest against my erection and like that, we sat eye to eye. Her scent thick with lust reminded me of a hot summer meadow, and I wanted to be surrounded by it. My hands roved her body as I pressed her against mine, and even through the many layers of gauze, I could feel the heat of her. Her hands roved under my shirt, before she expertly pulls it off around my antlers. I was thoroughly impressed she managed it without undoing the snaps along the seem. I parted from her mouth, and when the shirt was free, I devoured her neck, her pulse skittering beneath my tongue.

"God, you taste like heaven."

She chuckled. "Oh, I doubt that."

I cupped her face in my hands. "You shouldn't doubt my truth. You are delicious."

Her eyes widened and for the briefest of moments, she smelled of fear. "Okay. Kiss me you fool."

My hand slid back into her hair. "Are you afraid?"

"Why?" She asked, resting one of her hands on my bare shoulder.

"Because for the briefest of moments." I inhaled deeply, the bitter smell gone, only that warm summer meadow remaining. "I could smell your fear. If you are uncomfortable with this," I waved my free hand in the space between us, "it doesn't have to continue."

I started to pull my hand from her hair, the stinging ache returning to my heart. She captured my hand and pressed it to her cheek. "In the beginning, when you purchased me, what were your plans?"

I ran my thumb against her cheek, my scarred wrist stark against her chocolate skin. Did I have plans? No, I just had instinct, desire. To pull whatever creature that carried that lovely scent, her lovely scent, out of that foul place and keep it. I just wanted that close to me. "I didn't really have any plans."

"Then why me?"

"Your scent led me from the dank back alley of the market. I still can't quite explain how or why, but I was drawn to you."

"All the way from the alleyway?"

"Yes." I pressed my forehead to hers. "And I would do it over and over again for you. For the gift that you are."

"Even this." She gingerly placed her hand over the gauze covering my chest.

I closed my eyes. "Yes. Even that."

She was quiet for a long moment; my body thrummed for her approval, her acceptance of me. "When we first met, what were those words that you said to me?"

"*Is liomsa tu?* You are mine. Why do you ask?"

"*Is liomsa tu.*" She said it lovingly. "In those moments did you say that solely because you purchased me or because of something else."

I pondered and again it had just been instinct that had driven me. "Something else. The same reason I went to that auction."

"My scent."

"No, there was a pull in here." I placed my hand over hers on my chest. "I couldn't tell you what it was, but you called to me deep in my very soul."

"So strange. Do you think our paths would have crossed had I not been kidnapped off the street?"

"There is a chance." There was a chance, I feel like we would have crossed paths at some point. "But I don't want to think of a life where you are not in it."

She wrapped her arms around my neck and presses her lips to mine. "Neither do I." She kept one arm wrapped around my neck and tried to slip out of her panties.

"Let me." I shifted my hand into long claws. Her breath hitched as I slid the sharp edge over her bare leg, hooking it under and slicing through the fabric. Her hand slid the remaining fabric away. She frowned but the expression didn't meet her eyes.

"I liked those."

"I'll buy you another." I said, running my clawed fingers delicately over her back. Delighted when she shivered, and gooseflesh alights her skin. "I'll buy you everything you could ever desire. You'll want for nothing."

"Everything? Doesn't that conflict with your overall goal?"

"Only a little bit. The satyr is the one who worries about the finances." Her hands started to wander over my side, "I just make the final decisions. Allipo says it's important because I lead this operation that I should have a say in where the money goes."

"I see. You'd waste it all on me?"

I kissed her forehead and trailed my nose down her cheek. "For you, it is never a waste."

Her fingers caressed over my throat, my jaw, then up into my hair. I pressed kisses against her pulse, soft gasps and moans falling from between her lips as she begins to rock against me, the friction near maddening. I bit her neck hard enough to bruise, but not to break the skin and she tugged hard on my hair. I growled against her skin, her other hand sliding down my side and coming to rest on the hem of my pants. She hesitated and pulled back to look me in the eye.

"You're sure about this?"

"Yes, my love." I groaned, looking at her through my lashes knowing hunger lay in my eyes. "Being with you will be the most healing experience of the last few days."

In answer, her hand slid beneath the fabric of my sweats, her finger wrapping around my length, moving in long, slow strokes. I let my head fall back against the headboard lavishing in the feel of her fingers on me. She leaned in and proceeded to kiss my throat and neck, biting down on my pulse. It took all my will to not buck against her as a loud moan exited my lips. She smiled against my skin, her breath cool against the spot when she speaks sends chills through me.

"You like that?" I groaned her name in response, she licked the spot causing me to shudder. "You taste good, too."

"The basilisk certainly thought so."

She leaned back to glare at me, her lips done up in a playful smile. "Well, the basilisk doesn't get to have you. *Is liomsa tu.*"

My heart clenched, skipping several beats as the primal part of me screamed. "Truly?"

She looked into my eyes, searching the swirling emotions there for answers. "Yes."

"*I gá duit.*" [27] My hands cupped her supple ass, lifting her. She held my gaze as she tucked me between her

---

[27] I need you.

legs and slid me into her. I groaned loudly, her body so tight and hot around mine. "You are heaven."

She rocked against me, grinding her body against mine. One of her hands rested on my uninjured shoulder, the other curled behind my neck stroking the knotted muscle there. I arched against her touch and fire-hot pain radiated from my chest, but it mixed deliciously with the pleasure I received from her. I must have made a face because she cupped my cheeks, concern furrowing her brows.

"You okay?"

My breath was coming in short pants. "Yes. I feel pain, but there is more pleasure."

"You shouldn't feel pain at all." She grumbled petting my cheek.

"You make pain pleasure, *amhrán anam*." [28] I said, captivated by her. She laughed, filling my heart with joy. She ran her fingers through my hair on either side of my head coming to rest at the base of my antlers. A mischievous glint entered her eyes.

"What?"

Pausing her undulations, she wrapped her hands around the base of my antlers, pulling my head to meet hers. She rested her brow against mine, perspiration slick between us. "What are we?"

I met her warm earthen gaze; if my heart hadn't already been pounding it would be now. "What do you want us to be?"

She pressed a light kiss to my nose. "I want to love and be loved by you. Without conditions."

My heart skipped at the prospect, but fear won my heart. "There have to be conditions. My world is too dangerous."

"I know. Mitta is teaching me how to protect myself."

"Being able to protect yourself isn't enough."

[28] Soul song

"Then teach me to be dangerous. Teach me so that I can—" She takes a shuddering breath. "So, I can protect you, too."

I watched her, searching those depthless eyes. She couldn't be serious, but I saw nothing there that told me she wasn't. "Why would you want to protect me?"

There was a ferocity in her eyes that warmed me beyond where our bodies were joined. "Why wouldn't I?"

Tears burned in my eyes, at the fear and joy that twisted in my heart. It was dangerous for her. I should be able to deny this request, but I could see in her a determination that I would not be able to hold back. "Okay."

Surprise brightened her face. "Really?"

"Yes." I pressed a kiss to her cheek. "When I am better, I will sit in on some of your lessons. Watch you learn and we'll go from there."

She kissed me, her grip tightening on my antlers. "Then love me with the one condition: that I become dangerous."

I chuckled, trailing my hands up her back. "You are already dangerous; we're just going to make you lethal."

She smiled lovingly. "Deal."

"Now, *mo grá.*" [29] I said as my hands traveled down her body and cupped her ass. "Love me without reason."

She understood, adjusting her grip on my antlers to use them as handlebars while she rode me. Her slick heat softly clenching me, the friction of our bodies together glorious. Her warm summer meadow scent maddened me; I let myself fall into it, drown in all that was her. Our mouths crashed together with a mess of lips, teeth and tongues and she tasted of flowers and honey. A keening cry of my name came from her lips, and I followed her lead over the edge into delicate spent bliss. She rested her head on my uninjured shoulder, her breath feather-light against my pulse.

"What did you call me?"

---

[29] My love.

My breath came in lurid pants as I rubbed her back, shuddering. "What?"

"Mo something." She said softly.

"Ah, *mo grá.*" I said kissing her on the temple.

"Yes that. *Mo grá.*" She says the words lovingly and she caresses the edge of my jaw, "What does it mean?"

"It means my love." I said, her hand stilling against my throat.

"Do you mean it? Completely?" She sat up to meet my gaze. I did, I wanted for nothing but her and her happiness. Fear twisted in my heart. To admit this would prove her my weakness, the key to bringing me to my knees. Did her love for me outweigh the threats that bombarded us from all sides? Was my love enough to keep her safe?

"Nira, what's wrong?" She stroked my cheek.

"It's nothing. I—" I take an unsteady breath leaning into her touch. "I just don't want to put you in danger."

"Loving me and being loved by me, will probably be one of the less dangerous things you do in your life."

I chuckled. "In my life, yes, but my loving you makes you a target. My loving you puts you in danger. My loving you makes you—"

"Your weakness." She said plainly, sliding off my lap and laying beside me.

I let my hand fall to her shoulder stroking it with my thumb. That horror locked in me for her. "Yes."

"Teach me so that's not the case. Make me lethal and we'll tell them all we're not to be messed with."

"I can do that." I said. "You amaze me."

She laughed curling against me before stifling a yawn. "Good cause you're stuck with me."

"*Is breá liom tú*" [30]

"Whatever you say, I agree." She mumbled against my side.

----

[30] I love you.

I chuckled as she drifted off into a deep restful sleep. I wondered how little she had gotten, fretting over me the last few days. I tucked her under the blankets and stroked her shoulder. I loved her. That dangerous realization rocked me, and the weight of my decisions sat heavy on me.

Chapter Thirty-Six

Shasha

I awoke alone in the bed, tucked in tightly and surrounded by his smell. I sat up, my heart pounding as I searched the room for him, the blanket gathering at my waist. He was sitting at the desk, an arm wrapped gingerly over his abdomen, Allipo beside him going over some papers. Both men looked up at the sound of movement, and Nira grasped Allipo by the horn and pulled his head down and into his side.

"Good morning, *mo grá.* I had Allipo set a robe on the bed for when you woke."

I saw the fluffy robe on the end of the bed. "Morning?"

"Yes. They decided to let us rest."

I pulled the robe on and slid off the bed tying the sash at my waist. "Are you well?"

"Yes." He said, releasing Allipo's head. The satyr huffed beside him. "Allipo insisted on assisting me to the desk. He wanted my input on whether or not I would feel up to the Samhain festivities at the end of the week."

"Samhain? Festivities?"

"Yes, the harvest season is coming to an end, and the time to honor the dead has come. It's an old-world holiday that men and the fair folk observe."

"Samhain, it's a lovely festival, both somber and full of debauchery." Allipo said, smoothing his shirt. "Dancing, a feast, a bonfire and drinking."

I smiled, "Sounds fun."

"It always is." Allipo beamed. "I just wanted to know if we were still going ahead as normal with all that has transpired."

"And I see no point in denying our friends their fun when I just observe anyway."

"What do you mean you just observe?" I asked, coming to his side.

"The lord sits out most holidays besides the feast. He says it's because he prefers to watch the rest of us get good drunk and make fools of ourselves." Allipo answered.

"I leave the frolicking to the fae of the house."

"Mitta won't appreciate that."

"I won't appreciate what?" Mitta said, coming through the door.

"Our lord has looped you in with the rest of us fae."

Nira gave Allipo a side eye as his cheeks colored slightly. "I was only saying I would leave the frolicking to the rest of you. I am too old for that."

Mitta smiled brightly, "Oh really?"

"Yes." Nira turned in the seat to look at her. "Far too old."

Allipo took a few steps toward Mitta. "Strange. From my understanding you are in your prime. You certainly rut like you are."

"That's what that smell is." Mitta growled though there was no hostility in her face. "I thought I said strenuous activity was off the table."

Nira's body went completely rigid, primed for violence. I placed a comforting hand on his shoulder. A jolt of electricity sparked between us, and he looked at me softly, his body easing under my touch. I found strength from the touch, to defend him and I said. "It wasn't strenuous for him. Why do you think I took a nap?"

Color returned to Nira's cheeks, and I pressed a light kiss on his brow as the other two laughed long and hard. Mitta straightened, wiping at her eyes before she spoke.

"Anyways, I have word from Bastion."

Niratap turned back to her. "What did he say?"

"He says he has been on light duty since the incident and is monitoring the scientists. He says it's hard pretending to not be interested in what they're doing, but he is being discreet and befriending one of the talkers. This scientist tells him that she is looking into the effects of basilisk venom in blood. He asked her specifically what kind of things she was looking at and she told him that her study is blind, so she doesn't know what kind of blood reacts how, but there is one sample that is very different from the others. She showed him that in the blood sample the red blood cells get swallowed for lack of a better term and then the venom slowly eats the cell. It also melts the white cells on contact. Instantaneously. She prattled on about how this sample also clots heavily which is different from every other sample. He has some suspicions, but without knowing what the sample is he can't confirm. That is all he sent."

"I wonder what species has that reaction?" Allipo asked, looking a little green.

"I can test what I have in the lab to see if it recreates that reaction, if that is something that you think I should look into."

"Please." Nira said with a nod. "I want to know if Dravin is trying to weaponize basilisk venom for his own gains."

Mitta gave a shallow bow. "Yes, my Lord. How is your pain?"

"Minimal at the moment. Thank you for your care, Mitta and your stubbornness."

She smiled. "As long as you appreciate it." Then she turned out the door.

Allipo bowed as well. "Do you require any assistance, my Lord?"

"No, Allipo." He replied placing a hand at the small of my back, "I think I have plenty at the moment."

Allipo smiled. "Very well."

He bowed once more before he left the room. We were quiet for several moments before he looked up at me.

"You have questions."

"Some."

He sighed. "Pull up a chair, my dear. What do you want to know?"

I smiled, pulling the little stool over to the desk. "Why do you sit out, really?"

"Next question."

"No answer me." I said sitting down.

He sighed again, quicksilver eyes catching mine. "Why must you know?"

"Because *mo grá,* I think we need to be forthcoming in what life is between us."

He held my gaze for a moment longer before looking down at the papers on the table, "I—I don't feel like I belong, and revelry takes me back to the many years I was a prisoner."

I leaned back against a wall. The horrors he must have faced beyond that night. I watched him flip through the papers on his desk not really seeing what was written. He was embarrassed by what parties meant to him, what they had come to be because of the things that had been done to him.

"Was that your only question?" he asked, sitting back in his chair, meeting my eyes. He had prepared for a fight. I could see it in the walls he had built around himself.

I spoke slowly, carefully picking my words. "How long will you let the darkest parts of your life overshadow the light?"

His eyebrows rose, the only indication that my words had hit home. "What do you mean, Shasha?"

"When will the darkness stay in the shadows so you can live in the light?"

"*Mo grá.* I am a creature of the darkness and nightmares of others. Shadow is my life."

I cupped his cheek; pricks of stubble along his jaw poked my fingers. "Be that as it may, you can't sit on the side lines forever, your family wants you to experience the good that you're fighting so very hard to create."

"The shadows are all that I have had." He said solemnly, looking back at the papers on the desk.

I pulled him to look at me again. "Then let me be your light."

He smiled, but it doesn't reach his eyes. "You make everything sound so easy."

"Because it is, Nira, you just have to let yourself."

He kissed my palm. "You make me want those things, Shasha."

I pulled away, walking toward the bathroom. "Then want them. Want them and do them. Live."

"Where are you going?" He asked, turning in the chair.

I paused at the threshold part of me debating whether or not I was prepared for what was about to come between us. "Nira, I want this. I want us."

He used the desk to push himself to stand. "But?"

I swallowed looking into the bathroom. "But I want to live, Nira. I want to dance around fires. I want to be in the world, not hiding from it."

"You think I am hiding?"

"I know you are. Why else would you choose to stay here in this house after all that happened here. Why else would you choose to stay in the mountains away from everything."

"Shasha, this world is dangerous—"

Something hot and dangerous rolled through my body. Tears threatened to escape. "Oh, don't tell me again that the world is dangerous! I know the world is dangerous. I have heard over and over again that the world is dangerous. The road is dangerous. The woods are dangerous. The city is dangerous. Monsters are dangerous. Men are dangerous. That is all I have heard my whole life, from teachers, my mother, my father, my friends and now my boyfriend. I don't want to live in a bubble, Nira. I—"

Arms wrapped around my shoulders, how did he come to stand behind me? "I'm sorry, *mo grá*. I'm not saying that I think that you are not capable of surviving this world. I am afraid of what is out there, what could happen and has happened to those I care about. I am afraid of the danger and even more so now that I have you." He kissed the top of my head. "I love you and it scares me."

My heart started pounding. "I—Nira, I want to live, beyond just being alive and being with you."

"I understand." He let out a shaky breath. "I want to give you that as best I can, but—"

"But the world is dangerous." I looked over my shoulder at him.

He frowned and closed his eyes in frustration. "I—I regret that my choices in life have caused you pain and continue to do so."

"Nira."

"Let me finish." He stepped back and braced his hand on the doorway running his free hand through his hair. "I regret that my decisions, whether involuntarily or not, have hurt you. I take the responsibility for Bastion's abuse. He wouldn't have been there if not for me. I have been stubborn and unwilling to compromise and that has driven us to fight, nearly killing both of us. I haven't been honest with you until now, and I realize now that it is a disservice to you. You make me want things that I have never considered for myself. I want to enjoy placid days and just exist. I want to wake up and not have to worry about the market anymore. I want to wake up and not have to worry about my family. I want you to be there. I want to settle into a kind of life where I don't have to fight."

I smiled. "That will take time though. I realize that. You can't just stop being what you are because of me."

We looked at each other. Me standing in a robe in his bathroom. Him leaning against the doorway in a button shirt that was half done and sweatpants. Light purple bruises danced on his neck and collar bone above the gauze. My cheeks heated, meeting his gaze.

"You really believe that?" He asked, his voice taking on a warmth.

"Nira. I love you. Whether it's good for me or not, I
do, with my whole heart." I took a step toward him.

"I feel the same." A smug look settled on his face.
"Boyfriend, huh?"

I swallowed, refusing to look away. "Yeah. Do you—
do you not like it?"

A smile brightened his face. "No." I looked down and
he stepped into the bathroom, hooking a finger under my chin
and lifting my face. "I love it."

I smiled. "So, you'll take me as your girlfriend?"

He cupped my cheeks, pressing a kiss to my forehead.
"If you'll take me as your boyfriend."

"I do."

It felt like a promise I would never break.

Two days later.

"You're healing well. Finally." Mitta said, after
unbandaging his chest, and indeed his flesh was stitching
together nicely, no longer raw and red, but taking on a baby
skin pink. "I think you should be fine to roam about the
manor. I still want you to take it easy, but you aren't confined
to your quarters anymore."

"That is good to hear." He said as she stepped away.

"Does that mean he can come watch my training
today?"

"If the lord is so inclined. After lunch still, correct?"

"Yes. Are we sparing today?"

"Well, it is just you and I today. Eloimaya went with
Allipo to town. We can spar if you like, or we can try a new
skill."

"Oo, can I think on that and get back to you."

"Of course. I'll see you guys after lunch. Be careful,
my Lord."

"Yes, Mitta." He said, buttoning up his shirt over his
gauze free chest.

I sat next to him on the arm of the chair, looking over his face. He looked much better; his skin had warmed in tone. "You do look much better."

"I was hopeful to spend less time down. Basilisk venom seems to stick to me, unfortunately. I am ready to enjoy things again, and not be in pain."

"How is your pain?" I asked, catching a strand of his silky hair between my fingers.

He smiled sweetly at me. "Almost non-existent, *mo grá*"

"Good." I leaned in to kiss him, but someone cleared their throat in the doorway.

Katrel entered with a deep bow and her voice shook. "My Lord."

"Yes, my dear?"

A dusting of rose covered her cheeks at the term of endearment. "I was wondering how you were doing?"

"I am well." He said with a warmth in his voice. "At least another week or so and I'll be one hundred percent again."

"I'm glad to hear it, my Lord. Do you need anything?"

His hand came to rest on my leg, as he hefted himself out of the chair with a grunt. "No Katrel. I have all that I need and then some. Is there something wrong, my dear?"

"I," she threw a look at me.

"Katrel, you can trust her." His voice took on that authoritative edge.

She looked down at her shaking hands, she was clutching a crumpled parchment in her fist. "I received a letter from my father."

Nira's brows knit together. "What does it say?"

With a shaking hand she offered him the letter. Nira cleared his throat and read. "Princess Katrel Gwendolyn Raloqen, last princess of the elven dominion. I'm writing to you to tell you that your jaunt of freedom must come to an end. The queen and I are entering our sunset years and require your immediate return to wed Lord Revan Cistern whom I have chosen for you in your absence. He will be a good king to our people. Your presence is required without the trash I sent away, by the summer solstice. Your father, King Cardoc Raloqen, third of his name. So, your father wants you home. What makes him think you will bend to him?"

"I—I don't know. My Lord, I don't want to go back to that place, not without my sister. Especially not so some knight can take the throne and force me to pop out Cardoc the fourth."

"You don't have to. However, you will have to answer the summons at least. Make an appearance."

"I know."

"Why does she, if she doesn't want to go back.?" I asked.

"Cardoc is blood thirsty, and if she ignores his ignorant demand, he will rain hell down upon us. I would like to avoid bloodshed if possible."

"I worry for my sister. He'd use her to get to me. He did the entire time we were growing up."

"I won't let that happen. We have time. We'll come up with a plan and address it close to midsummer."

Katrel bowed. "Yes, my Lord."

"Don't be afraid, Katrel, I won't allow him to hurt you girls further."

"Thank you, my Lord." She said, turning out of the room.

"So, princesses?"

"Yes. They are from the last royal line of elves. Though neither of the girls want the title of queen. Not after the abuse they suffered. Not after Cardoc sold Tummi."

"Why are parents like that?"

He placed his hand on my nape. "It's not all parents. Some parents are just bad people, some are just trying their best."

"Are you doing, okay?"

He pressed a kiss to my forehead "Fancy a walk?"

“If you’re up for it.”
“I am.”

Chapter Thirty-Seven

Niratap

The luster of fall blanketed the land in honeyed golds and burnt reds. As we walked through the slumbering garden, the breeze kicked around the scent of early decay. The garden had already been prepared for winter; hay spread across the beds to protect the soil. We didn't talk as we wandered the grounds, but I kept her close as the neighbors roamed, setting up for tomorrow. We stopped by the stables to see the horses. Guinness neighed the loudest for affection; it had been a long while since I had made time to ride. He warmed to Shasha instantly. One day I would take her on a ride, but I was certain that Mitta would disapprove of the idea, now or anytime soon.

"Oh, can we go see the dryads?" She asked out of the blue.

"We can, though I don't know if they have started their hibernation."

"The dryads hibernate?"

I smiled. "Well, the girls are all tree spirits and they, like the trees, tend to sleep through the coldest months. I would not be surprised if we got snow here shortly."

"How do you know?"

I scented the air, tapping a finger to it. "The nose knows."

She giggled, grabbing my hand and tugging me along. I let her, enjoying her childlike wonder and joy in the sleepy land. She was so beautiful wrapped in the glow of autumn. She belonged amongst the foliage and spice of the season. A tightness coiled in my chest. So close. We had come so close to losing one another, solely because we were trying to avoid what we were feeling for one another. No longer was I going to hold myself back, not when it came to her. She had listened to all the terrible things I had done and understood that terrible things are part of my future. She chose me.

The grove the dryads favored was heavily blanketed with leaves in every shade of the sun possible, but instead of giggling a slumber-deep silence held the grove.

"They must be in hibernation, my dear."

"Darn it. When you were gone at the market earlier this month the girls said they had a surprise for you. Then, well everything happened."

"I understand." I walked into the grove knocking on Hawthorne; she was the easiest to wake. I took three steps back as leaves rustled around us, the trees shaking.

With a mighty yawn Hawthorne stretched, berries falling from her branches. The others following suit, save Oak.

"Lord of shadows, are you well now?" Hawthorne questioned.

"Yes, are you alright to be roaming the grounds?" Willow whimpered.

"Lady tiger would be very upset with him, if he was out here breaking her orders." Rowan said and the others nodded. Shasha gave a curious look and mouthed 'lady tiger'.

"I am getting better every day, and Mitta has cleared me to wander. I wanted to check on you ladies to see if you were good for your hibernation, and I was told you had a gift for me."

"Oak has a gift for the lord." Maple said, going to the still slumbering tree. "Sister Oak! Sister Oak! The lord is here to see us!"

Birch joined her sister, "Sister Oak, the lord is here and the young lady."

Leaves fall from her mighty boughs, she stirred.

"Sister Oak! Sister Oak! Sister Oak!" The girls chime.

"Okay, little ones, I am awake." Oak groaned, stretching her arms into the boughs of her branches. "My, my, my. The Lord of the Shadows casts gloom through my grove and he has brought his lady of the seasons."

"Oak." I bow my head in greeting. "My apologies for waking you this close to the frost, but I wanted to make sure you were well off for your slumber."

"Well, one who is the fear of the forest, we are well covered, the trees have given us many warm leaves this year. The ground is still warm from the summer suns and the late rains have hydrated us for our longest sleep. We are well off. The roots tell me that it will be a mild winter for us. However, I believe your lady of the year's bouquet has told you that I have something that the lord of things shrouded would appreciate."

"You have caught me." I smile gently, cautious of what she had to say. "My flower has told me you have a gift for me."

"A gift of knowledge, a tidbit of the truth. A creature not much unlike yourself is lurking in our woods. Hunting those that live between the knots and twigs. The littlest of beings whisper that it is searching for you. Hunting for you, lord of shadows." Oak gave me an accusatory look. "Why would a shadow hunt another? What darkness have you brought to our home?"

Shasha's hand curled around mine, whether she felt the looming cloud Oak cast over me I was uncertain. "I assure you, Oak, I have no inclination on what this shadow is or why they are here."

"Mystery, I suppose." Oak turned. "What does the scariest thing in our forest fear would be a better question then?"

I pulled Shasha closer and growled, her words both ominous and threatening. "Much more than the last time we spoke."

Oak eyed Shasha before casting a look at me that made my skin feel tight. "The shadow has plucked a bloom. I wonder how long that shall last. My sisters, we must slumber."

The girls gave us a curious look before they returned to their places around the grove. Falling quietly into their slumbers. Oak frowned at me. "Lord Bondbreaker beware the shadow. It brings me a sickness in my heart and that is something that I fear."

Her cryptic words wound tightly around my own heart, as she turned once again falling into slumber. Tugging Shasha from the grove I pondered Oak's words. What was this creature encroaching on my home?

"Nira."

Why is it here now?

"Nira, stop."

How close is it to breaking through?

"Niratap, stop."

I needed to get ahead of this.

"Niratap stop, you're hurting me!" Shasha shrieked.

I froze at the terror in her voice. Looking over my shoulder, she had her fingers clawing at mine on her wrist, her brows pinched together. I released her, and she clutched her wrist to her chest. Blood seeped from between her fingers, the iron and floral scent attacking my nose.

"Shasha I—"

"No. It's fine. I'm fine."

I sank to my knees and reached for her. I expected her to run, but she let me take her hands in mine. "It's not. Let me see."

"I just need a bandage, it's not that big of a deal. Is Oak always so cryptic?"

"You bleeding because of my lack of control is a big deal." I growled, turning her injured wrist over in my hand. Four puncture wounds from my claws dotted her wrist, my stomach flipped at the sight. I did that to her. "Yes, she is. Age makes it so."

"The shadow creature she was talking about. Is it the creature we saw in the surveillance footage right after I—" Her voice trailed off as I pressed my tongue to her wrist. I used my tongue to clean away the blood, while I drew upon my magic to stitch her skin back together.

She tasted; unlike anything I have ever had on my tongue. Her blood was sweeter than blood should be. Something about it hummed through my veins and made me feel like I was falling. It was all flowers and earth, moss and rain. It went straight to my head in a euphoric rush, and even when her wounds had closed, I nipped at her freshly healed skin. My pulse raced, my body coiling tightly. The euphoria faded just as quickly as it had set in, but my body was alert to hers. The sounds of her heartbeat was in my ears, the summer scent of her arousal. I pulled back in confusion. She cupped my face and kissed me before a coherent thought could pass between my eyes. Her tongue danced with mine and over my teeth.

When she pulls away, she asks. "What did it taste like?"

"What?" My voice came out breathy.

"My blood. What did it taste like to you? It just tastes like blood to me." Her tongue danced across her lips and teeth.

"It tastes—" How to even begin to describe the place that just a taste of her had taken me.

"Like?"

"It tastes like a warm spring meadow on a warm day after it rains. It tastes like cool summer forests blanketed by moss. It tastes like flying. No, like free falling."

She stroked my cheek. "You going to eat me then?"

My eyes searched her for fear, like the fear that had settled in my heart at her words, but there was nothing but warmth and love in her eyes. "No."

She tugged my hands, urging me to my feet. "I know. I was just teasing."

I pressed my forehead to hers. "I'm sorry."

"Don't be. I understand."

"I know," I cupped her face. "But I should control myself better. It shouldn't have happened at all."

"It's okay. You're too hard on yourself." She folded her body against mine. "Hard everywhere it seems."

I coughed, feeling my cheeks heat. "Apologies."

Her hand slid between us and cupped me, making me hiss. She cooed. "Don't apologize. I like that my very essence riles you up."

"*Mo grá,* do you intend to take me here in the garden?"

"How very Old Testament of you."

"Sex with a monster in a garden, don't you think it's a little cliché?" I asked, already thoroughly embarrassed at how my body was reacting.

"Take me to a secluded spot where you can have the fruit of the garden." She urged, giving me a firm stroke through my pants.

"You want this after what just happened?"

"I want you." She whined. "Regardless of what just happened. Actually, what happened might just be fueling the euphoria."

I scooped her wrists into my hands. "Blood and sex are supposed to do that."

"Really?" She asks dreamily. Her cheeks were rosy-toned, and her scent was thick and muggy.

"Yes." I pulled her flush to me, lifting her so she was standing on her tiptoes. "When my kind mate we share blood, share our souls, it's a sealing to one another, a claiming, and not something I take lightly, my dear." But that would explain my reaction to her blood.

She wiggled against me. "Sounds exciting."

My body was running on instinct. Just one taste of her blood had whipped it into a frenzy to set the bond. I couldn't. Tempting as it was to keep her forever, she was too young, too mortal to bind herself to me that way. I set her down and pressed a kiss to her cheek.

"As inviting as that sounds, my sweet, I will have to opt for a time with cooler heads. The euphoria should subside shortly."

"Why does it have to subside? I never want it to stop."

"Because neither of us are ready for that kind of commitment to one another."

Lunch consisted of butternut squash and parmesan risotto with prosciutto served with a glass of Chardonnay. It was decadent and filling while not being heavy. Shasha chatted happily with the Days about the dish. Durgash spoke about the subtle flavor changes between different kinds of Chardonnay. Shasha nodded, taking in all the information, asking questions, and was invested in every word the orcs spoke. Her enthusiasm warmed me.

"How quickly things change." Rogmesh commented, clearing my plate.

"What do you mean?" I asked.

She smiled at me and nodded at Shasha. "That girl has pulled you out of some of your darkness. She brightens you, brightens the whole manor actually."

"Does she? I hadn't noticed." I said watching her laugh with the Orc.

She swatted me with her towel. "I think you have noticed the most. It is good to *see* you, my Lord."

Pulling my gaze from Shasha I looked at her. "I'm still the same monster, shadows or not."

"Yes, but you are not the same man." She said walking off into the kitchen, her words sinking into me.

I was a different man with her. I felt deeper or at the very least acknowledged my emotions. With her I was more thoughtful, more considerate, more reckless, and somehow more responsible. With her I was just more. I finished my wine and stared at the glass. Had I really grown so distant from my family in recent years? Had I really changed so much with her in my life, enough that it was noticeable?

"What are you thinking about?" Shasha asked, touching my arm lightly.

I smiled softly. "You."

She chuckled. "I doubt it, you don't get the little line in your forehead when you're thinking about me. I affect you in other ways."

I raised my brows leaning back in my chair. "How do you know how you affect me?"

"Oh, I've felt how I affect you." She croons seductively. "Many times."

"Now, lovebirds." Rogmesh chided, coming back to the table. "No fornicating on my dining table."

"I'm fairly certain you live in my house, dear." I said smugly. "Therefore, my table."

"Besides that, my love." Durgash said behind her. "Isn't the table how we conceived Bastion?"

"Durgash!" She turned to swat at her husband, but a large toothy smile sprouted on her face.

Laughter bounced around the room. I joked. "Bastion will never eat at this table again if you tell him."

"No, he already knows." Durgash chortled. "Lost his lunch right then and there."

"Fairly certain that was because he had the stomach flu, dear." Rogmesh scolded her husband. Their laughter resonated about the space. If all my days could be this moment, that would be a perfect life. Alas, danger filled every turn. Mitta and the girls filed into the dining room, both Katrel and Tummi looked spent as they flopped limply into their chairs. Shasha and I exchanged a look before she asked.

"Rough training day?"

"It was exactly what they wanted." Mitta said, sitting opposite the girls.

"We need to be ready for Midsummer." Katrel mumbled, throwing a sad glance at her sister.

"What is happening midsummer?" Rogmesh, asked concern tightening her face.

I sat forward. "We'll discuss it at length at dinner. However, Katrel received a summons from her father to return home by midsummer to marry. Don't stress girls, we have time to plan."

"Time travels fast for those in darkness." Katrel said coppery eyes full of warrior's fire.

"That it does, but I won't let you fall back into his hands to do his bidding. Much less to marry some knight."

"What makes you think he'll listen to you?" Katrel snarled as her sister dished food onto her plate.

"Katrel." There is an edge to my voice, a demand for respect.

"My kind hunted beasts as well. My father very well could have been the killing blow to your mother or sister. He will not respect your self-given title or fear your name."

"I know your father won't listen to reason." I growled, fisting my hand. "All the same you both know that I will fight to keep you free."

Katrel settled in the seat, looking intensely at her plate, her voice a near whisper. "I know. I apologize, my Lord, I am—"

"Afraid." I said matter-of-factly.

She nodded thanking her sister for serving her food. Tummi smiled brightly. "My Lord, we know you won't let our father enslave us. No matter the trappings. Katrel is just worried that we won't be enough to assuage him."

I shrugged. "I will not allow him to take advantage of you girls. He sold one of you into slavery and abandoned the other until he saw her as his only option. That is not how a father treats his children. That is not how men should treat women. Period."

Tummi beamed. "Thank you, my Lord. My friend."

I nodded and Mitta added. "We'll be ready. When it comes time, we'll be ready. Shasha, if you want you and the lord can go into the gym, and you can start your warmups. I'll be up after I eat. Shouldn't be too long."

"Okay." She said, lacing her fingers through mine. "Come on."

Standing, I smiled softly at the girls. As we passed, I squeezed Katrel on the shoulder. "You are stronger than your adversity."

In the gym, Shasha sat on the mat to start her stretching. She looked up at me. "Is their father really that terrible?"

I sat in the chair that Mitta had no doubt left out for me with a groan, my legs feeling less and less sturdy as the day progressed. A little frown dawned on her face. "Don't fret about me, the walk just tuckered my legs. Cardoc is a good king to his people, just and fair."

"Just not with his daughters?"

"Cardoc never wanted daughters, he comes from a long line of men bearing men. He's old-fashioned at best and I don't know the whole story." I crossed my ankles. "Old world elves are very set in their ways. It doesn't matter that he could just choose an heir, he wants his bloodline to hold onto the royal title."

She stood and folded forward giving me a glorious view of her ass. "I think it's silly. Both of them are strong individuals and shouldn't have to bend to anyone's will." She peers at me between her legs. "No one should be put in that kind of position. stop staring at me like that."

"Like what?" I smirk at her.

"Like I'm a snack."

I huffed a light laugh. "You're my favorite kind of snack."

She stands and twists glaring at me playfully. "You're terrible."

"It's a natural thing." I say as she twists the other way. "Even if we weren't a couple, in any proximity to you I would find you attractive. Beyond your scent, you are very beautiful."

She stretches her arms and sticks her tongue out at me. "Beyond my scent acting like a magnet. Ha."

I scowled at her. "I'm being serious. I find you visually appealing."

She turns away stretching over her head. "I'm not that attractive. I'm disproportionate, my hips and thighs are too full, and my boobs are too small. My stomach isn't snatched enough. I—"

I stood. Spun her around and loomed over her. "Stop. You are beautiful. I love all the softness of your curves. Society's mold for how women should look is unrealistic and not achievable. You are beautiful."

I cup her face in my hands as she speaks. "I will agree on one condition."

"What my flower?"

"That you accept that I find you dazzlingly handsome. Scars and all."

I opened my mouth to object, but Mitta came through the doors. "Okay lovebirds knock it off. Shasha and I have a rigorous regimen today."

"Mitta." She queried between my hands. "Do you think lord Niratap is handsome?"

Mitta's eyes widened a bit before a toothy grin lit her face. "As handsome as any male could be."

"What do you mean?" She wiggled loose from my grip.

"Well, I would say the lord is handsome. If I preferred males, he would definitely be a contender."

"Oh." Stunned surprise lights up Shasha's face. "Is there someone you fancy?"

Mitta chuckles. "Oh, there definitely is, however, they are definitely not into me the same way, but even so I want their happiness and friendship."

"Who is it?"

"Now, just because you and the lord are out in the open doesn't mean that everyone else has to be."

"I know but—"

"Earn it." Mitta shifted into a fighting stance.

Shasha matched her gracefully. "Oh, I will."

Chapter Thirty-Eight

Shasha

My head spun as Mitta planted me on the mat again.

"You're favoring your right side." Niratap said from his seat, those silver eyes piercing as he watched me get my ass handed to me repeatedly.

"Oh, thank you, my Lord, I didn't realize." My voice dripping with sarcasm.

"I'll remember that tone."

"Oh, I bet you will." I said as Mitta offered me a hand.

"He is correct though." Mitta said, hefting me up. "You do favor your right side; it comes from being right hand dominant. It makes your left side open, even when you defend. You forget your other side exists. Again?"

I sighed. "Let me get a drink and we'll go again."

Mitta nodded. "My Lord, how are you feeling?"

I walked past him to grab a glass from the pitcher behind him. "My legs are tired, but I am well."

"No pain?"

"No, just the healing itch."

I chugged the glass of water, refilling the cup and sipping from it. "Good. That is a good sign."

He smirked at her. "A contender, eh?"

"Don't let it go to your head my Lord." She patted him on the shoulder.

"Oh, I won't." He chuckled.

"So." I pressed. "Who is it?"

"You didn't earn it, blossom."

"I have to win to earn it?"

"Show me you can, and I'll tell you who I fancy." Mitta turned back to the ring. "However, you can't make it weird."

As I walked past Nira he said. "Remember your left side."

"My left side. Got it."

I planted my feet across the ring from Mitta, her feline smile an invitation to try as she raised her hands. We circled one another, two predators sizing each other up. I swung first, but Mitta was faster than me and jabbed me in the ribs, the blow enough to make me stagger a little. Mitta swung again at my left. I ducked and shifted my feet, throwing a low punch to her stomach. She dodged and came back to center. We exchanged a few more blows. She swung at my left again and I caught her arm. Her brows rose as I swiped her legs from under her, like she had the past three times she had knocked me down. Mitta hit the mat with a thud, laughter bubbling up from her throat as she laid there.

"So?"

Mitta stopped laughing, but the feline smile was plastered to her face. "A certain stressed-out princess but drop it. She has more than enough on her plate without worrying about me. That was a nice combination, by the way. I wasn't expecting you to grapple me from your left side. Impressive. Maybe the lord should sit in on your training more?"

I offered her my hand. "Nah, he stares at my ass too much."

Nira coughed from his seat but didn't deny it.

"Maybe, but you seem to understand his advice better." She said, taking my hand. "I think the lord could teach you some other skills, things he does better than I do."

"Like what?" I asked curiously.

"Well, if he felt up to it, he could teach you how to shoot. He is a much better shot than I am."

"Would you teach me?"

He eyed Mitta cautiously before he said. "I could. If that is something, you are interested in learning?"

"We were making me lethal, remember?"

He smiled, chuckling to himself. "I did say that didn't
I?" He stood with a groan and offered his hand. "If you are
done for the afternoon, Mitta, I would like to take her."

Mitta raised her hands, "As you wish, my Lord.
Please don't give her a tank of a gun."

"I won't. Are you ready for tomorrow?" He asked her.

"For drinking, socializing, and dancing? I couldn't be
more ready."

"I may need your backup, with all the leaders."

She waved a dismissive hand at him. "Allipo is your
courtier not me, I'll be around if there is some bloodshed."

He chuckled as we walked to the door. "Good to
know, Mitta."

We curved down the stairs hand in hand, and as we
walked down the dark hall to the basement hall, I paused.
Trepidation. Maybe even a little fear permeated my skin. He
paused before the door question on his face.

"I'm not supposed to go into the basement."

His brows knit together, and he looked at the floor. He
looked up suddenly, guilt floating in those piercing eyes,
realizing something, "I am sorry."

"It's not your fault." I said too quickly. "I just—"

"But it is, had I not lost my temper—"

"I also lost mine."

We stared at each other for several moments. He
sighed. "We don't have to do this today. If you don't want to
go down."

"No." I huffed a sigh, blinking back tears. "I want to
do this. I need to do this."

He gave a small nod pulling me to him. "When you're
ready."

I took a few steaming breaths. "We will not fight?"

"No."

"There will be no bloodshed?"

"You are safe with me, wounded or not. I command these halls."

I swallowed, wrestling my fear down. "Then lead the way, my Lord."

He opened the door, and cool underground air coiled around us like mist. My heart fluttered frantically in my chest. "I won't let anything happen to you."

Together we crossed the threshold, and he led me down the stairs. At the bottom there was a small foyer with three branching halls.

"To the left is the gun range at the end of the hall. The right is the library annex and the vault. The straight hall leads to the menagerie; it's dangerous to go alone."

"That's where I ended up last time?"

He nodded. "It's a maze intentionally. In case something tries to escape."

"Like the wraiths?"

"Yes." He tugged me down the right hall. "There are worse things in the menagerie than shadow wraiths."

"Like what? I thought we were going to the gun range."

"We will, but I want to show you the annex and the vault. A show of trust after this morning."

"Nira, I trust you and I understand why what happened happened. You don't need to offer me an olive branch."

"I know," he said softly. "I decided that since you are going to be part of this house and this is part of what I do, I should show you. And maybe the library annex will have something for your studies."

I smiled cautiously. "Okay but stop feeling guilty over this morning. I know what you are and what you do. They don't scare me, because I love who you are. Scars and all."

He paused before the door, his hand hovering above the handle. "*Is bronntanas thú.*"

"What?"

"You are a gift. When you say things like that, I stop breathing. It makes me feel like you see me under all the masks."

"Because I do." I said looking up at his stoic face. "You are good."

His eyes found mine and in their vast depths I saw so much regret and sorrow, but as quickly as it set in, it was gone, and warmth settled there. He bent, kissing me softly. "You are too kind."

He opened the door before I could correct him because despite all the kindness, he had offered me, despite his humility when it came to his shortcomings, he didn't see himself as kind or good. Only thought of himself as a shadow.

Through the doorway, a large room was lined floor to ceiling, wall to wall with shelves of books and scrolls. Straight down the center aisle along the back wall was a large vault door.

"You are welcome down here and in the gun range, though I hope you will have someone with you in the range while you're starting to learn."

"And the vault?"

"I will give you a tour, however, only Allipo and I have access to the vault. Beyond that door are catalogs of mythical creature parts, cursed objects, and magical items that should not be in the hands of mortals." He had piqued my interest as I followed him between the stacks of books.

At the vault door, he lifted a hand and pressed it to the center of the door. His palm glowed a vibrant lavender color, bright runes lit across its surface as spelled locks clicked free. The massive door swung in, and the lights of the room flickered on. Along the walls were glass shelves with diverse items in jars, vials, and boxes.

"There are a variety of items in here ranging from basilisk fangs to a genie lamp to necromancy spell books. All are kept here to protect those who can't protect themselves."

"All of this has been purchased off the market?"

"Or stolen." He said, letting me walk in front of him.

"For the greater good."

"Yes." He watched me as I examined the items on the shelves. I pointed to a bottle with swirling purple liquid. "What is that?"

"Manticore venom. Nasty stuff."

"And those?" I asked, pointing to a jar of black feathers.

"Thunderbird feathers. They are charged with the might of thunderstorms, even the smallest amount of static can set them off."

I pulled my hand to my chest and moved past the shelves of glass. Spying a crate that was the size of a loveseat, I asked. "What is in that crate?"

"Three mummified hydra heads."

I turned to look at him. "Just three?"

His eyebrows rose. "Were you expecting more?"

"I mean three just seems like a small number."

"Hydras are monstrosities from antiquity. They were hunted to extinction long before I was born, somehow those heads ended up on the market. No one thought they were real."

"Are they?"

He surveyed me. "They are locked in this vault for a reason."

"What is the most dangerous thing in here?"

He walks past me, his fingers shifting into claws as he drags them over the crate containing the hydra heads. "Why do you want to know?"

Something in his tone makes me uneasy. It was like this knowledge was something that could unravel everything. "Curiosity."

He sighed, taking a shaky breath. "Follow me."

He led me past crates and bottles, vials and jars to a small door along the back wall. "What I am about to show you cannot leave this room, for what is behind this door could ruin many lives and endanger many more."

He wouldn't meet my eyes. "I—I understand."

He swallowed. "Very well."

He pulled a key out of the air, magicked it from smoke and shadow. He bent, unlocking the small door and slipping through, folding his towering frame through the opening into the darkness beyond. Stagnant cold cavern air rolled past me. I hesitated, the pure black of the room beyond reminding me of another room on this level. A room with a screaming door. His hand appeared at the entry, an invitation to follow. I swallowed, what could possibly be so dangerous, that it was sealed away thrice over? What terror could be waiting beyond that threshold?

"Take my hand, it's dark and I don't want you to trip down the steps." His voice soothed my nerves. I took his hand and followed him into the darkness.

He guided me down a narrow stairwell, no lights to show the way, just his preternatural vision in the blackness. In the dark, only the sound of our footsteps down the dirt steps and the warmth of his hand filled my senses. He stopped and I stumbled into his back, blind to what was ahead. I heard the click of another lock, and he tugged me through another door. This new room thrummed with an otherworldly power that reverberated through the soil, the air, and my very bones. A ball of pale white light blinded me as it appeared.

"Apologies." He said softly, his breath clouding in the stale air.

"Where are we?" I asked, sneaking under his arm and against his warmth.

"Deep under the house. This was the only place that felt safe enough to keep her."

"Keep who?"

He led me around a bend in the tunnel. "Her name is Saabraa. She has been in hibernation for a very long time. When I had found her and rescued her from the church, we had both agreed this would be the best way to keep her safe from traders and hunters."

At the back of the room, floating freely in the air was a mass of sable and grey feathers and within that mass was a devastatingly beautiful woman. She was an olive-toned statue of antiquity that takes my breath to behold. Her soft, summer wheat hair contrasted against the feathers, which I realized were wings upon closer inspection.

"What is she?"

"Some say a harbinger. Some say an angel of death. I would call her lost and lonely. I rescued her from an abandoned church after one of the wars. She had been locked in a gilded cage; her feathers used to perform miracles for the congregation. Though I view her as kind, when she interacts freely with the world, she has a tendency to cause more death and destruction than either of us wants to manage. So, we agreed that she should remain dormant, sealed away from humans."

"But why lock her away?"

"Oh, she is not trapped at all, if she woke, she could get out of here with less than half a thought. The many locks are to keep others from disturbing her. Keep her away from the influence and grasp of the churches."

"She is very beautiful."

"She is."

I peered at him in the dim light. "Does she ever wake?"

"Occasionally she shifts, but she hasn't woken since Bastion was born, though it was brief. Rogmesh had a hard labor with that boy, he was breached and folded. Got stuck in the birth canal for far too long. When we finally got him out, he wasn't responsive." His words felt distant. A story from the past that was both full of trauma and wonder as I took in the soft ethereal face, the full lips, the delicate sweep of her lashes against her cherub cheeks. "Then Saabraa appeared and pressed her lips to his forehead, blew a breath into his face and he cried. Durgash thinks that's why Bastion is fair-skinned, he entered the world through death and not life" He shrugged, the light bobbing with movement.

"And she hasn't woken since?"

"No." I looked at him again, his features unreadable as he watched her float there.

"What would happen if she woke again?"

"I would assume either something miraculous or something terrible." He met my gaze. "We should go."

I only nodded as he took my hand and led me from the darkest place in the manor. When the vault door was shut, the magic locks clicking back into place, I asked.

"Are you afraid of it?"

He turned curious eyes at me. "Afraid of what?"

"Of death."

He offered me his elbow, his face solemn. "I am and am not."

I wrapped my hand around his offered arm. "Why is that?"

"No creature wants to go swiftly into death's waiting arms. However." He said thoughtfully. "If death was easy to avoid there would be more of my kind. More of other beasts around. The world is about balance. No matter how fair or unfair that seems to be. If death didn't come swiftly, it would be unbalanced, the cycle of energy broken. Death is just the final destination for our bodies anyway. The soul travels farther. Whether that be to a great beyond that the religions of the world say or the soul being reborn, born anew. I do not know but knowing that there is more beyond this is a comfort in the decay. Why ask me such a complex question?"

"I was just curious. Mortality is something that no one thinks about unless they are faced with it. I wanted your thoughts. That is all."

Passing the apex of halls, he said. "Mortality only scares creatures who have too much time to think about the end that they may face, instead of living in the moments that they are given."

"Do you think of death often?"

There was a long silence before he said. "I didn't use to."

I looked up at his face and it gave nothing away. "What changed?"

He was quiet as we continued through the hall, pondering his answer. We stopped before a metal door when his gaze shifted to me, a bittersweet smile curling upon his face. "I found something that I wanted to live for."

The words squeezed my heart and I said. "Did you not have anything like that before?"

"Not for a long time."

We entered the gun range, and it was like every single one I had seen on TV and in movies. Four stalls with targets at the end of the hall. He turned me into a center stall and summoned a pistol from his shadows.

"This is a Glock 26, it's a semi-automatic pistol. It is a lightweight 9mm, with a variable capacity. I think this will be a good gun for you. Especially given what you said a couple of months ago about your mother not being fond of guns, I assume you have never fired one before."

I shook my head. "Not once."

"Watch closely." He said. "Safety is my first concern with firearms. Never point a gun at anything you don't want to shoot. Here, always point it down range. I want you to know how to check to see if a gun is loaded, or clear. Whenever I pick up a firearm, I check it and have been called neurotic for it. So, to check, you eject the magazine. Most modern guns are semi-automatic and have a release button on the side, like this." He showed me the button and ejects the magazine.

"Now, without the magazine in the gun, it can no longer feed bullets into the chamber. To check to see if the chamber is clear, you rack the slide back. If there is a bullet in the chamber it will be ejected." He smoothly pulled the top section of the gun back and showed me where a bullet would be ejected.

"That's how you know that it is safe. You're not going to accidentally shoot yourself or others if you do that. Only in that order. If you rack the slide back with the magazine loaded, you can load a bullet into the chamber. It makes it dangerous to carry in pockets, your pants, or even in a holster."

I nodded and he reset everything back to how the gun appeared before then he offered it to me. "Now you try."

I repeated his motions, ejecting the magazine, pulling the slide back, peering into the chamber, then putting it back together. He had me repeat that several times, before nodding. "Good. Now stance, like fighting is important and very similar. Feet shoulder-width apart and offset, non-dominant side slightly forward. Bend forward at the waist. This is so that when you fire, your whole body is prepared for the recoil, and it doesn't knock you back. Alright, take up your stance and point the gun down the range."

I did as he instructed, being conscious of my foot placement, and then brought the gun up. I cradled it with my other hand. He curled around me, his hands covering mine, his breath against my ear. "Not terrible for having no experience, but you want to hold it like this. Dominate hand fully engaged, trigger finger off the trigger until you are ready to shoot. Then bring your non-dominant hand here, press the ball of your palm here, wrap your fingers around, and keep this thumb like this. This way the slide doesn't hit you when the gun fires. Lock your elbows, which will keep the gun from coming back and hitting you in the face."

"Okay." I said feeling the heat of his body coiled against my spine.

"When you look through the sight, keep both eyes open, and stay aware of your surroundings. You never know what could come out of your periphery." I nodded, his calm breath tickling my cheek.

"To sight, you'll look down the top of the weapon. There are two sight finders, the back dip and the colored sight at the front. You'll line the colored sight into the center of the dip. Focus on that colored sight, because that is where the bullet will go. Then when you're ready to fire, inhale to prepare your body for recoil and exhale as you pull the trigger it lessens the tension which is what causes you to fire off sight and miss, especially with rifles. Practice that.”

I turned my head, and my mouth was dangerously close to his. “Breathing?”

“Breathing while you fire.”

“But the gun is not loaded.”

“Exactly, it's called a dry fire.” He stepped back.

“Okay.” I inhaled. steadying the nerves that seemed to rise. I exhaled, my finger sliding to the trigger and pressing. The gun clicked.

“Good again.” I did, moving to set the gun down. “Clear it before you set it down.”

“How?”

“Just like you did to check to see if it was loaded.”

I went through the motions and set the gun on the table. “I have a feeling this is something I will have to practice repeatedly before I fire an actual bullet.”

“Oh no, you will fire live rounds today.” He said, eyeing me. “I stress safety; you have to respect firearms because they are high-power lethal weapons. I feel like you can't do that without firing.”

“You're going to trust me with live rounds on my first day?”

“Are you? Because if you don’t trust yourself with the weapon, you will make more mistakes. Mistakes in the real world get you hurt. Those you are trying to protect hurt. Or worse, killed.”

I swallowed. “This is more intimidating than I thought it would be.”

“Using a gun should be. Practice it all for a few rounds. Check the weapon, load it, get into position, dry fire, and clear.”

I obeyed, Nira watching my every move, occasionally correcting my stance or my hold. When I had done the whole rotation several times with no mistakes, he came to my side again.

"Good. Here put these on," He offered me some earmuffs and some clear plastic glasses. "Eye and ear protection, important for practice."

I took them and watched as he donned similar protection. "Does it hurt you? The sound?"

"Firing without protection in the range can, it echoes and reverberates more. Personally, I don't like being deafened, which happens regardless, the protection just minimizes the duration. Hand me the magazine."

I handed him the magazine and watched as he carefully loaded bullets in a smooth motion, transfixed by his deft fingers. He handed it to me. "Now, you cleared the gun to give me the magazine. Load it, check to make sure the bullet is in position and go through your stance and fire."

He stood behind me watching carefully as I loaded the gun and shifted into position. The nervousness settled in faster with the live rounds in the gun. I took a few steadying breaths, trying to get my heart to stop racing and my hands to stop shaking. Nira's arms wrapped around me covering my hands.

"It's okay to be afraid. What is in your hands has the power to take life away. It's not something to be taken lightly, but whether you take the shot today or tomorrow or in a few months I will not be disappointed in you."

I took another breath and as I exhaled, I pulled the trigger. The force of the gun knocked my hands back, but I didn't drop the weapon and it didn't come flying back at my face.

"You missed the target, but it's okay. Fire again. Remember to focus on the nose sight and keep your arms locked."

I did as he instructed and fired again.

"You hit the target that time, you want to try to keep your shots clustered. You'll get better with practice. Clustered at center mass."

I gave a subtle nod as his hands came back to rest on my shoulder, support if I needed him. I fired again and again and again. The power of the weapon became an extension of my body, my soul. With this, I could protect him. I fired until the gun clicked, the magazine empty.

Nira pressed a button at the edge of the stall. "Check the gun to make sure it's clear."

I did so as the paper target came forward. He leaned over me pointing at the target as he spoke. "Good. You fired eleven rounds. One outright miss, two near misses, the rest of your shots hit, and like I said your cluster will get better as you practice."

"How often can I practice?"

He smiled looking down at me. "As often as you like. Mitta keeps all the weapons locked away. So, you can always ask her to retrieve it for you. Everyone in the manor can shoot. Echo will probably be the least willing to come and be your firing partner."

"Can I watch you shoot?"

"Would you like to today?"

"I would."

He summoned his weapon; the same gun he had taken into the city the day he'd been shot. "This is my favorite gun. I like the way it feels in my hand, it's lighter than yours but just as powerful."

He went through the motions of checking the gun, then he stepped into the stall next to mine. His skill and preternatural grace made his coming into stance stunning; he steadied himself easily, his breathing smooth as he settled. Then he fired rapidly the gun going off until the clip was empty, the recoil bouncing tufts of shadows off his body, always present even when he wasn't using them to conceal himself. He cleared the weapon and set it on the table before he took the ear protection off and shook his head. He summoned his target, and I noted the two tight circles of holes. One at the center of the target and one in the head of the target, it was amazing to watch him.

"Wow."

"Practice, *mo grá,* and you can do this too."

I took a step toward him. "It'll be years before I'm that good."

"You never know." He turned to face me.

"Is it possible for me," I pressed my hands against his abdomen. "To practice knowing you?"

His brows rose, before he tilted his head predatorily. "And how, my flower, do you want to know me?"

The deep rumble of desire in his voice caused my skin to goose, a shiver running down my spine. I slid my hands up his chest, "Fully and deeply. Preferably right now."

His hands came to rest on my ribs. "Right here. Surrounded by gun smoke?"

"Yes." It came out like a sigh, my fingers tugging the buttons of his shirt.

His hands traced along my ribs, "So eager. How should I get to know you? Shall I lay you on the floor and bury myself inside you? Bend you over a gun bench and take you from behind?"

Shadows slithered across the floor and up the walls as his tail uncoiled from his waist and stroked up my thigh. "All of it. I want all of it and all of you."

He leaned in, kissing the spot where my neck met my shoulder. "You smell like the perfect afternoon snack."

I started to untuck his shirt, hunting for contact. "I'm still sweaty from training."

He ran his beastly tongue over my pulse and up the side of my throat causing me to shudder. His voice was thick with desire. "I like a good salty snack."

"You're disgusting." I said playfully, running my hands over his abdomen, tracing the panes of muscle there.

"You enjoy it. I can scent that on you my dear." He locked eyes with me, his gaze making me molten. He kissed me softly as his claws climbed up my back. "Like a warm summer day."

I hooked my fingers into the waistband on his pants, pulling him close, the hard generous length of him pressing into my stomach. "Do I always smell like summer?"

"No." He kissed my throat and purred as I stroked him through his pants. "Just when you're aroused."

I released him from the trappings of his zipper, the silky feel of him in my hand. He growled as I pumped him twice. I watched as a bead of liquid came to the head. "I like the way you smell too. Like fresh rain and moss."

I shifted, lowering myself to take him into my mouth, but he caught my chin pulling my face to look up at him. His eyes shined with dagger sharp intent; his voice quivered with restraint. "Shasha, you do what you're thinking, and I am going to lose the very thin hold I have on my control."

"All the more reason to." I pulled, but his hand-held firm.

His emotions shifted in those steely eyes so quickly I couldn't catch them all. Finally, he said. "You are dangerous."

I let a coy smile dance over my lips. "I like when you tell me that. Now let me worship you."

Slowly, he released my chin and set his palms against the wall behind him, his breath coming in heavy pants. I held his gaze as I sank low enough that his proud member was before me. I wrapped my hand as far around the honeyed shaft as I could and in agonizing slowness, I stroked him. His eyes fluttered as he watched me, his cheeks flushed, lust softening his gaze. He watched as I pressed my tongue to the tip of him wicking up that bead of liquid. The salty taste of him caused a rush of heat between my thighs.

I pulled him into my mouth, watching him as his eyes closed and his head fell back against the wall, his antlers clattering against the stone as a guttural sound came out of him. His fingers splayed as he fought to keep his instincts at bay.

I worked him with long strokes and sweeps of my tongue, loving the view of his resistance as I eased him deeper into my mouth. His musky rain scent filled my nose, and I rubbed my thighs together, craving an ounce of friction as I took him. I dragged my teeth along the underside, and it was his undoing. Just as I cleared the head, he had me pinned to the ground with frightening gentle grace, a snarl reverberated through the room.

He had shifted partially, his fur tickling my cheek, his maw of teeth wrapped around my throat applying pressure, but not breaking skin. I must have gasped because his eye found mine and ever so slowly released me from his grasp.

His tongue trailed over my rapid pulse. His inhuman voice, both rough and musical. "My apologies. I did not mean to startle you, my flower."

"I like you like this." I panted. "Wild and unhinged."

I ran my hands up his arm, iridescent dark scales cover them. He growled. "I did say my restraint was thin."

"You did, and I love it." I arched against him, earning a snarl.

"You test my resolve, pretty one."

"Then let go." I murmured, his canid ears folding back. "Take me."

"Shasha." My name a purr in that monstrous voice, his clawed fingers slid beneath my shirt and wrapped around my waist. "You will be my undoing."

I rake my hands down his chest, finding his clothes had been magicked away. "I wish I could do that."

A deep-throated laugh came out of him. "But then I would lose out on the unwrapping of my snack."

"Then unwrap me so we can play."

"So eager."

He licked my throat as his hands trailed up my ribs, sliding my shirt free. Then they slid down my body, his claws make fireworks dance across my skin before they snagged my leggings and freed my lower half to him. I tried to reach and unzip my bra, but he snarled at me.

"I want the pleasure of undressing you, and I mean completely."

His tongue traveled up from my navel. I groaned, rising up to press his fullness between us causing him to hiss. With a singular claw as he licked and nipped at my stomach, he pulled the zipper down, with the same slowness at which I had stroked him. His eyes devoured me as the garment fell away exposing my breasts to him. He traveled up my body, his tongue and teeth delighting in my flesh. He bit my nipple ever so gently as a clawed hand claimed the other breast, his utter worship of me had me writhing on the ground beneath him, his name a prayer on my gasps. My hands tangled in the soft fur around his neck.

"How do you want me?" His question, an ask for permission, for guidance and it made my heart swell with emotions I couldn't fully register with the searing heat growing in my gut.

"Like this." I whimpered.

A clawed hand traveled down my side, my body goosing at the sensation of him. He hooked my knee, opening me to him. He rubbed that beastly length of his across the slick heat of me, and a growl of anticipation echoed through me and off the walls as he prepared himself to enter me. He didn't make me wait long for that monstrous size of him. Ever so gently he eased into me. I gyrated against him; a low guttural sound puffed from him in my ear. He tentatively stopped and with his depth stretching my body, he stroked my face with his velvet soft muzzle as he pushed the last painful bit to fully seat himself within me. I cried out, the sharpness of his intrusion into me stealing my breath, but I wrapped my legs around his waist holding him to me.

"Are you well?" His voice tentatively soft, afraid that he had hurt me.

"Yes." I am well. I am shattered. Destroyed by him in all the ways that matter.

"Did I hurt you?"

"No." Tears welled in my eyes at his care of me. I ran my hands through his fur. The sable strands as delicate as the shadows that slithered across the floor. "Please."

He huffed in my ear as he pulled his body from mine, the agony of him sent me quivering. His teeth and tongue at my throat as he buried himself deep, sent the very tendrils of thought from my mind. His savage gentleness tortured my core, and I was lost. Shattered by him. My body was not wholly my own as he set a heart racing pace. I clung to him. My body reached its peak as he continued, my breath coming in soft pants. A satisfied growl came from him, and he sought his own release. And when he laid himself bare, shuddering as his seed spilled inside me, I peaked again, crying out his name.

Claws and fur faded, my fingers resting on the hammering of his pulse, those silver eyes heavy lidded and full of all the emotions that I could not express. There was joy. Devastation. Concern. Hunger. Most importantly I saw love. A love that went deeper than what we were. It felt so deep. Soul endingly deep.

"I love you." I whimpered, cupping his cheek in my hand.

A sweet smile danced across that beautiful face. "I love you, too."

Dinner was a simple dish of roast chicken, potatoes, and carrots that smelled heavily of rosemary and garlic. We did not serve each other, but rather Nira poured everyone's wine and we passed that around. Allipo prattled on about the most recent interaction between him and the sheriff, who absconded their return for thirty minutes.

"Rodger just doesn't understand how we're not involved in all the weird stuff going on around town and I told him that just because we are the only beings around that are different, doesn't mean we're doing every weird thing around here."

"The sheriff is just a busybody in a sleepy town." Katrel growled, tonight's main topic of discussion had a battle waging inside her.

"Be that as it may." Nira said, folding his hands in front of him. It took my breath away when that grace glazed simple aspects of him. "I am in agreement with Rodger that whatever is preying on the deer and cattle around us needs to be dealt with."

"So, do we have any clues as to what that mysterious shadow may be?" Allipo asked.

Darkness clouded Niratap's eyes. "Unfortunately, I haven't found anything about it."

A harsh silence settled over the table and for the first time I really sat and ran a tally of all the things that stood against us. Something that I hadn't really taken time to do in all the trials and tribulations these was really think deeply about all that had happened. Firstly, just how badly had Niratap painted a target on his back when he purchased me? He already had enemies before me, but how sharply had that number grown since? Second, this growing threat of the shadow that had the forest disturbed, and had local law enforcement breathing down our necks, looking for anything to launch an assault. Third, this talk of one of his kind on the market. What kinds of terror and trauma had that triggered in him, though he didn't let it slip into his face? Lastly, the distant worry about the elf king who wanted to use his daughter as a broodmare to carry on his line. Not to mention all the aspects of the world I hadn't gleaned yet. So, I said:

"What are we going to do?"

Nira's eyes found mine as his brows rose. "Take it one day at a time, plan, and prepare for the worst."

Eloimaya spoke quietly. "Why do I get the feeling that this is about more than the shadow creature?"

"Because it is." Katrel said from across the table; all eyes shifted to her. She swallowed, searching Nira's face for something that she must have found because she took a breath and began, casting a glance at Tummi. "Our father has requested that I return home to marry a man of his choosing. Without my sister and without resistance."

Dheg said coolly. "And this is a vast concern why? Just tell him no if you don't want to. I know elves are backwards, but he can't force you."

"You don't understand." Katrel half snarled, and I realized then that the vast collection of them didn't know.

"Well, explain it then," Dheg said with no contempt in his voice, "because noble or not, no man can force you into a marriage bed."

"Our father," Tummi took the reins from her sister, her voice soft, tentative even and it broke my heart, "is King Cardoc Raloqen, third of his name and the last-born king of elf kingdom, Babylos."

That caused the table to pause, wide eyes from everyone except from Nira, Mitta, and myself. No one else had known or figured that the two lovely elf women who had shared their tables for many, many years were royalty.

Allipo cleared his throat. "You mean to tell me that I have been dining with royalty all these years, and they sit farthest from the head of the table? Father then me?"

Niratap chuckled. "Neither of the girls has ever claimed their royal blood, both of them disowning their heritage from the moment Tummilia was sold into slavery. They have fought and prevailed. Though Cardoc is a beast of a man and the Raloqen name runs deep in the ties of the world, he believes himself owed his daughters time and grace. Even if Katrel deigned to reply to her father to tell him she refused to come home and for him to instead seat an heir of his choosing, he would send an army to bring her to him, and we would be fodder at that kind of onslaught. She has no choice but to present herself. Showing up might be enough to reason with him, but we will not know if it will be until we try."

"Our father is a cruel and vain man." Tummi said with a frown. "He won't take kindly to her refusal. He more than likely will try to force her into those bonds. To be quite honest I would not be surprised if he tied her to the marriage bed, to fruit the next of his name."

Echo made a sound of disgust in her throat, and I saw Katrel flinch at it. She still saw herself weak, even after all that she did, all she fought for. It wasn't enough against the mountain of authority that was their father.

"What are your ideas then, my Lord?" Durgash asked with a haunted, hateful gleam in his eyes. The look mirrored in his wife's eyes?

"We train and plan. All I have planned for now is that we will go to Babylos for the summer solstice. We will see this battle head on and do our best to stay alive and stay free."

Chapter Thirty-Nine

Shasha

The neighbors came and went often through the evening, building the bonfire and preparing the yard for dancing. Niratap kept careful watch over them, the shadows dancing across his skin whenever they were near. Not so much to hide himself, but to warn them of the beast that lurked within. After the sun had set, I had not been allowed out of the house. I had waited for him to return to his room. Finally, Mitta's voice filled the hall loudly as she scolded him for pushing himself.

"I release you from bed rest and you go and put in a full day. Are you mad?"

"I promise you, Mitta, I am not in any pain, just tired."

"You need to be careful, my Lord. If you push too hard you could set yourself back. Your wound may have closed, but you are still healing slowly. Infection could still set in."

"I will rest most of tomorrow before the festivities. I promise, my friend."

Mitta sighed. "Go to bed, my Lord."

"Goodnight, Mitta." The door opened and closed. He walked across the room deep in thought and added a log to the fire. "Are you staying with me again tonight?"

I shifted on the bed. "Unless you want me to go."

He shook his head and sighed as he unbuttoned his shirt. "I may have overdone it today."

I frowned, sliding out of bed and going to him. "Why?"

"It's my nature. I get tied up in how things are running, and I forget to care for myself."

"I do similar things when I worry." I crouched down before him and untied his shoes. "That first day you were down, I didn't eat. You were unconscious and had a fever and I was so scared that I would lose you."

"But you didn't. I am here, *mo grá*." he said toeing off his shoes.

"I know that now." I stood and wrapped my arms around his waist. His tail wrapped around me, securing me to his body. He was warm and solid. The scar from the basilisk was large and soft, but it was a scar. "But I didn't then, and I fear for you again. So please, keep your word to Mitta and rest tomorrow. Sleep in and rest."

"Yes, my love." He released me. His hand stroked my face before he finished undressing.

In bed I curled against his form, his strong arms holding me close. Wrapped in each other's scent was exactly where I wanted to be. There were so many emotions that flowed through me as I listened to his heart beat, listened as his breath slowed and he drifted to sleep. We had been so close, so close to losing everything before it had even had a name.

"Nira?"

"Hmmm."

"I know you don't want to hear it, but I am sorry."

He gave me a squeeze. "No."

I placed a gentle kiss on his chest. "You need to rest, my love."

"Your heart is full of worry."

"You are weary from the day. Rest. We can discuss my worry later."

His hand traced my cheek, and I gazed up at his luminescent eyes. "You will not rest well if you go to bed with a worried heart."

"All too often your heart is heavy with worry when you come to rest."

"A worry for a worry then we can rest."

I sighed, resting my head against his chest. "We could have lost it. Us. before we were even an us."

He stroked my back. "And the fact that it could happen at any time now that we have put a name to what we are, it is weighing on you."

"Yes and no. It was my foolishness that was weighing on me."

"You are not foolish. You are determined, much like myself, and didn't want to take no for an answer. I have done similar things, in different situations."

"Have you?"

"The auction is one such moment where I would not take no for an answer. Nothing and no one would keep me from you."

I nodded, stifling a yawn. "I understand, Your worry?"

He pulled me close, curling around me protectively. "That this is just a long nightmare, and I will wake without you."

The next afternoon we were still wrapped lovingly around one another. I didn't want to leave his embrace. I ran my hand over his ribs, and goosebumps crawled over his skin. He curled tighter around me.

"I am not ready to leave here." He whispered into my hair.

"Neither am I, but I believe you have an obligation to uphold."

He made a long-suffering sound before he uncoiled and stretched his long body beside me. "Unfortunately."

I chuckled to myself as we both got out of bed and went to ready for the day. After a shower and the tedious care of my hair, Dorilody spirited me away to dress me. In a few hours, we had gathered in the foyer, Echo delightedly chatting with Dheg about the dances they would share and the food they would eat. It was intoxicating to hear, the ecstatic joy that came off them an effervescent claim to excitement brewing in my heart.

As I excitedly followed the others out the doors, Niratap caught my wrist and spun me around. He pressed his lips to my forehead, the press of his lips and body against mine was a show of claiming that I knew was for our neighbors. So, they knew who I belonged to.

"I know you are excited, *mo grá;* I have three rules that are non-negotiable."

"Are they fair rules?"

He smiled cupping my cheek. "Listen. One, do not drink the wine the neighbors try to give you because they will try. Two, don't dance with anyone you don't know or didn't know prior to tonight. And three, do not wander off into the woods. Fair?"

"Fair, but why can't I dance with the neighbors?"

"The last thing that I need is for you to be spirited off by them. Half of them would love to have you in whatever way they can. Even though I am getting better, I won't be fast enough to stop them." He ran his thumb over my bottom lip, his brows furrowed with concern. "Please don't break my heart, because losing you, even briefly might do just that."

I stood up on my tip toes and kissed his lips. "I don't plan on it."

He kissed my forehead again before taking my hand. "Okay."

Outside the bonfire was already roaring to the sky, fighting off the October chill, and many fae roamed the yard. Pixies and fauns, satyrs and centaurs, trolls and gnomes, and many more I didn't know. So many had gathered on the grounds to celebrate; the numbers were staggering. A large table was laden with copious amounts of food and drink. A large oaken chair lay at the center of the table, and that was where Niratap led me. Many of those in attendance gave bows of varying degrees, and most tittered between each other.

"What are they whispering?" I asked him as we neared the table.

"A variety of things from my appearance to how good you'll dance to how you may taste." He threw a glare toward the group of dark-skinned, scaled fae at the edge. "Stay clear of the naga, they only whisper of the taste of your flesh."

He sat wrapping a steadfast arm around me, the honey color of sunset casting a healthy glow across his skin. A hush fell over the crowd. He gave me a reassuring squeeze before he spoke.

"Welcome friends and neighbors to this year's Samhain feast. This year has been plentiful for all of us, both in company and in harvest. Let us remember those who passed this year and honor them in dance and feast. I only ask that you respect my home and my family, so we can meet again after the long dark."

There was a cheer as the crowd went back to their milling, our family intermixed with them. Most chatting with others, smiles plastered on their faces, except Mitta and Allipo who were stoic talking to a dark-skinned man, who had ethereal blue eyes that glowed.

"Who's that talking with Allipo and Mitta?"

Nira looked in their direction and his brows furrowed. "Someone I did not expect to be here. His name is Ventris, an air elemental, he works for the magic bureau branch of the government. He's an ally most of the time, but sometimes our organizations don't see eye to eye. He's a good man though."

The man looked our way, his brows raising at me before he nodded at Niratap. "Should I avoid him?"

"That is your call, my dear. I don't think Ventris will try to harm you in any way, at worst he will question my reasons for having you in my company."

"Okay." I watched the man as he smiled warmly at me, but something about him was off. "So don't dance with him."

"If you want to, I'll let you."

"So, he's an exception." I smile sheepishly.

Nira sighed. "He is someone I trust, and he will neither spirit you away nor try to eat you."

I giggled. "Okay, when does the dancing start?"

"Soon, the fae like to catch up, then the leaders will present gifts to the host—"

"Which is you?"

"Yes, my dear. After that you can dance."

"How many leaders are there?"

Niratap scanned the crowd. "Well, you met Windflower. She is the leader of the wild fae and pixies." She was as I remembered her, fair-skinned, wrapped in a flowing gossamer gown, and her large ethereal blue eyes. "Over talking to Dheg is Staspar. He is a Satyr and watches over the local satyrs, fauns, and centaurs." He was a few inches taller than Dheg with pale skin, his cheeks and shoulders kissed by the sun. He had light red hair that curled around his sand-colored ram horns. A circlet of gold leaves sat between them. "There by Durgash and Rogmesh is Thegguma Hillchest. She is the head of the mines in the area and looks after the mine workers; things have been much better the last few decades with her in charge." The butch dwarven woman had fawn colored hair braided in a thick rope down her back, the sides of her head were shaved, and she sported dark tattoos over her olive skin. "Lastly is Creseda; she's a kelpie and is the keeper of the shifters in the area." He tilted his head at the pale woman, with long, deep teal colored hair that trailed behind her. "I'd suggest you stay away from her. Out of all of them she I trust least to be respectful of rules and boundaries."

"Noted." I sat on the arm of Nira's chair, the split in the leg of the flowy copper pants—that I had told Dorilody would be too cold for an October night—flared open showing a vast expanse of leg. The pants were paired with a matching shirt with a deep v-neckline that exposed the top swell of my breasts. Niratap made a noise in the back of his throat at the sight. "Yes, my Lord?"

He cleared his throat. "Who suggested this beautiful outfit for tonight, my dear?"

"Dorilody suggested it and said it would be good for all the dancing I wanted to do."

He leaned in close, his breath hot on the shell of my ear. "I will very much enjoy tearing you out of it."

I threw my head back to laugh. "Is that a threat or a promise, my Lord?"

"It's both." He said his voice full of heat, that wicked smirk cresting his beautiful face.

"That is quite the delectable prize you have found yourself, Lord Bondbreaker." Said voice that lapped against my skin like cool lake waters. The owner was the kelpie Niratap had just warned me about. She bowed her head toward him, a serpentine smile on her lips, as she eyed me with a dark swirling gaze that conveyed only hunger.

"Creseda." Niratap's voice took on an icy edge. A threat of violence. Whether it went unnoticed or ignored, her smile did not waver.

"Lord Bondbreaker." She purred with a bow, spreading her arms wide as two other kelpies came pulling carts. "The shifters bless your home with a bountiful harvest of freshwater fish and three mighty harts to fill your coffers."

"Many thanks to yours, Creseda; I'm sure the Days will appreciate your generosity as much as I do."

"Of course, many thanks to your continued efforts to free our brothers and sisters in bondage and to the protection of your shadow."

"Oi!" Staspar honked as he stormed up. "Why yous alway gos be firs Cresda? Is ain' ike yous needin be cener ovhe room."

"It is pronounced Creseda, Staspar. And I have already said my hellos to those I need to. Glad to see hybrids still follow a bumbling halfwit."

"Creseda." Niratap growled, violence no longer merely a threat.

She bowed at the waist. "My apologies, Lord Bondbreaker, I forgot my tongue."

I saw the irritation muscle twitch in Niratap's face. "Mind it, Creseda. You are dismissed; let the other leaders have their space."

"Yes, of course, My Lord." She and the other kelpies left, leaving the carts.

"I don't like her." I said at last, noticing the faintest smile on Nira's face.

"You are not alone." He said. "But the shifters chose her to be their voice."

"She's rude."

He chuckled. "Most of them are. Do you wish to present, Staspar?"

"Yessur, me lord Bondbreaker. We hybreds 'ave culivaed he 'arth an' 'ave brough yous dems fruis of our labors." He waved over a centaur pulling a cart. "Oi! Wevs brough haery veg for ye shores. adoes, carrus, onins, gerlic, durups, begas, parnips, and sun udder thins as well. We thank ye for avin those who need avin and yer pertecshin."

"Many thanks to you and yours, for sharing your bountiful harvests." Niratap said smoothly, as I stifled a giggle.

Staspar bowed deeply, his nose nearly kissing the ground, the centaur following suit after unhitching themselves from the cart. When Staspar rose, he gave us a warm smile.

"Oi, yous gos youseves a perddy lass, me lord." I straightened at that.

"That I have." Niratap gave me a squeeze; it was for show more than anything. I belonged to him in their world, I was off limits. Staspar gave a less dramatic bow, before he and the centaur returned to the fray.

"He's interesting."

"He's missing part of his tongue; he used to speak quite elegantly, like most satyrs do. Now all that elegance goes into making music. His family always makes music at these kinds of events."

"Okay. Why do they, beyond how I smell, look at me like I'm dinner?"

"To Creseda you are dinner, same with Windflower. Staspar has a different kind of hunger in his eyes."

A shudder rolled through my body. "So, stay away."

"Yes." He looked up and gave a nod to Windflower. Across the table from us I could see her dress was made of spider silk and flowed lightly about her lithe body.

"Lord of shadowy places, your wild neighbors have brought gifts of the forest, many gathered herbs, nuts, berries and mushrooms." Five baskets appeared by the table on a spring scented breeze, heaped with the many items. "A thanks for your efforts to continue our freedom and your protection from those who wish to end it."

"You and yours have outdone yourselves this year. Mitta will be pleased with the medicines she can make."

Windflower gave a sweeping bow and fluttered her wings, before she flitted off. Thegguma came forward, the Days flanking her and laughing loudly at something the dwarf had said. Before the table both the Days gave deep bows to Niratap, Thegguma kneeled before him keeping her head low as she spoke.

"Lord Niratap Bondbreaker, I thank you for your hospitality and generosity, for your continued support and safety in the mines and for your efforts to free us all from bonds of slavery. From our toils underground," she stood pulling a pouch from her waist band as an orc came forward, two hefty bags on one shoulder. "Salt of the earth to season your other wonderful gifts and some herkimer diamonds and garnets from the gem mines." She set the pouch on the table before him, the top opening to reveal gleaming, snow-white gems with blood red ones scattered throughout.

"Many thanks to your earthen folk. I hope to keep the mines as safe as possible for you."

"Many thanks, my Lord." She returned to kneel before us as the Days began to collect the offerings. "And my apologies, but a fine young woman you have found for company. She must have cost you a hefty sun."

Nira unwrapped his arm from around me and leaned forward in his seat. "Thegguma though you are correct that I paid a hefty sum of funds to free Shasha from slavery, your insinuation that she was purchased as a plaything I find quite offensive."

"My apologies, my Lord." I didn't think it was possible for her to sink lower to the ground.

"Furthermore," Niratap raised his voice as he stood so all could hear. "If anyone is thinking such things, I would like to remind you that all I demand of you is respect to each other and to my household. That respect covers her for she is part of my household. Now if any of you wish to continue your sniping at her, you will quickly meet with my claws. Understood?" The entire crowd, even those who lived with us, bowed deeply to him. It was the only confirmation that was needed, and Niratap sat back down. "Thegguma you're dismissed."

A couple of young satyrs came forward and assisted the Days in ferrying the gifts to the storehouse as everyone went back to milling about and chatting.

"Did you feel that was necessary?" I asked seeing the tension coiled in Nira's shoulders.

"Yes." He exhaled a long breath. "However, it will still probably paint you as a possession to them."

"Even when they know what you do?"

He shrugged, leaning forward and pouring a glass of rose-colored wine. "It's complicated explaining what a relationship is to most fae. Wild fae mate, and if the female doesn't eat the male, they stay mated forever. Centaurs court each other, fauns and satyrs rarely settle down. Really, only humanoid class creatures date or marry. The concepts are lost on the others."

"So, what of you, *mo grá?*"

"Bitarogs mate, but our numbers are so few that I fear by the turn of the next millennium we will be extinct."

"Are there really so few?"

"I know four others of my kind that are alive. All males. All single. Some say that there is so few of us left that there may be only ten or twenty of us, some say around a hundred. Either way the genetic pool is quite small. So even if there were a hundred of us all gathered, we would still die out." He shrugged while taking a drink of the wine. He wraps an arm around my waist. "The power of fear in the masses."

"Quite the pessimistic one." I said as he offered me a sip of wine.

"I'm being realistic." He sighed. "The music will start soon."

There were satyrs and fauns tuning instruments in a small circle, "What will they play?"

"Usually, the *Federkleid* is a favorite to open the dancing." Allipo said, coming to stand on Niratap's other side. "It's about growing wings and flying away. After that they go with the flow of energy. Are you excited to dance, my flower?"

"I am. If the lord will allow me from his side, that is." I smiled at him coyly and his expression flattened. "He is very protective of me today."

"I heard. My Lord knows I will keep you from harm."

"I know that you will keep her safe, that was not a question in my mind. However, I am curious as to what Ventris is doing here?"

"He came to observe and to discuss some matters of the market with you."

"I'm guessing he will only speak to me when the music is going, and the company is distracted."

"You are correct, my Lord."

Niratap uncurled his arm and pressed a kiss to my shoulder. "Very well. Take care of our girl."

"Yes, my Lord, my honor." Allipo stepped forward and extended an elbow to me.

I slid off the arm of the chair and moved to cross in front of Niratap. He caught my wrist, pulled me against his chest, and pressed a hot kiss against my pulse. "Remember my rules?"

"Yes, my Lord."

Another kiss, this time against my cheek. "Good, return to me when you tire."

"Yes, my Lord."

He pressed one last kiss to my forehead and then rested his brow against mine and in the quietest voice possible. "I love you, *mo grá*. Return to me."

"I will, *mo grá*."

Niratap released me and as I lay my hand on Allipo's arm letting him guide me to the fire, warmth sailed through my body. We came to stand before the band, and Allipo sketched a bow for me, offering me four ribbons with bells sewn onto them from his pocket.

"What are these?"

"Bells, for dancing. 'Tis customary for women to wear bells. May I?"

"You may."

He gently scooped up one leg behind the knee, his hand sliding down my calf and resting my slippered foot on his thigh, delicately tying the bells around my ankle. He then repeated the very deliberate show on the other leg and followed by tying the remaining ribbons around my wrists. I wiggled them when he was done and laughed at the whimsical sound.

"Why the bells?"

"So, you can be found if you wander from the dance." He said mischievously. "But probably more so that you are also an instrument. I enjoyed bestowing them upon you, as a jab at the lord."

"How wicked of you." I smiled, looking toward Niratap who sat, eyes glued to where I stood. His face was neutral, but I felt the heat in those eyes even over the fire.

"Are you ready, my flower?" Allipo asked as others came forward to dance. Dheg came to my other side and Echo beyond him, the tinkling of tiny bells echoing my own. Was I ready for this?

I swallowed, butterflies tickled my stomach and my heart started pounding. I took a shaking breath and tried to find the excitement that had had me rolling in the sheets with Nira and working extra hard in the practices we had done.

"Yes," I said, still shaking. Allipo and Dheg both smiled at me, holding their hands out palms up. I set my hands on top of theirs.

"Then let the dance begin."

"Just follow our lead, Shasha dear."

An awe-filled silence fell over the crowd, a collective breath before the first strum of a harp. The men raised our hands slowly overhead as pipes played a light tune. I looked at Dheg who had closed his eyes, a dreamy expression and lurid bliss resting on his face. I turned back to Allipo who smiled in his most satyr way as our hands came down.

'Ready' he mouthed.

I looked toward Niratap who had a sly smile on his face; I looked back at Allipo as everyone prepared to dance. 'Yes.'

And the dance began with a jilting run of drums that filled the air, and we stepped to one side in a hop stomp around the fire. Female satyrs and fauns began singing and we stomped with the drum. The drums picked up again and we danced the other direction. My belled feet excitedly fell into the spell of the dance, and when the next verse started, Allipo took my hand and spun me to the beat of the song, a heartbeat through the earth. We joined back into the ring around the fire and continued stomping around, first right then left in time with the music. With each verse everyone paired off and spun and stomped and hopped in a flurry of colors and smiles. At the last verse Allipo spun me and lifted me above him and on instinct I spread my arms, soaring through the song and then we were in the ring once more, spinning faster and faster to the beat.

The song evolved into another, and we broke off in smaller groups or couples, spinning and clapping along. The next dance had the men bowing to the ladies to dance. I had to turn to Allipo or Dheg multiple times as other satyrs, fauns, and fae men tried to get me to dance with them. There was many a sad face, but I wasn't going to give Nira a reason to worry. After several dances, I bowed out of the revelry and went to Nira on aching feet. He was talking to the elemental when I walked up. I plopped in his lap, and without turning his head or stopping what he was saying he offered me a chalice of cool sweet juice then wrapped his arm around my waist.

"So, what do you want me to do V?"

"Niratap, you can't be so reckless on the market. There are big players out there hoping to get their hands on you. I think you should back off the market for a little while." The man named Ventris said.

"And I disagree." Nira said, pulling a plate of sliced cheese and thin meat before me. "Not that there aren't beings out there that want me enslaved or dead, but stepping out for a while won't help either of our goals. I freely let you track my movements and be an integral part of my organization, but stepping out isn't an option. I know you are coming from a place of concern, V, but I can't. Especially now."

"The bitarog rumor."

"Yes. I got hold of Howen not too long ago; he's moved his operations farther East. Europe's market is, well, on a witch hunt for him, but he didn't know anything about one of us being thrown on the market. He did tell me that he was sure Casrian was dead, which isn't surprising given how he was."

"Casrian. He was the 'blaze of glory' one, wasn't he?"

Nira nodded as he buttered a roll and set it on my plate. "Yes. He was reckless Howen, and I both told him being that way was going to get him killed."

Ventris sighed, but I felt his stare as Nira continued to set things on my plate to eat, "My bureau has rules we have to work in. Even with spies, techies, and undercover agents our black market is evolving rapidly. The players are rapidly gaining or losing power. I just don't want you and your family getting swept off the table. Things are volatile."

"What do you know of Dravin Cirano?"

"What? Fat Cat?" Ventris shook his head. "Probably about as much as you. He's low priority. Dealing in prostitution, he's gained some power and recently hired a bunch of scientists. We have eyes and ears in there but there hasn't been much movement beyond that."

"He's experimenting with basilisk venom."

"How do you know?"

"My eyes and ears."

"That's concerning, but it has been sometime since D reached out."

"Who is this D?"

Ventris sighed again and I wondered if he was always so begrudged. "I can't tell you that, just like you won't tell me who you have in there."

"Precisely." Nira said softly. "But I'm sure you already know who isn't here."

"Is the kid, okay?"

"He's getting better. He was shot a little while ago. He's tough like his parents, V."

"That was a hard job, the mines. We lost a lot of beings in that raid."

"We did." Nira placed a kiss on the crown of my head, pouring water into my empty glass from a carafe. "I don't want there to be a mass casualty event again, but I think we need to keep a better eye on the sleaze ball."

"I'll get some things organized, and I'll loop you in when I know more."

"Thank you, V. I know you skirt the line a lot for me."

"I'm just trying to keep as many of us alive anymore as I can, both of us have too many enemies."

"And both of us make them too easily."

Ventris chuckled as Nira reached for a tray of dried fruits and nuts and pulled it closer. "You going to keep stuffing her with food?"

"As long as she keeps eating it, yes." I felt the smile in his voice.

I swung my elbow back gently into his stomach. "I can feed myself, my Lord."

He leaned forward and kissed my cheek. "I know, *mo grá*, but humor me."

I locked eyes with Ventris, his steely eyes seemed to peer deeply into my soul and his eyebrows raised with curiosity. He asked me. "How did you come into the lord's life?"

I felt Niratap go rigid beneath me, something in Ventris's tone that alerted him. I asked cautiously. "Why do you want to know?"

Something flickered in his eyes. "Curiosity. Niratap doesn't really gravitate towards humans. I just wanted to know, why you?"

"Do you question all of the lord's decisions on the company he keeps?" My tone is dagger sharp. Niratap chuckled as shock settled over Ventris's face. I popped a dark grape in my mouth. "I find it quite rude to ask such things and not expect backlash."

"I only ask because this whole night from what I have witnessed he treats you more like a possession than a companion. Which for the duration of the time I've known the lord, is very much out of the ordinary. I want to know why."

Niratap paused as he was reaching for another tray. "Commander, though I do consider you an ally, I will defend her and side with her. It is quite rude to question, but I'll humor you." He said sitting back and possessively placing his hand on my thigh. "She was kidnapped off the street by Fat Cat and went up for auction the night I ventured into the August market. Now the reasons why I was there don't matter because they are need-to-know. I purchased our girl and broke plenty of underground rules to get her. Even so, she is neither a prisoner or a servant, nor a bedmate. Shasha is free to do as she pleases."

"Within what you lay down as rules." There was something in his voice that rang like anger.

If I had not been sitting in his lap, I'm sure Niratap would have stood. He spoke slowly and deliberately. "My rules only exist for her safety."

"She is not safe with you." The words landed heavily on us.

Niratap fisted his hand, his voice taking on the promise of violence. "What concern is the girl to you, V?"

Shock flared in his eyes, mixing with the rage. He closed them and turned. "It seems I have overstayed my welcome. I wish you well, Niratap. Young lady, I hope you are sure of your choices; the man who you are defending is a monster."

I made my voice sound as bored as possible "That sir, is something I am very aware of, and it happens to rank very low on my list of concerns regarding the lord. Safe travels."

"Blessed Samhain to you both." He turned, storming away towards the forest. Once past the revelers, he disappeared on an autumn breeze.

"Do you get the sense that was weird?" I asked.

"What? The conversation or him turning into air?" Nira asked, sitting back in his chair.

"Surprisingly, I figured him just disappearing into thin air was an elemental thing. The conversation. Something about it set you off and then after you said my name, something in him changed."

"I agree, there was an edge of distrust to his voice and there was a possessiveness I've never heard him use."

Niratap took a grape from my hand and chewed it thoughtfully.

"How long have you known him?"

"A hundred years or so. He has worked hard to build the bureau and even harder to prove that we creatures are worth saving."

"Does he have secrets?"

"Yes. He's done a fair bit of undercover work the last forty years. If I remember right, he was in that town you grew up in at one point."

"Really? He did look vaguely familiar, but I can't place it."

"He wouldn't have used his real name. I don't remember what his alias would have been. They tend to blur together."

I turned in his lap. "I missed you."

He smiled wistfully. "You missed me while you danced?"

"I did. Allipo and Dheg are great dance partners, but I would prefer you to be my partner. I know you're still recovering."

He pulled my chin toward him. "I don't dance, my darling, but I love to watch you."

I smiled but rolled my eyes. "You're impossible."

He pressed a kiss to my temple. We sat there for what could have been a few minutes or an eternity watching the revelry, listening to songs from long ago, while the bonfire crackled in unison. I could live thousands of nights like this, as long as he was beside me.

Chapter Forty

Niratap

Time has a funny way of flowing when you fall in love. Days and nights spent by her side, made it stall for long moments, but at the same time, they flew by faster. A night felt like an eternity, a few days a moment. Three days after Samhain she was curled against me, working on her schoolwork while I went through my emails and reports, the first fine snow falling outside the windows.

"And done." She said, saving the document she'd been pouring over. "My paper is finished."

"I'm glad." I said, wrapping an arm around her. "What was this one on?"

"It was a research paper on the history of satyrs, faun, and centaurs and the worship of Dionysus. How much longer until you're done? Mitta is going to come by to check you again soon."

"Just a few more minutes I think." I said, pulling my eyes from an email of stock balances. "I just have to sign off on this allocation report from my accountant and I will be all yours."

"After Mitta gives you the all clear."

"Of course." She beamed at me practically wagging a tail. She had been waiting for Mitta to clear me to train. Shasha desperately wanted to spar with me.

I finalized the report and sent it off as my phone rang. The number was Bastion's burner. "Bas, you clear?"

"Hey bud."

"Understood."

"So, there's a get together happening next week in the city and I wanted to see if you were coming."

Mitta opened the door after a quiet knock. I held a finger up to my lips. "No, I didn't hear about that. Where is it at?"

"The usual fancy bigwigs spot on Saturday night. I hear someone's going to bring a bit of a prize."

"Anyone I might know?"

"I'm not sure, like I said I was just checking to see if you would be there."

"Sure, sure, and I might bring some candy of my own."

"Usual suspects I suppose."

"Possibly." I cast a glance at Shasha. "Maybe someone new, too."

"Nice, some fresh faces will be nice."

"True, true. See you then, man."

"Ciao."

He disconnects. Shasha arches a delicate brow. "Did Bastion just invite you to a party?"

"No, it's code." Mitta said, "Another market?"

"Yes, next Saturday, it's the market they're planning in auctioning that bitarog."

"You shouldn't go." Mitta barked at me. "It's dangerous."

"Mitta." My voice demanding respect.

"Apologies, my Lord, but I don't think you are in a condition to go prowl the market alone."

"I don't plan on going alone." I cast another glance down at Shasha. "Would you like to be my arm candy, my dear?"

"I—" She began.

"Absolutely not." Mitta snarled, and I gave her an incredulous look. "I mean no disrespect, but she isn't trained enough to be your bodyguard."

"This I know, and she won't be going as my bodyguard, that is your job Mitta."

"Then why take someone untrained with you? Why risk it?" Mitta demanded.

"She is going as a distraction, but I want her to learn how to walk the market like a predator."

"You're insane." Mitta groaned. "This is insane, she will just become a target."

"For now." I snarled. "I understand the risks involved, but she will pull attention from me. Shadows can only hide so much. Regardless that I have been eating well, I have lost weight since I was injured. It is noticeable enough to be a cause for concern. The flower of the market will distract from the healing monster beside her. You are also one of the most lethal creatures alive; your face is known on the market, and you will keep them away."

Mitta's face was flushed with anger, but she didn't say anything as I closed my laptop and eased myself out of bed. "Besides, she fully accepts what we do in theory." I said unbuttoning my shirt as I strode toward her. "She may as well see it in action. Then decide how far she wants to take her involvement. Whether she wants to be part of that aspect of life here. We're putting all the effort into training her to be a player, she should see what the underground is capable of." I sat on the stool that had become too close a friend. "It is her choice whether or not she comes anyway, Mitta, but regardless I am going. I'm not going to miss an opportunity to rescue one of my own kind."

Mitta focused on peeling away the remaining bandages left over the worst of my injuries. Her hands were cool and gentle against my chest. Lucky. I had been so lucky. Had that fang sunk any deeper, had my magic failed me any earlier, had they not reacted swiftly; I might not have made it. She poked at the pink flesh that had finally knitted itself back together. A dark scab sat over where that fang had entered me.

"Your wound is sealed. I'll clear you to go back to regular activity, but unfortunately Shasha won't be able to spar with you. I need you to be careful not to open this scabbed spot. A secondary infection would be disastrous. Unfortunately, I do think you will be left with a significant scar."

I grasped her hand as she pulled away. "Thank you. For all your care, Mitta. I know your focus is safety for both me and Shasha, but I know you understand why."

"I do, my Lord."

"Alright then. *Mo grá?*"

"Yes?"

"Do you wish to accompany Mitta and I to the market next Saturday?"

"I would, my Lord."

"Then it is settled. I'll have Dorilody find a fitting outfit for the venture."

Mitta sighed. "Scant I assume."

"You would be correct. It will sell the image. The market thinks I bought a plaything and that is what they will see."

Mitta gave me a sharp look as I released her from my grasp. "I don't agree with this, but as you wish, my Lord. Be kind to yourself for a couple more days please."

I gave her a small smile as she turned for the door. "Yes, Mitta."

She let loose a long-suffering sigh, before she walked out, the door clicking quietly behind her. Shasha spoke as she came in front of me to examine my wounds for herself. "She is only concerned."

"I know." I said watching her eyes take in what was definitely going to be a hefty scar on my body. She gingerly placed a hand over the scabbed flesh, over my heart. Many emotions dancing through those endless autumnal eyes. "I am alright, my flower."

Her eyes met mine and whatever shadows had been there had floated away. "I know."

Somehow, I had a feeling she questioned it, but I said. "What do you wish to do with our day. *mo grá?*"

She smiled brightly, her fingers tracing the line of my collar bone. "well, we can't spar like I wanted, but we could go shoot, maybe go for a walk."

"It will be chilly, and we have been to the range everyday save Samhain." An idea sparked me. "How about we do something different today?"

"Like what?"

"How about we go for a ride?"

Dheg was happy to saddle Guinness, the shire with a coat of such dark brown it was almost black, who was finicky enough that he only preferred one rider. He was getting older now and soon enough I would have to retire him to pastures and lazy days.

"Hello, my friend," I spoke to him softly. "We're going to our favorite place."

His ears twitched with delight.

"We won't go full send, however."

He snorted indignantly.

"We have precious cargo today, my friend."

Shasha giggled at the doors of the barn at something Dheg had said. She was dressed against the chill in fur lined, caramel-colored boots that covered the bottoms of her grey leggings, a light puffy yellow jacket and a burgundy scarf wrapped around her neck. She really was all the joy I needed in life wrapped up in one smile. Dheg sketched a bow to her, before he slipped back out into the gentle snow. What a wonder she was, to have slipped fully into all their hearts, without fear of our scars, our survival. A marvel indeed. She walked up to Guinness with the same amount of openness that she approached me all those weeks ago, offering him a handful of oats.

"Hello, my mighty, wild friend." She crooned, stroking the softest part of his nose. Guinness let her touch that most sensitive spot and munched happily at the oats in her hand, content to let her do as she wished. "I'm surprised by your connection to him, you being a predator and all."

I watched her scratch him gently. "Horses have an innate sense of knowing. They are loving creatures of the earth; they can see the depths of a person's soul and know when one means them ill will. I think they also have their own magic that helps heal those who need it. Those of us with fractured souls."

She looked up at me, some shadows drifting in those earthen depths. "Your soul is not fractured."

She had heard it all and still she held my gaze with such warmth. "Yes, my dear, it is, but perhaps not as fractured as it once was."

"Because of Guinness?"

"Some of it. He is one of many friends I've had in my time free. Mostly it is because of you."

She smiled. "Where are we going?"

I ran my hand over Guinness' mane, gently grabbing the halter to lead him from the barn. "To a place where I find peace."

"You mean to tell me you don't find peace in your home?"

I glanced at the manor and helped her up onto the saddle. "Scoot up on the horn."

I hadn't ever found peace in this place, so many of those dark shadowy nights stained the grounds, the walls, the room where I slept. All of it was dark. I hopped into the saddle behind her, adjusting for both our comforts. She sank into my chest as I eased Guinness into a steady trot through the flurries of snow.

"You didn't answer my question." She said softly as the falling snow.

"No." I said plainly. "I have never found peace in those walls."

"Then why stay?"

Her soft question clawed at the cracks in the soul she didn't see as fractured. Knowing my story. Knowing the things that I had done in that house. How the faces of the innocent people I had killed in those halls haunted my nightmares as often as I watched Deirdre die. Almost as often as nightmares of Shasha under the basilisk or that shadow that hunted me, pulled me from sleep, even with her soundly breathing beside me. Why did I stay? We could have razed the whole place to the ground, left it smoldering and found somewhere else where we could have built something better. All the blood spilled on these grounds, laid beneath a heavy blanket of ash. I felt her shift in front me, her body a warm anchor against the cold, pulling me from my thoughts.

"Nira?"

I took a breath at the concern that laced her words. "Honestly, *mo grá,* I don't know."

We were quiet the rest of the ride, contemplative as we passed through meadows and glades following beside the river. Guinness' hoof-beats through the snow a comforting sound as we traveled. As we neared the place where I found the most peace, I took in the glade of birch trees we passed through, the trees naked for winter. How easy it was to compare to the nakedness of my heart. Dangerous were these moments just me and her, alone with just love between us. I had given her access to all those shadows, and she did not balk. I found myself in awe of her, my free hand tracing idle circles over her thigh.

"This is far from the manor." She observed, pulling me from my circle of dark thoughts.

"Yes. I stumbled upon it during one of the wars after." After I slayed the household that had held me.

"It is definitely peaceful." She mused not needing me to finish my thought. "I bet it is glorious in the spring."

"Yes, it is. The glade is full of life then. Wildflowers and spring grasses that sway in the breeze. I will bring you back here when the seasons change again."

Her head rested lazily against my chest; eyes bright as she gazed up at me. "I would like that, very much."

We could plan for the future, even though it still astounded me that she would consider one with me. The monster who owned her. How had I fallen from where I stood for the last few centuries? I gave everyone choices, options with the promise of my protection, but Shasha. Shasha, I wanted to hold on to. I wanted to keep her close to me. Did that make me a villain then or now that she had fallen in love with me?

The waterfall clearing came into view as we rounded the bend. The waterfall roared into the crystalline pool below, moss still verdant against the light dusting of snow. Coming here helped ease the tension I could feel gathering in my heart. Would she love my place of repose?

I eased Guinness to a stop and slid off the saddle, then reached up to help her off. I said, "This is my little slice of peace."

Once her feet were planted and she scratched Guinness behind the ears she turned and took in the clearing. Would she hate it? Would she think me simple that in all the grandeur that the manor was, this would be my peace? She stepped into the clearing, taking it all in and I felt vulnerable. Her sharp eyes seeing in every nook and cranny of my peace, from the soft grass meadow dusted with snow that come springtime I would love to bed her in, to the roaring tumbling cerulean waterfall, the bright pops of color in the water caused by koi and fairy fish. When she faced me and smiled broadly full of light and joy, I knew she wouldn't condemn me for the simplicity.

"This place is beautiful."

Her praise made me feel weak in the knees and I held onto Guinness to keep from falling. "Thank you."

"Does it freeze in winter?"

"No, the water comes from a hot spring. The water doesn't freeze until it's by the manor."

"So, it's warm?"

"Yes."

She spun, dancing in the falling flakes, then stopped to beam at me with delight as she undid her scarf. "So, you're telling me that we could swim here?"

I cocked my head. "I've never thought about that before."

She skipped to me, unzipping her jacket. "And why is that?"

My blood heated, little vixen. "Well, I mostly come here with Guinness and just have a relaxing sit."

"Well, I think we should." She says laying her jacket in the snow followed by her top. She toed off her shoes and danced about while she shimmied out of her leggings. "Join me?"

I chuckled as she took off running. "Be careful."

She dove into the water with the grace of a swan. I laughed then paused shuck my own overcoat on her pile. I waited for her secondary splash and the gasp for air. My heart started to skitter. I tossed my phone into the pile and kicked off my shoes. My legs ate the distance from the edge of the clearing to the pool, my fingers tripping over the buttons of my shirt in a panic. I almost tripped sliding out of my pants, abandoning them on the bank as I dove into the pool.

Water rushed past my ears. Once the plunge had stopped, I opened my eyes searching for her. The water was calm, and the roar of the waterfall sounded far off. The pool was much deeper than it appeared above, tall water weeds swayed in the current. I wanted to scream her name, but I didn't want to surface without her. Mad panic swirled in my heart. *Where are you? Where are you?*

There. Floating face up, smiling brightly as a magenta colored fae dancing in front of her. I kicked down to where she was, my heart thundering, my lungs starting to burn. She beamed at me as approached, bubbles coming out of my nose. I pointed to the surface, and she nodded, waving at the small fae and swimming to the surface. I sputtered as we close in on the sky, my lungs screaming for air. Shasha grabbed my elbow as the bubbles explode from my mouth. She helped tug me to the surface. I gasped, coughing violently as I inhale water.

"Hey just take an easy breath."

"How?" I coughed violently as she eased us to the shore.

"I like to swim."

I huffed. "No. How can you hold your breath for so long? I thought you had hit your head on the bottom, I—"

"I'm sorry, I didn't mean to scare you. I always have." She said leaning against the smooth stones next to me. "Mom never said much about it. She was a swimmer in high school, and she thought I might do something similar."

The ache in my lungs began to fade. "I'm glad you're safe. Why didn't you do something similar?"

She smiled, looking towards the waterfall. "I did it my freshman year, and don't get me wrong, I love good competition, but competitive swimming wasn't something I loved."

I pressed my forehead to the cool stones, taking a couple deep breaths. She was fine. Safe. I was the one who almost drowned because I had panicked. I panicked. Something that many years of instincts and living should have told me to avoid in this type of situation, but my heart and brain fought for dominance when it came to that beautiful woman beside me. Had she actually been in danger, would I have made it to her in time? Would I have earned her love and then lost her? The thought made me shudder.

"Are you okay?" Her voice pulling me again from my shadows.

"I'm," scared, lost, scattered and shattered with you, "okay."

She gave me a pensive glance, before she pushed off the rock and swam to the center of the pool. Droplets of water fell from her cloud of curls as she stared up at the sky. My love who was an observer of all the seasons that clung to her scent. The water fae danced around her legs, their varied colors glowing in the water. I swam toward her, my shadows skittering across the surface, drawn to her light like a moth to flames. I needed her, I realized. She was a balm to those cracks in my soul. I wrapped my arms around her, and her head fell back against my shoulder continuing her survey of the world.

"Do you think that time is strange?"

I leaned my head against her. "What do you mean, *mo grá?*"

"I mean do you think time is strange, the passage of time to be specific?"

"With you I do."

"How so?"

"With you, moments like this one seem to last forever. I think it's because I never want to leave them and then when these moments are over everything seems to happen so quickly, I feel like I've lost my footing."

"Hmm."

"Hmm? That's all you have to say?"

"I was just thinking the same thing." She twisted out of my arms and ran her hand over my chest. "I'm sorry for scaring you."

"It's okay. You are safe and ultimately that is all that matters to me."

"I wish we could stay here." She murmured softly.

"For now, we can. A few hours just you and me and the water."

"And then what?"

"We go home, prepare for all the things to come."

She pressed a kiss to my lips so soft and feather light. "Okay. And we'll face them together."

"Yes."

Chapter Forty-One

Saturday morning came too fast and Niratap was already out of bed when I woke. I stayed there thinking about the risks and dangers of tonight. Mitta was right. I wasn't prepared to be his bodyguard like I wanted to be and even with her going with us, I was uneasy. I wasn't sure I could be just a plaything. My cell phone chimed on the bedside table. Rolling over, Niratap's rainfall scent fluffing up from his pillow, I picked up the device to read the message from my mother.

Hey baby girl! I know it's not our chat day, but I wanted to know if you will come to visit me for Thanksgiving. We talked about it before you went to school, but I wanted to know so I could prepare. I love you.

I sighed. Moms for thanksgiving in less than two weeks. I stared at the ceiling, contemplating. I would have to ask Niratap. Visiting my mother made my stomach turn angrily, and I wouldn't want to go alone. I wondered if he would come with me. A gentle knock sounded from the door, and I slid into my robe.

"Come in."

Dorilody entered the room with a box in her hands. "The lord wanted me to dress you in your outfit tonight so you could get a feel for it and see if I needed to make any adjustments."

"Okay." I came around the bed to where she stood. "What did you find?"

"The lord had a vision for what he wanted, so I made the gown."

She took the lid off the box and a glittering swath of gold fabric that lay within. "You made this?"

She smiled, lifting the dress out of the box. "Yes. Are you comfortable with the role the lord wants you play?"

Her question threw me. "I understand it."

Her smile fell and something akin to disgust took its place. "A plaything. A cruel thing to be, not as completely unsavory as some things that the world denotes for those that are other."

"Dorilody." My voice a near whisper, gingerly placing my hand on hers.

"It was a long time ago, child." Her eyes glittered even as she smiled. "Come now off with the robe and let's get you dressed."

I pulled off the robe very conscious of the cellulite and rolls of my body. The glittery gold dress fell over my head. The main body of the gown was snug and accentuated the dip of my waist. The flowy gossamer skirts wrapped around my hips, the sides of the gown were split, connected to the back by fine gold chains. Dorilody adorned my arms with delicate chains that hung from the dress collar over my shoulders, bangles of gold at my wrists, three thin gold rings on my fingers, and two large gold hoops in my ears. She painted my eyes with gold and glossed my lips; I looked like a gem gilded in gold.

"No necklace?" I asked, taking in my adornments.

"You are still bound to the lord." She said with disgust plain on her face. "That will be the necklace that you wear."

"Why does that upset you, aren't you all bound to the lord?"

"No. We serve the lord out of gratitude for our freedom and his protection. You are the only soul bound to him with magic."

"Why me?"

"That is a question Allipo has hounded the lord about from the first day you came here."

"I'll have to ask him then?"

"Yes, though I don't know if the lord will openly tell you, his reasoning."

"Why do you say that?"

"Because when Allipo confronted him—" The door creaked open, and Nira entered the room. Dorilody bowed. "My Lord."

He stalked around me, appraising my outfit. He was dressed in a fine black suit with delicate gold pinstripes. The glint of topaz in his cufflinks caught the light. He stopped and smiled hungrily at me. "You have outdone yourself, Dorilody."

"Thank you, my Lord."

He snapped his fingers, and the familiar tang of magic filled my nose and the cool brush of the gold collar fell against my throat. He came close to me, pressing his body against mine. His hand captured my chin with gentleness and pulled my face up to look at him.

"You are very beautiful."

Heat filled my body under his stare. "Thank you."

His nostrils flared, but he stepped back. "We'll be leaving soon. You should eat."

"Okay, have you?"

"Yes, I was letting you rest, while everyone else berated me about tonight."

"Berated you about what exactly?"

He took my hand, Dorilody following after us as we exited the room. "Mostly about me taking you in this role. Others are concerned for our safety because I am not fully healed. Some are concerned that it is a trap. Mitta is angry that I'm not going in armed."

I stopped. "Why not?"

"I am weapon enough."

"Yes, but you're not healed completely, you should at least have some kind of small arms. A firearm."

He eyed me curiously. "I will be fine."

"No. You arm yourself. If not for yourself, do it for me, because I can't hide a single weapon dressed like this."

One eyebrow rose, but he submitted to my request. "Fine."

I caught Dorilody's eyes widen and then her face settled into a satisfied smile as she skirted past us and down the stairs. I wondered what had passed through her thoughts to cause such a shift.

In the foyer Mitta was talking with Allipo, who was tucking a gun into the waistband of his dress shorts. He had chosen to wear a dark plum ensemble today and seemed to have shined his horns. Mitta was dressed how I would assume an assassin would dress. Head to toe in form fitting black with straps and holsters all over her. From the bandolier of black knives at her chest, to the two pistols at her hips, she was dressed to kill.

"My Lord." Allipo bowed and Mitta gave a bow of her head. "We are ready when you are to head into the city."

"We'll leave within the hour, let Shasha eat some breakfast."

"Very well my Lord. Also, I called the craftsman when you informed me of the auction, and I put a rush in on this." Allipo presented Niratap with a canid skull mask. "I will say that it is some of Thaegan's best work. He said if you break this one, he'll charge you double for the next one."

The mask was similar in build to the one that I broke, but upon its surface there were whorls inlaid with a fine silver thread.

"Of course, he would. Send him my thanks."

"Of course."

"My Lord, have you thought about my request?" Mitta asked.

"With some convincing, Mitta, I will accept your demand of me." I elbowed him in the stomach as I walked towards the dining room, and his chuckle followed me through the door.

"Well don't you just look like a treasure." Durgash said as I came into the kitchen.

I smiled brightly. "Thank you, Durgash. Dorilody did a fantastic job."

"She always does." He smiled, stirring whatever he had bubbling on the stove. "What would you like for breakfast, my dear?"

"Fried eggs and toast will be fine. I can make it myself if you're busy."

"No, I can make it for you." He adjusted the temperature on the stove. "It will be my pleasure. Would you like some fruit, my dear?"

"That sounds lovely."

He ambled about the kitchen. "Are you prepared for tonight?"

"Yes. I'm nervous, but the lord will be with me and Mitta. I'm sure we'll be fine."

He flipped my eggs. "I know you will be fine, but you do realize what the lord is asking of you? To play the part of his plaything, an adornment of pleasure?"

That much I had been told. "Yes. I understand what he wants me to be." The subservient bed mate, compliant and only his.

Durgash gave me an evaluating gaze as he buttered my toast, "None of us are fond of this idea of his."

"That is what he told me. I accepted it because I want to know, I want to understand. I wasn't there very long, and yes, I am scared. I don't know how I'll react, but with him with me I can be strong."

Durgash smiled, as he slid my eggs onto a plate and handed it to me. "The lord is a lucky male indeed."

I took the plate, matching his smile. "I really think that I am the lucky one."

In the car, a tightness danced across my skin; both Mitta and Niratap watched out of their respective widows as we traveled through the woods. Hunting for the shadow that was hunting Nira. I took in his rigid posture and how his eyes ran back and forth over the horizon, shadows licking up at the collar of his shirt and cuffs.

"Have you gotten any closer to figuring out what it is?" I asked, trying to break the tension.

Nira's hand curled into a fist in his lap. "No, I haven't. Whatever this creature is, I haven't found anything."

"We'll figure this out, my Lord." Mitta said. "One way or another."

"And it needs to be sooner rather than later."

The tense silence settled and stayed as we entered the town. Grahamsville was similar to my hometown, with its quaint main street full of colonial houses that had been turned into businesses or made to look like them. Little cafes and boutiques lined the street. It was cute like home. We had just passed an intersection when I saw the sheriff's blue and white car pull behind us.

"This won't be pleasant." Mitta grumbled.

"He only wants to argue with me some more. It's a waste of both our time." Nira growled, donning the mask and pulling his shadows over his skin.

"Is he going to pull us over?" I asked, irritated. "We didn't do anything though."

"It doesn't matter." Mitta said as blue and red lights reflected through the windows as we exited the town proper. "He'd find a way to cause problems one way or another."

"But—"

Nira held up a hand as Allipo pulled to the shoulder.

"Apologies, my Lord."

"It's not your fault, Allipo. Rodger just wants to bust my balls." No sooner had the words left his mouth, the sheriff knocked on his window. Niratap took a breath before he lowered the window. "Rodger."

"Where are you off to, beast?"

"Mind your tongue, sheriff." Mitta snarled.

"Mitta." Niratap's voice held a firm command.

"Apologies, my Lord." Mitta shifted in her seat, and I knew it was an act.

"Where are you going, beast? I won't ask again." The sheriff's stony face leering into the cabin at us. His eyes lingering on me for an uncomfortable amount of time. Niratap marked the stare his knuckles popping as he clenched his fist. "Interesting to see you are still with this monster."

"He is more of a man than you'll ever be." The words are out of my mouth before my thoughts can solidify.

"Playing the devil's toy, girl?"

I looked at Niratap. He bobbed his head, placing the ball in my court.

"Sheriff much like last time, I am perfectly content with where I am. The lord has been nothing but kind to me in the time I have been with him. However, I find your disrespect of him atrocious and tiresome."

The sheriff's eyebrows rose but addressed Niratap. "Well?"

"My comings and goings from my own home are none of your concern, sheriff."

"The safety of the community is my concern."

"And if you recall, Rodger, my household comes down the mountain and patrons this community."

"What have you brought to the mountains that's killing the cattle and deer?"

"I assure you if I knew what was killing the deer and cattle it would be dealt with by now. I'm looking into the issue, but we both know that this is a waste of both of our time. So, if you would let us be on our way, we have an appointment in the city."

"Planning on selling that scantily clad young lady?"

"I am not for sale." I placed my hand on Nira's thigh dangerously close to his groin and leaned, giving the sheriff a good view of my outfit. Nira graciously followed my lead and wrapped an arm around me, his fingers dancing across my skin. I poured honey into my voice. "I only belong to Lord Niratap, and I will not allow a smaller man the joy of our time. You have become tedious, sheriff."

Rodger's face turned a bright shade of red. "I'm going to figure out what monstrosity you are Niratap, and when I do mark my words, I will hunt you down and find justice."

A predatory growl reverberated through the cab. "Is that a threat, sheriff?"

The sheriff was wise enough to back away from the window. "Don't bring any beasts home."

"Mind your business, Rodger; you'll live longer that way." With that Nira rolled up his window, ignoring the glare the sheriff shot him in response.

Allipo chuckled in the front. "Those are some blades you have for a tongue, sweet flower."

Mitta smiled over her scrunched nose. "She called him what he is: a lesser man who is tedious. Allipo, I'm going to come up there before we take off."

"Be my guest."

"Why are you going up front?"

"Because even though I care deeply for both of you, I'm not going to sit in his scent for two hours."

Nira growled, but shifted in the seat, in male discomfort. "I can't help that she makes me feel this way."

"Yes." Mitta said, sliding out the door, "However, there is a time and place for those kinds of things, and if you hadn't dressed her as a toy, maybe you would have better control of your instincts."

Allipo rolled up the privacy screen as Mitta shut the door, chuckling between themselves. I stroked his thigh, feeling him tense beneath me.

"So, my Lord." I brought the honey back into my voice. "Do you desire me?"

Shadows exploded covering the windows and encasing us in endless night. I stared at the glowing stars that were his eyes in that shroud of darkness, unfaltering under their blazing intensity. He laid me down across the seat his claws delicately tracing over the cutouts of my dress.

"Remind me when we come home." His voice guttural. "To thank Dorilody profoundly for this dress."

My heart skipped a beat as he looms over me. "Noted, however my love be careful with it, it has to survive the night."

A growl shuddered through my chest. "Pity."

He leaned against my throat, licking my pulse. I arched beneath him, letting my legs fall open, another growl as my body rubbed against his.

"To answer your question, *mo grá*. Yes, I desire you. Every part of my life has desire for you threaded through it. When I am away, I think of you. When I am lying next to you, I hunger for you. When I dream, I dream of you and your scent fills my nose and I want to be buried inside you."

I felt my body flush, his warm, rain-filled scent filling my nose. "You make such promises."

He coughed a chuckle. "Oh, it's a threat, my dear. Right now, I will be gentle with you but when we get home—"

I kissed him sweetly. "I expect to be ravaged."

His answering growl was all I needed as my hands found the button of his pants. Releasing him into my hand I stroked him; the sounds that escaped his throat caused me to go molten with need. His hands gathered my skirts around my hips quickly, but with the lightest of touch as he exposes me to him. He whispered in my ear as he thrust into my hand.

"You are my light. The air in my lungs. The water of my blood. The fire in my soul. The earth of my bones. The desperation in my all-consuming desire. You have power over me, that I will give no other."

"Prove it. Make love to me that fulfills all those things."

"With pleasure, *mo grá*."

He pulled free of my hand and thrust into me. The feel of him filling me was a blessing that made stars dance in my vision. He was gentle and soft as he kissed me, his hands shook as he traced the lines of my body beneath his. He slid an arm under me and pulled me to his chest before he sat up and I sank down upon him, shattering completely in his arms with his name upon my lips. He shook with his release, filling me with his essence.

"You are a gift to me, *mo grá*." He murmurs against my neck.

"No. You were the gift, Niratap."

He chuckled, "How so?"

I wrapped my arms around him, pulling the mask away as the shadows melted from around us. His face was so breathtaking, scars and all. I let my hands trail over his defined features, committing them to memory like I always wanted. He smiled at me, and my heart twisted at the sight. I thought about all the places I could have ended up because of my foolishness. All the terrible things that would have happened had he not been at the market that night. Those were the thoughts that kept me from sleep, even when I was safely tucked next to him. I never wanted to lose him.

"How am I a gift, my flower?"

"Not so much a gift as you are my everything. My savior. My heart. My home."

Something flashed through his molten eyes. Is it shock or maybe awe? I wanted to dive into that look and find what part of what I had said caused it, but words didn't exist between us then. Just our bodies thrumming with release, still connected to one another. Just our breath tangling between our mouths with the weight of all the things we both wished to say but were holding back. Just our souls softly pressing against one another.

He pressed his forehead to mine, "*Conas ata tu chomh foirfe?*[31] You are my gift. Sometimes I ponder if you are my salvation after all life has hurt me with. I want that, you for eternity."

"You have me as long as you wish."

"Forever is not long enough."

"I'll take what I can get."

He chuckled and pressed a kiss to my cheek. "You smell like me."

---

[31] How are you so perfect?

"All the better." I said, sliding from his lap. "Lest the beasts of the market forget who I belong to."

New York City was just like it was the first time I had been here. The hustle and bustle of people running about catching my eyes from food cart vendors to people frantically hailing cabs on the sidewalk. Nira had pulled the mask and shadows back into place as we had entered the city, the tenderness of the time we had spent wrapped around one another fading as the deep anxiety of what we were doing here settled. I stood, rolling the privacy window down.

"Gah." Mitta groaned. "Do you have to open the window? It smells like a barn back there."

"I would say that the smell of sweat and sex is a familiar scent. Reminds me of my childhood." Allipo said smiling.

"The debauchery of satyrs." Mitta groaned.

Nira chuckled from behind me as I asked. "Where are we going?"

"We are heading to The Langham hotel."

"A hotel? Isn't that conspicuous?"

"The benefactor of this auction." Niratap said as he watched out the window. "Is an eccentric trillionaire that enjoys rubbing elbows with the seedy underbelly of society. He books the Langham out completely."

"Isn't he afraid of—" I ran my finger across my throat.

"No, the bonus of being financially available to the underground means that he is safe from the wrath of said players. Enough of them are in his pockets that anyone taking him out would cause an all-out war. Which is something everyone in the underground would like to avoid."

"Why is that? I would think knocking off a couple of your enemies in a war would be advantageous."

"That it may be." Allipo said. "But all-out war in the underground would be fraught with casualties. The people in power stay that way because they know how to manage risk."

"Now when we get to the hotel, Shasha dear." Niratap said, I turned to face him, the silver eyes that gazed at me were pinched with worry and guilt. "You will have to be silent, obedient. No asking questions. Do not stare, don't even make eye contact. Once we are seated, I will tell you who is there and what I know. Knowledge is how you survive in the underground."

"So were laying out rules."

"Yes." He looked out the window.

"So, rule one stay silent. Rule two no questions. Rule three no staring. What else?"

Niratap didn't speak, just stared out the window.

"My Lord." Mitta called from the front seat.

Niratap sighed. "Apologies. What I am asking you to do doesn't sit well, but it is the easiest and safest way for us to be at this auction. For a chance—"

"At freeing one of your own."

He sighed again. "For the possibility of finding one of my own, but I don't treat people, how I am going to have to treat you tonight."

"And how will you treat me?"

"Like a possession. I will not ask you to do things. I will demand. If you hesitate, I will have to force you to act. I you make a mistake. I will have to punish you. I do not treat people this way and it doesn't sit well with me."

"It took you this long to realize that it wouldn't sit right." Mitta scoffed from the front seat.

"It hasn't sat well from when I suggested it, the danger of this is—"

"Frightening." I offered.

He finally looked at me. "Yes."

"We're coming up on the hotel, my Lord."

"Thank you, Allipo." He lifted his hand, and the fine gold chain branched the space between us. With a gentle tug he brought me to him. "I need you to listen explicitly to me tonight. Do not acknowledge anyone else. Keep your head down."

"Okay."

He swallowed. "They may touch you, examine you, appraise your worth, and you must stand there and let them."

It clicked then; he was speaking from experience. Hard lived experience. "Yes, my Lord."

"When we get sat at the table, you will sit in my lap, and you will listen to my every breath because it may be the only thing that keeps you alive."

"I understand."

We pulled into the hotel parking lot, the car falling deathly silent, as Allipo gave over a card, and we proceeded into the darkness of the garage. We parked on the second level down and when Allipo and Mitta exited the car Niratap pressed me against him.

"Regardless of what happens tonight, regardless of what I say or do, know that I love you, and I will not let any harm come to you."

"I understand, *mo grá*. I love you."

"I love you." He kissed my forehead then opened the door.

In the hotel we were greeted warmly by the hotel staff and servers wandering between small groups of people. Out of the corner of my eye, I saw in the small groups only one or two people holding flutes of champagne. A hostess greeted Niratap warmly and led us through the dining room that had tables and chairs draped with fine white tablecloths. We stopped and the hostess handed Niratap a glass of champagne and only him. We stood there in front of our table and Niratap scanned the room eyes hunting and searching.

I dared a look through my lashes, taking in the faces of humans and creatures alike, all dangerous unknowns to me. I never wanted a dagger more than I did now. Never felt fear like I did now. Niratap shifted a half step in front of me, my fear must have permeated my scent. Niratap wagged his fingers at me, to get my attention.

"Look at me, pet." His voice was quiet, but full of demand. I looked up at him cautiously, my eyes meeting his over his shoulder. "Only at me."

I didn't nod. Didn't speak. The danger of it all hit me, and I wanted to cry. I felt myself tear up.

"Breathe." He commanded.

I took a shuddering breath.

"Again."

This time it was smoother.

"Again. Settle."

His eyes softened as my third breath was easy and calm. He turned back to the room, watching the vastness of enemies and allies.

"I see more enemies than allies, my Lord." Allipo said quietly.

"Agreed. V is here with his team, too." Niratap said, tilting his head to Ventris across the room. I found him past a group of elves, those electric blue eyes locked on me with a look of disgust on his face.

"Do you think he will come and speak with you?" Mitta asked, taking in another group chatting to one side. "He looks mighty pissed for an undercover agent."

Niratap sighed. "Let's hope not."

"Seager is coming this way." Allipo said, straightening next to him.

"Great." Nira groaned, pulling me directly behind his back.

"Lord Niratap." A young, jovial sounding man, who looked around my age approached. "I was hoping to see you here." I peered around Nira's arm. The man had shoulder length black hair that sliced through the air around his pale neck, he was dressed in a plain black suit. He had his arms folded behind his back. I would have thought he was human except for the red color of his eyes.

"Seager." Nira bobbed his head in response. "Why were you hoping I would be here?"

The jovial young man smiled viciously. "Aaron said that you caused quite a ruckus in August at Nocturnal. Paid way over market for a plaything that smelled like heaven. I wanted to confirm his tales myself, but I can smell the delectable creature." He bent at the waist to peer at me behind Nira, the motion was almost childish. Those red eyes, the color of fresh blood, took me in, I couldn't look away from his gaze, he smiled that viscous smile again and that was when I saw them. Twin sets of fangs crowded his mouth. Vampyre. "Did you bring her just to warm your lap or is she to share."

"Aaron was correct, and she is just for my lap I suppose. She was very expensive."

"I can see why she caused quite a stir in the market. With that scent any creature with moderate sense of smell would be starved." Seager stepped back appraising my body. "She is easy on the eyes. Do you make her beg?"

"She begs enough for me that I don't have to force it."

"I wonder what her blood tastes like?" He mused while staring at me.

"And you can keep wondering, Seager."

"Oh, come now, friends, a taste won't hurt her." He reached a long-fingered hand in my direction.

Niratap snatched his hand with a snarl. "I already said I'm not sharing, Seager. Take the warning, and you will live another long lifetime."

"Unhand me."

"Leave what is mine alone." There is a lethal edge to his voice.

"Understood." The vampyre looked at me again as Niratap released him. "She may look like a rabbit, Niratap, but she is a wolf hiding in the rabbit's skin. Be careful with that one."

Nira growled, but Seager was already slinking away when the voice full of fake warmth reached my ears. "Well, well, well, Lord Niratap Bondbreaker." Dravin crooned. "At least one rumor is true, there is a bitarog at the auction tonight."

Nira huffed a breath. "Fat Cat."

The man was in front of me before Nira could turn, he grabbed my face roughly and examined it then my outfit. "She is quite the beauty. Shame someone bought her."

I felt the air go staticky as Niratap turned to face Dravin fully. "Yes, it's a shame."

My jaw was going to bruise with the force of his hold. I hissed. "Sucks for you."

Dravin glowered at me. "Seems you need to train your toy better. Maybe a muzzle. What do you think, wife?"

"A muzzle would suit that one." The matron said from behind her husband, giving me the side eye before she gave Niratap a critical evaluation, running a hand down his chest, "I would love to see you muzzled, Bondbreaker."

I bristled, but Mitta was at his side in a half a breath, the point of her blade pressed against the matron's throat. "Back off."

The woman to her credit didn't flinch even as the rivulet of blood trickled down her skin. A hush fell over the room, and Dravin broke it by saying. "Call off your beast, Niratap."

His eyes narrowed. "Call off your whore."

Dravin released my face. "Christiana, enough. They're not worth it."

Mitta tracked her as she moved back to her husband's side. "Mitta."

Mitta eased her position but did not sheath her dagger. Dravin offered his wife a handkerchief before speaking. "You are floating dangerous waters, Bondbreaker."

"Don't threaten me, Dravin."

"It's not a threat. You do realize the sea in which you stand. Dark waters for you."

Through the speakers in the room, a man cleared his throat. "May I have your attention, my friends." On a stage at the back of the room a tall, lean, blonde man, with sweeping horns that pierced the air above him stood in his periwinkle blue suit. He was handsome and his voice tickled the back of my mind.

"Now, I know we can play nicely with each other." The man said pointedly at where we stood. "I am your master of ceremonies tonight, and it is my pleasure to open this gathering of darkness. Now if you would please find your seats, meals will be brought to your tables. I am a generous man, so your entourages will also be fed, toys and all. After food is served the floor will open for the first items on the docket for today."

"Watch your back, Bondbreaker." Dravin said, passing Niratap. "You may find a knife in it."

"You don't scare me, Dravin."

"Well, that is where you are naive." He and his wife left us at our table.

"Disgusting." Mitta growled as Nira sat at the table. He tugged me roughly to him and I fell onto my knees between his legs. Pain barked up my legs causing tears to sting my eyes. I knew it was for show, a show for all eyes watching him, trying to find a weakness, something to exploit. I kept my head down, waiting for him to address me, I would not be that weakness. I braced my hands on his thighs.

In a death's quiet voice. "What happened to staying silent?"

I said nothing, waiting. Knowing his words were not for me but for the others.

He rolled his shoulders, neck cracking. "You are an embarrassment."

Allipo and Mitta took their seats on either side, and Nira's hand threaded through my hair, pulling my head back to look at him. His eyes were hard, but pleading. Begging for forgiveness.

"You will have to earn your meal. Do you understand?"

I kept my voice soft. "Yes."

"Yes, what?" Pain flickered through his eyes, and I knew what we needed. What would make this believable.

"Yes, master." Mitta looks away and Allipo flinches from the words.

"Tonight, you will prove to me your worth. Now sit pet."

I rose, knees aching, and crawled into his lap. Blood welled on one of them, rolling down the outside of my calf. He pressed me against him, his body a wall of stone behind me. He rested his head against mine, his teeth grazing my ear even with all the eyes watching us. Seeing if I was the key to capturing a legend on the market. His hands skirted over my hips and across my thighs, my body responded to his touch, heat dancing across my skin. Mitta shifted in discomfort as the scent of arousal danced around us. Chatter grew back up as the servers flitted about the room dropping off trays of food.

"I'm sorry." He said in a whisper that I could barely hear, his hand traveling to my injured knee.

I squeezed his arm in response. A toy, I had to remember that right now, I was a toy. Not his girlfriend. Not a fighter. A toy.

"Across the way, the man in the atrocious yellow suit." My eyes went to where he spoke, his lips grazed my pulse. "That is Theador White; he runs a drug trading ring that specializes in hallucinogens. Mainly acid, but he also deals with fairy dust. The next table over is Omar Causta; he is also a drug dealer dealing in Devil's Breath, enslaves lesser fae to cook for him. Darkath and Kharis Pageiros, the elves by the stage; bounty hunters that capture rare beasts, but they like to collect them as well. The man on stage, Voxviraz Penn, an incubus who slept his way into power, now runs a fortune five hundred company and is the eccentric trillionaire."

A dozen more names, faces, proclivities from a whore trader to monster breeder to an assassin. I tried to file away all the information he purred into my ears in his soft honey voice. His hands traveled over my exposed skin, across my stomach and over my chest. No one paid us much attention, casting glances our way only when discussion of us rounded their table. When meals had been dealt to all the tables, a finely spiced chicken dish that I didn't dare touch, Voxviraz purred through the microphone to begin the auction. Drugs. Women. Harpy feather knives. Venoms. A dybbuk box. Guns. Servants. Whores. Dragon scales. The lots went on and on like that for what felt like forever, then a brilliant white blade made of bones was purchased.

"That is all, my friends." Voxviraz announced. Outrage echoed about the room.

"Things are about to get dangerous, my Lord." Allipo said.

"Go grab the car; we'll make an exit soon."

"Understood."

Shouts rang from the tables about the big-ticket item. Where is it? We were promised a bitarog for purchase. The screams of protest overlapping one another, demanding answers.

Voxviraz was a bit shaken as a sea of armed underground bosses and their cronies crept to the stage. "My friends, the bitarog female that was to be the big ticket was purchased this morning, by a private buyer."

More cries about the promise of a bitarog for purchase. Voxviraz glanced at our table, and I knew. "He's going to sell us out."

"Time to go." Niratap stood scooping me into his arms.

"This was a set up from the beginning." Mitta hissed.

We were halfway to the door when Voxviraz spoke, finally making his decision, "Where are you off to, Bondbreaker?"

The room fell silent as all eyes fell upon us.

Niratap didn't turn to face the room. "My business is done."

"Oh, I think it has only just begun."

Niratap peered at Voxviraz over his shoulder. I heard knives being unsheathed; guns being cocked. "You are mistaken."

I felt the shadows, as they exploded around us. Blocking us from bullets and I heard the screams as the underground panicked. Niratap shuddered a breath; I felt him stagger before we fled.

Allipo had already pulled the car up to the front. Shots rang behind us, a bullet whizzed past my head, shattering a window. Mitta flung the door open to the car and returned fire, covering Nira as he dove onto the floor of the car with me in his arms.

"Go, Allipo," Mitta roared as she dove onto the seat and slammed the door. Allipo peeled away from the curb and Mitta watched out the window as we disappeared into the night. "This was a trap from the beginning. Dravin intentionally put a target on your back. You took his bait. We could have gotten killed because of a rumor."

Nira's heart was pounding, his breathing shallow and when he spoke his voice was thin. "I am sorry, Mitta."

"You better be sorry! You took us in there to become prey because you were foolishly chasing after finding more of your kind."

He was shaking, pulling me closer to his chest. "I'm sorry."

"I can't believe—"

"Are you hit?" I asked him. Mitta turned to us, sprawled across the floor.

A heavy breath. "No."

I reached up my palm finding his cheek, his skin was clammy with a sheen of sweat. At my touch the shadows slid from his body. His breaths were slow.

"What's wrong?" Mitta was at our side, the mask sliding from his face. He was pale and sweat dampened his forehead, his eyes unseeing.

A few shaky breaths later he swallowed. "I pushed too hard, expended too much with that shield. My reserves are low."

"Damn it." Mitta snarled, turning to the opposite side. "You should know better than that."

"It was instinct." He said, trying to sit up. "If I was fully recovered that would have been nothing."

"Shasha, lay him back before he strokes out on us." Mitta growled, rummaging through the first aid kit. I started in his arms.

"Can that happen?"

"No." he said weakly, but he eased his hold on me so I could sit beside him and he laid flat on the floor. "But it is likely that I'll pass out."

Mitta came to his side. "Chills, sweats, tremors. Anything else?"

"It hurts to breathe."

"Got it." She pulled a pen-like object out of the first aid kit and kept digging. "Shasha, will you get his pants off?"

"Yeah, what's happening to him?"

"It was one of the things I was worried about. He hasn't fully recovered from the basilisk attack and that cloak of shadow overtaxed his capability."

"What does that mean?"

"Magic wielders can draw magic power one of two ways, either from physical stores of energy in their body or from outside stores of energy in nature." Allipo said from the front as I slid Nira's pants down his legs. "The lord pulls from internal sources of magic. Not being fully healed has depleted those stores of energy, probably because his body has been using that magic to heal, since rapid healing is one of his race's natural magical attributes. The cloak he used to get you out was more than what his stores had, and when that happens, the body uses other forms of energy."

"Like hormones or nutrients in the body." Mitta said, pulling a glucose meter out of the first aid kit much like the one my mother used occasionally. "Which can throw the user into attacks. I'm going to give you some epinephrine then test your blood sugar, okay?"

Nira gave a weak nod. Mitta slammed the epi injector into his leg. The force makes me cringe, but Niratap barley flinched.

"Hey." She snapped her fingers in front of his face. "Niratap. I need you to stay conscious, okay?"

"I know, trying." His voice took me back to the cold shower floor.

She pricked his finger and squeezed until blood welled up on the pad. The meter beeps and she frowned, grabbing two little pouches and opening them.

"Open your mouth," she squirted the liquid in his mouth, "Swallow."

"His blood sugar is low?"

"Yes, it's hanging around fifty. The glucose gel will help that rise, but it will take time."

His eyes were heavy. "I hate this."

"Play dumb games, win dumb prizes." Mitta snapped, as she shifted, helping me pull his pants back up over his legs. He offered a small chuckle.

"We'll be out of the city soon." Allipo said.

"Good, I hate this place." Mitta said, moving to sit in the seat.

"Why?" I asked, wiping the hair stuck to Nira's face away.

"Enemies at every turn and beings just trying to one up each other constantly, like history never taught them anything."

"I wonder if V's team made any arrests." Allipo mused.

"I'm sure he's going to call before the night is over." Nira said, shivering.

"Are you cold?" I asked him.

"Just chilled, I'll be okay." I look at Mitta.

"It's just a natural reaction to low blood sugar and adrenaline. He will be fine, but there's a blanket in that compartment under the seat behind you." Mitta said gently, her ire running out.

I turned to retrieve the blanket, covering him with it. "Thank you."

"Your color is starting to come back."

"Well, at least I'll live." He grunted, halfheartedly.

"We got lucky." Mitta grumbled staring out the window. "Self-sacrificing bullshit."

"There's no cure for that, Mitta." Allipo said from up front.

She laid down across the seat. "I've tried to cure that too."

Nira chuckled, turning his head slightly to look at her. "The girls would be displeased if you hadn't."

"Rest, you oaf. Like I am, because caring for you and you alone is a full-time fucking job, with way to much overtime."

"At least I pay you well."

She huffed and draped an arm over her eyes. "Well, there is that."

He smiled rolling to his side to curl around me. "I'm sorry."

"You don't have to apologize to me." I said brushing stray hair behind his fine pointed ear.

"No." He murmurs. "I put a target on us defending you from Seager and Dravin."

I traced the lines of his handsome face. "And I should have kept my mouth shut."

Mitta puffed, rolling over into the seat. "Just please refrain from make-up fucking while I'm back here."

His eyes opened, glancing up at me with a crooked smile coming to his features. "She's abrasive don't you think?"

"And you're stupid my friend." was her muffled reply.

Allipo chuckled. "Will you catty people just calm down and sleep? I'll get us home safe."

Mitta flung him an abrasive gesture through the window. I laughed, then curled against Nira on the floor, his arm wrapping around me, tucking me under the blanket with him.

"You can lay on the seat, my dear."

"And miss out on monster cuddles? No way."

He laughed sleepily, pulling me against his chest, our legs tangled together. Soft rain danced in my nose, and it took me to swaying meadow grass and a bed of pine needles. My slice of peace when everything wasn't peaceful. I pressed my nose against his throat and inhaled the balmy memory. I wanted to show him that slice of peace, wanted to lay with him in the pine needles and watch clouds roll by. I wanted to take him in the sweet grass that I went to for solace.

I inhaled his scent again, taking in the warm damp stone and finding that feeling again. The centering strength to keep going. The deep-seated sense of safety. Home. He felt like home. He was home for me and my heart. Home.

"Nira."

"Hmm."

"I have a request."

"Ask away, my love." He shifted to look at my face.

I bit my lip. "My mother wants me to visit for Thanksgiving."

He blinks. "Do you wish to go?"

I looked down. "Yes and no."

He pulled me to him. "Why do you want to go?"

"I—I miss her, and I want to make sure she is okay."

"But?" He knew me too well.

"But." I said, snuggling into his chest. His heart beat had returned to normal. "I don't want to get trapped there. I love her, but—"

"She loves you too hard." It was the truth. The cold hard truth, that my mother loved me too hard.

"Yes."

He kissed the top of my head. "You are allowed to see your mother, if that is something you want."

"I do, but—"

"What, *mo grá*?"

I kissed the line of his jaw. "Would you come with me?"

"To your mother's house for thanksgiving?"

"Yes, if you want to."

"Your mother won't take kindly to me."

"I know."

"She will probably say things about me."

"Probably."

"And mean them."

"Affirmative."

"You sure you're up for that?"

"With you I am up for anything."

"Then my heart I will brave a holiday with your mother."

"You're probably going to regret that."

"With you I can withstand anything."

Chapter Forty-Two

Standing in the driveway of the dull yellow house with the green metal roof made me wish I hadn't agreed to this, that I hadn't asked Niratap to come with me.

"Yes, Allipo, we'll be fine. No, I will not scratch the paint. Yes, I will call you when we're coming home." Niratap growled into the phone, grabbing bags out of the car. "No, we were not followed. Tell Mitta to relax. Afton is the last place anyone would look for me. I have my firearm. We will alert you to anything if something happens."

"You know." I suggested. "We can, you know, just go home now."

He gave me a searing look as he hung up. "I will remind you that you already accepted your mother's invitation to dinner and to stay for a couple of days."

"I know but—"

"You didn't tell her you were bringing me, did you?" He frowned.

I sighed. "No, I didn't."

"Given what you have told me, your mother will not be impressed. One because you brought the man who purchased you on the black market, two that we are now a couple and three because I am not human. Not to mention the age difference there. Why did you not tell her you were bringing me with you?"

"I panicked, okay!" I covered my face with my hands and leaned against the car. "She's so demanding when it comes to literally everything. I figured that if I agreed, it would pacify her, but coming alone was never an option for me. She would hold me hostage in the little town and I—I don't want to be trapped here. I wanted to try and bridge the gap, have her meet you and see that you're different."

"Different than what, Shasha?" His voice was tight. "Than other men? Because I'm not. I bedded you as soon as I got the chance against my better judgment. And yes, though I love you and want the world for you, it does not mean that I am different."

"I'm sorry. You don't have to stay with me if you don't want to?"

He cupped my face with his free hand. "No, I'm here with you and I am staying. Your mother will not appreciate my presence, especially unannounced."

"I know, I just thought with you here I could leave."

He pressed a kiss to my forehead. "I understand. Are you telling her the whole story?"

"I mean I kind of have too. I can't lie to her face. She has a sixth sense for it. I will probably leave out what you are and your age, because my mother is very opinionated about things. Are you sure you're okay showing your face?"

His eyebrows raise. "She has a sixth sense for lies right?"

Smiling, I kissed him. "Are you ready?"

"Are you?" He asked, offering his hand.

I took it. "With you I am."

Together we walked up the steps of my childhood home, steps that felt different with him beside me. He ducked under the awning as we approached the door.

"Your poor neck."

He leaned in and knocked. "It's fine. You are worth it."

"I'm coming." My mother called beyond the door.

I took a breath as the lock clicked and the door swung open. "Shasha?"

"Hi, mama." I waved sheepishly, letting go of Nira's hand.

"Oh, baby girl." She wrapped me in a tight hug, then held me out at arm's length. "Oh, let me look at you. Have you been eating enough? You're looking slim."

"Yes, mama I'm eating plenty, I've been working out and doing some fight training, kickboxing and the like."

"Fight training? What for?"

"Mainly as a precaution, but I'm enjoying it. Self-defense, small arms."

"It's not interfering with your classes at all is it?"

"No, mama. Professor Vrorlin said if I stick with it, he'll use it as my Phys. Ed. credits. So, it's a win-win."

She smiled, but it didn't touch her eyes. "Okay. Who is this, baby girl, you didn't tell me you were bringing anyone with you."

"It is a pleasure to meet you, ma'am." He bowed deeply then offered his hand. "I am Lord Niratap Bondbreaker."

"You're that lord that has been holding my daughter against her will." Realization coming to her. She shrieked as she pulls me against her. "Who—who purchased her. What kind of vile things have you done to my precious baby?"

I pushed out of her hold and came to stand in front of him. "Mama, that's rude. I plan on telling you the whole story, but you will not disrespect him. I swear I will turn around and leave right now if you do."

"Shasha. This—" She gave Nira a once over. "Creature, purchased you and has been holding you hostage, keeping you from me."

"No, mama he's been keeping me safe and not against my will."

"Safe?" She shrieked. "Shasha, I can't even with you. Who in their right mind would hold you against your will to keep you safe."

I was about to lose my cool. "Mom. This man saved my life multiple times at this point. He has given me amazing opportunities because of his status and kindness. He has treated me with respect and care, even at my worst. Mom, if you're not going to calm down and be kind to my boyfriend, we'll just go."

My mother's brows rose. "Your what?"

"You heard me." I fisted my hands at my side. "Niratap is my boyfriend, and I won't stand for you being cruel to him."

"Shasha Dion, never in all my days would I allow you to date a man, let alone a monster!"

Niratap cleared his throat. I looked up at him, his face was flat, unreadable as he spoke, "Ma'am. You do not have to like me, and to be fair you are correct in the assumption that I am in fact, a monster. I mean no disrespect. However, I will not listen to you berate your daughter over her decisions. She is an adult and fully capable of making those decisions for herself. Now if we may go inside so she can tell you the events leading up to this point, because she wants to be honest with you."

My mom blinked several times before she looked at me. "O—okay."

I grabbed his hand and followed behind my mom. "This will be okay."

"Of that, I'm not worried." He said, ducking through the door.

Through the door was the living room. It was spacious and comfortable with its dull yellow paint, but the ceilings were not nearly high enough for Niratap, who held himself hunched, bent at the waist so as to not scratch the ceiling with his antlers. To one side was the coat closet and the door to the garage; the other had the stairs to the second floor and the doorway to the sunroom and the kitchen. Beyond the living room was the dining room where a simple table that had four simple chairs sat off the kitchen. After shrugging out of his winter coat and taking mine to hang on the coat rack Niratap went to the stairs. He set our bags on the floor and stood to his full height in the alcove. Mom looked between us and scurried into the dining room, grabbing two of the chairs and setting them in front of Niratap. She sat awkwardly, trying not to stare.

"Did you want a chair?" I asked Niratap.

"No, I'll stand for now, it is quite a long drive from the manor. It feels good to stretch my legs."

"If, you're sure."

"I am, *mo grá.*"

"I—I don't want to be rude." My mother started. "But how tall are you?"

Nira gave her a pleasant smile as I took my seat. "I am eight-foot four heel to crown; the antlers make it ten."

"My heavens." She held her hand to her mouth. "How do you find clothes?"

He chuckled. "I have a very fine tailor."

"Do you only wear suits?" She asked, staring at the burgundy suit he had chosen to wear to meet her. He had paired it with a black silk shirt, tie, and loafers, he was sharp with his hair done back in a low braid.

"No, I have some casual clothes as well, also made by my tailor. I do tend to dress more professionally in my day to day though. Antlers make t-shirts a bit of a struggle."

"I can only imagine." My mom genuinely smiled at him.

I cleared my throat. "So, mom, are you ready?"

She cast a glance between us. "Well, I'm already sitting down. How bad can this story be?"

"It's not a great story." I told her. "I made mistakes that cost me. I'm not going to lie to you and tell you that everything was fine and dandy. I have been in some very scary situations that lead to where we are now. I want to get through the whole story, then answer questions, is that okay?"

"I think I can do that."

"Okay. The week before school started there was a summer rain in the city—"

And just like that I told her everything. I told about my capture in all its facets, she cried, but didn't speak. I told her about the natural draw between the two of us that started with scent then hearts. I told her of the terrifying parts. How one fight led to the basilisk attack, the fear of losing someone that made me feel whole, that we weren't just a happy couple, that I wasn't suffering from Stockholm syndrome. I told her about each of my friends that I had made, even the orc who had hurt me who was just playing a part in a bigger plan, of training to be stronger not only to protect him but also myself. I told her of shared kisses, shared meals, shared stories, shared bodies and when I was done, I looked down at my hands which were shaking.

"Do you have any questions?"

"So, you have experienced all this in the three months you have been away from home?"

"Yes, ma'am."

"Niratap." She began. "I want to thank you for being there, for saving my daughter from being sold as a sex slave, and then asking nothing of her."

I looked up at her, she had streaks of tears rolling down her face. "Mama?"

"You were there for her, you kept her safe and at great cost to yourself. I want to know why, after saving her from that place, you kept her?"

Nira had shifted to leaning against the banister and he considered. "Initially I just wanted to keep her scent near me. The beastly part of me was drawn to it like a moth to a flame. Against the much better judgment that I have made in the past I wanted to know why in my soul. In the beginning it was nothing but that. Now it is because I love her, in all her beautifully frustrating facets. In hindsight, it was probably wise of me to keep her, knowing how Dravin Cirano is. He would have gone after her if she wasn't with me. I'm sorry that her subsequent disappearance and concealment of the truth until now has caused you distress, but it was for both your safety and hers. She is well cared for. She is loved immensely by both me and my family."

She nodded thinking over the dump of information that she had given. "I guess, well I will have to process all this. Is pizza acceptable for dinner tonight?"

I smiled. "Pizza, will be fine mom."

"Okay, I'll run and grab a couple pies." She said standing. "Get settled."

"Okay, mom."

"You remember where—"

"The extra blankets and pillows are in the linen closet; towels are in the cupboard by the bathroom."

She smiled kissing my cheek. "Pepperoni and pineapple?"

"Is there any other way to have pizza mom?" I asked, Niratap chuckled.

"Do you have a preference?" she asked him.

"No, ma'am."

"Alright. I'll be back in a little bit. You didn't park behind the garage, did you?"

"No, I was told to park in the driveway closer to the grass, just in case." Nira smiled at me.

She kissed my cheek again, "Okay."

Mom left, her little old 2002 Honda Accord whining down the road into the main part of town. "Well, that could have been worse."

He smiled as he bent to pick up our bags. "We'll see. Show the way?"

"Of course." I said starting up the stairs. "Please don't judge me."

"*Mo grá*, have I ever?"

"No, but this is my childhood bedroom, and it hasn't changed a whole lot in my life."

"A deeper peek into your youth."

"It really isn't that interesting."

"I beg to differ." He said, catching my hand at the top of the stairs and kissing it. "Anything about you, I find interesting."

"How is that?"

"What?" He asked, ducking his head.

"That the big scary Bondbreaker is such a cheeseball."

He laughed a deep, happy sound. "Only for you, my darling. I thought you found the cheese endearing."

"I do." I stopped before my door, my name still spelled out in gold letters. "I just find it funny that one of the most feared players in the black market is pro-cheese."

He planted his hands on either side of my head, his breath hot in my ear. "I would call myself a romantic, but I can prove otherwise."

"Nira we can't."

"I like when you defend me, it makes me want to taste you." He runs his tongue over the nape of my neck.

My knees felt weak, and it took all I had not to lean into him or the door. "You make being good hard."

"That is fine with me; I don't want you to be good."

My heart fluttered, a trapped bird between him and the door. "What do you want?"

"You spread wide open for me."

"We can't—"

"Why not? It's just you and me. Thirty minutes is more than enough time for me to enjoy you."

"But it's not enough time for me to reciprocate." I turned leaning against my door. "That's not fair."

He caressed my face, the scars and calluses of his palms reminding me of how they felt all over my body. "Okay."

"That's it?"

He smiled wickedly. "Yes."

I swatted him playfully. "You tease."

He chuckled, turning the knob to my door. "So are you."

Entering my room, it was just how I had left it. Pale pink walls covered with posters from music groups from all parts of my life. Fairy lights glowed on one wall that held pictures of my mom and I as I grew up. The small twin sized bed was not going to be big enough for both of us. "Shit."

"It is fine, your mother said there were extra blankets in the linen closet." He kissed the top of my head coming into the room. "I can sleep on the floor."

"But."

He set the bags at the base of the bed and sat down the bed groaned under his weight as he stretched out his legs. "Really, love, I wouldn't fit in your bed if I wanted to. Fitting in you, however, is a different story."

I scowled as he smiled at me. "You're incorrigible. I'm going to grab blankets."

He laughed as I walk out of the room into the hall. "You know you love it."

"That's beside the point." I shouted back.

I pondered how interactions with my mother had gone thus far while grabbing an armful of quilts. Would she accept him? Would she accept my choices to stay? Back in my bedroom, Niratap had laid back diagonally across the bed; his long body would never fit comfortably on my tiny bed. His antlers were suspended above the small space on the opposite side of the bed, his legs were planted on this side, the long lines of his body drawing my eyes.

"Do you think she likes you?" I asked, setting the blankets down in a pile by my bed.

"I think she doesn't trust me, which given what you have told her, I don't blame her."

I stood before him planting my hands on his thighs. "Really?"

He opened one eye and peered at me. "A monster bought her daughter for a large sum of money for very little reason beyond instinct. I'm not really boyfriend material for anyone at that."

"Don't say that." I say, coming to my knees. "You are my boyfriend material. You are everything I've ever needed."

I slip my hand under his tail to the button of his slacks, undoing it and slowly descending his zipper. "You are flirting with danger, my dear. Thirty minutes isn't long enough for both of us, that is what you told me."

"It isn't." I said pulling his hardening length from his shorts. He sucked his teeth, his head falling back over the edge of the mattress. "But you always get the first bite, so now it's my turn."

I ran my tongue along the underside of him. He arched off the bed. "Fuck."

I fisted him. "You know I love this, taking you here in my room."

"You are devious, you little minx."

I chuckled taking him in my mouth again. His skin was velvety soft on my tongue, salty on my pallet. He groaned and bucked up into my throat, it hurt bringing tears to my eyes, but I wanted this. I tried to relax and take him deeper. He sat up, threading his fingers through my curls.

"Shasha, you don't have to take all of me. I won't fit down your throat."

I pulled back letting my teeth drag, his hands tightened in my hair. I looked up to him through my eyelashes as I released him with a pop. "But I want you. All of you."

His stare was heated and intense. "Let me take you then, both of us would enjoy that."

I smiled at him. "Oh, really."

He pulled me up by my hair until I was facing him. "Yes. I do enjoy your mouth on me, but it is only fair for you to enjoy me to."

"That's what I was saying before."

His hand traveled gently over my neck. "You're acting out, aren't you?"

I glared at him. "I am not."

He gave me a knowing look. "Shasha?"

I sighed. "How do you know?"

"Well, though I enjoy your enthusiasm." He said righting himself. "And you do want me, that much I can tell, but this is not what you want. You don't want it for us. You're trying to make a statement to your mother who by the way just pulled back into the driveway."

I started shaking. "I—I—"

He guided me to sit beside him. "It's okay, *mo grá*."

"But it's not, I—I was trying to use you to get to my mother. I'm sorry. I didn't mean to do that I—" Tears rolled down my face and he pulled me into him.

"It's okay, love. I understand you want to prove to her that you're not a child, but her walking in on us mid-coitus won't prove to her that you're an adult, love. It will only solidify what she thinks of me. Don't cry, everything will be okay."

"But I was trying to use you. How can you not be mad at me?"

"Because I understand. She has been controlling and demanding. You just want to show her that you can handle the world, especially after telling her your story."

"That woman, I love her to death, but I want her to see me and—wait, what does my mother think of you?"

He smiled sadly at me. "Based on her body language and scent she thinks that I'm predatory, that I'm only using you for my carnal needs. She doesn't see what we feel for each other. She's afraid for you. She's afraid of me."

"But she doesn't have to be, you have been nothing but kind to her."

"True, but I am also the man that has kept her daughter from her. I am the man who has been sleeping with said daughter. I am the man that locked her daughter away."

"But you didn't lock me away, really. You gave me access to the world. You pulled strings so I could stay in school. You've protected me even when I've made an ass of myself."

"Be that as it may, your mother doesn't understand what we are. She doesn't trust me. Trust is something that takes time, which isn't something we have the luxury of." I nodded as he stood, bending forward. He kissed me sweetly. "Let's go down. Tonight, will be awkward, but hopefully tomorrow's formal dinner will not be."

"Okay."

Downstairs mom had set dinner in the living room, pizza boxes open on the coffee table, a two-liter of cola in between them. Mom was in the kitchen opening and shutting cupboards.

"Go ahead and sit on the loveseat, I'll go help mom really quick." He kissed me softly before I walked into the kitchen. "Do you need any help mom?"

"Sure, baby, will you take the plates and cups into the living room."

"Yeah." I walked into the kitchen to collect the plastic plates and cups from the counter.

"I didn't know what soda to grab, so I just grabbed a regular cola."

"I'm sure it's fine, mom, I can get a pitcher of water or make some lemonade too if you're worried."

"Well, what does he drink normally?" I pondered all the things that Niratap drank, knowing my mother would disapprove. I opened my mouth to speak.

"A high-shelf scotch is my preferred, but I'll drink anything." I spun around to see him leaned against the door frame. I shot him a glare to which he responded with. "What?"

"Scotch?" My mother's tone told me exactly what she thought. "You won't find anything harder than coffee in this house."

"Cola is fine, like I said I'll drink anything. Can I help?"

"Here." I handed him the cups and plates. "Go sit, I'll be right there."

"Okay." He frowned but turned away, into the living room.

"Scotch." My mother whispered.

"Mom, he was being funny."

"Alcoholism isn't funny." She turned, the ranch bottle in her hand.

"He's not an alcoholic." Though I knew he drank more than occasionally.

"Mm hmm."

I took the dip cups from my mother. "He's not."

In the living room, he sat in the loveseat at an angle to accommodate his long legs. His face was stoic. "Did I say something I shouldn't have?"

"No." I sat the dip on the table and snuggled next to him. "My mother just has strong opinions on the way things should be."

"That's where you get that from." He joked and I swat at him playfully.

"What kind of pizza do you want?"

"What is there?"

"Pepperoni pineapple, and mom likes supreme, which has sausage, mushrooms, olives, onions, and green peppers."

"I'll try both. I'm intrigued with pineapple on pizza."

I dished him up, handing him the plate, then poured him a glass of cola, setting it before him on the coffee table. "Have you never had pizza?"

"I have had pizza, but it was on a trip to Greece and about fifty years ago."

"Oh." I smiled putting two slices on my plate with dip. I dipped my pizza in the ranch and took a bite, wiggling happily as the creamy salty sweet flavors danced on my tongue. He chuckled, his thumb sweeping the ranch off the corner of my mouth.

"*Tu ta inoraic.*"[32] He said lovingly.

"What?" I asked around my pizza.

"You're adorable." He said, taking a thoughtful bite of my favorite pizza.

"Do you even notice when you do that?"

"Do what?" My mother asked, coming to sit on the sofa.

"Oh, he randomly flips into Irish, and I can't understand what he is saying."

[32] You're adorable.

"Irish is my first language." He said, leaning to dip his pizza in my ranch.

"That is where you're from, right?" Mom asked, dishing her own.

"Yes, I was born on the green isle." He said before taking a bite, nodding.

"Why did you come to the US?"

He passed a glance at me, and I nodded. "I didn't have much say in the matter."

"What does—"

"Thanks for pizza, mom. I've missed this."

"You're welcome. Have you not had pizza in a while?"

"No, the manor isn't really a place where you can order pizza."

"Why is that?"

"The manor is fairly isolated." Niratap said, reaching for his cup. "In the mountains and the people in the town nearest us are afraid of the forest surrounding the manor as well. Not that I can fault them, there are dangerous creatures sheltered there."

"Dangerous creatures?" My mother asked, a slice of pizza suspended between her plate and her mouth. I shot him a scathing look.

"Think of the land around the manor as a sanctuary for threatened creatures."

"That's how you were injured recently."

"Yes." He took a drink.

"Why keep dangerous creatures close to your home?"

"To keep them safe."

"At risk to you and your family?"

"They understand the risks and so do I."

"Does my daughter?" Her tone became sharp.

Nira tensed, and I felt it though the loveseat. "If she didn't, she does by now."

"The risks seem unnecessary. If I recall what my daughter told me, you could have died."

"It was worth the risk." He said, setting his plate on the table.

"Almost dying was worth it?"

"Your daughter is unharmed and alive." He growled. "So yes. It was worth the risk, and I would do it again."

"How did you get that scar on your face?"

"Mother."

"No, it's okay. It was an injury I received a long time ago."

My mother just stared at him, looking into the depths of his soul. Finally, she shook her head and looked at me. "This is what you chose?"

Nira just shook his head and leaned back against the cushions. He was accustomed to people judging his actions at face value. He was accustomed to abuse. I swallowed. "Mother, please."

"I just don't understand. Why a monster? Is it Stockholm syndrome? He *saves* you and takes you home and lures you into a sense of safety for his pleasure. It doesn't sit right with me."

I hissed. "I don't care if it sits right with you mother. He is the man I choose, for however long I can have him, and he'll have me. Your opinion on his species doesn't mean anything to me."

My mother gave me a wounded look. "You have never spoken to me in this manner. I don't agree with this match you have chosen for yourself. There are plenty of boys, closer to your species, that would suit you better."

"In your opinion." I said, a hollowness entering my chest, because I knew. I knew every moment of this weekend would be a fight. I knew because in her mind I had been spirited away by a monster to warm his bed. A princess trapped in a tower. I wished she could see that he had rescued me from such a fate or worse.

My mother took a bite of her pizza, her eyes bearing down on Niratap, who did not balk from that intensity in her stare, if anything he matched it. We discussed this, that my mother was opinionated, that she had already spun a tale from her fears and worries that would damn us. Regardless of the truth. Regardless of if we presented it to her gilded in gold and silver. She only saw the towering monster, not the man in its skin.

"Is there something that you need to say, ma'am?" Nira spoke smoothly, not breaking my mother's stare as he crossed one leg over the other.

Daggers were thrown with her eyes. "You are not good enough for my daughter."

Nira blinked, and I glared at my mother shifting to snap, but he said. "Of that we agree."

My fire died instantly. "What?"

Nira placed a hand on my knee, to steady me, but his eyes never left my mother's face. "I am not good enough for your daughter. She is kind and good. Open with her feelings and her views on the world. Loving to a fault, and she sees good in every living thing. I don't hide that my life is fraught with danger and my hands are not unclean from those dangers. She sees that, and it astounds me every time she chooses me."

"Then why hold her hostage."

He looked at me, finally, breaking from her ice. "Because I love her and the only way, I can keep her safe from those who wish to hurt or hunt me is to keep her at my side."

"Doesn't that put her at even greater risk?"

A wicked smile came across his face, showing his fangs. "I can be very convincing otherwise."

My mother frowned, but just continued to eat her pizza. The rest of the meal was done in silence, the tense air thick enough to cut with a knife. In silence, I helped mom clear the coffee table, Nira offering to wash the dishes. Mom didn't say anything, just went back to the living room to watch the evening news. Nira rolled up his sleeves, the expanse of his forearms covered in small scars, the magic burn bright against his honeyed skin.

"Well, that went well." I said drying the dishes next to him, sarcasm lacing my voice.

"Give her time."

"I shouldn't have to."

"I know, my flower, but you won't be able to convince her otherwise if we are constantly at each other's throats."

"I just want her to accept it. Us. You and me."

"You can't force her, and she may never accept what we are to one another."

I huffed, putting the plates back into the cupboard. "It shouldn't matter."

"I agree, but that is the hand the world dealt us." He said, rinsing the cups. "There are many who wouldn't approve of you and I. We are too different from one another for it to be 'natural.'"

"What we are biologically has nothing to do with how my soul sings for you."

He smiled. "I agree. My heart called to you and now I feel lost without you."

I smiled as I dried the glasses. "Why can't that be enough?"

"I've asked myself that for a millennium."

After we finished the dishes, I told my mom that we were going to bed, she gave a halfhearted non-committal response. We went up to my room and I leaned against my door as Nira sat on the bed, his tail uncoiled from his body, and he began undoing the buttons of his shirt. The dress shirt slid off, showing his black shirt underneath, which he tugged apart, and I heard the tiny pops of the snaps. He glanced up at me as he slides out of his shirt.

"Yes?"

"I always wondered how you got into the t-shirts."

"Dorilody is a clever tailor." He said, coming to stand. His body a testament to the life he had lived, scars of varying ages crisscrossed across his body.

I smiled. "That she is."

He examined my face for a moment, tracking my visual exploration of his body. "I am alright, *mo grá*."

I wiped a tear from my face. "I know. It's just that your life has been hard enough, and she just doesn't understand."

He gave me a sad smile as he slid his legs out of his pants. "Time heals all wounds eventually. I am okay."

I crossed the room as he folded up his slacks and plopped down on the bed, laying back across it. "I don't understand how you can be so calm when she or anyone for-that-matter digs at you."

"I have lived a long life already, and in comparison, her words are just that. Words." He slid into pajama pants and sat next to me. "It warms part of my heart to know that you wish to defend me."

"Why is this so hard?"

He placed his hand on my stomach. "Because you love her, and you want her praise and approval. Which makes her resistance difficult to process."

I looked at him, catching the end of his tail and stroking it. His fur bristled, but he didn't pull away. "Why do you always have an answer to my questions?"

"Because you ask for advice, and I have lived more than you. It's easy to find some kernel of wisdom in my years." His fur bristled again, and he tugged his tail from my hands. "That tickles, my flower."

I smiled. "Oh really?"

He chuckled, sliding to the floor to fluff out the blankets. "My tail is very sensitive."

"Do you think that she will? Accept you I mean?"

"It's up to her, *mo grá*." He said sitting down in his nest.

I stood then and went to the suitcase to dig out my pajamas. "I wish she would just listen."

"I know, but listening to what you have to say doesn't mean she'll change her opinions."

I sighed as I slipped out of my jeans. His logic was spot on, and I knew it, but that didn't make it easier to swallow. I felt his eyes watch me as I changed, his gaze always seemed hungry, like he couldn't get enough of me. I liked his attention, but I didn't understand what he saw when he looked at me. I crawled between the sheets and rolled to face him.

"Other than how you have been treated, what do you think about my hometown?"

"It's quaint, but I can see why you wanted to get away."

"You don't think I'm Podunk?"

He chuffed, scooting down into the blankets. "Never."

I smiled at him. "Thank you."

"What for?"

"For coming with me. For being kind to my mother even when she wasn't."

"She is important to you, and I know you struggle with how your relationship is with your mother. I figured for you I could try to not be the monster that I am."

"You're not a monster, not to me."

"I think you are the only being on this planet that thinks that."

"I think that that is not how things are supposed to be."

"Perhaps. Get some sleep, my love. I'll be right here if you need me."

"I love you, Niratap."

"I love you too, Shasha."

I draped my arm over the bed, twisting my fingers between his. I fell asleep like that, curled up in my bed holding his hand.

I awoke surrounded by his scent. Sometime in the night I had crawled out of my bed into the nest he had crafted and into his arms, finding the most comfort there. Now, he was nowhere to be seen. Quickly I pulled on my sweats and opened my door to the hall, peeking down its length, I saw that mom's door was closed telling me she was still asleep. I rushed into the bathroom, hoping to beat her down the stairs. I trusted Niratap not to intentionally push my mother's buttons, but I didn't trust her not to be rude. When I was done in the bathroom, I saw that the bedroom door was now open, and the soft pad of my mother's slippered feet going down the stairs hit my ears. I swore to myself and stealthily followed down the stairs after. She paused at the doorway into the dining room, pulling her robe snugly around her.

"Oh." She chirped in surprise, before stepping into the room. "Good morning."

"Good morning. I made coffee if that is alright." Niratap spoke clearly, devoid of his normal growly sleepy voice that was my second favorite to hear. "I hope I didn't wake you when I came down. Crouching down the stairs is a bit tricky. Antlers make me top heavy."

"You didn't wake me and thank you for making coffee." Mom said, voice still heavy with sleep.

"I'll go. Give you some peace." I heard the scrape of a chair on the well-worn hardwood of the dining room as I crept down the stairs.

"You don't have to leave." Cupboards opened and closed as mom grabbed a cup. Mom gasped. "You have a tail."

He laughed gently. "Yes, I have a tail. Your daughter had a similar reaction when she saw it as well."

"I don't mean to sound rude. It just I didn't notice it yesterday."

"Most of the time outside of home I have it wrapped around my waist. it doesn't get stepped on that way."

It was my mother's turn to laugh. "Please, please sit. I have some things I'd like to ask you."

"I didn't find what you said rude, either. I'm not human and that can be unnerving for some." He grunted sitting back down. "Go ahead and ask your questions, though I can't guarantee that I can answer all of them."

"Shasha said that you purchased her from a black-market auction."

"I did."

"Is that how you fund your lifestyle? Buying and selling things on the black market?"

"It is a small part of a much larger organization. Our largest income comes from investments, stocks, and bonds, all legal. I do occasionally sell on the market, but I'm not in the trade of selling creatures."

"What do you sell?"

"Mostly rare plants that my gardener and groundskeeper grow. They are prized by alchemists and fetch high prices. Sometimes art or jewelry, on rare occasions a non-lethal artifact."

"So, you don't sell beings?"

"No." There is a sharpness to his tone. "I purchase beings out of the market. Buyout debts, try to conserve rare creatures, or at the very least keep their body parts from being used for nefarious things."

"My apologies, I am just seeking to understand the—" I could practically see my mother searching for a word. "Being that my daughter has chosen for a partner."

"You don't need to apologize. My irritation isn't directed at you, it is at that insinuation that because I am a player on the market that I prey on those who cannot defend themselves. I don't want others to suffer as I suffered."

"You were—" the end of her question hung in the air.

"Yes." He answered plainly. "For a vast portion of my life I was a slave to evil men. I was beaten, abused, and starved into submission."

"But you were freed?"

I peered into the dining room at them. They sat on opposite sides of the table from one another. "I escaped. It is not a highlight of my life, in order to survive I did terrible and cruel things. All of my closest companions would say that it was necessary, but not all of that blood needed to be spilled that night.”

“You killed your captors?”

“I slaughtered the entire house, took all that he owned and claimed it for myself. Dug my claws into the young American soil and worked hard to protect it.”

“Why my daughter? Why buy her?” My mother’s tone was incredulous.

“Be it a surprise to you, I don’t make a habit of patronizing brothels. She’s special. Her scent is special. It drove me from the streets to her. She is beautiful, especially decorated in gold. Exotic even, but I don’t even have an answer for the whys. I don’t know why she smells the way she does. I don’t know why it captivates me. I don’t know why I purchased her beyond instinct. I didn’t give her options like I give others because I still need to understand why.”

“Why do you think that is?”

“I don’t know, but she is special to me.” Niratap looked up at her and pinned me with his gaze past her. “More so than I would like to admit at times. Yes, she is frustrating and pushes me from my comfort zone, but she also brings such joy to my life. Joy that I haven’t had for a vast majority of said life and I can promise you that even though I’m not what you want for your daughter, that I’m not perfect. I love her. I want her joy, her health, her safety. Above all else.”

I smiled. My mother set her cup on the table. “You sound like you care for her, but what happens when she ages, and you don’t? What happens if she gets sick? What happens if she gets hurt?”

Nira's' nostrils flared and he stared into his cup. “We will cross those bridges if and when they come. Worrying about what-ifs with her is something that takes away from what we have now. If she gets sick or gets hurt, we have a medic on staff, and if it goes beyond her scope, I have money to pay for hospital bills.”

“I want to know if she is cared for and protected.”

Nira's tail swished across the floor in cat-like irritation. "And I am telling you that there is nothing to worry about. I have things handled."

"What if you get her pregnant?"

His brows rose. "We would deal with it then. I will say again I'm not going to worry about the future what-ifs. I choose to be with her, and she chooses me and that should be all that matters. Dislike me all you desire, but I'm not planning on hurting your daughter."

"Whether you plan to or not doesn't prove that you have her best intentions in mind." My mother's tone was sharp as a blade.

I walked into the kitchen then, faking a yawn on my walk to the cupboards. "Good morning."

The viper turned to honey. "Good morning, baby girl."

I poured myself a cup of coffee, "I must've been really tired, I didn't hear either of you get up. Thanks for the coffee mom."

"Actually, he made coffee."

I poured cream into my coffee. Taking on my mother's earlier viper tone. "He has a name mother, and I would appreciate you using it."

"What kind of name is Niratap, anyway? It isn't Irish."

"No, it's not. It's Bengali, my father's tongue." Nira said.

"Irish and Bengali, how did they even meet?"

"After the hunt for my kind in Asia, my father had migrated and eventually made it to Ireland and met my mother. My sister was born about a year after that."

"What? How old would that make you? Monster hunts haven't been a thing for several hundred years." She stood and backed several steps from the table. "What are you?"

He looked at me as I came to stand by his side. We had intentionally not told her his age or what he was, knowing it would only aggravate and cause her to fear him more. "He is a bitarog and he's a little over a thousand years old."

"Impossible."

"I can assure you, ma'am, that it is indeed true." He said as his hand wrapped around my waist.

"Bitarogs are man-eaters, Shasha. Man-eaters. That was why they were hunted. He's dangerous. Get away from him." She squawked at me.

"Mom, I will do no such thing. He's not a threat to you or me. Stop acting a fool and sit down."

"But baby, he musta brainwashed you or something because my child would never speak to me that way. Let alone pair up with a man-eating monster."

There was a subtle shift in his face, a swish of his tail. The only indication that her words had cut deeply. I placed a hand on his neck rubbing softly against his pulse. He leaned into my touch, like it anchored him. "Mama. I love you, but this is going to be the last time I ask, please respect him. You don't have to like him. You don't have to be his friend. You don't have to do anything but respect him because regardless of if it is in ten minutes or tomorrow night, I will be going home with him. The when is up to you. Now I don't claim to be blissfully ignorant to the man I chose. I know what he is, what he does for work. I know what he's done to survive. He has a temper and is standoffish and it blew me out of the water when he agreed to come to dinner here. Where he knew he wouldn't be welcomed because you're so against anything not human enough."

"That is unfair, Shasha."

"Is it, mom? Why did I grow up only knowing two non-human families and farm fae? Why is Afton still mostly human?"

"Fine, I am afraid. Deathless, ageless things should not exist."

"Long-lived is a better term. Given the opportunity to live, most races would eventually die of old age." Nira half growled, before taking a sip of his coffee. "If humans didn't hate everything but their own kind, senseless death could always be avoided."

"I don't hate beings that aren't human, God tells us—"

"No." Nira slammed mug down, coffee splashing over the side. "Your god has nothing to his name but cruelty and bloodshed."

"How dare you!" My mother hissed. "How dare you tell me what my god has done."

"No, your god is kind and giving, it's his preachers who twist the word to serve their needs. Who take and take and take without remorse, who kill whoever is not worthy of their god in their eyes." Nira stood as far as he could. "Don't tell me how great your god is, when he has done nothing but take and kill from those who have no voice or use their voice to disagree."

He took a shaking breath before he turned to the sliding glass doors. "Nira, don't."

"I need a moment, *mo grá.*" He whispered, pressing a gentle kiss to my temple. He was shaking.

I watch him exit and lean on the banister outside cradling his head in his hands. Fire burned in my heart as I turned into the kitchen to grab a rag to clean up the spill. "I hope you're proud of yourself."

"Excuse you?" My mother seethed, coming around to the counter after me. "What was that supposed to mean?"

"You know exactly what I mean. You goaded him, made him relive all the terrible things that happened to him."

"I don't know those things. I can't be held responsible for his sensitivity." She hissed at me over the counter, as I wiped up the coffee and collected the mugs.

"Your ignorance isn't an excuse, mother. We will be leaving when he is ready; I don't care if you are worried about me or scared for me. I'm fine."

"He's a monster." She shrieked. I knew he could hear her and the ache in my chest screamed.

"No. He is a man." My voice came out hard as I started the water to wash our cups. "A good man at that."

"Shasha."

"And I love him regardless of what you or anyone else thinks." I snapped. My mother's face was akin to a fish on dry land, painted between rage and shock.

"Shasha Nicole Dion. I can't believe you would choose him over me."

"Mom, you're not listening to me. I didn't choose him over you. I'm defending him because you're being unfair."

"I'm being unfair. That monster purchased you on the black market and has been holding you hostage."

"Hostage? He saved me. I still get to go to school. I am fed, clothed, and warm. I'm learning to defend myself. I still get to call you and visit you."

"I would have preferred—"

"What would you have preferred, mother? Would you have preferred him not to have purchased me? Would you have preferred me disappearing completely, swallowed whole by the market, forced to turn tricks for food?"

"Shasha."

"Or better yet sold to a vampyre, perhaps, and used as a midnight snack. Maybe a kelpie even; I would make a fine meal for them." Tears rimmed my eyes, but I was too angry to let them fall.

"Stop." She whimpered over the faint sound of the patio door opening.

"Or I could have just been raped and killed just like you said I could living in the city." I was shrill in my ears.

"Shasha, please stop."

"Dead? Dead, is that what you would have preferred?"

His arms wrapped around me, his voice a whisper in my ear. "Enough love. Enough, that's enough."

"But she—" I looked up at him, tears finally rolling down my cheeks. There was such kindness in those eyes.

Kindness and sadness that caused that ache in my chest to grow.

"I know." He said just as soft. "But you are being cruel."

I looked at my mother and she was crying. Shame coiled in the hot spot in my heart. "Mama, I—"

"No." She whimpered. "I don't want you gone, or eaten, or dead. I want you home."

"This isn't my home anymore, mom."

"What—what do you mean?"

I took a shuddering breath. "Mom, I love you. Truth is since I've been fifteen you have smothered me. I couldn't do the things normal kids got to do, because you were scared and tried as you might to instill that fear of the world in me. You did the opposite. I thirst for adventure and new experiences. I compromised so much to go to school, to experience life. As naive as I am, I needed it. What happened to me was terrible, but I have grown so much, learned so much because of it."

"Ma'am, not to be forward." Nira said stepping in front of me. "Your daughter has become a force to be reckoned with, she is loving and fierce and I would not have her any other way. I know you love her. I can see that you do, but she is not a child anymore. She is a full-fledged adult who is capable of making her own decisions."

My mother sniffled, but she nodded. "I'm sorry, baby girl. I didn't mean to; God I didn't mean to make you feel trapped. I just wanted you to be safe."

"Making me afraid of everything wouldn't teach me to be safe."

"I know." She wiped her face, taking a shaking breath. "I guess you'll be leaving then. I should call Decan and let him know dinner is canceled."

Nira looked at me over his shoulder, it was my choice whether we went or stayed. I took a breath. "Mom don't cancel dinner. We'll stay."

My mother looked at us with her eyes wide. "After all of this all the yelling and fighting? You'd stay."

He smiled softly at me. "And help, if you'll have us."

For the first time this entire trip my mother smiled at me, truly smiled at me.

We did help. Niratap even showed my mother a trick for keeping the turkey moist but giving it a crispy skin. Things were still tense, but they were interacting without daggers shaped like words being thrown across the room. We had pushed mom out of the kitchen to rest her feet, while we finished everything for dinner. I was mashing potatoes when he came to my side, kissing my temple.

"You know you have to put a little force into mashing those potatoes or they'll be lumpy."

"I know how to mash potatoes, you ass." I said leaning into him.

"Who is this, Decan?" He asked, leaning against the table.

"Old man Decan? He's the neighbor. He was friends with my father at one point and he has helped mom with fixes when she didn't know how to. Just a good neighbor."

Nira nodded. "You're not going to have to defend me from him too?"

"Decan? Gods, no. He used to be a cop and his partner wasn't human. He has nothing, but good things to say about the integration of other beings, especially in law enforcement. Fae hearing and scent helped him, and his partner solve a lot of cases."

"Interesting." There was a knock at the front door that mom got.

"Decan, welcome"

"Hey, Jazzy girl." Decan said as he entered the house. "That's quite the car that's parked out there."

"Yes, Shasha brought someone with her for dinner. He drove."

"Shasha brought a boy home?"

"Yes."

I looked at Nira. "Here we go."

He chuckled, going back to the oven to check the turkey. "We'll be fine."

Mom and Decan came into the kitchen. Decan was a lean man in his sixties, his hair once blond had gone grey. He smiled warmly at me, but his eyes swung behind me as Nira put the turkey on the table.

"Well, I'll be damned. Niratap, is that you?"

"Decan Castiglione." Nira smiled wide, coming around to shake Decan's hand. "I wondered what hole you had crawled into to retire."

"Afton has very little crime for me to stress about."

Nira chuckled. "Fair enough."

"How's V? I haven't heard from him since he got that fancy promotion."

"He's V. He doesn't loop me in unless it's necessary."

"He still a prickly bastard?"

"Twenty years isn't going to change that."

"Hold on." I said, breaking out of my shock. "You two know each other?"

Nira smiled at me. "Decan here used to be Ventris's partner when he was working on integrating the NYPD."

"The work I did with V got me fast tracked to detective. We solved hundreds of cases together and some of those cases were interwoven with Niratap's vigilante cause."

"Vigilante makes me sound like, Batman." Nira said.

"Well, I just call them like I see them, Batman. How is everyone?"

"Everyone is good."

"That's good, you look just like I saw you last."

"Well, being long lived does have its advantages. Age looks good on you, Decan."

The men laughed. This dinner was going to be easier than I had thought. Decan and Nira sat across from one another chatting about my friends. Mom and I sat next to them, eating up every word they spoke about old cases, old enemies, who was still kicking from the old days and who wasn't.

Dinner itself was delicious, the turkey was moist with crispy skin, the mashed potatoes were, in fact, not lumpy and it was surreal. That the man who had purchased me, loved me fiercely, could kill if he needed, was just a man who walked a dangerous path. Who sacrificed when he needed to. He gave too much, too much. They were talking about the last big case that they had worked on before Decan had retired, it had been the first time Bastion had been working with Niratap in the field, while mom and I cleared the dinner dishes.

"—I thought I was done for, and that crazy kid ran up on the *vato* with a two by four. Ballsy kid. I'm glad he is doing well."

"Me too, Bas is a good kid. He'll be happy to hear you're doing well."

"I bet. You can tell him that crusty Italian he saved his first time in the field hasn't kicked the bucket yet." Decan looked into the kitchen at us. I smiled at him. "So, the big question Niratap. How'd you meet our Shasha girl?"

Nira sighed. "I was hoping you weren't going to ask, my friend."

"Well, you can't expect me to think she met you at school."

"Niratap purchased me off the black market." I said plainly, ripping the band-aid off. "He saved my life."

The heaviness that had been missing all of dinner settled in again.

"I see. Someone I know?"

"Dravin Cirano, he's been a whore trader for a long time." Nira offered.

"He's that mob boss's kid, right?"

"Yes."

"God, I was hoping that POS was dead, at least in jail."

"No, he's low priority with the bureau. Bas, is looking into him, but that was all I heard last."

"Makes me want back in the fray, if just to put a bullet in the fuck."

"Decan!" My mother hissed.

"What? Anyone brutalizes my girl, I'll kill them." Decan said vehemently.

"I second that." Nira growled. "Dravin will get his comeuppance soon enough. Man keeps putting targets on my back."

"Be careful, Niratap. The last thing you need is to be targeted for a hunt."

"Well, we were shot at last week." I said offhandedly, I slapped my hand over my mouth as my mother raised a brow at me.

"We got out unharmed." Nira said, before taking a drink. "Besides, Mitta is a better shot than any of those that were there."

"That she is." Decan agreed. "That woman could outshoot all the marksmen when I was in the force."

My mother seemed to ease at Decan's praise. "Dessert anyone?"

"You can't have a Thanksgiving dinner without it." Decan mused. "I don't know where I'll put it, but yes please, Jazzy."

Mom laughed. "I have pumpkin pie and cake."

"Cake?" Nira asked, turning in his chair.

"Yes, Ice-cream cake to be precise."

"Mom, you didn't." I said, turning to her.

"I know it's your favorite."

I hugged her tightly. "Thank you."

"Happy Birthday, baby girl."

Niratap's eyes widened. "I didn't know that your birthday was today."

"It's not; my birthday is Monday the thirtieth."

"We used to always celebrate on Thanksgiving though. That was when all the family could get together.

Now everyone's moved away, and my mother passed away." Mom said, smiling sadly.

Decan stood with a grunt. "Candles still in the junk drawer?"

"Yes."

"We don't have to sing." I said, as Decan dug in the drawer.

"No, no. We sing happy birthday in this house, young lady." Decan said adamantly. "And we blow out candles."

Niratap chuckled. "I agree. I'll have to let the house know. They'll be upset you didn't tell them."

"No. No, you will not." I said, turning to him.

"Rogmesh would be heartbroken if she couldn't make you a cake."

"But I'm not big on being the center of attention."

Nira smiled. "You will always be the center of my attention, *mo grá.*"

I stuck my tongue out at him. "You're not helping."

He shrugged. "There are far too many cooks in that kitchen."

"That's not what I meant."

"Semantics."

"Decan and I got this, baby girl, go sit."

"But."

"Go sit with him." She gave me a gentle push out of the kitchen, there was a pause. "Niratap, would you like pie or cake?"

My heart stopped and Nira beamed. "Both would be fantastic, Ma'am."

Chapter Forty-Three

Niratap

When we returned home to the manor Monday afternoon, we were greeted by a thick layer of snow. Our goodbyes with her mother were much better than our hellos had been. Jazzera wasn't entirely my friend, but I now believed we could exist without hatred for one another. She asked if she could visit, meet the beings that had become her daughter's family. In the spring we could get something sorted, the snow would be less treacherous and the manor more in order then. She frowned at the response but didn't argue and neither did her daughter.

Everyone greeted us warmly when we came home, happily chatting to Shasha about her birthday. Something I had, in fact, told the household before we had left. They showered her with gifts and sang to her loudly. It warmed my heart that my family accepted her as one of their own. How could I have gotten so lucky to have her fall into my life? I left them to their merry making and went to the study. I had emails to pour into, research to do. Solitude. It was something that I had grown accustomed to. I wanted to enjoy it with them, but many weights had settled on my shoulders, and I didn't want to darken Shasha's day with my worries.

I checked my email. I could see that Allipo had kept up with business in my stead, starred messages that needed my attention, but it was the new message from the occult professor from NYU that caught my eye.

Greetings Lord Bondbreaker,

My name is Berengarius Seri. I am the Occult Arts professor at NYC. Vrorlin gave me your email so that I could reach you on the interesting specimen you have captured on your trail cameras. At first glance I would assume that you had caught a shadow wraith, then Vrorlin slipped me the information you gleaned from the kill site. So, I did some digging and reached out to some of my peers around the world, and my friend in Europe sent me some information on a necromancer spell that may have created the creature that is hunting you. It is something called the malice, a rough translation of a text that is several thousand years old. I will continue looking into this for you and reach out if I can confirm that it is indeed this.

    Regards Professor B. Seri Occult Arts

    Interesting. If the creature was an occult summon, that would mean that there was someone behind it, someone was hunting me. I ran an internet search for myself, finding nothing on the occult creature called the malice. Frustrated, I opened the cabinet behind my desk, pouring three fingers of my favorite scotch, the warm spiced smell of it filling my nose, before I downed it in a single swig. There was a knock at the threshold of the study.

    "Did you run away to get drunk alone?" Shasha stood in the doorway, smiling softly.

    "No, my flower. I had things to look over since I have been gone."

    "You seem stressed. Tell me what's bothering you?"

    "Many things bother me." I said, turning back to the cabinet, pouring another drink.

    "Well, what things are bothering you to the point that you came into the study to be morose by yourself?"

    I sipped the liquor. What should I tell her? Maybe I should just show her. I leaned over the desk and clicked into my email again. "Come see."

    She came to the desk, sitting in my chair to read the email. I leaned over her and inhaled her scent into my nose. Lavender and sweet grass laced with sugar, no doubt from the large pink cake that Rogmesh had made for her. I wanted to curl up in her scent, bury myself in all that she was.

    "So that thing that is hunting you might be this thing called the malice."

"Yes. Seri says he will look into it for me. I'm curious to see what his research will uncover." She watched me for a moment. "What, my flower?"

"You've just been quiet since we left mom's; I just want to make sure you are okay."

I took another sip of the scotch. "I've been thinking about a lot of the things that your mother said."

"So, you 've been stewing over something that she said since we left this morning?"

"Not stewing." I smiled at her. "Some of the things that she said, though spoken from a place of fear, did have some valid concerns about us that I have been mulling over."

"The what ifs that you didn't want to worry about?" She crossed her arms.

"Well, one in particular." I said, my heart fluttered uncomfortably in my chest.

"What?" She sounded irritated; her mother's cruel words cut her much more than they did me.

I took a breath, finishing my scotch. "About pregnancy?"

Her face softened. "That has been what you have been mulling over?"

Her tone was flat, like she wasn't in the least bit concerned. "Why do you sound so unbothered by that?"

"Because it isn't something I'm worried about. Firstly, I'm on birth control. Secondly." she said with a shrug. "Yes, I'm not ready to be a mom, but babies happen when they happen. It's not something that is terrible, it's just a life change. I'll cross that bridge, when it happens, regardless of who it is with."

I bristled at her words but let a heavy breath out. We were in a relationship, yes, but she was not my mate or bound to stay mine. I sat in one of the chairs on the opposite side of the desk. "I just. I haven't been—I've never had to—I mean."

"You're worried because I've let you just destroy me and cum inside me?" The vixen smiled at me.

I glowered at her, but my cheeks heated. "Exactly that, you minx."

She leaned back in my chair. "You're cute when you're flustered."

I laughed, the ache easing in my chest. "Must you tease me for my concern?"

She came to me, straddling my lap. "When you're being silly yes. If it happens it happens, and we'll cross that bridge then. No need to worry about it now."

"But if it does happen?"

She pulled the elastic from my hair, running her fingers through it, "Well, what do you want, my love?"

"I've never thought about children. My species is quite particular about how those things come together, with the state of our kind." I shook my head. "It wasn't something I thought would happen."

She cupped my cheek. "Would you want to keep them?"

I leaned into her touch. "I would."

"Then it's settled, if or when it happens, we'll bring them into the world, no matter what and I know you will keep them safe."

"How are you the calm one when it comes to us."

"Because we as a unit are not complicated. We were universally drawn to one another, and I don't plan on going anywhere. If by chance I do get pregnant it will be a blessing to be a mother to your children. Whether it happens tomorrow or in ten years. I don't plan on leaving you."

I searched her eyes, finding nothing but conviction. "I love you."

She kissed me. "And I you. Now stop your moping and come with me."

I chuckled as she slid from my lap and clasped my hands, pulling me from the chair. "Where are we going, my love?"

"I want my gift from you."

"I wasn't able to get you anything for your birthday."

"Then I want you. Fully and wonderfully."

I scooped her into my arms, kissing her. My gift. "Very well."

In our room, for it had become ours, I tossed her on the bed. She grabbed me by my tie and pulled me closer. She kissed me deeply, her tongue dancing with mine and tracing over my fangs. I felt her undo the buttons of my shirt as I laced my fingers against her scalp. I could drown in her. Her mouth tasted of buttercream and spring, welcoming and warm like I expected her body to be. She pulled the snaps free on my undershirt, her hands pressing and exploring my chest. Her fingers delighted over my nipples, a growl slipping from me as she pinched them. I pulled back to look at her, her summer scent filling my nose and clouding my head. She licked her lips and smiled, her breath coming in huffs like my own.

"How do you want me?"

She slid off the bed and grabbed me by the waistband of my pants, leading me to where the stool sat against the wall. She sat and gazed up at me with her heated eyes.

"Put your hands on the wall and leave them there. Then give me your tail."

I did as she commanded, my tail sweeping between her fingers. She ran her pointer finger along the underside against the grain, causing me to bristle and goosebumps to sing across my skin.

"I told you my tail was ticklish." My voice has a feral edge to it.

"I know." She set my tail in her lap, a playful smile on her face. Her hands returned to the waistband of my pants. It was agonizing to watch her slowly free me from the clothing. Her hands light as she cupped me, and her fingers wrapped around my length.

A choked sound comes out of my throat. "Shasha."

"I want to taste you, *mo grá,* and I want you to watch me."

This woman was my undoing. I was already unhinged. "I don't have the control for you to torment me."

She stroked me gently. "Too bad. I want you to stand there and watch."

With that her mouth closed around my head. A shudder ran up my spine as her tongue roved over me. I groaned as she took me deep into her mouth, as deep as my size would allow. Stars glittered in my vision and claws dug into the plaster.

"Allipo will not be impressed when he has to paint this room again." I gritted through my teeth. Her answer was to take me deeper in her mouth, I brushed the back of her throat. "Oh gods."

I felt her smile around me as she squeezed my nuts in her other hand, dragging her teeth along the bottom and my head lulled back. My vision was going hazy as she played with me. Her mouth left me, the chill of her breath, a new exciting sensation that exploded across my skin, making me dizzy.

"Do you like that?"

"Woman, if you keep this up—"

"What will you do?" She stroked me with each word. "What. Will. You. Do."

I was shattered. Destroyed at her touch. "I will take you, and I will not be in control."

"Sounds fun to me." Then her mouth closed around me again, taking me deep into her throat in quick motion.

"Fuck."

Her mouth. Her tongue. Her eyes. Her scent. The sight of her wrapped around my cock. All of it took me to the edge, I tried to pull away, but she dug her nails into my thigh holding me to her.

"Shasha, if you keep this up, I'm going to cum."

She pulled back to the tip in agonizing slowness, the tip of her tongue slipping over the slit. That she-devil smiled wickedly around me as my eyes fluttered beneath her touch. My legs shook and heat and lust coiled tightly in my gut. My body was losing to her; I loved it as my vision blurred and a shudder ran down my spine.

"Shasha." I panted her name. It leaves my tongue like a prayer, "Shasha. Shasha. Fuck. I—"

She pulled back and flicked the head with her tongue and it was over. My body became molten as I released into her mouth. She took it all, swallowing as I came so violently my vision was full of fireworks. My body quivered there. I was in awe as she pulls away and wipes her lips with the back of her hand, a satisfied feline smile resting on her face.

"You taste like berries." She said.

Undone. Destroyed. I can't string thoughts together. "Shasha."

"Do you desire me?" Her voice was velvet in my ears. I did desire her. I wanted to be buried deep inside her and fill her with my seed. I wanted her begging for me. I wanted her.

"Yes."

"Then take me how you want to."

I scooped her up, my claws slicing through the fabric of her leggings so I could plunge into her wetness. Deeply seated in one thrust and she cried out her nails scraping down my chest. I carried her to the bed. Her body shuddered against mine.

"Nira."

"Shasha." I groan shredding her blouse and exposing her to me, her skin soft beneath my hands. "I love you."

"I love you." She sighed as her hands trailed down my stomach. "Scars and all."

I leaned over her, hands fisting the blankets, her legs wrapping around my waist. I kiss her chest, her neck, any inch of skin that was there to explore. I devoured her with my lips, my teeth, my tongue, and it was my name she whispered like a prayer, begging me. I buried my face against her neck. Her hands found purchase on my antlers, holding me there, bound in her scent. I stilled, my soul crying out for her. It wanted her forever. Instinct was about to override every part of me.

"Shasha. I'm going to lose control."

She panted and rocked against me. "Please."

I let a harsh breath free. "You would take me, like that?"

"Nira, I want you like that."

The beast clawed at my heart, demanding access to her. I swallowed, "I want you like that as well."

"Give me your wild, Niratap."

I pulled from her, flipped her as my body gave in to the beast. With her bent over the bed, I ease my large knot into her. She moaned my name as I eased into the depths of her. Both of us were panting my body both hot and cold and lost. I was so lost in her scent. Once I was seated, her body quivered around mine, almost sending me over.

"Shasha," I murmured against her pulse, nipping and sucking at her tender flesh, "I'm going to fuck you."

"Please."

I retreated and thrust, leaving her gasping beneath me.

"I'm going to fuck you with all my wild."

"Yes."

I thrust into her again and her cry had fur and scales taking over my skin.

"I'm going to take you, with all that I am."

"I want you."

Another thrust and she keened, her body shattering around mine.

"Fuck, how are you so beautiful." I picked her up off the bed, my body still deep inside her. I lay her face down on the soft carpet before the fireplace. Half shifted; I captured her hand in my claws. My voice was no longer human sounding at all. "This is your last chance to tell me no. To tell me to stop, because I will be lost if we continue."

"Please. I want you unhinged; fuck me, *mo grá*. Fuck me wild and true."

I was undone, clawed paws took over my hands and she was pinned underneath me. I am sucked into myself as my body became animal. As I pounded into her, driving into her hard. Under me, she submitted, crying out in wanton pleasure as the beast of me took her. My massive body stretching and claiming her. I was wild. I was a monster. I was undone. Lost. Shattered. Uncontrollable. My soul wept for her. I wanted her, in all ways I could. In all the ways she would have me. I wanted her unyielding love. I wanted her as my wife. I wanted her as my mate. Mate. Mate. Mate. She screamed my name as my heart screamed mate. Mine. I exploded. Filling her with my essence, with my scent. I poured into her, unleashing everything I had.

I settled over the top of her, both of us shattered. Broken. Trying to order my thoughts enough for my body to settle. For me to settle back into my body, I rested my head next hers. Her breath dances across my fur, twining through the strands into my very soul.

"You are magnificent." She murmured onto the carpet.

I chuffed. She was the magnificent one. Transcendent really.

"I never thought you would let go."

She wiggled beneath me eliciting a growl as my animal body denied her freedom, pain climbing through my groin.

"Are you going to hold me hostage, like this then? With you knotted up inside me?"

I tilt my head toward her, my eyes pleading. *Just wait for a few minutes please.*

Her intelligent eyes searched the depths of mine. Her voice haggard, but gentle. "You need to settle first, huh?"

I nodded once.

"And when I move it makes that harder? It hurts?"

Another nod.

"Have you ever done this before?"

I folded my ears back; we had utterly destroyed each other, and she wanted to ask questions.

"I'll take that as a no."

I sighed. Damn her and her curiosity, my back is burning being coiled so tightly. Relax, damn it.

"So, this is what it's like to be taken by an apex predator. World ending."

I chuffed; my body finally released its hold on me. I tried to gently pull myself from her. She winced and I froze.

"I'm okay." She reassured me with her hand cupping my cheek. "You are just very large."

I snorted, shaking down the wild and shifting back into a half beast, so I could ease out of her. My voice was carnal. "I'm sorry."

She rolled, gripping the hard lines of my maw between her hands. "Don't apologize. I love you and that was life altering."

She threaded her fingers through the sparse fur. "You are life altering."

She chuckled, continuing to pet me gently. "So never before?"

I took a breath and eased into my human form with a sigh. "No." I never wanted to be with another. I pulled her against me.

"What was it like for you?"

"So full of questions." I sighed into her hair.

"I'm just curious."

"I am destroyed."

She pressed a kiss to my throat. "Mutual."

"Did I hurt you?"

"Not in any way that matters."

I shook my head. "That makes no sense."

"That's fine." She purred, kissing my throat again.

"You vex me, girl."

"Do I now." She ran a finger over my collarbone.

"Yes." I buried my face into her cloud of hair, inhaling her scent.

She yawned and snuggled against me. "You owe me a birthday gift."

I chuckled as I scooped her up in my arms and walked to the bed. "What would you like, *mo grá*?"

I tucked her in on one side of the bed. "I want to go dancing, at a club in the city."

"I can arrange that." I said slipping in on my side of our bed.

"And I want to dance with you."

I kissed her temple, curling my body around hers. "My flower, I don't dance."

"That's why it's a gift. I want you to dance with me."

"I will think about it."

"You better." She mumbled, falling asleep wrapped in my arms.

I chuckled. "So demanding."

Sleep evaded me as thoughts of her tormented me. I wanted to claim her. Wanted her forever and always, but how could I ask her to bind her very soul to me. She was so young. So wild. Why on earth would any being want to be wrapped up in my darkness? Why would she choose me so completely? Her scent covered me and my scent covered her. Would she want that always? Being marked by me? Who would want that?

Chapter Forty-Four

Niratap

"My Lord."

I sighed, sifting through the paperwork on my desk. "If you're here to admonish me for bedding my girlfriend you might as well turn around and rethink it."

Allipo cleared his throat, and I looked up at him dressed in a grey suit that didn't fit the satyr's natural ban on boring colors. His face also held none of his usual vitality, his hand held a small black box.

"What happened?" I said standing.

"Taegan was compromised."

"What happened?" I roared. Taegan had been so young, a satyr who Allipo had taken under his wing to teach, who saw the vast good we were trying to do and wanted to fight too. "What is in the box?"

"My Lord."

"Tell me what happened."

Allipo came forward and set the small black box on my desk. "Taegan called while you were gone. He told me that he thought he was compromised. That he was getting pushed off and left out of meetings about products. He said he was going to try and get out before anyone could mark him. I booked him a flight out of Coeur D'Alene, but it was Thanksgiving weekend, and the airports are a nightmare. My last communication with him was twenty minutes before his flight was to board. I told him to call me when he landed here, that I would be waiting. He never showed. Yesterday before you and Miss Shasha returned, Eloi and I went to get gifts, check the mail, and all that. The box was in the mail. I had to sign for it. It—just look for yourself."

With shaking hands, Allipo lifted the lid of the box, and I saw red. Resting in the black satin lined box were two slate-colored eyes and two satyr ears. I sank back into my seat. A note was nailed to the top of the box for me. It said:

You can have your eyes and ears back. Bondbreaker.

"Was anyone else compromised?"

"No, his handler reached out this morning. Kallin is twisted up, but he's alive and they don't know he's dirty. Kallin was there when they tortured him. He only gave them your name."

I slammed my hand on the desk and stood loosening my tie, which seemed to tighten unbearably on my throat. I needed to run this off. "Burn the box."

"Yes, my Lord."

"Tell Kallin to exercise caution, the soonest whisper of him being compromised, I want him out." I tossed my jacket over the chair and undid the buttons on my shirt.

"Yes, my Lord."

"Ventris will call sometime in the day; take notes of the call and report to me."

"Yes, my Lord. Are you going off?"

"Yes, I need to settle my mind. I'm going for a run. I'll go over your report when I return; I'll be back by nightfall, if not by morning." I said toeing out of my shoes.

"What do you want me to tell Miss Shasha?"

I paused, sliding out of my pants. "Tell her I needed to find some peace."

Allipo nodded and bowed. "As you wish, my Lord."

I shifted as I exited the study doors, plodding down the hall, through the solarium and out into the snowy mid-morning. I sniffed the air and even the mountains couldn't soothe the smell of blood and death in my nose and the ache in my heart. I took off at full speed. Pushing my body until my lungs and eyes burned. I didn't see the lands around me, the sleepy glades of trees or quiet meadows, where the wildflowers grew in the spring. I only saw sweet hearted Taegan. I only saw the starved, young satyr who I had rescued from a slaver. He was younger than Bastion; they had been friends, sparing, and playing together. How was I going to tell him his best friend was dead?

Allipo had breathed life into him with their heritage and took him to the Satyr village where Staspar showed him the love of food and music and women. Dorilody had smoothed nightmares and clothes. The Days fed him extra out of the kitchen, helping him put back on healthy weight, and nurtured his sweet heart. Echo and Dheg dragged him to the garden so he could fall in love with the sun again. Mitta taught him to defend himself. The sisters gave him a thirst for justice.

Then he swore fealty to me. Healed and happy, he kneeled before me, caught me off guard and swore to serve the cause, to free those who were trapped like him. I was so shocked I accepted his oath. So young. I had sent him off to Idaho to watch over the dragon scale trade there. It wasn't high risk, but I needed to know how and where they were supplied. I had sent him to an early demise. Allipo would never blame me for his death, but I did.

In the clearing I collapsed by the pool, my legs screaming in protest. I had sent Taegan there and had been confident that he would be safe. It was a simple operation, small but growing. How had he been compromised? How had I failed him?

I roared at the sky. Life was unfair and cruel. It should have been me I wanted to scream. It should have been me. Taegan was so full of light. It should have been me and my shadows to cross the threshold, not Taegan. I wept. Time passed differently as I lay there in my misery. Letting the snow dust my fur. Hoof beats pulled me from my sorrows and there she was atop Guinness, face wind kissed and wrapped up warmly.

"I thought you'd be here." She said sliding from the saddle and coming to my side to bury her face in my fur. "Allipo told me you needed peace."

I chuffed laying my head back over my paws.

"Guinness made sure I was safe. Allipo told me you guys lost someone, that you would find peace in your own pity party." She sat next to me, her hand coming to rest on my head.

Fucking satyr. I huffed; my heart achingly heavy.

"Allipo is wearing grey today. That should have been my first clue. When I saw him first thing this morning, I didn't even doubt it as he paced about the dining room. Rogmesh actually told me that he was just a kid. That this death would rock the whole house for a time."

I placed my head in her lap, and she stroked me between the ears. Her scent anchored me.

"Durgash said that we would have been friends. That he was friends with everyone."

Taegan was friends with everyone. I let loose a heavy sigh.

"Whenever you're ready to talk about it, I'm here."

I leaned into her touch, her scent, just her. Warmth and love in every breath for a monster that sent a child to his demise. My heart cried. I hated myself. This was my fault. Knowing the risk or not, Taegan's death was my fault.

"It's not." She murmured into the falling snow. "His death. It isn't your fault."

But it is, *mo grá*. I am at fault. I sent him there. A shuddering breath left me. She ran her hands across my muzzle.

"It's not your fault, love. He knew the risks when he went under. He knew what could happen and accepted it."

But I should have thought. I shouldn't have let him sacrifice himself for my cause. I—

"I know what you're thinking. He made the choice, Nira. He knew what he was getting into. You don't have to beat yourself over his decision."

I lifted my head, staring deep into her eyes. I let my beast fall away, fur and scales becoming flesh again. I wrapped my arms around her, burying my face into her neck.

"He's gone, and I sent him out there." A sob cracked my voice. "He's gone."

She stroked my hair and held me lightly, "My love, it's not your fault. It's not your fault."

I sobbed, my heart cracking open, spilling into her hands. She let me. Let me sob and cry. She let me break. I knew everyone who I had lost in this fight to keep our freedom. Every face that I had saved. Every face that had walked away with my protection. Every face that swore to fight with me. They all had a piece of my heart. They all had me with them and losing any of them wounded me. She didn't know that, but still she held me.

My skin was chilled when the sobs had subsided. A shiver brought me back to the present.

"You must be cold." I said to her, pulling away.

"I'm fine." She smiled. "I brought some clothes if you want, but we can always dip in to warm up."

I gave her a half-committed smile and my heart wept. "I want to talk to you about something."

"Anything. Wait one second." She ran over to where Guinness pawed at the snow, munching on the winter grass beneath. Pulling a blanket from one of the saddle bags, she wrapped it around my shoulders when she returned to me. "I know it's not much, but it should help with the chill."

I kissed her cheek. "Thank you."

"What did you want to talk about?"

"I—" How do I tell you? "I told you not long ago, that my species is particular about how things are done. A biological directive if you will."

"Yes. Bitarogs mate. I remember."

I sighed. "I want you."

She smiled at me. "You have me."

"No. I don't think you understand."

She frowned. "Enlighten me."

I took a breath to find my nerve. Another breath and my heart screamed. "I want you the way a male of my species wants. I want to be wrapped in your essence and you

411

in mine. I want our souls linked. I want you as—" I swallowed, looking into the depths of the water. "As my mate."

Seconds pass, maybe minutes, before she spoke. "You want me as your mate?"

A breath shuddered from me, and I didn't dare look up. "Yes."

She was quiet. My heart screamed please say yes. Please be mine.

"I know it's wrong of me to ask. You are so young and wild. I've argued with myself for days, wanting you so completely, wanting you as my mate, binding our souls together. It's wrong of me to want that." I fisted my hands. "It's wrong of me to put the weight of that on you."

"What does it entail, becoming your mate?"

I swallowed; I couldn't look at her as I felt the weight of her definite rejection. I said. "We exchange vows, bodies and souls, fully like we did last night. Share our life's essence. You take my blood and I take yours."

"Then what?"

"Then we exist with one another. Your scent will be a part of mine and my scent a part of yours. We will be linked. There isn't much information on my kind; it could do anything since you are not like I am. It could extend your life, or it could shorten it. There is no precedent for what it would do."

Her hands cupped my face, pulling me to look at her. The warmth I found in those depths caused my chest to ache with all the things I was afraid of wanting. She smiled. "I would be honored."

My heart stopped. "What?"

"I would be honored to be your mate, Niratap."

Tears anew streamed from my eyes. "I must be dreaming."

"Nira." She spoke my name like a song. "I would love to be and honored to be yours."

"You wouldn't feel trapped? Tied down to me forever."

"No, it would be fulfilling. You are my life, whatever comes."

I threw my arms around her. "Truly?"

"Yes." She laughed softly. "I wish to be yours as long as you are mine."

"You have had my heart from the moment I met you. I would have waited another millennium for you."

"When do you want to do this?"

"Whenever you want, whatever you want."

"Right now."

My heart pounded wildly. "You can't mean."

"No, I do. Why wait a millennium if we have found peace with one another?"

I kissed her hard, my mouth and body pleading, begging for her. My heart screamed for her. I lifted her into my arms and carried her back to the hidden cave by the waterfall. Guinness knickered at me, bringing me to a halt.

"Yes, my friend?"

He stomped the ground impatiently.

"Right." I returned to him and took the two saddle bags off the back. "You are free to return home, friend. I have her."

He bobbed his head before turning and trotting away towards home.

"You really have a connection to him, don't you?"

"He is a good horse." I said, walking us into the shelter of the cave. "I was blessed to call him friend."

I set her down on the cave floor and laid the blanket out on the soft loamy soil, "It's warm in here."

"It's the heat from the spring. It warms this whole cave."

"You didn't show me this the last time we were here."

"I was a bit preoccupied with the thought of you drowning."

"But I didn't."

I chuckled, cupping her cheek. "No, you did not. You are a gift."

"So, were going to be mated when we leave here?"

"Yes." The notion still caused my heart to sputter.

"You said we exchanged vows, what should I vow?"

"Whatever you wish, they are like marriage vows, promises to one another."

"Then we have sex."

"Yes."

"And we exchange blood."

"Yes."

"Then I am yours completely."

"Yes. You will be mine and I will be yours."

"Mine." She whispered full of devotion; her voice almost dreamy.

"Yes. I will be yours, until the day I cease drawing breath for good. Only yours forever."

Her arms wrapped around me. "Mine and yours forever."

"Yes." I hadn't thought that she could shatter me any more than she already had.

"Then I vow to love you. To cherish you. To honor you. I offer myself to you, soul and all. I will be your shoulder to lean on in times of need. Your home to return to when you are away, for you are my home and the home of my heart."

My heart swooned at her. I kneeled before her, holding her hands in mine and bowed my head. "I vow to love you, honor you, cherish you, protect you. I give myself to you completely on bended knee and with bowed head. You are the master of my heart. My safety. My life. My home."

She cupped my face, tears streaming down. "You are my safety. My heart. Home. I have known that for longer than I wanted to admit."

I kissed her tears away. "After we bed, there is no going back. Are you sure you want to do this with me?"

"It's the surest I have ever been."

I laid her down over the blanket. I searched her eyes and I only found love. No regret. No fear. No doubt. Just her unending love for me and somehow that was everything I had ever wanted. She slid her clothes away and wrapped her legs around my waist. I slid into her. Our gasps and sighs echoed off the walls of the cave. I made love to her there. Slowly. Lovingly. True. She shattered beneath me, and I kissed her deeply before flipping her over. I shifted to the monster that struck fear in the hearts of so many but her and slid into her. Her sweet supple body yielding to me with a grace I would never understand. I rested my head over her shoulder, her hot breath gliding through my fur and shadows. I would give her everything and anything she desired, the keeper of my soul. Again, she was lost to pleasure. Lost to me. I nuzzled against her, deep body purrs radiating through me. She was accepting me, accepting a monster as her mate. I fully shifted, filling her beyond what her body should have allowed. She cried out my name, her voice echoing over me, a song as I bed her. She shattered a third time, pulling me beyond with her. I dumped my seed, my heart, my soul into her. We stayed there for a few moments, while I settled back into my skin. Settled my soul against hers.

She panted into the blanket. "How is it that I can still take all that I am and lay it bare before you, again and again? How is it that you chose me?"

I came back to my human skin and kissed her shoulder. "I wonder the same thing."

She turned to face me. "I love you."

"I love you." I lifted her from the blanket, and she groaned as I slipped between her molten hot flesh, having her straddle me. "I will always love you."

"We share blood now?" She asked, trying not to squirm, her body demanding friction.

"Yes." Claws overtook my fingers. "I will cut myself for you and use magic to keep the wound open. Then I will cut you or bite you, it is your choice."

She bit her lip. "You would bite me?"

"If that is what you want."

"Yes." The word was breathless.

I took a breath to steady myself. To calm my fear, my doubt. I pressed my brow against hers. "I am afraid that you will regret this. Regret me."

"Never." Her eyes held mine with the determination that they held when she shot, when she defended me with her words. It was the truest word in the world to her. She was mine. I was hers and nothing, nothing, would take her from me or me from her.

"Very well, *mo grá*." I dragged a claw over the left side of my neck wincing at the pain.

She places a hand on my shoulder as the blood slid down my neck. "I'm ready."

She tilted her head to the side exposing her delicate pulse to me. My fangs felt heavy in my mouth. "No going back."

"I don't want to."

I kissed her pulse. "I'll be gentle."

She giggled, kissing my jaw. "I don't know why."

I smiled. Then I sank my teeth into her throat, a small noise escaping her. My body wen rigid as her essence filled me. Summer rain, winter ice, fall winds, and spring grass assault my senses, and I was in free fall. Falling into her taste. Falling into the depths of her being. Into her soul. I was tossed by an internal wind. Lust beyond anything that I felt for her urged me to fuck, breed her. Then her lips met my throat. Electricity slammed through me, and I could taste moss, Irish rain, cloves and smoke on my tongue. My essence mixing with hers, our souls wrapping tightly around each other. I thrust into her, a choked groan coming from her, and she dug her nails into my back. Everything. She was everything. My air. My water. My sustenance. My heart. My soul. My home. Everything began and ended with her. We tumbled to the floor, and she released my neck to cry my name. I licked her throat, using magic to heal the wound close. Enough to stop the bleeding and seal the punctures, but not enough so the deep purple bruise would stay. I wanted the world to know that she was mine. She was transcendent below me glowing, really glowing, pale blue light dancing over her skin and crawling over mine as my shadows dance over her. Her head lulled back, face painted with pure ecstasy and lust. Pure joy. And mine.

I captured her mouth with mine, I tasted my blood on her tongue, the mountains, the rain, the spice of me as she tasted me. I pounded into her wantonly and with each thrust my heart cried. Mate. Mine. Driving us to the edge and diving right over it. A free fall into bliss. A toss and tangle of limbs, mouths, tongues, and teeth. We worshiped each other. I devoured her skin, with kisses. She explored mine with her mouth. We were not two separate beings anymore. We were a single soul frenzied with lust for everything. A single being discovering its body for the first time. Discovering divinity.

Shattered. Utterly destroyed. Spent and satiated. We curled against each other, no space between us, between our breaths, between our souls. She was mine. I was hers. That was everything that would ever matter again.

"*Is liomsa tu agus is leatsa mise.*[33]"

"What."

"You are mine and I am yours."

---

[33] You are mine and I am yours.

Chapter Forty-Five

Devastated. I felt whole. I was home. That was the only way I could describe what he had done to me. With me. Mine. He was mine. Mate. The word warmed my heart, my soul, in spite of it being so foreign. I wanted him. All of him. Scars and baggage and all. His face was so peaceful as he slept. Tomorrow we would go home anew. Tomorrow we would address all the questions and concerns. Tonight though, tonight it was just him and I and the bond between us. I could still taste the smokey rain on my tongue, could smell him laced across my skin. Feel him in the pleasurable ache of our joining. He was everything. My sun. My moon. My sky. Everything.

When the sound of winter songbirds danced over me that morning, I was snuggled into his soft furred body. In the night he must have shifted to keep us warm against the chill. I ran my hands through the silky stands, and a purr resounded through the cavern walls. I buried my face into him and blew a raspberry.

A growl was my greeting.

"Good morning to you, too, my love."

The fur faded into skin, that I kissed quickly, before he snatched me in his arms.

"You minx. That is not how one wakes their mate."

"And how would one wake their mate?"

He rolled on top of me, kissing the tender spot on my neck. I wrapped legs around him, finding his hard length pressing against me. I groaned, my head falling back. "Like this, *mo grá*. Like this mate. Mine."

He slid into my bruised body, the pain twisting with pleasure. My body arched against him. "Nira."

"Shasha."

He was gentle with me, so gentle. His thrusts were soft and loving. He kissed me and where his lips and tongue met my skin, fire erupted. I was consumed by him, his gentle love. His tenderness. I cried his name as I fell off the edge. He roared as I pull him over with me. It felt like we're flying, wrapped up in one another's arms. Floating on the ocean of our bond. Home. I was home.

He rolled off me and laid at my side, staring at the ceiling. He was always so transfixed by the goings on in his brain. I rolled onto him, my fingers dancing over the pink scar on his chest. "What are you thinking about?"

His eyes settled on me. "About us."

"What about us?" I asked, laying my head on his chest. Listening to his heart beat, my heart beat.

"That I don't want to share you."

"We can't stay here forever."

He sighed. "I know."

"What now?"

"You are mine and I am yours."

"And as such I am more of a target. A way for our enemies to you."

He closes his eyes, the point causing him pain that ached in my own heart. "Yes."

"And our friends?"

He ran a hand through his hair. "Allipo would give me grief. The women of our house would probably skin me alive."

I laughed. "I don't think so. I think they would celebrate us."

He ran his other hand down my back. "You're probably right, but still, I think we should keep this to ourselves for now."

"Won't they smell the bond though?"

"No, you already had my scent on you, and I already had yours on me. If we spend a decent amount of time apart the scent won't fade, and that would be a tell for those who know what our scent is separate from each other."

"I see and you want to keep it from our friends for now—"

"As a means of safety. For both of us."

"You're not trying to tell me that you think our friends would turn on us?"

"No, but the less they know the better it will be for you and I. At least until things settled down."

"Okay. If it will ease that worry line in your face."

He chuckled, looking at me with such warmth and joy.

"You're mine that is all that matters."

"I couldn't be happier to call you mine."

Chapter Forty-Six

Shasha

Winter at the Manor was beautiful as heavy snow blanketed the ground and weighed down the branches. I felt comfortable here, especially since semester finals were done and I could spend all my time with Nira. My mate. It was still foreign to me, how it sounded off my tongue. However, having him with me always as a part of my soul was comforting when he was busy. And for the first time in my life, I felt whole.

He didn't give me a role or a title with the bond. He said I was free to be whatever I wanted, spend my time however I wanted. He was so afraid to be a shackle, and yet I hadn't found the courage in my heart to ask about the binding spell that still lingered around my neck. Why did it still linger when I had proven I wasn't going anywhere?

The house was full of activity as winter fae brought gifts for the house in the form of holly and mistletoe. Niratap had been accosted for the majority of the day out in the cold with a spirit, an old man with a long beard and antlers that weighed down his head. The manor was so isolated, but the man had shown up alone and without transportation. He did not shudder in the cold, even as Niratap had shoved his hands deep into his coat pockets. When he bid the spirit adieu, and came into the house puffing breath into his hands. I was waiting to greet him.

"Who was that?"

"A winter spirit who goes by many names. Father winter is his most common, jack frost I think is another colloquialism for him. He is a being who is about to be reborn to continue the cycle of time."

"Why was he here?"

"He visits us every year, only asks that the guardians listen to his tale of the year, and he offers blessings for the next." He smiled at me, taking off his coat, which was frosty.

"Why did you stand out in the cold, why not invite him in?"

"Because inviting beings that are the cycle of life into your home, usually has ill consequences."

"Like what?"

He kissed my cheek, his face icy to the touch. "So many questions. Though I enjoy his tale of the year, winter is a dreadful time of year. I would rather it not hang around beyond its welcome."

"That could happen if you invited him in?"

"That's what the stories say." He offered me his arm. "I could use a hot cup of tea after his visit. Would you join me?"

"What else is there to do to prepare for the season?"

"Well, Dheg and Durgash are out getting a tree, and I'm sure the evening will be filled with threading popcorn and cranberries." He said softly.

"You sound like you're almost excited to have a family filled evening of stabbing your fingers."

He chuckled.

"Almost. What's wrong?"

"The holidays are hard for me. They are hard on the Days."

"Because Bas won't be here."

The worried crinkle came to his face. "No, he won't be."

"Hey, don't beat yourself up."

He sighed. "It's hard not to."

"Bas knows what he signed up for, he knows the risks. He knows the danger. He knows, and you treating yourself poorly because you're technically his boss doesn't change that. You're also family. He made a choice; you can't fault him for making a choice."

He gave me side-eye. "How do you do that?"

"I just listen and give you wisdom that I have gleaned from you."

He smiled, as we turned around the kitchen. "I'm glad you are so intelligent and wise."

"You better not be bringing sass into my kitchen, my Lord, or you will be stringing cranberries and popcorn by yourself." Rogmesh hissed.

"Never." He said with a laugh, and she flipped her towel at him.

"Just tea, Rog. I just want some tea to warm my bones from old man winter." I loved when he was like this, their friend. Not just the man who saved them and gave them choices, but the person they claimed as family.

"Tonight's the night, then?"

"Yes, it is, the hunt is on."

"The hunt?"

"The wild hunt. Yuletide is when they go off through the world capturing lost souls roaming about." Nira said, opening the pantry.

"So, we stay inside and decorate the house." Rogmesh said, filling the kettle with water.

"To avoid the hunt coming after us." Durgash said from the doorway.

"Did you guys find a good one?" Rogmesh asked him.

"Why of course we did, my fearless one. Dheg was a mighty help felling this one." He said, wrapping his arm around Dheg's shoulders as he came into the doorway.

"A fine evergreen it is." He said with a smile. "The winter neighbors also dropped off more garland and holly. Was that old man winter we saw spiriting away?"

"It was." Nira said, setting a jar on the counter and reaching into the cupboard. "The hunt will be out tonight. I want everyone inside at sundown."

Dheg and Durgash bowed. "Yes, my Lord."

"Now, you guys must be chilled. Tea?" Nira offered.

"Yes please, my Lord." Durgash smiled.

"Sounds amazing, my Lord." Dheg agreed.

"Durgash, now that you're done playing in the woods, would you help me finish the meal for tonight?"

"Yes, woman, I will help you, let my old bones warm first."

"Your bones are not that old. Your disposition on the other hand."

He wrapped his arms around her and nuzzled her neck. "Woman, you hurt my pride."

"That's not all that's going to hurt if you don't unhand me, you brute." I laughed at their banter.

"You love me."

"Be that as it may Durgash, I will wound you."

"I love foreplay." He kissed her cheek. "Is it a promise?"

"Durgash." She chuckled.

"Now, please save us your bedroom shenanigans." Nira said as he spooned tea into the cups.

"Like you do, my Lord?"

Nira cleared his throat. "I have no idea what you mean."

"Oh, really." Dheg said, walking past Nira into the pantry and coming out with a box of chocolate cookies. "The dark cloud that was cast over the gun room tells a different story."

I slapped a hand over my mouth and Nira's ears pinked.

"Not to mention the noise. Mitta was sure something had gotten out down there." Durgash grumbled.

"The worst part was the smell." Mitta said coming to stand at the door. "You two really exude the scent of arousal all the time."

Nira coughed and I broke, doubling over in a mad cackle. Nira poured water into the cups. "I'm glad you find our public shaming funny."

I wiped tears from my eyes. "How many of you were in the hall?"

"Mitta, Durgash, and myself. Just the three of us." Dheg said, taking a cup from the counter.

Rogmesh laughed as she walked through the kitchen. "I can't believe you three eavesdropped on the lord and young lady."

"There was no way that was eavesdropping Rogmesh, I heard them in the security room." Mitta groaned. "With the door closed."

"They were in there moaning and groaning and snarling all over each other." Dheg said, making kissy faces at us.

Nira groaned, stirring sugar into our tea. "Please stop."

"Sex, that would explain his rather pleasant mood the last couple months." Rogmesh said, snatching the box of cookies from Dheg and returning them to the pantry.

"A good rut will do that." Dheg agreed, a fae-smile brightening his face.

Nira stared up at the ceiling and sighed. "This is divine retribution for something."

"Just think of it as comeuppance for your normally shitty moods." Mitta said.

"Did you need something, Mitta?" He said handing me the warm mug. "Or are you just here to pick on me."

"I do have something that requires your attention, my Lord, but poking at you is also fun, friend."

He leaned against the wall beside me and drank his tea. "What is it this fine afternoon that requires my attention?"

"Bastion sent me a correspondence while you were preoccupied with old man winter."

Nira paused, lowering the mug. "What did he say?"

"He wished us a blessed holiday; said he was going to miss his mother's cookies."

"The holidays are not the same without him." Durgash said.

"You remember that time we got him drunk on eggnog, and he nearly burned down the house throwing up in the fire."

A small bittersweet smile crept onto Nira. "That wasn't all that was in his message."

"No." Mitta frowned. "Dravin was the private buyer for the bitarog."

A feral snarl came from his throat. "That fucking snake."

"Agreed." Mitta said, picking at her nails. "They're moving her somewhere; he does not know where."

Nira's knuckles cracked as he fisted his hand. "So, we wait."

"Yes."

The ease of the kitchen conversation prior to the news from Bastion was gone. Nira sat beside me, piercing popcorn and cranberries on the fine thread, his face drawn as the others chatted quietly. His shadows danced along his fingers, twining over the decorations. His shoulders were tight, his brow furrowed.

"You're worried."

"Hmm." He didn't look up.

"I can see it written all over your face. You're worried."

He sighed, setting the garland in his lap. The room went quiet. "I am, *mo grá*. That bottom feeder Dravin is plotting something and I don't know what. Bitarogs are rare. Females even rarer. What is he planning on doing with her? To her?"

"He could take control of the market with a bitarog. As weapons, they made kings." Mitta said, not turning from her scrutiny of the evergreens she was trying to hang on the mantle. "There were several used by the church for the crusades and the inquisition."

"And most of them died because of it." His hand slid to his side just below his ribs, where I knew he had a faded, wide scar. "I was almost one of them, during those crusades."

"My kind were used the same." She said, shifting the boughs.

"I have not forgotten." He said, glancing at where she stood fussily shifting the same bough for the third time. "You won't get it any straighter than it is, Mitta."

She glowered at him, but Allipo asked. "What else could he gain?"

"Leverage will probably be his first aim. Money, power, allies." Nira said leaning back on the sofa. "Then he will probably start going after his enemies."

"And we're his number one target right now." I said looking down at the garland in my hand. "Makes sitting here making decorations feel kind of silly doesn't it."

"It's not silly." Echo said sadly.

"We are sitting at the brink of what might be a war on at least a couple fronts. How is sitting here not silly?" Eloimaya asked, her brows furrowed.

"Because it's not." Tummi said.

"Why?" I pushed.

"Because there is plenty to be thankful for." Dorilody said.

Niratap smiled, but I asked. "What is there to be thankful for?"

"Because we are here." Allipo said, wrapping an arm around Eloimaya.

"Because we are alive." Rogmesh said.

"Because we are free." Dheg said.

"Because we have each other." Durgash said.

"Because we will fight." Katrel said standing.

"Because we will triumph." Mitta finished.

Niratap beamed at them, his family, his staff, the leaders of whatever armies he would lead. I wondered if he knew. Knew that the people around him, even I, would go to

the ends of the earth for him, bleed for him, die for him.
"Blessed winter to you, my friends. Yule-tidings indeed."

I grasped his hand. "Whatever may come, *mo grá*."

He eyed me, still smiling, but a great sorrow filled his
eyes. "Let us enjoy this Solstice season, live each day like it's
our last, until it is. Whatever may come."

And we did. Making music and dancing with the men
of the house, save my mate who refused me the joy of his
hand. We drank wine and decorated the tree and halls with
our garlands and evergreen. We ate a hearty dinner of roasted
meat and vegetables and drank brandy. It was fun and full of
laughter, but when we went to bed, I couldn't settle my
thoughts even as Niratap breathed lightly on the bed beside
me. Eventually I moved to stand by the window and watched
as a pageant of ghosts astride mighty red eyed steeds flew by
in an eerie fog. The wild hunt searching the forests for lost
souls. I wondered if they collected those who did not know
about their yearly ride or if by some ancient instinct everyone
stayed inside on this cloudless winter night. I watched them
through the trees, hounds crying death knells as they hunted
for the lost. I wondered if they would reap my soul one day.
Would it be in a millennium if I stood at Niratap's side, if the
magic that spun our souls together would keep me alive with
him? Or would it be in the next few months in the battles that
we were sure to face, the war we would no doubt have to
fight in? Would I be strong enough then to protect him like I
vowed? Only destiny knew what the future had in store for
us.

Yule was a beautiful morning and fresh snowfall
made a blanket for the earth. The day itself was like the night
before, dancing, merry making, delectable snacks and
everyone piled gifts around the tree. Rogmesh made
Bastion's favorite cookies, because there was no way to
celebrate without his spirit there. Fresh cookies and hot
chocolate warmed the cold bones after playing in the snow

with everyone, building snowmen and forts, throwing snowballs at each other and running amuck through the fresh undisturbed blanket of snow. As the sun began to dip, Nira was sliding back into his coat when I slid away from the dining room.

"Where are you going?"

He smiled. "I'm going out to witness the mother travel by. Would you like to accompany me?"

I scampered past him into the coat closet. "Yes."

He chuckled, wrapping his scarf around his neck. "Dress quickly against the cold my dear, we have little time on the longest night of the year to see her."

"Who is she?" I queried, coming out of the closet in my coat. He wrapped a scarf around my neck pinning a spring of berries to it. "What are those?"

"She is the goddess of life, living the cycle of time. She is journeying to the farthest horizon to give birth to the sun god so the cycle can continue. Those are yew berries, to keep you safe from winter spirits lingering about."

"The hunt?"

"It's possible. I have never tested it to see." He said with a mischievous smile.

"Let's not." I took his hand as he stepped to the door.

"Stay quiet, stay close."

I nodded and we were off into the snow that glistened in the moonlight. The only sound was the crunching of the snow under our boots. Our breath curled and danced through the air, wispy white shades in the night. Into the forest we roamed, and I pressed closer to him.

"Have no fear, *mo grá*. The beasts of the forest rest tonight so that the lady may pass through undisturbed. To interrupt her journey could be the end of days."

"Why is that?"

He smiled. "Because to interrupt the mother, to stall her journey to the horizon could mean the sun does not rise tomorrow or again. So, we may watch, as the passage of time continues."

"So cryptic."

He chuckled as we came to the edge of a clearing. "Here we are, and now we wait."

"Will she make us wait long?" I asked, shivering.

"No." He said looking up at the sky, "She'll be here soon."

He pulled me close to him as an icy breeze tore through the meadow before us, tickling the tall grasses that fought through the winter snow.

"She's here." He pointed across the way, and I saw her.

A lovely woman clothed in gossamer, heavy with child, was astride a mighty white hart, whose antlers were adorned with bright silver bells. She had summer tanned skin and long earthen hair the flowed behind her in ethereal waves dancing on a phantom wind; her hand lay lovingly over her mountainous belly. A denizen of fae carrying lanterns of blue fire flanked the beautiful woman on all sides. The procession traveled towards us, the faint bells tinkling with every step the hart took. As they passed, Niratap bowed, his head lowered near the ground. I bowed too, but my eyes peered up at the beautiful woman before us. Her eyes were bright like stars, glittering in the blue fire light.

"The shadow of the forest has come to see me travel by. Pray tell who is that that keeps your company?" Her starlight eyes finding mine, her voice both young and old.

Nira's hand came around me again even as he did not rise. "She is my mate, dear mother."

"Milady, we shouldn't doddle." The creature at the head of their winter procession said.

"I know will-o-wisp. A blessing for you and yours, dear shadow." She lightly tapped the longest point of Nira's antlers. "May light find you when things are the darkest."

"Milady."

"Of course." She cupped my face pulling it to meet her stars. "Fierce wind, guide his sails true. Bright fire, warm his soul. Soft water, ease his wounds. Gentle earth, anchor him. Strong spirit, guide him home."

"Blessings to you, mother." Nira bowed lower.

She released me, a delicate smile dancing across her lips. "Onward."

They disappeared between the trees, and when the last wisp crossed our path, we stood. The tinkling of bells faded; the sound swallowed by the snow at our feet.

"I thought she wouldn't stop."

"Normally she doesn't." He said, eyeing the threshold of trees where the light bobbed to and fro. "Peculiar indeed. Let's go home."

Back at home Nira retired for the evening, told me to stay and listen to the tales that Allipo would spin of winter solstices old. I would have pushed for him to stay, to sit with me by the fire, but the forlorn look about him had stilled my tongue. I worried if the blessing the mother had bestowed upon us had actually been a curse. Tales were spun for hours, until just before dawn. We ventured out to the eastern side of the gardens; evergreens glittered with frost in the predawn light. His hands rested on my shoulders as he joined us.

"I didn't think you would join us." I said softly.

"I never miss the birth of a new sun." He said with equal hush as pale purple kissed the sky and stars started to wink out of the sky. "Did you enjoy his stories?"

"Allipo definitely knows how to tell a story. Although I think he embellishes a bit."

"It's the satyr's nature." He said with a smile, predawn gold dancing against his skin.

Red and bronze grew across the sky, banishing the coolness of the night. "Is it always so bright, the first sunrise of a new sun?"

"It depends on the strength of the earth and the mother of the year. Sometimes the sun is like this bright, and full of the life-giving warmth we need. Other times the sky is grey and pale when the sun rises. Those years are ones full of hardship, longer winters, dry summers; the animals don't produce, and populations fall. Years full of pain for the earth usually cause grey suns for the next year. When the creatures of the earth massacre each other, when men go to war and tons of wasted blood is spilled in the earth."

"I see. So, the way the sun comes in after the longest night of the year kind of determines how the earth is the following year?"

"Something like that, it's more complicated than that, but it's a simple explanation for a bigger cycle."

I leaned into his warmth, his strength. "How are you feeling?"

"That is a loaded question, *mo grá*."

"Is it?"

He sighed. "I am fine."

"Fine is a dirty, four-letter f word."

He chuckled. "Later, my dear. I will let you explore how fine I am."

"Oh, is that right?"

"Most definitely. A threat even."

"Could you guys not flirt within fifteen feet of me please?" Mitta growled just as a bright flash of yellow light cleared the horizon.

I smiled as the newborn sun kissed my face. A cheer echoed from the woods, the neighbors welcoming the sun to the earth.

"I think coffee is in order." Rogmesh said.

"As long as there is whiskey in it." Allipo agreed.

They laughed at that and began to file back into the warmth of the manor. Nira held me in place as the others passed, wanting a moment just for us.

"This day is special for me."

"Is it now? Because of the blessing?"

"No, because of you, getting to experience everything with you. My life suddenly has a new set of firsts, and it makes me happy."

I looked up at him. "Cheeseball."

He smiled sweetly at me. "I love you."

"I love you too."

"We should head inside."

"For coffee?"

"No, for presents."

"You are the only gift I need."

"Now who's the cheeseball." He chuckled, guiding me back toward the manor.

"I hope you like what I got you."

"As long as you didn't have Allipo or Mitta help pick it out I will be fine. I do not need another tie or dagger any time soon."

"Oh no, I picked this out all on my own. However, you have to open it when we're alone."

His eyebrows rose. "Oh, now I'm intrigued."

I danced out of his hold and scampered ahead. "How long do you think it will be before they notice were not in the great room with them?"

"If Allipo has whiskey in his coffee, at least a half hour."

"That should be enough time to unwrap your gift. If you can keep up."

"Minx." He called after me as I dashed into the manor and up the stairs. He was on my heels as I made the last couple steps and tried to dart down the hall. He caught me before I reach the first door of the hall. I giggled wildly as he hauled me over his shoulder.

"This gift you chose must be mighty fine."

I laughed, snatching his tail in my hands. "Not as fine as you."

"Hey now, that is sensitive."

"Oh, I know." I ran my fingers against the grain of his fur.

He snarled and I could have sworn I heard faint laughter from downstairs.

"We are putting on quite the show, don't you think?"

"All the better, they know to leave us be." He eased open the door to our room and set me on the floor. "Now go fetch this gift you have for me."

I smiled, backing into the bathroom. "What about my gift?"

"All in good time, darling."

I clicked the bathroom door shut and opened the cabinet where I had stored the delightful honey-colored lacy underthings. I had tried to be conscious of what I purchased, not wanting to spend too much on something that would probably be sliced off my body faster than I could put it on. But when I saw this, I couldn't resist, knowing how he worshiped me gilded in golds. I painted my eyes and lips with a similar golden color. I bought this with him in mind, but as I was staring at myself in the mirror, I wondered. Would he see me as his mate, a goddess for him to devour, or a cheap whore. I turned from the mirror and walked to the door before I could lose my nerve.

He stood by the fire, his back to me, a silhouette that should have struck fear in my heart, but only love was found there. The man before the fire was all that I needed. Time was so strange when you were in love. In four months, I had gone from college student to lover to mate. Strange, indeed. When you have someone to roll with lazily in the sheets when it snows outside. Frenzied joinings caused by heated stares or words. When someone worships you and all that you are. When you can worship them in return. Loving him was honey and dreams that were fed by his devotion to my body and mind. I was just so happy to have him.

He turned to me, his eyes going wide at first and then filling with that hungry fire. I walked to him, no words were needed, no words could encapsulate who we were to one another. He set a small box on the mantel before he stalked around me. The appraising eye of one who had fine taste. He stopped before me, lifted my chin to meet that heated gaze. Then he lowered his head, so it hovered mere inches from my own.

"You are a goddess, and I am half tempted to rip you from these lacy items, worship you as only I can worship you."

"But?"

"But another part of me wants to slowly peel these delicate items from your body, to torture you slowly before I worship you."

I kissed him deeply, remembering that he was all of my firsts. My first. My first hero, my first lover, and most importantly he was the first man I loved, the only man I ever wanted to love. What would the year bring us, with the blessing from the mother goddess, with the looming possibility of war? But today it was just us. Just me and him and this kiss and this room.

His fingers knitted into my hair, pulling my head back farther so he could plunge his tongue deep into my mouth. My hands came to his chest, the strong corded muscles underneath the fabric just out of reach. His other hand traveled down my back, cupping my ass and lifting me flush against him. I wrapped my legs around his lean frame; he groaned into my mouth at the pressure of me against him. His cock was hard against me, and I didn't care how he undressed me. I just needed him.

I pulled against his hold in the kiss. "Nira."

His mouth moved to my throat devouring me. He growled between kisses and nips. "Yes."

"I want you."

"I know." He said, dragging his tongue over my flitting pulse. "I want you to, but I'm going to worship you first."

My head fell back, and he licked my pulse again. "Gods."

He laid me atop our bed, stepping back to look at me. Taking in my skin under the golden garments, which always seemed to be covered in small fading bruises, whether from training or from him I never knew. He knelt before the bed, before me, his hands snaking up my legs over the delicate lace of my stockings.

"You are a beautiful feast to behold." He murmured, kissing the sensitive spot at the crook of my knee.

His fingers slipped under the garter clips, undoing them. With agonizing slowness, he rolled the stockings down one at a time, kissing his way down the soft flesh of my inner thigh. When he reached the end of my leg he kissed his way back up, paying extra attention to my most sensitive spots, pausing to suck or lick at them; eliciting moans from me.

"You smell delicious."

I just panted in response, and he smiled against my skin, pressing a kiss to the apex of my thighs. The texture of the lace and his pressure caused me to arch against him. A feral masculine growl crawled through him, a promise that his worship will be rough.

He nipped at my hips, catching the ties and pulling them free. He slid the fabric away and pocketed the panties. His breath was both hot and cold against my sensitive skin as he spoke.

"I'll save those for later."

"You're being cruel." I groaned, arching off the bed, spreading my legs for him. He made a satisfied male noise.

"I think you're enjoying it. You're already so aroused and wet for me."

He kissed my hips, traveling up my torso, leaving a trail of kisses in his wake. His body covered mine, and I thrashed against him. I just wanted him. I needed him.

"Nira, please."

"I'm enjoying unwrapping this gift," He pressed a kiss between my breasts, "and I want to savor this."

"This is torture."

He licked the swell of my breast, and I moaned pressing my head back into the bedding. He licked the other breast. I reached for him, and he collected my hands and pinned them above my head, his other cupped my waist.

"No, you are going to take me at my pace, not yours."

"Nira."

He looked at me, watching my face as he bit down on my nipple through the lace, sucking on it. I arched against him, crying out as his free hand slid up my back, to the back of the top, pulling the clasp open. The garment sighed off my body. He slid it up my arms, out of his way, so he could devour my chest freely. Each nip and suckle pulled me to the edge. I was begging him, pleading with him, but he just kissed me on the mouth, silencing me.

He whispers against my lips. "Stay right here. Don't move." Then he was gone.

I looked down to where he stood, his eyes a blaze with heat as he unbuttoned his shirt and unsnapped the undershirt, exposing the canvas of his skin flecked with the sorrows of his life, but all of that skin was mine. His lips glinted in the firelight from my lipstick. I watched as he released himself from his pants, heavy, mirroring the desire that was in his eyes. He smiled at me as I stared at him in all his beauty, because despite what he thought, he was.

"Do you want me?" He asked thickly.

"Madly."

He closed his eyes and took a breath. He placed one hand on his stomach and one on his chest where his scars were the starkest. He looked at me again, "Do you—do you like what you see?"

I sat up with sorrow in my heart. "Why wouldn't I?"

"You don't find me to be damaged and unsightly?"

"Damaged, yes, but you are beautiful to me too. Like I told you before, I want to commit every inch of you to memory, scars and all." He seemed frozen as my eyes ate up the skin that was his and mine. "Come here."

He came to the edge of the bed, his gaze holding mine, still heated, but there was something else there, maybe awe floating in those silver pools. Maybe fear. I grasped him in one hand, a little snarl of shock coming from him. With my other hand I ran a finger down the largest scar on his chest, the basilisk scar, the scar that was my fault.

"This is from me." I said. He opened his mouth to object, but I continued on and to the long scar across his stomach just above his navel. "What caused this?"

"Someone tried to gut me during one of the wars." He said softly. I stroked him and a soft groan came from him.

My hand followed the delicate line and cupped his side, where that wide faded scar sat just below his ribs, "This?"

"A spear during the crusades." Another stroke, another groan, his head falling back, "Gods."

My hand drifted down his side where a thin line was raised around his hip. I ran my finger over the line he shuddered at the touch. "This?"

He didn't answer. I looked up at his face; it had gone stoic and there was shame in his eyes, "I was lashed, by that lord for not performing for him. He wanted me to bed and kill a young fairy. I refused."

I stroked him again, my hand resting on his hip. "All these little ones?"

"Arrows, bullets, stabbings, all too numerous to remember."

I kissed a few of the tiny marks, stroking him as I went. "Thank you, for sharing those wounds with me."

I sucked his nipple between my teeth, a feral sound coming from him. I looked up at him, his eyes glazed over. He asked. "May I have you?"

"You don't have to ask."

He eased me back down into the bed, kissing me, his tongue doing large sweeps against mine. He parted from me and kissed a long slow trail down my body, stopping at the apex of my thighs. His breath tickled me as he spoke.

"My goddess, I wish to worship you and only you forever. I want to drown in all that you are forever."

"Yes." I said spreading my legs for him.

"My sweet goddess." He moaned before his mouth descended upon me.

His tongue lapped at the sensitive flesh before him, and my hand threaded through his hair holding him to his feast. He sucked on my clit causing me to buck into his waiting mouth. He slid two of his fingers inside, thrusting them in time with his sucks. I cried out, coming undone at his hands, and he plunged his tongue into me, his purr of pleasure vibrating through me. He pulled away, licking his lips, eyes ravenous as if I am his only sustenance.

"You are divine." His voice was feral.

I smiled softly at him. "I need you."

"I know."

I scooted back as he came to kneel on the bed, an Adonis kneeling before his goddess. "You're magnificent."

He tilted his head in the predator way. "No, my dear, it is you who is magnificent."

He guided himself in, slowly and so gentle. He groaned as he pulled back, leaving just the tip inside me. He hooked my leg and twisted my hips to one side. He buried himself and the angle forced a moan from me. He leaned over my body, his hands roving my ass and my breasts, and kissed me deeply as he gently fucks me.

He pressed his sweat slick forehead to mine. "I have been searching for you my entire life. My salvation. My home."

"I think I was looking for you too." I whimpered, my body already coiling to fall. "I have never felt more complete, than when I am with you."

"My mate."

"Mine."

He smiled. "Mine."

I felt myself slipping off the edge, and I begged him. "Cum for me, mate of mine. Fill me with all that you are."

Devastated. He roared as he spilled into me, my body lost, my mind too. His name was a repeated prayer off my tongue. Niratap. Mate. Mine. Forever.

He pulled away, kissing down my side as he went. "I'll be right back."

I lay there, destroyed by our joining, my heart already calling for him.

He returned, easing my legs apart and wiped a warm rag over my sensitive skin. I gasped.

"I'm sorry."

I looked down at where he was crouched. "Don't apologize. It just shocked me. I'm sensitive because of your thorough devotion to your goddess."

He smiled, kissing my inner thigh. "Am I a good devotee?"

I smiled. "The only devotee I will ever need."

He tossed the rag aside and scooped me into his arms, pressing a tender kiss to my lips. He tucked me into the bed and crawled in behind me, wrapping those arms around me, and pulling me close. His warm rain scent ushering me into a sleepy yawn.

"It's the middle of the morning, we can't go to sleep." I said wistfully.

"It's a holiday. We can sleep; the others will occupy themselves."

"It's a family holiday though."

"It is and our family will occupy themselves. They will all probably nap while we nap."

I twisted in his arms to face him, kissing the underside of his jaw. "I love you."

"I love you."

"When will we go dancing?" I asked as sleep tried to drag me under.

"After the new year, we'll venture into the city. Did you have a place in mind?"

"I might." I yawn settling against him. "I'll show you after our nap."

He chuckled, kissing my brow. "Okay, my flower."

Chapter Forty-Seven

Niratap

It wasn't often the whole house piled into the car, but Shasha was worth sitting with these fools that I called family for several hours. Gods grant me patience, so I didn't murder all of them. Shasha had chosen a club, The Machina, in New York City. It was what I expected when it came to a dance club: lights and smoke, scantily clad waitresses and patrons that wove around each other in the heady fog of sweat and sex. My senses were already overloaded by the time we were led to a VIP table. The girls all took a shot together before they left to the dance floor, Dheg already bouncing in the center of the floor. I caught Shasha's hand as she went to follow them and pulled her close to me to whisper in her ear, so quiet that only she could hear me over the din.

"You are mine. My mate."

"And you are mine." She mirrored my quiet tone, her hands wrapping around my neck.

"Only dance with our friends, okay?"

"I really only want to dance with you, but I will stay with them."

"I'll think about a dance." My nerves were already shot. "Go have fun."

She pressed a kiss to my shadowed cheek. "I love you, Bondbreaker."

I chuckled as she left me, bouncing off into the throng to where the group was already gyrating. The Days had wandered off, so it was just Allipo, and I left the table. I watched them, transfixed as the girls danced with each other and Dheg frolicked around them. Shasha was gilded in the glow of neon, reflecting off the gold of her dress. Rogmesh and Durgash chatted with the orc barkeep, laughing like they were old friends. A strange feeling settled on me.

"Do you think that it is fun, Allipo?" I asked curiously, I had never been a free spirit since Deirdre but maybe.

"I would assume that it is, my Lord." He said with a smile in his voice.

"Don't mock me," I growled.

"I'm not mocking you. It has been an age since you allowed yourself that luxury, to frolic and dance like it calls our blood to do."

"If it calls to your blood, why are you sitting with me instead of out there?"

"Patience, my Lord. Soon the night's beauty will beckon us."

"Us?" I shot him a skeptical glance.

He smiled. "Just wait."

And we did, the thudding bass of dance music thrummed in my head causing an ache behind my eyes. The sounds, the laughter, the moans, the music, the clink of glasses, the pops of corks from bottles, the clack of heeled shoes on the concrete; the smells, the sweat, the sex, the variance of alcoholic concoctions, the grease; the visage, the artificial mist that strobe lights and lasers danced though, beautiful males and females of all races dancing in fanatic movements of sways and grinds and shakes, the hustle and wisps of waitresses with trays; the whole of this place was near suffocation.

I wanted to run from it, to go out into the endless night, but then she came towards the table, a glittering goddess of the richest earth and gold. Allipo lifted his head, his eyes finding the lithe figure beside her, the dress a glove of shadow against porcelain. They were laughing and breathless. I stole a glance at Allipo, the edge of his mouth lifting in satyr mischief as the girls came to the table.

Eloimaya slid into the booth seat next to Allipo, resting her sweat-slicked head on his shoulder, a wicked satyr grin on his lips. Shasha leaned against the table, sprinkled in dew, breathing in happy pants. My chest became tight with the yearning for her to fall to my side like that.

"Eloimaya." Allipo said, his voice full of that satyr charm. "You are ravishing."

She chuckled. "No, I'm sweating like a whore, but dancing is a much more enjoyable affair."

"I don't think that." His voice sincere, his deft hand swept a loose strand of her sunlight hair behind her ear then drug the digit along her jaw to the tip of her chin, directing her eyes to his. "You are the dawn, day, and dusk to me."

Had her face not already been flushed she would have blushed, and Shasha smiled a knowing smile over her shoulder before she turned to look at me.

"Come dance with me." Her voice was husky and lovely to my ears. Alcohol and dancing had given her dark skin a rosy glow.

"My sweet." I said, her sweat an alluring draw. "I told you that I don't dance. Besides who will watch the drinks,"

Most of the drinks were gone, save my own glass.

She pouted a little, reaching across the table and grabbing my glass of scotch, she downed its contents in a swift three swallows. She winced as the liquor burned the back of her throat. She hiccupped when she opened her eyes and grasped my hand giving a gentle pull.

"See? There are no drinks to protect. Come dance with me."

I took her hand and followed her sashaying hips to the dance floor. The music's bass reverberated through my chest, the sound in my ears a roar that was deafening. I gave my head a shake, trying to ease the rising panic that causes my heart to flutter as she pulled us through the crowd to the center of the dance floor. She wrapped her arms around my waist, pressing against me, as she swayed her hips. The world seemed to slow as she smiled up at me, as I started to sway with her.

"I love you." She shouted over the din.

I leaned so I didn't have to shout. "And I you."

“I know this isn't your kind of thing, but I appreciate you being here with me.”

“Only for you.”

“I never asked you why.”

“Heightened senses, my dear. The lights, the smells, the music, all of it is a lot on my senses.”

She cocked her head to the side. “So, it's not that you don’t dance? All of this is just painful for you?”

I gave a small nod and she frowned.

“But what about at Samhain? You didn’t dance with me then and it wasn’t like all of this.”

“A different kind of pain, my dear.”

A worried line creased between her eyes. “Why didn’t you say so? We could have stayed home.”

“You wanted to come to the city. You wanted to dance. I didn’t have the heart to tell you no.”

“But if it—” She shook her head and pulled me from the floor, down the narrow hall to the exit, and into an alcove. The sounds of the club muffled, and she sighed. “I wish you had told me, and we could have done something else.”

“But—” She pressed her fingers to my lips.

“I can dance anywhere. If being here hurts, you we can go somewhere else, granted I am quite tipsy after downing your scotch.”

I chuckled. “How about a compromise?”

“You have already compromised for me, Nira. Let's go.”

“No.” I said, pulling her close. “A compromise, for my mate. We will go dancing for three songs. Then if you are satiated, we can leave. If not, I'll let you dance on your ass off for two songs and we can leave after.”

She looked up at me, her deep earth eyes wide with amusement. “Deal.”

I let her pull me back onto the dance floor but picked a far edge a little off from the main crowd. She turned to the beat of the bass and shimmied and sashayed before me. I swayed to the beat, running my hands over her waist and shoulders. The song had a strong bass line that I could feel in my bones; it was easy to move with. The second song was much faster, and Shasha bounced to the beat, throwing her hands in the air and singing along. Her joy was contagious, and it had me smiling to myself. I bobbed and rocked to her beat, not caring if it matched the music. The third song had her swaying against me. the words carried this song. They spoke to me, and Shasha must have seen it in my eyes because she tugged the lapels of my jacket, so I would get closer to her.

"You like this song?"

"It makes me think of you."

She giggled, breathlessly. "I would have never thought you would like Ed Sheeran."

"Is that the artist?"

"Yes. The song is *Shivers* I think." She let go of my lapels and clapped along with the song.

I followed suit. Enjoying the energy, she brought into my life. A light I wanted every day that seemed to slip into the darker parts of my heart. I didn't even notice when the song ended, and the next song began. She smiled warmly up at me as she danced, enjoying my presence in her life. I hoped that I was worth all that she gave me. The others had drifted our way, laughing and cheering as they reveled beside us. Two more songs passed and somehow the din of sound and the cacophony of smells didn't feel like a suffocating weight. Not when Shasha was there to ground me with her touch and her light. At the start of the next song, Shasha pulled me from the floor, laughing and giddy with delight. Back at our booth, she pushed me into the seat and kissed my cheek.

"You're bad at compromising."

"I guess I am." I said, pulling her between my knees and kissing her. "You made it enjoyable."

She laughed. "If you want me to shake my ass for you, I can do that at home too."

“There are many other things I would like to do with you at home.”

She giggled again. “I’m going to go to the restroom. Then you and I can go, okay?”

“Okay, if that is what you want, my dear.”

“What I want is for you to bury yourself in me, but we can't really do that on the dance floor. But in the car.” She winked at me before she sauntered away.

Chapter Forty-Eight

Shasha

To my good fortune there wasn't a line at the restroom or even anyone inside when I rounded through the door and dove into the first lit stall. Things that they don't tell you when you dress up to go to the city; heels hurt a lot and although dresses are easy to pee in, they tend to want to hold on to your lower half when you don't want them too. Fixing my dress and flushing, I heard the door as it squeaked as someone entered, darting into a dark stall and shutting the door.

I made it to the sink to wash my hands, hoping that in the silence they weren't going to start retching. I kept my eyes focused on my hands in the sink. I was a little tipsy, and the pink neon around the room made my head swim a little, the room carried a clean laundry like perfume. I felt a presence behind me, wondering if it was the other occupant debating whether they were going to be sick or if they were free to go back to the sway of the club. I splashed my face, not really caring if the gold of my eyeshadow ran, just needing to cool my flush. I reached blindly for the paper towels and blotted my face, before looking up into the mirror. My heart stopped.

"Well, hello, little whore." The ogre, Mandrake, said behind me. He was faster than me, cupping a hand over my mouth, before I could move. "You can scream all you want, darling, not even that beast will be able to save you."

He plunged a needle in my neck and my head spun as he let me go. "What did you just inject me with?" my tongue was thick in my mouth and the world teetered.

The ogre smiled. "Versed, it's a sedative. It will be easier to haul you out of here kind of pliant, don't you think?"

My vision went fuzzy around the edges, I tried to call out to him, but my tongue felt heavier with each passing second. "Nira."

I took an uneasy step to the door; the ogre grabbed me around the waist. "He'll come for you, but right into the boss's hands."

"No." My legs felt foreign and far away.

He laughed. "Come on, babe, let's get out of here."

The world spun as he led me to the door. "No."

The door opened and a couple girls stopped dead. "Sorry ladies, my girl just had too much to drink."

The girls smiled sadly at me and let him cart me past the doorway. Words abandoned me as he hauled me down the hall. The opposite direction I'd come, away from Niratap and my friends.

I pushed weakly against him. "Stop."

"Come on, darlin', let's get you home."

"Imna yer darlin." Fuck.

He eased us through the back door. "Night, love."

Unconsciousness found me hard.

When I came to, I was laying in the back of a van, my arms tied behind my back. I struggled to sit up; my mind foggy. How had I gotten here? I had been at the dance club, with Niratap and the others. I had gone to the bathroom. Then the ogre opened the back doors, and I remembered. It was starting to rain.

"Good morning, sweetheart."

"Where am I? Where did you take me?" I hissed.

"Right where I need you to be." Dravin came into view.

"You just signed your fucking death warrant, Dravin."

"Oh, I don't think so." Dravin pressed a hand to his ear. "Understood. They just left the club and are on their way. Grab her."

I snarled scooting back. "Don't you fucking touch me!"

"You are feisty bait, that's for sure. Bondbreaker should have kept you closer to him if he wanted to keep you both safe."

"What do you mean?"

"Well, my dear. You weren't my target. You were the bait to draw the prize into my trap."

My blood went cold as the ogre pulled me from the van. "What are you going to do to him?"

"We're going to trade, and I know he values you enough to concede. Once I break, him he will make me a lot of money."

"It will take a lot to break him. He's stronger than you."

Dravin just smiled his grotesque smile. "He has been broken before, my dear. It won't be too hard to do again."

"You won't break him."

Dravin tied a gag in my mouth as the ogre held me in place, "I will, and I will take great pleasure in crushing the wild right out of him."

Chapter Forty-Nine

Niratap

Something wasn't right. I sat at the edge of the VIP booth; my eyes glued to the hall where the restrooms were. I knew that sometimes there were lines, but in the twenty minutes that she had been gone no women had exited the hall, and only a pair of girls walked down the hallway. My skin felt prickly. Something was most certainly wrong. Mitta and Dheg came up to the table laughing with one another, and Mitta marked my gaze instantly.

"What's wrong?"

"Shasha is taking too long. Something doesn't feel right." I said my eyes not leaving the hallway.

"There's probably a line." Dheg said leaning against the table.

"No one has come out of that hall since she went back there."

"There is another dance floor at the other side, maybe she wandered that way on accident." He said.

"No, something is wrong." The couple of girls that had walked down the hall resurfaced, and I stood.

"You can't seriously think that barging into the women's restroom in a club is going to be a good idea." Dheg growled.

"Something is wrong." I snarled. I nodded to the small group of girls. "Go asked them if they saw her."

Both of them looked at me cautiously before he nodded, and Mitta said. "I'll go with you."

She followed me as I stalked toward the hall. Her scent was there, but there was something else familiar in the hall.

Mitta ran to get in front of me. "I'll go see if she's in there. Wait."

Mitta pushed into the bathroom, and I tracked the scent in the hall. Where are you? My skin was crawling. Mate where are you?

"She's not in there." Mitta said as she exited the bathroom.

Dheg ran down the hall. "My Lord, those girls said that Shasha was in the restroom when they went in, said that her man took her out."

Fear coiled in my chest; rage coiled tightly through me. "Obviously he did not."

Dheg held up his hands. "My Lord, they said she was with an ogre, that they went out the back."

"My Lord." Mitta said gingerly, placing her hand on my arm. "The shadows."

My shadows were crawling over the walls, hunting for what was stolen from me. The others were standing at the end of the hall, eyes wide. I took a breath and then another. "Find her. I need to find her now."

Her scent was muddied by all those around us, the filth and decay, the sweat and drink, but I could smell her. I turned, following the muddy scent, the other familiar scent I knew now. The ogre that had taken her, Dravin's third. The ogre that had kidnapped her to begin with. My blood boiled. I would take great pleasure in tearing him apart. Her scent led out a rear door; I followed her, and I didn't care if anyone else kept up. My mate was in danger, and she was all that mattered right now. It started to rain, and my body threw itself into finding her before it washed away her scent. Onto the street where people began to run, shielding their hair and faces from the wet. He had carried her down the street and no one had looked at him and questioned; no one had tried to save her, my mate.

Under a bridge and down another block. I could hear Mitta, Allipo, Dheg, and the Days following behind me; the girls must have gone to get the car, a closer escape. I smelled him before I rounded the corner into the alley, red neon light staining the concrete like blood. I held up a hand to the others stalking forward. Rage had me uncoiled, my tail swishing behind me, and wrathful fear twisted in me, as I took in the sight of them before me. Dravin with a dozen cronies behind him, Bastion to his right, the ogre on his left who had my mate held tightly against his chest. Her arms were tied behind her, ankles bound together and a gag in her mouth. They would pay. They would all pay.

"Finally, you found us." Dravin said smugly, Shasha thrashed in the ogre's hold.

"Dravin. Release her." I snarled; vengeance was the only thing he would get out of this. The only thing he would get to walk out of here with if he hurt her, my mate. Mine.

"So, possessive of your plaything." Dravin purred. My hands shifted, not fully of my own control and claws took the place of my fingers.

"I'm not asking." It was a death's promise.

"Now, now put the claws away, kitten, you won't be able to fight your way out of this one. Who would have thought that you," He pointed at me still smiling like he was going to win, "failing to practice auction etiquette six months ago would pay off for me. Who would have thought that the college girl off the streets would be the key I would need to further my goals."

"My patience is gone, whore trader." I hissed. "Release the girl, and I might let you leave this alley alive."

"No. You see, we won't be conducting this encounter on your terms, Bondbreaker."

"Release the girl." I shouted. "Or you will meet your maker today."

"Hear me out. Wouldn't want to scar her pretty skin now, would we?" The ogre pulled her tighter against his chest, pressing a knife against her throat. The scent of her blood called out to mine for retribution.

"Let. Her. Go." I forced my instincts down, retracting my claws. The knife left her neck. Fuck.

"I am only reclaiming property of mine. The girl is human, she is nothing in your grander schemes." Dravin cooed though his voice didn't give anything away.

My growl reverberated off the concrete. "Let her go, Dravin. Your fight is with me, not her."

"Very true, but I also have grander schemes than whores, Bondbreaker. How about a deal?"

I scoffed; he couldn't be serious. "A deal? What is it you want? Money? My Monsters?"

"You."

Everything in me went tense and then loose in surprise. Why? "Me?"

"Yes, her freedom for yours. Her life for yours." Dravin smiled. Me for her.

Allipo stepped closer. "My Lord."

"No." I snapped. Allipo stopped his push. I closed my eyes. This had been a trap. They had been watching us. They knew, he knew, what she meant to me. "Why?"

"Now, I can't show you all my cards, can I? Take off the mask and let us actually talk face to face."

I reached behind my head and Shasha screamed, finally free of the gag. "Don't do it, it's a trap!"

"I think he's figured that much out, my dear." Dravin purred, grasping her chin. "Such a pretty thing, it's a shame I have to give you up."

"Fuck you." She hissed. Fire and ice incarnate was my mate. Mine.

The mask came off and I let the shadows slide away. "Happy?"

"Very, but also disappointed. I was expecting something much more grotesque if I am honest."

I huffed a sardonic laugh and handed the mask to Allipo. "Sorry to disappoint."

"Do you concede to my terms?"

"Don't do it, Nira!" Her shriek broke my heart. Anything for her safety. Anything.

"I'm sorry, Shasha. I do."

"My Lord you can't be serious." Allipo's voice broke with fear I had never heard from the satyr. He turned to Dravin. "There has to be another way."

"There is, but I don't think your master wants your blood cooling on the concrete."

I clenched my jaw. "No, I do not want my family hurt."

"Then we are in agreement. You and your advisor can come forward, but know I only have to say the word and my snipers will take care of your family. So, no funny business."

We moved forward as one. My mate's fear, piercing my soul.

"Stop. Now, Bondbreaker, I want you to kneel."

My stomach flipped, and Shasha lunged, still held back by the ogre. "No."

I took a breath; I would bend for her. For her and for my family. Everything and everyone I cared for was in danger. I slowly descended into the cold, dirty puddles before me. He wanted me to be subservient, pliant to his will. I would give him that, until I had the chance to shred his soul from his body.

"Now, knowing how I float about the city, I know that you're armed. Advisor, disarm your master."

"Don't call him that." Allipo barked. Handing Dravin, a weapon out of fear; he didn't want me doing this.

"Allipo." I snapped, but the order in my voice was painted with defeat. Allipo reached, pulling the weapon free. I whispered. "You will listen, do as he says. Get Shasha safe. Contingency V."

Allipo gave a slight nod, the only confirmation that he understood.

"Bring the weapon forward, satyr. Mrak will meet you halfway and collect it."

Bastion walked forward his expression hard, playing his role as he collected the gun, clearing it as he spoke under his breath. "I will contact you when I know where we are going, I haven't been privy to everything as of late. I think

Dravin suspects a rat. I have to keep my profile low. They figured that the lord felt something more for Shasha since the auction but had to wait to act on it until you came into the city again. They were watching in the club. They have had people watching all over. They will shoot when they get what they want. They will shoot first for fun and then to kill. You have to be fast. I will put on the dramatics. I apologize for pretending to shoot you."

I paled; Dravin was going to try to take her from me regardless of the price. I spoke, pulling everyone's attention, "That is my favorite gun, just so you know."

"It's a nice weapon." Bastion said, turning back to face our enemy, "Beretta APX 9mm, fast and reliable, low capacity though."

He turned suddenly and pressed the nose of the gun between Allipo's brows, and I tensed. Allipo didn't even flinch. "This isn't the first time I've had a gun pressed to my head."

"It won't be the last if you're lucky." Bastion painted a wicked smile as he rocked the pistol back. Allipo feigned a flinch. "Bang."

"Mrak, quit playing around."

"Of course, sir." Bastion returned to just behind Dravin's right side, crossing his hand over his wrist with the gun pointing down, at ease, but there was tension in his eyes. He glanced at Shasha and grinned his most wicked grin.

"Release her." I growled; I didn't want to play these games anymore.

A sniper sight centered on my chest. Dravin was also done playing. "Send the satyr forward. Don't move. I would rather take you minimally injured, but either way you'll serve your purpose."

I gritted my teeth, raising my hands above my head. I would submit for her, my mate. Mine.

She cried. "Nira, you have to fight."

Pain and heartbreak shook me. "I can't."

She begged me, salt hitting my nose through the rain. "Nira, please fight."

I looked at the ground. "I can't."

"Submission looks good on you, Niratap. That's close enough. You I recognize; you were once property of my great-grandfather, back in the day. He ran a black-market fighting ring. He switched over to prostitution after he lost his best dollar, a black-horn satyr."

Allipo denied him. "I don't know what you're talking about, but it sounds like the apple didn't fall far."

"Oh, but I think you do, I wonder what my granddaddy would say to see you here. Probably whip out his moniker-breed of ass-whooping. Blackdagger beatings were always the hardest. You stay right here. Dolan."

They were facts from over a hundred and fifty years ago, I had stolen Allipo from the Blackdagger, a mafia boss in a near-lawless New York, who enjoyed carving into his enemies. I looked up to where a mage cleared the ranks, two others with him; the boxes of slavery never changed. I was shaking; going back into bondage was the cost of her safety. A cost I would pay a hundred times over, no matter if it cost me my light.

Dravin stalked toward me casually. He paced around me as he spoke. "Now. I spent a lot of time and resources to come to this moment. Dealing with all sorts of people in our beautiful underground. I found these lovely cragstone manacles and had them modified so that I could control you magically. I found myself a skilled mage who could write me subjugation spells that would be stronger than those that have existed up to now. I have played the last decade very strategically, so that I could acquire the legendary Bondbreaker and—" he stops behind, me pausing for some dramatic flair, "and because of you, young lady, I have expedited my plans by almost a year."

I huffed. "The moniker should be enough to tell you that you won't keep me long."

"We shall see."

The men approached me cautiously; the mage opened the boxes and stood between them before he spoke. The magic swirled around me, tasting of battery acid on my tongue and burning my nose. "Servant of shadow, creature of darkness, stalker of the night, I cast you into the bonds of servitude to your master and their blood."

The mage spoke the words in Irish, the language of my home. He looked me in the eye as he cast his spell. The chains floated out of the box, encircling my neck, wrists, ankles, and around the base of my antlers. "Theirs are the words to which you kneel. Theirs are words to which you bow. Theirs are the words to which you yield."

I shook, but took deep chested breaths, squashing my instincts to run. The air crackled with magic. My body felt the fire of the magic burning my flesh, slicing into my soul. Trapped. I was trapped again. "To them you are bound, to their terms and shall remain. Until they release you from these or they are broken by another, these are the bounds to which you obey."

What? What did he mean, *broken by another?* I stared at the mage. Who are you? I wanted to ask. Dolan was his name, but I didn't know him or his face. Who are you? Why put a loophole into a binding spell? A loophole spoken in a language that Dravin didn't understand.

"He is yours, Dravin."

"Good." Dravin purred from behind me. "You see, Niratap, I win. I will enjoy breaking your spirit."

I was still focused on the mage, but I laughed. "It will take a lot more than chains to break me."

"Perhaps, but I have an ace."

A needle plunged into my neck, and I arched back with a roar. Acid flared through my veins, and I doubled over clawing at the hurt, the roar fading into a whimper as the acid ate my strength. The sound of a rifle going off and its ricochet were distorted and echoed in my head.

"That will be your only warning." Dravin hissed at my family as he leaned over me, "Stings, doesn't it? I had my people develop this, just for you."

"What did you inject me with?"

"I can't give that away. Advisor, you can take the girl. Be quick, because my generosity has just about run out."

"Allipo, let me go!" Shasha shrieks against him.

"I'm sorry, Shasha, we have to go. We are free to go, correct?" Allipo sounded so far away. Don't fucking question him. Just go. Take her and fucking go. A groan was the only sound I could make.

"I mean, I have what I want, so I don't see why not." Dravin's voice is unnervingly friendly. A bullet rand out and I heard my friend gasp. Hit. Allipo was hit, I tried to shift, to lift my head and scream, to fight, but my body wouldn't listen.

"You just have to be quick."

Hooves beat past me. Yes. Get her out of here, get her safe. She screamed. "We can't leave him! Allipo, put me down! We can't abandon him! Nira! Niratap no!"

Her screams haunted me, and my breathing was ragged. I was a prisoner again; for her I would be a slave. Dravin squatted down in front of me, lighting a cigar. He grabbed an antler and pushed my head back.

"Pity she had to go." He puffed the sweet smoke into my face. "I am a man of honor, but Mandrake was growing rather fond of her."

I growled, but it was a pitiful sound.

"You will make me a lot of money."

"Fuck. You. You will pay for this."

"No, Niratap, you are the one who is going to pay." He stood, stepping away. I felt his cronies surrounding me, pressing in. "Checkmate."

They jumped me. Fists, boots, bars, and pipes collided with my body. I roar, but it is snuffed out by a boot to my throat. I wondered if this was the kind of servitude I would be in again. A toy for entertainment. A weapon. Who

knew what Dravin's plans were with me. The pain
disappeared as soon as I lost consciousness. At least my mate
was safe. At least Shasha was safe.

Chapter Fifty

I could feel him before he rounded the corner and was standing at the end of the alley, painted red in the glow of the neon that reflected off the puddles starting to form. He held up a hand to the others, who rounded the corner behind him. He stalked forward, expression hard and his tail swished with rage, but there was something I couldn't help but see in his eyes. A vast undercurrent of fear beneath the rage.

"Finally, you found us." Dravin said beside me. I wished that it was Bastion holding me back against him and not this ogre. He would have let me slip free and escape. He would have played it up to make it seem like I overpowered him.

"Dravin. Release her." Nira snarled; it was too much. He was falling right into Dravin's trap. I would have warned him if I could get this gag out of my mouth.

"So, possessive of your plaything." Dravin purred, and Nira's hands shifted in response.

"I'm not asking." The lethality a promise in his voice.

"Now, now put the claws away, kitten, you won't be able to fight your way out of this one. Who would have thought that you failing to practice auction etiquette six months ago would pay off for me. Who would have thought that the college girl off the streets would be the key I would need to further my goals."

"My patience is gone, whore trader. Release the girl and I might let you leave this alley alive."

"No. You see we won't be conducting this encounter on your terms, Bondbreaker."

"Release the girl, or you will meet your maker today."

"Hear me out. Wouldn't want to scar her pretty skin now, would we?" The ogre pulled me tight against his chest and pressed the knife against my throat, slicing my skin and I felt a bead of blood roll out my neck.

"Let. Her. Go." He said, his voice carrying that sharp edge, but his claws receded. the blade against my throat softened in answer.

"I am only reclaiming property of mine. The girl is human; she is nothing in your grander schemes."

A growl vibrated off the walls of the alley. "Let her go, Dravin. Your fight is with me, not her."

"Very true, but I also have grander schemes than whores, Bondbreaker. How about a deal?"

Nira scoffed at him. "A deal? What is it you want? Money? My Monsters?"

"You."

Surprise lit Nira's face; he hadn't been expecting that. I struggled against the ogre trying to push the gag from my mouth. "Me?"

"Yes. Her freedom for yours. Her life for yours." Dravin smiled, and I shook with rage.

Allipo took a step forward. "My Lord."

"No." He snapped, and I knew then he would do it, he would fold to this whore trader for me. Panic slammed through my heart as Nira closed his eyes. "Why?"

"Now, I can't show you all my cards, can I? Take off the mask and let us actually talk face to face."

Nira reached for the tie just as I got the gag out of my mouth. I screamed. "Don't do it, it's a trap!"

"I think he's figured that much out, my dear." Dravin purred at me, grasping my chin. "Such a pretty thing. It's a shame I have to give you up."

"Fuck you." I snapped.

The mask came off and the shadows slid from his face, brilliant orbs of moonlight settled in a beautifully devastating face. It would always take my breath away. "Happy?"

"Very, but also disappointed. I was expecting something much more grotesque if I am honest."

Nira huffed as he handed the mask to Allipo. "Sorry to disappoint."

"Do you concede to my terms?"

"Don't do it, Nira!"

He looked at me. his eyes sad. "I'm sorry Shasha., I do."

"My Lord, you can't be serious." Allipo's voice broke with the panic in my heart, and he turned to Dravin. "There has to be another way."

"There is, but I don't think your master wants your blood cooling on the concrete."

A muscle ticked in Nira's face. "No. I do not want my family hurt."

"Then we are in agreement. You and your advisor can come forward, but know I only have to say the word and my snipers will take care of your family. So, no funny business." Pain flashed on Nira's face as he came forward, Allipo at his side. "Stop. Now, Bondbreaker, I want you to kneel."

I lunged at him, almost kicking free of the ogre. "No!"

Nira closed his eyes as he descended to his knees. I watched as Allipo throat bobbed and he looked away as if the idea of Nira submitting to anyone was making him sick.

"Now, knowing how I float about the city, I know that you're armed. Advisor, disarm your master."

"Don't call him that," Allipo barked. Allipo had unthinkingly given Dravin verbal ammunition to use, not only against us but also Nira. Knowing the sensitivity of the word gave Dravin more power.

"Allipo." Nira snapped, but his voice had taken on a haunting quality of resignation. Allipo reached into the back of Nira's waistband and pulled the weapon free. Nira said something to Allipo so only he could hear and Allipo gave a slight nod.

"Bring the weapon forward, satyr. Mrak will meet you halfway and collect it."

Bastion walked forward; his expression hard as he passed. He collected the gun. I watched from behind as he cleared the weapon and checked it. Allipo's eyes darted between me and Nira, paling at something.

"That is my favorite gun, just so you know." Nira said, pulling everyone's attention to him.

"It's a nice weapon." Bastion said, turning back to face our enemy. "Beretta APX 9mm, fast and reliable, low capacity though." Bastion turned suddenly and pressed the nose of the gun between Allipo's brows. and even though I knew he would never shoot one of us, by choice, panic flew through my body at the same time as it alights the faces of his parents, who stood at the mouth of the alley. Allipo's pinched stoic expression didn't even flinch.

"This isn't the first time I've had a gun pressed to my head." He announced.

"It won't be the last, if you're lucky." Bastion painted a wicked smile as he rocked the pistol back. Allipo flinched and closed his eyes, and I couldn't tell if he was acting. "Bang."

"Mrak, quit playing around."

"Of course, sir." Bastion came back to stand just behind Dravin's right side, crossing his hand over his wrist and pointing the gun at the ground. He appeared at ease, but I could see the tension in his eyes when he glanced at me.

"Release her." Nira growled.

"Send the satyr forward." A red light centered on Nita's chest. "Don't move. I would rather take minimally injured, but either way you'll serve your purpose."

That muscle in Nira's jaw twitched, he held his hands above his head. This couldn't be happening, my man submitting to these thugs. "Nira, you have to fight."

Pain laced his expression. "I can't."

Tears welled over my cheeks as I lost my fight to keep them at bay. My heart cracked and I begged him. "Nira, please fight."

He hung his head. "I can't."

"Submission looks good on you, Niratap." Dravin pulled a dagger and pointed at Allipo, "That's close enough. You, I recognize. You were once property of my grandfather, back in the day. He ran a black-market fighting ring. He switched over to prostitution after he lost his best dollar, a black-horn satyr."

"I don't know what you're talking about." Allipo's hands fisted at his side. "But it sounds like the apple didn't fall far."

"Oh, but I think you do. I wonder what my granddaddy would say to see you here. Probably whip out his moniker-brand of ass whooping. Blackdagger beatings were always the hardest." Allipo blanched at his words as a red dot appeared in the center of his chest. "You stay right here. Dolan."

"Yes, sir." The mage that had bound me in the beginning parted from the ranks; two others followed, each with a briefcase that I knew held chains of subjugation. Nira was shaking, and I knew that he would be back in those dark places that I had tried so hard to fill.

Dravin walked forward as he spoke. "Now, I spent a lot of time and resources to come to this moment. Dealing with all sorts of people in our beautiful underground. I found these lovely cragstone manacles and had them modified so that I could control you magically. I found myself a skilled mage who could write me subjugation spells that would be stronger than those that have existed previously. I have played the last decade very strategically so that I could acquire the legendary Bondbreaker and," he came to a stop behind Nira and spun to face me, "and because of you young lady, I have expedited my plans by almost a year."

Nira huffed. "The moniker should be enough to tell you that you won't keep me long."

"We shall see." Dravin sheathed the dagger and nodded to the mage. The men approached Nira cautiously. The mage opened the boxes and stood between them.

"A sheirbhíseach an scátha, créatúr an dorchadais, a stalcaire na hoíche, chaithim thú faoi cheangail na seirbhíseach ar do mháistir agus ar a gcuid fola. Is leosan na focail a nglúineann tú. Is focail iad a gcloíonn tú chucu. Is leosan na focail a thugann tú leo. Dóibh tá tú faoi cheangal a dtéarmaí agus fanfaidh tú. Go dtí go scaoilfidh siad uathu seo thú nó go mbrisfear iad ag duine eile is iad seo an ceangal lena ngéillfidh tú." [34] As he spoke the chains floated out of the box and toward Nira, encircling his neck, wrists, ankles and around the base of his antlers. He shook, taking a couple deeper breaths, but did not fight. The air crackled with the magic, and I felt pinpricks of it along my skin. When he spoke the last line both Nira and Allipo shifted towards the mage. Something was off in Allipo's expression as he turned back to face me completely.

"He is yours Dravin." Said the mage.

"Good. You see, Niratap, I win." He pulled a syringe out of his coat, and the ogre covered my mouth so I couldn't warn him. Allipo's face paled as another dot appeared on his chest. "But I will enjoy breaking your spirit."

Nira laughed "It will take a lot more than chains break me."

"Perhaps." He drove the needle into the crook of Nira's neck. "But I have an ace."

Nira arched back, a roar coming from his mouth before he fell forward clawing at his neck. The sound faded into a whimper. Rogmesh took a step into the alley, a step toward us, and at the bang of a rifle she froze. The bullet left a hole in the ground before her.

---

[34] Servant of shadow, creature of darkness, stalker of the night, I cast you into the bonds of servitude to your master and their blood. Theirs are the words to which you kneel. Theirs are words to which you bow. Theirs are the words to which you yield. To them you are bound to their terms and shall remain. Until they release you from these or they are broken by another, these are the bound to which you obey.

"That will be your only warning." He said to them as he leaned over Nira, "Stings, doesn't it? I had my people develop this just for you."

"What did you inject me with?"

"I can't give that away. Advisor, you can take the girl. Be quick because my generosity has just about run out."

Allipo reached for me as the ogre released his hold. I tried to duck under his arm and run to Nira, but Allipo caught me around the waist and hefted me onto his shoulder.

"Allipo let me go." I thrashed against his hold.

"I'm sorry, Shasha. We have to go." Allipo turned towards the mouth of the ally. "We are free to go, correct?"

"I mean, I have what I want, so I don't see why not." Dravin's voice was unnervingly friendly. Bastion's brows raised, the only warning before a bullet rang out, grazing the top of Allipo's other shoulder. "You just have to be quick."

Allipo took off running, and Dravin laughed. I screamed and fought against him. "We can't leave him! Allipo, put me down, we can't abandon him!"

"I'm sorry, Shasha, I was given specific instructions."

"Nira!"

As we came to the end of the alley, Dravin's men circled Niratap. He was still laying in the dirty water of the alley. I screamed, but the sound was swallowed by his roar.

Allipo set me down by the car and I leaned against it, so I didn't fall over. Echo opened the door and people shuffled past me to get in. Durgash offered to drive us home. Mitta agreed that was a good idea. My throat burned from screaming and sobbing and when I spoke my voice sounded wrong.

"We have to go back." Mitta and Allipo just looked at me, neither responding. My voice was shrill when I glared at them and tried again "Didn't you hear me we have to go back."

"We heard you." Mitta said softly, turning back to Allipo and inspecting his wound. "But we can't."

"Flower, it's not that we don't want to, it's just that—"

"That what? He sticks his neck out for all of us and I'm the only one trying to go back for him. How can you guys just load up and talk about going home? Niratap was just imprisoned before us. He was degraded. He was bound to that maniac for gods only knows what. And he fucking injected something into him? How are we just standing here we need—" a hand swept hard across my face. Shocked, I looked up at Eloimaya. "You hit me."

"I did."

"You hit me."

"I did. You're not being rational. You're letting your emotions get the better of you, and that's not what we were taught."

"Well, I'm sorry, but it wasn't your lover that got taken." I snarled.

"No, but mine did get shot rescuing you." She shrieked before covering her mouth with her hands. "I'm sorry. I—"

"No, love, you're okay." Allipo soothed. "It's just a flesh wound, and I'll be fine. We're all shaken up over the lord's capture."

Tears rolled over Eloimaya's cheeks. "This is terrible."

"Why didn't he fight? He could have taken them easily."

Mitta sighed. "He didn't fight because he wasn't going to risk you because he loves you."

I flushed, embarrassed for being the one thing that I would always be to him. His weakness. "But how would they know that?"

"They were probably already tracking our movements." Allipo said. "They must have seen you and the lord dancing. They probably suspected when he defended you at the auction, took that as an indication that you meant something to him. They were probably already looking for an opportunity to take you.”

Tears welled in my eyes as I lost the fight with my emotions again. “How could he just let them? I don't understand. He never wanted to be a prisoner again. He said he would fight to keep that from happening. That he was never going to be under someone ever again.”

“He wasn’t going to risk us.” Mitta said sadly. “We were in danger. We all saw the bullet that was fired at Rogmesh. Dravin meant business and he made sure that he didn’t leave that alley without the lord.”

“We need to save him.”

“And we will, darling, it will just take time.”

“What if he doesn’t have time?”

Mitta wrapped her arms around me in a tight hug. “Listen, sweetie. I don’t think Dravin wants Niratap dead. Firstly, the bastard said he had plans for him so I think it’s safe to assume that he will be alive when we go for him and secondly if he had wanted us dead, he had ample opportunity in the alley. Thirdly we have contingency plans for this kind of thing.”

“A contingency plan?”

“Yes.” Allipo said. “And the sooner we get home the sooner we can enact that contingency.”

“What is it?”

Mitta looked around the dark street. “Let’s get going. Who knows who's watching us now.”

I nodded letting my tears roll down my face as the rest piled into the car. I sat next to Dheg who wrapped a comforting arm around my shoulder, and Mitta rolled the privacy window down.

“Let's go.” She said. “Don’t drive like a maniac. I'm going to treat Allipo.”

“I’m a decent enough driver.” Durgash grunted from up front. “People are just slower than me.”

Mitta sighed. “Just don’t get us killed.”

He chuckled as we pulled away from the curb. Mitta grabbed the first aid kit and sat next to Allipo.

"Take your shirt off." She said digging through it. Eloimaya knelt between his legs and helped with the buttons, gently peeling him out of the silk. His chest was marred with scars that crossed and pocked his skin through the salt and pepper hair on his chest. His eyes met mine and I looked away quickly, tucking against Dheg who gave a gentle squeeze.

He said a quiet thank you to Eloimaya who moved to sit beside him. He cleared his throat. "It's a sight, the things that were done to me. The things I survived." He smiled sadly, his honey-colored eyes half closed, he placed his hand over the three largest marks that started just above his heart and slashed down his abdomen to end at his opposite hip. "A chimera got me, I won that fight, but it almost killed me." His hand shifted to the pocked skin on his other hip, "wrong end of some buck shot."

"I remember that, took forever to pull that out of you." Mitta said pouring some antiseptic on the wound.

He chuckled. "Yeah, you had me on a table for hours and I still had some lead in me."

"Yes, and then you got sick and spent even more time on the table." She glanced at me as she pressed gauze against his shoulder. "We all have scars from our lives, both before and after we came into the lords care."

"I—" I took a deep breath to find my nerve. "I realized that was a possibility, but seeing it and hearing it is shocking, and I don't mean to stare or sound insensitive, but I'm just curious and then I'm shocked that you all are so—"

"Adjusted." Dheg finishes beside me.

I flushed. "Yeah."

Everyone gave a tight smile as Mitta closed the kit and she looked at me again, "So the contingency plan involves an ally that for mutual benefits we try to keep separate from. The FBMI, the Federal Bureau of Magic Investigation. They do exactly what we do, just less of the dark-sided stuff. I'm assuming he told you to get in touch with Ventris?"

Allipo nods. "Yes. Ventris will be our contingency. I'll call him as soon as we get home, meaning there is a possibility that we will have a lot of people at the manor shortly. So, I need everyone to be prepared. They may be our allies; however, they do work for the government and as such are not to be fully trusted."

Everyone nodded.

"Bastion will get a hold of me as soon as he is able, and he will tell us some of the whens and wheres."

"We will get the lord back." Mitta said. "That I can promise you."

Chapter Fifty-One

Niratap

Everything felt heavy. My shoulders ached. My throat felt bruised. I tasted blood. My skin goosed cold against the air. My clothes gone save for my briefs. At least it was me and not Shasha here. I attempted to wipe my hair from my face, but my arms were the only things holding me upright, suspended from the walls. I tried to pull free, my strength nonexistent.

"I was wondering when you'd wake up." Dravin said.

I opened my eyes. He sat causally before me in a dark suit, one foot kicked over his knee. Bastion and the ogre stood behind him.

"Where am I?" My voice sounded garbled.

"Somewhere hidden." He smiled that vulpine smile of his. "You are going to make me a lot of money, Niratap."

I let out a sharp bark of a laugh. "No, I'm not. However, I will bring death upon you."

The smile faded. "You sure about that?"

"Positive. In one form or another you will not live past this."

"Would hate to have to go hunting to get you to behave. Granted it's not like the manor house is a secret either."

I snarled. "Leave them alone."

"Then behave. My scientists are curious about your species. There's not a lot of information on your kind. So, answer their questions and maybe I'll reward you." I didn't give him an answer. "Mrak will watch after you and make sure you behave today."

"Yes, sir." Mrak took a station against the wall.

"I'm excited to see what makes you tick. Maybe I *will* go after the girl."

I snarled, pulling as hard as I could against the chains. "You touch her—"

"And you'll what, Niratap? As things look right now, you're in my custody. What are you going to do snarl at me?" He laughed as he rose and left.

We stood in the quiet for several moments before Bastion spoke. "My Lord, we can speak freely, but there is surveillance. I will get word to Allipo as soon as I can, we will get you out of here."

"Bas." I said, keeping my head down. "Where are we? How long have I been unconscious?"

"Four days. A warehouse in the meatpacking district. Grungy looking place. I wasn't able to get here until light duty. I've never been more thankful to be shot." He grimaced. "That sounds bad, don't tell my mom."

I tugged on the chains again and shook my head defeatedly as I chuckled. "She'd kick your ass that's for sure. What's his game anyway?"

"I'm not entirely sure. He has the other bitarog in a cell a level below. She's passive. Let's the scientist prod her and poke her. She is fitted with an injector collar just in case she decides to fight back. They'll probably stick you in one, too, my Lord."

"What's in it, the injection?"

"At first I thought it was a sedative, but I think it's whatever the lab coats have been working on."

I twisted my head, not finding relief. "You said they were experimenting with basilisk venom. That would explain the sensation of having acid injected into my veins."

He crossed his arms and donned a smile on for the camera. "I'll pry a little more with the girl I've been working, maybe they've been making some kind of synthetic venom. Resistant to antidote. All the weakening and pain without the death."

Footsteps sounded beyond the door. "Guess our chat is over for now, we have company."

Bastion nodded as the door opened and four scientists walked in. The man leading the group approached me, head held high and proud. "My name is Dr. Foltar Paloka. I am the lead scientist employed by Mr. Cirano. We're going to fit you with an injector collar today for our safety and your compliance. We are also going to draw blood and take some measurements of your anatomy. You don't have a choice; I am letting you know out of courtesy. Any questions?"

"I have plenty, but I think you are asking me out of courtesy, and I doubt you'll answer them."

"You are correct."

I chuckled. "Very well."

The other three scientists came forward. A slight young woman bearing a collar with silver tubes around it, came to stand before me. She eyed me carefully as she tapped her keycard to the lock.

"I won't attack you." I said, shifting my feet slightly, trying to ease the tightness in my shoulders. "Besides, I'm not very capable of that at this moment in time."

"I just don't want to get bitten as I put this on."

"My dear, I may be a captive beast and a monster, but I am a gentleman." I gave her a flash of a smile.

She gave a tentative one back as she closed the last bit of distance between us. "If you say so, but please don't bite me."

"I won't." I meant it.

She wrapped her arms around my neck, clicking the collar in place. She spun the collar around my neck and typed on the small keypad. The collar cinched snugly around my throat. "The collar is made of a similar material as the binding chains, you won't be able to claw it off. If you do manage to damage it, one or more of the injectors will activate. The collar has a remote detonator, and all the science team has a programmed trigger which they will activate if they feel threatened in any way. Understood?"

"Yes, my dear." I purred in her ear. "What is in this delightful contraption?"

"That's classified. They're going to lower you down so we can examine you."

She stepped back. Levers clicked behind me, and I was lowered to the ground. My knees gave out, buckling underneath me. I sat on the ground as the mechanism came to a stop. My arms tingle as they come to rest at my sides, I hissed as pins and needles took up residence in my extremities.

"Now then, some questions."

I flexed my fingers and sharp pain exploded up my arm. "Carry on."

"How old are you?"

"One-thousand-one hundred thirty-two give or take five years."

"In human years?"

I huffed a laugh. "Twenty-nine to thirty-two."

She nodded as she jotted down notes. "How tall are you?"

"Eight foot four without the antlers. With antlers ten."

"From tip to tail?"

"About thirteen."

"How much do you weigh?"

"Umm three-sixty in this form."

"That seems quite heavy for how lean you are."

I looked up at her and smiled. "I'm all muscle and dense bones, my dear."

Her cheeks colored slightly. "How healthy would you say you are?"

"Our resident doctor gave me a clean bill of health a couple of weeks ago."

"No communicable diseases specific to your species we need to know about?"

"None that even I know about."

"Do you have any health conditions?"

"PTSD I'm told, but physically no."

She stepped closer. "Alright, given your history we've been told to sedate you for examination. Which is sad because I find you charming."

I gave her a toothy grin. "My girl would agree with you."

She traded her clipboard for a large syringe. "I don't think this will knock you out, just dull your senses and strength." She cupped my chin and lifted my head, "A main vein will make this set quicker."

"It's not like I have much choice in the matter." I said and she poked me expertly. The sedative was icy in my veins, and I could feel it travel through my body. My head spun and my weak arms couldn't catch me, as I flopped to the ground.

"Are you okay?" Her voice had a hidden frantic edge to it.

My tongue felt like cotton. "Yes."

"Okay, we are going to do a physical exam." My eyelids fluttered, failing to stay open.

They spoke in hushed tones that were hard for me to decipher as I felt their hands running the length of my limbs, unlocking the manacles, measuring my antlers, and drawing several vials of blood. One of them left the room, and when his footsteps echoed back down the hall. The main doctor tapped my face a couple times and my eyes opened partially.

"I figured the heavy sedation would have this kind of effect. I am going to give you a couple more injections. The first is a shift stimulator, it will force your body to shift. I hear it is quite painful to force a shift this way, but the sedation should keep you passive."

"D—don—don't—" I forced out my tongue stuck in my mouth.

The doctor eyed me before he continued. "After you've fully shifted, I will inject a long-lasting inhibitor which will hinder your ability to shift back. It coats the neurons responsible and nullifies the ability. We have found that large shifters are easier to control in their beast forms."

He took a prepared syringe from one of the others. "This will hurt."

The injection itself did not hurt; nothing hurt as it traveled through my body. The tightness started at the base of my skull and skittered down my spine. My back arch and lightning strikes of pain exploded over my body. My muscles seized and spasmed. My movement was still restricted by the sedative, so I rolled as every bone in my body snapped and reshaped under my skin. I couldn't get enough air into my lungs and my head was stuck in a bone-splitting vice. Fur ripped through my skin with enough force to bleed. Everything was on fire. I moaned, hot tears rolling down my face as a snout took place. I lay on the cold concrete floor panting, wishing to be anywhere else. The doctor approached, and I didn't even feel the other injection, my body still trembling with the force of the shift. I watched them leave in single file until it was only Bastion and I in the room. He kept his face neutral, but I could see the unhinged panic dancing in his eyes.

I tried to stand but my legs give out beneath me. Fuck. How long would this sedative last? I felt my consciousness teeter on the edge. If I slept, I would be vulnerable, and hot panic stabbed me in the chest. I gave my head a shake, laying down fully. Sleep would clear these cobwebs, maybe ease the aches in my body. I cast a glance at Bas, his arms causally crossed over his chest, his hands in white knuckle fists.

"I'm not going anywhere." He said clearly. It was both the threat a true guard would make it to be and also a promise to me. He would be here for as long as he was allowed. I let my eyes drift closed. For now, I could rest. For now, I would have protection, even as minimal as it was.

A soft curvy body was pressed against mine. I leaned into her, taking a big inhale of her hair. Sweet-grass, lavender, sunflowers, oakmoss, she smelled like home. I pulled her closer, because I knew she was not here, and I was not with her. She stirred in my arms.

"Nira." She said groggily. "I must be dreaming."

"How fascinating." I said, kissing the top of her head. I wanted to commit her to memory.

"What?"

"We're *ag brionglóideach*. Dream walking."

She pushed against my chest to look at me. "You mean to tell me that we met up in our dreams?"

I cupped her face. "Yes, *mo grá*." I pressed a kiss to her brow. "Are you safe?"

"Yes, we're back at the manor. Allipo and Mitta told me to go to bed because I was making them anxious. I spent an hour after we got back practicing my shots. Then I paced for an hour while Mitta, Allipo, and Ventris discussed what the game plan was while we waited for Bastion to get a hold of us. Are you—no of course you're not. Have they hurt you?"

"Not really. They forced me into my beast form, which was painful, but other than bumps and bruises I'm okay."

"They can force you to shift?"

"Yes, it's a chemical process that was developed by the Lycans to help youngsters through their first and help them learn control."

"Will you be able to shift back?" She asked, cupping my face.

"Eventually. They have given me an inhibitor, to keep me in my beast form. For whatever it is they are doing."

"Do you know where you are?"

"Bastion said we were in a warehouse in the meatpacking district in New York City. I don't know exactly, but I'm sure Bastion will give Allipo coordinates as soon as he can."

She nuzzled her face against my chest. "Every second without you breaks my heart."

Her words broke mine. "Regardless of what happens to me—"

"Nothing will happen—" I pressed my finger to her lips.

"Regardless of what happens to me. Whether I am freed or not. Sold or not. Killed or not." She tried to protest again. "Listen to me, *mo grá.* Neither of us can guarantee my safety. But you," I ran my fingers across her cheek. I wanted to always carry her softness with me. "I can protect you, from where I am and if anything happens my magic will keep you safe. That is all I want, for you to be safe and cared for."

"I am coming for you."

I sighed, my anger at the declaration was only because that was the exact opposite of what I wanted. "I know, even though I hate it. This is the last place that I want you to be."

"But it is what I signed up for when I chose you and I will continue to choose you."

"I know." Footsteps on concrete were coming closer. The rattle of chains. "I'm going to have to go soon, *mo grá.*"

"No." Her arms wrapped around me tightly. "Please don't go."

Tears stung my eyes. "I'm sorry, dear. I don't have a choice. I'll come back to you." There was a creak of the metal door. I kissed her again. "I love you, Shasha."

"I love you, Niratap."

My eyes still burned from uncried tears. My joints still ached but I didn't feel like I was weighed down. I lifted my head as the metal door of the cell opened. The ogre that had held a knife to Shasha's throat. I would make him suffer, of that much, I was sure.

"How's it been, Mrak?" The ogre nodded toward me.

"Hey, Mandrake. After the scientists, he slept. Been a pretty quiet eight hours." Bastion said.

"Well, it's awake now. Think he'll give me trouble?"

"If he does, take this. The lab coats only gave me one guess we'll have to share."

"Thanks. Ask them about it your next shift."

"Break hours I take it?"

"Yeah. They pulled Dolan onto rotation. He has the coats right now. To be honest I wouldn't trust a mage with shit, but hey, whatever the boss says I guess."

"True. Well, good luck. I don't know how he'll be awake. He gives you trouble just use the transmitter. I'm going to catch some shut eye."

"Night."

Bastion left, not looking back as he shut the door behind him. Damn, I was proud of that kid. He walked the walk of a ruffian well. I laid my head down and watched the door. Escaping on my own was out of the question. I had to plan carefully.

"You won't be escaping on my watch. So don't even think about it."

I huffed and laid my head between my talons. *I will definitely be killing you.*

We sat in silence for some time before he broke it with his atrociously rough voice.

"Gods this is boring. Back-to-back babysitting is dumb shit."

You, sir, are dumb shit.

"If only I had a hot girl to enjoy."

I rolled my eyes. *Like any woman would go for you.*

"We have the same tastes, you and I. I like curvy women, but I prefer them to have bigger tits. Your lady is also too feisty. I like them submissive and begging."

Disgusting.

"I bet your sweet little piece of ass will beg for me if I get her right. You're a big dude; I bet she likes it from behind."

I growled, pulling my lips back from my teeth.

"Possessive. That's fine. Good pussy is a thing to be possessive about. Maybe after we're finished with you. I can hunt her down and fuck her. She obviously has a thing for monsters. I'd love to have that pretty mouth around my cock."

My hackles rose and I stood. My joints ached still but if this creature kept talking about Shasha, I would make a poor decision. She was mine. My mate. Mine.

"I wonder if she tastes as good as she smells. I would love to have her sit on my face. That would be nice. I'd also love to fill her full of ogre babies."

Enough! I launched myself across the room with a snarl. It was a bad decision, but I wasn't going to sit and listen to him prattle on about my mate. Mine. I snapped my jaws, narrowly missing him and ramming into the wall.

"I knew that would get a rise out of you. Ain't no pussy good enough to throw your freedom away. Come at me again. See what happens."

I'll enjoy ripping you limb from limb. You dumb fucking ogre.

I lunged, and he pulled the transmitter out of his pocket. I couldn't slow down, and everything else seemed to. The press of a single bottom would activate the collar. Would it dispense all five vials or just one? I heard the sound of the injector release, felt the needle puncture the back of neck. I yelped as the sensation of acid lit my blood on fire. I lost my footing on the landing and rolled several times before coming to a bruising stop against a post. I huffed and panted. Fuck. I scratched at the collar; the needle did not retract from my neck. It dug deeper making me bleed. I rolled on the ground, but nothing gave me relief. The ogre laughed, an atrocious sound that filled me with even more loathing.

"You think I'd actually let you get hold of me? Damn no wonder you let yourself get captured." He walked closer and hovered over me. "I should have just slit her throat in that alley. I should have fucked her when I knocked her out. Either time. I was the one who pulled her off the street during that rainstorm. She was so soft then, so easy."

I lashed out, my claws tearing into his arm, his slimy flesh flaying easily beneath my talons. He screamed and pressed the transmitter again. The second dose hit me hard. My breathing slowed and my vision blurred around the edges. I was going to pass out. My legs felt like Jello. I moved away from the ogre who was still screaming, blood dripping down his arm which hung limply in front of him. The injector fired again, and even though there was pain, it didn't quite register in my brain. Whatever this shit was, it was going to do a lot of damage to more than just me. I flopped against the wall, my legs giving out. Blackness surged like a dark sea, swallowing me whole.

Chapter Fifty-Two

Waking up surrounded by his scent without him was hard. Without his arms wrapped around me was heartbreaking. Five days without him felt like an eternity. I untwisted the blankets from around me and sat there. The dream stuck to me; the weight of his arms around me rocked me to my core. I sighed, hopping off the bed to tend to my needs. I needed to go downstairs and discuss what Niratap had told me. About where he was and what they'd done to him.

After getting dressed I padded barefoot down the stairs, poking my headfirst into the security office before heading down to the study. I could hear Allipo and Mitta talking as I entered the library.

"I don't like this." Allipo growled.

"It's the only way. We have to." She answered.

"No, we need to lead the recovery of the lord. You're asking too much."

"That's what my superiors want, Allipo." Ventris.

I came around the doorway, Allipo was pacing the length of Niratap's desk worrying his goatee. Mitta sat in one of the plush chairs watching him; she looked my way as I entered and gave a tight-lipped smile. I came and sat beside her on the arm of the chair. Ventris's face was on screen a video call on Niratap's monitor; his brows rose when we made eye contact.

"What is it they want to gain?"

"I already told you, Allipo. I don't know what they are planning beyond wanting control of the raid. My superiors are humans; I can't vouch for their plans. They may seize assets, execute arrests, and everyone may be arrested regardless of who they are. I can't tell you for sure."

Allipo slammed his hands on the desk. "That's not good enough!"

"I'm sorry."

Allipo glared at the man on the other side of the screen. "What good is having you as an ally, if—"

A ringing came from the computer as another call came in.

"I thought you said your lines were secure."

Mitta glowered as she leaned forward to add the caller on. "They are. Only our eyes and ears have access. It's probably Bas."

Bastion came into view, eyes widening at the sight of Ventris. "Well, that's not what I was expecting."

"Is your line of communication secure?" Ventris barked.

"It is. I'm calling through a spoofer. On our end, it looks like I'm playing a shooter game. Nothing about this will reflect back or break my cover."

"Is Niratap okay?" I asked before the hellos could be said.

Bastion gave a sad smile. "He's a little roughed up. When we jumped him, a couple of the guys went a little heavy. Some bruises and possibly some muscle tears. They fitted him with an injector collar. I don't know what is in the vials; I'm assuming it's whatever they have been experimenting with. They sedated him pretty heavily when the lab coats were in there."

"Is it true you're in the meatpacking district? What did they do to him?"

Bastion's brows rose in surprise. "How did—yes, we are. I sent Allipo the coordinates for the warehouse. The scientist took measurements and asked him questions about his weight and age and what that equates to in human years. Then did what Dravin wanted them to do, so he would be easier to control."

"Forced him to shift into his beast, so he couldn't charm his way out."

"Wait a second." Bastion said. "How do you know this?"

I opened my mouth but shut it again. We hadn't told anyone, and I wasn't sure if they would catch on about us being mates. "The lord and I were dream walking, and he told me what was going on vaguely. I—"

"That's not possible." Ventris said with something akin to rage on his face. Allipo, Mitta, and Bastion all smiled. They all knew what dream walking meant.

Allipo whispered to himself. "That sly devil."

"When?" Bastion asked.

"Between Thanksgiving and Yule. We—"

"This is unacceptable." Ventris growled, interrupting me.

"To be honest, Ventris." I said, taking on that lethality that Niratap had taught me. "I don't know you and I don't care about what you think about my relationship with Niratap. Bastion, do you have any idea of how we can get both of you out safely?"

"Realistically." Bastion began. "I don't have an exit plan to get both of us out. I think the best course of action would be a full-on raid. Which I am sure is why Ventris was looped in. A raid would guarantee Dravin getting knocked down but doesn't necessarily guarantee the lord and I getting out unscathed."

Allipo began pacing again. "I need something better. Your parents will kill me if you get hurt because of this, and we can't risk Lord Niratap that way. I need a promise that he won't be harmed, Ventris."

"And like I've been saying my superiors only want control of the raid. Claim the glory, but that doesn't come with any guarantees."

"So, what you are saying," I said, locking eyes with Ventris, "Is he could go from being the prisoner of a trader to a prisoner of the government?"

Ventris sighed. "It is a possibility. Lord Niratap has been an asset—"

"However." Bastion added. "Dravin's idea of studying bitarogs isn't a bad one. Not a lot is known about them. The government may want that."

"Bas," Mitta queried. "What do you know about the other bitarog?"

"Her name is Nessa, and she's a little older than the lord. She's got a mouth on her which, is probably part of the reason that they forced the lord to shift. She was living in the wild. She's not very friendly."

Mitta considered for a minute. "You don't think Dravin is planning to try to breed them, do you?" Everyone's eyes widened and a rock settled into my stomach. "I mean think about it. Why else would you hunt down a rare male and female monster."

"Dravin did tell the lord that he would make him a ton of money. It is a lot to risk, but the profit margin on bitarog pups would be astronomical."

I chewed my lip. "There's no way Niratap would go along with that."

"No, he wouldn't." Allipo said. "Mated males are true to those they are bonded to. They would force them."

"Bitarogs are canid. They have heat cycles." Mitta said. "That is a lot of waiting for something that may or may not come soon. You can't force that."

"No." Ventris said. "They'll simulate it. In vitro. Hormones."

"The lord wouldn't give up a sample willingly." Mitta said.

"He won't." I said the heaviness nearly taking my breath away. It sunk in that I had seen what they were planning a thousand times in my life. "In his beast form they'll treat him like an animal. They'll collect it like ranchers do cattle. Electroejaculation."

"That sounds painful." Bastion said grimacing.

"It's widely regarded that way, but not everyone can afford artificial mounts for bulls. There's really nothing that you can do to guarantee Niratap's safety?"

Ventris sighed. "I will talk with my superiors and see if I can get something for you guys. I don't want to see Niratap a prisoner any more than you."

"Trying is better than nothing." Mitta said.

"Fine." Allipo said. "When can we expect to set up a base? Are you going to do central here, or do you have a place in mind in the meatpacking district."

"Send me the coordinates, and I will let you know."

"No." I said. "Talk to your bosses, then we'll discuss the coordinates."

"Shasha." Bastion positioned. "You can't give him nothing; there is no way our family could take Dravin. We need the bureau's help."

"I understand that. But without the guarantee of both yours and Niratap's safety, I don't feel comfortable sharing that information and them going in without us."

"I am offended that you think I would sink to that." Ventris said.

"Again." I said pointedly at him. "I don't know you. I know Niratap trusts you, but I also know he doesn't trust your organization."

Ventris sat back in his chair defeated. "Fine. I—"

An alarm sounded behind Bastion. "Shit. Shit. Shit."

"Bas." Mitta stood alarmed. "What's going on?"

"It's a containment alarm." He said, sliding a gun into the back of his pants. "God dammit. The lord probably got into it with fucking Mandrake. The ogre is a piece of shit though, he probably deserves it. I've got to go help with this. I'll try to keep the lord in one piece. I'll call you back when this blows over."

Bastion disconnected and fear coiled in my gut. "Ventris, talk to your superiors. We need to get them out of there."

I glared down the sight of the pistol. I needed to get him out. I needed him safe. I exhaled and unloaded the clip.

"Your form is looking good."

I sat the gun down and looked at Mitta, who was leaning against the door of the shooting range. "Thanks."

"Practicing distracting yourself?"

I turned back and pushed the button to pull the target up. "I might be. I—I can't sit idly by while he's trapped."

"I understand. That's a nice spread." She said, indicating the tight circle of chest shots.

"It is, but I missed my head shot."

"That's fine. You've only been shooting since November; that's quite impressive."

"It's not good enough."

"Shasha, if the lord hadn't taken you under his wing there is no way that you would be this good a shot. Hell, I wasn't even that good a shot that early."

"It's still not good enough." I slammed my hands down on the counter, tears falling down my face. "It's not enough. It wasn't enough that night. I wasn't lethal enough. I wasn't dangerous enough. I wasn't strong enough, and they took him. They chained him up, Mitta. They beat him. They bound him to that monster. They are doing gods knows what to him, and I am still here."

Mitta placed a hand on my back "Shasha. The lord wouldn't want you beating yourself up over the decision he made."

"But he shouldn't have had to make that choice. I wasn't paying attention and the fucking ogre snuck up on me. If I had been paying attention. If I had—" tears rolled down my cheeks.

Mitta pulled me against her chest. "You can't blame yourself for what-ifs love."

I sobbed into her. "Why? Why did he do that, Mitta?"

"You don't need to ask me that. You know why. He loves you. He's mated to you. He chose you, and he will continue to choose you over anything, even his freedom."

"I shouldn't trump his freedom."

I could hear the frown in her voice. "But you do." She pulled back, holding my face in her hands. "Keep practicing. I'll let you know when Bastion calls back." She turned to leave.

"What if we can't get to him in time?" I asked, afraid of the what ifs.

She stopped in the doorway. "Niratap wouldn't leave you. I can guarantee he is doing everything he can to get back to you. Don't focus on the 'what-ifs' Shasha, just the goal and getting him." With that she left.

I don't know how long I practiced. My arms ached when I finally traveled down to the kitchen to find something to eat. I could hear someone crying, tucked beyond the patio doors. I opened the door to find Echo sitting on the bench, Dheg holding her hand and kneeling before her.

"Is everything okay?" I asked.

Echo turned to me, her pearlescent skin casting rainbows through her tear tracks, "Oh, I'm sorry, Miss Shasha. I'm just so distraught by the lord's capture. I was with Dheg in the barn helping him tend the horses, and the lord's horse looked at me so sullenly, I started bawling. Forgive my weakness."

"There's nothing to forgive, and please, Echo, you can just call me Shasha. I understand. I have cried a lot the past few days worrying about him, but we will bring him home. Come hell or high water."

She cracked a small spritely smile. "Yes, we will. I have faith in that. The grounds just feel different without him."

Dheg nods. "Guinness understands too. Please come back to the stables with me, lovey. Other than the lord, you're the only one he lets untangle his mess of hair."

She let out a bell-like giggle. "You just don't do it right, Dheg. He's tender headed."

"Only between his ears." Dheg grumbled.

I chuckled.

"You should join us mi—Shasha. It will help take your mind off missing the lord while we wait."

"I'm going to grab a bite to eat. I've been practicing all morning, and I think I'll go read after. I have homework I should work on, too. Though the thought of answering comprehension questions on the history of earthen people feels mute."

"Okay, eat a good meal. The lord would be unhappy if you didn't." Dheg smiled.

I returned the gesture. "That he would."

I sat, curled into the blankets on our bed, all my homework and reading caught up for my classes. Vrorlin and I had exchanged some emails about what was going on. He would shift me to an independent study type situation for the semester, understanding that Niratap meant more to me than classes and grades. He told me Niratap was tough, that he had survived hundreds of years in captivity, a few days or few weeks would not be his downfall. I knew he was right, but something hollow had taken up residence in my heart, chilling me to the core. I left the bed, deciding a shower might ease the unsettled part of my soul.

Hot spray danced over my skin, but the chill only sunk deeper, drawing tears to my eyes. They stung, but the water washed them from my cheeks. What was going on? What is this feeling? I curled up under the spray and for the first time in what felt like forever, I prayed. I didn't really believe in God as my mother did, but whatever divinity was out there, I wanted them to hear me.

"I know I haven't spoken out to whoever you may be in a long time, but I want you to know that I love him. That it isn't just a crush. It isn't just a fling. He is the air in my lungs. The blood in my veins. The fire in my soul. No one has ever held such a prominent place in my heart. Please. Please. I'm begging you. Don't take him from me. I know you shaped him to be a fighter. A protector. I am asking you to keep him safe. Keep him alive."

The chill, hollow feeling faded as quickly as it had set in and soon the water felt cold against my skin. I don't know if that higher power had heard me, but I hoped it would keep him safe.

After a very quiet dinner with my new family, I curled into the sheets, his scent clinging to them faintly though they lacked his warmth. Sleep evaded me, the unease at the feeling of him missing from me still twisting in my gut. Eventually I opened my eyes in that honey-kissed room of our dream from last night. I sat up, his warmth still missing. He wasn't there.

Chapter Fifty-Three

Niratap

My body felt like I was hit by a train. I grimaced trying to roll over. The rattle of chains greeted me, a momentary jolt of panic made my heart flutter in my chest. I was a prisoner. I had been pushed, and I had lashed out. I hoped that disgusting ogre bled to death.

"He's lucky the boss got to him in time." A familiar voice said.

"He's going to be feeling that beating for a while." A female voice thick with my homeland's accent.

I let out a shuddering breath, pretty sure at least one of my ribs was broken, or maybe it was just the bars that I felt digging into my ribs. I was back in my human form. What happened? I try to lift my head and chains rattle in my ears.

"He's awake." The female voice said.

"That he is. Niratap, don't try to move too much. You were beaten to near an inch of your life." The male voice said footsteps approaching. Light flooded my eyes as a cover was pulled off the cage I was in, the mage stood next to the cage with a friendly smile. "Good morning."

"What happened?" I asked, my throat scratchy.

"You attacked Mandrake, to be fair though he probably fucking deserved it. Nasty one he is, but he hit you with the injector collar three times, sending your body into shock. You blacked out, and he went to town on you with a pipe before he called for help. You stopped breathing when the coats were looking at you, and they decided it would be best to shift you back and treat you. Dravin is pissed and Mandrake is only allowed to babysit the coats now. Fitting punishment, if you ask me. So, it will just be Mrak and me in twelve-hour shifts."

"How much damage did he inflict while I was unconscious?"

"Two broken ribs, bruised liver, fractured wrist, and a bunch of contusions."

I shifted enough to look at myself, |I saw dark bruises crisscrossed over my abdomen and chest. I sighed. "How long was I unconscious and why are you being kind to me?"

"You've been out for a couple of days, and believe it or not, I'm on your side."

"Forgive me, I don't."

"I can prove it."

"Then do so."

He pulled a pendant from underneath his shirt, an over-sized red stone. He hovered the pendant before him, and a glamour so expertly woven slid away and fell to the floor like thrown glitter. Black dog tags took the pendant's place. They read:

McCallum

Dolan A Neg

1585622593

USMC Spec Ops L

Catholic

"I've been under cover with Dravin for a year and half. I'm part of commander Ventris's division." He reapplied the glamour, hiding his identifiers.

"Why trust me with information like that? I could use it against you."

"You could, but it wouldn't help you get out of here and get back to that girl."

I push myself off the floor, almost falling back down at the jolt of knife-sharp pain in my wrist. "Damn it."

"I would take it easy on the wrist there, *dearthár leanbh*." [35] The familiar female voice said, causing goosebumps to travel rapidly over my skin.

---

[35] Baby brother

I looked at her over my shoulder, my eyes widening at the sight of her. A knowing wolfish smile dawned on her pale honey face dotted wildly with freckles. Endlessly long, straight, black hair much like my own draped over her body acting as a curtain to hide her. Her bright silver eyes were filled with the same mischief and maturity that she had always had, shining with glee through the bars of her cage.

"Nessa?" My voice doesn't raise above a whisper.

"Hello, Niratap. It has been a very long time."

Tears welled in my eyes as my heart swelled. "I thought-I thought I'd lost you."

Her face softened with warmth and love. "And I you."

"Nessa told me you were her brother." Dolan said. "That's not going to stop Dravin and his plans."

The shock of seeing my sister faded quickly. "And what are Dravin's plans exactly?"

Dolan swallowed uncomfortably, but it was Nessa who spoke. "He's planning on trying to breed us."

"Never gonna happen."

Dolan stood returning to his chair. "Dravin's not going to give you a choice."

I laughed an ache radiating from my ribs. "Fat chance. I love my sister but that is disgusting."

"Niratap, you see the position that we're in, right? It's not like we'll have a choice until we're released. Dolan has been telling me that he knows you have someone on the inside too. Have you seen them? Have they gotten a message out?"

I eyed Dolan, still not trusting. "They said they were working on it, they were going to get the coordinates to my people, I don't know if they were successful."

"You don't have to trust me, Niratap." Dolan said, "I know what being undercover is like. I know it's dangerous, even with other undercover operatives—no, especially with other undercover operatives in the mix. I understand you don't what to compromise his identity."

I cocked a brow at him. "You already know who my operative is?"

"I do." He smiled smugly.

"What do you want?"

"Niratap." My sister scolded. "He's trying to help us out."

"Be that as it may, Nessa. If he puts that kid at risk—"

"You mean more at risk than going deep cover for a monster trader kingpin?"

"Bastion chose to go undercover." I growled. "His parents didn't want him to, I didn't want him to. Dravin was a low priority until—"

"You bought the girl."

I took a breath. "Yes."

"Shasha Nicole Dion, twenty-four born November thirtieth to Jazzera Hardy-Dion and Xaevean V. Dion, in Afton, New York. She's a freshman at NYU majoring in monsters and mythology. She was picked up by that nasty ogre and sold on the market for just shy of three million."

"How do you know that?"

"It's amazing what happens when you work for the government, right?"

"Explain yourself." I snapped.

"Temper. Temper. Don't you find it interesting that Commander Ventris was undercover for six years in Afton?"

"I know that he was stationed there, to monitor underground sales of faery dust. Why does that matter?"

"He met a woman when he was undercover, and married her, but she only knew him, by his undercover role. They had a kid together."

"What? Impossible. He would have told me he started a family undercover."

"Shortly before he came out of that role, the bureau rolled a bust on that ring of faery-dust dealers. Ventris left soon after that and cut ties completely to protect them. The ringleader wasn't part of the bust; he was here at the market when it happened."

"What you're insinuating is—"

"She is Ventris's daughter."

"Well, fuck."

"Why is this important information?" Nessa asked.

"Because even though Ventris and I are friends, I've been sleeping with his daughter for seven months."

Nessa opened her mouth and closed it, glaring at me as she scented the air. "It's more than that, isn't it?"

I sighed. "Nessa."

"You're not just fucking her, are you?" Nessa snarled, gripping the bars.

I looked down at my hands. "We chose each other."

She scoffed. "Leave it to my irresponsible brother, literally fucking away our rescue."

"Are you going to blame me for everything?" I sighed.

"Regardless of how available you are, mate. Dravin is working on forcing that interaction. If you don't consummate, he's going to simulate it. Force you to part with a specimen and force her into heat."

"Fuck." I groaned, leaning back against the bars.

"Indeed." Dolan said as he eyed me. "You both should rest. Dravin is out in Texas meeting someone. He'll be back in a few days."

"What then?" She asked.

Dolan grimaced. "Then I assume Dravin will see that things are set in motion himself."

Sleep was hard to sink into, but I needed to see her. It had been days since I had seen her in my dreams. Just over a week since I had actually held her in my arms. Since I'd danced with her. Since I had kissed her. Everything was weighing heavy on my mind, making it even harder to find our dream space. I had many things to tell her, though I did not know how to tell her that Ventris was really her father. I should allow him that, but I held fear in my heart that he would try to tear us apart.

Songbirds sang overhead, and a warm summer breeze blew strands of my hair over my face. I opened my eyes, I was sitting against a tree in a meadow, summer grasses danced with wildflowers scattered among the blades. The ground was warm, and everything was so peaceful. A small town was visible down in the valley, wheat fields beyond it. I had never been here before.

"I was hoping you would find me here." Shasha's voice came from behind me. She was dressed in a butter yellow dress that flowed with the breeze.

"*Mo grá.*" I smiled at her. "Where are we?"

"That is Afton down there. This was my favorite place to hide growing up. Every time I ran off alone, I got in trouble, but nothing could keep me from this place."

I chuckled. "You are quite a handful, aren't you?"

She smiled, but it didn't touch her eyes. "I was hoping to see you sooner. You know, since we figured this out. Are you okay?"

I debated telling her. She must have seen the internal war in my eyes.

"The truth *mo grá.*"

I sighed. "No. I let my anger get the best of me."

"What happened?" Her voice had a hard edge that promised violence.

"Shasha, I'm alive, and I will be fi—"

"Niratap." She snarled. "Tell me what happened or so help me I'll—I'll—"

"You'll what love?" Rage boiled under my skin, like it did in her eyes.

"Tell me, my mate. Don't lie."

I looked away. "That ogre baited me; He was saying all the horrible things he would do to you. I lost my temper and attacked him, collar be damned. He pushed too much of whatever is in the vials into my system, and I blacked out. He beat me with a pipe afterword. I'm battered and bruised with a couple broken ribs, but I am okay.”

“You’re leaving something out.”

“I’m in a cage now, in the same cell as the other bitarog. She’s my sister.”

“Before that. I don’t know what it is, but something felt weird the other day right after we shared the dream space. It was like you were missing from my heart.”

I swallowed. “Shasha, I—”

“Please.” She came to kneel in front of me, tears in her eyes. “Please tell me why you were missing.”

I took a deep breath. “Apparently, while I was unconscious, my heart stopped. It took them a few minutes to get it beating again.” She stood and pressed a hand to her mouth. I could see the heartbreak at my words in every fiber of her being. Tears rolled over her cheeks. I stood, pulling her into my arms. “My love, I am still here. I am sorry my recklessness causes you pain.”

“You need to be more careful. Don’t give them a reason to kill you. Please. I can’t—” She took a shuddering breath. “I can’t carry that weight of losing you.”

“Shasha I—”

“Promise me that you will keep your head down.” She slammed a fist against my chest. “Promise me!”

“I can’t promise, my love.”

“Promise me!” The breeze whipped past me as she yelled. The truth of what Dolan had told me, the truth about her father, sank into me. I relented.

“I will try, *mo grá.*” I kissed the top of her head. “I will try.”

She wiped her eyes with the heels of her hands. “Bastion got a hold of us; we know where you are and we're coming to save you as soon as we can. Ventris is trying to negotiate with his superiors so we can guarantee Bastion’s and your safety. Mitta proposed that they are trying to breed you and the female.”

“They are, and she is my sister.”

"What?"

"The female bitarog is my sister."

She stared up at me with both excitement and fear flooding her eyes. "That complicates things, doesn't it?"

"It does. Dravin is gone for a few days in Texas. It will give me time to recover."

"Have they been feeding you?"

"Well, I have been unconscious the majority of the time I've been here, but hunger hasn't been an issue. I assume they've been tube feeding me while I was unconscious."

She frowned. "That's cruel."

I shrugged. "I have been given water recently, too. I can't serve Dravin dead."

Her brows furrowed. "I don't like this at all."

"Neither do I, my love, but I will try to keep my head down. I can't guarantee that I will be whole when you find me. I have a feeling I'm going to pay for flaying that ogre's arm open."

She pressed her ear to my chest, listening to the steady thud of my heart. "I miss you."

"And I you. I never imagined that I would miss someone like I miss you." Mate. Mine.

She looked up at me. "This is going to be dangerous, isn't it?"

"Very."

"A raid is the only answer, isn't it?"

"More than likely, and you will need Ventris's forces. Dravin has only trusted our guarding to his top three men. Ironically apparently two of the three are actually undercover."

"Who else?"

"The mage. He says there is another operative from the FBMI in with the scientists. That is a lot of people to try to free in a raid."

"Five is a lot?"

"Plus, whatever other creatures he has held here. I don't know what exactly he's experimenting with beyond the basilisk venom."

"We need to know what he's doing so we can prepare."

"Bastion told me he was working on it, but I might be able to get information out of Dolan."

"Just tread carefully, my dear, and know I'm coming for you. Nothing will keep me from you." A knock echoed through the meadow, and we clung to each other.

"I will see you soon, *mo grá.*"

"I love you."

"I love you."

She faded from my arms slowly, leaving me alone in her meadow. I looked over the valley, my chest filled with hollowness. I needed to stay alive for her, but I didn't know what Dravin was going to do. I did know that the scars I would get from this would be worth every breath she took.

The days that followed were strange; both Bastion and Dolan made sure we were fed and had water to drink. My sister and I got a shower. Though the water was cold, getting the dried blood off my skin and out of my hair was a relief. I watched my bruises fade and it became easier to breathe.

Nessa told me of her life back home, running through the wild moors of the green isle. Even though Ireland had grown like the rest of the world, it was still an untamed place. I told her the cliff notes version of captivity and the life I had built for myself. Mostly I told her of the recent months with Shasha.

"She sounds like a treat, brother." Nessa said, idly combing through her hair.

"She's feisty." Bastion added. "You'd like her."

"And she gets feistier by the day, Bastion. I reckon she shoots better than you already."

"Lies." He growled.

"No. I'm serious, she's got a wicked eye with her pistol."

"What gun is she shooting?"

"The Glock 26."

"You gave that girl a handheld mini turret?"

"She only has a fifteen-capacity magazine."

"It's still basically a turret. How's her long range?"

"We haven't had a chance to take her to the outdoor range, not with the recovery from the basilisk attack. Mitta wanted me to be careful, so I didn't tear healing muscles, though the point is moot now that I have been imprisoned and hung from chains. Mitta has been teaching her the bow; maybe we can go on a hunt after all this is over."

"You sound so confident in us getting out of this, brother."

"The family I have grown over the years won't rest until I'm free. Shasha wouldn't let them give up on me, even if they were lesser."

"Steel bars kind of keep hope at bay little brother."

I hear footsteps. "Bas there is no way has it been twelve hours already?"

"No." He straightened in his chair.

"We have company then." I said sitting up.

The screech of the metal door grated against its hinges. Dravin walked in, his face a mask of bored disinterest as he undid his cuffs. He was flanked by several scientists and soldiers. "How has it been while I've been gone, Mrak?"

"Uneventful sir."

"The love birds getting along?"

"*Muc nimhneach tú. Bainfidh mé taitneamh as féachaint ar na cuieoga ag piocadh ar do chuid iontaoibh.*"[36] Nessa snarled.

"In English, you dumb bitch. I don't speak whatever heathen tongue that is."

---

[36] "You vile pig. I will enjoy watching flies pick at your entrails."

"It's Irish, you ass." I growled, but a smile twisted my lips. "Don't speak to her like that. Though I would gladly translate it for you if you wish."

"That's not necessary. Whatever she said was vulgar based on the expression on both your faces."

"*Briseadh agus bru ar do chnamha.*"[37] Nessa spit on the ground before him. "*Go ngearrfaidh an daibhal an ceann díot agus go ndéanfadh sé obair lea de do mhuineál.*"[38]

I laughed.

"Really? I am so very curious. Mrak, do you speak Irish at all?"

"No, sir. I don't."

"Very well." Dravin looked at me with a searing hatred in his eyes. "Obey."

The searing bite of magic cut into my skin. "Fuck you."

"Submit."

My body shook as I fought. "And you know my answer, Dravin. Fuck. You."

"*Fag mo dhearthair leat fein carn farae peisteanna.*"[39] Nessa snarled.

He turned his eyes toward her. "Bend to my will, whore."

Nessa screamed; I roared. "*Fág mo dheirfiúr ina n-aonar.*[40] Leave her alone!"

"You don't want the bitch to suffer? Obey. Tell me what she said."

Fire raced down my spine, causing me to buckle forward. Panting I glare up at him. "She said 'you vile pig. I will enjoy watching flies pick at your entrails.' 'A breaking

---

[37] "A breaking and crushing on your bones!"

[38] "May the devil cut the head off you and make a day's work of your neck."

[39] "Leave my brother alone you pile of worm fodder."

[40] "Leave my sister alone."

and crushing on your bones!' 'May the devil cut the head off you and make a day's work of your neck.'"

"Tell me everything." Dravin snarled, storming toward the cage.

I cast a glance at Nessa, I had to lie to keep us safe, Dravin was already using us against one another.

"Don't look at her! Obey me you fool what did she say!"

Lightning courses through my body, and my body writhes involuntarily. "She said to leave me alone, you pile of worm fodder."

Dravin laughed. "Maybe I should have Mandrake take care of that mouth of hers. Though I guess he only has one arm to hold on to her with."

I lunged against the bars of the cage, clawing at the space he had left between us. "Leave her alone, Dravin."

He held up his hand, a chain materializing between us. He pulled me against the bars, a sinister grin coming across his aged mug. "I'll spare her today, for a cost."

"What?" A promise of violence on my tongue.

"You will not fight what is to come."

"And what is to come, Dravin?"

"Your punishment, of course. You didn't think that you would get away with flaying my third like that, did you?"

"What's my punishment?"

He pressed his finger against the scar that ran down my cheek. "One of you will taste the whip. Will it be you or her? Complete bloody submission at my hand."

I stared into Dravin's eyes. I didn't need to look at Nessa to know she was afraid. The acrid scent of it stained the air. I closed my eyes and took a breath. "I will accept the punishment."

"Good." Dravin dropped the chain and it dematerialized before it hit the floor. "Let him out; he won't fight me now."

Two armed men came forward, unlocking the cage and the shackles at my wrists. I crawled out of the low cage and the men chuckled before I stood, towering over them. They backed away guns pointed center mass. My blood boiled in my veins at how truly powerless I was.

"Come stand over here, Niratap." Dravin directed me to a spot close to the center of the room. I faced away from him, knowing what was to come.

"Kneel."

Everything in me wanted to fight, to reject the command. Pride was my downfall now that I had been free. Pride slowed me from descending. I took a couple of steadying breaths.

"I said kneel." Dravin's voice is laced with venom and command. Fire dripped down my spine again as I brought my knees to the floor, wrapping my tail around my thigh and lowering my head. Dravin walked rounds past me.

"I'd never thought being in control of such a creature would give me this sense of euphoria." He ran a finger over my antler. "Your submissiveness pleases me, Niratap."

His footsteps paced behind me, and my heart skittered unnaturally in my chest. He wasn't going to warn me when the whip would kiss my skin. The anticipation itself was a kind of torture of its own. I wanted this over. I wanted the pain. The pain was better than blindly waiting for it to happen. I tried to calm my heart. Make my body relax. The damage wouldn't be as deep if I could relax, but I couldn't seem to find the serenity needed.

The whip cracked the air as it came across my skin. The sting of it across my back was both foreign and familiar. My breath left in a rush. Fisting my hands on my thighs, I forced myself to focus on bringing air into my lungs. The whip came down again and again and again. Some caught me sharper than others, causing me to scream. I had lost count when the whip finally sliced through my skin, and blood wept down my back. My body shook, but I couldn't yield.

There was a pause. My breathing had become labored, my knuckles white, and Dravin came to stand before me.

"I'm impressed that you could withstand that." Dravin praised using the handle of the whip to tilt my face back. "I thought you would collapse."

He looked past me and nodded. The clank of metal being locked into place as they assembled something. He smiled down at me with cruelty on his face.

"Have you figured out my plans, Niratap?"

A breath shuddered into me. "You plan on breeding us."

He frowned at me. "Yes, that is a large part of what I want to do, but—"

"That will never happen." I sneered.

The smile returned. "That's the best part. You don't have a choice."

"I won't lay with her."

"Again, you don't have a choice. Now shift. I have been told that forcing the shift could hinder production."

I growled. "I will not lay with her."

He struck me with the handle, blood filling my mouth as he spoke. "Shift before I lose my patience."

I spit, but didn't argue, crouching forward and letting the aching flesh grow fur and stretch around my form. Blood quickly matted my fur, dripping onto the ground.

"Come, beast." Dravin called, and as much as I hated myself, I obeyed. Turning around, they had set up a cattle chute. Soldiers had ropes and chains at the ready, and the horror that I really didn't have a choice sunk in. I shook, blood splattering over the concrete.

"I don't have all day, Niratap. Get in the chute."

I didn't want this; the wild in me screamed to fight, to run. I turned into the chute, soldiers flanking the sides slid the bars closed in around me. My heart fluttered once more. The wild cried in my blood. The wild in me wanted to lash out as a heavy muzzle was quickly dropped and fastened around my head. Panic had me backing up against the bars that had closed behind me. I reared back as the magic chain materialized through the head door pulling me through. I thrashed against the hold and tried to fight as the men tied my legs to the sides of the chute. I was trapped. My world spun, becoming so small and tight.

"Enough." Dravin snarled at me, hitting me again with the handle of the whip. I was shaking but fully immobilized. Dravin observed me for several long moments that cruel, amused smile taking up its home on his face. "You're afraid."

I growled in response, and he just smiled more, waving the scientist over.

"What are you doing to him?" Nessa's voice quivered with rage, and she sounded so very far away.

"Electrostimulation. I figured when I went on this journey to breed bitarogs that they wouldn't be willing to breed with one another. So, this was the simplest way of achieving that. You see the scientists are going to insert an electrode stimulator into the rectum and electrically stimulate the muscles and glands until ejaculation."

"That doesn't mean his seed will take." She growled.

"No, it doesn't." Dravin turned toward her. "They are also working on forcing you into heat so we can get this money bun cooking."

Nessa snarled and lunged at him through the bars. "Fuck you!"

He laughed as they inserted the probe and I struggled against it.

Pain lit up every part of my being. I snarled. I yelped. It was unlike any pain I had felt before. The tight coiling in my gut was nauseating. My brain was spiraling the drain; pain, and stress taxing all that I had reserved after healing. I clawed at the floor, nearly begging for this to be done. Begging for it to end. My muscles were beyond my control, had I not been restrained as I was, I would have ended up on the concrete. Time slowed there. Almost froze completely.

"Dravin, we have a good-sized sample now. The color is good, and it's clean."

"Good. Mrak, how much longer is your watch?"

"Another four hours sir."

"Sometime before you switch over, get him back in his cage. He won't fight you at all. I'm sure his spirit is broken, at least for today."

"Yes, sir."

They left, and silence haunted me. My body was still spasming, blood dripping onto the ground around me. I had recoiled all the way into myself. I didn't know how long I stayed there. Trapped. Weak. Shaking. Gentle hands slid up my face, undoing the muzzle. It fell away, and I just stared at it there while whoever it was untied my bound legs. They were speaking in a soothing voice as they opened the door and lead me back to the cage. Once inside I looked at the gentle person who had moved me. Bastion's face was full of worry as he locked the gate.

"My Lord?"

I laid down; existing was painful, but I let the beast slide away. My voice was not my own it came out choked and gravelly. "Bas."

"We're going to get you out of here."

"I—I don't doubt that, Bas." I brought my arm under my head. My back screamed as I curled in on myself. "Everything hurts."

"I'll try to get you something for the pain. I can't promise anything, but I'll try."

"Thank you, Bas."

He stepped away, and eventually I heard Dolan come in. They exchanged some words before Bastion left. Sometime after that, I faded into the darkness of unconsciousness hoping that maybe I would find her beyond it.

Chapter Fifty-Four

Shasha

I was getting ready for bed when my phone rang, for some reason it caused my heart to skitter wildly. Bastion's name came across my screen.

"Hey, are you guys, okay?" I said in greeting.

"Hey, Shash. Um, fuck this is hard. Today has been hard. I had to watch them do that, and I had to tie him down, and I—I just needed to talk to a friend. I know he's your mate, but I just can't believe my hands were involved with that."

"What happened?"

"What you said would happen."

My stomach turned. "They treated him like cattle, like a dangerous stud."

Bastion swallowed and a shaky breath came from him. "Yeah."

"Is he—" okay? Hurt? I wanted to ask, but I was afraid of what would come from voicing those questions.

"He's in a lot of pain. Dravin—he—he whipped him, and his healing is being suppressed by the synthetic venom they've pumped into him. Dravin used Nessa against him. Threatened her and he folded. He let Dravin take him to the ground, whip him. Then they bound him in that chute and," Bastion took a sharp, shaking breath. "The terror I saw in his face, Shasha. It broke a part of me."

"He's tough, Bas. You did good. You kept your cool and did as you were told. I can't fault you for doing your job." I felt my lip wobble. "I don't want to have to find you in a ditch somewhere because they broke you."

"This is so hard, Shash."

"I know." I did. After the basilisk attack, I knew. Feeling utterly hopeless as toxins rendered Niratap helpless. How it had taken months for his body to recover. How long would it take him to recover after this? "Was he awake when you left him?"

"No, he curled up and passed out. He's in so much pain and I don't know how any being could withstand what he did today."

"He's strong, and he's been in this position before."

"I know. I just—I'm sorry that I couldn't do anything."

"It's okay, Bas, my only request is that you keep the both of you alive until we can get to you, okay?"

"I swear."

"Thank you." I yawned.

"I should let you go to bed. I know it's late."

"No, it's okay if you need to talk."

"No. Oh, but I had something else to tell you."

"What is it, Bas?"

"Dravin is holding a masquerade in two weeks, to show off his prizes. I overheard him talking to Christiana about it. How he was still waiting on the scientists to figure out a way to force Nessa to go into heat and might as well show off what he has. He's going to let the lord heal for that. I sent Allipo the information about the masquerade already."

"Okay, I'll talk to Allipo about it tomorrow."

"Dravin also said he was going to work on him. I don't really know what that means, but it can't be good."

I swallowed, knowing Dravin was going to try to break his spirit. "No, it won't be."

"Okay. I'll see you soon, Shasha. Be careful, and if you see him in the dreamscape, tell him I'm sorry."

"I will, Bas. Get some sleep, bud."

I hung up, settling into the bed of pillows and blankets. His scent clung to the sheets, but just barely. He was starting to fade from around me and my heart seized at the thought of waking up and him being gone.

The room I woke up in was not warm and soft like the bed where I had fallen asleep. Hard cement was underneath me and at my back, the only light came from a single exposed bulb by a red metal door. In the dim light I saw two cages halfway between me and the door. A heavy iron-rich smell stained the air, but I could smell him too. The rich scent of petrichor woods, of home.

With bare feet I walked to the cages, afraid of what I would find. A cold, viscous liquid squelched between my toes. I knelt down, the half brown half red liquid was stark in the pale light against the white of the concrete. Blood. Chains clanked on the metal bars of one of the cages. I knew whose blood had been left to dry here. He was in one of those cages. He was in pain. I swallowed, following the trail of blood.

I looked at the other cage first, not ready yet to see him, even though my heart screamed for justice. She was beautiful, his sister Nessa, though her face was pinched in a permanent scowl. Pale honey-porcelain skin, raven dark hair, and a light dotting of freckles danced across her shoulders and cheeks, full lips and a straight nose. I wondered if they took after their parents. Nira's skin was closer to honey and though his hair was dark, it was much coarser than the fine curtain of his sister's. I sighed, turning to whatever horrors lay in that other cage.

The other cage was shadowed by a pillar, but I could see him there and my heart cracked in my chest. His back was to me, blood had dried and scabbed over him. The lashing must have been brutal, to leave so little of him unbloodied. I knelt beside the cage. In the shadows I can see the rope burns and bruises from them restraining him. I cast a glance around the nondescript concrete room, I needed to get in there with him. A chair sat under the light, the kind of spot I would assume a guard would have sat, and top the chair was a ring of keys. I smiled, if only this was real, and I could free them. I collected the key and unlocked the cage, where Nira slept.

I crept in and lifted his head lightly into my lap. He was shackled to the cage, a prisoner. I stroked my fingers over his face, brushing hair back behind his ears. He had a bruise along his jaw that was a deep purple. I gingerly ran my finger over it, and he flinched from my touch, his eyes opening.

"Shasha." His voice had a haunted quality that only made the ache in my chest worse.

"Yes, my love." I stroked his cheek gently.

He shifted and winced. "You shouldn't be here."

"Well, I'm not really here. We're in the dream space."

"This isn't a dream, *mo grá*." He shifted groaning.

"If this is not a dream, love," I said with a bittersweet smile. "What could it be?"

"You being here, with me like this." He winced, sitting up, his face contorted with pain as his torn skin stretched. "Tells me that this is a nightmare, and knowing how my nightmares go, you don't want to be here."

I frowned at him; his movements were stiff. His hand cupped his throat, and the shackles clinked around his wrists. He coughed. "Well, nightmare or not, I am here."

His eyes were sad, and his voice broke when he spoke. "I—I never wanted you to see me like-like this."

I cupped his cheek and he winced. I felt tears well up in my eyes. "I told you a while ago that I wanted all of you. Even your darkness."

He looked thin; his shoulder bones were poking through his skin. He huffed. "Though I appreciate that you love me, you really shouldn't be here."

"I needed to be here. I needed—" I felt the tears slide over my cheeks.

"What. *mo grá*?" He cupped my cheek.

"Bastion called me. He told me what they did. What caused this." My fingers brushed his lip right above his bruise.

"I see."

"He told me to tell you that he was sorry."

He sighed. "I don't fault the boy for what happened to me. If anything, I'm proud of him for keeping his cool."

I stroked his cheek lightly. "That's what I told him."

We sat there staring at each other. The light flickered and he murmured. "Don't cry for me, Shasha."

"I can't help it." A sob broke from me. "I just miss you and I hate this. I hate that I can't rescue you now. I hate that I don't know where you are. That you are being treated so terribly, and I can't do anything to get you out."

The light flickered again, and he narrowed his eyes, past me. "I know, love. I know you guys are trying your hardest to get organized. To get us out. You need to leave now love."

"No." I pulled his face to mine. "No, I have things that I need to tell you. Questions I need to ask."

"I know you all are trying your hardest to get organized and get us out. It's time for you to leave."

"No," I pressed my forehead to his, "I have things I need to tell you and I have questions."

"Quickly, my love, I don't know how long you will be safe here."

I frowned again but pressed forward, "Bastion told me that Dravin is planning a masquerade in a couple weeks; he plans to present his prize at the event."

"That was something we talked about after the auction, making allies by using me."

"As a pawn or as a weapon?"

"A pawn, with how injured I am, regardless of if he lets me heal in the time between or not. Pain has never been a motivator for me; it will not make me bend. Unless he breaks me, I will not be his weapon. I refuse to be used that way again."

I looked to the other cage. "Do you think that they will succeed?"

"Nessa is fierier than I am. It won't be pleasant if they do manage to get her into heat. She'll fight them the entire way."

"But if they succeed?"

He frowned, his eyes going to the flickering light. "We'll cross that bridge when we come to it, I guess.

I stroked his cheek. "Bas also said that he was planning on working on you. Does that mean he is going to try to break you?"

"Yes." The light flickered again and felt him bristle. "He can try. He can beat and bend my body, but he will not break my spirit. You have that, and as long as you are safe. So am I."

"I am not your spirit."

"No, you are not, but you are the key to breaking me. Dravin knows that you mean something to me, and I need you to stay away and stay safe."

"I'm not going to abandon you."

"You're not abandoning me. You staying safe is keeping me safe. You are my mate and my sole reason for existing now beyond my own survival. I cannot lose you." He clutched my face, wiping away tears with his thumbs. "I cannot."

"And you know that I will not sit by and let other people save you. I will not sit by and risk you."

He frowned, opening his mouth to retort when the light flickered out, and he growled. "You need to leave."

"How?" I asked as the threads of moonlight barely illuminated a curtain of black smoke.

"You need to wake up, you have to get out of here."

"Bondbreaker." A hiss of a voice, reminiscent of the shadow wraiths whispered across the room.

I turned as a fanged mouth smiled at us. I scooted back into Niratap's chest, as undiluted fear ran through my body. Niratap wrapped his arms around me, pulling me as close as he could. He snarled.

"Fuck off."

"Now." The smiling maw shifted, taking a face I'd only seen in my dreams, Deirdre, "That's no way to talk in front of a lady."

"Fuck you." I hissed.

"Hmm." The creature pondered, tilting its head like an owl at an unnatural angle for the form it has chosen. "Not much of a lady then."

"You are not welcome here, creature." Nira hissed over the top of my head. I felt scales against my throat as his body prepared to attack. "That form is not yours."

"Oh this?" the creature returned its head to a normal position. It smiled too wide with far too many teeth. "What is wrong with this form, Bondbreaker? Do you not want to watch her die again? Watch her bleed out and be able to do nothing?"

A thin line sliced through the creature's throat. Blood trickling down the pale porcelain skin. "What a horrible fate, to have one so precious taken so viciously."

"Stop it." I barked. The creature's eyes shifted to my face again.

"Or would losing this one hurt you more?" It shifted to a mirror-image of myself, naked. "What would be the most horrible way to watch her die? Raped and bleeding out like the last girl?"

Blood pours from the creature's neck and wrists, pooling on the floor, dark purple handprints streaked across its body. My body. Nira's breathing hiccupped and he squeezed me closer, a sharp pine scent cut through the petrichor. He growled, but his voice lacked the ferocity, "Enough."

"Oh, is she the key to your fear?" The creature jerked an arm, and it cracked as the bone broke, flaying the skin open.

"Stop." His voice wobbled, even with me actually wrapped in his arms.

Another bone snapped. "Delicious. Your fear."

"That's enough!" I shouted.

"What about you?" The creature's eyes shifted to me. "Bondbreaker fears losing you, but what do you fear?" It shifts its shape into the jorogumo. "You have met many terrifying creatures since you entered this world." It shifted again into a basilisk. "Things that would scare anyone." It shifted into Dravin. "People who strike fear." It becomes shadows. "What do you fear?"

"That's none of your concern." I hissed.

"You may be right." The shadow smiled that tooth-filled smile again. "You will be just as delicious."

The shadow lunged at us, I threw up my hands and I screamed.

Sitting up with a cold sweat over my skin, I took in our bedroom cast in an eerie moonlight, panting. That was the thing that was hunting him, even in his dreams, exploiting his fears and trauma to dig at him. It used me against him, to torture him. What was this creature called? Why was it sent after him? How did they stop it? All of those questions would have to be answered at a later time. After Niratap was free. After Dravin was dealt with. For now, they had to plan for the masquerade in two weeks' time. Who would go with me and who would stay behind? Because they were not going to lock me away and keep me from him. I needed to see him, not just in my dreams.

Chapter Fifty-Five

Niratap

After the nightmare I couldn't sleep, Shasha's scream echoing in my mind. My body ached and there was tension in my back that I couldn't stretch out for fear that I would reopen the wounds, now that I had finally stopped bleeding. So, I just laid there listening to the sounds of Nessa breathing and the snores of Dolan asleep in the chair, and contemplating what was to come. Who knew what Dravin would do in his process of trying to break me. Branding smelled terrible and usually led to infections. Waterboarding was highly likely, so was electric shock. Chemical torture was doing enough to keep me weak, but being physically pliant, though being beneficial to his end goals, wasn't what Dravin wanted. He wanted me to bow before him willingly, and that was something that would never happen. When dawn eased into the sky, I heard them walking down the corridor.

"Dolan. We have company." I said.

He yawned. "Damnit, I was having a good dream. How are you feeling?"

"I'll live." The footsteps paused outside the door. "They're here."

Dolan twirled the keys in his hand as the door creaked open. A group of scientists slunk in before Dravin, Bastion, and Mandrake entered. The ogre's arm was still in a sling.

"Morning, boss."

"Dolan." Dravin tilted his chin in recognition. "You'll be watching the bitch while the scientists do their thing. We're going to work on my friend here."

Nessa hissed. *"Fág ina aonar é."* [41]

---

[41] Leave him alone.

Dravin scowled at her but turned to me. "I'm excited to start this process."

"Fuck off, Dravin." I didn't even raise my head to acknowledge him. The keys jangled in the lock, the sulfuric smell dancing over my skin as the binding magic activated. I took a breath, then was wrenched from the cell by the chain around my neck. Nessa shrieked in her cell, banging viciously against the bars as I coughed on the ground.

"Watch your tone, Niratap." Dravin said coolly. "Bind him."

Bastion pressed me face down onto the concrete, and I felt my back begin bleeding again. He folded my arms behind my back; my heart fluttering and I thrashed as he bound them together at the elbows. He whispered. "This won't be pleasant for either of us." He bound my ankles together. Mandrake hooked an arm under one shoulder and Bastion the other, they drug me to a trough that was being filled with water. Let the breaking begin indeed. Dravin leaned against the wall with a cruel smile on his face.

"You will be mine in every way I can own something eventually."

I laughed. "Not going to happen."

The smile didn't fade as Mandrake shoved me against the trough. "Shut up."

I snarled. "Watch, its ogre, or I'll make your arms match."

Dravin cocked a brow. "Mrak."

I looked up at Bastion who stood opposite me. There was sincerity in his eyes, but his mouth crooked into a wicked grin. He grabbed my antlers roughly and forced my head under the water, and immediately instinct had me, thrashing trying to get free. It was ice cold, and I felt a large hand press into the back of my head. My lungs burned needing oxygen. The hand at the back of my head fisted my hair and pulled me back; the rush of air into my lungs caused me to sputter and cough.

Dravin and I locked eyes, as I huffed air. "You will break."

"Never."

He just nodded, and I was plunged under the water again. I fought the bonds and the hands that held my head below the surface, but they held. I was sputtering and my lungs ached when they pulled me out again, oxygen and water entering my mouth all at once.

"You will bend." Dravin said eyes locked with mine.

"Eat shit."

I don't know how many rotations of this we did. Dunked until my body protested, him telling me I was nothing, I was property; I was weak; I would break, and me telling him I wouldn't. I felt the restriction of air in my limbs. They screamed, my body going limp under the onslaught, but my mind stayed firm. I would not break. Even as pain screamed behind my eyes, and the world spun when they brought me above the water.

"Do you submit?"

I wheezed when I sucked in the precious air. "Never."

My body shivered from the cold water. I knew I was bleeding from my wounds. The world was fuzzy at the edges. My eyes stung, my chest ached. I panted in Mandrake's hold.

"Do you want me to dunk him again?"

Dravin eyed me momentarily. "Paloka."

I heard footsteps as the doctor approached. "Yes, Mr. Cirano?"

Dravin pointed at me with his chin. "Can we continue, or should we stop?"

The doctor leaned over me checking my eyes; they wouldn't focus. Shit. "If you want to keep him alive, my advice would be to stop, before hypoxia takes a full hold."

"In your medical opinion?"

"Correct."

Dravin nodded. "Again."

I saw the doctor back away eyes wide as the boys plunged my head back under the water. I didn't fight, I just let them hold me underwater. I just let the air leak from my mouth and bubble over my eyes. It was surreal, like floating meets flying, a transcendent euphoria hit me before the world went dark.

I awoke in my cell, an oxygen mask on my face. I reached for it, but a hand swiped mine away.

"Leave it." A feminine voice said. I forced my eyes to focus on the girl before me. She was the scientist from before, the one who had put me in the collar. She was counting my pulse; satisfied, she pressed a stethoscope to my chest. "You're really lucky, I hope you know. You could have died."

"What happened?" I wheezed.

"You were tortured, nearly drowned repeatedly until you finally blacked out in the water. Dr. Paloka resuscitated you." Bastion said, coming to loom over the cage. "Dolan took a six-hour security detail, so we don't have to worry about the cameras. Nikki here works with Dolan outside and offered to give you some care."

I glanced at her. "Thank you."

She gave me a soft smile. "Your lungs are going to be achy for a few days. Normally I would tell you to take it easy and rest, but I don't think Dravin plans on giving you even one day."

"We'd be lucky if he gave him a few hours." Bastion grumbled.

"Nessa." I said.

"I'm okay, brother." Her voice sounded from her cage; she sounded so tired. "Poked and prodded, but okay."

"Can you sit up, Niratap?" Nikki asked.

"I think so." I shifted forward, wincing as my back protested.

"Good job." Nikki said, assisting me the rest of the way. "I'm going to put a salve on your back that will aid your healing and protect against infection. It won't be obvious as soon as it's absorbed into your skin."

"Dravin is trying to break my spirit so I'm subservient to be used as a weapon. He wants to breed bitarogs to sell as weapons to the highest bidder. He plans on announcing such things at this masquerade."

"Correct." Bastion said, his voice only slightly shocked. "He wants the scientist to try to find the longevity gene and see if he can synthesize it. That's what I couldn't share with you when we were chatting."

I chuckled. "You're telling me, the chatty scientist that you were squeezing information out of was an FBI agent."

"Pegged me as easy, but I'm really not. I knew he was digging for information debated on trusting him. I took your vitals one time after the ogre beat you. He asked how you were doing, and I knew he was more than just a grunt for Dravin." Nikki said.

"That's what tipped you off, my asking how he was?" Bastion asked.

"Yes, because you actually cared. I could hear it in your voice. You weren't asking for Dravin or just for curiosity's sake, but because you cared."

"I have known the kid his entire life." I mused.

"Practically was a second dad." Bastion said then coughed as if realizing he had given too much away.

"It's okay, Bas. I think of you as mine, too. Closest thing I've had to a kid of my own." The feeling was bittersweet. "How close are they to forcing Nessa into heat?"

She paused in her mission of applying the salve. "Dravin is pushing, but your race has complex hormones, things that have to work in the right amounts to trigger a heat cycle. The science team is going to try in a few days with a synthetic trigger. I haven't been on that team, just genetics."

Nessa hissed, but I said. "Do you know if there will be any adverse reactions?"

"I don't know." She finished with the salve, collected her medical supplies and the oxygen mask and handed the jar of salve to Bastion. "Rest while you can, Bondbreaker. Who knows when Dravin will come back. Use the salve if you can; it will work on either of them."

"Thank you, Nikki." I said again. "For your kindness."

"Thank you for not biting me in half." She said, smiling at me.

"I told you I was a gentleman."

She dipped her chin and left through the door, leaving the three of us. Bastion reached in and helped me down to the floor of the cage, his brows knitted with concern.

"I'm sorry."

"You don't have to be Bas. We both know that what you've had to do is part of the job. I do not fault you for staying undercover. Even for me."

"Rest; heal as much as you can. We're getting you out of here."

"I know."

Sleep was easy enough to slip into. It was dreamless even though I wanted her for comfort. My mate was safe and far enough away, protected by my friends and they must know now where we were. What was she doing right now? Practicing her shot most likely, but maybe she'd taken Guinness for a ride today and she was in our slice of peace or maybe she was just curling into our bed. Those thoughts helped ease the vast sense of loneliness that had settled in me without her.

I was dragged out of the cage by my antlers by two soldiers. I hissed, swiping out at them with my hands, but fire danced through my veins and had me choking. Dravin smiled cruelly at me, in his hand was the control button for the collar.

"I hope that we didn't wake you."

I growled, but the acid kept my tongue at bay. The men dragged me to a table, and I barked in pain as they hefted me on top of it. They grabbed my wrists, pulling them to the corners as I fought, arching off the table. Terror made my heart pound wildly in my chest. I was stronger than they were, but between my injuries and the acid in my blood, they overpowered me. Dravin's hand pressed on the center of my chest holding me down as they latched my hands, his face a mask of cool indifference until he smirked at me.

"Behave. I don't want to have to push more of the serum, but I will if I have to."

I knew he felt my racing heart. I knew he saw the spike of terror in my eyes before I closed them to try to settle myself as the men shackled my ankles down. Confinement like this scared me. Having no way to move, no way to defend myself, made the world shrink in on me drastically.

Dravin ran a finger down my body, over the patchwork of scars, my hip bone, and down my leg; it was almost a lover's touch. The act sent my stomach rolling, my skin goosing, I looked away from him.

"You know, you're attractive enough. If you didn't have all these scars, you could make me money other ways. Maybe after I've broken that wildness from you, I can still make a decent profit off you that way as well."

"You're disgusting." I hissed.

"I figure you wouldn't be a willing participant in such an activity," Dravin eyed me, a merchant examining a fine product, "but there are ways around that."

Nessa hissed from across the room. "You leave him alone! Haven't you done enough?"

Dravin just glowered at me, slamming his fist down across my hip. I arched off the table trying to roll away from him as he slammed another fist down across my knee. I cried out as his fists came down again across my stomach and chest. He wailed on my body until dark purple rose across my skin; Nessa screamed the entire time, tears streaming down her face as I thrashed against the bindings digging into my skin. When he stopped, he glared at her, panting with rage or exertion I did not know.

"Ask me again, question me again, whore, and the whip will grace his skin." Dravin grabbed my face. "Now that that is done. You're not comfortable here chained down to this table. Being at the mercy of others makes you to be afraid, makes you realize how weak you are. So, I think I'll leave you here just like this to stew. See how long it takes for you to snap."

"You won't break me."

He ran a hand up my arm, grabbing my pinky finger and wrenching it back with a snap. I screamed. "We'll see about that."

He left. My hand was throbbing; broken bones were the second worst kind of pain. Bastion stalked around the table like a predator. Playing up the interaction, so he could set my finger.

"You really had to say something didn't you?"

I jerked my arms and arched off the table, "I will not break for that bastard."

"I know." Bastion said grabbing my finger and jerking it straight. I roared, settling back against the table. "You shouldn't try to bait him."

I panted. "I can't let him win."

"Your pride is not a reason to get killed, little brother." Nessa snarled.

"It's not pride. If I didn't fight back, he would be suspicious."

Bastion frowned. "Don't get yourself killed before we can get rescued."

"Not my intention."

I spent two days on the table, before Dravin returned. My wrists and ankles bled from struggling against the bindings and the strain had my joints screaming with each movement I attempted. He and the scientists crowded around Nessa.

"Leave her alone."

They ignored me, pulling her back against the bars of the cage, she thrashed wildly and eventually they captured her hands to pin her down. She shrieked and I thrashed in my bonds.

"Leave Nessa alone!" I shouted.

"Niratap!" She screamed.

I roared against the bonds as acid slid through my veins. Her screams became sobs and finally they left her. The scientist came over to me and took some measurements and blood. I growled at them, but it was Nikki who took my blood, and after her kindness, regardless of the fact she was undercover, I wouldn't snap or snarl at her. Dravin came to the table as they parted from me. He smirked cruelly.

"Will you bow?"

"Fuck you." I snapped, lunging for him.

He tsked at me. "Very well, stay there a couple more days and think about it. However, after those couple days are up, the scientists need another sample."

He smiled at me as my heart raced in my chest. Helpless was the only thing I could feel, and I thrashed until I was exhausted. Nessa moaned quietly in her cage the rest of the day.

Sometime in the night, after exhaustion had won and I lay there almost asleep, Nessa screamed. I heard Dolan leap from the chair and was asking her what was wrong. She screamed again, and I smelled the blood.

"Nessa." I roared.

"*Gortaíonn sé deartháir. Gortaíonn sé.*" [42] She moaned.

---

[42] It hurts brother. It hurts.

"What hurts, Ness?" Dolan asked.

"My body. My stomach. Everything feels like it's on fire."

"Nessa, you're bleeding." Dolan said, his voice faltering.

"Fuck, Dolan, help her!" I snared.

He was on the phone then, whoever he had called must have been asleep as he whispered what was going on. He hung up quickly. "Nikki is coming."

I thrashed, panicked for my sister, my heart pounding wildly in my chest. A bird crashing against a cage. I was just like my heart, caged and screaming and beating myself up trying to get free. I stared hopelessly at the ceiling as the door opened. Nikki came in, her voice was full of worry and thick with sleep. I jerked my wrist pathetically against the binds as she spoke.

"The formula they tried wasn't balanced right is my only guess. They gave her too much of one hormone and not enough of another. She's bleeding pretty badly, but I'll have to have the others figure it out. I'm not on the breeding team." I could almost hear the frown in her voice. "I gave her a sedative and something for the pain."

She came into my view. Her hair was in a messy braid and her eyes fatigued, "Do you need anything?"

I huffed. "Don't put yourself at risk. Is Nessa going to be, okay?"

She frowned. "I don't know. I'll check back after my shift."

I gave a curt nod as a shuddering breath left me. "Thank you."

She nodded, gently patting my shoulder before she left, the door squeaking behind her. I stared at that plain white ceiling the color of bones, and let that overwhelming hopelessness swallow me.

The ceiling was my only companion the following two days. I watched the shadows crawl across it as the sun rose and fell. The scientists came and went, repeatedly tending to my sister. Under their chatter of hormones, all I heard was her moaning in pain, which sometimes rose into keening cries, each one cutting me to my core. I was powerless. I was helpless. We were helpless and waiting for a rescue that may not come. Was this what breaking felt like? It had been so long I had forgotten. Dravin stood over me the third day, smiling.

"I was told that you have been rather quiet the last few days."

I didn't respond and he nodded to the soldiers who undid my bindings. My shoulders ached as I brought my hands to my chest gently massaging my wrists.

"Get up."

I obeyed, collapsing as my legs failed to hold me and my face kissed the concrete. Dravin's brown leather loafers entered my vision.

"Being strapped down made your muscles forget how to work, didn't it? Kneel, you remember how to do that?"

My body screamed in protest as I pushed myself on to my knees. I didn't need to see his face to know he felt as if he had won. I wanted to deny it, but I was numb.

He grabbed my face, angling it up. "My, my, so subservient. Have I broken you?"

I couldn't muster my face into a scowl. I warred with myself, but it stayed placid. Maybe he had won. Maybe he had broken me.

"You remember what I told you was going to happen today?"

I nodded. I didn't want this, but I was tired. I just wanted to rest. After this I could rest.

"Shift."

I eased into my other shape, fur and scales covering my skin. There was murmuring and a gasp that sounded from the scientists that were gathered. Was it Nikki who had gasped? Surely, she had seen my wild shape before.

"Into the chute."

I made my way across the concrete, a walk of shame, as I entered the chute without being forced and I knew some of the men around me were disappointed that I didn't need motivation. I braced my legs against the bars, as they used ropes and chains to secure me. Bastion. My Bastion. Slipped the muzzle over my face. His eyes were hard, like something about all of this was breaking him in two. Did I look haunted? Did I look lost?

They beat me. Tied down and defenseless, they beat me with batons. I yelped as some zapped me with a cattle prod, the crackling sound my only warning before it collided with my skin. Then they milked me. The pain was the same, electricity climbing my spine, stabbing nauseating pain in my gut. The scientist took blood and did measurements and they left. Dravin spoke with Bastion about the masquerade in a few days before he left as well. I felt broken, parts of me scattered across the floor, aspects of who I was trying to blow away, but was I actually broken?

Bastion gingerly freed me from the chute. His face filled with questions, but I just trudged past him. Past his fear, his concern, his care, his guilt, and curled up on the floor of the cage. He squatted in front of me, opposite the bars and spoke promises of rescue. He reached through the bars and caressed the top of my head; a shudder crawled through me. The beast fell away, and I was a man once again and I felt the hot tears roll over my cheeks, as silent sobs rocked me to the void of sleep.

I was a broken man.

Chapter Fifty-Six

Shasha

In the two weeks since the nightmare, I hadn't found Nira in my dreams. Two weeks of planning. Two weeks of figuring things out. Two weeks of negotiations with the government. Two long weeks of training; Mitta handled the physical and Allipo prepared me for the market: how to walk, how to talk like I owned it. Two weeks of fighting over who should go and who should stay. Mitta didn't want me to go, and I refused to be left behind. We had agreed that Mitta couldn't go to the masquerade, that the market knew her too well, knew she was dangerous and even with the invitation they might not let us in with her. Dheg volunteered to go; he had kept mainly to the manor since he had been rescued. Allipo would go because he wouldn't let me go without him. We had traveled into the city the day before the event, staying the night in a hotel to rest and mentally prepare for the things that we would see. Allipo and Dheg took turns showering, and I laid on the bed, staring at the ceiling as Allipo dried his horns and hair.

"I still haven't seen him." I said into the void, unnerved. I had told them about the nightmare, about the malice attacking us. Chasing me from his dream. I updated them every day that I hadn't been able to find him again, my mate.

"But you still feel him?" there was fear in the question.

"Yes." I placed a hand over my heart. It felt heavy and sad, but he was still there. "He just feels so sad; our connection is sad."

Allipo sighed, both with relief and sadness. "We'll get him out, Shasha dear."

"But will he be whole, or will Dravin have taken a part of him and destroyed it?"

"I don't know, love."

Dheg came out of the bathroom with a towel wrapped around his waist. "He'll be okay, lovey."

I sighed, returning my eyes to the ceiling as Dheg dressed. "I feel lost."

I saw them exchange a look, but neither of them said anything. Where are you, my love? I curled onto my side, staring out at the city. The neon and streetlights twinkled like stars, but I just wanted to be under the stars in the clearing with him. The city had lost its magic. It wasn't the brilliant glow of neon lights and vastness of culture that had called to me once. Now it was a prison, a land of concrete and steel that had my mate trapped within it. I wondered if he could see the stars where he was. I wondered if his wounds had healed. I wondered if he could feel that I was closer. I reached for him, hoping I would find him when I slept.

A spring breeze blew across me; long grasses and bunny tails tickled my face. I heard the cascading of the waterfall and the sighing breath of the weeping birch trees. The sun warmed my face and the ground around me. I felt him near me, could feel his heart beating all around me. Where are you? I sat up in the sunny spring meadow, hunting and searching for him.

"Nira!" I walked around the meadow, searching for his sleeping form in the tall grasses.

"Niratap!" I checked the shore of the turquoise pool.

"*Mo grá!*" I dipped into the cavern. My breath puffed more the farther in that I traveled.

I used the wall to travel farther and farther into the cold darkness of the cavern. I felt his heartbeat through the earth around me. The hot smell of burnt hair coiled through my nose, followed by the irony tang of blood. Where are you? I pushed farther into cavern, and it finally opened up into the cold concrete room I had been in before. Nessa wasn't in her cage, and neither was Nira. Dried blood lined the floors of both. How poorly were they being treated, that even in his dreams he was trapped here?

There was a ringing sound that carried through the room, and I finally saw him. He was strapped, spread eagle, to a steel table; his body was covered in fading yellow bruises and he was pale, so pale. His arms were streaked with blood from him trashing and pulling at the cuffs. He was staring at the ceiling, occasionally pulling at one wrist or the other. He seemed so sad, so defeated. Broken. Tears burned my cheeks as I approached.

"Nira?"

He breathed deep and exhaled, but he didn't say anything, just stared at the ceiling.

"Niratap." I reached out and gingerly touched his chest, but he recoiled from me a snarl echoing around the empty room. His eyes were wide, his pupils blown. Fear. He was afraid. Of me. I held both my hands up.

"Mate, it's me."

He panted, eyes blinking and unfocused.

"Niratap." My heart was breaking. "*Is liomsa tu agus is leatsa mise.*" [43]

He closed his eyes and shook his head. His voice was rough, ragged from screaming. "You're just a ghost. A memory. My mind playing tricks on me."

I felt that sad, lost feeling coil in my heart. "No. *mo grá* it's me. I've been searching for you. I—"

He blinked again. "You can't be real. You can't be."

Very slowly I reached my hand out and stroked his cheek. "I'm coming for you."

Tears flowed softly over his cheeks, his eyes starting to focus. "Shasha?"

"Yes."

He tugged against the bonds to lean in close, pressing his forehead to mine. "Mate."

"Mine."

---

[43] "You're mine and I am yours."

He choked a sob, kissing me his arm straining against the bonds.

I cupped his face, pulling back. "Let me help you out of these."

He eased back, laying back on the table. "I—" A shudder tore through him.

"How long have you been kept like this?" I asked, unbuckling the cuff.

"I—" he shuddered. "I'm not, right now. I just keep coming back here in my sleep. He kept me like this for five days, maybe six."

I moved to his other side. "Why?"

"I think he was going to torture me, but I—" he swallowed, closing his eyes, "being restrained like this, it takes me somewhere very dark and very lonely. Dravin saw that, felt it, and he left me there."

I dropped the cuff, and he sat up, slowly undoing the cuffs around his ankles. "I was fine the first couple days, but then they tried to force Nessa into heat. It failed, but that night she was screaming and bleeding and I could do nothing. She whimpered and cried and bled and I could do nothing."

I eased him to the edge of the table, pushing myself between his legs and wrapping my arms around his waist. I pressed my head against him listening to his heartbeat in my ear.

"He left me to listen to her for three days. I—" He took a breath, dropping his face in his hands. He was so thin and weary. I needed to get him out. "I think I might be losing it. I feel so lost and broken. I'm no longer strapped to that table, but I'm stuck there listening to Nessa scream and sometimes it's you I hear screaming."

He choked on a sob, and I rubbed soothing circles on his back. "You crying for help, and I can do nothing because I'm stuck on this fucking table, staring at a bone white ceiling."

"I'm coming for you, mate. I'm coming for you."

"I know. I know you are coming for me, but I am terrified that I will be too lost, too broken to find you."

"Do you love me?"

"Always."

"Then you will find me." I looked up at his worried face, "You are mine, and I am yours. Forever. The masquerade is tomorrow, if it goes according to what the FBMI wants then we will be getting you soon."

"You came to a consensus with them?"

"Yes. Any undercover agents and prisoners will remain unharmed in the raid. You and Nessa are priorities." I would take my pound of flesh then. I kissed the panes of his stomach. "I will see you tomorrow."

"You don't mean that you are coming to the masquerade?"

"I am."

"No. My only solace in this was knowing that you were safe at home. My freedom is not worth your safety."

"No. You do not get to tell me I can't rescue you. You do not get to tell me that I mean more than you. You are mine, Niratap. My mate, and I will burn the world to get you back."

"Shasha."

"No." I growled. "I am coming for you. Tomorrow night I will have Dheg and Allipo with me. Nothing, absolutely nothing will keep me from finding you and bringing you home."

"Shasha." He frowned down at me. "Please be careful."

"I will."

He strokes my cheek staring down at me, clarity finally back in his eyes. There was fear and uncertainty, anger and pride. The emotions danced through the moonlight pools. Depthless and beautiful and mine. I pushed up on my tip toes, pressing my lips to his. Dravin would suffer for what he had done to my mate. Whether it be by my hand or the laws, he would pay for the permanent marks he'd left on Nira's mind, body, and spirit. A keening cry echoed around us, and the world whooshed out from under my feet.

"I love you, but I have to go." Nira's eyes were filled with pain.

"I love you." I pressed hard against his mouth in a demanding kiss wrapping my hands around his neck threading my hands through his hair. The world of dreams is fading around us and I pressed my forehead to his. "I am coming for you."

I woke to the crest of dawn on the horizon with a renewed sense of vengeance. I was going to get my mate back.

I walked out of the bathroom in the backless, flowy, pale-champagne dress that hugged my curves with a slit up the side that showed off my leg. Both of the boys smiled when they saw me. Both were well dressed in dark colored suits, Dheg in a deep burgundy and Allipo in plum.

"I thought masquerades were all poofy skirts and big hair?"

Dheg laughed and sketched a bow. "Maybe a hundred years ago. Modern times, modern garb, milady."

Allipo stood, bowing as well before he straightened his suit. "Milady."

"You guys don't have to bow." I said a little flustered.

They exchanged a look before Allipo said. "As the lord's mate, you outrank us in the household. He would be displeased if we didn't show you that respect in the outside world."

"I know it probably makes you feel uncomfortable." Dheg added with a smirk. "But you are the lady of the house."

I didn't know what to say or think. Allipo spoke tenderly as he came to stand before me. "As lady of the house you have as much say as the lord does. You get to make financial decisions, a say in how things are planned and managed in the house, and if the lord sees fit, you will be able to organize operations as well. May I?"

He had a thigh holster for a dagger in his hand. "You may."

He kneeled before me, running his hands up my calf, the holster sliding up behind them. He tightened the straps, so it was snug and slid the translucent black stone blade in. "Black cragstone, sharper than obsidian and as strong as steel. *μάσκα από τη θέα, μανδύα τη νύχτα, ώστε να είναι έτοιμη να πολεμήσει.*" [44]

I looked at him quizzically as he stood. "What was that?"

"Greek and a glamour spell to hide the dagger."

"Why? Both of you have firearms in your jackets."

"Black cragstone is for one very rare and two very illegal. Not a big deal on the black market, however it makes you the most dangerous creature in the room. It can kill the unkillable; hydras, vampires, werewolves, and the like."

My heart seized in my chest. "Bitarogs?"

His brow furrowed. "Yes. It interferes with the rapid healing."

"Those are dark places to go, milady." Dheg said, checking his firearm and the long silver stiletto in his jacket. "The lord is tough."

"I worry after last night. He recoiled from me." I blinked back the tears that threatened to fall.

"Don't cry. It will ruin your makeup, and it doesn't serve you in the dark." Dheg frowned as he wrapped me in a gentle hug. "We're going to get him back."

"Will Ventris be here tonight?"

"He should be. If not him, one of his undercover agents will be there." Allipo looked out the window. "We aren't from the House of the Bondbreaker tonight. Tonight, we are from the House of Dion, and we are just here to

---

[44] "Mask from sight, cloak at night, so she is ready to fight."

observe. No matter what, we do not engage our enemies and there are bound to be more of them than friends."

Dheg released me and fixed the wrinkles out of my dress. "We cannot react to how he looks or how he's treated. We'd paint a target on us as his allies, and this is the night where Dravin tells the world that he is in possession of two bitarogs."

I nod. "This is just to see him."

Allipo looked at me sadly. "Confirmation of life. Then at the end of this week, the raid."

The two men looked at me with determination as they slid on their black masks. Allipo tied mine onto my head; it was the same color as my dress with wispy feathers on the side.

"Let's do this."

"Wait." Dheg said, pressing himself tight against my body. His hands cupped my neck and rubbed a thick oil into my skin. They trailed up and down my spine, and around my arms and wrists. "This will hide your scent."

"How?"

"This musk will make you smell like a faun. At worst, if some of your scent slips through you can just claim to be a half-faun if anyone asks."

"Alright then." Allipo said, pulling me a step away from Dheg. "Let's go."

Allipo drove us to the event, handing our invitation to the valet who waved us through. I was nervous walking into that den of snakes with only the two boys at my side. If this went sideways, I didn't want to lose either of them.

Inside all sorts of creatures milled about in elegant gowns, well designed suits and a flock of feathered masks. Champagne flutes were danced around the room on silver trays by women and men in fine gossamer outfits in varied shades of deep blues and green. More barely clad women danced in cages to sultry club music.

"Not what I expected." I said softly to Allipo as he surveyed the room.

"Nothing is to be expected. We are surrounded by enemies, not friends."

Dheg pressed against me, "Teyren is here."

"Who?"

Allipo answered with a nod to a willow-thin elf woman who bobbed her chin in response as we moved to a darker secluded corner. "She works with V."

Something vicious shifted in me, drawing my eyes to the stage. "He's coming."

The two men didn't question me as they looked to the stage, and Dravin walked out in a royal purple suit, his hair combed back to create dark grey and silver waves. He smiled smugly over the crowd, enjoyed flaunting his success to his friends and enemies.

"Welcome to my event, my beloved underground." He boomed over us. "I have not one, but two surprises to show you. Many of you have purchased from me. I am known for my fine wares, and it is through your many years of patronage that I have acquired a piece for my personal collection. She is subdued for your safety, but she is a feisty beast."

He stuck his hand out and a heavy chain appeared which he gave a sharp tug. The pale skinned woman, paler than I remembered, tripped through the curtains, draped in troves of pale green gossamer that did nothing to shield her body. She had a silver muzzle bit in her mouth and her hands were bound behind her back. Her fine black hair swished across the floor as her knees slammed down beside Dravin. She hissed and glared up at him.

"I present the beautiful female bitarog I purchased before the Christmas season. Apologies for buying her outright."

"That is the—" Dheg started.

"Yes." I shushed. My eyes were not leaving the stage as cries of rage rose from the crowd. Dravin frowned.

"Like I said. Apologies." He hooked the chain in his hand to the stage and whispered something to Nessa that caused her to lunge, blue light glowing around her manacles, holding her back from him as he walked across the stage.

"Now I know we have not always agreed on how things are done. How we hunt our prey. How we sell. However, many of us have had a similar thorn in our side, many have adopted this enemy from their parents or organizations. Some have been his enemy for hundreds of years." A chain appeared in his hand. "In August this enemy slighted me in etiquette, paid me a hefty sum for the key to his undoing." A hush fell over the crowd as if they were holding their breath, trying to figure out which one of them was missing. "Now I present my newest item to my collection. The Bondbreaker."

With a tug of the chain, my mate came through the curtain. He was thin, with faded bruises all over his chest and stomach. A scrap of cloth was pinned around his hips. His face is on display for all our enemies. He glared at Dravin as voices of the crowd called lies. Our eyes locked instantaneously as I made it to his face. He was tired, haggard from lack of sleep and torture. I grabbed both Allipo and Dheg's wrists as they collectively tried to move forward.

"No, you'll give us up. We have to stay back; we have to watch. I know it's hard. There is nothing more that I want to do than run to him, but we can't."

They fisted their hands but eased beside me as Dravin brought Nira to his knees. No one in the room believed him, that he had captured the Bondbreaker.

"Silence." The room hushed. "What proof do you desire that I have him under my thumb?"

"Have him speak." A feminine voice pierced the room. Ventris's spy.

"Beasts prove your identity to the crowd."

Nira glared up at him but did not speak. Defiance. Dravin frowned, leaning in to whisper in his ear and Nessa fell forward, writhing on the stage. She whimpered. The sound broke my heart, broke my mate.

"Dravin stop." His voice was quiet, but it carried across the room. There were some gasps around, but the silence was thick. "Leave her be."

Dravin smiled. "Very well. Now that that is cleared up. I have a proposition for you all. With these two specimens I plan on producing pups. Think about it, my friends, owning and raising a bitarog for your own purposes. Weapons to take what is yours. Ferocious defenders for your troves. Predators subdued to hold all others." There was murmuring excitement and fear charging the air.

"But before then, I know many of you have grudges against this one." He gripped Nira's antler and moved his head about loosely, "I will give you a pound of flesh, no weapons, but feel free to wail on him."

Dravin kicked Nira forward off the stage and he landed face first onto the floor below where the crowd had parted. My hands tightened on the boys, holding us all back. I didn't want to watch as the vultures circled him. I didn't want to watch as he spit blood from his split lip, blood coating his teeth as he hissed at them, cornered before the stage. I didn't want to watch as they began to hit him. Men and women slammed their ringed fingers into his face, kicked him in the stomach and chest, thwacked him with canes and bags. A large wave of crowd that seemed hellbent on taking their pound of flesh.

"Breathe." I whispered to them. To myself. I had let my emotions get the better of me the last time I had been in the underground. I would not make that mistake again.

"I can't watch this." Allipo snarled through his gritted teeth.

"You have to, and you have to pretend that you enjoy it. Leaving now would put targets on our backs. Acting now isn't the plan and would put them both in danger. You just have to watch, my friend."

"This is barbaric." Dheg said, his body tight.

"It is." A voice said beside us. I turned, my body settling as I saw Bastion standing there, under a simple black mask. "Dravin is earning their favor by letting them wail on him."

"Is he?" I couldn't help asking.

Bastion laughed, because he was playing a part, because Dravin had looked our way. "He's in a bad way. I worried that he is starting to lose himself. Would you like to dance, milady?"

A couple walked past and nodded at Bastion. "I would after the presentation."

"Very well." When the couple was out of earshot. "Dravin is getting closer and we're running out of time."

"I'll meet you on the dance floor." I made my voice sound bored, as a man in a fine suit walked by.

"Yes, ma'am." He sauntered off to wait for me on the dance floor.

Alone in our dark corner, I took a steadying breath. "Dheg, do a social lap, listen in to conversations. Plant some doubt just for fun. Allipo, get the car ready; we'll be leaving soon."

"Shasha, what are you planning?" Allipo asked, sounding offended that I was sending him off.

I smiled sweetly at them, "I'm going to dance and give him some hope to hang onto."

Dheg grabbed my arm. "Be careful."

"I will."

We scattered. The beating had finished, and Nira leaned against the wall of the stage. Welts and bruises lit his skin; a black eye was starting to set. There were a couple women chatting beside him, and Dravin was chatting with a group of gentlemen about Nessa on the other side of the stage.

"I don't think my husband would be foolish enough to purchase a beast like this. Wild and unruly." One of the women in a pewter dress said as I approached.

"Dravin is a mad man but think of what you could do with a bitarog. You could raise it and bend its will to your own." The other one in bronze said.

"A weapon you raise." I said passing them, drawing their attention.

"But look at him. I don't think a scarred creature could produce offspring that are fine and fair. Any weapon should be a fine accessory." Said the first woman.

"And Bondbreaker himself is such a hateful creature. Would the offspring carry that wild disposition? Hideous creature."

I cupped Nira's chin pulling his face up. His eyes were full of rage and fury and fear. I knew he was angry with me being here, but there was no way I wouldn't come to see him. I was risking it all because I couldn't stay away. "I don't know, I think he is rather handsome to look at. I wouldn't mind him fanning me on a hot day." Nira's eyes softened and I turned his head inspecting his wounds, in a way that looked like inspecting a product. "I think he would be a mighty fine accessory."

"You must have a death wish, child, bitarogs are dangerous." Bronze hissed.

"The men will probably use them to wage war on each other." Pewter added.

"More than likely. You wouldn't get to keep him to fan you." Bronze said snarkily.

"Pity." I said while playing the game. "I find him beautiful because of the danger."

"Foolish you are." The two huffed and walked away, and I took that opportunity to lean in close to his ear.

"I am coming for you." I whispered, brushing my lips against his bruised cheek. "At the end of the week the raid will take place. I need you to be ready. I need you to be strong."

"*Mo grá.*" He pulled his head from me for show, Dravin was watching us. "You need to go."

"Be ready." I stroked his cheek before I turned away to find Bastion. Leaving him was a knife to my heart as I approached the dance floor. Bastion caught me off guard as he swooped in.

"May I have this dance?"

"Most definitely." I said letting him lead me onto the floor.

The next song started up, slow and melodic and he led me through a simple waltz. "What you're doing is dangerous."

"I know."

"Speaking with him was probably the most dangerous."

"I know, but he needed it. The raid will be in a week's time, make sure our allies inside know. Make sure you're ready."

Bastion spun me out, with the lift in the music and then brought me back in close. "Yes, milady."

"Be ready."

"We will. I'm ready to come home." Bastion said, coming to a stop.

"Milady," Dheg offered his hand in a bow. "It's time we take our leave."

"Very well." I smiled at Bas, "Thank you for the dance, orc."

He smiled a genuine smile. "Anytime, milady."

I let Dheg guide me from the party, and even though my heart wanted me to look back at my mate, I held my head high, forced myself to move by without a glance. It was a punishment of its own, knowing that we had walked the razor's edge. I hoped he wouldn't pay the price for it. Please keep them safe.

In the car I let the tears roll down my face; I let all of it go as we left the city. As we left him behind again. I promise you, *mo grá,* I am coming for you, and nothing will keep me from bringing you home alive. Nothing. Those that have hurt you do not know the wrath that I will unleash upon them.

Chapter Fifty-Seven

Shasha

I had fought to be here, and they knew I wasn't going to sit back on this one. Even so, the car was terribly quiet as we rolled into base camp. Dorilody, Eloimaya, and Echo had stayed back at the house, not wanting to be part of a raid. The rest of us were dressed in tactical gear, bullet-proof vests, cargo pants, and weapons strapped to various parts of our bodies. Dheg balanced his stiletto on his fingertip in the tight air. We were going to get him back.

"We're going to get him back." I said confidently.

Dheg sheathed the knife and smiled. "Yes, we are, wildflower."

"What is the plan?"

"We'll meet with Ventris, and we will see what his organization wants. That will determine what happens, who goes in and when." Mitta said, peering out the window.

"He won't keep me out of this."

"We all might be benched." Durgash said. Outside the window we were waved through the guard gates into the throng of hundreds of operatives milling about, stretching, chatting, waiting for the command to go.

"No one." I said steadfast. "No one is going to keep me from him anymore."

"None of us are going to stand in your way, darling." Rogmesh said smiling. "If anyone deserves a pound of flesh, it's a mate."

"You have us at your back." Allipo said, pulling into a spot in the parking garage that had become ground zero. "No matter what, we will all be going home at the end of this."

"Agreed." Katrel said with the utmost confidence.

"Let's go." Tummilia said standing, "let's get this over with and go home."

Filing out of the vehicle, we stood together. All of them looked at me, faces a mix of hope and fear and rage. Allipo smiled before bowing. Then Mitta bowed. Then Dheg and the rest followed suit. I felt both in awe and incredibly shy as my family gave me this kind of honor publicly. Agents eyed us, some even dipped their head as if they were unsure where they stand to me.

"Come, milady." Allipo said, extending a hand. "You are our leader, lead us."

I walked through them and took Allipo's outstretched hand. He gave me a squeeze as I walked, head high, into a different kind of den, the mission control tent. Ventris stood hunched over the large map with several men and women in uniforms: fire, NYPD, paramedics, and the FBI. Ventris paused in his talking as we entered, Mitta and Allipo at my side.

"What are you doing here?" Ventris said, looking back at the map.

"Ventris." Mitta hissed.

"No, it's fine." I said to her, stepping forward, squaring up to him at the table. "You don't like me very much, do you?"

Ventris sighed.

"Well, that's too bad. I am here. Niratap is my mate, and regardless of what your feelings about us are, I am going to get him out of there."

Ventris clenched his jaw, before I looked down at the map. "You do not have the skills to be here. You are a liability."

I stared up at him through my lashes. "You don't know my skills, so I would keep your opinions to yourself. Now, if you would, introduce us to those who are gathered and fill us in on what this is going to look like."

Ventris's eyes flared, his voice tight as he spoke. "These are the task force leaders. Commander Kris Tongee of the FBI." A tall black man with a shiny bald head to the right of Ventris bobbed his head in greeting. "Fire Captain Sarah

Vega." A lean blonde elf woman smiled warmly. "Chief of Police Luis Maroto." A broad-chested Hispanic man who didn't move. "Captain Vega's lead paramedic, Crystal Reed." A broad-shouldered brunette who also nodded. "They will be our back up for the raid, crowd control, fire if it breaks out, and medical. Most of you know Mitta Rask, Lord Niratap's Tactical and Security Specialist. This is Allipo Comotis, his Head of House, and this is Shasha Dion, Lord Niratap's mate."

Commander Tongee eyed me cautiously before turning back to the map to speak. His voice was husky and low. "Team one will go first through sector one." He pointed to a section of the map that was labeled simply as "entrance." The map was the blueprints to the building where Niratap was being held. My heart raced as I scanned over the list of labeled rooms, finding "laboratory" and "prison" highlighted. "Team two will cover the rear and side entrances. Team three, Ventris's team, will make the main push through the floors to acquire the captives and undercover operatives. It will be a flash bang into a tidal wave scenario."

"Where do you want us?" Mitta asked.

"What do you have to offer?"

Allipo came up next to me. "There are the three of us; our group also consists of two orcs, a faun, and two elves. The Days would be good for the initial push with team one. I would like the other three with team two for security. If Ventris will take us, the three of us should be on his team to retrieve the lord."

"I am not opposed—"

"I don't want her on my team." Ventris cut Commander Tongee off, lifting his chin at me.

"Excuse me." I hissed rising to face him. "You will not keep me from him."

"This operation is too dangerous for a novice. You're out, Shasha."

"You will not keep me from him." I shouted, feeling my entire body prepare for a fight.

"No. You are a liability. I don't care how rigorously you trained with Mitta in the last six months. I know she is good, but no one is that good."

"I wouldn't have brought her if I didn't think she could handle it." Mitta growled.

"My answer is still no."

"I don't have to prove myself to you." I fisted my hands.

"To be on my team, yes you do."

"I am getting my mate back. You know what being mates means? Nothing is going to keep me from getting him back. Not you. Not Dravin. Nothing."

Ventris scowled at me. "You are not going in."

"You won't stop me."

"Chief Maroto, could you escort the young lady to somewhere safe so the rest of us can get on with it?"

"You are out of line, Ventris." Allipo growled.

"Am I?" He said standing straight. "Teyren told me you were at the Masquerade Allipo. I explicitly told you to stand down. That we would handle the confirmation of life. You didn't listen and you put someone inexperienced in the field, and she almost cost the entire mission by approaching Niratap fifteen feet from our enemy."

"It was a masquerade." I said incredulously. "I was glamoured one, and two, my face was covered, Dravin didn't know it was me and I don't need you telling me that it was risky. I knew it was risky, but I had to give him hope. Give him something to hold on to so he didn't fall apart. So, he was ready for today."

"You're still not going in." Ventris said, wanting to be done with the conversation.

"You don't get to tell me that."

"I do as rush commander, and you will listen to me, child."

"Don't talk down to her, Ventris." Mitta snarled. "She has the skills for this and has just as much at stake."

"I know how shock and awe goes. Smoke screen, flash bombs, and charge using the element of surprise to subdue your enemies. Tidal wave is the use of five-man teams to overwhelm the enemy. Tactics have been part of my training for a while, not just because of what's happened." I said with all the calm I could muster, even though a lethal edge crawled down my spine.

"We could argue this all day." Captain Vega interjected. "But as I see it, we don't know her skills. And yes, without knowing, that she is a liability. However, she is going to storm in that building with or without us. Whether you agree or not, V, take the girl on your team. I would rather not incur Lord Niratap's wrath for denying his mate."

"We would incur his wrath if she was injured or killed during the raid." He snarled at her.

"I am capable." I snarled back at him.

"Take the girl." It was the Fire Captain.

"Sarah."

"Just do it."

He glared down at the map. "Fine."

"We charge in thirty." Tongee said. "Be ready."

"We are." I said confidently.

"Fine." Ventris hissed as he walked past. "Mitta, you're the most skilled out of all of us; she is your responsibility."

"Noted." Mitta glared at his back.

"What's his damage?" I growled.

"Inexperienced people in the field can cause lots of damage." Chief Maroto said. "You are untested and emotionally involved. It can cause you to make mistakes. That can cost you and others their lives."

"Untested or not, I promised Nira, I would get him out, and I plan on doing just that."

"Well then, let's wrap this up and get people organized. We have thirty minutes. Make arrests. Hit them hard and fast. The UC safe word is cerulean. All agents have been informed." The captains shuffled out of the tent, until it was just the three of us and Tongee.

"Even—"

"Yes, Bastion was looped in." Tongee said with a soft smile as he started past me. "He's a good kid. Durgash."

"Tongee! They haven't decided you're too bull headed yet?" Durgash clapped hands with the commander as the Days came into the tent.

"No, not yet. I take it you and Rogmesh are okay with being battering rams?"

"Haven't we always?" Rogmesh said clapping a hand on his shoulder. "Couldn't disappoint you now."

They walked off chatting, and Mitta placed a hand on my shoulder. I asked. "Do you know why Ventris is like that?"

"No, but if he lives through this, I will find out." She was staring after him. "Come on. Let's get into formation. We are going to get the lord out and then we can deal with this."

"Agreed."

Chapter Fifty-Eight

Niratap

My vision swam. Someone was calling my name. How many days have I been stuck here? Since the masquerade? How long ago was that? A week? Two? No, Shasha said in a week's time they were coming. Coming to save us. I wish I could remember how many days it had been. Bloody saliva dripped onto the ground in front of me. My shoulders screamed for relief; they were the only things holding me upright against the post.

A rough calloused hand gripped my face and Dravin spoke. "Have you given up yet? Who was the woman at the masquerade?"

"I don't know." It was the lie that I was sticking to. I wouldn't put her at risk. "Some aristocrat."

A fist connected with my gut, and the air wheezed from my lungs.

"Still sticking to that story, huh?"

"It's not a story." I panted.

"Leave him alone." Nessa snarled. "Haven't you done enough?"

"Shut it, bitch, or do you want me to drown him again?"

"Just leave him alone." My sister sobbed. Another secret I'd kept close to my heart; he couldn't know that we were siblings. His fist connected with my side again, and a rib audibly cracked.

"I'm going to break you. I had a feeling that the long days strapped to the table had done it, but since the masquerade you have been resistant again. Though I do enjoy wailing on you." He pushed my head back and our eyes met; I poured all my hate and malice into the glare I sent him. "Maybe I should put you back there. Maybe I should go find that sweet girl of yours that the non-human men are all drooling over."

"Leave her alone, Dravin." No. No. No.

"Mandrake would love to break her. He talks often about how he would love to destroy her sweet-smelling body."

I snarled, pulling against the bonds.

"Temper, temper." Dravin stepped back out of range of my teeth and depressed the collar control button. I thrashed against the binds, the fire in my blood not easing. I slumped against the pillar panting, my body going weak and my already strained shoulders, strained even farther. "Maybe that will be my next move. I'll go and kill your little found family."

"No."

"And I'll bring back their heads and the sweet little girl."

"Leave them alone." The conviction was missing as I teetered on the edge of consciousness.

"I'll let Mandrake break her like he wants. That would destroy you, wouldn't it?"

"Stop." The rage boiling in my blood fought against the acid and lost. "Just stop."

"She means so much to you, doesn't she?" Dravin pushed my head back by my antlers. "Your little girlfriend could make me a lot of money, too. She's definitely pretty, but even at the auction she had all the non-humans drooling for a chance just to be near her. Why is that?"

"I wonder the same." I seethed as the door opened and the Dr. Paloka walked in.

"Mr. Cirano, there is something I need to show you in the laboratory."

Dravin dropped me. "Very well, Paloka. Lead the way."

They left. I stared down at the drying and smeared droplets of blood on the floor. If he went after Shasha, I could do nothing. I felt the cracks in my soul deepen. I was trapped again in that darkness that roiled inside me. I had been too young and untested to protect my mother. I had been paralyzed with fear and unable to protect Deirdre when it mattered. Had barely been able to protect the girls. I couldn't protect Nessa as we were. Trapped. Utterly trapped. Dolan pushed through the door with Nikki in toe. He latched the door behind him.

"It's time?" Bastion asked standing.

"Almost. We have about twenty minutes before the raid actually starts. I wanted to get here sooner, but Dravin was in the middle of his—" He paused, throwing a glance my way. "Interrogation. I don't have enough time to undo the spells that hold them both."

"Nessa." I rasped. "Take care of Nessa."

Bastion and Dolan exchanged a glance before Bas tossed the keys to Dolan. "I'll get him down."

"I'll help." Nikki offered.

Bastion handed her a long hunting knife. "If you'll cut him down, I'll catch him."

"What? Don't think I could hold him?" She shot at him.

Color-stained Bastion's cheeks as she took the knife. "No."

I chuffed as he cradled me against him. "Girls are your weakness, Bas."

"I might drop you for that." He didn't smile, but it was in his voice.

"I may not be able to kick your ass now, kid, but it's coming if you drop me."

"Okay, well let's get out of here alive and you can beat me up whenever." He said as Nikki sawed away at the ropes while Dolan chanted over Nessa.

Bastion braced as the last of the ropes gave way. My body sagged against him and with a grunt he eased me to the floor. Pins and needles traveled down my arms as my muscles and joints could finally rest. Nikki pressed her access card against my throat and the collar beeped.

"This will probably sting." she said as she undid the collar and lifted it away. The back of my neck felt raw, and the smell of iron and pus filled my nose. Nikki rubbed a thick salve on the back of my neck; though it did sting it didn't have the bite of the venom. Bastion swore.

"What Bastion?" Dolan asked, helping Nessa out of the cage and to her feet.

"These cables around his wrists are laced with cragstone. I can't cut through them with my knife and Dravin has the key to the locks."

"Can you not bust the locks?" Nessa asked, crouching beside me and pushing back my hair.

"No, it's also cragstone. We need Dravin's key to get him out of here."

"Fuck." Dolan hissed. "Bastion, can you support him so we can make our way out of here?"

"Yeah." Bastion looped his arm through my bound arms. I hissed at the movement of my arms. "Sorry. On the count of three, 'kay?"

I gave him a small nod.

"One. Two. Three." Dolan helped guide me to my feet. I leaned against Bas and closed my eyes as my head swam.

"I think he might have a concussion." Nikki said.

I chuffed. "Most definitely."

"Let's get going." Nessa urged. "I don't want to be found before we can get out."

We had made it down three halls and down a flight of stairs before the sounds of flash bangs and gun fire rose from the floors below. We ducked into a room just off the stairs, Bastion easing me to the floor. We were shielded from sight. Dolan pressed his back against the door and peered through its small window. Nikki knelt in front of me checking my eyes and fretting over the small wounds that she could clean.

"Looks like the action has started."

"That it does." Bastion moved to the other door.

"How far until we're out of here?" I asked. My body felt ungodly heavy, and I just wanted to sleep.

"We have three floors. Agents will probably meet us on floor two or three." Dolan said as Bastion poked his head out the other door.

"Hey. Hey. Hey." Nikki said gently patting my cheek. "I need you to stay awake."

My lids fluttered and I struggled to focus on her face. "I'm so tired."

"Niratap. I need you to stay awake."

I blinked a couple times, clearing the cobwebs away. "I know."

"Shit." Bastion growled, pulling into the room. "Shit. Shit."

"What?" Dolan's hands glowed as he summoned ether.

"Mandrake and Christiana are coming this way."

"Shit." Dolan dropped his magic, opting for his sidearm. "This is less than ideal."

"Mandrake will take his pound of flesh if he sees us." Bastion eased the door shut and locked it. Together we held our breath as the ogre's shadow covered the frosted window in the door. He rattled the handle.

"The doors locked." Mandrake said surprised.

"It shouldn't be, I was just in there." Christiana's voice said behind him.

Shit. Their shadows left the door window, and we listened intently as their footsteps rounded the corner. I pressed my body hard against the wall just behind the door, I was in no condition to come face to face with the ogre. Nikki braced her feet against the door and waited. Bastion leveled his gun at the doorway, focused. Dolan shuffled silently around the doorway and pressed against the opposite wall. I could see him through the crack in the door, his gun pointed at the entry. Mandrake turned into the room; gun pointed into the darkness.

"Who's there?" He called. "Show yourself and I won't shoot."

Doubtful. When he had stepped into the room, Nikki kicked the door with all her strength, knocking the gun from Mandrake's hand. It fired into the room, and I heard the bullet ricochet off the floor. Dolan fired three shots into the side of the ogre. Mandrake snarled as he fell to the floor. He was still alive but immobilized.

"Who goes there." Christiana said from the hallway.

"Drop the weapon." Bastion hissed. "I don't want to have to shoot you, but I will."

"Mrak." She feigned surprise in her voice, but I heard a twist in it that felt like oil on my skin. "Never would have thought you would betray us. Dolan, I expected, you can't trust magic users with your life. I wonder who you have smuggled into this room with you?"

"That's not my name." Bastion said, his hands steady.

"A shame." She said, tucking a hand into her pocket. "I would have loved to get to know the real you, child."

"Christiana. Hands where I can see them."

"Drop the gun, Christiana." Dolan barked.

"Now why would I do that?" she asked, pointing the gun toward the crack in the door. "When you're trying to smuggle out my husband's newest toy." Her malicious gaze met mine as I heard two clicks. I shifted forward, shoving Nikki clear of the bullet's path and it sliced through my tail and into the floor. I hissed. Another shot rang out, and there was silence.

"You fucking killed her, jackass." Mandrake hissed.

"She was given ample warning." Bastion came forward and tied Mandrake's arms behind him. "You, however, were just a threat to be neutralized. Thanks for making my job easier, dick-weed."

"You'll pay for this. You and Bondbreaker."

"Sit here and think about all you've done."

"Fuck you, orc."

Bastion came to where I was sitting. "My Lord, are you okay."

"It just grazed me." I said. "Nikki, are you okay?"

"Yeah." She said coming to stand. "Thank you."

Her and Bastion lifted me from the floor, Bastion taking most of my weight. My legs still felt like Jello. How long did the effects of the acid hold me back? Dolan pulled the ogre to his feet and stood at the doorway when a deafening sound shook the floor. An explosion radiated through the stairwell, the force of it knocking Dolan and Mandrake back into the room and onto a glass table. My ears rang.

"Dolan!" Nikki screamed as she left my side.

"I'm okay." He groaned, shoving Mandrake's unconscious body off of him. "Ogre took the majority of the blast. My ears are ringing, that is all."

She helped Dolan to his feet. Nessa frowned, smelling it when I did. "You're bleeding."

A piece of table was jammed into his thigh. "Fuck."

"Nikki take the fire escape." Bastion said. "Get him some help quicker."

"But what about you guys?" Dolan protested.

Bastion eyed me, there was no way I was going to be able to take a fire escape ladder, bound as I was. "I won't make it through the fire escape. Go get him help so he doesn't bleed out here."

"What about the ogre?" Nessa asked.

"Leave him." I said. "He's not dead, so if he's lucky the other agents will sweep this floor. Nessa you should go with them."

"No." she said. "Bastion will have to take too many breaks. Especially down two flights of stairs."

"She is right. Having someone else will make the stairs easier and we can get out of here faster."

"I don't like splitting up." Dolan said.

"Neither do I, but we don't have much choice if all of us are going to get out."

Dolan gave a forlorn nod. "Be swift."

Bastion nodded. "You too."

We made it down the hall that branched in three separate directions. Bastion panted and Nessa wrapped her arm around me.

"Take a break Bastion. I have him." Nessa said, easing me against a wall.

"We need to keep moving." He panted.

"I know, but this floor is a maze and even though you know your way around it doesn't mean carrying the extra weight around makes this easy." I ground out. My limbs were still weak and tingly. "I'm not in the condition to be running any marathons."

Bastion chuckled, catching his breath. "Duly noted."

"Well, well, well." The arrogant voice traveled down the hall to the right of us. "Never thought I would be betrayed quite this way."

"Dravin." Nessa hissed, shifting in front of me as he came from the shadows. His hands tucked behind his back.

"You have found yourself in a pickle, huh, Niratap?"

"Give us the key, Dravin!" Bastion shouted pushing forward past Nessa.

Dravin pulls the silver key from beneath his shirt. "This key? Sure. Come get it, I know when I'm out gunned."

"Bas." I cautioned as he took two steps toward Dravin.

"Bas?" Dravin purred. "What an interesting name, Mrak."

Bastion reached for his gun, tucked into the small of his back. "To be honest Dravin, I never liked working with you."

"And I thought we had an understanding. You were like a son to me."

"I have a father, and he is more of a man than you'll ever be."

"No, he isn't because he's an orc. A grunt for war and mine work as it should be. You were a good grunt, obedient, willing to do what I needed."

Bastion tensed. "I only needed to get close so I could get information from you."

"Bastion." I snarled, forcing myself to stand on my own. "He's trying to get a rise out of you."

"Don't take the bait." Nessa said.

"Oh, I don't have to bait him." Dravin said. "He's as good as dead anyways."

Time slowed in that moment as I pushed forward into Bastion, knocking him off balance. Dravin pulled his pistol from behind his back and leveled it at us, firing. Nessa screamed as the bullet careened through the air, slicing across my chest and boring into Bastion's shoulder, his own gun skittering down a hall. The pain was whip-like to my senses. I lost my footing and hurtled into the opposite wall. Dravin laughed.

"You know what the doctor told me as we walked to the lab?" Dravin said as Nessa fussed over me and then Bastion who had fallen backwards onto his ass. "The doctor told me that the two bitarogs I have in my possession shared DNA. I laughed at him of course, because there's no way that is statistically possible. Then I looked at his printouts of the DNA and sure as shit, there are too many common genes for there to just be a coincidence. He speculated that you two were siblings."

I panted and chuckled through a wince as I straightened. "Kind of ruins plans on breeding us, doesn't it?"

Dravin frowned. "Inbred creatures always run the risk of being damaged, but I still have two bitarogs. Kneel."

The word held the power of the spells that still bound me to him. The blue fire cracked around my neck, pulling me to the ground. Dravin's frown only deepened as Nessa stood, tall and proud, unaffected by him.

"Well, it seems, I have been betrayed in more ways than I originally thought. Seems my mage has also betrayed me, but I'm guessing that you ran out of time before this little raid started. Speaking of the current state of my operation, have you run into my lovely wife at all? I wonder where the viper has slunk off to." Dravin took two steps closer.

"She's dead." Bastion said with a wince.

There was a twitch in his face. "Dead?"

"You heard me." Bastion snarled.

"Bend. Now tell me. Is it true, what the doctor told me?"

Lightning flashed through my body, taking my breath away. I pressed my forehead to the floor, waiting for the pain and nausea to ease. Tremors shook through my body. We were so close to being free.

"Enough, Dravin." Nessa hissed but made no move toward the man.

"Well, beast, tell me."

I panted. "Nessa—is my—sister."

"Hmm. Inbred indeed it seems. Oh well, I can make do. Not like my buyers will know."

"You've lost. Let us go." Nessa snarled. "Let my brother go."

"Lost." I looked up at Dravin, a cruel smile giving his face an unhinged quality. A chain appeared between his outstretched hand and my neck; the heavy cold metal tight against my throat. "By the looks of it I still have the upper hand. I still have the Bondbreaker. I still have a gun."

He pointed the gun at Nessa, who tensed, but made no move to run.

"Dravin. Take me; let them go."

"Why should I do that?"

"You can use me as a bargaining chip for your life." I said, hating the words on my tongue. "I can't fight you. I'm too weak, but I can be your ticket out of this."

Dravin considered my words, before he looked at Nessa with cold hatred. "Five."

I twisted toward my sister. "Nessa! Bas! Run!"

"Four."

Nessa helped Bastion off the floor and then bolted down the hall at full speed.

"Three."

I roared at him as he aimed the gun at their backs. Time. They didn't have enough time.

"Two."

I pushed from the floor quickly, launching myself at Dravin.

"One."

My legs wobbled, but I stood before him as Nessa and Bastion turned a corner, heading to freedom.

"My, my, that self-sacrifice is going to get you killed, Bondbreaker."

"Oh, it will eventually, but you won't be the one that kills me, Dravin."

Chapter Fifty-Nine

In tight formations, we followed behind Tongee's group as they charged forward. I took a breath. As they burst through the door, and the initial gun fire broke, out we swept in. Mitta pressed to my right and Ventris in front of me. He had shifted the teams around, so we ended up in team three with him and one other agent. It felt like time slowed as we waited for the rush team to clear the first floor.

I followed behind him, keeping my head low as we swept the rooms. It was a chaos of smoke and flashes, gunfire and shouts. Somewhere, hidden in this chaos, was my mate. I felt him. The draw that he had on me only intensified with his absence. There was a familiar feminine scream that I had heard in the dream space that came from our left.

"Wait." I shouted peering over into the room. One of the FBI agents stood over a pale orc and a woman who had long, elegant, spiraled antlers and fine-boned features. I had seen her in my dreams and knew who she was. The agent had his sight centered on the orc's chest as he tried to cover the woman. Blood oozed from one of his shoulders.

"Stop." I shouted, coming to stand in front of the agent. "He's one of us."

The agent's eyes were wide as he stared at them. "But he didn't identify himself."

"If you had paused two seconds to listen, I would have told you." Bastion snarled. "Bastion Day, Bondbreaker, the color of the day is cerulean."

"Bastion." Rogmesh had been behind us following close behind after the initial push. "My baby!"

"Ma." It was a happy and annoyed sound as she came to his side and helped him up.

"Medical evac." Ventris growled into the radio. "One male orc, a female bitarog. and Rogmesh are coming down."

"Where's Niratap?" I asked Bastion as he leaned on his mother.

"Dravin has him." Bastion's face fell. "We tried to get him out, but Dolan didn't have time to get him out of the binding spell. Dravin still had cards to play and the key."

"Key?"

"Yes." Nessa spoke her voice was lilting with a thick Irish accent. "Dravin has him bound in cragstone lined ropes and lock. Dravin had the key around his neck."

"Niratap defended us from Dravin, but he's weak from all that's been done and the poison in his body." Bastion looked at me solemnly, his brows pressing together in anguish. "Fucking jackass doesn't know when to let anyone help him."

"He did what he thought he had to."

"Where's Dolan?" Ventris asked from the doorway.

"Dolan was injured by one of the upper floor blasts. He went out the back way with Nikki. They are probably already out at base camp."

"Where was Dravin heading?" I asked.

"Up. The top floor is just cells for holding creatures. He is probably planning some last stand."

"Perfect."

Ventris hissed into the radio reporting back to incident command as Bastion and Rogmesh passed him. Nessa stood beside me, she was tall and slender like her brother. Her hair the same sable black and her eyes the eerie silver, but that was where similarities stopped. Where Niratap had honey skin she was pale porcelain. Where his hair had a natural wave to it if he let it have a mind of its own, hers was pin straight and cascaded behind her like a curtain. Where his body was etched with his battle tough life, hers was unmarred unless you counted the dusting of freckles across her shoulder and cheeks. She tilted her head in that predatory way, her nostrils flaring before she spoke.

"What are you?" She asked.

"Human."

Her head tilted the other direction, "No, you are not. Though I can't place the scent."

I scowled. "As far as I am aware both my parents are human. Other than the mate's claim, I only smell like me. Though I am told it is a transfixing scent."

"Most definitely. I can see why you drew my brother to you, how any creature with a sense of smell could be. How curious."

"Nessa." Ventris spoke firmly behind me. "You should go. The medical team can treat your minor wounds and check you out for worse ones."

"Save my brother." She said as she passed me. "Save your mate."

I followed behind her. "What do you mean by curious?"

"I mean you are not what you seem. I think Niratap realizes that as well."

"Is he—" I couldn't finish the sentence.

"He is in rough shape. Dravin beat him repeatedly today. Trying to find out who you were."

"Dravin knows me."

"He wanted to know who the woman at the masquerade was. That was you."

Another team pushed past us and into the room where Ventris was, going over the plans for the rest of the floors. "Yes."

"You risked much to give him a sliver of hope."

"I couldn't let him lose himself."

She smiled sweetly. "You must love him very much."

"Love doesn't describe what I feel for him."

Nessa glanced back at the room. "You want to find him more than the rest of them. Go. Find him. Bring him home." My heart fluttered as she moved past me. "If you want your pound of flesh, go now."

I drew my pistol and pushed forward without anyone. Nessa's words had rung too true in my heart. If I went with the team, Ventris would see that Dravin was arrested. Taken alive to be interrogated, and he would get released because money got you good lawyers. Dravin would be inconvenienced at worst and not held accountable for all the terrible things he had done to my mate. He wouldn't be held accountable for the things he had done to me.

The second floor was a bunch of hallways and doorways. The first set of stairs I found to the third floor had been blown apart and I had to backtrack down a series of halls to find another set. I paused at the top of the stairs listening. I could feel him there in the space of this floor. I heard the snarl echo off the empty halls. Mate. Mine. I wanted to run to him, but I knew I had to be cautious. I couldn't risk this when he was so close. Down two more halls and around a bend, I heard them. Keeping close to the walls, I crept down the hallway to the door where their voices were coming from.

"You think you're gonna get out of this, but you're not." Dravin's voice came through the doorway.

Niratap laughed, but it sounded weak. "You going to kill me, Dravin? After you bound me as a slave and drugged me? Tortured me? I didn't take you for a weakling."

I peeked around the corner as Dravin rammed his boot into Niratap's stomach. He was already bloody, his arms bound behind his back. There was blood all over the floor, probably from the slash-like wound over his chest.

"Shut up. They're only here because of you. I should have just killed you."

Niratap spat. "I wouldn't be any good to you dead, though."

"Between you and the bitch I thought I had it made. Bitarog pups would make me so much money."

"Too bad we're brother and sister, then." Niratap laughed again.

"I was going to make it happen." Dravin snarled.

"Trying to simulate it without having any knowledge of the species. That's a fantastic idea. You almost killed her with that concoction." Niratap snarled. "She almost bled to death."

"I fucking know," He smacked the nose of the gun across Niratap's face. "Jesus. Do you think that I wanted this? For my people to be killed and arrested? My wife shot? To be betrayed by my second and my mage?"

Niratap spat blood on the floor, his eyes met mine and I saw fear in the pools of moonlight. "No."

I closed my eyes and stepped around the doorway and raised the pistol. "Drop the gun, Dravin."

"Shasha, don't be stupid run!" Niratap snarled and Dravin laughed as he turned to face me.

"That's hilarious. Girl, put that down before you shoot your eye out."

"Let him go." I edged toward him.

"Or what? You'll shoot me."

"Shasha," Niratap pleaded, fighting against the ties at his back. "Go. This is too dangerous. Go."

Dravin kicked him again. I adjusted and fired, the bullet just missing his face. "That is your only warning. Drop the gun and let Niratap go."

"I don't think so." He growled hefting Niratap up, a surprise given Niratap's size. He held him close, a shield of flesh. He was pressing the gun into his back. "I control this. If you want to live, you'll leave while you have a chance."

"I'm not leaving without him." I yelled. Fuck I didn't have a shot.

"Too bad. I need him to get out of here alive."

"Dravin let her go, your fight is with me."

The bang of the pistol startled me. Niratap cried out. Dravin had shot him just above his hip. It had gone through him, the hole wept blood. "Shut up."

"Niratap." I fight with control over my emotions, panic trying to take hold of my heart. The nose of my pistol wobbles.

He panted against the pain. "Shasha. Run."

"Shasha. Run." Dravin mocked, laughing. "God, I can't believe this nightmare that I have been thrust into. All because of you." Dravin leveled the gun at me.

"How is it any of my fault?" I asked, edging deeper into the room.

"What makes you so special? What draws them to you? The Fae, the beasts, men they all are drawn to you. Why?"

"If only I knew. Not that I would tell you." Booted footsteps came down the hall. I flicked my eyes that way, Ventris has his back pressed against the wall, Mitta behind him.

"Who's there, little girl?" Dravin asked.

"Does it matter? You're trapped, Dravin. Now let him go."

Dravin pressed the gun to Niratap's shoulder. "I want a guarantee that I will walk out of here."

"Dravin, let Niratap go, and we can talk about this." Ventris said around the corner.

"That's not the answer," He fired into his shoulder.

Niratap screamed. the sound breaking my heart. The gun quivered in my hand; I took a breath. "Let him go."

Ventris swung into the room. "You heard her, Dravin. Let Niratap go. No one else has to die today."

"That's where you're wrong, Commander." He placed the gun against Niratap's' back.

"No!" My scream is swallowed by the gun firing through his chest. Dravin laughed as he dropped Niratap to the floor. Niratap wasn't moving, blood pooling on the floor.

"He wasn't going to get out of this alive if I wasn't." Dravin said laughing. "He's weakened by my synthetic venom. He'll die if you don't get him to a medic. He'll die if you don't let me go."

"Niratap!" I took a step towards them, lowering my gun to the ground.

"Stop. If you come closer. I will blow his brains out. Make a choice. Tick tock."

Ventris held his hands up. "Okay, Dravin. Give us the antidote, and we can all walk out of here. The warehouse is on fire, Dravin; we can't dilly dally. We can all go."

"Ventris." Mitta growled, "We don't have time for this. Niratap." She poked her head around the doorway. "Fuck. Niratap doesn't have time for this."

"Tick tock, tick tock."

I closed my eyes and took a steadying breath. "You're wrong, Dravin."

"About what, child? I have all the cards in my hand."

"No, you don't. We have a wild card."

Dravin dropped his gun to his side. "Oh really, and what is that?"

I took another breath, raising my gun, "Me."

I fired.

Chapter Sixty

Shasha

From the moment I pulled the trigger, time seemed to slow to a crawl. The bullet hit Dravin in the head just under his right eye. Shock filled those eyes just before they rolled back into his head and he fell backwards, the gun skittering across the floor.

The distance between Niratap and I seemed to grow as I ran to him, tucking the gun back in its holster. There was so much blood pooled around his body. I came to kneel beside him, the lukewarm crimson seeping into the knees of my jeans. I had never noticed but his blood was a few shades darker than mine and Dravin's, which had started to pool behind his head.

"Nira! Nira!" I shrieked, turning his head into my lap. "*Mo grá,* please don't be dead. You can't. I can't lose you. Please open your eyes."

"Shasha." Mitta put her hands on my shoulders. "Let me check him okay."

I nodded, scooting back from his body, remembering the key. I fetched the small silver key from Dravin's neck. Mitta pressed her fingers to his neck, closing her eyes to focus. They flew open and she shouted "Ventris, we need medical. Now!"

"He's alive?" I asked, terror easing slightly as I unlocked the cragstone. bindings.

"Yes. His pulse is weak, but he's alive."

"Central." Ventris spoke into the radio, "I need medical pick up in sector seven."

"Negative Commander. Fire has consumed sectors two and three. You'll have to evacuate via sector twelve."

"Fuck."

"What does that mean," Tears were pouring down my face. "How did a fire even start?"

"One of Dravin's men tossed a Molotov between us and the rest of the rush team."

Mitta wrenched her backpack off, then pulled medical supplies out. "And it means we have to get out here on our own. The chest wound is through and through, so I won't have to go fishing for a bullet, however his breathing is shallow, and his lung was punctured." She handed me gauze. "Pack that bullet wound on his back. Then I'll try to reinflate his lung."

My hands quickly caked in blood as they staunched the flow. Mitta took a knife and a bottle of alcohol out of the pack, poured some on the blade and made a small hole four inches from the wound. She pulled a length of tubing out. Dropping one end of the tube in the bottle and pushing the other end of the tube in the incision. She lifted the bottle over her head; bubbles and blood tainted the alcohol. He gasped and coughed; blood coloring his lips.

"Nira." I stroked the sides of his face. "Stay still, *mo grá*, you were shot."

He took a shuddering breath. "That explains—" Another raspy hollow breath. "The pain—" A string of coughs. "At least."

"Don't talk." Mitta barked. "Focus on breathing, we need to get you out of here. Ventris sector twelve is on the roof, right?"

"Yeah, it is. He can't walk, so that will slow us down."

"We need to get him out. He doesn't have much time." Mitta growled.

I pressed a kiss to Niratap's forehead. "Mitta, he's so cold."

"Ventris, radio Tummi, tell her to be ready for me. I have an idea; can you get Shasha out?"

"Yes, I can. What are you going to do, Mitta?"

Mitta removed her weapons, holsters and clothes, shoving them all into her pack and handing it to me. She had an intricate tattoo of a white tiger on her back. "I'm going to shift and run him out of here. If there are enemies, most men run when faced with a twenty-foot tiger, battle armor or not."

She smiled before standing and taking several steps away. She shook her shoulders and took a steady breath. She took three more steps as a shimmering glow covered her body as she shifted. Her brown eyes were beautifully set in her moon white furry face, which was cut with dark stripes.

"Beautiful." I said in a whisper.

She chuffed at me in a laugh then spoke, her voice full of gravel, but still Mitta. "I'm glad you think so. It has been a while since I shifted."

"Tummilia, be ready for Niratap. Medical be ready. We're coming out."

"Yes, sir." The answer came through the radio.

"Shasha, help me get him on her back." Ventris said going to Niratap's side. "This is going to hurt like a bitch, my friend."

Nira gave a small nod. We looped our hands under his arms, hefting him up onto Mitta's back. Ventris took a length of rope and tied Nira down, securing his wrists around her neck.

"Get him out of here, Mitta. Be safe."

"I plan on blowing through here and getting him to the girls."

"We'll be right behind you."

"Ventris." Niratap wheezed. "Keep our girl safe."

"I won't let anything happen to her."

I pressed a kiss to his forehead. "We'll be right behind you. I love you."

He gave me a small smile. "I love you."

"We'll meet you down there." Mitta said before she turned and ran out the doorway.

I took a breath before I asked Ventris. "Okay, how are we getting out of here?"

He held out his hand, "The way air elementals travel."

"I'm not an elemental."

He gave me a curious look. "He didn't tell you, did he?"

"Who didn't tell me what?" I queried, drawing back my hand.

"Niratap. You are half air elemental. I will explain later. Let's get out of here."

"What? How do you know that? How is that possible?" There is a shrillness in my voice.

He swallowed. "Because I—I am your father."

"No. That's impossible because my father was human. My mother would have told me if I was half anything."

"Shasha, it's the truth." He barked exasperatedly, casting a glance at the doorway where black smoke started to hang in the hall. "Now, the fire is climbing the stairs and will be here soon. When we are safe on the ground, I'll explain everything, but until then I need you to trust me." He extended his hand again.

"After we're on the ground and I know Niratap is safe, you'll tell me everything. I want the truth."

"I will. Now take my hand."

I eyed his palm, calluses that could be so foreign and so familiar within reach. "Promise me."

"I swear on my breath in my lungs." He groaned. "Now, sweetbreeze, let's go."

The words struck up a memory. A warm spring day on the hilltop meadow with my dad. Tears threatened to well up as I took his hand, and I drew in a shuddering breath. He gave me a soft smile. "I—I can't believe—" I started, feeling overwhelmed and dizzy.

"I know. Neither can I. I need you to take a deep breath for me. Find your calm again; if you start to panic you can get hurt, okay?"

I nodded, taking a couple deep breaths. "Okay."

"Ready?"

"Yes."

"Okay, we're going to walk to the doorway. Right before we cross the threshold, I need you to take a deep breath and hold it. Do not look down. Do not panic. Do not let go of my hand. Understood?"

"Yes. I understand."

He took a breath to steady himself. "Okay."

Together we walked purposefully to the hall.

With five feet left to go he asked again. "Ready?"

"Yes."

With three feet to go he squeezed my hand, and I squeezed back.

With two feet he said. "Okay. Take a deep breath, baby-girl."

With one he did the same.

At the threshold wind whipped my ears, drowning all other sound out. I felt my feet lift from the floor, weight and gravity ceased to exist. We flew through the building in a twisting and rolling storm, wind blowing through the first door or window to the outside. I closed my eyes as we plummeted to the concrete as a gust of wind. Then just as suddenly as I had become the storm wind, I was solid again. I was pulled tightly against Ventris's chest, his breath level and calm. His scent was that of salty sea air and summer sun. Warm and familiar.

"Sweetbreeze, you can breathe now."

I took a shallow, almost haunted-sounding breath. My voice shook as I asked, "What was that?"

I could hear the smile in his voice. "Wind walking. I don't know if your air elemental blood is strong enough for you to do it on your own though."

I look up at his face and in the foggiest parts of my memories I saw a man much like him. Eyes less vibrant. Dreads instead of the close cut. But his smile was one I would never forget. "You really are him, aren't you?"

He nods. "I am."

He looked past me, and I turned, Mitta was prowling toward us, Niratap still tied to her back. "Ventris."

"Right, the medical tents are this way. They should be ready for you. You okay?" He asked, pressing a hand to my back.

"Yes. It's just a lot to take in."

He nodded and led us to the medical tent. Katrel and Tummi stood anxiously waiting at the mouth of a tent, ready for anything, but I saw the fear that danced in their eyes as they saw him. I kept pace with Mitta's long strides, tucking a strand of his hair behind his ear.

"We're getting you help. You're going to be okay, love." His eyes found my face and that was the only indication that he heard me. My heart started racing again.

Once in the tent Allipo and Ventris came to Mitta's side as she shifted back, into her human form. The girls had shut the flaps of the tent, giving us privacy.

"You got him?" Mitta asked as they grabbed his arms.

"Yes." Allipo said. "We got him."

They ease him onto the medical bed as Mitta came to stand and I handed her the pack with her clothes. "Katrel, start the transfusion and IV, while I get dressed. You will probably have to hit a main vein in order to get it going."

"I got you." She said quickly busying herself with the task.

"What can I do?" I asked. "I want to help."

Mitta gave me a tight smile as she pulled her shirt overhead. She quickly began to braid back her hair. "Stand up by his head. Keep him conscious; if he blacks out it'll be hard to get him back."

I wet a rag as Mitta washed her hands and pressed the cool fabric to his forehead. His eyes were cloudy, as he looked up at me. He wheezed. "Hi."

"I'm glad I found you."

"I'm glad you found me, too." The smallest hint of a smile.

"Shasha, roll his head that way so I can poke him," Katrel directed.

He tried to take a steadying breath. Feeling him tense under my fingers as Katrel drew near, I pressed a kiss to his forehead. He instantly relaxed and she inserted the IV with no issues. The lack of fight stilled my heart all the same.

I eased him back to center. "Thank you." He rasped.

"Anytime, *mo grá*."

"Okay," Mitta came beside the bed. "I'm going to clean these wounds, dig the bullet out of your shoulder, and stitch you up. I'm going to give you some local anesthetic, while I do that. I'm fairly certain your shoulder is broken. Ventris, do we have a portable X-ray at base camp?"

"I'll go see." He said, dipping out the flaps.

"It looks like you've pretty much stopped bleeding, too. Which is good." She looked up at me as she spoke. "How are you doing, Niratap."

"Cold. Sore." He replied.

She took a pen light and shined it in his eyes. "Pupillary response is good; your color is already starting to come back. Tummi, will you find me a blanket for him?"

"On it."

Mitta pulled a tray of supplies to the right-side bed. "Hold his head."

I grabbed his antlers and pressed them down into the padding. He looked up at me with a sultry look in his eyes despite everything. I asked. "What?"

"Just remembering how you like to hang on."

My cheeks heated and Mitta cleared her throat as she gave him the local. "He's going to be fine."

Ventris, Tummi, and the mage, who was limping slightly, walked through the flaps, I moved around the table standing between him and Nira. Tummi shuffled past and draped the blanket over Niratap. My hand went to my holster on instinct, "What is he doing here?"

Both men held up their hands and Ventris spoke. "Hey, baby girl. This is Dolan. He is part of the mage Corp and works in the bureau. He was working undercover in Dravin's network."

"Shasha, I know you don't trust me. We haven't had a chance to talk. I just want to help if I can."

"Dolan has a spell that will help Mitta see the damage in his shoulder. He's really just here to help."

Cool fingers rested on my hand, but my hand did not waver. Niratap's strained voice tried to soothe me. "*Mo grá. Let him help, he doesn't mean us any harm.*"

"Show me the spell." I spoke firmly.

"Shasha is that really—" Ventris argue, but I interrupted.

"If he wants in here, if he really wants to help, then yes, it is necessary, no one is getting near him, unless I can trust them. Now show me."

"Very well. *Taispeáin dom cad atá taobh thiar den bhalla.*"[45] he held up a hand, brushing the other past it. The spell, though not an x-ray, showed a window into the grotesque mechanics of muscle, tendons, and bones. He dismissed the spell. "Satisfied?"

I forced my body to relax. "Anything funny and know that I will shoot you."

Dolan gave a small nod. "I understand."

They came to the side of the bed as I returned to my station at his head. Nira smiled up at me as I pushed back his hair. "What?"

"You are just a beautiful, lethal creature."

Ventris chuckled. "Mitta, how can I help?"

"I'm about to sew him up, but—"

"I can use my magic." Tummi interjected, and everyone's gaze pinned the fair elf where she stood. "I know that I have a limited store of magic, but I could try and then you can focus on pulling the bullet out of his shoulder."

Mitta smiled. "Less poking for him, and less chance of my getting bit. I like it. Dolan, you and Tummi come to this side of the bed; we're going to roll him on his side."

[45] "Show me what is behind the wall."

Tummi smiled as she and Dolan came to stand beside Mitta on either side, Dolan stood closer to me. He eyed me for a moment before turning to Mitta for guidance.

"On the count of three." Everyone around the table, with free hands, grabbed his right side to roll him. Katrel handed me a rolled-up towel to place under his head. "One. Two. Three."

Niratap groaned at the motion but did not protest. With the makeshift pillow in place, I came to stand in front of him to observe. Dolan and Tummi's magic cast colorful lights across the tent. Mitta took a long pair of forceps and probed the wound. Through Dolan's spell, Mitta guided them to where the bullet lay jammed into the joint.

"This is going to hurt." Mitta warned, "Allipo will you and Ventris hold him down?"

They came to stand in front, Allipo grabbed his arm and Ventris wrapped his arm around his waist. "We're ready."

"You got his head?" Mitta asked.

"Yeah," My hands wrapped around the base of his antlers.

"Okay."

She tried to pull, leaning her weight against the bullet. A roar rocked the ground, Nira gripped the edge of the bed, trying to keep himself controlled. "Damn it."

"Mitta." The growl from him was feral, a snarl taking up home on his face.

"I'm sorry. You're healing around it; I'm going to have to use more force." I peered through the spell, amazed as the bone and cartilage were steadily trying to swallow the slug.

"Mitta, I would tell you to hurry, but I think we can all agree that is a must." Allipo scolded, adjusting his grip.

"Right, I'm going back in. Hold him still."

We braced as she tried again twisting, breaking the growing fragments away. Nira roared again; it was a deafening volume and the silence that followed after, was as if the world held its breath. Mitta wrenched backwards, the slug coming free. She stumbled, Katrel catching her before she fell.

"Tummi, flush the wound before you heal him." She gasped.

"*Mo grá* it's over. She got the bullet out. You're going to be okay." He didn't respond and my heart started a gallop, "Nira?"

Ventris came to my side, leaning in against Nira's mouth. "It's okay, sweetbreeze, he's just unconscious. It's a natural response. He's still breathing."

"You guys, okay?" Bastion's voice came from the entrance. His forehead was wrapped and his arm in a sling.

"Yeah." I said, wiping my eyes. "How are you?"

"Beyond being shot, tore my rotator cuff, a cut on my forehead, and bruises. Nessa is in the tent next door. She's resting. The IV seems to dilute the synthetic venom."

"That explains him trying to heal around a bullet." Mitta growled as the guys rolled Nira onto his back. "I'm glad you're okay, kid. Your mom will be proud of you."

"Ah shucks, Mitta, I knew you cared."

She glared at him but smiled. "Don't test your luck child, your mother would be rather cross with me if I had to kick your ass."

Allipo came to my side, dropping a little vial in my hand. "That should rouse the lord. Just uncork it and run it under his nose."

"Thank you."

He smiled. "My money is on Mitta."

"Damn satyr! Why do you got to do me dirty like that?" Bas whined and they all laughed, moving toward the entrance of the tent.

"We'll give you two the tent." Mitta said as she passed. "He's probably missed you. Hey Allipo, you get the first guard."

He whined playfully as they exited the tent.

"Dolan, can I talk to you?"

He froze at the door. "You're not going to shoot me, are you?"

"Not at this particular moment. I have a question for you actually."

"Okay." He approached cautiously. "You not going to wake him?"

"No, I don't want his input on this just yet."

"Okay, What's your question?"

"Is there a way to keep him from being bound again? To keep him safe? Watching that happen to him again was heavy, and no I don't fully trust you, but you bound him to that monster. I—I just want to know if there is a way to prevent that from happening in the future."

"For right now he's not at risk; he can't be rebound to another authority while he is bound to Dravin's bloodline. That is currently not a cause for concern either as his child is currently in prison."

I frowned. "That doesn't ease my fears."

He raked his hands through his hair. "I can do some research, but the easiest way would be to bind him to someone you trust."

"I wouldn't trust someone to not abuse that kind of power."

"Yourself then? I mean you guys are mated, right?"

"Yes, we are."

"It would keep him safe from poachers that want his hide, especially since the masquerade put him on display and because I know the raid made national news. Niratap has plentiful enemies that wish him harm. Dravin proved he can be caught, it's only a matter of time until someone tries again."

I chewed on my lip, mulling over his words.

"Look, I know it's a lot to think over. Talk to him and see what he thinks." He angled his head at Niratap. "It might surprise you what he thinks, but rest now. You both deserve it."

Dolan left the tent, his idea weighing heavy on my heart. Nira had told me the purpose of keeping me bound to him was to keep me safe. Would he allow me to do something similar? Would he allow himself to be shackled to me? I dragged a stool next to the gurney. I could have used the smelling salts on him, roused him and asked, but he looked so peaceful like he was finally resting for the first time in months. He must have been so tired. I had the feeling that fighting for your life did that. I stroked his face trying to soothe his pinched features. That was softer than his cries of pain had been on my heart. I pulled the blanket over his chest and laid my head against it listening as his heart thudded in his chest.

Dolan was right though; Nira was at risk. In danger now that his enemies knew he could be captured, held against his will, bent to their own. Fear coiled in my chest, knowing that even with everything that had happened, he wouldn't back down. When he was healed and able, he would be prowling those dark denizens again, looking for those that he could save from the terrible fate he had endured and kept enduring for them.

"Self-sacrificing fool." I muttered.

Chapter Sixty-One

Shasha

A buzzing woke me, I had fallen asleep on the stool, my head firmly anchored to Nira's gently rising chest. The buzzing kicked up again and I dug through the many pockets of my tactical pants to find my cell.

"Hey. Mama?"

"Where are you?" There was a lot of background noise.

"With Niratap. Mom, where are you? Is it very loud?"

"I'm standing on the opposite side of a police barrier in the meatpacking district."

I stood. "Mom, what are you doing?"

"Are you guys, okay? These cops won't let me through."

"We're fine. Nira was injured, but he's resting. Wait, what are you doing in the city? You hate the city."

"I was visiting a friend, and we watched the coverage of the raid on TV. I saw you. Now come and get me before I push through these barricades and get arrested."

"Okay mom, don't get arrested, I'll come grab you."

I hung up with a groan.

"Your mother is a beast of a woman." His voice was weak, but a small smile rested on his exhausted face. I gave him a small smile in return.

"She is definitely a nuisance."

He shifted with a groan. "You love her though. Go fetch her before she hurts someone."

"Will you be alright? Are you in pain?"

He rolled away from me with a sigh. "Yes, to both, *mo grá*. I am just going to go back to sleep while things settle down. Mitta I'm sure will appear with medicine soon enough."

I pressed a kiss on his cheek. "I'll be right back."

"I'm not going anywhere on my own power anytime soon, love. Go."

I smiled softly at him, before I left the tent to go find my mother.

An officer had pointed me to the barricade where my mother was screeching to be let in. She was getting side-eye from many of the agents that were scattered about. I pitied the officer that was standing before, her not letting her pass, as he was being berated by the woman. As I came into earshot, I pitied him more.

"You listen here officer Nicks I will be reporting you to the chief of police. My daughter is in there and she needs me. What if she is hurt? I need to get by."

"Sorry, no can do, ma'am."

"That's not good enough. My daughter will not stand for this. She is with the Bondbreaker, and I need to get through."

"Yeah, right." The officer said crossing his arms. "She's not with Bondbreaker."

"Yes, she is."

"Do you want to get arrested? I've told you a dozen times now that you're not getting past. No press without a pass. No media without a pass. No civilians period."

"I need to get through to my daughter—" She saw me as I finally approached. "Shasha. Tell this officer that I can come through."

"Mom, what are you doing? Why are you here?"

"I told you on the phone. I was in the city visiting my friend, you know you Aunt Cylia." A vague inclination of a boisterous round woman I had met once in high school flashed through my mind. "We saw the news coverage on the raid, and I saw you. I had her rewind the coverage so I could see it again. What are you doing here? Raids are dangerous!"

"It's okay, officer. I'll claim this crazy woman."

"I was told no one in without a pass."

I frowned, grabbing my mother's hand and pulling her behind me. I said over my shoulder. "If you have a problem with it, take it up with Lord Niratap or Commander Ventris."

The officer called after us, but I didn't want to be away from Niratap for long. We wove between congregations of all sorts of agents and officers, my mother protesting loudly behind me.

"Shasha, slow down."

I stopped and rounded on her. "Why are you here? What in god's name possessed you to show up here at a multi-organization black market raid? Other than to hover over me and tell me that I'm making horrible decisions about my life."

Her eyes were teary. "No. The news said the raid was a rescue mission. To rescue several undercover operatives and Niratap. They shared on the news that he was a black-market kingpin to some and a savior to others. I know I wasn't very warm to him when you visited and the last few weeks you've sounded sad. You didn't tell me that he was taken. You just said he was not around."

"It's not like you cared about him."

"No, but you do, and I love you. Is he okay? The coverage didn't say, but—" her brows furrowed as her eyes drifted past me to where Ventris was talking with Commander Tongee. "Xaevean?"

Ventris froze at the sound of her voice, eyes going wide as he saw us together. His mouth opened and closed like a fish on a dock. It clicked into place in my head that they hadn't seen each other in nineteen years.

"Xaevean Dion!" My mother shouted, and I felt rather than saw the rage on her face. Ventris's face paled visibly as he started toward us.

"Jazzera."

"How dare you!" She shrieked, surging past me.

"Jazzy. Let's not—"

"Don't you Jazzy me!" She snarled. Jabbing him in the chest. "How dare you! How dare you! You left me alone for twenty years to raise our daughter and then what? You decide to show up randomly when she's grown. How dare you!"

"Jazz, I didn't have a choice. I—"

"Don't give me excuses! You left, Xaevean." Her voice broke, the fiery rage quenched by heartbreak. "You left."

Ventris wrapped his arms around her as a sob rocked her. He kissed her forehead. "I know, Jazz, baby. I know. I didn't want to leave you and Shasha, but I was undercover and when we went through with the bust, the ringleader escaped. It was in your best interest that I disappeared. I didn't want him coming after you guys."

"You could have taken us with you. You could have told me. You could have—"

A roar of pure agony shook the ground beneath my feet. Sweat pricked my skin as my heart began to race. Mom turned to me with terror in her face, and I started running. My parents followed behind me as I charged into the tent to my mate.

Niratap was sprawled on the floor, his body covered with a thick sheen of sweat, and he was breathing heavily. His clawed hand was coated in blood. He glared across the tent at a man who was being restrained by Allipo and another agent, a pool of blood growing around him. There was shouting all around us. My mother screamed. I went to him, crouching by his head. His pupils were almost nonexistent. The muscles in his back were coiled, primed to strike, but his hand shook.

"What did you inject me with?" He rasped.

The man laughed. "You really thought you'd get out of this. The Bondbreaker will be no more."

Mitta and a tawny haired woman came into the tent as Nira snarled. "What did you inject me with?"

The tawny haired woman crouched next to Niratap. Her eyes went wide. "I need Narcan right now."

"Do you know what he was injected with?" I asked my free hand hovering over my knife.

She shifted, waving a hand in front of his face but didn't react. He was fighting for every breath. "Niratap? Can you hear me?"

"Something's wrong." He said. "Sotings ong."

"Shit." She looked at me. "He's been dosed with an opioid, help me roll him into his side."

"What?" I helped her roll him. "Why roll him on his side?"

"In case he starts to seize." She turned and shouted. "Where's my Narcan?"

"Nira." I said stroking the hair from his face. "It's okay. It's going to be okay."

The man laughed again. "I did my master right. I hope you die, beast."

"If Dravin wasn't already dead, I would kill him again."

The man chuckled; he was fading. Really looking at him for the first time, I saw that Niratap's claws had disemboweled him. "Cirano isn't my master. He has grander ideas than making money. I hope you are at home with the shadows that are coming for you and your mate, little girl."

Rage burned through me as I rounded on the man, grabbing him by the collar. I screamed. "Who do you work for?"

He laughed. "Endless night is coming."

A shudder went through the man and with a gasping breath. He died. Who was he talking about? I knew that enemies would be coming for him now. Knew that the target on his back had grown exponentially. Knew that he had always been and would always be in danger. I just had never thought that they would come for him so soon.

"Shasha." Mom's voice whispers behind me. "Shasha. He's gone."

I dropped the man. I wanted to shake him for answers. I wanted him to come back to life so I could kill him myself. I felt tears roll down my face, so angry that I was crying.

"Baby." She tried to pull me into her arms, but I avoided her advances.

"I'm fine."

"Honey, you just watched a man die; it's okay to be upset."

I rounded on her and I knew it was bad to take the fire in me out on her, but I was so angry. "Mother, I'm fine. I killed a man today, if anything I'm angry that he bled out without giving me answers. I'm angry I didn't get to kill him myself."

Her eyes went wide, and she took a step back. "I—"

"Niratap. Hey, I need you to answer." The girl said, snapping her fingers in his face. His body jerked stiffly, and I went to grab onto him. "No, just make sure he doesn't hit his head, we can cause more damage restraining him. Just talk to him consolingly and I'll time the seizure."

"Nira, it's going to be okay, *mo grá*." I murmured, cradling the back of his head.

"I have Narcan, Nikki." Dolan said, pushing through the tent flap.

"Give it here. Do you remember his weight from the last measure?"

"Two ninety."

I look at him shocked. "In two months? He lost that much in two months?"

Dolan frowned. "They weren't fed anything I'd call substantial. Do you need me to hold him down?"

"No." she said, snatching his tail. "Hold please."

Dolan took the tail in his hands as it spasmed. Nikki drew the medicine into the syringe.

"Pull it towards you, Dolan. Thank you." She brushed the fur back before she pushed the Narcan.

"Why there?"

She withdrew the needle and rubbed the spot in his tail. "There is a vein there that runs directly to his heart. The tail was just the easiest to restrain without causing him injury."

She checked her watch and frowned. "V. We're going to need a bus."

"I'll grab one." Ventris said, ducking out of the tent.

My mother's bleary eyes darted between us and after him. She was scared, for who I didn't know, and honestly I didn't really care. I looked at the tawny haired woman named Nikki as she measured my mate's pulse through the muscle spasms, which were starting to slow. I asked. "Who are you?"

She looked up at me when she was done counting and smiled tightly. "Agent Nikoloa Hammel, FBI inter-species science specialist. Nikki for short. I was undercover with Dolan working the science side of things. Researching mostly. I treated Niratap's wounds when I could."

I looked back at my mate, his body eerily still with an occasional twitch. She touched my hand gently. "He's going to be okay, dear. He's made of tough stuff."

"Bus will be here in five." Allipo said. He was covered in blood, though it only showed on his olive-toned skin, though his black tactical gear was shiny. He smiled tightly at me. "You ride with him. If he comes to, he'll panic without you."

"Backboard." Mitta called, dropping it behind him.

"Roll him gently." I said as they ease him onto the backboard and strapped him down. My heart fluttered. "Are the straps necessary?"

"It's so we don't drop him. It's okay." Mitta said gently. She rubbed my shoulders, and I realized I was shaking. "It's okay, Shasha."

Tears fell anew. This was scary. Scarier than the shadow wraiths, than the basilisk, than fae, than being kidnapped and held hostage, than going into the raid. After all this, I could lose him. After fawning and fucking and fighting and falling in love, I could lose him. A sob rocked me, and strong arms pulled me in tight.

"Shh, sweetbreeze. It's okay. It's going to be okay. He's going to be okay."

"Ventris."

"Stodden! In here." Ventris called and two paramedics came in.

"Where do you want us to take him?"

"Take him to St. Hubert's hospital. I have a physician there I trust. They already know you're coming." Allipo, Dheg, and Mitta helped lift Niratap onto the gurney and the paramedics rolled him out of the tent.

"I have to go with him." I cried.

"I know." Ventris pushed me back to look me in the eye. "He's in good hands. I have to tidy things up here. When I can, I will meet you there, okay? Stodden, he only goes with Dr. Kozran."

"Yes, sir."

"Okay." He gave me a tight, fatherly hug before he let me go to follow the paramedics. In the back of the bus, they had already started an IV and put an oxygen mask over his face.

"Are you okay?" One of the men asked me.

"Yeah." I looked down at myself, following his gaze. I was covered in blood. "It's not mine."

He gave a terse nod and turned back to Nira. "How long has he been unconscious?"

"Umm, about fifteen minutes." I answered.

"Eight of those minutes were spent in a seizure because of opioid overdose." The one Ventris had called by name, Stodden, said to his partner, a fine-featured blonde man.

"I'll push another dose of Narcan to see if that brings him around. Does he have any allergies?" The blonde asked, turning around. I caught a glimpse of pointed ears tucked under his hair.

"Not that I know of."

"What's his age?"

"One thousand one hundred thirty something."

"In human years?"

"Um, around thirtyish I think."

"How much does he weigh?"

"Dolan said two ninety. He's normally in the three-fifty, three-sixty range."

They nodded. "Pushing Narcan."

"What's going to happen when we get to the hospital?"

"They'll probably have you fill out paperwork. Medical history and whatnot. He's stable, but they'll probably take him back for some scans. CAT scan, MRI, blood tests."

The other paramedic rubbed his sternum vigorously for several moments with the knuckles of his fist. "No response to sternal rub."

"What does that mean?"

"He is just unconscious and unresponsive. His vitals are stable. It may mean nothing, given all the pain he's already endured. We'll leave it to the doctor."

Chapter Sixty-Two

Shasha

We pulled in and backed up to the bay. The doors opened and a gaggle of nurses stood ready. Stodden exited and met them.

"He's only to be seen by Dr. Kozran."

"We were told. Commander Ventris called ahead." An older nurse said, stepping forward, she bowed to me. "We were told the lord, and his mate were coming in and to put them in a private suite. Come now, we'll transfer him out here and get him to imaging. Dianna here will take the lady to his room to wait."

Stodden helped me out of the van, and I stepped to the side. "Patient is Lord Niratap Bondbreaker around one thousand one hundred thirty years old and weighs two ninety. Forcibly overdosed on an opioid of unknown origin which led to an eight-minute seizure and unconsciousness. Patient has been given two doses of Narcan and has remained unresponsive. His vitals are stable and he's breathing on his own."

"Thank you, we'll take him from here."

The nurses pulled him into a bed with surprising ease and rolled him into the hospital. A petite brunette smiled at me. "Come with me, and I'll take you to his room."

She led me through the hospital and into a large room without windows. "This will be his suite. There's a bathroom through that door and the couch is a pull out. Please make yourself comfortable while you wait."

"How long will they be doing tests?"

"It could be anywhere from thirty minutes to a couple hours. It will just depend on the images the doctor wants. Is there anything I can get you?"

"No. I'm alright."

Her warm smile faltered a bit. "Just press the call button if you need anything. I'm sure your families will be here soon."

She left, the door shutting in near silence. It was that silence that made my chest ache. Pulling my phone out of my pocket, I called the only person I could think who would listen, even though I had been so cruel to her not even thirty minutes ago. She answered at the second ring.

"Baby-girl?"

"Hey, mama."

"You at the hospital?"

"Yeah, they put me in his room while they take images and run tests."

"We'll be there soon. Your father is—"

"Please don't call him that."

"Shasha. He is your father."

"Have you guys even talked? Has he explained himself? Explained what he is?"

"No, we haven't had the opportunity. He's been giving orders and managing the press. I know we're both angry with him, but I never stopped loving him."

I sighed, pacing the length of the room. "Even without him saying a word? Even without him checking on us?"

She sighed. "I have loved your father from the moment I laid eyes on him. I could never hate him."

"Okay."

She was quiet for a moment. "If one day, Niratap left. No word, no explanation, just gone. Would you hate him?"

Tears welled into my eyes and rolled over my cheeks. I could never hate him. Never wish him ill. I choked. "No."

"Love does that my dear. Now I know we have a lot to talk about, but it can wait. We'll be there soon. I have a feeling that there is more that you want to tell me."

"Okay. I'm sorry, mama."

"For what?"

"For being so angry that I took it out on you. For being so caught up in everything that I didn't think."

"It's okay, baby girl."

"And I'm sorry that I didn't tell you."

"Tell me what baby?"

"About him being taken. For not telling you about the raid. About us being mates."

"We can talk about it later. We'll see you soon, okay?"

"Yeah. Okay. I love you, mama."

"I love you too, baby girl, and whether you want to believe it or not, I am proud of you." Someone spoke to her on her end. "Okay. I'll see you soon, baby."

"Okay."

The line disconnected and everything over the last eight months crashed over me in waves. I slid down the wall and curled my knees to my chest and let myself cry. Terrifying things had happened to me over and over again since I had left home. I had been kidnapped, sold to a monster, attacked by all manner of creatures and men. I had done what I had set out to do and expanded my understanding of the world. I had lived vigorously, found strength in myself, and above all else I had fallen in love. I had fallen in love with a monster who lived a dangerous life, where he stood mostly in shadow trying to pull others into the light. He was light in the shadows. Kindness in a cruel world. Hope when all else seemed to have been lost. Without him, I was lost. I hadn't realized it in the two months that he had been taken from me. I had been so focused on getting him back. So driven to get stronger and tougher and faster. Desperately reaching for him in our dreams. I hadn't realized how lost I had become.

The door to the room opened. How long had I been asleep? I heard her gasp before her hands cupped my cheeks and lifted my face.

"Baby-girl."

"Mama." I wrapped my arms around her, and she rubbed my back in soothing circles.

Behind her was Ventris and Allipo, both were in clean clothes and free of blood. Outside the small window, I saw Mitta talking to an over-sized man with ashen skin. Allipo bowed deeply at the waist, a department store bag in his hand. He smiled sadly.

"Milady. I took the liberty of collecting you some clothes that would be more comfortable for a hospital stay."

"Thank you."

"A pleasure."

"Where are the others?"

"Everyone else is set up at a hotel down the street. We figured you would want to be here the entire time, so we'll take turns checking on you two."

"Who is that talking with Mitta?"

"That is Dr. Kozran." Ventris says softly. "They're going over his medical history. You should go take a shower my dear."

"Where's Niratap?"

"They're still doing tests."

I frowned but took the bag from Allipo's hand and went into the bathroom. It was a simple bathroom with squat fixtures. I started the water and stripped out of my clothes. Allipo had gone above and beyond as he always did. The bag contained sweatpants with a matching flowy tank and hoodie, and my favorite brand of underwear. It also had my favorite body wash, toothpaste and lotion. Stepping under the spray I watched the dried blood melt off my body, and swirl around the drain. I let the water wash away the salt of anger and sorrow and fear and once I was clean and comfy, I went back out into the room to face what was ahead.

Like a moth to flame I was at his side, before anyone could say anything. I took his hand in mine, and he looked almost peaceful. The crinkle he got when irritated, situated at home between his brows. The monitors beeped in time with his heart, steady and even. His breath a soft whoosh of air. He was alive. He was stable. He was here. He was—

"Why is he still unconscious?" I asked, feeling the eyes of everyone in the room fall on me.

The doctor cleared his throat, opening the file in his hands. "To be honest, milady, I'm not sure why. His scans came back normal, imaging showed no signs of atrophy or damage, and other than being dehydrated and malnourished which is to be expected with his most recent experience, there is nothing clinically wrong with him."

"But if there's nothing wrong, why is he still unconscious?" My voice is firmer than I expected, holding authority that I had never thought myself to have.

"As I said, milady, I am not sure. It could just be his brain prioritizing healing. It could be a hibernative sleep, which is common in long-living beasts. I honestly can't give you an answer as to why he is still unconscious. We'll keep him on an IV and monitor him, but that is all I can offer you at the moment."

I frowned but looked back at his mostly peaceful face. I stroked his scarred and calloused hand as I spoke. "*Mo grá,* I need you to come back to me. I need you to wake up."

The doctor said a few more things to Allipo and Mitta: it sounded like finalizing guard rotations. My father, Ventris, volunteered for the first watch. They pressed that he had been up too many hours and needed to rest, but eventually relented. We needed to have our discussion. I looked at them and gave a small wave as Mitta and Allipo left. I knew they wanted me to rest and take a break, but I had already been away from my mate for too long.

Ventris cleared his throat. "I have to fully explain myself, and so do you, my dear."

I gave a nod. "Your wound is older."

He cocked his head but sighed, sitting down on the loveseat next to my mother. He took her hand and smiled sadly at her. "Okay. I haven't been honest with either of you. I am Xaevean Ventris Dion. I am an air elemental and I work for the Federal Bureau of Magical Investigation. When I met you, Jazzera I was undercover trying to infiltrate a faery dust smuggling ring. I had an old friend in Afton, my old partner Deacon from when I worked for the NYPD.”

“Xaevean, how old are you?” She asked, her brows crinkling.

“One hundred sixty-seven.” He said sheepishly. My mother huffed but didn’t say anything else. Ventris continued. “However, he introduced me to the girl who worked at the post office, said the perfect way to integrate into the community was to date a local girl everyone knew. He also hooked me up with a job.”

“So, I was just your cover?” My mother hissed and pulled her hands away.

He looked down at his hands. “At first. It wasn’t my intention to get attached, but after a few dates I knew you were the girl I wanted. I was never a purist like my father, but I knew there would be risks involved with just being with you. I couldn't stay away. I was using my real name and then that night we were up on the hill talking about our dreams. How you told me you wanted as many nights like that as you could get, and I agreed. I meant it. I want that. I still want that.”

He reached for her hand, and she pulled away. “You lied to me.”

“I did.” He said rising to pace. “I lied about what I was and where I was from and why I chose Afton, but when I asked you to marry me, that was real. When you told me you were pregnant with our baby, those tears of joy were real. Falling in love with both of you was real, Jazz.”

“Then why did you leave?” She almost whispered, I could see the tears beginning to flow in her eyes.

“I didn’t have much choice.” He said defeated. “When we executed the bust, the ringleader escaped. We didn’t know how or why because we had him dead to rights. He slipped through our fingers, and I left on the advice of my superiors at the time. That was to cut contact with my cover even if I had made them family."

"Why didn't you tell me? Why not take us with you?" She yelled.

"I was afraid." He shouted back.

"Stop." I hissed. "Or you can both leave."

They both murmured an apology and my father continued. "I was afraid. I didn't want to uproot you; I didn't want to scare you. I didn't want—fuck—I didn't want this to be convoluted or weird, but it is."

"Why didn't you ever call? Why didn't you come to celebrate your daughter's achievements?"

"I couldn't put attention on you, that is why I never called. But don't think for one minute I didn't hear about all the amazing things our girl did. Deacon forwarded me every Christmas card. Every report cards. Every milestone and achievement. I celebrated. I made it a point to be there when she graduated, because I needed to be there." He looked between us. "I wanted to be there, but I wanted you to be safe more."

"And now?"

"The ringleader is in the wind. Shasha is grown and is in very safe, capable hands. If you'd have me, I'd like to pick up with you, Jazz. I'd like to be a husband and father again if you girls will let me."

"Well, that explains your attitude problem." I said my attention going back to Niratap.

"Excuse me?" He asked.

"The way you acted at Samhain and over the video conferences to organize the raid. Both Niratap and I thought it was strange. I understand now because you weren't going to tell me who you were, but you don't approve of my choice in a partner."

"It's not that I don't think it's a good match." He said reclaiming his seat next to my mother. "It was the pretense that you were property that I didn't like. Even though he doted on you, it didn't feel right."

"It was for my safety at the time. I had only been training with Mitta for a month at that point, and regardless of them being Niratap's allies, he didn't trust the fae not to spirit me off."

"He still shouldn't treat you like property. The auction was a disaster after that. He brought you as a plaything and claimed you as more. That public defense marked you both."

"If it suited for both of our safety at Samhain or the auction, I would have let him fuck me on the table to stake his claim."

Both my parents bristled at my words. "Shasha, I didn't raise you to be a harlot."

I shrugged, caring very little. "I'm not a whore, but if a public display offered us both protection it would always be an option. Lucky for both of you, he doesn't like to share."

"Shasha Nicole Dion!" My mother shrilled.

"What?" I turn, giving her an indignant look. "I don't live in your bubble of the world anymore, mother. I'm mated to a monster who is a back-alley denizen. That alone is dangerous. Not to mention him being hunted constantly. I can't be soft or meek anymore."

"Both of you have tossed that term around. What does *mated* even mean?" She asked and my father eyed me.

"Between Thanksgiving and Yule, we mated."

"You had sex." She said indignantly.

"Yes, but we had already had sex at that point."

"A mate bond." My father said with his own indignant look. "Is a soul bond between two beings. It's a common practice in beastly creatures and some wild fae. It's deeper than being married. It's a 'til death kind of thing."

My mother paled as she looked at me. "Don't tell me that you—"

I nodded, my only confirmation.

"You bound yourself to that—that—"

"Think really hard about what you're about to say." I hissed standing square to her. "You shame him, swear at him, belittle him without him being conscious to defend himself. I will kick you out of this room, and you will not be allowed back in our life."

"Shasha." My father said softly. "Don't you think that is a tad harsh?"

"No. I don't. I have experienced more terrifying things in the last eight months than she has in her whole life. She wants to be this voice of reason that I can't accept. She wants to tell me my choices are flawed and dangerous and to be honest, I don't care. I have always wanted to live, and Nira has given me that. Has given me a choice."

"Except your freedom." He said coldly, glaring at Niratap's prone form.

"What are you even talking about?" I hissed ready to throw them both out.

"When Niratap purchased you, he bound you to him." My father spoke as if he understood everything. "A master and a slave. That magic still holds and I wonder why you weren't given a choice like everyone else who is with him. Loyalty and a sense of justice binds them, but you. He had to keep you locked to him. He didn't give you that choice. A fundamental choice he gives everyone."

My heart was beating erratically in my chest. "What are you trying to say?"

"I'm saying you were magically bound to him, it's not a far stretch that he magically had you bent into the position you find yourself."

"He would never." Flashes of that terrible fight stomped my racing heart.

"Yet you are still bound to him. Why?"

"For my protection."

"A whole lot of good that has done you. You were held hostage for bait."

"I had gone to the restroom alone. I had been drinking. I wasn't paying enough attention to my surroundings."

"But he could have protected you better." He said pointedly. My mother was ashen and just staring at me, still trying to comprehend the fact that I had bound myself to him so deeply.

"It's not fair of you to try to plant seeds of doubt in my heart when he can't explain himself. That's cruel."

"But you have wondered why, haven't you?"

I sat on the stool by the bed. I had wondered initially when I had been told that no one else was bound to him like I was, but he loved me. He worshiped my body, soul, and mind. Maybe in the beginning it was to keep me close, but even then, he said I could continue my schooling and talk to my mother. He hadn't cut me off. Hadn't secluded me like a slave, it was and always had been for my protection. Just as I was now considering asking him to bind himself to me for his own safety.

"You're wrong. Niratap has only kept me bound to him by magic for my protection. I bound myself to him with love. You can't twist our story to suit your late-blooming paternal need to be a protector."

"Shasha." My mother hissed, finally coming out of her shock.

"No. I said what I said. Now if we're done, I would like it if you left. Stand your guard outside if you must, but I'm done with this discussion."

"We are not done having this conversation." My mother seethed charging forward, yanking me from the stool. "You need to free yourself. You can't bind yourself to a monster. I won't allow it."

I pulled my arms from her. "I am an adult. I can make my own decisions and I will never sever the bond between Niratap and myself. Never. Now please leave."

"Shasha."

"Leave." My mother cast me a shocked glance. "Leave. I won't have you here attacking me and him. Just get out."

I heard my mother break down into her crocodile tears as Ventris eased her from the room. He said something as he left, but I was done listening to either of them. I laid my cheek against Niratap and stroked his hand softly.

"Would you please come back to me? I need you."

I awoke curled in soft blankets, a steady clicking coming from behind me. I shifted, my world coming back into focus as I scrubbed at my eyes. I was in Niratap's hospital room, the beeps of the monitors still a constant hum. I rolled over on the pull-out loveseat. Rogmesh sat in the soft chair, knitting.

"Good morning, lovely." She said, not looking up at me. She bobbed her head to a silver bell cover. "You should eat."

"When did you get here?" I said sitting up. Niratap was still in the bed, breathing evenly.

"A few hours ago. You passed out sitting on the stool. A nurse helped make up the bed and I moved you over. You didn't open an eye as I moved you either."

I uncovered the plate under the bell; steam rose and made my mouth water. Poached eggs, toast and a bowl of brown sugar oatmeal. "I didn't know that you knit."

"I don't get a lot of time to do it when I'm feeding the whole house." She smiled at me and held up the project she was working on, the bright yellow glistened in the light. "I like you in yellow, so I figured I would make you some comfort items."

I smiled softly, picking up my spoon. "Has there been any change?"

"The doctor was in about an hour ago." She looked back down at her project, picking up where she had left off. "He said that the lord had been dosed with tramadol and based on the dilution in his blood he had been given twice the lethal dose for his weight. The doctor expressed some concerns over the lord's liver and kidney function. He drew some blood to run more tests. Other than that, the lord has shown no change."

I frowned, spooning the oatmeal into my mouth. I was still angry that I hadn't been able to snuff the life from that man. I was angry that Dravin hadn't suffered, and my mate had. I ate, contemplating what we were going to do. With Niratap unconscious, everything was paused, except the upcoming deadlines. We only had a couple months to prepare before we had to travel to Babylos and deal with Katrel and Tummi's father. He sounded like a terrible man, a really terrible man like how my parents had tried to paint Niratap. I sighed at the empty bowl, taking a slice of toast as I looked toward Rogmesh.

"I'm surprised you're not fretting over your son."

"Oh, I've fretted plenty." She said, working through her stitches. "Silly child can't seem to pull his head out of his ass. He's going to get arthritis in both his shoulders when he's older. Stupid boy." Her voice didn't carry any malice.

"He survived and got Nessa safe. That's what mattered. He was brave."

She nodded, pausing in her stitch. "You were mighty brave too. Dravin could have killed you."

"I know." I said, grabbing another piece of toast. "I would do it again if I had to. He is always worth that risk."

She smiled at and opened her mouth to say something, but a grunt and a murmured "no" stopped us both. Nira had shifted in the bed slightly; his brows pinched his jaw tight. I shifted off the pull out and went to his side as a nurse came into the room.

"Is everything okay?" She asked as I hopped onto the bed and straddled my mate, cupping his face.

"It's fine. He's just having a nightmare, but he might wake up."

"I'll go grab the doctor." She rushed from the room.

"*Mo grá* I need you to open your eyes. It's just a dream, love."

"Leave her alone." He groaned through gritted teeth, arching underneath me. His body tremored.

597

"I'm right here, my love. I'm okay. I'm safe. I need you to wake up." I stroked his cheeks.

"No. No. No. No. No. No."

"Nira. Niratap. I need you to wake up." Nurses rushed in trying to pin down his arms and legs as he thrashed.

"Let me go." He hissed.

"No, let him go. You're only going to make it worse." I tried not to yell it.

"Get off me. Let me go." He snarled, thrashing.

"Stop it. You're just making him panic. Let go." I was growling the words at them.

His eyes opened, but they were unseeing.

"Watch out for his claws!" A nurse lost her hold, his clawed hand grasping my waist hard.

"Niratap. It's me." I swallowed my small fear of pain and leaned in, pressing my lips to his. "You're safe. It's me. I'm right here."

His hands slid up my back, claws scouring my skin, but his tremors eased. I watched as his eyes focused the silvery pools with their slit pupils met mine as clarity and awareness came back. He pulled me close to him and kissed me back deeply.

Chapter Sixty-Three

Niratap

I felt like I was floating through thick warm water, everything going in slow motion. I watched as Shasha screamed at the man who had stabbed me, watched her shake him and drop him as the light left his eyes, dying in her hands. The sounds vibrated the vision in pearlescent waves. I watch my own eyes roll back into my head and my body jerk on the floor. I was having a seizure. What had I been injected with? What was going on?

"Tá taithí gar do bháis agat, a leanbh."[46]

I turned to the voice and saw the soft face of my mother so much like Nessa's. *"Máthair?"*[47]

"Aye." She was bleary eyed but didn't reach for me. *"Gheobhaidh tú a roghnú cá háit a dtéann tú anois."*[48]

I frowned. *"Cad atá i gceist agat?"*[49]

My father appeared behind her. He was as stoic as I could remember. *"Beatha nó bás? leanúint ar aghaidh nó síocháin a aimsiú? Géilleadh don rud a tharla duit nó lean ort ag troid? Is leatsa an rogha."*[50]

"Síocháin?"[51]

"Aye. Is féidir leat teacht ag fánaíocht linn."[52]

"Fuaimeanna sin go deas."[53] Shasha called out. Ventris was holding her, he was her father, comforting her.

---

[46] "You are having a near death experience, my child."

[47] "Mother?"

[48] "You get to choose where you go now."

[49] "What do you mean?"

[50] "Life or Death? Continue on or find peace? Succumb to what has happened to you or keep fighting? The choice is yours."

[51] "Peace?"

[52] "You can come roam with us."

[53] "That sounds nice."

"Ní mór duit mo mhac a roghnú."[54]

I looked at my mate, her face pinched angrily and tears rolling down her face. My heart ached that I couldn't comfort her like Ventris tried. Like her mother tried. I couldn't leave her.

"Chomh deas leis sin ní féidir liom mo chara a fhágáil i mo dhiaidh. tá sí ag teastáil uaim agus tá sí de dhíth orm."[55]

They smiled and my mother dipped her chin in a graceful nod, and they began to fade. *"Nuair a bheidh tú réidh beimid ag fanacht."*[56]

I smiled. *"Is breá liom tú"*[57]

Darkness swallowed me, it was thick and warm. Suffocating shadows slithered over my body and into my mouth and nose. I was drowning but still able to breathe. I clawed at the muck thick darkness. Where was she? My light? My hope?

I heard voices talking about me, but I couldn't make them out. They were rushed and hushed, and I couldn't make out what they were saying. I was trapped in my own mind. I tumbled as the shadows shifted wildly. Am I moving? I cried out but the sound was swallowed by the shadows.

I used to find comfort in the dark, but now it was only holding me back, keeping me from all that I wanted and all that I loved. I reach for her beyond where I am stuck within myself. Shasha you are the salvation that I have been searching for my entire life. The safety from the deluge of terrible things that have crashed against me as the surf crashes constantly against the rocks. I needed her desperately. I knew that before this, but she was the guiding light.

[54] "You need to choose my son."

[55] "As nice as that sounds, I can't leave my mate. She needs me and I need her."

[56] "When you are ready, we'll be waiting."

[57] "I love you."

The shifting sea of shadows seemed to settle. The scent of all the seasons flooded my nose and I just wanted to curl into her, but my mind was trapped within my body, banging and thrashing against the wall between us. Voices slipped through the darkness and the steady beeping of machines.

"Why is he still unconscious?" Her voice pierced the swarm.

A male cleared his throat and there was a rustle of papers. "To be honest, milady, I'm not sure why. His scans came back normal, imaging showed no signs of atrophy or damage, and other than being dehydrated and malnourished, which is to be expected with his most recent experience there is nothing clinically wrong with him."

"But if there's nothing wrong, why is he still unconscious?" My mate near growled, stepping into her role that I had failed to tell her about. Something to rectify when I was free of this mental cage. My mate. Mine.

"As I said, milady, I am not sure. It could just be his brain prioritizing healing. It could be a hibernative sleep, which is common in long-living beasts. I honestly can't give you an answer as to why he is still unconscious. We'll keep him on an IV and monitor him, but that is all I can offer you at the moment."

I felt her hands stroke mine and so softly she pleaded. "*Mo grá,* I need you to come back to me. I need you to wake up."

Shasha. Mate. Mine. I screamed into the ether, but her light was yet to find its way into my darkness. I can't get to her. Trapped in a prison of my own making. Time doesn't exist here.

Her voice pulled me closer even though it is hostile. "Think really hard about what you're about to say. You shame him, swear at him, belittle him without him being conscious to defend himself, I will kick you out of this room and you will not be allowed back in our life."

"We are not done having this conversation." Her mother matches her tone. There's a scrape of chair legs and her constant warm hand leaves mine. Mate. "You need to free yourself. You can't bind yourself to a monster. I won't allow it."

This woman was so divided when it came to me and her daughter. Shasha must have enlightened her on the mate bond. She said adamantly, "I am an adult. I can make my own decisions and I will never sever the bond between Niratap and myself. Never. Now please leave."

"Shasha." She sounded wounded.

"Leave. Leave. I won't have you here attacking me and him. Just get out."

A sob, footsteps, a door opened, Ventris's voice cut through. "You need to think hard about what you are willing to risk being a belonging."

A click sounded and a gentle weight settled on my abdomen as she took my hand in hers again, stroked my hand softly. She murmured. "Would you please come back to me? I need you."

I clung to the sound of her breathing and the feel of her hand in mine. I can't wait to hold you again. As soon as I can sneak fully back into my body, I will hold you. Shasha. *Mo grá.* Mate. Mine. I clung to her scent in the dark place, as the shadows plunged me deeper into the sea of myself. Sleep is a possibility, but everything feels so foreign. The shadows eased as I relaxed into their embrace, the twisting controlling hold oozing into dark waters to float in.

I drifted. Floating over an ocean of shadows. Alone in darkness. How long would I stay stuck in this darkness, floating in this sea, trapped with my own thoughts? Would it only be a few hours or would I be stuck here for days, with only her scent and warmth to keep me sane. The door cracked open, and a woman tuts, her footsteps stopping beside the bed.

"Silly girl. You'll get so sore sleeping like that." Rogmesh.

"How is everything?" An unfamiliar female voice
asked.

"Its fine. That loveseat pulls out into a bed, right?"

"Yes."

"Would you help me get it set up for her. If she sleeps
like that, she will be in so much pain."

"Of course." Their voices fade away and the darkness
laps against me.

"Shasha, love, I'm going to move you now."

My heart seizes, as she sleepily says no. The monitors
beeps barely skipped a beat.

"Come child. You'll be hurting something fierce if
you keep this up." Shasha's weighted warmth lifted away,
and I reached for her in the shadows. A heavy calloused hand
meets mine in the dark.

"I know you can hear me, my friend. Our girl is safe,
so don't you fret one second. Rest and come back to us." She
pressed a motherly kiss to my brow. Rogmesh.

I sank beneath the surface of the black waters that
churned all around me. Succumbing to all that it had in store.

I sat up in our bed, in our room. Home.

"Shasha!" I hollered and only silence greeted me.

I stood, expecting my legs to fail me, but they held as
I began my search. She wasn't in our room or in her personal
suite or in the gym. Downstairs no one was there, not in any
of the common areas, the kitchen, my office, not a sound or
scent was anywhere.

"Shasha!" Mate. Mine. My heart started racing, but
cautiously I began the descent into the basement. If no one
was here, anything could be loose. Where was everyone?

Through the countless halls there was no one. The
beasts locked away in the menagerie. Shadow wraiths
whispered in their tomb. In the library she wasn't stashed
between the stacks, the door to the vault sat open and the seal
to the angel's resting space sat ajar. The vault was in order,

nothing out of place or missing, but why was Saabraa's cavern open? An eerie iron scented breeze rose from the bowels of the angel's cavern and my stomach dropped.

Down the earthen steps I traveled, my eyes adjusting quickly to the darkness, the scent of iron thickening with each step. I slipped at the bottom of the stairs, my hand sliding through a viscous slime on the wall. I willed a ball of pale light into the dark space. The wall and floor were covered in blood. It led down the hall and around them bend where Saabraa slept.

"No." I murmured into the cavernous space.

In Saabraa's space, feathers littered the ground between the bodies of my family. Bodies broken. Faces contorted in screams of agony and fear. Eyes cold and lifeless. I scrubbed my face roughly trying to erase the image.

"This can't be real. It can't be real."

"I mean it could be." A voice both of now and then that had haunted and hunted me crept from the cavern. The malice in the form of the Atton casually walked towards me. "Or maybe this is just a nightmare. Where is that pretty mate of yours?"

I rounded, fully pinning the monster to the wall. "Why?"

The cruelty in his smile sent shivers down my spine. "Now, now my prey I can't tell you that. It takes the fun out of the hunt."

"Why are you hunting me?" My claws gouged the earthen wall.

"My master wants you. That is all. I don't ask questions, I just serve those who have summoned me, but I know they have grand plans for you."

"Who are they?" I snarled through gritted teeth.

It shifted into Shasha's form and laughed her bright sunshine laugh. "I wonder what my master will think of all this? The Bondbreaker, almost his. So close yet so far away."

"What do you mean?"

"The longer days are coming. Harder to hunt without my shadows, but soon, Bondbreaker. Soon."

"Soon what, you cur?"

The creature laughed and blood poured from my mate's throat. "You'll see. But I will enjoy stealing your happiness until then. Slowly tainting everything you love, with darkness."

I brought my claws down over the form of my mate and the creature laughed, dissipating into smoke. "Now where oh where is that sweet little flower, blessed by all the seasons? Master is curious about her; I wonder what he'll do when he finally has her."

"Leave her alone!"

The creature laughed as it disappeared back to its master. "Enjoy your friends, Bondbreaker. Who knows when they will meet their end."

"Come back here." I roared slamming into a wall of earth that didn't belong, sealed inside a tomb. Slimy fingers wrapped around my wrist. I wretched my hand from the grip pressing against the wall.

"My Lord, why did you leave us?" Allipo's corpse asked, half the skin of his face hung limply. "Where were you?"

"Yes, where were you?" Tummilia's corpse said from where it crawled, leaving its legs behind.

"Stop it."

"You abandoned us." Bastion's corpse said from where it leaned, twisted and bent in all the wrong angles.

"I didn't. I—I—"

"You let us die." Rogmesh's corpse cried.

"No. No. No. no." I was trapped. The corpses grabbed at my clothes, trying to drag me down. "Let me go."

I screamed.

"No, let him go. You're only going to make it worse." Her voice pierced the darkness, but my eyes couldn't find her.

I arched up trying to wrench my limbs from the hands that held me down, corpses still clawing at me. "Get off me. Let me go."

"Stop it." She hissed. "You're just making him panic. Let go."

I thrashed again, the hands leaving my limbs. My eyes opened, but nothing was in focus.

"Watch out for his claws." Someone unfamiliar said and there was a sharp inhale.

A kiss was pressed against my lips, the scent of iron still clinging to my nose. "Niratap. It's me. You're safe."

"Shasha, you're bleeding." Rogmesh's voice says softly.

"I'm fine, I just need to wake him up." Hands cupped my face. "*Mo grá. Mo grá.* it's me, love. It's me."

Mate. Mine. I still couldn't see, but I could feel her, and I kissed her fiercely. I blinked, trying to clear my eyes and my voice ragged in my own ears. "Shasha."

"Yes. Yes, it's me. My love, it's me." Droplets of water fell onto my face.

"Shasha." Mate. Mine. Her teary earthen eyes finally came into focus. It was her floral blood that I smelled, my hands start shaking. "Shasha, I'm sorry."

She pressed a kiss to my brow, stroking my cheek with her thumbs. "Don't. A little blood doesn't bother me. You're awake now, and that is all that matters."

"Let me check him out real quick, let the nurse look at your wounds, milady." A male voice said behind her. I growled as Shasha slid gracefully from my lap.

"It's okay, *mo grá.* I'm okay. It's just a scratch. This is the doctor that's been taking care of you."

"I'm Dr. Kozran, I just want to look you over really quickly." The male gargoyle said, holding up his hands.

"Kozran?"

“So, you do remember me.”

“It’s been a few hundred years.” I said.

Kozran chuckled. “I never got to thank you for that either, so let me check you out. I’d recommend that you stay a couple days for observation.”

I chuffed as he shined a pen light in my eyes. “I think I’ll be fine.”

“Of that I have no doubt, but I’d rather be safe than sorry. I know you can take a beating, but you’ve been through some severe trauma, and you should let your body heal.”

“What even happened?”

“My understanding is,” he said pressing a stethoscope to my chest. “That someone outside of all the organizations snuck into your med-tent and injected you with a lethal dose of tramadol, an opioid, which caused you to have an extended seizure. Thankfully the medics that were there were able to give you large doses of Narcan to counteract the tramadol, and the drugs don’t seem to have caused any adverse effects to your liver or kidneys, which was one of my concerns. Your family filled me in on what they knew to have happened to you while you were captured, but I have a feeling that you have experienced more than what they’ve told me.”

“Aye. How is my sister?”

Kozran’s face didn’t change as he wrapped the stethoscope around his neck. “She's okay. Anemic and slowly regaining minerals she lost. If she’s anything like you, she’ll probably want to charge up here soon to visit. Though I would also like her to rest.”

I smiled. “The lass is worse than me. There was a reason she was born first.”

Shasha’s worried face broke a little letting a smile creep to her lips, but I saw the hard-edge determination. Her voice was firm as she spoke. “I want you to listen to him.”

“Shasha—”

"No. I want you to listen." Her voice broke on a sob. I saw a group of our family hovering at the door pausing to listen. Everything quickly was lost, and it was just the two of us facing off. "I lost you. You gave yourself up in my stead and I lost you. You were still in my heart, warm and whole, but I lost you. Then I felt you die. Not once Niratap, but twice. Knowing that you were so close yet so far and I could do nothing. Everyone was trying to protect me, telling me to stay away, telling me to do nothing. You told me to stay away, but I couldn't. You told me to do nothing, and I couldn't. I felt you die. I felt. You. Die."

Tears began to roll down her face and my heart cracked at her sorrow. Thoughts of her had kept me mostly whole in those dark places I had been. She had been so resolute and determined and angry in the dream space. that it hadn't occurred to me that she had broken like I had so long ago. After Deirdre had died because I had been young and scared and stupid. Fuck.

"*Mo grá.*" I started as her mother wrapped her arms around her as she cried. The viper shot me a glare, and vaguely I recalled them arguing about me while I had been unconscious. "I would raze the entire world to the ground for you. I would break any law of the land, the earth, and my own to get you back. I was frantic when you had been taken from me and if that filthy scum hadn't had his hand around your throat and a knife in your back, I would have slaughtered them all right then and there. I didn't go uninformed into Dravin's hands. I know what that kind of slavery is like, I have lived it many times. I have been a pawn, a weapon, entertainment, a punching bag. I have experienced those things repeatedly in my long life and do not think that for one moment I wouldn't do it all over again for you. I would sacrifice everything that I am for you and your freedom."

Tearily, she stared at me, pulling from her mother's vice grip. She came back to my bedside with fire burning in her eyes. "No."

I held her gaze, met her fire with my own. "Yes."

"No. I cannot have you do that."

"You are my everything." I said with all the softness in my heart. "I would give anything I have and everything I am for you." I reached for her hand. She pulled it away. That rejection stung, but I pressed forward, needing all who were present to hear this deepest of declarations for her. "You are my mate. Mine. Mine Shasha and I am yours. I give you anything and everything I am. My heart. My soul. My body. My anything is at your disposal to use, to love, to hate if it comes to that. I would not stop to keep you safe. It is a promise, an oath to the depths of myself."

She swiped the tears from her eyes with the back of her hand, her eyes hard with determination and will. "I would do the same for you. I would go to any end to keep you from harm. Your life has been hard enough, dangerous enough, cruel enough, to warrant you to rest. I was beside myself with fear and sorrow and hopelessness, but there was also this burning rage that you were suffering again, and it was my fault. That after everything you have been through and everything that you have done the universe decided to kick you down, using me to do it. If I had been paying attention—"

"Don't." I said with all the hardness I could muster. "Don't blame yourself for what happened."

"But if I hadn't—"

"No."

Tears anew flowed as she grasped my hand. "But—"

"You are not at fault. I don't care about how you think you were too drunk or how you think you went into the bathroom without someone or how you think you wasted time trying to get answers. You were attacked, held hostage, and used as bait, because I painted a target on both of our backs with my carelessness."

"No, Nira—"

I took a shuddering breath as my heart started to race, the monitor beeping rapidly. "If I had followed the rules, you wouldn't have been in danger. If I had shook that fucker's hand that night, he wouldn't have felt slighted. If I hadn't fought with you because I wanted to teach you a lesson, I wouldn't have been injured, which made me visibly weak to our enemies. If I hadn't defended you at the auction, Dravin wouldn't have known that you meant everything to me. And lastly if I had gone with you, waited in the hall for you, that fucking ogre wouldn't have slunk in and taken you from me. I am to blame, I'm too old to be as reckless and brash as I have been for the past eight months, but you bring out a coltishness in me that I didn't have the opportunity as a young male to have. You make me want things I haven't envisioned for myself in over a millennia."

Her gaze softened. "Like what?"

I swallowed. "I want to live peacefully. I want you heavy with my babe growing in you. I want to live with you, for as long as time will let us."

She kissed my knuckles. "I like the sound of that, but after."

"After?" I queried, as our family moved into the room.

"After we deal with things. After Raloqen. After the malice. After we bring down the market."

"That is an ambitious after." I said, smiling at her.

"I want us to live peacefully as long as time will let us. I want to have your babe growing inside of me." She said the words so tenderly, placing a hand to her belly. "I want them to grow up not being afraid that they could lose one of us because of who and what we are. That's not the life I want my children to live. I don't want them to be afraid."

"I like that."

"No." Her mother growled.

"Jazz. Let them be." Ventris gripped her wrist, holding her back.

"No, he can't have our daughter." She hissed. "He can't father children with her."

"Jazz that's not for us to decide."

She pulled from his grasp and charged at us. Shasha swung around, bracing against her mother. "Stop."

"Break it. Whatever hold you have on my daughter, you break it."

I swallowed. "That is not possible."

Her voice went shrill in my ears. "What do you mean it's not possible? She is not a possession."

"We are bound to one another beyond the laws of the earth."

Ventris rested his hands on her shoulders. "Their souls are intertwined."

I nodded, looking at my mate. "I vowed, gave her my body, my soul, my life."

"I did the same." She looked at me lovingly as the fight seemed to disintegrate from her mother. She smiled and spoke our vows aloud to our family. "I vow to love you. To cherish you. To honor you. I offer myself to you, soul and all. I will be your shoulder to lean on in times of need. Your home to return to when you are away. You are my home."

I bowed my head but held my mate's gaze. Mate. Mine. "I vow to love you, honor you, cherish you, protect you. I give myself to you completely on bended knee and with bowed head. You are the master of my heart. My safety. My life. My home."

She abandoned her mother, cupping my cheeks and pulling my face up to crash against hers. "Mate. Mine."

My chest ached with a flutter. "Mine."

Chapter Sixty-Four

Shasha

I had missed him. Having him in my hands, having him whole overrode anything else. I didn't care that my mother was there gawking at us. I didn't care that Rogmesh ushered the rest of the family out of the room, tutting away. I didn't care about anything, but him. His rough hand wrapped around the back of my neck and held me to him, deepening the kiss. Mine. He was mine.

The doctor cleared his throat. "I know you will make a full recovery with proper care. So, rest for now, my friend."

Nira rested his brow against mine. "Thank you, Kozran and at the behest of my heart, I will stay and let you care for me."

"As you wish. I will leave you in the care of your mate for now. I will check back this evening."

"Thank you, doctor." I said, trying to look at him, but a possessive rumble kept me from moving. "Thank you."

"Anything, milady. Call if you have a need."

"Will do." Ventris said dismissing the doctor, from where he guided my mother to sit on the pull out.

"Not going to leave us in peace, V?"

"No. My wife and I have questions." She had forgiven him that fast then.

Niratap eased his hold on my neck, but his body was coiling with a different kind of tension. I settled next to him as he adjusted the pillows behind him. His arm curled protectively around me. "What are your questions?"

Ventris eyed my mother who took a deep breath. Her hand went to her throat as she met his gaze. "How did that happen?"

Nira straightened his free hand resting over the stark burn scar across his own throat. His eyes going a bit hazy. "Ventris doesn't even know the whole story there."

I interlaced my fingers with the hand at my hip giving him a squeeze. His gaze focusing on me. "It's your choice."

"Do you think it will help?"

I looked at my mother, who leaned into Ventris for support, her hand resting on her throat and her owlish eyes watching us. "I don't know."

She frowned, but it was Ventris who spoke. "I know a lot about your past. We have discussed the things I know, the roles you took in the market, how we met."

He looked at my mother. "Would knowing my story help you? My full story? We only shared what had happened since your daughter came into my care."

"I don't know." She mirrored my response, holding Nira's gaze. "At the very least it might help make my decisions on the two of you."

I frowned, but Nira nodded. "Very well. I was born in what is now known as—"

And thus, his story was told again. The loss of his family. Separation from Nessa. Deirdre the first woman he had ever loved and how she was taken from him. His imprisonment and abuse. The dark night that gave him his moniker. His fight for freedom and survival and the freedom of others. Then he told them about us, about the auction that started this.

Ventris interrupted. "Why is she still bound to you magically? Why was she not given the choice that you give everyone else?"

If the question bothered him, Nira didn't react. "Initially it was solely to keep her close. My instincts overrode my reason and only wanted to keep the source of that mesmerizing scent close to me. I wanted to understand why it had such a pull over me. It shifted at some point to being just to keep her safe."

"When did that shift?" My mother asked, her face streaked with tears.

He pondered looking down at me. "Before Samhain, but the exact moment I'm not entirely sure. It could have been when she brandished a branch against Murdoch, the basilisk that attacked me, or when she cradled my burning body in the cold shower as the venom wreaked havoc, or when she demanded to clarify what we were, but at Samhain I knew I needed her to be safe, regardless of what we were to each other."

"Do you love her?" Ventris asked.

Nira chuffed looking down at me. "What I feel for your daughter is deeper than I can explain and loving her is only a small part of it. I want her to succeed in everything she does. I want her to chase whatever dreams she has. I want her sunshine laughter to light the night sky like fireworks. I want her to be happy, regardless of my role in that. If she decided tomorrow that she no longer wanted me, it would break me, but I would let her go wherever her heart decided to go."

"Break you?" My mother asked.

He looked up to her slowly. "She is my everything. My heart. My soul. The air in my lungs and the blood in my veins. What I feel for her is all consuming and losing it, losing her, would kill me."

Mate. Mine. I leaned into him. "That isn't going to happen. I feel the same way about you. You are my everything."

"What happened when you were captured? Shasha said she felt you die?" My mother asked and I felt Nira tense again.

He sighed. "The first time I lost my temper when I was at a disadvantage and paid for it. The second time Dravin was trying to break me."

"What do you mean, by disadvantage?" Ventris pressed.

"Dravin had us fitted with remote collars that injected a synthetic venom. The ogre was watching me, and he kept prattling on about all the things he would like to do to Shasha. The possessive male part of me saw red. The collar sent that acid into my veins and when I blacked out, he beat me with a pipe. The combination of those two things caused my heart to stop."

"The second time?" I asked.

"Dravin was trying to break me."

I narrowed my gaze. "How?"

"He restrained me and had me held below water until I ran out of air. Repeatedly. I went hypoxic and blacked out. I assume that repeatedly being drowned like that can cause your heart to stop."

"Hypoxia does that." Ventris said.

Anger boiled in my blood. How dare he die so easily, but my mate had been at risk. "If that monster wasn't already dead, I would hunt him down and kill him again. Make him suffer."

"Shasha, you don't mean that." My mother said sharply.

"Oh no, I do. I would torture and kill him slowly. For all that I experienced and for everything my mate suffered." Nira gave me a squeeze, his gaze sad and tired. "You should rest."

He pressed a kiss to my forehead. "I'm alright, my dear."

"I should feed you." I said, he was my sole focus. "You probably haven't had a proper meal in a long while."

"Not since we went dancing." He said. I felt the ache in my chest as he brought his palm to my cheek. "It's not your fault."

"It feels like it is."

"You are not responsible for the cruelty of others." He stroked my cheek. "Don't take on that kind of burden."

"Nira." Tears welled in my eyes.

"He's right, sweetbreeze." My father said standing. "You are not responsible for what others do, only how you react. With that, I would like to apologize to both of you for how I reacted. I was out of line. I'm sorry."

"You are forgiven, V. I'm glad the mystery has been solved," Nira said, easing back against the pillows with a groan. He waved off my fretting. "I am alright."

"I'll run down and grab some food. There's an Italian place up the street. They have pretty good stuff." Ventris offered.

"Carbonara sounds fantastic," Nira said as I tugged the blanket over his waist. "Stop love, I'm alright."

"No. I'll never stop because you are mine and I love you." I smiled at him.

"What would you like, darling?" He asked Mom.

"Oh, just spaghetti. I'm easy."

"Shasha?"

"Chicken Alfredo."

"Alright, I'll be back soon. Be kind to one another."

I frowned at him as he walked out the door. I clung to Niratap's side, and my mother chewed on her nail deep in thought.

"Are you going to scream at us some more?" I asked not looking at her. Niratap's eyes narrowed.

My mother cleared her throat. "No. I'm trying to digest a thousand years of history. I'm trying to come to terms with what my church and by the sounds of it most churches have done in the false name of my god. I think I can come to terms with you two being mates easier than rethinking my views on the world."

I turned to her then. "You mean?"

She lowered the hand she had been favoring for her thoughts. "I still have to ponder over the age difference. That is still bothering me, but I can see now that there is something very deep between the two of you. I can see that even after all the hardship of your life, Niratap, you can still love deeply with your soul. Not many beings can do that."

"I appreciate the compliment. I love your daughter and don't wish her harm."

"I know."

"Then why have you been so mean when it came to him?" I said, staring at her as Nira collected my hand in his and kissed it.

"I didn't know any better. I had been raised that way. Watch out for other species. The fae will steal your children and eat them. That was the world I grew up in."

"Hate was the go-to for many years, *mo grá*. I can't fault her for her upbringing. It is something she has to grow past." Niratap spoke softly into my knuckles. "Kindness is always the hardest option. Kindness when all you know is hate is impossible sometimes."

"It shouldn't be. You are a good man."

"I am, but my species was hunted down for a reason. In the wild times bitarogs were predators. They competed with Basilisks and hydras for food and sometimes that food ended up being humans. Fear and misunderstanding killed my kind and fueled the entrapment and slavery by those in power."

"Until that night," My mother started, "you never killed or hunted humans."

"No. I was very young when I lost my parents, but we were very isolated in those mountains. It wasn't until they started expanding into our territory and mining the mountains that we interacted at all. My father was more afraid of humans and my mother was kind to a fault. She was more than likely killed because of fear, not because she had done anything to warrant it."

My mother nodded. "I will come to terms with it all. I know that. I can see that nothing I say or do will wedge between you two."

"Never." I said and she just nodded again.

"Do you mind if I nap while we wait for your father? I haven't gotten a good amount a sleep the last few days."

"Go ahead." Nira said.

She curled up on the pullout and was asleep in a moment. My heart hurt for her. She must have been frantic about the raid and then our fights the last couple of days must have taken their toll. Niratap shifted over and pulled me up into the bed next to him. I chuckled as he tucked me close to him. No words were needed. Home. We were home with one another. Nothing would keep us apart and whatever tried, hell hath no fury. My father returned after a little bit with hot food. Nira was grateful for the act of kindness and devoured his food and then what was left of mine when I was stuffed. My parents left soon after, my father saying he was going to take my mother home to Afton, but they would be in touch soon. Mom wanted to see where I was living and Niratap agreed it could be arranged soon. He pulled me against him as we settled in for the night.

"You were very brave." I whispered into his chest.

"What do you mean?"

"I know your story isn't one that is easy to tell. Your struggles and loss."

He shifted pressing me closer. "With you I feel like I can do anything."

"That feeling is mutual." I laughed and we settled into a heavy silence.

"This all feels like a dream." He whispered.

"I promise you. This is real. I'm real."

He pressed a kiss to the top of my head as we fell asleep, but he held me tighter to him like I might disappear, and he would be back in a dark cell alone. Time would be the only thing that would ease those fears. The only thing that may heal that wound.

A week later.

We were home and I needed him in more ways than I wanted to ask. The ride home was filled with lust, but the confined space of the car was even smaller with the Days sharing the space. Instead of diving headfirst into me, he dove headlong into work, saying he needed to settle things and shift people around, and left me to my own devices. I meandered by the kitchens where the Days fretted over their son who kept trying to lift heavy things to help. Through the gardens where Echo dug beds for spring readying to plant our food and was watching over Nessa who was recovering but had a sun-kissed glow about her. I was home but my body felt off. In the stables Dheg was brushing Guinness, who whinnied gleefully at the sight of me.

"Hello, my friend." I said petting his nose. "Good morning, Dheg. You jumped back into work quickly."

"Everyone has. We feel weird if the lord is and we're not milady."

"What should I do?" I asked. "I haven't been charged with a task or had any fulfilling skills beyond stubbornness."

Dheg cocked an eyebrow. "Milady you are much more than stubborn. You are kind. You are gracious. You are fierce. Loyal."

I rolled my eyes. "Dheg those are just aspects of my personality. They're not skills."

"But they are. You are gracious and willing to help anyone. You are kind even when most of the beings you have met have wanted to eat or fuck you, and the ferocity at which you defend those you love astounds me, for someone so young. All of those are skills."

I didn't agree, but I didn't want to argue semantics. "Do you think I could take Guinness for a ride?"

Dheg gave a knowing look but didn't comment. "I'll saddle him up for you, milady."

"Thank you." I said scratching Guinness behind the ears. "We're going to our favorite place."

"When the lord comes searching for you, what shall I tell him?" Dheg asked with a grunt, throwing the saddle over Guinness's back.

"Tell him I went for a ride." I said as I slid the bridle over his nose. Securing it place behind his ears. "Tell him I went to find peace."

I hefted myself onto Guinness's broad back. Dheg twisted his hands nervously. "Be careful, milady. It's springtime and things are starting to wake out there."

"I'll be fine, Dheg. I have my knife and my pistol."

Guinness took me from the barn, ready to ride. "Just be careful. The lord would be upset if you were hurt."

"I will be. Let's go, Guinness."

Dheg and the manor faded as we rode through the pastures and forest trails. Spring alive with wildflowers coming back and growing between the small piles of snow. My heart sang when the meadow comes into view. Crocuses, jack-in-the-pulpits, wild geraniums and many other flowers I didn't recognize bloomed across the expanse of tall, swaying soft grasses. I could understand what Nira meant about the spring as the early bird twittered overhead. Home. Peace.

I dismounted and found a soft place to lay and listened to nature's orchestra of insects. I wondered if when night fell there were lightning bugs. I wondered if in the blistering heat of summer, cicadas would sing with the crickets and bullfrogs happily. I wondered how beautiful the stars would be here with him next to me. It occurred to me then that we wouldn't be here for the summer.

We had discussed in depth when we would leave for Babylos and mid-May was the best option. We would go, together, much to each other's objections. I wanted him to recover, he wanted me to be nowhere near Cardoc. Not going wasn't an option, so both of us would go. Katrel and Tummi would go face their father and fight for Katrel's freedom. Mitta and Bastion would come as extra muscle if it was needed. Katrel didn't want anyone to be put at risk but understood there was no other option if she wasn't folding to her father. Katrel and Tummi were scared of the man that fathered them. What kind of long-lived male had such an archaic focus? What kind of father could be so terrible to his children?

A wet nose pressed to my cheek, startling me awake. When had I fallen asleep? Nira shifted laying down beside me in the soft grass. "I thought I'd find you here."

"I figured it was pretty obvious, when I said I was going to find some peace."

He smiled, reaching out to stroke my cheek. "It was trusting of you to fall asleep in the meadow. Even this place of peace sees plenty of the roaming beast and fae."

"It wasn't my intention." I said rolling to face him. "I was lost in thought and fell asleep. Guinness was keeping an eye on me."

Guinness knickered from where he was grazing and Niratap smiled warmly. "Be that as it may, please try to refrain from casually dozing away from the manor."

"Noted. I missed you." I said cupping his face.

"I missed you, too."

"Are you done with work for the day?"

"I have things in motion, both in the aftermath of the raid and to prepare for while we're gone, though I don't want to extend our visit to Babylos longer than we have to."

"Why is that? Is their father really that terrible?"

He sighed, rolling onto his back. "Cardoc Raloqen is an old-fashioned brute, however he has made great strides in protecting his people that I can respect. His treatment of his daughters is abhorrent and if I hadn't seen it first-hand, I wouldn't have believed it."

"What do you mean?"

He looked at me sideways. "After we had healed from that night, I went with them back to the elf kingdom. Their mother greeted them and told them they needed to leave. That if their father saw them or me that he would kill them; dead children were better than a whore and a traitor."

I frowned and rolled back over, watching the clouds coast through the sky. "That's deplorable."

"Aye. Cisceri is good and kind, but she didn't have a choice in marrying Cardoc. She just wanted both of her daughters to live long, full lives. Cardoc knew, of course. He attacked us as we were leaving. Fired an arrow through my shoulder, the basilisk scar has covered that one. He was aiming to kill."

I glowered at the clouds. "Then I hate him, and he will feel my wrath."

He chuckled, rolling on top of me. His beautiful face blocking out the clouds. "I love that fire in you."

I smiled at him, reaching up to stroke his cheek. "Good. You're stuck with me now."

"I wouldn't have it any other way."

I traced down his neck and chest. "I mean, I would."

Ever so slightly his gaze shifted, from loving to predatory. I parted my legs for him and delighted in watching his nostrils flare. His voice was guttural. "Right here?"

"Right now."

He pressed a starved kiss against me, and I matched him stroke for stroke, my arms wrapped around his neck as he shifted between my legs, bracing his weight on his elbows, burying his hands into my hair. My leggings acted as a barrier from him taking me like I wanted. I moaned into his mouth, rocking my hips against his.

He hissed. "Mate. I want you."

"Please." I whimpered.

His hands traveled over my shoulders, his touch feather-light, his eyes burned with a passionate heat. "*Mo grá,* I have thought many times about how I wished to take you here in my meadow." He tore the shirt, exposing my breasts to him and the sky, his graze devouring the panes of my skin. "I want to be consumed in my love for you. I want to make love to you. I want to fuck you. I want to rut you until we are both comatose."

My heart was thudding erratically. His appraisal of my flesh caused me to shiver in the warm spring air. "I want that."

He growled but his hands continued in slow fashion down my body. His fingers hooked into the waist of my leggings and panties. He kissed the soft swell of my stomach and palmed my ample hips before he slid the garments away, freeing my legs. Hunger glowed bright in his eyes. "You smell like paradise. May I taste you?"

I arched as his breath danced over my heated flesh, eliciting a moan from me. Breathlessly I cry out. "Yes."

Fur sprinkles down his spine and his tail swished as he descended upon me. His tongue lapped at my core in luscious strokes, before he sucked that sensitive bundle of nerves between his teeth. I arched against him, staring down my torso and meeting his silver eyes as he plunged his tongue into me. I cried out as his arms wrapped around my thighs holding me to him, as a growl grew, vibrating through my body.

"My sweet little snack." His breath cool against my raging core. "I love how you taste weeping over my tongue."

I'm curious. "How do I taste?"

His tongue flicked over my clit, pulling a groan from my throat. "Like home."

I reached out, grasping his antler. "Nira. Please stop teasing me."

He smiled wolfishly. "I've only started my dear."

He crawled up my body, capturing my lips in a searing kiss. His whiskey-tinged mouth was coated with a honeyed floral musk. He pulled back, staring deeply into my eyes, asking. He was always asking. I pulled him back into a kiss, my tongue sweeping over his canines. He bit down on my lip, sending rabid shivers down my spine. He rubbed his member against my core spreading the slickness over both of us. He panted as he eases himself inside me.

"Nira."

He groaned as he seated himself, nesting his head in the crook of my neck. "Shasha."

I rocked my hips against him, his breathy gasp warm against my pulse. "I missed you."

"I missed you, mate." He kissed my pulse, his body retreating from mine, causing me to cry. "You are my home."

"Please." I writhed beneath him. "Please."

"Patience, *mo grá*." He slams into me as his teeth grazed my pulse, ecstasy ripping from my throat. "I plan on enjoying you. Fully."

"Mate."

He sat back, clawed fingers gliding across my ribs. His eyes bore down my body with heat that fueled the lust in me. He rocked ever so slightly. "Look at us, mate. You fit me so well. Your sweet body is ready to take all of me. Willing to stretch to accommodate me."

I look down as he withdrew and sank back into me to the hilt, my flesh goosing at his appraisal. His tail swished with excitement, before he dragged it over the swell of my breast, the velvet soft fur tickled my nipple, pulling a gasp from me. I arched my back from the ground and Nira wrapped an arm around me, pulling me up to his face.

"I wish to claim you."

I panted deliriously already lost in him. "Claim me."

His brows raised and that lupine grin graced his lips, exposing his canines. "I wish to taste you."

I let my head fall to the side exposing my neck. "Taste me."

His lids fluttered and his heated gaze caused a spasm through my body. His grip tightened on me. "I wish to drown in you."

"Drown."

Then we were lost. He leaned into the soft juncture of my neck, his fangs finding their marked home. The pain turned pleasure rocked my body into a tailspin. Tipping me over the edge. He pressed my body to his as he thrusts into me at a languid pace. Riding the waves of that orgasm.

He pulled himself free and spun me, planting my hands and knees on the ground. Euphoria and glee tightened my core and the heat for him returned, at the sight of the bright glossy droplets of my blood on the soft meadow grass. He folded over me, his long beastly tongue cleaning the wound, sealing it with magic.

"Mine." His voice took on that carnal sound. His middle shape. A shape of nightmares that enveloped me. His fur tickled along my spine as he rubs his massive, ridged length between my legs. "Beg for me."

I whimpered, as I rock back against him, the friction lighting fireworks through my body. "Please mate. Mark me in all your wildness."

"You want me, feral and wild."

"Yes, mate." I was at his mercy. "Fuck me in this shape. Hurt me if you must."

I sense the predatory tilt of his head, before he wrapped his arm around my waist lifting my hips to his jowls. His bottom teeth grazed my belly, and his long canines press into the top of my ass. His tongue violated me, in sweeps and penetrations, pulling an illicit cry from me as he worked me over the edge again. I squirmed in his hold, his sharp teeth cutting into me, the pain twisting hot pleasure through my body.

He eased my quivering body back to the ground before he inserted the massive length of himself in me. I felt so full of him, my body and his becoming one. His clawed hands dug into the ground beside my head. He growled as I rocked against him.

"Careful, little flower, I don't want to lose control just yet."

I peered at him through my lashes, the sight made my heart skitter. Taking in his elongated lanky body, a body made to kill. The skin pulled tight over his muscles and bones cause deep shadows to contrast with the barely restrained need in his bright eyes. Those eyes were the only things that anchored me to my mate in this form, as he panted between exposed jaw bones filled with jagged canid teeth. Of all his forms this one scared me the most.

I grasped his wrist. "I want to taste you."

Those eyes widen as he lowered his maw of teeth between my face as his arm. Fear lightings through me as he dragged his tongue over my arm causing me to pull it back. "You wish to taste me, mate?"

My heart hammered against my rib cage; I managed a nod. A predatory sound reverberated through the meadow as he sliced his wrist for me with those savage fangs. He braced on his elbows, pulling the cut wrist to my mouth.

"Then taste me while I fuck you, mate."

My lips folded over the cut, his thick blood coating my tongue like maple syrup. First tasting of iron then his essence seeped over my senses wild rain, primordial forests and the sharp bite of aged whiskey and tobacco. He growled as I sank my teeth into his open skin savoring the taste of him. He hooked his other arm under my waist and pulled me up deepening his thrusts. The combination of him filling me with his body and his blood was too much. I plummeted over the edge of pleasure again. I released him in a shrill cry that echoed across our meadow. He panted as he withdrew from my body and flipped me to face him, his eyes glowing with restraint. He runs his tongue over my small cuts, soothing small hurts before it drifts to my breasts and causes me to arch into him.

"Your body is so willing for me, my mate." He panted over me as his jaws wrapped around my neck. The spike of adrenaline made me whimper. "May I continue?"

"Yes." A breathless whisper from my tongue.

He rolled me back onto my belly. His tongue trailing over my spine. He pulled my ass into the air, his claws pricking my skin deliciously. "Keep this ass in the air, mate. I don't have much control left and I don't want to hurt you."

I planted my feet and look back at the beast who was mine. "I don't care. Pain from you is pleasure. It pushes me past my limits and the ecstasy I experience is out of this world."

He purred pushing back inside me. "Very well, mate. I will not be gentle."

I braced myself as he shifted, growing larger inside me, stretching me. His clawed talons landed over my hands and a thrilled jolts through my body. He pressed his muzzle against my shoulder as he pushed deeper inside me. My legs shook at the intrusion and even though he said he wasn't going to be gentle, his pauses to let me adjust to him, fully seated inside me as a beast.

"Nira. Mate. *Mo grá.*" The words tumbled from my lips breathlessly like a prayer.

He retreated and thrust, slowly at first as if he was testing how willing my body was to take him. The tempo built, the force knocking me forward. He wrapped a taloned forelimb around my waist to hold me back, his talons pricking my skin lightly, goosebumps erupting across my skin. He growled as I reach between my legs to tease that bundle of nerves, both of us so close. I wanted to be so full of him that the universe could not tell where I ended, and he began.

"Nira." I pleaded as I took a nosedive into another orgasm. "I need you to come. I need you to fill me with you so completely that we can never be apart. Please. Mate. Mine."

He roared my words pushing him off the edge behind me. I was giddy with the dizzying satisfaction that he finished, when I had asked him to. His copious seed leaking down my legs, tinged pink with blood. The sight should have appalled me, but I felt satiated.

He panted in my ear, his fur tickling my cheek. He eased us to the ground to let us settle into one another. My body spasming around him all knotted up inside me, the pressure was amazingly pleasurable. Beneath him I felt safe, protected, and loved. Whole and home.

I didn't know how long we laid there in the meadow grass lost in each other, but when his body relaxed and he shifted back into the man, sliding himself from me in a slurp, the full feeling didn't leave. He rolled me into his chest, and he kissed me sweetly.

"Mine." I murmured into his chest.

"What?" His voice was ragged and spent.

"You are mine."

"Yes. Forever, mate."

"And I am yours forever." I traced my fingers over his many scars.

"Yes." He said softly.

"Welcome home."

"It is good to be home."

Epilogue

Jazzera

April 30th

I was nervous. This whole drive I'd been nervous. Xaevean kept reassuring me that nothing bad was going to happen to me, but I was unsure. I let him drive us because I would have probably chickened out and never left Afton. I needed to see where she lived, and actually meet all those beings who were filtering in and out of Niratap's hospital room. The female orc Rogmesh was kind and soft natured, even if it didn't match her hulking appearance.

Pulling away from the small town at the base of the mountain, red and blue lit up our window. Xaevean sighed heartily next to me as he pulled to the side.

"I was hoping he wouldn't stop us."

"Xaevean, he's a police officer."

"Yes, and he's a nosy prick who won't leave the lord be in peace. He stopped us because this road only goes to the manor."

"That's ridiculous."

"Yes, it is." There was a knock at the window, and he rolled it down. The man is probably not much younger than me with deep smile lines that were nearly covered by a bushy tawny mustache. "Rodger, is there something wrong?"

My eyes bugged out of my head at the bluntness of my husband. "Xaevean."

The sheriff peered at me, then back at him. "Ventris, why are you taking this lady up into the mountains?"

"Not that it's any of your business, but we're going to visit our daughter." Xaevean grumbled his knuckles going white on the steering wheel.

The officer ignored him and looked to me. "Ma'am are you okay? He's not dragging you up there against your will, is he?"

I mean, yes. Xaevean gave me an annoyed look. "No. We're going up to see our daughter. Why did you stop us, officer? We aren't doing anything wrong."

The officer, Rodger, glowered at us. "It's dangerous in those mountains, ma'am. Beasts, monsters, wild fae not to mention that false lord and all his shady friends."

"You do realize that I am one of those shady friends, officer, and I'm a federal agent." Xaevean growled.

"What is he up to? He was gone for two months and then suddenly the whole house pretty much up and leaves. The last month so much coming and going. Government officials, city doctors, and all sorts of beings coming and going."

"Lord Niratap's affairs are none of your concern."

"I saw the news. Was he really being held prisoner or was he the jailer?"

I didn't know if the steering wheel could withstand Xaevean's grip. I placed my hand on his knuckles, a motion that the officer marked. "Officer, I don't know what the tension is between you and my daughter's man or my husband, but they are expecting us, and we need to get there before the sun sets. Right, babe?"

Xaevean's eyes swung to me, his face tight and his tongue sweeps out over his full lip. "That's right, baby. So, Rodger, if you please, may we go?"

I didn't think it was possible for the man to frown any deeper, but he did, then turned away without a word and returned to his car. We waited until he flipped around and drove back towards town.

"He was pleasant."

Xaevean chuffed as we continued down the road. "I'm honestly surprised he didn't heckle us more. Granted you are human, and my race is humanoid, so I think he has less of a problem. It's my understanding that he stops Niratap every time they go through town."

"Couldn't he just push him out?" I asked, watching as fields shifted into thick woodland.

"Niratap could kill him easily if he wanted to, or chase him out, but Niratap tries to spare as many lives as possible. The sheriff is just full of hot air, but he isn't a threat to Niratap or his operations. An annoyance more than anything."

"But why tolerate the annoyance if he is so powerful?"

Xaevean smiled as he watched the twisting road. "For that very reason. Niratap was appointed as a lord by two very grateful elf princesses, and his title, though well-earned, has little bearing on how he interacts with the world. Most of calling him a lord is out of respect for what he does. He is far nobler than some of the men and women I work with, and though I don't always approve of his methods, our goals are the same."

"Which goals?"

"We both want to end inter-species slavery, the use of dangerous creatures as weapons, the skin trade, magical drugs production. He works outside of the law in the underground and feeds us intel when he can."

"Is it really dangerous what he does?"

"Most of the time I think Niratap's job is more dangerous than mine. He puts his whole soul into it sometimes and sometimes he puts himself in precarious situations. He isn't covered in scars for no reason, babe."

"Our daughter chose him, but I still don't understand the why."

"You really haven't seen much of their interactions and to be honest neither have I, but there is something about how he dotes on her that I approve of."

"What do you mean?"

"You'll probably see some of it tonight. Oh, that reminds me, tonight is a festival, Walpurgis Nacht or May

Eve. There will be quite a few beings milling about the manor tonight and tomorrow.”

“Why did they invite us then if they're having a festival?”

“I think it was because it was the soonest that they could accommodate us before they go on their journey. The festival is a sacred night for many beings. Niratap offers the manor grounds to those he cares for and their families to have a secure place to have their larger celebrations. Usually at least twice a year, but more often than not it’s much more frequent. Niratap is fairly private overall and usually observes the festivities and speaks with the clan leaders. In the fall. at Samhain, they pay him a tithe for his continued protection. He doesn’t enforce it, because on its own the manor produces enough food to feed its occupants.”

“If he doesn’t enforce it, why do they do it?”

“Respect. Gratitude. Tradition.” He shrugged. “Fae and old-world creatures are like that.”

“Should I be worried?”

“It is always wise to walk with caution around fae. Most will leave you be. The carnivorous ones are the only ones you really have to worry about. Kelpies, pixies, trolls. Niratap wouldn’t let them hurt you. He’s very strict when it comes to the treatment of everyone. Creseda the Kelpie clan leader is notorious at pushing that boundary.”

“I wonder how he’s doing?”

“Niratap?”

“Yes.”

“Hopefully well. Bitarogs heal rather quickly when they aren’t hindered. He has probably spent the last month rebuilding his strength and putting weight back on. He needs to be healthy for their upcoming journey.”

“You mentioned that earlier. What journey?”

He cast his cerulean blue eyes at me, uncomfortable. “From what I was told, Katrel was summoned back home by her father to wed an heir. Katrel has maintained her freedom from her father for a few hundred years, but you can’t tell the elf king no. They are going to try and convince him to let his daughter keep her freedom."

"That's terrible."

"It is. Elves are very traditional, painfully so. Katrel is expected to marry the man of her father's choosing and quickly produce a suitable heir for the throne."

I frowned. "That's disgusting."

"I agree. However, that is their tradition. Many species are like that, very few creatures interbreed. Bloodlines die out like that noble blood quickly gets diluted when that happens. Elementals are the same way. Purists. Believing that nothing should taint their magical lines." He shrugged noncommittally. "My father is like that, which is why we haven't spoken in twenty years."

I watched him, looking for signs of remorse. "Do you regret that?"

"Fuck no. When I told him that I had married a human and we were having a child, he demanded that I end it and abort the '*abomination*' promptly. I valued you and Shasha more than my father's opinion."

I peered out the window digesting his words. He chose us over tradition. It was just another thing for me to process. I had learned many things over the past month, and I was questioning more, looking for answers from my god that priests and scriptures hadn't been able to answer. I loved my daughter, and her partner seemed kind given his past, but I felt so lost now.

"Do you think they'll like me?"

"I think they will make their own decisions."

I glowered at the trees. "Thank you, Xaevean, for the vote of confidence."

"I'm sorry, Jazz. I adore you, but I can see you, Shasha, and Niratap have a tenuous relationship. Though I doubt that they have spoken ill about you. You will just have to wait and see."

"I guess."

The manor house was an ostentatious eyesore of exuberant wealth, and though beautiful, it twisted my gut. A satyr with black horns, salt and pepper hair, and finely dressed in a periwinkle suit stood before the stairs to the entrance. He idly picked at his nails, but smiled when we pulled up.

"Allipo." Xaevean supplied without me asking. "He is Niratap's house manager and his right hand. He's a good man, but a satyr through and through."

"What do you mean by that?"

"You'll see."

We exited the car and the satyr bowed to us both with a large sweep of his arm. "Welcome, welcome."

"Only you to greet us?" Xaevean asked, grabbing our bag from the trunk.

"Yes." He rose, his honey-colored eyes bright. "Lord Niratap was accosted by Thegguma and Staspar to discuss a new mining operation and an expansion on the care for the hybrids coming out. Lady Shasha is still getting ready for the evening. Dorilody was fussing over her hair the last I checked."

I cast a glance at Xaevean. "Thegguma is the earthen people's clan leader and Staspar is the hybrid clan leader. Dorilody is his head housekeeper and seamstress."

I looked at the satyr. "Lady Shasha?"

"As the lord's mate she automatically earns his rank." The satyr smiled warmly, but I could see the mischief in his eyes. "Not that she hasn't earned the respect she is given."

"Are you going to show us to our room?" Xaevean asked.

"Yes. Follow me." He led us into the grand entry, warm mahogany floors and opulent soft yellow walls with a grand stair. "This is the main foyer. To the right is dining room and kitchen, behind the stairs is the ballroom to the right. Down the left hall is the library, the lord's study, and atrium. You will have free access to the house and grounds, except for the basement levels, back garden and aviary. The forest is also off limits without the lord."

"Why is that?" I ask curious as we a started after him up the stairs.

"For safety, the forests around the manor are full of creatures, many of which are coming out of hibernation and cranky in the simplest of terms. The basement is where the menagerie is and the creatures there are sealed away for a reason. The back garden is where we cultivate poisonous plants. The aviary is just because harpies are fucking nasty vicious creatures that shouldn't be messed with. Now I'm sure V here told you there are festivities tonight, from what I have been told you are—" He paused at the mouth of a long hall before continuing. "Uh, hesitant about others. Rest assured that no one is permitted into the manor without the lord's knowledge. You are welcome to join if you are so inclined, but it's not expected."

"What happens at these festivities?"

Allipo chuckles softly. "Dancing. Drinking. Feasting. Walpurgis Nacht is really just a large party to welcome the spring. There will probably be a righteous amount of debauchery."

Xaevean let out a long-suffering sigh.

"What does he mean?"

"Public displays my sweet."

I looked between the two men. "What?"

"Excuse my language, dear." Allipo said, mischief glowing brightly in his eyes. "But fucking. There will be lots and lots of fucking."

I felt my face heat and Allipo cleared his throat.

"Well, this is the aqua suite. It's close to the stairs so it is easy to find. There is an on-suite bathroom and a balcony. The festivities start at sunset."

The room was painted in a soft sea-foam blue green with cream colored furniture spread throughout and accents matching the room to a T.

"Thank you, Allipo." Xaevean said brusquely. "Though you are the most over-the-top prick I know."

"X."

"Who do you think designed this, babe."

"Well, whoever did has exceptional taste."

"Thank—"

"Don't bloat the satyr's ego or he'll never leave us alone."

Allipo folded his hands behind his back, his face pleasant but there was tension in his voice. "Well then, if you have a need for anything just let one of us know. You are both guests."

He smiled tightly at Xaevean before he turned and walked back down the hall. Xaevean flopped down on the bed with a sigh.

"I'm sorry, Jazz."

"What do you have to be sorry for?" I hissed walking to the balcony doors. Outside there were all manner of creatures milling about, but I spied Niratap talking with a satyr and a dwarf woman standing by where the others are building a bonfire. His face was serious, but he nods listening intently.

"For being an ass. Losing my cool." He grunts rising from the bed and coming to stand behind me. He wraps his arms around my waist. "Allipo has a way of getting under my skin, always has."

He pressed a kiss to my temple. "Why is that?"

"Well, for the most part because we have the same taste in liquor and women. Especially at the same time."

I turned to glower at him. "I'm not going with the satyr anywhere."

He pressed another kiss to my cheek. "I know, Jazzbaby. I know."

"You must be tired. It's a long drive here."

"A bit I could use a nap. Lay with me?"

"I don't think so. I think I'm going to try and be brave and look around. Maybe find our daughter and have her give me a tour."

The manor was expansive to say the least. I got turned around twice trying to find the stairs. I was looking for my daughter, but without knowing what room hers was I was lost in the long halls of matching doors. Downstairs there was a group of orcs sitting at the dining table drinking tea. Rogmesh smiled warmly at me as the men chortled about something. I assumed the large burly male was her husband and the fair-skinned younger man was her son. When we had been chatting, she had said she was going to break both the boy's legs to keep him out of trouble. The boy groaned a long-suffering teenaged sound that I was very familiar with before he got up and walked out the open patio doors. Guess she hadn't followed through with that threat.

Walking down the hall opposite the dining room, again more and more doors until I came to a large set of double doors that stood open to the library, and Niratap's rich-toned voice came from within. He was sat at his desk speaking with someone on the phone, his back to me. I leaned in the doorway listening.

"Yeah, I know Saara. The first year is always the hardest. He was a good kid and a valuable member of the team. No, don't worry at all or apologize for calling. You are family, love, and I take care of my family." He turned in his chair, his brows raising as I stood there. He held up a finger signaling me to wait. "Whatever you need. Blessed May Eve to you too, darling. I'll have Allipo deliver that all to you after the holidays. You too, love. Goodbye."

He hung up, sighing before he stood and directed me with a hand to the seat across from him. "I apologize for not being available to greet you when you arrived. It wasn't my intention."

"It's okay. Allipo told us you had been commandeered."

He chuckled moving to the cupboard behind the desk and pouring himself a dark amber liquor. "Yes, a couple of the clan leaders wanted to run some expansion ideas by me."

"Who were you talking to on the phone?"

He watched me for a moment swirling the liquor in his glass. "Before the winter months one of my associates was compromised on the west coast. It—" He cleared his throat then downed the glass. "It cost him his life. I was on the phone with his mother."

"How old was he?"

"Taegan? He was forty-five and would have been forty-six tomorrow, but still young by satyr standards. She wanted to make sure she wasn't a burden for me." He sighed, again setting the glass on his desk and sitting. "Losing Taegan is hard. He just reconnected with his mother before he went under. They had been separated in a capture raid and we pulled him out of a fight pit. When he found his mom, she was destitute, and he asked me for money to get her out of the slum and into better housing. She's disabled and isn't able to work."

My brows furrowed. "Why would she feel like a burden?"

"Because I personally have paid for her expenses the last five years and plan on continuing to do so." My eyebrows must have crawled into my hairline because he scoffed. "I may be a monster, but I'm not evil. The death of her son is a personal loss for me, and it would dishonor him if I failed to keep her comfortable."

"I never said—"

His silver eyes bore into me full of anger and something else. "You didn't have to."

I swallowed. Sorrow. There was such sorrow in his eyes. I needed to change the subject past the boy. "Your home is lovely."

He watched me, considering. "Thank you. Have you met everyone yet?"

"Allipo is the only one that I've officially met. Rogmesh and I talked at the hospital; I saw her and her family in the dining room, but I didn't intrude. Their son was upset by something."

He nods. "The Days are a raucous bunch. Durgash likes to incite conversation but isn't always eloquent with his words. Bastion is young. He's as brash as his father and as strong willed as his mother. They're good people."

"Anyone we should be worried about?" His lips quirked to one side.

"No. Katrel has a sharp tongue. Bastion a morose drunk. Allipo is mischievous. But none of them will cause you harm."

"Good to know. Where is my daughter?"

"Well—"

"I'm right here, mother." I turned to see my daughter in a deep evergreen outfit. It was billowy but cinched at the wrists and ankles with gold bracelets that warmed her skin. Her midriff was exposed, and her hair had been braided down and had gold ribbon woven in. She walked past me sparing no glance and went to stand between his legs. She had slimmed a bit and built muscles I hadn't noticed the last time I had seen her. He smiled warmly at her as she spoke. "I hope she hasn't been causing you grief, *mo grá*."

"No. I am the master of my own grief, mate."

"Mine." She pressed a kiss to his cheek before she turned to me sitting in his lap. "Please be kind to my family."

"Shasha, I—"

"Don't feign offense, either. You are a guest in our home and will be treated well by those who live here. Don't treat them less.

I swallowed. "You look very beautiful."

She smiled. "Thank you. Dorilody would not let me go before she did my hair."

"You look like a warrior." He rested his head against her shoulder, kissing the exposed skin. She smiled at him, and I could see how much they loved each other.

"Well, I hope I don't have to fight anyone today. I want to have fun and dance." She turned to face him. "You're going to dance with me tonight."

He chuckled. "Your wish is my command. One dance as compromise."

She pressed another kiss to his check as someone knocked in the doorway. The woman, who I remembered from the raid, bowed deeply to them. She had skin sun-kissed with deep chestnut hair and eyes, dressed in a flowy tunic shirt and black leather pants, a knife strapped to her thigh. "My apologies, my Lord and lady, but we might have an issue."

Niratap growled; the sound startled me. "What did Creseda do this time, Mitta?"

Mitta smiled as she stood. "I'd happily handle it for you if you'd let me. The kelpies can find a better leader."

"What did she do, Mitta?" Shasha asked, sliding from Niratap's lap so he could stand.

"She's picking fights with everyone. Especially Thegguma and Staspar because and I quote '*how dare you steal the lord away for a private meeting on a holiday. What if I had an opinion on whatever it is you spoke about. Or even worse you speaking ill of me to the lord.*' Blowing smoke as usual but the fauns and satyrs are gnawing at the bit to retaliate, that is the only reason I came to disturb you while you were with our guest."

"No, that's quite alright, Mitta. I will go deal with Creseda." He grabbed Shasha by the chin and tilted her face to his. "Remember, *mo grá*, you outrank all of them. Do not let them treat you as anything other than the lady of this house. If blood is needed for that lesson to take hold, so be it."

"Yes, my love." She smiled as he kissed her.

"You'll take care to introduce everyone to your mother?"

"Yes."

"Alright." He came around the table and gave me a nod. "Mitta, lead the way."

"Yes, my Lord."

When they left, Shasha came to my side. "Let's go meet the family."

I sat on the soft plush couch with a sigh. Shasha sat beside me with a smile on her face. She had dragged me all over the house and the back parts of the yard, avoiding the courtyard where everyone else was. The Days had been in the kitchen and were warm and welcoming. The Raloqen sisters were night and day to each other; Katrel did have a sharp tongue and her sister was the salve. Dorilody was polite and enjoyed talking about the colors she would dress Niratap in if he'd let her. Dheg and Echo had been in the stables. Both were kind and smiled sweetly while Shasha introduced me to Niratap's horse.

"Well?"

"You have found quite the family. I didn't expect that they would be so kind and loving. I—" I took a breath. "I never thought that beings could coexist like this."

Shasha sat forward resting her elbows on her knees. "Yeah. They're great. Sunset will be here soon. You should come out tonight."

"You don't think I would be in the way?"

"Heavens no. I know it's way out of your element, but I think it will be good for you to see. The fun. The dancing. Nira and I."

Xaevean came into the sitting room and smiled at us. "There's my girls."

"Hey." She said, giving him a little wave before she stood. "Give it some thought, okay mom? I'm going to go and find my mate. I hope to see you there."

She smiled at X as she left; they had been talking, but their relationship was tense. In person they seemed to circle each other like predators not blood. He took her spot on the couch taking up the same position.

"So?"

"You two are definitely related." I smiled laughing at them.

"Well, yes." He smiled. "I meant about the festivities."

"Well, I was brave and didn't get eaten in the house and out to the stables. So."

"Neither I nor Niratap will let anything happen to you."

I smiled. "Okay. I'll go, but at the first sign of trouble I'm running back inside."

He chuckles. "Okay, babe."

X held my hand tightly as we walked to where Niratap sat chatting with Allipo and another satyr. A bonfire glowed hot in the fading light, drums were pounding, and a wild dance was already taking place. Shasha smiled at me as we came up beside them, a bench was sat next to the table for us.

"M'lord you ars de mos gracious."

"No, Staspar." Niratap said, irritation evident in his voice. "You were elected to be your people's leader and you do a fine job meeting their needs. Creseda just likes to be the center of attention and the only way she seems to be able to capture mine is by attacking you for something you had no choice in. It's appalling, however, she is just like you chosen by her people, and the shifters are always doing well under her leadership."

I leaned into my daughter and whispered. "I take it she didn't take kindly to whatever it is that he said to her."

Shasha laughed and I saw the corner of Niratap's mouth quirk into a smile. He answered me.

"She got the kind of attention she deserved and threw a mighty fit." He angled his head at a gaggle of beings on the outskirts. "She's complaining more but has cooled from the sound of it."

"You can hear them from here?" I was shocked.

"Over the din, yes. It's faint, but I can pick out what they're saying for the most part. She will probably try to butter up to me at some point before the night is over."

"Aye. Wes eaves you be m'lord. Ejoy de evenen."

"You as well." The satyr bowed and took his leave. Niratap watched after him as he returned to a group by the fire making music.

"Do you want me to watch Creseda, my Lord?" Allipo asked.

"Watch her people, Creseda isn't foolish enough to act on her own; she'd want the deniability. Let me know if anything happens."

"Of course. Are you going to speak?"

"No. I think the fact that we can gather is testament enough."

"Very well. I will report to you if I see or hear anything."

"Thank you, my friend."

"Always, my Lord." He swept into a deep bow. "Milady, enjoy your evening."

"Would you like me to spy as well?" X asked from where he stood behind me.

"If you feel inclined, I won't object." He said leaning back in the large carved chair. Shasha shifted from the spot by his chair and sat in his lap facing me. He wrapped his arm around her as he buried his face into her neck, she laughed.

"Stop." She grabbed him by the antler, pushing him away. "My mother is watching us."

"Fairly certain she'll see all kinds of sights of a debased nature tonight, my dear." He pushed against her hold.

"Yes, that is what you told me. However, you and I will not be on display."

He made a deep-throated sound. "No, I don't feel like sharing you with any of our friends. Though many of these males think they could land a chance with you."

"Hardly. I only have eyes for you, mate."

"Remember that while you dance. Take care to remind them that you are mine."

She smiled and pressed a kiss to his cheek, before climbing free of him. "And you are mine."

"Return when you tire."

"Same rules as Samhain?" She asked, stepping back.

"For the most part. Dance with whoever you please but be smart about it."

"Remember you owe me a dance." She smiled before she practically skipped down to the fire, X trailing behind her casting me a smile.

Niratap grabbed a glass of wine from the table before he settled back into his chair. I asked. "What were the rules for Samhain?"

He sipped the wine. "She wasn't permitted to dance with anyone from outside of the house, to drink the faerie wine, or wander off with anyone. I would suggest similar guidelines for you as well. You are safe here; however, I would not be overly trusting of those who do not live here."

"I don't know if I'll be as adventurous as my daughter."

He smiled warmly. "All is well."

"Will you go and dance with her?"

"I'll let her, and the party tire out a bit. I am still recovering, and my joints are still quite sensitive. If I overdo activity, I get tingling in my hands. Kozran says it is caused by pinched and compressed nerves most likely from how I was bound."

"Won't it heal?"

"Time will tell." He poured himself another glass of wine and another then offered me the second glass. I took a careful sip; it tasted of roses and honey. "Kozran is hopeful, but it could be something I have to live with for the rest of my life. Annoying at best, life threatening at worst given my occupation."

"Is my daughter in danger?"

His silver eyes considered me before he spoke. "Yes. That was established long ago though. Players on the market know what I intend to do and up until recently they were afraid to fight against me. Now, however, it has been shown that I can be captured. That I can be bent. That I have weaknesses. I don't want her to get caught in the torrent coming for me. She has no such compunction."

"Sounds like my daughter." He quirked a brow. "She always excelled. She always wanted to be smarter. Tougher. Braver than the rest of the kids in her class. I guess I shouldn't be surprised she would continue to want to excel."

"Aye. She definitely likes to excel." He swirled the wine. "Her shooting rivals mine, she wins about half her sparring matches now, and she can work a room like royalty. I am always worried that she will push too far in a situation where she is ill equipped, but she proves herself more resourceful than I give her credit."

"You fear for her." I said, setting my glass down on the table, looking out at where my daughter danced with Dheg. He spun and lifted her up into the air, her face alight with glee.

"I do." He smiled though there was pain in his eyes as he set the glass down. "Rest assured though I will do everything in my power to keep her safe."

"Is that what you did when you got yourself imprisoned?" He clutched the arm of the chair, the wood groaned in protest, but I continued. "Is that what you were doing when you got beat so badly your heart stopped or when you were being drowned and it stopped for a second time?"

He looked at me, his eyes gunmetal severe in the firelight. I swallowed, looking back out at the revelry. "I have never seen callousness in my child except when that man died in her hands, and she wanted to spill his blood herself. I have never heard my daughter scream like when you were stabbed in that tent and started to seize. I have never heard her break like she did confronting you about dying. Niratap, you love my daughter, don't you? You say you'd raze the world for her, but in the venture where you burn it all for her, do you include yourself in that? Do you think that by keeping her physical form safe that you won't damage her heart and soul when you take those blows? I don't think your life is valued less or more than my daughter's, but I do value her happiness more. The mere thought of losing you kills her. Love my daughter, Niratap. Love her in all the ways a monster and a man can love her, but don't break her heart. Love her, but without sacrificing yourself."

He huffed a choked smokey laugh and I braved a glance at the man next to me. He smiled lovingly out at the party, but I knew where his eyes rested. Watching the wild woman in green and gold dance around the fire with his heart in her hand. It was from those loving eyes that tears streamed over his cheeks, which he wiped away on his sleeve. "Is this your way of giving your blessing?"

"You could say that." I said, eyeing the food strewn across the table. "I want her to be and have all the good things; she wants them with you. I've thought about it, you and her. I've thought a lot about this being part of not only my life but the world at large. I've thought a lot about my relationships with God, my husband, my daughter and the man my daughter chose, and I want to have a better, more understanding relationship with all of them."

He considered me again, both of us sizing the other up. Finally, he smiled and shook his head, reaching for a dish that looked like a quiche and serving some along with bread and potatoes. "I see where she gets that logical mind from. I would be honored to have a relationship of better understanding with you, Jazzera." He set the plate before me and refilled my wine, raising his glass to me. "To a better future."

I smiled. I could see how my daughter fell in love with him as I clinked my glass to his. "A better future and bigger family."

His smile broadened at me, taking a drink as Shasha returned, straddling his lap and stealing the glass from him, downing it in two large gulps. He laughed heartily.

"Come dance with me, mate." She crooned, kissing along his throat.

"I will soon, *mo grá*. Your mother and I were having a discussion."

"About what?"

He looked at me. "We were talking about my thoughts on things."

"What things?" She hissed at me as I took a bite of the quiche Niratap had served me, it was rich and pillowy full of mushrooms and greens.

"Now, now, love. She hasn't said anything of ill intent."

She glowered at him her hands cupping his cheeks. "You've been crying."

He clasped her hands. "She shared a hard truth that I hadn't thought about. It wounded me, but it was only because I had made missteps and didn't realize the full scope of how some of my decisions could hurt you."

She frowned.

"She gave us her blessing and wants to build a relationship with us."

Shasha gave me a disbelieving look. "No way."

I smiled at her. "Just don't go popping out babies right away."

Niratap's cheeks pinked and cleared his throat as he stood. "A dance, my flower?"

"Coward." She mocked as he tugged her behind him.

"I am not." He chuckled, giving her a gentle spin, before he bowed to me. "We'll return in a moment, enjoy your meal."

"Thank you."

I watched them as they slowly danced out of tune with the music playing, until the band noticed them and eased into a slower melody. Shasha glowed gazing at him, full of love and promises that they passed between each other. He leaned his head back and belly laughed at something she said. They reminded me of a simpler time. When I was young and falling in love. Someone sat next to me in Niratap's chair. I felt their gaze, a chill shooting up my spine, but I did not move to meet it.

"You don't belong here." The smooth feminine voice says.

I swallowed. "And you don't belong in that seat."

She laughed. "Probably not, but the lord and his half-human whore are dancing."

"Excuse you, that is my daughter you're speaking about." I faced the woman, her skin is corpse pale, long teal hair flowed like underwater grass and pitch-black eyes that sneered at me.

"You think just because you're the whore's mother you belong here? Makes me miss the old days where my kind had the free reign to eat your kind. There aren't many of us left that remember the taste of man-flesh."

"Well, I can assure you that the lord and my husband would kill you faster than you could attack me." I said looking back out at the dance.

"Is that a challenge?" She hissed, her voice taking on a reptilian quality.

Niratap's eyes met mine and I swallowed as his brows lowered in concern. I couldn't find X and a rock settled into my stomach. I was in danger. "No, it's just a fact."

"Hmm. I wonder where this husband of yours is?"

I clutched my hands in my lap to hide their shaking. Niratap started toward me, and my chest tightened. "What did you do to him?"

"Oh, I didn't do anything. I've been here talking to you, in plain sight. It's a shame though Ventris has always been so very handsome."

I tried to slow my fluttering heart, halt the tears that wanted to run down my face. Niratap was stopped by Allipo. Please No. No. No. Xaevean can handle them, he's made of tough stuff. I need you. "You have a lot of nerve. Creseda, I presume?"

She smiled at me with a too-wide smile with far too many jagged sharp teeth. "Oh, you know of me; that is a fine development. At least I know I'm spoken of, but I do hope there was fondness on their tongues."

I force a tight laugh. "More like annoyance. I was told you like being the center of attention."

"I belong in the spotlight." She twirled her hair around a claw. "Silly male could have anyone as a bed mate, but he chose a half breed."

"You know being a pick-me bitch doesn't ever get you far."

"Excuse me?"

"You heard me." I said glaring at her as I took up my half full glass of wine. "Being a pick-me bitch doesn't get you far."

"Why you filthy human scum—" She lunged for me, and I threw my wine in her face, backing off the bench to try to get away. She hissed, a snake cornering a mouse. "You will be a satisfying treat before I feast on that whore of a daughter of yours."

She leaped at me with her gaping maw of teeth wide. I screamed covering my face with my hands.

A deafening roar echoed off the forest. Then silence.

"How fucking dare you." A guttural sounding voice snarled. "How fucking dare you."

"Mama." Shasha asked, pulling my shaking hands from my face. "Are you okay?"

My daughter's face was contorted with worry. I swallowed, shaking my head. Words were beyond reach at the moment.

"Shasha, is she harmed?" The monstrous voice asked.

"No. She's not hurt." She shifted out of my line of vision, exposing the beast that the voice belonged to. My heart stopped at the grotesque looking monster before me. Shadows whipped about its limbs that were long and lanky the back legs covered with grey fur, the front were clawed and scaled, a long tufted tail, the skin on its body was pulled tightly over the muscles and bones giving it a hollowed look, the skin on its face was peeled back from the gaping maw of jagged canid teeth. I was horrified and strangely at ease as I met the creature's silver eyes. Niratap.

"Good." He turned his attention back to the kelpie woman under one of his clawed hands. She thrashed against his hold, a gurgling scream coming from her throat. "How fucking dare you. Not only have you disrespected me and my home. You have disrespected my mate and her family. What gives you the right Creseda? Where does this innate need to be the center of my attention come from."

He eased off of her so she could answer him. Her voice quivered in fear. "I meant no disrespect to you, my Lord. Humans don't belong at the revelry of the wild things. I did not know that she was the mother of the lady of the manor."

"Liar." I hissed.

"Kelpies do not lie." She hissed at me, Niratap growled. "I didn't know."

"Liar." I snapped with more gumption. "You called my daughter a whore, threatened me, and my husband."

A deep growl resonated throughout the space. "I don't care that you disrespected me, I've grown accustomed to it. However, I will not stand for you disrespecting my mate or her family."

"I meant nothing by it, my Lord." She pleaded, unable to wriggle free of his claws. "I did not know."

"Liar." He snapped his jaws in her face, and she whimpered.

"My Lord." Xaevean spoke from behind me.

"Xaevean." I turned wrapping my arms tightly around him, his familiar sea scent grounded me.

"Are you well?" Niratap asked.

"Yes. A little rough for wear, but I will be fine." I peered up at his face a black bruise rimmed one eye and a slice oozed on his right cheek.

"Very well. Explain yourself, Creseda. You will only get this one chance. Lie to me again, and it will be your life that is forfeit." There were cries of outrage scattered throughout the crowd. "Silence! Speak, kelpie."

"Why?" She shrieked. "Why did you choose her? A half-breed and a human at that to be your bedmate. What does every other female lack that she has? Is it just that suffocating floral scent that attracts you to her? Why her and not me?"

Niratap removed his claws from around her and sat back on his haunches. He still towered over her. "You sound like a jilted lover, Creseda."

"Why love the human half-breed and not one of us of the wilds."

"Is it power that you are looking for, Creseda?" He asked with a tilt of his head. "Is being the leader and spokesperson for your peoples not enough?"

She swallowed, scooting away from him, streaks of muddy tears rolled down her face. "What does she have that other beasts do not have?"

"I don't have to answer that, Creseda, for it is none of your concern. I will let you keep your life and your station, but you are out of chances. Slight me again, disrespect the members of the council, my family or my mate again and it will be your life you give up for the transgression."

"But."

"Enough. Go home, Creseda. Take your family and go home." His voice sounded heavy. "Everyone heed that as a warning. I will not be questioned about my mate or why I chose her. My reasonings are my own, and that will be your only warning."

He shifted further, grey fur and black scales overtaking him, part wolf, part dragon, part wildcat. His bright silver eyes locked with mine. He approached me, let me run my fingers through the soft strands of his fur. He turned and pressed his cold wet nose to my forehead, I felt a magic pulse around me, weaving itself into my shadow. When he pulled away, he gave me a cursory once over.

"I am fine. Thank you."

A silent nod as he turned to my daughter, her fingers weaving into the thick, soft fur about his face. She whispered, deep understanding in her face. "You are fine. We can retire."

"Bondbreaker!" Creseda snarled from down the hill. "I will not forget this."

He snorted, lips pulling back over his teeth, but my daughter spoke in his stead, drawing a long black knife. "Creseda, I suggest you heed the warning you were given. He may have decided to be merciful, but I will not. I will gladly carve my own pound of flesh for how you treated my mother and how you disrespected my mate."

"You shouldn't place yourself on a pedestal, girl. How long will you warm his bed before he bores of you?"

"He is mine and I am his. We are one soul in two bodies, woven together by choice and fate."

I didn't think it was possible for the pale creature to become any ghastlier. "You are mated?"

"Under the wild night sky." She said, taking a step forward a fierce wind whirled around her. "Mates. Mine. He will never be yours to claim."

"The Bondbreaker has bound his very soul to a mortal woman. How interesting." She smiled, before turning away and waving behind her.

Niratap growled, as she and her ilk flitted into the forest, disappearing from sight. A tightness settled over him as he turned from all of us and loped to the manor. Shasha watched the tree line expecting them to return, eventually her shoulders slumped, exhaustion rolling off her. Allipo approached and bowed deeply to her.

"Milady, would you like me to send the others away?"

She sheathed her blade, but her eyes were still watching the trees. "No, they may continue to dance and celebrate the spring, I know that it is important for them."

"Aye."

Xaevean's breath tickled my ear. "Do something with me?"

"Anything."

"Bow to her."

I looked to the ground, Xaevean's strong arm guiding me into the motion. Shasha made a small, surprised sound. I peeked over the crowd and the whole of them, the mix of creatures and fae bowed to my daughter. Xaevean's voice boomed.

"Long live Lady Bondbreaker."

There was a cheer in response. It was in that moment when we stood and I saw her framed in the light of the bonfire, that my daughter was so much more than my baby and it was something I hadn't seen happen. She was a warrior, a fighter, a survivor, a lover, a lady of station, and a beacon for those like her, beings who were in both worlds because of their lineage. My daughter was a beacon of strength to those who were in between both worlds. A beacon of hope.

Acknowledgments

All my friends and family who have been pressuring me for years to get something done. I did it!

The authors, artists, creators, and musicians that fuel my creativity. I devour content like its water so the list of you is beyond comprehension but thank you.

My husband, Allen, for being just as invested as me and pushing me to live my dream. My springboard of thought, my foundation, my rock, my everything. I love you.

Amanda, my soul sister that I clicked with faster than anyone should ever click with someone. I love you more than words can express and even now I miss you terribly. Thank you for volunteering to edit my books like the savage that you are. Thank you for making time to visit and running to hug me. Two hours will never be enough time. Thank you for being my friend.

Katie for being the best new edition to my tribe. Thank you for being the love, support, peer pressure and motivator that you have been for me. You push and push and push and I love you for that.

Alexis for being both chaos and calm when I needed it. Thank you for also pouring love from your cup into mine and supporting me beyond measure. So sure, that you would be one of the first to call me your favorite author. I couldn't wish for a better friendship.

And to my readers, who, however few or many, are cheering me on. Who have fallen in love with my spicy half-elemental and my fae beast and want to go on more adventures with me.

Author Bio

S. R. George is a witch and storyteller who grew up loving to read. From a young age she has wanted to tell the grand adventures her mind takes her. Love stories are a favorite of hers, especially if they have fantasy aspects to them. Now she wants to share her chaos with the world. She currently lives in Idaho with her husband and two cats.